Thirty Days Has September

THE LAST TEN DAYS

James Strauss

Geneva
Shore
Publishing
GENEVA SHORE PUBLISHING, INC

Geneva
Shore
Publishing

Geneva Shore Publishing, Inc.

www.genevashorereport.com

Cover art by Lee Wheeler.

ISBN-13 979-86776289-1-7

I would like to offer this work as a tribute to all the men who came home only to find a place for themselves on that shiny wall in Washington, D.C. I offer it to their survivors, as well.

contents

Thirty Days Has September

THE LAST TEN DAYS

ninety-eight

THE TWENTIETH DAY : SECOND PART

I hit the flattened fern leaves and shoots on my left side, trying to hold my right arm free in case I needed to get to my Colt, and also stay away from having my strapped-on pack catapult me out of the chute. My attempt to control the descent was totally wasted as soon as I fell around the first bend and over the first cliff. Only the angle of the descent and the thickness of the packed ferns saved me from injury. I was thrown everywhere, frightened of going over another cliff. The first violent drop had been about six feet but the next was ten. I plummeted down the chute, no longer in doubt about why the Marines before had screamed all the way down. I didn't know or care if I was screaming. The speed of my descent was beyond calculation, with everything around me seeming to form a dark hole through which I moved, with the moist misery of jungle never giving me anything to focus on. Slush, rush, roll, toss and drop again. The chute seemed without end, although I knew the peak was only nine-hundred and seventy-five meters high. Three thousand feet or so, but every meter of that distance was a meter down through the different layers of hell.

I didn't know where I was going and that was the worst part. Was there a team of NVA soldiers, having predicted our descent, waiting with butcher knives at some turn where the chute evened out, or would there be an unseeable drop-off of a couple hundred feet somewhere along its route? Had the Army guys, that we had seen at the bottom been killed by their bullet wounds, or had the chute killed them with its brutal furious descent and severe damage from unforeseeable and terminal drop offs?

Shivers of fear burst inside me like artillery flares, staying and wagging their way back and forth through my torso and mind. My body accelerated to what I thought had to be the end, and it was. I came out of the chute flying, my helmet seeming still in the air just forward and to the right of my head. Suddenly, I was down. Not into the pond I'd seen earlier, but into the waiting arms of my Marines. They were laughing, as they must have at the others who'd preceded me down the chute. I tried to laugh with them but couldn't make anything happen. The shivers of fear had turned into shaking and quaking, and I had to hide that effect at all cost.

They put me down and plopped my helmet back on my head. From the trip down I'd picked up another dent in the side of the damaged thing. I silently hoped I'd still be able to get the liner out of the metal shell so I could at least use it as a basin to wash my hair and face. But there was no time to scrub by scooping the water from the pond or tributary. Most of the company lay hunkered down, probably to watch the arrival of the others before I came out the end looking like a giant and terrified muddy gerbil, which I no doubt resembled.

"Move," I yelled. "They know we're down and they'll be coming."

I took off running toward the Ontos, sitting on the mud about four hundred meters in the distance. The sun was so hot and, with the moisture mostly gone from the air, turning my exterior coating of mud into a dark hardening and cracking plaster. I looked back over my shoulder at the end of the chute. Flying down Tantalus on ti leaves as a kid back then had saved my life today. There was no way I could write about that in a letter home. My wife wouldn't believe me, could not believe me, much less anyone else.

Although there were no gunshots coming from the hillside jungle I felt and then saw an RPG round hit not far from where the Ontos sat. A direct strike would take the little machine of death out. I ran as fast as I could toward the Ontos, my ears ringing from the explosion. It would take half a minute at least to get the tubes around to face a new threat, and the turret wasn't moving. Had the crew been taken out with the shock of the explosion? The double doors of the Ontos were closed and locked when I got there but I didn't need to get inside to figure out what was happening.

Fessman, who'd stayed with me pushed the AN/323 headset against my shoulder, as I heard the heavy rumble and drone of big radial engines punching through the air above. The Skyraiders were back.

"Cowboy?" I said, hopefully into the small microphone, hoping the radio still worked after its run down the sluice.

"Flash, how you doin' down there?"

"They've got some RPG shit down near the base of the hill just to the north of our perimeter," I replied. "I can't pull artillery rounds into that defilade."

Cunningham and Firebase Ripcord were the closest artillery

outfits and both might be close enough to fire their howitzers at a high angle and actually reach the back side of the hill, but the indirect fire was less accurate and more difficult to adjust, especially when the hillside's changing altitude was taken into consideration.

"We only got four of us for fun this fine morning, Flash," Cowboy said. "Took a peek at the peak and there's no joy up on top of that mountain today."

"Twenty-seven, we lost twenty-seven," I blurted out, not knowing why. It didn't matter how many we lost. All that mattered was what supporting fire Cowboy had brought to support us in our position.

The Skyraiders roared over us, one after another at low altitude.

"We're just a pair of deuces today, but let's light the place up with everything we got with one pair. That'll leave the others to hang about and cover your six until we can get back from a quick turnaround. Twenty-seven. Maybe we can fit in twenty-seven round trips in one day. Let's give it a go."

That was the longest I'd ever heard Cowboy speak. I knew that the number had reached him and cut deep, although I couldn't feel it myself. I'd liked the look of the Army guys. No mud. They'd been clean shaven and looked tough as hell compared to the mess of Marines I was among and was myself. Clews had been so enthusiastic and his men so committed it was almost impossible to consider that they were gone forever. That was the worst part, aside from the fact that I would never forget how badly I hadn't wanted to accompany him on his mission, and that such great young guys had gone into their deaths following such a distant and damaged drummer.

"Don't go," I whispered to myself, remembering vividly what I'd told him.

"Say again," Cowboy said, before adding to the others, "get your Marine Corps girly asses down into the mud."

The Skyraiders came out of the south, straight up the river, seemingly only a few feet above the water. One after another, they strafed the bottom of the hill with their twenty-millimeters. The spacing of the planes was about twenty seconds apart. By the time the fourth one was angling away and pulling up into the air hard, the first one was coming back. I pushed myself into the mud, face down, my hands clutching my helmet to press my head even further down.

Bombs started exploding, as the second run was a carpet bombing at a low level. I could tell they were dropping two-hundred-and-fifty-pounders because I wasn't being tossed upward by the concussion the five hundreds would have caused. I could stay flat, the earth only seeming to wrinkle under me a bit with each explosion.

Over on the hill, a couple of hundred meters away, the effect would be as mind and ear-ripping as it was deadly.

The Skyraiders flew off, one after another. I pulled my face from the mud to look at the smoking pyre they left behind them. The planes could stay on station for most of the day but had to return to base if they were to stay fully armed. That trip could take vital hours, leaving our situation untenable. We were trapped between two enemy forces, both of which were well dug in and outnumbering us. What they didn't have was artillery. Their 122mm long-range guns did not reach as far north as our location, or at least I didn't think so because we hadn't been hit by them since leaving the southern part of the valley.

I got up and ran for the Ontos, covering the ground without any shots being fired that I could hear. Some crew member had opened the rear double doors but nobody was inside and I wasn't going in either, even if the guns were pointing the wrong way. I shrugged my pack off and struggled to cram my body under the armor protection, in fear of what I knew had to be coming. The next enemy move was as predictable as it was terminal. They would attack from up on the hillside, establish a base of plunging fire down upon our position and then come at us from the south with the real force. We'd be pinned down by the base of fire and then eventually overrun by the numbers of the attacking forces from downriver. The guns we had faced south but was that the right way?

It was almost impossible to figure out who was jammed under the machine's protection, as the passage down the slope had covered every Marine with layers of mud. The mud was the cloying volcanic kind that was more red than brown or black and nearly impossible to remove without rinsing with large amounts of water.

The Gunny stared into my eyes. I didn't need to see the features of his face clearly in the diminished light or through the layers of mud. The Gunny's eyes were darkly distinguished and identifiable, and they were filled with anger.

"Now that was a ride," the other man, lying prone and facing me said, and I knew him to be Jurgens by the sound of his voice, which continued on.

"Holy shit, everyone's going to be talking about this one for some time to come, Junior. Disneyland doesn't have that ride."

I was trying to adjust to Jurgens not being pissed off because I'd pushed him over the edge while at the same time attempting to understand why the Gunny was obviously so angry.

The Gunny pushed against my right shoulder, so I leaned toward the left tread as far as I could to let him by, but he wasn't having any of that. He pushed harder until I understood what he was communicating, and began crabbing backward out from under the covering armor. Although I didn't want to be in the open without supporting fires dumping ordnance around us, I couldn't deny the Gunny's insistence. I backed slowly from under the Ontos, while the Gunny slid by and came up to a crouch near the back of the machine. He lit a cigarette with his special Zippo, before clicking it shut loudly, and then returning it to one of his chest pockets.

I crouched next to him, not saying a word, for fear of setting the obvious high bar of his anger even higher.

"You didn't know shit," he whispered over at me between taking and blowing puffs of smoke from his cigarette.

There was no way to answer this question, so I waited. I didn't know what? Of the many things I didn't know shit about, what particular thing might he be talking about?

"That chute, or channel, down the face of that mountain, could have ended anywhere," the Gunny finally got out. "All of us could have gone over a fifty-foot cliff, or run right straight into a machine gun nest, and you didn't have a clue.That was what I was going to tell you when I saw the decision to go forming inside of your head."

I had no answer that made any sense. My time in Hawaii and my experience with tea leaf sliding down Tantalus, seemed ridiculous to tell him about and use as an excuse. I hadn't known where the channel was going to lead and there was no lie I could think of to cover that rather obvious fact.

I held out my right hand to accept his cigarette instead of talking. My hand sat in mid-air for almost half a minute before he moved the cigarette close enough so I could accept it. I took one puff and returned it. The gesture meant everything to me. The Gunny was mad as hell, I knew because I'd made the decision and then committed him to it, and I'd done it in such a way that my physically pushing him had been taken, by him, as some sort of macho male affront.

"Our position was hopeless," I finally said.

"Our position here is hopeless," he shot back, flicking his unfinished cigarette out across the mud. "We lost a shitload of equipment on the way down, and here we are stuck between two unbeatable NVA forces dug in down to God knows where."

I looked down at the mud squeezing up over the sole of my right boot. There was no sound or movement from the Marines under the Ontos, but they were only a few feet away. There was no covering noise, except the whispering tributary waters to our back, to keep them from hearing every word the Gunny and I were exchanging.

"Fussman," I whispered, my mind racing to devise a new plan before the heart of the company was eaten out by despondency and fear.

Fussman appeared around the side of the Ontos, accompanied by Zippo and Nguyen. I recognized them more by their body sizes than their appearance since everyone in the company resembled the mud men from Flash Gordon when it came to facial appearances.

I reached out my hand and Fessman placed the arty net microphone into it, as I knew he would. I looked up at the swirling clouds circling the top of the peak and reached out to Lieutenant Howell, the duty battery officer at Cunningham. I was thankful that 'Howler' was on. I knew we were still too distant from the firebase for high angle indirect fire, which meant I couldn't touch the near slope we'd come plummeting down. I laid out two zone fire areas. One to cover the rest of the hill that was reachable and the other to carpet the jungle down below where the old airstrip ended. Howell came back after plotting the zones and offered the addition of Cunningham's 155 battery for depth since I'd asked for a mix of concrete piercing and high explosive. He also wanted to know if Firebase Ripcord could join the party. I knew by that unasked addition Howler understood we were dealing with tunnels, how many Marines were likely in trouble. I figured he'd probably followed some of the command stuff over the past few days, as well. The double payload of the 155s, and whatever Ripcord could throw, would extend the underground radius of tunnel crushing shock waves tremendously in both zone areas.

I gave Fessman the handset back. I'd need the air radio in a few seconds but I had another job for him first. I looked into the Gunny's angry eyes. I knew he was more embarrassed about being pushed than upset about the risk I'd taken. The risk had worked, and success was hard to argue with. I knew the Gunny had to secretly enjoy the established fact that he was the accepted leader of the company. I had no reputation to protect. He did. The Gunny was a much more powerful name to be addressed by than Junior, and everyone knew it.

I motioned to Zippo and Nguyen. "Jurgens is under the Ontos. Help him get out here to join us."

I knew Jurgens was listening to every word we were saying, and the other men down under the machine with him. Almost instantly, before either Zippo or Nguyen could even bend down, Jurgens scurried forward and then stood to join us.

"Our situation is hopeless," I said.

There was no sugar-coating the fact that, even though we had massive artillery and air support, if something didn't change, our position would eventually be overrun and all of us would be killed.

"We've got to make a move, and we've got to make it fast."

"Back to the runway, it's the only way open" the Gunny replied, immediately.

I hadn't expected an answer at all since I hadn't phrased my statement as a question. I knew the old airstrip was no more survivable than our current position, except for the small hole the river had eaten into the bank under it. That the Gunny hadn't figured that out or was still so angry that he wasn't thinking clearly, was more problematic from his presenting the idea out loud rather than just between us. With the enemy on both the north and the south flanks, and the other two sides blocked by an unscalable cliff and a raging river, the situation, if we successfully made the move back to the abandoned airstrip, would be as impossible to defend, for any period of time, as our current one.

"We're going north," I said, hoping that my calling in of artillery support would carry enough weight to keep me from going against the Gunny again in front of the company and also motivating everyone listening to accept the fact that our situation was only hopeless if we made it hopeless.

I stopped talking and waited. The Gunny pulled out another cigarette. I could tell from his movements he wasn't likely to be sold on anything I recommended, his anger over being pushed into the mud, and then screaming as he plunged down the hill, still affecting him deeply.

"Shot over," came out of the small speaker on Fessman's Prick 25. My head snapped around to look at him.

Fessman smiled weakly.

I tried not to smile. The corporal deliberately set the switch of the small external speaker on for everyone to hear, since by activating it he cut out any ability to communicate using the handset. I nodded at him, as he reached his fingers over to shut it off. Fessman knew I needed help and was giving it to me in the only way he knew.

"Shot, out," he responded back to the battery.

"Down," I ordered. "Zone fire," I said, "we don't know exactly where their shit's going to hit."

In training, the size of the area to receive fire was set at about a square kilometer, but when firing into an area with different elevations receiving that fire, wide disparity in rounds impacting could be unpredictable and deadly.

I never heard the response to "Splash," as the rounds came in early, hundreds of them. Howler had laid down a zone on the hill like I'd never seen or heard in training. I squeezed under the Ontos, where everyone else up top had retreated. Those Marines in holes I knew would be digging deeper as they pressed down. Shells were impacting too close for the indirect fire to be raining down on the near side of the hill until I realized that Ripcord was off at a northeasterly angle further north. Their high angle fire was tearing the southern slope apart making me glad that, for once, I'd registered in our true position before they opened up.

Fessman was next to me, his Prick 25 down and next to him, as the Ontos armor hung too low to let him wear it on his back.

"Give me the 323," I said, as the explosions continued to blast away in the near distance, the shattering blasts not so severe as to affect hearing, but the shock-waves bouncing everyone uncomfortably about. I wasn't ready to call Cowboy and his Skyraiders just yet, but I wanted every Marine cowering under the Ontos with me to be thinking about taking fire to the enemy rather than the possibility of ground forces slowly but surely pinning us down and killing us off one by one.

"When we'd occupied the hill earlier we got up there by climbing the rip-rap angled down from the top lip of the cliff on the east face. The plan is to do what we did three weeks ago. We don't attack the hill, we go around it. Instead of climbing the rocks and debris to reach the top and, then hook back toward the southern peak, we turn and head through the trees up there toward the north until we're well away from the area."

I waited for any comment that might be forthcoming from the Gunny. The area under the armor was dark but daylight filtered in from every direction. The Gunny had another cigarette out and was working the smoke slowly in and out of his lungs. We lay with one of the crewmen between us, but I could distinctly see the Gunny over the Marine's flat shoulder blades. He looked across the short distance at me, his muddy head backlit against the light from the outside.

"Bait," the Gunny said, picking a piece of tobacco from his lips and snapping it away. "Battalion's not going to like it. This hill's here for a reason, and us with it. I'll bet they're sitting back in the rear devising some huge muscular operation, supposedly to support the dire mess we've gotten ourselves into, when all along they caused us to be here. Exactly here."

"A stalking horse," Jurgens replied to the Gunny, his voice coming from the other side of the tightly massed bodies, surprising me, not by his agreement with the Gunny, but because he knew what a stalking horse was. "We're a stalking horse to see if an operation can make it down here. If we hold out then they come in force and they have a victory that can go into Stars and Stripes. Probably why those film guys were here earlier. Background. Stock footage."

"We move without battalion," I said, the Gunny's response having just enough agreement built into it to allow me to proceed.

"What's the plan going to be called?" Zippo asked, in the short silence that followed.

"Run to Daylight," I said, off the top of my head, knowing I had assigned that name a few days ago. Vince Lombardi used to repeat himself.

I was from Green Bay and Vince Lombardi was the coach, and that had been one of his expressions. I didn't like the 'run' part of it but we would certainly be climbing up into daylight if we made it that far.

"Like in football," Zippo replied, his voice quiet, while he considered the merits of the plan's name, if not the plan itself.

The artillery barrages were finally over and everyone climbed out from under the Ontos. I noted quite a few of our Marines, who'd been dug in, up and wandering near their holes, as well. Such heavy munitions coming in for so long was deadening to the minds that survived, even when they were not the targets.

The Gunny came close, his cigarette still lit and dangling from his lips.

"I don't like it and I don't know why," he said, taking the cigarette from his mouth. "Somehow we made it without any real casualties so far. But what if they figure this new move because they can sure as hell see down the side of that hill?"

I watched his muddy face closely but could see no more animosity in his features.

"They didn't occupy the hill from the plateau that strings out behind it," I said, laying out the foundation of my plan with as much rationality as I could. "They would have come in hard from that plateau if they'd been there and our line of light machine guns strewn across the saddle of the ridge wouldn't have stopped them for long, either."

"What about the Ontos?" the Gunny said. "We can't just abandon it down here for them."

I hadn't thought about the Ontos, but I was too embarrassed to admit it, especially not in my weakened position with the Gunny. I tried to modify the plan in my mind to include splitting our forces, with one force making it up the old highway running next to the river while the other took to the high ground of the plateau, but I didn't get far in doing anything but think about the modification.

The whole hillside, supposedly beaten half to death by artillery fire, opened up, literally spraying our entire area with high-velocity small arms fire. An RPG exploded not twenty feet from the Ontos, tossing, even more, mud on the Marines standing around after the barrage. I had the headset on but didn't key the microphone. I didn't have time.

"Get Cowboy on the air and get the Skyraiders back as soon as you can," I said, tossing the headset to Fessman and plopping my helmet back on.

Our own artillery fire from Ripcord had been particularly accurate, although obviously ineffective at reaching inside the mountain and killing the NVA buried down in their deep tunnels. The slope was registered, and more fire would quell some of the incoming but I was worried about something more immediate and threatening.

I clambered out from under the armor, crawling quickly through the mud until I could stand. I slithered into the back of the machine, the heavy armored twin doors gaping open. The crew was under the machine not inside it. I screamed back toward the mud.

"I need the Ontos crew on station now," I yelled at the top of my voice, as I left mud everywhere in my attempts to get into the firing officer's metal chair.

The Ontos was pointing the wrong way. I hit the battery switches and slammed right track in reverse and left track forward nearly simultaneously. The turret began to whine and the Ontos turned 180 degrees.

It seemed to take forever, so I slid off the seat and peered out through the doors. Fear shot through me as my imagined possibility was being realized before my eyes. The hill was close to our position. Too close. There had been no way to establish a perimeter far enough from the beginning of the slope, to allow enough stand-off distance to react, or even for some of our weapons to properly arm. The NVA had figured that out even before me. Although the tributary feeding the Bong Song wasn't nearly as dangerous as the full river in flood, we were backed up to it and it could only be crossed safely by using either the Ontos, as we had in the prior crossing, or by laying ropes that were not yet laid.

We had no wire. We had only about a hundred meters of open mud between our defensive holes and the heavily forested bottom of the slope. It was across that area that they came, and the sight was a shock. I'd seen dead bodies, and an occasional single enemy or two, but never a mass of them, all dressed in black, all wearing the strange conical hats, and all running at us with wild abandon.

I jumped back to the seat and stopped the turret's movement. I breathed deeply, having no time to check the crew to see if they were standing by or whether the deadly area behind the barrels had been cleared. I thought we'd loaded all six barrels with flechettes. I didn't even know what standoff distance the rounds required before exploding, but I hoped and prayed it wasn't much. I knew the 106 barrels had to be numbered or identified in some fashion, but I didn't know the codes or the system of fire.

"Fire the one-oh-six, one on each side," I screamed down through the open doors. I knew the doors should be closed in case of a closer rocket strike or ricocheting bullets but I didn't know how to use the intercom. Yelling was my only way of communicating. I had no other plan to stop the attack. If the NVA over-ran our position with infantry then I wouldn't need another plan, but that fleeting thought was blown from my brain when two of the 106 rounds launched together. With the doors open, and barrels so close, the sound of the explosions immediately deafened me. My world reduced down to the gun sight my right eye was plastered to.

I didn't see the rounds go off, all I saw was four large groups of men go down as if their legs had been sliced off at mid-thigh. I hit the turret button, guiding the movement by what I could see instead of any of the instruments spread out on what resembled a small boat's helm in front of me at lap level. I could not take my eye off the scene. I stopped the turret's movement when the crosshairs lay just above another clump of the enemy. Somewhere in my mind, a tiny voice whispered that the NVA troops had a hard time staying properly spread apart in combat situations, just like my Marines.

"Fire the one-oh-six, one on each side," I screamed downward again, this time with more confidence that the rounds would actually be launched, but with less confidence that my voice was actually being heard. I could barely hear myself, which meant that the Marines outside the Ontos had to be having problems too.

I hit the turret button again and let the slow-moving mass of metal move back across the scene until I found more black-clad bodies. This time they were not running at my sight. They were running back toward the mountain for their lives.

"Fire the one-oh-six," I yelled, knowing that the crew knew what it was doing. "Reload," I added, wondering if that was a necessary command to a crew facing charging infantry in the open.

Two more rounds went off and I knew it because the running figures dropped away from my eyes. It was like magic. A brilliantly conceived killing magic. I slid off the seat and moved to the back of the machine. The Gunny rose up from where he'd stayed for the attack, Tank, his radio operator next to him. I heard thrumming engines I knew so well buzzing in the far distance. Cowboy was coming. The Corporal had gotten through.

"Never seen that before, "the Gunny said, softly, getting another cigarette out of his chest pocket. "It's like they don't die. They're just gone."

He looked up at me and then smiled, as he let out a deep inhalation of smoke. "Now that was some mighty fine shooting, Junior," he said.

The other Marines comprising the two companies were once again starting to gather, and every one of them nearby smiled back at the Gunny, including me. The Gunny was back. I would not have to go it alone. But I needed a new plan because I wasn't about to give up possession of the Ontos after what I'd seen and made happen using it.

ninety-nine

THE TWENTIETH DAY : THIRD PART

There were fifty bodies, and right away everyone in the joined companies knew that the enemy soldiers were not NVA troops, or really soldiers at all. The uniforms were wrong and the ages were wrong. The bodies were of very young men and women dressed in peasant attire, carrying AK-47s with mostly empty magazines. Their bodies all looked the same, like nothing had touched them. The only thing out of place was the tiny little x marks all over every inch of them. The 'x' marks had no blood. There were no entry and exit wounds from the flechettes, like would have been normal to witness from almost any bullet passing entirely through any human body. But the flechettes weren't traveling at bullet speed when they struck the peasant's bodies. They'd been traveling about ten times faster. Twenty-two thousand feet per second instead of around twenty-two hundred. Hundreds of nearly microscopic darts had gone through each body, regardless of uniform, clothing or bone.

"They took the farmers and made them charge us," the Gunny said, examining the bloodless penetrated corpses as closely as everyone else.

"Why?" I asked, kneeling at the Gunny's side, no longer curious about the damage the Ontos had wrought but instead beginning to worry about the odd move on the part of the NVA.

"In preparation?" the Gunny asked back.

"I know," I responded, "but preparation for what and when?"

The Gunny didn't answer. I got up and made my way back to the Ontos. Whatever we did we had to do it quickly. No matter what the NVA were planning it was evident that they were planning something. They'd just tossed a hundred human beings at us as if they were worth nothing, which to them they must have been.

I pushed my back against the front of the Ontos slanted armor plate and stared up at the front face of Hill 975. The side of the mountain to the east, where I'd considered scaling the rip-rap to reach the highlands before heading north was no longer a consideration. The NVA surveillance from their tunneled in mountainside positions was too pervasive to risk having all my Marines exposed, first in single file getting to the rocks and then more exposed making the climb up. We were going to have to go around Hill 975, as planned, but we were going to have to use the riverbank and the hard-crusted dirt road called Highway 548. The maps showed the road as passable all the way to the DMZ. Resupply would have been easier once we reached the highlands but we would have to make do with the Highway 548 plan as best we could.

The Ontos had 15 rounds of flechette ammo and five of high explosives. How far could the companies get with artillery support and the Skyraiders until we reached some secure position to be resupplied could not be calculated. The A-Shau Valley was twenty-five miles long and we'd come only about six miles north since dropping down from the mountains separating the valley from Ga Noi Island. The valley would not climb out of the lower elevations for about ten more miles, in checking out the contour intervals on the maps I had. In truth, my maps didn't go far enough to reach the DMZ itself. I'd need more at the next resupply.

The choice to move in toward the river and move north between the rushing water and the old damaged highway wasn't a difficult one. It had some of the same downsides of heading north the other way, with the exception that we wouldn't be moving up a dead-end valley with a difficult climb into an unknown fire at the end of it. The surveillance by the enemy forces drilled and tunneled into the very body of the mountain outthrust of Hill 975 would be the same, however. There could be no surprise move on our part, not in the daytime, and not in the night with the Ontos growling its way up what was left of the old highway.

The idea of building another likely-to-fail firebase down in the very bottom creases of the valley had been abandoned by the command in the rear, but the fact that Hill 975 had not been taken and held would not go down well, if at all. We were heading north for no good reason I could figure out and I knew neither the Gunny nor anybody else had a good idea either. For the time being, moving anywhere but where we were made sense, and the north flatter terrain and area of operations would allow for full use of the whole arsenal of artillery supporting fires.

The Gunny came running across the open, followed by Sugar Daddy, Jurgens, and Obrien. When they went down into the mud it was almost impossible to tell what or who they were, other than higher lumps than other lumps nearby. The rain returned in earnest, pummeling down on my helmet. It wasn't entirely unwelcome, except for the fact that it was too warm. The mild rinsing effect it had made a dent in the mess we'd all become, although nothing was going to clean us off entirely without some sort of full immersion.

"What's the butcher's bill?" I asked the Gunny, pulling back as far as I could under the raised front edge of the Ontos' armor.

"Can this shit get any worse?" Jurgens asked, to no one in particular.

As if he'd hit a switch the drums began beating again. They were louder than they'd ever been before and caused every Marine in our combined unit to go silent and listen. The beat was strangely attractive but it came with a message of deep fear. I now knew that the NVA only used the drums when they thought they had us in a weakened position. They were doing what the professional football teams did when a field goal kicker was about to make his effort. They were icing us. Which also meant that they were getting prepared to hit us again, although, with the losses they'd taken from the flechettes, civilian as those losses were, they'd probably wait until after dark to set up some bases of fire before attacking under their protection.

"We didn't lose anybody, amazingly enough," the Gunny replied to my question, "But they sure as hell took it in the ass."

"I still don't understand why they used the villagers?" I asked, the feeling of helpless sorrow almost overcoming the winding fear the drums recreated and send coursing up and down the insides of my torso.

"So you'd feel the way you feel," the Gunny replied instantly. "The way you look. The way we all look. And maybe they wanted to see what we had and quite possibly to get us to spend our inventory because we aren't getting any more supplies until we get out of this hell hole."

I looked down at hundreds of small leeches, their thin bodies searching upward in waving curves from the mud. I realized that the leeches were fighting for space, air, and to survive. They were a lot like us.

I laid out my plan to move the Ontos up the highway with the rest of us accompanying the machine, covering the miles north move by using the brush and light jungle terrain between the road and the bank of the river. The 175s could safely fire over our heads to cover the rear, at least once we were a couple of clicks north of where we were now. Artillery from both Army firebases would be able to reach out and hit the highlands on either side of the valley, and Cunningham could even adjust fire up and down the eastern face. Hill 975's entire length could be kept under near-constant fire while we passed by while Cowboy, and whatever other Skyraiders he could gather together, could orbit and drop down from above. The only real safety we would have, however, was in moving. Staying where we were would lead to our eventual annihilation.

00:00

00:00

The drums were horrid, the sounds seemed to come through the rain in waves, and the malevolence in their constant beating was impossible not to feel and concentrate on. We needed to get away from the drums as badly as we needed to leave the area for tactical reasons, and we needed to do it immediately.

"What position do we need to arrive at up north and when?" I asked the Gunny, still feeling a strangeness in the asking. I knew that feeling was never going to leave me as long as battalion command chose to ignore me as the only officer commander it had in the unit. Command still called to talk to Gunny on the combat net, as if he was the six-actual and not me.

"Just a grid coordinate that will become an LZ when we get there. The 1st Air Cavalry is going to be flown in to spearhead an operation heading back down here into the southern part of the valley to clear it out once and for all."

Jurgens started to laugh and was quickly joined by Obrien and Sugar Daddy, with the ancillary radio operators and my own scout team joining in.

That they could laugh at all with the drum beats rolling over us like shifting clouds of doom, surprised me and I wondered if I was anywhere near as tough as any of the Marines who'd managed to survive to be where and when we were.

The Gunny and I looked at one another, neither of us even cracking a smile. The rear area, whether of Army or Marine Command, just could not accommodate that fact that the A Shau was riven with tunnels, split by a ferociously powerful and deep river and populated by a supplied NVA force that most likely was as large as the entire allied military structure available to I Corps in the northern part of the country. Even if the Army division brought in all of its men it wouldn't be enough, and it wouldn't bring in all of its troops. The Gunny wasn't laughing because he knew what I knew. A lot more Marines were going to die in such an operation, although they wouldn't die alone because they'd have plenty of Army company.

"Give me the grid position where we're headed," I said.

The Gunny read off the numbers he'd somehow, even with the heavy rain and miserable humidity, written down on his palm and managed to keep legible.

I memorized the number, knowing the map of our area so well that I had a good idea of where we were headed. From the way the photo/contour map was displayed when I had it out earlier, I knew that we'd likely be gathering together on a flat and level plain pretty far from the river. A great field of fire for the enemy but also well chosen for being dead center at close range for at least four allied artillery firebases, if not more when I included the 155s and eight-inch guns bunkered in closer to the DMZ. I knew that, at least if the Army was involved, then resupply was going to be heavy and qualitative. We needed 106 ammo and Claymores if we were coming back south again.

"I'll take a couple of minutes to lay out our defensive fires," I said, without further comment on or preamble to my plan. "I'll call in Cowboy and then start to soften the east side of this hill for our departure. We should be able to depart in twenty minutes with Sugar Daddy's platoon walking point, with the Ontos taking the lead."

"No fucking way," Sugar Daddy said, even before I finished my last sentence.

The syncopation of his words was somehow linked to the drums. The 'no,' followed by a drumbeat, and then 'fucking,' another drumbeat, and then the final word.

I didn't have to move my right hand. I'd kept it on the handle of Tex's .45 automatically. I kept the cover of his closed-style holster folded open unless I thought I might go swimming again. I wondered briefly what it would be like to serve in a stateside Marine unit and not think about shooting any of my own men as a response to either threats, denials or other rotten conduct.

I realized that there was nothing to be said that might lead away from a violent confrontation that could only compromise the plan. We had to get out of where we were and we had to do it quickly, not be mired down in some sort of intra-company firefight. Instead of saying anything, I slowly got out from under the Ontos and stood in the full press of the heated rain. The thousands of drops striking my helmet acted like a melody to the dull hateful lyrics of the enemy's death song.

Fessman, Zippo, and Nguyen moved with me, as I walked toward the back of the armored vehicle. I glanced behind and noticed that Nguyen was walking backward, and I realized at that point that the Montagnard's trust in Sugar Daddy was even lower than my own.

I called in the zone fire I thought we'd need to the front of our moving position and also the 175s to chew up the rear. That left only the problem of the jungle-covered side of Hill 975 and the wall of the plateau that extended miles back from it. Cowboy would arrive in an hour with his wingman for additional support. Before we moved I wanted 105s and 155s to churn the side of that hill to a mess of chewed vegetation and crushed tunnel entrances. Nothing could reach down deep enough into the mud and rock to destroy the body of subterranean chambers and paths the Vietnamese had dug down there over generations of occupation and fighting, but if the NVA couldn't use the entrances and exits until they did more digging then we'd be gone by the time they came out. Nobody was going to live if trying to remain above ground protected only by the dense, but by no means impenetrable, ground cover.

The Gunny came around the back of the Ontos and stood next to the three of us. I handed the AN/323 air radio headset back to Fessman.

"Sugar Daddy has a point," the Gunny began, taking half a minute to light a cigarette before he went. "There are only two ways to go. The NVA know we can't stay here so we have to move north. South is a dead-end street. We won't be going up the cliff, and they probably know it. That leaves the highway, and the Ontos and all of that."

I watched the Gunny masterfully keep his cigarette burning in spite of the mildly blowing wind and rain. I also noticed that the more it rained the more I could begin to make out facial features as the mud from our slide down the mountain continued to wash off.

"So, what's your point?" I asked, taking a puff from the cigarette the Gunny held out like an olive branch.

He was in a bad position and I knew it because I'd left him in it. My reputation as 'Junior, the miracle artillery and map reading expert' didn't extend to allowing me the full leadership of the outfit. Sugar Daddy knew it and used it or the Gunny wouldn't be sharing a cigarette with me and trying to come to some accommodation that would satisfy Sugar Daddy and his Marines.

"Kilo's with us and has almost three full platoons," the Gunny said softly, before looking away.

He waited, using the time to accept his cigarette back and snap the remains off toward where the river still ran so strongly. Even the beating of the awful drums could not overpower the sound of that deep rushing water.

"Can't work," I said. "Sugar Daddy and his guys have endangered the company twice if not more times than I know. I'm not personally concerned about this disobeying orders or even the cowardice of abandoning posts under fire. We're the United States Marine Corps and we have only that to get us through. We get artillery, supplies, air power and even the Ontos because we are that. We're not throwing Kilo into the charnel house. They don't have a clue. We're going to act like Marines this time, and Marines fight when they have to, not when they want to. Sugar Daddy takes the point or I'm calling in the first 105s on his unit over there by the river. You want that grid number because the battery has no idea we're this close to the slope of the hill?"

The Gunny stood and stared at me through the falling rain, his expression more dead-flat expressionless American Indian rather than whatever extraction he was a combination of.

"They know where we are," the Gunny, replied his voice low. "They won't fire that close, knowing where we are."

"Fine," I replied, getting ready to pull my pack down from the rear of the Ontos and prepare for departure.

The Gunny was right. I was bluffing. The batteries knew exactly where we were, if not from my own registration, then from monitoring the air support frequency.

"Give Sugar Daddy and his platoon the tail end Charlie position. They should be safe there, and the batteries will never really know where their exact position is, once we get moving."

"We need that platoon," the Gunny shot back, shaking his head.

"As you said, we now have Kilo, and they don't seem to have the racial mess we're dealing with, at least not after we allowed eight more blacks to come under Sugar Daddy's control."

We'd made no attempt to guard our conversation against the Marines around us. The Ontos team was under the belly of the armored beast, but they could hear everything, even over the sounds of the river and drums. My scout team was right beside us. I'd not taken the Gunny aside on purpose. Sugar Daddy needed to know what I might be planning, not that I was caring as much as I might have at one time. Was my threat a bluff? I wasn't sure myself, although mentally I had already begun to calculate just where the optimal beaten zone might be set up to excise the racial problem once and for all.

The Gunny walked away and I turned my back. Zippo helped me with the straps on my pack.

"They ain't all bad, sir," he whispered into my left ear, as he worked.

"Who?" I replied, knowing exactly what he was talking about but not ready to recant on my announced decision.

Zippo didn't answer. He continued to help me adjust the heavy pack.

"It's not about that," I said with a sigh, not expecting Zippo, even though he'd come out of Sugar Daddy's platoon at his own request, to understand at all.

"It's about leadership, isn't it, sir?" he replied, surprising me.

He was right, but in a different way than I thought about the problem.

"Inside the wire, Zippo," I said, thinking about the complexity of the mess the entire unit was in. "Those inside the wire are friendlies. Those inside the wire maximize the survival of all those around them. Outside the wire is the enemy, no matter what uniform they wear or what they say."

"So, if they won't do what you tell them to do they're outside the wire?" Zippo asked.

"You missed that part about maximizing survival," I said, after taking a few seconds to try to put the words in a form he could understand. "If they won't fight they then threaten everyone else. It's their choice. I call supporting fires on the enemy, whomever that enemy might be. Everyone doesn't have a choice here. I didn't' make it that way, the Marine Corps did."

The Gunny came back down through the small rivulets of water that had begun to form and run in every direction through the mud around us.

"The Ontos needs to fire up and get to the point. Sugar Daddy's platoon is going to lead us past the worst part and then be relieved once we're clear. They want to form up behind the Ontos and have it loaded with those flechettes."

The Ontos started before the Gunny was done speaking. The driver had been listening to everything.

I looked at the Gunny, but he wouldn't meet my eyes. A compromise had swiftly been worked out behind my back. The company had run on compromise too many times in the past, I felt, but the drums, the river, the mud, the hula dancing leeches near my feet, all beat me down. Once again, Sugar Daddy had been warned and once again, I knew in my fear-shivering bones that he would try to take me out at the earliest opportunity. After my threat, and the Gunny's compromise, I couldn't exactly drop artillery in on his platoon without losing the rest of the company in the process or even having them kill me in retaliation. Sugar Daddy wouldn't be so open or constrained.

"Wait for Cowboy, before we pull out," I said to the Gunny. "The first artillery should be impacting at about the same time. Cunningham and Ripcord are both firing for suppression, so the planes will be coming up from the south to stay off the gun target line."

I hunkered down next to the idling Ontos. It would only take the beast about five minutes to get to the point and start the move up the valley. The driver stuck his head out of the hole in the armor plate. I nodded at him, thankful that someone in the unit, other than my scout team, was accepting direction. The Ontos surged forward, spitting mud out the sides of its tracks, as well as behind them. More mud covered me. I wiped what I could away, more to make sure I hadn't collected any leeches because I wasn't going to get any cleaner. I'd been clean all my life and hadn't really known or understood that it was part of this life. Being abysmally filthy all the time wasn't something I knew I was ever going to get used to no matter how long I lasted in Vietnam.

I moved toward the river with my scout team. Zippo and Nguyen kept their distance, as I'd taught them. One grenade was not going to get all of us, or one booby trap unless it was really huge. Jurgens appeared out of a bamboo thicket near the rapidly passing current.

"We've got your back, Junior," he said, with a big smile.

"I don't need your protection," I shot back, still angry with the compromise and the seemingly dense and stupid men who had caused it.

"I meant that we're covering the rear for the move, sir," Jurgens corrected, his smile wiped from his face.

I almost rocked back in shock. Jurgens hadn't meant what I thought he'd meant and he'd called me sir.

"Ah, thanks, got it, move out," I replied, shaken by how badly I'd misunderstood him and also how much of a mess the race thing might continue to grow to be.

I was being made to think in terms of black and white Marines and I didn't want to go there. We were dying. Our losses could not be sustained and allow any of us to survive even a fraction of whatever time the rear area command intended for us to be in the field, yet old and stupid prejudice permeated the unit from one end to the other.

I moved forward as quickly as I could. The Skyraiders approaching thrum behind us radiated up the valley, overpowering the drums, the river and the constant beating of the rain. I had to get far enough upriver to adjust the first artillery rounds. The Ontos was ahead on the highway, but too far up it to be heard. The Ontos was the company's key to close in survival. None of the firebases would fire within two hundred meters of the highway, no matter what I called in. The officers in those batteries had their own careers to guard, and dropping friendly artillery on Marines in combat was a quick road to a court-martial and even prison time if it could be determined that they violated the rules of engagement. The batteries accepted my lies about our fictional positions because that data could be used to defend them if things went wrong. There was nothing to defend me, however.

The first artillery rounds came in, just as the Skyraiders hit the jungle with their twenty-millimeter cannons. The artillery rounds didn't need adjusting. Cunningham and Ripcord knew exactly where Hill 975 was and understood that we were moving up the highway. The Skyraiders were always a relief to have on hand. They swooped away after making one run and disappeared up through the low hanging clouds. I had no idea how the pilots could see through their canopies, with the rain being fairly heavy and the light so limited.

Our first casualties didn't come from the jungle or an ambush up near the point. It took a couple of minutes, once the sporadic firing began, to pin down what had happened. The western wall of the valley, the one that rose up high above the swirling river that ran right up against its stone face had been left out of my calculations. The NVA had put snipers up on top of the wall. There was no place for us to go. From sniper positions up on the wall, there was no cover. The snipers didn't have to be that good since they could simply load and fire as endlessly as they pleased.

I'd gone down deep into the riverbank mud at the sound of the first shots. I knew where the drums were. The snipers were firing from whatever position they'd selected on the far wall to locate the drums for maximum effect. The snipers were succeeding where the drums had not. I knew Marines were being hit from the screams upriver.

I reached out and Fessman filled my hand with the artillery net microphone.

"Call Cowboy and get them on it," I said, as calmly as I could.

I took no time to re-orient myself using the map in my pocket or my compass. I knew where the last rounds had come in up the opposite side wall of jungle cover. I called in a spotting adjustment in white phosphorus instead of a new fire mission to Ripcord. I asked for 'right two thousand,' hoping the explosion would be close to the top edge of the opposing wall and the blooming phosphorus visible from where I was.

The round impacted the side of the cliff, about three hundred meters up. It hit the wall so low that phosphorus bits and pieces cascaded down and across the river.

There were more screams. But there were no more sniper shots coming from the top of the wall.

I didn't see the next round when it went off somewhere back from the upper edge of the cliff, but I heard it. The Skyraiders strafed the top of the cliff in the same area, but they were gone in seconds. I called in for a battery of six and waited. The rounds came in, and there was no missing their impact. Thirty-six rounds of forty pounds each. Some outer explosions were visible from my position, and I knew the remainder were impacting in a circular pattern approximately two hundred yards from the edge. It was all I needed. I adjusted fire up and down along the top of the wall, knowing that we'd probably take more casualties from the stone and rock that had to be flung outward by some of the impacts.

Cunningham was still firing on the jungle side of the wall. I heard the roar of the Ontos as it built up to top speed. Everyone was moving. There could be no slowing or stopping again. We had to get out of the beaten zone we'd somehow gotten ourselves into. Sugar Daddy's platoon had taken casualties, I was almost sure. I didn't know about any of the other platoons, although there were plenty of Marines running and walking while carrying the corner of a poncho cover.

"Steeped in blood," I whispered to myself, handing the microphone back to the Corporal.

"Sir?" Fessman replied.

"Steeped in blood," I repeated. "I never named the plan. That would have been an accurate one, and we have a long way to go."

"I don't think that would have been a good idea, sir," Fessmanr said, "and don't say that out loud, anymore."

one-hundred

THE TWENTIETH NIGHT : FIRST PART

The mess of stationery I carried was a collection of soggy, semi-wet and dried water stains holding strands of paper together. The envelopes were in the best shape because I'd rolled them into a tight tube and used one of my extra trouser springs to hold them together. I released the spring and carefully pulled out an envelope in the very center, unfolding it as I went while making sure the pack of stationery and envelopes stayed guarded under the tipped-up edge of my tilted helmet. I was under my poncho cover, and the wet mud of the river-bank wasn't really all that wet, but still, I fought to maintain as much moisture security as I could cage together. The sun had fallen behind and above the clouds that poured drizzling rain down into the heart of the valley where the company, and what was left of Kilo, had gone down following the debacle of taking out the cliff top snipers. Blowing the drums along with them had been a great positive bonus.

It wasn't quiet by any means but at least the night would not be owned by the NVA.

I smoothed out a whitish-blue sheet of the only stationary I could get from resupply. I tried to ignore the envelope that was unfurling itself next to the sheet of paper, but I could not. There were two printings on the left face of the blue-shaded envelope. The first was in the upper left corner, making it difficult to put a proper return address in that traditional area. The printed symbol was in gold and white with little black lines. It was the Marine Corps globe and anchor. Below that was the worst part, a half-envelope-wide and two-thirds-envelope-high rendering of the American flag being raised up over Mount Suribachi on Iwo Jima. The two symbols together illustrated everything that was wonderful about the Marine Corps and being a Marine, and especially being a Marine Officer. The images wouldn't let me write to my wife. I wanted to throw up, instead.

I leaned closer to the envelope and picked up my cheap U.S. government pen. I clicked the little tab on top and exposed the tip through the small hole at the other end, conscious of each tiny move the pen and

I made together. My right hand moved slowly across the paper and over to the envelope. Very intently, right next to the globe and anchor symbol, and very close to the very corner, I wrote two numbers. They were both twos. Twenty-two. Twenty-two Marines had died, a dozen from falling rocks blown outward from the face of the cliff by my short round and then ten more burned to death from the inside out by chunks and pieces of white phosphorus when the ranging round I'd called to correct came in too short and exploded too low. I'd gotten the adjustment location wrong and the battery had followed up by getting the elevation from the bottom of the valley up to the altitude of the round going off. I would never tell anyone back home about what the two numbers signified. Never. My wife would never guess or know either.

I thought my emotions were gone but suddenly they were not. My eyes filled, forcing me to look around intently. It was still light enough to see me, although only my scout team was nearby. Fessman messed with the Prick 25, constantly rubbing and cleaning it, using the rain as his solvent. Zippo sharpened his K-Bar knife with a piece of stone taken from the river. He said the stone was some sort of special Indian sharpening stone but nobody believed him. Nguyen sat in his usual bent-knee crouch, staring out toward the area of the river but not really. I knew he was watching me. I knew in my heart of hearts that all three were making believe they weren't watching me. The Gunny had told me many days before that if I could not act like the commander then I should at least look like the commander.

I pushed my poncho cover back over my shoulders, making my writing space almost too dark to see anything. It was wet and raining outside of my small little-protected cleft. The tears came. I'd held them back like a drunk trying to find a place to vomit but unable to until, at last, it didn't matter. I'd killed twenty-two of my own men in seconds, some in the most awful way possible. I'd been fifty meters off. I'd been fifty meters off twice in a row. It was unforgivable.

I didn't make any noise or show any sign that I was crying like a baby, and I was proud of what was left of my self-respect for that discipline.

I could still see the Marine Corps symbols in the poor light. They were right there in front of my face, but I knew down to my core, to the depth of my soul that I was not a real Marine. Real Marines didn't cry. Real Marines did not kill their own men, much less so many of them that he could not keep count. Real Marines sucked it up and moved on.

Adapt and survive. Fire and maneuver. Any decision is better than no decision.

The men at the flag raising could not see me, even if they came alive. Not one face in the flag raising photo reproduction was turned in my direction. They stared straight ahead, at the pole they were fighting upward. Intent. Mission-oriented. Real Marines.

I had to write. Later in the night, we'd reach a position further up the valley. We'd stopped far enough from the jungle outgrowth of the east wall, as the canyon wall had grown ever lower in elevation. We were far enough to escape ambush or attack from that direction. Close enough to allow us to gather our dead and wounded and prepare for a move that would now allow us to get medevac choppers in to pull them all out. We'd suffered the worst losses since I'd been with the company and the casualties were all my very own.

I wanted to write letters home to all the survivors, but how could I write twenty-two letters and how many on top of that for the badly wounded. The Gunny had come to get what little morphine I had left, but not to end any Marine's misery by taking him out, but instead just to ease the burns of those still living. The Gunny had said that the sound of the wounded crying and whimpering was worse for the men than the drums. He also wouldn't let me go forward to view the havoc I had let loose.

"It wasn't you," he whispered. "It's just what happens in this kind of shit. The men understand, better than you think. Don't quit on me. You've lived longer than any company grade officer we've had and God Himself can't call better-supporting fire than you."

I hadn't cried in front of the Gunny. The cigarette and matches he'd left me lay across the top of the sheet of stationary I was trying to write on. The cigarette was a Pall Mall, I saw, reading the elegant tall black printing on the white of its tobacco tube. It still had the long filter still on it. The Gunny always pinched the filter off but had either neglected to do so or maybe thought I'd be more likely to find some solace in the gesture if he left it on. The Gunny was too inscrutable to figure out which it was.

I lit the cigarette with shaking fingers. My shakes were back although I wasn't in terror this time. I smoked the cigarette, breathing in and out deeply until the area under my poncho cover became fully dark from the dense smoke. My eyes hurt but they stopped dripping tears. Maybe the Gunny's wisdom extended to fixing crying officers, as well.

I crushed out the cigarette halfway through. Whatever value I was expected to receive had already been imparted. I checked the matches and wondered how the Gunny could keep them so dry in the awful hot and wet conditions they were living in.

I picked up the pen again and started to write. I wrote about my world, but not the reality of that world:

"My world is a shrunken husk of a thing, all green, wet and filled with teeming amounts of animals and plants I've never seen or even heard of. I eat my C-rations and nothing else. I drink water from re-supply containers or that which frequently flows down off my poncho cover. My Marines are my humans, with the enemy being either almost unseen or dead. My Marines are grunts who scorn everything and everybody. My sense of smell is gone. My clothes are a tattered collection of dirty dish rags and the aroma from it must be awful, but none of us notice. My wallet has fallen apart, as have all my pictures from home. Only laminated stuff survives for very long. I only carry two weapons. My .45 I got from one of the other officers and two M-33 grenades I keep in my pack so the pins won't come out accidentally. I have my scout team of about fifteen Marines who guard me all the time so I am pretty safe except at night. Nights are hard, especially in the rain because you can't hear anything. Can't see and can't hear, like when we are in contact. All flashes and darkness, with more flashes. I wonder if my hearing will ever be as good as it was before I came here. I never thought about how loud it could all get but I should have known with Dad being on the pistol team, and all. A kid named Fessman is my radio operator and he does everything for me that I need to be done."

I reread my work. It was legible, and I'd said nothing that might worry her. My scout team was a mere whisper of what I'd written but she couldn't know that.

I thought about crossing out Fessman's name but then realized I was falling into the superstition trap so many of my Marines lived in. Mentioning another Marine's name was supposed to mean that that Marine would soon die. The government pen wasn't erasable, or I might have taken him out just as an afterthought, but I didn't. Maybe, one day, if I made it home with any kind of decent health I'd be reading the letter with Fessman's name in it and laughing. Hopefully, with him.

I examined the envelope closely. It wasn't the normal 'Marines raising the flag on Iwo' thing. Instead, it had a small map near the left edge. The countries of North and South Vietnam were inset in white against the blue window under a place for my return address. I wondered how my return address could be "F.P.O. San Francisco" when I was so far away. I checked out the tiny map and realized it was the only map of the whole country I had or had seen since landing at Da Nang so long ago. The A Shau wasn't on the map but I knew it was located just a bit east of the Laos border and down from the DMZ, which was printed there with two dotted lines close together. The map told me that I was directly inland from Phu Bai, a place I'd heard of, but knew nothing about. I sealed my wife's letter into the sticky envelope and put it into my thigh pocket, noting the fact that my morphine supply was gone. I wondered if I'd be resupplied with syrettes later on. I hoped that wouldn't happen but I was past feeling the kind of dull regret I'd had the first times I had to use it.

I pulled out my artillery one to twenty-five thousand and oriented it easily because the direction of the valley extended almost exactly from the north down to the south. I checked the contour intervals, as the valley wall to my east lowered to the north. A faint idea came into my head. I looked at the envelope again and then back at my 'real' map.

"Barnyard chickens," I whispered to myself, "we have to eat so the chickens have to die."

I knew the analogy was idiotic but, in a strange way, it made sense. I was not in control, other than to very marginally try to steer my way through the nightmare without end as best I could. That I might become attached to the chickens under my farm care made sense, just as it made sense when they had to be killed and put into a soup pot. It was just the way it was.

Sugar Daddy appeared before me, his dark face, muddy utilities and purple glasses making him all but invisible. His bulk had been the giveaway that it was him.

"You saved our ass," he said, his voice low before I could react to his presence in any way. "You had to know. You always fucking know. That's why you're Junior. That's why you didn't put a name on the plan. We owe you."

And then he was gone, retreating backward in near silence, back into the looming stygian darkness of the wet darkness, only the rivers slushing current and ever-present mud letting me know exactly where I was. I lay with my head up, my helmet blocking the rain, its drops coming down so soft they didn't even patter against my helmet cover. I tried to take in the meaning of what Sugar Daddy had said. Somehow, his

unit on the point had passed far enough beyond the beaten zone where
the rocks and white phosphorus had come down to escape casualties.
And somehow, Sugar Daddy and his Marines had it in their heads that
I'd planned the whole thing that way. I breathed in and out, wanting one
of the Gunny's cigarettes, although I knew in working with the casualties we had taken he'd be smoking everything he had. Another thought
occurred to me. If Sugar Daddy thought I'd save him and his men then
what must the others think?

I got to my hands and knees and moved to where Fessman sat
huddled under his own poncho cover.

"The Army has to extract the bodies up on 975," I said. "Call
it in. We can't help them but with a significant force of gunships they
shouldn't have too much of a problem."

"What about our own," the Corporal asked, not reaching for the
radio handset.

"Some of our own are up on that mountain," I reminded him.
"We're going to have to carry our own down here but the terrain is going to flatten, as we head to the north, and then to the east."

"We're not going north or east," the Gunny said, from behind
me. "The 9th Marines out of Phu Bai are coming down the valley to
clear the area. They'll take 975 and everything else up here. We're headed back down to secure the flank."

The Gunny pushed a cigarette through the soggy air at me. I took
it, inhaled once and then passed it back, my mind a jumbled mess of
confused thoughts. I realized my thoughts had little to do with my Marines. I was frightened again, down to my core, and it seemed only my
own men could induce that kind of deep shaking terror that ran from
the bottoms of my wet boots all the way up to the top of my head. What
we had to do was move. Timing was everything if I was somehow to
avoid Jurgens or anyone else from easing through the density of darkness to pay me back for whatever I was found to be at fault for.

"Back down where to secure what flank?" I asked, suddenly giving full import to what the gunny had said. "We can't go back down
there," I continued when he didn't respond, my voice beginning to rise.
"They're waiting for us back down there, and what of our wounded and
the dead?"

"Those are the orders," the Gunny replied, his voice dropping
almost to a whisper.

"Where's Tank?" I asked, noting that the Gunny's radioman

wasn't present.

"He got hit," the Gunny said, squatting down. "We've got nineteen injured, twenty-two dead and the twenty-four still left up on 975."

I motioned for Fessman for the radio, not wanting to ask the Gunny if Tank was among the wounded or the dead. I knew there would be no move to save me, night or otherwise. Once again, we could not go forward and we could not go back, not and have any chance of survival at all. My own situation with the men was suddenly in a distant second place. If we marched through the night back down the river then we were dead men walking or dead men upon arrival back near the old airfield.

I had Fessman switch the Prick 25 to the command net and contacted battalion. It took almost ten minutes for the six-actual to come on the line. I hadn't spoken to the colonel in many days, as his preference for dealing with the Gunny personally was self-evident.

"Sir, we're not moving north or south from our current position," I reported; we've got sixty-five casualties, forty-six being KIA, and need resupply and medevac in force at dawn before we can do anything."

I let go of the transmit button, wondering if sixty-five casualties in such a short period of time was a lot of where we were in the war.

"What are the enemy numbers?" the colonel asked back, without any delay.

I thought for a moment, looking at the Gunny, who could only shake his head and shrug. "A hundred and twenty-one KIA," I said, approximating the civilian farmers the NVA had sent against the Ontos. A brief moment of silence ensued while I wondered whether they'd buy the numbers as I'd sent them.

"My orders were pretty clear, Junior, in spite of those numbers," the colonel replied briskly. "Leave your casualties with a rear element and get back down the valley, as ordered. I'll send choppers at dawn. You can leave the Army gear with the holding force."

I held the handset out away from my body like I was gripping the head of a poisonous snake. I looked over at the Gunny. The 'Army gear' was the Ontos, the only piece of equipment we could not afford to give up. If a hold at all cost defense was coupled with Zippo's use of the Starlight Scope, the Ontos and artillery the colonel's order almost sounded reasonable.

"I'll stay with the wounded and then come down the river once the choppers are gone at dawn," the Gunny said, taking out a cigarette and lighting it. He cupped one hand over it to guard it against the rain. Then he handed his special lighter to me.

"Hang onto that for luck until I make it back down."

I clutched the lighter. I knew he wasn't giving it to me for luck. There was no way a small security element could guard the dead and wounded. The Gunny didn't think he'd be coming back. The wounded were bad off, unable to remain silent from the phosphorus burns. I knew I was far from them but their sounds still came through the soggy air and rain, accompanied by the ever-present sound of the river's rushing waters. It was like their sounds of agony were being deliberately delivered by the river. The smallest units of NVA in the area would make short work out of any unreinforced force, particularly one not covered with supporting fires. There was no air support at night. That meant artillery fire, no matter how many casualties we'd taken earlier. And I was the only artillery our company had, and the only one able to handle the Starlight Scope to take advantage of the Ontos.

"Remember what we did at the cliff face before?" I asked, pushing the lighter back at him. "You're not staying out here alone with anyone. We're moving to the eastern wall through this mess and digging in. I can carpet the bottom of the valley along here with fire from both Rip Cord and Cunningham. I'll send cascades of 175 rounds down the valley to put a cork in that. All night long.

Cowboy will be back in the morning. We can decide what to do when the day comes.

"What about battalion?" the Gunny asked. "And last time digging into the cliff only served us for a very short time."

"Fuck battalion, and we've only got to worry about a very short time," I replied, accepting the cigarette and taking a deep inhalation before exhaling to talk on the radio again.

"Colonel, we're not moving," I said into the microphone, making the words distinct and saying them slowly. "We're digging in and waiting for resupply and medivac choppers in the morning, or whenever they arrive."

I waited, as seconds marched by, finally motioning for Fessman to switch on the Prick 25's small external speaker.

"You'll obey orders Junior or I'll have your ass relieved on the spot," the colonel shouted, his bellicose tone converted to a mechanical whine by the inadequate speaker.

"Well, yes sir," I shouted back into the handset, unable to keep from smiling coldly when I said the words.

"So, you will proceed south as ordered?" the colonel came back, his voice returning to a more normal level.

"No, sir. I'm ready to stand relieved, sir."

"Put the Gunny on," the colonel said, after a short pause, his voice beginning to rise again.

"Can't do it, sir, he's wounded," I replied, watching the Gunny begin to slowly shake his head in disgust. "If you can't fly the resupply and medivac then I'll call up Army air," I added.

I wasn't at all certain but I knew the Army would come and battalion would hate the idea.

"Stand by on this frequency for further orders, and I don't believe one word of what you've said," the colonel ordered as if none of what had been said had been said at all.

"God damn it but we're fucked," the Gunny said, snapping his cigarette butt out into the rain. "Every time I start thinking about making it back home the whole idea is snatched right back like Lucy and the football in Peanuts. I'm not wounded and what if they don't send anybody? What then? We can't stay alive without support from the battalion."

"We've got water, food, and ammo," I replied, calmly. "We could use more 106 flechette rounds for the Ontos, but I don't really think the enemy's going to come at us in the night. We'll point the Ontos down the river. That's the only place we'll likely see trouble from. Zippo can sit up with the Starlight Scope and the crew. I'll begin night defensive fires when it's full dark. I'm worried about what Jurgens and his men might do because of the casualties." I said the last words with some reticence and trepidation. After twenty days, and part of one night, I was still unsure of how the dynamics of relationships in the company worked and who was really loyal to whom.

"Let's worry about the big stuff," the Gunny replied, "we've got to get through that mess of jungle and reach the base of the cliff to establish any decent fields of fire. We could just stay along the river."

I looked at the Gunny, standing to his full height, facing the river as full dark was coming upon us. "Might work, except for snipers at daybreak," I said, "they'll be moving along the upper ridge and the river's too close to the other cliff face. I don't want any more friendly casualties from the artillery I'm calling tonight."

I had no idea how long we might be required to hold the position we were stuck in. It could be days, depending on the weather and what else was going on in the combat area. The jungle growth would not be able to be cleared completely, thereby providing concealment, if not effective cover, from sniper fire. The narrow pass by the east side of the river assured that the NVA would not be able to bring a fifty caliber and spray up and down our line, and if they stayed south with one then either the two batteries or the 175s would do them in with punishing high explosive or variable time fire.

"What's the name of this plan?" Zippo asked, from the edge of the darkness.

I knew he was asking because of superstition. I hadn't named the last plan and a lot of Marines had paid a big price, the way some saw it.

"Snoopy and the Red Baron," I replied, with a small smile, thinking about the Peanuts comic strip the Gunny had mentioned. 'We're going to shoot every Red Baron we see until we're relieved."

I knew I wasn't being relieved, and the company wasn't either. There was no one to relieve me, and no unit would be sold on taking the kind of losses we were suffering to relieve the company. I was learning that real combat didn't work that way. I also knew that fate was casting me back into the south of the A Shau Valley, the very worst combat charnel house I'd ever read or heard of. I could not escape it, and no matter how I twisted and turned I knew our company wasn't going to the DMZ or getting to take a break at any of the firebases so tantalizingly close along the western highlands beyond our position. The 9th Marines might come down the valley but they would not come far, even with our own combined company unit waiting with some sort of semi-safe perimeter near the end of the highway.

I got to my feet, Zippo dragging my pack along, as we moved to the edge of the jungle outgrowth. It was less dense than I'd thought but still took real work to move through, the wet branches and bamboo pushing back as if to let us know just how unwelcome we were. The Gunny hadn't seemed worried about what Jurgens and his men might do. I knew I would not be sleeping through the night, and I suddenly worried about the fact that I was still covered with mud from my slide down the mountain, and my Colt was filthy too. I had to break it down as soon as I could. I had fifteen rounds, and they were as filthy as the automatic.

We reached the lower edge of the cleft at the bottom of the cliff wall. It was similar to the one we'd taken some quarter in days ago when we were further down south.

With some digging with E-Tools, a decent area could be dug out of the base, providing cover from the never-ending rain, the ever-present animal predators and waiting along the bottom confines of any jungle terrain. I pushed into the cleft Nguyen cleared out, barely able to see anything. I lit a chunk of Composition B for light, more than to heat some water. I was five feet under the edge of the cliff and Zippo and Nguyen had piled the dirt and plant matter to form a low berm out from the front lip. But I had run out of time. I spread out my map and began designing the rippling night defensive fires I'd planned in my head earlier, but not put to actual numbers because I hadn't known where we'd end up.

I called for Fessman to raise the artillery net and made the necessary contacts before I boiled a canteen holder full of water, not to make coffee out of, but to pour over the parts of Tex's .45, bringing the dull blue of its surfaces back to bright cleanliness for potential use. I threw all my ammo in the cover and sloshed the rounds around. I hoped the factory loads wouldn't leak, but I really didn't have much choice. If a round failed to fire I would have to manually eject very quickly. Fortunately, the Colt did that seemingly small operation neatly, as well. Holding the loaded .45 gave me my first feeling of real security since I could recall.

"Snoopy and the Red Baron," I said out toward the night jungle. I was ready. Except for one more duty, I could not avoid. I had to move from my little haven of security and visit every wounded Marine, and then view the dead. They were my Marines, living and dead, and my own feelings of guilt or the injustice of it all was meaningless to them.

"Snoopy and the Red Baron," I whispered into the uncaring and unforgiving jungle in front of me before I slowly moved into its clutching grasp.

one-hundred-one

I holstered Tex's Colt .45 automatic that I had used half my canteen water to boil clean earlier. I had no oil but I knew there had to be some kept by others in the company I could get later. The Colt would operate just fine with no oil at all but only as long as it remained clean, which wouldn't be for long if the last twenty days and nights were an example.

The brush was thick and wedged well back into the cleft but, working with Fessman and Zippo, while Nguyen faced outward to watch for trouble, it took less than twenty minutes to clear a space where we could all lay down our poncho covers and get through the night. The rain had lessened somewhat but, since it was monsoon season, the rain was never going to leave entirely, for at least the remainder of the month. I'd seen to the wounded and the dead. Morphine had made the visits not quite so agonizing, as the pain from the burns of white phosphorus were dulled to the point where those Marines that had them just breathed so slow and deep it seemed they were as lifeless as the dead.

Real help and relief would have to wait until the morning, when the sounds of helicopters, and the simple fact that there was no other convenient time to fly resupply and pick up the casualties, would mean that the enemy would be waiting. My refusal to proceed back down the valley and face almost certain annihilation would not go down well back at battalion, I knew, but I didn't care. What were they going to do? Send me out to a worse unit or field of combat?

I took off my helmet and rummaged inside my pack and found a can of ham and mothers. I had to eat, I had to drink, and I had to get some light to set up the night defensive fires before arranging combined artillery and air support to cover what had to be coming in with first light. I ate from the grease-filled can with gusto, tipping it and waiting for the mess to slide into my mouth, not bothering to find and break out my little set of utensils. When I was done I wanted a drink but didn't want to use my slippery hands to get my canteen out. Then, an idea came into my head. I carefully worked the flap holding the Colt into my holster.

With two fingers, I pulled the weapon free, dangling it in the dark in front of me, before grasping it firmly and then rubbing every exposed piece of its metal surface with both of my greasy hands. I worked with a slight smile. The smell would attract bugs, maybe even leeches if the leeches had as little taste as I did, but the action would be smoother, at least for awhile, and I lived only from one 'awhile' to another.

With the pork-lubricated Colt secured back in its holster, and with only the sounds of the rushing water from the nearby river penetrating the brush in front of our cleft, I pulled out my stationery from the plastic bag I kept in my right front thigh sewn pocket. I rummaged about but could not find my flashlight or my binoculars in the complete darkness. For some reason, I didn't want to tell Fussman, or any of them, that I'd misplaced some of my gear. I knew the lack of sleep, and the intensity of what we'd been going through, had to be affecting my mind in strange ways. A shiver of fear went through my body at the thought of losing my mind or my memory, however.

My memory was keeping me alive, along with being able to create strange and unexpected plans and moves that had to be keeping the NVA from wiping us out. My wife would have to wait. My brain felt like a sponge anyway, and I wasn't at all sure that I could conjure up a bunch more lies to make it all seem like I was okay.

I drank the other half of my canteen water down without stopping. It wasn't enough to slake my thirst but I wasn't at all sorry that I'd used half of it to clean the Colt. I pushed back into the very back of the cleft, half my body able to jam itself into the crack where the cliff wall encountered the hard rock plane of the grounds level surface. I wondered if I could sleep, knowing that I didn't know when I slept anymore. Reality would fade and then come back with none of the relief or comfort, or even vague sleepiness I used to feel upon waking that I'd experienced back home. At times of seeming rest, I was there, not there, and then there again. I worried some more about how that might be the way I would sleep for the rest of my life if I somehow made it back home.

My left side was jammed into the crease and my eyes were closed for only seconds, I knew, before the sounds of bodies approaching caused my right hand to automatically unsnap the flap of my holster. I didn't get a chance to crawl out of my space before I felt the presence of several men arriving and stopping only inches from me. I couldn't see anything in the dark. Fear crawled across the surface of my skin like cobwebs being dragged by giant spiders. I knew if I took my hand off the Colt's handle that it'd be shaking again, so I didn't move.

"Junior," Jurgens whispered.

I didn't respond verbally, only breathing in and out heavily. I waited.

"It's Sugar Daddy and me," Jurgens continued. "We think you saved the Gunny from getting killed and, well, we wanted to say thanks for that."

I wondered if I should laugh at the idea that I was saving anyone but myself but kept breathing in and out deeply in silence instead, wishing I had one of the Gunny's cigarettes.

"He's coming," Jurgens whispered, like we'd shared some confidential conversation and should be afraid someone coming might find out.

I eased myself out from the crack so I could sit up. I heard the sound of ruffling poncho rubber in front of me before I was blinded by the light. I blinked rapidly, trying to recover.

"Your flashlight, sir," the Corporal said.

I noticed that I was sitting up inside a roughly thrown together tent. Fessman and Zippo had no doubt, created it with a couple of poncho covers while I was lost in whatever reverie passed for napping in the A Shau. The Gunny slid under the side facing outward. I grasped the flashlight with most of my left hand over the lens, to hold down the brightness. At least I had that instrument to plan the night defensive fires I'd been about to blow off from fatigue and the effect of the ham and mothers hitting my system like a ton of bricks. One more mistake and we'd all be dead, just like my Marines who'd been standing in or laying in the wrong place when the cliff and Willy Peter had come plunging down.

Jurgens and Sugar Daddy surged in again behind the Gunny but hung a few feet back. The three men lay on their stomachs, elbows extended to keep their heads up, as they faced me.

"We can't stay here and we can't head up the valley north," the Gunny said, taking out a cigarette slowly and getting ready to light it. He spoke with a casual tone, almost as if he was talking only to himself. "So, we can't go down river. You were damned straight about that. If we stay here, what's to stop those assholes from coming out of the caves and tunnels they've got to have drilled all through this wall we're up against?"

The Gunny blew smoke out his now lit cigarette, and a layer of it immediately began accumulating just under the top of our 'tent.' I liked the aroma. My wife was my idyllic home back in the world, and the Gunny and his cigarettes were my dysfunctional form of 'home' in the valley.

"Nope," I responded to his tunneling question, wanting a drag from his cigarette but not going to ask.

I pulled out my map of the area and unfolded it. I pointed down at Hill 975 with the flashlight. With my other hand, I pointed at our position well up the flank from the tip of the hill.

"The hill's not a hill at all as you know. It's a finger of commanding high ground that juts out, looking over the river and down the valley to where the airstrip is. The end of that finger of land is tunneled through because it controls all cover and concealment in this part of the valley, and it's composed mostly of mud and loose rocks, as you'll recall."

I tapped my flashlight on the top of our poncho cover tent. The metal cracked harshly against the hard surface above.

"That's solid rock. No tunnels. Not even spider holes. And there's no need for them, anyway. No one would pick this place to stop and make a stand for any other reason than the one we have."

The Gunny held out his cigarette as if rewarding me for the explanation I'd provided. I took it gratefully with my left hand, still holding the flashlight with my right.

"What's the reason we have?" Jurgens asked, as I puffed on the cigarette.

"What the Gunny said," Sugar Daddy replied, his tone one of near derision.

"We've got nowhere else to go."

"We've got another problem," the Gunny said, accepting the cigarette back from me.

I waited. It seemed that the company was always in the same situation, with only the weather and geography being different. We had nowhere to go that would let us stay alive, and we always seemed to have 'another problem.' I knew the Gunny had waited to bring the new problem up until he could find some plan to get through the night. I also knew that he'd accepted my plan of staying where we were, which was more of a relief to me than I'd realized. I could not go directly against the Gunny, and he was damned hard to convince about doing anything I came up with.

I thought he was going to bring up the obvious fact that, even with our supporting fires being maximized and air likely to show up just after dawn, the medevacs flying up to the top of the hill and down near our location, along with resupply, we were going to be a nearly impossible mess to coordinate and also to provide protection for.

The Gunny looked at me directly for the first time, taking a long drag on his cigarette, before speaking.

"They want to insert a Lurp team on top of the hill to get their bodies out."

A Lurp (LRRP) team. A Lurp team was the Army version of Marine Force Reconnaissance. An elite Army force of company size. The word stood for Long

Range Reconnaissance Patrol.

I breathed out a sigh of relief. I'd been frightened of being sent back up to the top of what I considered a hill of death. My relief was short-lived, however.

"They want the team to supervise the evacuation but then stay to occupy the top of the hill," the Gunny said, his voice going so soft I almost couldn't hear it.

"Ha!" Jurgens said, overly loud, before settling down. "The Army wants to do the job the Marine Corps failed at, and they probably want to do it with less men. Idiots."

The Gunny looked at me again, his dark eyes unblinking. I knew there was more, and that I wasn't going to like it.

"They'll let them take the bodies out," he said. "The NVA isn't stupid. They know we want that hill. When the choppers leave it'll happen all over again. They'll come out of those holes and tunnels and that'll be it."

"So, it'll be just like before," Sugar Daddy said, his tone more one of a question than of restating the Gunny's conclusion.

"And we'll be ordered to go up there and find out what happened when they don't respond," Jurgens replied, "because we're the only ones here."

"So, what do we do?" he finally asked.

"We do our job," the Gunny said, his voice going hard. We convince battalion to get the Army to send the smallest force possible. We convince them that we cleared the hill before we came down. We tell them we're remaining in position to help secure the hill and we'll back up the Lurp team. They'll believe us because they have nobody else."

"Just how in hell does having a smaller Army force up there help us?" Jurgens asked, before going on. "Isn't it the more the merrier down in this shitty hot wet hell?"

The Gunny stared into my eyes. I averted the flashlight to avoid looking at him. I knew the Gunny knew. I knew we'd arrived at the part where he knew we had to finally get to.

"They're going to order us to go get the Army guys when they're dead," I said, slowly. "We want the least number killed because they won't fly in another medivac up there after losing so many. The Gunny's saying that we'll have to carry or slide them back down and we'll have to do it damn fast or die up there with them."

"Jesus Christ," Sugar Daddy said, his voice a hiss. "We're supposed to write those guys off, just like that? And then lie to make it all happen nice and easy?"

"They're not Marines," Jurgens whispered into the silence that followed.

"Why aren't they sending us back up?" Jurgens asked.

"Because of Junior," the Gunny replied, his words hard, but I caught a thin glimmer of a smile on his lips. "They think he won't go. They think he's gone rogue from the combat losses. He refuses orders openly."

"Oh," Sugar Daddy said, his tone indicating that he didn't mind my being considered to be a dishonorable nut case officer. "I thought it was because they think we're a mess of fucked up units who can't do jack shit right."

"Well, there's probably a good bit of that in there too," the Gunny answered, before laughing gently.

Sugar Daddy and Jurgens began laughing with him. It was my turn to stare, wondering what kind of gallows humor was driving them, and why I couldn't find anything funny about some Army guys, probably decent fucking new guy Army guys, being sent up the hill of death to never return. I thought of Tex. My hand touched the Colt, but not in fear or anger, or as a threat.

"We don't give the orders, Junior," the Gunny said, reading my expression, finishing his cigarette, and snapping the short butt out from under the poncho cover.

I knew the Gunny's math and logic was correct. The fewer bodies we had to pack out and down the faster we could move, and the more likely we would live. Anybody sent up to the top of Hill 975 for any period of time was going to die. Keeping the body count down was a weirdly humane thing to do, although our own survival was all that any of us were really worried about unless we sat and thought about it, and I knew none of us wanted to do that.

"They need to come in when its dark," I finally said.

"Who?" the Gunny asked, getting ready to pull out and step back into the night rain.

"The medevac and resupply," I said. "We can't support them coming in with artillery, and firing early would simply alert the NVA as to what was coming. They can fly this far on instruments, orbit too high to allow for location, and then drop in at the very crack of dawn. With everyone ready, they can be in and out of here in less than ten minutes. When they drop the Lurp team up top, well, time is not going to matter for those guys."

The Gunny, Jurgens and Sugar Daddy pulled back out from under the poncho cover tent. Fessman, Zippo, and Nguyen replaced them, all three shedding their own ponchos, but wet through, anyway.

"What's the plan?" Zippo asked with his tone one of expectant enthusiasm.

I thought quickly about what we were doing.

"Parade Rest," I replied, with only a slight delay. "We're going to stand fast and keep our mouths shut."

"Rumor has it that we're being sent back down the valley, sir," Fessman said, not sounding like he'd fully bought into the plan.

I knew that the radio traffic had to be filled with stuff about my disobedience of orders, but there was nothing to be done for it so I simply waited to hear what he had to say further.

"They say we couldn't take the hill, sir," Fessman said. "The Army 75th is being sent in while we get sent back down the river. Resupply is going to be filled with new officers and FNGs to replace all the Marines we've lost."

The information Fessman was giving us from the rumor mill might be all true, or almost all of it could be nothing more or less than a fable, I now knew.

"We took the hill," I replied, thinking about what it would be like to be fully back to T.O. strength and with a whole suite of officers commanding both companies. "We just didn't hold the hill, and nobody else is going to either."

After being in the country only three weeks I no longer held out any hope that wholesale replacements would be sent in to fill all open positions. Nobody in the rear wanted to come out into the bush if they knew anything about it at all. The only result a combat unit could expect was to receive replacements who'd just come into the country and knew nothing about what might be ahead of them. I'd come to terms with why nobody would talk, or even answer me when I was in the rear and fresh from the states. They knew where I was going and nothing they could tell me would help me at all in staying alive. I was already dead to them.

There was no point trying to explain everything to my scout team, so I put them to work.

"Fessman, arrange for the medevac and resupply 46s to touch down from a high low drop out of altitude at the crack of dawn. Tell them it'll be a secure landing zone until just after light. Zippo, get to the Ontos and have them move back down the valley until they have the southern flank guarded. We'll be going south before snaking around to head back up to the top of 975. Nguyen, you're with me."

"We're going back up there again?" the Corporal whispered, his voice filling with disappointment and fear.

"Not if I can help it, but we've got to be ready for anything," I lied. "Get on the arty net and let me lay in the night defensive fires. Call Cowboy when and where you can. We'll need them just after dawn, once the NVA figure out we landed our stuff in the night. Or damn near."

I went to work on my map, memorizing the codes and grids and then calling it all into both firebases. I didn't expect to fire in the night simply because of the security of our current position. The NVA could not come at us from across the river, they wouldn't attempt the high cliff above it after the devastation I'd rained in on them earlier. Up there they were fully exposed, with only hard rock to dig into and sparse cover from artillery. They could come up the river on our side and encounter the Ontos, but I didn't think they'd do that either. They knew that with their overwhelming troop strength and underground positions they only had to wait. There was no waiting when it came to orders pouring out of the rear areas of the Army and Marine Corps, however. For whatever reasons, the guerrilla war we were involved in required constant movement no matter how meaningless to the troops and Marines out in the field implementing those moves and orders.

When I was done I pulled out my package of stationery and wrote a brief letter to my wife. It would have to get delivered the following morning if all went well. I wondered what it would be like to go home and tell her about what had happened the day before. I pushed myself into the cleft of the rock, staying just far enough out of it so not encounter the trickle of water flowing down it from north to south. I explained to my wife what a 'Lurp' was and how reconnaissance was supposed to be these special guys who went behind enemy lines and did heroic things. I did not tell her that there were no lines and that heroism was all fiction brought to the field of real combat, and then hopefully taken home because the real thing was too awful to contemplate or discuss. I sealed the envelope and stuck it back in my pocket before laying back on the hard rock.

Fessman was pulling on my upper arm. I opened my eyes but it was too black to see anything at all. I knew it was the Corporal because of his clawing grasp and insistent forever-repeated phrase; "It's time, it's time, it's time…"

Time for what I wanted to yell but didn't because I knew exactly where I was. I wondered if I'd ever wake up again and not know exactly where I was.

"What's the situation?" I asked, shoving Fessman's hand away and working sideways to escape the crimped-in wall's grasp.

Fessman was waking me for a reason, I knew, but the detail of what that reason might be would not come into my groggy mind. Very distantly I heard the distinctive sound of a Huey helicopter. My brain came alive. The choppers were up at altitude waiting. They would stay up there fooling any listener below. They couldn't fly much higher than ten thousand feet without oxygen for everyone on board, which they didn't have, but even at that altitude, the enemy would know they were somewhere above but would not be able to pin a location as to where they were or where they might be coming down. No altitude would allow for the complete silence of a Huey, however, since they were so loud they could be heard coming at sea level almost ten miles away.

"The lead pilot wants to talk to you," Fessman said, pushing the air headset into my neck.

How the Corporal saw anything in the stygian blackness was beyond me.

"What does he want?" I asked, mildly irritated, but happy that I'd not had to call in any night defensive fires.

That meant that the batteries unless they'd fired for somebody else, would be fully stocked for whatever the day brought. Unless we went back down the valley where their guns couldn't reach us.

"Who is he?" I asked.

"Lieutenant Blackbird, sir," Fessman replied.

I waited for a few seconds for him to laugh at the humor of a helicopter pilot flying at night being called Blackbird but nothing came back to me. If a lieutenant was the flight leader then the choppers had to be Army. Marine chopper pilots were mostly captains and majors, the ones flying in the left seats, anyway.

"Six actual," I said, hitting the tiny transmit button.

"Blackbird, over," the lieutenant replied instantly.

"Time on target is one three minutes unless the LZ's hot," Blackbird said. "Can you give me some assurance?"

I almost laughed out loud.

"What's he talking about Fessman? He wants some assurance that the LZ isn't under fire? Are they flying too high, or what?"

"The LZ is secure, quiet and likely to remain that way," I transmitted, shaking my head in the darkness.

"Are you the one they call Junior?" the lieutenant asked back.

"No," I transmitted in anger. "This is Gunny Socorro." Evidently, the word about me was getting around, and the word wasn't good.

"Got it, Gunny, and thanks," Blackbird replied. "Touch down is in one minute. Be prepared to offload two 47s and a single Huey."

The 47s were good news. The Army twin rotor carried twice what the Marine Corps 46 could haul. Resupply would be no problem and they'd be able to get all the wounded and dead to the rear.

"What about the Lurp Team?" I asked, crawling out from under the poncho cover tent where there was the faintest glimmering of morning light.

"That's a separate operation," Blackbird said. "The team is touching down at the same time as we are, using the gunships we've got, except for the C.O., Captain Victor Chase. He's coming down with me."

I pulled the headset off and handed it to Fessman.

"Victor Chase. What kind of weirdness is that? An Army captain, fighting a war in Vietnam, has the initials V.C.?"

"Zippo went to the LZ to get our stuff," Fessman replied, ignoring my question. "Why's the commander of the Lurp unit not going up there with his men? Did he find out something?"

I didn't know what the underground radio rumor mill was generating, but I wasn't confirming anything to Fessman or anyone else.

Some good men were being sacrificed for nothing and the responsibility for that was beginning to resemble a game of musical chairs, even before the event occurred. I hadn't asked Blackbird about who or what was in the choppers because it didn't matter. Both big birds together could bring in more than sixty Marines, depending upon what else they brought along for resupply. I was almost certain there would be a full complement of officers to replace me. There seemed little doubt that the nightmare of our A Shau operations were being viewed as almost entirely due to my incompetence, by our commanders in the rear area.

"How's the captain, if he's coming here, supposed to get up that hill?" the Corporal asked.

I put on my battered and ragged helmet, looked at my Gus Grissom watch and tried to ignore Fessman. I hadn't thought about how the Lurp leader was going to get up to his men and I didn't want to think about it. There were forces moving around me that seemed to make no sense and that I had no control over, just as before. I pulled the two letters home I had ready to go. Both were a mess of smudged ink and wrinkles. I tried to press them against my thigh but it was no use.

"We need to get to the LZ and make sure everything goes the way it's supposed to," I lied to Fessman.

In reality, all I wanted to do was get the two letters into a chopper crewman's hands and then see if I could do anything to help the craft survive out of the valley to get the letters home. The sound of the descending choppers was drowned out by the heavy roaring thrum of bigger engines and huge spinning propellers. The Skyraiders were back. Cowboy was once again coming through. I started up the bank toward where the only cleared area existed that was big and flat enough for the landing.

Except for the Ontos crew and some of Jurgen's Marines, everyone would be there to make the coming exchange happen as fast as possible. I moved as quickly as I could, my feet making sucking sounds that I could barely hear, as I pulled one boot after another up from the rain-soaked mud. I didn't bother with my poncho since the rain had turned into a mist that penetrated everything no matter what I might wear. I kept my left hand with the letters shoved inside my utility blouse, my right hand naturally falling to the butt of Tex's Colt.

"Can I turn my radio on?" Fessman asked.

The question surprised me, since usually he turned the little transistor thing on whenever he felt like it.

"Why not?" I replied, over my shoulder.

The LZ was going to go hot or it wasn't. Making noise on our part wasn't going to make a bit of difference about that, and what the new officers coming down might think, if they were really coming down, I didn't give a damn about.

"Here's one for you," the deep voice of Brother John, coming out of the tinny speaker all the way from Nah Trang, said. "Now don't you Marines out there take this one too seriously on this fine morning."

The song began with a very light drum roll, and I recognized it even before the lyrics began. I clutched the letters to my wife more tightly, as the country western singer began singing: "You've painted up your lips and rolled and curled your tinted hair... Ruby, are you contemplating going out somewhere? The shadow on the wall tells me the sun is going down..."

one-hundred-two

THE TWENTY-FIRST DAY : FIRST PART

The sounds of the Bong Song's nearby rushing waters, the whap, whap, whap of the descending chopper's supersonic blade-tips rotating, and the rest of the valley background sounds all faded into non-existence, as four Skyraiders came down the valley from the north, no more than fifty feet off the surface of the river. It was like the jungle peeled back to let them pass, the deep quaking thunder of their huge radial engines spitting out life-threatening noise even a close-mounted fifty caliber machine gun could not compare to. When the Skyraiders were on top of us and the thunder didn't seem like it could get any louder, Cowboy and his wingmen opened up with their twenty-millimeter cannons and swept the A Shau's lower surface like four brooms shaking the sawdust to pieces on an old saloon floor. Dust, dirt, and debris sprayed from one side of the narrow valley to the other before the monster planes were gone. There were no Marines still standing when that occurred.

I stood up and brushed myself down, knocking the crap from my helmet with one clenched fist, but avoiding hitting the sharp chunk of shrapnel that was sticking out of it. I still didn't like having the word "Junior" written under the single magic marker black bar on its front surface, but there was little I was willing to do about it. What was, was, and if I'd learned anything at all it was that the only way I had any chance at survival was to go along when I could, and adapt at every opportunity I was given, and forget about the fact that I was a valuable or a valued human being. I was just another jungle creature trying to get by, no better or worse than a venomous viper, the crocodile we'd killed earlier, or even the leeches and mosquitos I'd so hated in the beginning, before life had changed.

The sound of the chopper blades grew and grew. I looked up to see the two big birds orbiting at about five hundred feet. It was a sight I was becoming used to. I looked lower down near the top edge of the jungle. They came right over that fake green horizon. Six Huey Cobra gunships didn't come like the Skyraiders, lined up and delivering a wall of rolling fire. Instead, they came as an ever changing interlace of dancing dark creatures. No fire came from their machine guns or cannons. They were clearing the landing zone by observation and reconnaissance. They'd only fire if they needed to or if they were fired upon, which wasn't likely, and that fact was the only reason I wasn't back face down on the vegetation with my chest pressed into the mud. It took several moments of intricate weaving, and near-magical flying, for the sleek predator choppers to assure that the supply ships could come down. There was only one regular Huey, so I knew it had to be flown by Blackbird, which meant that Captain V.C. had to be aboard. My replacement officers would be in one of the 47s.

I crept closer to the only clear area of the riverbank that adjoined a slight bend in the river. The Huey dropped out of the sky but pulled up abruptly just above the mud. It then gently and brilliantly settled on its long tubular skids onto the surface, like a giant dragon faintly brushing the earth.

Macho Man stepped out, turned, brought his Thompson up to parade rest and faced. I could not help smiling. The unreal character was still alive, and so was I. I hunched over under the blades, and scuttled forward to deliver my two letters. He let his right come down from the Thompson's forward barrel guard to receive them. I could tell he was working hard not to smile and possibly fall out of his combat imaged role. I nodded, and he nodded briefly in return, the chopper's turbine howl making it too loud to speak over or through.

The two big 47s came skimming in behind the Huey, dropping the rears of the aircraft down to touch before the fronts settled into the mud. I knew their turbines would remain spooled up, just like the Huey's own. Even though there was no enemy fire, the only kind of landing zone in the A Shau was always to be considered a hot one.

V.C. crouched next to the machine gunner, just inside the Huey's side opening. Instead of jumping down and out of the machine, the Army captain dropped onto his butt, bounced once on the flat aluminum surface of the chopper's floor, and then landed to stand fully upright in front of me with a smile on his face. I liked him. Without a word, and not knowing a thing about the man, I liked him. His clean pressed and starched utilities, his bounce, his smile… all of it reminded me immediately of the kind of hard but clean and fair training I'd left behind forever.

Taking one last passing look at Macho Man, for my memory

banks, although I knew I would never forget him, I turned, and crab-walked back in the direction I'd come, hoping V.C. would follow. As soon as I was out from under the blades, Fessman, Zippo, and Nguyen joined in close at my side. I stopped when I thought we had enough jungle cover and distance from the Huey to talk. The Gunny, whom I'd thought would have been greeting the new officers bound to be aboard the 47s, appeared, as if out of nowhere. I was surprised, but I had no time to ask him anything.

"I'm reporting in," Captain Victor Chase said, his voice overly loud, even respecting the chuffing and whispering sounds of Huey's spinning rotor blades. "Where's the OIC?" he asked, as I turned to take him in.

He stood with his right hand out. I moved forward immediately and shook his hand. I wanted to say the words: "welcome to the Nam," like I'd first heard that day so long ago, but it wasn't appropriate, I knew. And "welcome to the A Shau," didn't have the same cachet.

"OIC?" I asked, feeling stupid.

"Officer in charge," the Gunny whispered into my left ear. "It's an Army thing."

I liked the captain even more. He had to know I was Junior. They would have told him, like everyone else who came to our company in the field. He'd chosen to 'report in' to an officer he knew was lower in rank, and he'd chosen not to call me by my nickname.

"They're going to be unloading the supplies and getting the hell out of Dodge, sir," I said, recovering myself.

"You came down here instead landing up on hill nine-seventy-five" the Gunny interjected, letting me know right away why he'd been waiting back with me instead of with the Marines unloading the choppers.

"Setting up a base for ingress and egress from that hill," the captain replied.

"And how in hell, sir, do you expect to get up and down that hill without a chopper?" the Gunny asked, surprising me by the cutting edge of his tone and in the nature of the question.

"Climbing gear," V.C. answered, his demeanor remaining one of openness and good humor, in spite of the Gunny's aggressiveness. "Two of my guys are with your incoming Marines. We're going to scale the face of this wall. I've brought in three small teams but we won't operate independently on this one."

I looked over at the Gunny, but he simply stood there. I wondered if he was too dumbstruck to respond. After a few seconds, he shook his head once, bent down and lit one of his cigarettes before walking away toward the waiting more distant choppers.

"Climbing gear, they brought climbing gear," I heard him whispering to himself as he went.

My own mind roiled. The thought of being five or six hundred feet up on ropes against the face of the bare cliff, with only a single sniper, like we'd had the day before, over on the top of the opposing ridge, made me feel a bit queasy. But my feelings about that were overshadowed by my sadness. I knew there was no chance that the wonderful-seeming young captain in front of me was going to live out the week, and then an ever-deeper sadness overcame me. I didn't want to die with him, near him or around him. I wanted to be away from him, for all the right survival, but wrong disciplinary reasons.

"You know, they all call me Junior, sir," I blurted out, trying to think of something substantive or clever to say.

"Yes, I heard that," V.C. responded. "A term of endearment. I wonder if my men will give me a nickname too. And, I heard that out here in the real shit you don't have to call me sir, either. I mean, if you're another officer."

The man's discomfort was palpable. I knew he knew that my name wasn't a 'term of endearment,' but I much appreciated the blasé ornateness of his lie. Mostly, my Marines didn't like me at all, any more than my fellow officers in the Basic School had. I'd spent many useless hours trying to figure out why that was but had never reached any acceptable or substantive conclusion. It was the way it was.

"It don't mean nuthin," I said, giving the captain as genuine a fake smile as I could manufacture.

"I've heard that expression too," he replied, "but I don't get it."

"That's easy, sir," Zippo unaccountably broke in. "It means everything's cool unless it sucks. And that's okay. It's just the way things are."

The captain looked away. All I could do was stare at Zippo and try to reflect on his comprehensible comment.

The Gunny came back through the low-lying jungle bracken, leading four Marines. None of the four wore the spotless gear the captain was wearing but all of them looked even younger than he looked.

"The new officers, ready to take command," the Gunny said, but in a tone that made it sound like he was saying anything but that. He backed off to light up another cigarette. When it was lit, and just before I introduced myself to the new officers, he added, "and I'll be right here if you want to have a smoke when you're done."

With that, he squatted down to begin brewing a cup of coffee.

I looked at the four young officers, knowing something was wrong, but not quite able to immediately place what it was. I looked at the rank designations on their collars, to determine which of them might be commanding my own company and Kilo, and then I got it. They all wore black single bars of cloth. They were all lieutenants.

Young lieutenants. New lieutenants. Brand new lieutenants

"Tell me you're not all second lieutenants," I said, the left side of my lips going upward in an uncontrollable tic.

"Same Basic Class," the leading lieutenant said. "Just graduated. Came in the country together. We're all MOS infantry and it's amazing they'd let us come out to the field together."

I looked at the black printing on the front of his blouse. The letters read: "LIGHTNER" on the small canvas tag.

"Truly astounding," I whispered, turning away to face the Gunny.

The Gunny worked with one hand to light his small deposit of composition B. He used his left hand only because his right was extended upward, holding out the burning cigarette he'd mentioned, toward me.

I slowly took a couple of hesitant steps, until I was close enough to take the smoking tube with my own hand. I inhaled deeply, and then coughed like I hadn't done since my earliest days in the country.

"Is there a problem?" the leading lieutenant asked from over my shoulder.

I shook my head, handing the cigarette back down.

"Coffee?" the Gunny asked, beaming up at me as if the universe had just played another of its tragically hilarious jokes on us. Which it, apparently, had.

I nodded but had to make sure about the seniority of the new batch of officers.

"Dates of rank," I said, "I'm going to presume that all of you are junior to me?"

"Junior," now that's funny," the leading man with the blackened name of LIGHTNER printed on the front of his utility blouse replied.

I squatted down by the Gunny, my back to the officers, and pulled the canteen rig from my belt. I took the thing apart and waited with my holder in one hand like I had all the time in the world. I didn't need their basic class or their dates of rank. It was all too obvious. I was still company commander of our company. All that could be done was to appoint one of the new guys to take over Kilo.

"Whichever one of you is senior by number, you get to take over as the C.O. of Kilo Company, or whatever's left of it," I said, not turning to face the officers. "Take your friends with you. I'm doing fine here. Divide up the fucking new guys and take half over there, and don't forget to pair up the Project Hundred Thousand Marines. They can't read or write so you'll know them right off the bat."

"What's that project?" one of the new officers asked, but nobody answered.

Zippo, Fessman, and Nguyen took off and began digging holes in the mud behind small chunks of the scrub jungle cover that grew close to the river. I watched as they worked, knowing they'd be careful to dig as far from the cliff wall as they could but not so close to the river as to have the mud around the holes cave in. None of them were going to forget the cliff coming down in huge chunks when my artillery call came in short earlier.

The Gunny poured half his hot water into my own cup holder, then threw down some sugar, creamer and coffee packets next to his small fire. I looked into his eyes. He said nothing, and all I could read from his barely expression-filled facial features was wry humor. I understood. The rear area was either laughing at our continuing deadly predicament or it was so out of touch that it had no idea what it was doing or why it was doing it.

"Ah, how do you tell who's who and in what company out here, Junior?" one of the officers, I presumed to be Lightner, asked.

"You don't call me Junior, lieutenant," I whispered, not caring whether the collected group of officers-waiting-to-be-dead behind me heard or not. "You call me sir. And you find out who's with Kilo by asking around. Everyone's all mixed together right now. If you want to make your company fall in then you better do it pretty quickly because we're about to take some enemy fire at any moment."

"How do you know that?" Lightner asked, his tone indicating his lack of belief.

"Mind if I join you?" the Army captain asked, squatting down next to my right side.

"Of course, sir," I responded. "If you want some coffee we'll have to boil more water though.

"You don't have to call me sir, and no I'm fine," V.C. said. "I won't call you Junior either, but I don't know your name."

"Hell, Junior's fine, as long as you say it with a laugh."

"Ah, okay, Junior," he got out, hesitantly, and then paused a few seconds before going on. "You think it's a bad idea to scale the wall?"

"Okay, V.C. here it is," I replied, after taking a long deep drink of my hot coffee. "We wanted as few of you up there because you're all going to get killed. Hill 975 is completely run through with tunnels. NVA tunnels. It's a beehive but a bee's sting is nothing compared to what those clowns deliver up there. They killed a whole brigade on top of that same hill a few days back. We wanted as few of you hotshot recon types up there again because we have to go up and get your bodies ready for medevac. You can climb that wall and probably get shot on the way up or you can call in a chopper and reach the top alive only to die in the night when the vampires come out of their coffins. Take your pick."

"Wow, that's pretty hardball stuff, Junior," Lightner said.

I turned my head to look back at the lieutenant. There was no use correcting his use of my nickname I knew, so I didn't bother.

"If I was you I'd get hold of an E-Tool and dig in like you see my scout team doing over there," I motioned toward the river with the cup holder, causing some of my coffee to spill over the lip.

"I've got orders," the captain said, his apparent enthusiasm not seeming to be one bit diminished by my lengthy and brutal comment.

"Do you have orders also, Lightner?" I asked of the lieutenant, who I knew had remained close behind my back.

"Kilo's supposed to move north," Lightner answered. "Kilo's eventually supposed to work its way over to the Rock Pile, but I didn't know I'd be commanding it. I'm supposed to be a platoon commander, not a company commander. I don't know how to be a company commander."

"Welcome to the Nam," the Gunny said, blowing out a puff of smoke from a newly lit cigarette.

"Welcome to the A Shau," he finished, putting the cigarette out in the mud with a flourish next to his small composition B fire.

"Sir?" I heard Fessman say in the distance.

I looked up and out toward the rushing water of the river. Fessman and the other members of my scout team were standing in their holes and looking up and back toward the cliff face. A light wind had picked up, and a drifting cloud of rain pattered down, making the cliff face look nothing more or less like just another cloud, albeit much thicker and grayer. Down the side of the face extended three bright yellow lines, running vertically from the top to the bottom.

"My Romeo must have called them to make the drop," V.C. said, climbing to his feet and gazing back through the misty rain with his left hand held up to shield his face from the rain.

"Romeo? Drop?" I asked, not understanding anything of what the captain said.

"Romeo Oscar, radio operator," he replied, surprise in his tone. "My guys up top dropped the climbing lines down so they can pull us up."

I looked around. I couldn't see any radio operators, other than the Gunny's and Fessman's digging away by the river. I wasn't fully conversant with the Army's military jargon or many of its other ways. In the Marine Corps, at least in my field experience, a radio operator was worn like a second skin, and he was called a radio operator, not by the alphanumeric of his title. Fessman was always in sight and hearing of my presence and it wasn't something I controlled. It was just the way it was in the Corps.

"They didn't have some ropes that were a bit darker?" the Gunny asked, taking it all in, as I was.

"I've got to get back to the LZ and get my stuff together to get up there with my men," the captain said, "with your permission, and all, Junior."

The smile on the man's face was difficult not to smile back at. I smiled. I liked the man and I felt bad for him. I wondered if there was the smallest part of God's heart that might be open to letting him live through the next twenty-four hours, but I didn't wonder for long. I knew deep down that God, if he was there at all, wasn't making his presence felt in the A Shau, except to take souls up to his side in great numbers.

The captain walked into the brush and was gone.

"You can't stop him, you know," the Gunny said.

"You stopped me," I replied, hopefully, but defeat coming through with a sigh at the end of my words.

"You're different," the Gunny replied.

I was afraid to ask him any questions about such a strange comment, so I changed the subject.

"Everyone needs to dig in," I said. "They need to make sure

they're covered when those Army types head up that cliff wall. I can get some arty on top of the other cliff, and Cowboy must be out there somewhere orbiting and waiting for the LZ to clear. The Ontos is no use at this low angle."

I listened to the varying whines of the distant turbines. The choppers were lifting off, and that meant the wonderfully deadly Huey Cobras would be leaving with them.

Once again, the capricious Skyraiders, what we could get of artillery support, and the Ontos would be all we'd have to hold back the NVA. My stomach churned as I recalled my conversation with Lt. Lightner. Kilo was going north where life would be found, while we were going back down into the south of the A Shau, where life flowed out and away from everyone like the water coming through the valley bottom sluice of the Bong Song River.

It was mid-day before my team finished the holes, and we set up close to them. The bottom of my hole was covered in three to four inches of water, coming up from the low water table so close to the river. And it was moving. The water was alive with leeches. I knew that there was no way any of us were getting in the holes unless enemy fire required it. Then Gunny, Jurgens and Sugar Daddy reported in. They were trailed by what I presumed to be squad and platoon leaders I didn't recognize. I hadn't seen the new lieutenants since I'd set them off to try to form a new Kilo company from the remains of the old one, and a good number of the fucking new guys. The lower clouds circulating through the valley abated, but higher darker clouds, dropping more water than the low little one, formed high above and slowly rolled across the distance between the two valley cliff faces.

A Marine crept close from the brush to drop off an envelope. At first, I thought it was one of the letters I'd given to Macho man for my wife. But it wasn't. It was a letter from the captain to be mailed home at the next resupply.

"He didn't seal it so you can read it if you want, Junior," the Marine I didn't recognize said, before trudging off to head back upriver.

I dried my fingers on my blouse and tucked myself back under the poncho cover Fessman had set up for me by my hole. I opened the flap of the envelope and pulled out three sheets of flimsy paper.

"Dear Alice," the letter began, "I met this really great Marine Officer. His men call him Junior. I haven't got a nickname yet…."

I jerked the letter down, slowly refolded it and carefully put it inside the envelope. I sealed the envelope before folding it and putting it into my special trouser pocket I usually reserved for my own letters home. I felt like I'd jinxed myself. I wasn't sure how. Reading the letter suddenly made me feel like I was reading a letter written about me after I was dead. I crouched inside my poncho, shivering, while the hot rain beat down on everything around me.

"Sir?" Fessman asked, holding out the Prick 25 handset.

It was time. I had to call in the defensive fires atop the far ridge, which wasn't that far away at all, as we'd discovered.

"Air?" I asked him, before taking the instrument.

"Rain's too heavy and the winds aloft too strong, sir," the Corporal replied, turning on his tiny Armed Forces radio.

I realized for the first time that Fessman didn't use the radio to remind him of home so much as he did because it helped with his own fear. The situation was making Fessman nervous, and I felt it through my own bones. It was the feeling of being among good and capable men but trapped inside a cage where the good and capable men could only run in place, keeping the cage going, with the cage always only going nowhere.

Cowboy and his magic wonder ships of ruin and destruction had gone home.

I called the first artillery mission using Willy Peter at altitude, in order to creep the fire back toward me, before calling in 'fire for effect' with high explosive super-quick fuses. I wanted to take no chances that there might be a short round, or a series of them, again. The first rounds exploded but their effects were blunted and invisible by the fact that the rounds were going off back from the lip of the wall, which was just the way I wanted to keep it.

I heard Fessman humming to whatever song was playing. I couldn't hear it well with all the other noises reverberating back and forth across the valley. I finally caught a stanza: "Come a little bit closer, you're my kind of man, so big and so strong. Come a little bit closer, I'm all alone and the night is so long"

I smiled a cold smile to myself. It was Bad Man Jose again. One of my favorites. "Come a little bit closer," I whispered out to the falling artillery rounds. Not too close, but a little bit closer.

I'd given my own Marines no warning, as to the barrage. There was no sense in everyone getting into the holes unless it was absolutely necessary. Secretly, deep down, I also knew that I wanted to prove myself to them again. I could call the kind of fire they needed to stay alive, and therefore they would consider keeping me alive, at least for another day. The drums started after the third series of fires for effect. The NVA was letting us all know, down below them, that they'd moved the drums and, therefore, probably everything else, to a more secure, or at least unknown new location. I knew that news was bad, but there was nothing to be done for it.

"They're going up," Zippo said, pointing at the wall with the yellow ropes hanging down.

I came out of my poncho cover into the rain in a hunched over position, putting my helmet back on and easing toward my hole. The cliff face was at least thirty meters away but that didn't seem far enough if any real fire came in. Fusner stayed with me, as I called in the zone fire I'd planned to run along the entire distance of the other wall's high ground.

It all happened in many slow seconds, or so it seemed later on. I brought the zone fire from three batteries at two firebases accurately in, glancing from the exploding top of one wall of the valley over to the other where the two men and one supply bag were being hauled up by the Army troops already stationed atop the hill.

The rain fell harder, and the drums seemed to beat louder, as their sounds interspersed themselves with the heavier thumps of 105 rounds going off, one after another, in rapid synchrony. Three fireworks arrows shot out from atop the far wall, somehow their launch points spaced perfectly between the exploding artillery rounds. It didn't seem possible, to my stunned eyes and brain, and my sinking heart. RPG round tracks across the sky were definitive and there was no missing what they were. The fireworks arrows arced silently across the valley, seeming to move in slow motion, the sound of their passage cloaked by the artillery explosions above and the drums reverberations everywhere. Whatever NVA ballistics expert was in charge of launching the RPG rounds knew his business. Three explosions impacted on the closer wall, as one, not a few feet from where the men and supply bag were being dragged upward. Rocks and debris rained down, but neither I, nor any of the Marines around me sought cover in our holes. We simply stood and stared upward in shock, watching what was left of two Army troopers, and their supplies, as they came plummeting down the side of the stone wall, like so much meaty confetti.

I sank back onto my poncho, not bothering to crawl under the edge of it to get out of the rain. The final rounds of my ineffectual barrage kept coming in, blowing the hell out of plenty of mountaintop foliage in the distance but accomplishing nothing.

I let Fessman pull the microphone from my hand. I turned into my poncho cover pulled it over me and removed my helmet. Very gently, I retrieved the letter V.C. had given me for safekeeping. I'd sealed it. I couldn't read it without opening it, and I just couldn't do that. I unfolded the letter and saw that the captain had used a Marine Corps envelope instead of some other. Maybe it was all he could get, I thought, but then thought again. The Army troops who worked with Marines had an inflated sense of how great the Marine Corps was, and I knew I was very likely seeing an indication of that again. I pulled my helmet slowly apart, placed the flattened envelope carefully against the helmet liner, and then slid the helmet over it. I put the helmet on and felt something better for having the letter right there right next to my face. I wasn't better. I knew I wasn't better because that would have required being better than something, and I wasn't something. I was Junior, a monster survivor at the bottom of a swirling pit that consumed everything around him, like the circling Coriolis water at the bottom of a bathtub. Alice's wonderful loving husband had just died before my eyes, as I knew he had to.

The very last lyrics of the Bad Man Jose song purred out of Fusner's radio nearby: "…I still hear her say…I still hear her say…" What would Alice say? What could Alice say?

one-hundred-three

The monsoon day wore on, its rain relentless, the river mildly rising in the volume of water passing, and in sound, but nothing we weren't used to enduring down in the bottom of our own private hell, known as the A Shau Valley. The new guys weren't ready, of course, just as the FNG's before them hadn't been either. V.C., and his Romeo Oscar radio operator had died only hours earlier.

I wished that the wind would stop or at least die down. I wished that there was some contact with the Army special teams up on top of Hill 975, but there was nothing. They had not pulled the yellow ropes back up to the top of the cliff. The yellow ropes, cut by the RPG explosives a little more than halfway up, blew up and then dangled back down as they danced against the wet surface of the cliff face. I wasn't concerned with the safety of the teams, as I'd already consigned them to death, I just couldn't stand looking up at the blowing ropes or trying not to look up at them, peering out from under my poncho cover and looking up at them until I couldn't do it anymore, which didn't seem to help.

The NVA had fired the three RPG rounds to great effect and then disappeared under the clouds of debris I'd rained down upon and around them. Whether they were dead up on top of the opposing valley wall or had successfully run off, I knew I'd never know. In real combat, I'd learned, if there was any risk to it all, nobody went out to check and see what the body count was from the effect of our fire. If forced to file an after action report I simply lied about it. It was like learning about 'confirmed' kills a sniper might make. Who was going to go out there, a thousand meters or more into Indian Country, to confirm anything? The sniper took the shot and his sidekick confirmed it. End of story. Dismount and move on to set up for the next shot.

According to Fessman, listening in to the combat net traffic, our company was verbally ordered down valley three times before the Gunny couldn't take it anymore. We hadn't moved an inch.

"We've got to move back down the valley," he said to me, kneeling like some sort of unwilling supplicant on the edge of my exposed poncho cover. His own poncho was being peppered with rain. The Gunny didn't wear any kind of head cover, his jet-black hair, with a few gray sprigs, looking almost like a helmet of its own.

"How long do you think Kilo is going to last with those children as their leaders?" I asked, sidestepping the fact that we had not responded to the battalion orders.

"You were one of them three weeks ago," the Gunny shot back, with a note of derision in his tone.

I stared into the man's dark eyes, hooded under his thick, even darker, eyebrows. The man seemed oblivious to the water running down his face. Occasionally he'd wipe his eyes with the back of one of his brown hands or swipe his hair back, but that was it.

I wanted to comment on the fact that he'd said I was special, earlier, but thought better of it. In truth, I was frozen in grief and terror. The grief was not over the death of V.C and his radio operator. It was over myself. It was Alice's letter and the premonition. I touched the outside of my helmet. The letter to her from V.C. that had so unsettled me was only micro-millimeters from my brain. I felt it was an omen, a premonition, and I was frozen in terror. In spite of the fact that I knew it was stupid, I felt like that if I didn't move then nothing could get me.

None of any of that could be discussed with the real warrior in front of me. Without that man's goodwill and help I'd have been long dead, and I knew I couldn't possibly go on without him. Another thought had struck me, the only thought that gave me any impetus to obey battalion's shitty orders at all. If the Gunny went with Kilo to help save them like he'd save me, then I would be alone and lost, and probably quickly dead.

I could see that the Gunny was just about reaching the point where he'd either say something really crummy to me or quite possibly hit me with some nearby object. I broke from my trance and moved.

"Head em up, move em out," I said, quoting the character Rowdy Yates from the television show called Rawhide.

I stood up, for the first time in hours, my body feeling like it had been put through one of those manual washing machine ringers.

"Those guys cut the Kilo Marines out?" I asked the Gunny.

"Still a mess," he replied. "Everyone wants to claim they're part of Kilo, of course, since they know where the rest of us are going."

I felt so relieved that my shoulders actually sagged. The Gunny was coming with me. He'd said the word 'us,' not 'you.'

"The bad news is we're going back down into the valley," the Gunny said, stepping back to allow me to gather my things. "The good news is that we can't go far because we've got the problem of those guys up on the hill."

The Gunny was right and I was cheered a bit. I could place artillery rounds all around the base of the hill, except for the hillside directly facing south, and for that, we had the fearsome Ontos, no doubt filled to the hilt with 106 beehive rounds from the morning resupply dump. I immediately began to pray that the guys up on the hill would last for a while up there. The longer they lived, the longer we got to hang around in the better part of the south valley. Moving further down would take us back into that killing hell where the snaking Bong Song, the predatory animal life, and the NVA waited with panting breath and drooling lips, whispering 'come my pretty' through the weeping jungle bracken.

I strapped my pack on, but not before pulling a can of Ham and Mothers out and working the tiny P-38 can opener around the top edge. The cans were dark green with black writing, no doubt designed for maximum camouflage, but making it impossible to read the writing in anything but the brightest light. I squatted down and poured the unheated greasy mess down my throat, gulp after gulp, knowing I was somehow being reduced to a lower order creature on the animal scale. I also knew that I wasn't thinking clearly. Not caring one whit about the lives of the Army troopers stuck up on top of Hill 975, but being badly hurt about losing V.C. on the cliff wall, didn't make sense, and I knew it. How had I become so calloused in such a short time, and would I change into the old me again if I made it back to the world? I finished the meal, not wiping what was left from the lip of the can for fear of cutting myself on its rough edge. I wanted to walk over to the river and throw the can in to watch it float away, like when I was a kid, but I knew I couldn't. I was the company commander. What I did might be copied and the company couldn't afford to have hundreds of C-ration cans floating downriver to reveal how many of us were left and where we might be on the river. Not that there was much mystery to our position, as far as the enemy was concerned. I put the empty can back into my pack and prepared to move out.

I followed the Gunny, and my scout team followed me down what vaguely passed for a trail. I looked at the fairly beaten mud path, putting one wet boot after another, making sure not to look back and up at the swinging blowing ropes I knew were still hanging down from the top of the plateau. I would have to write my wife about Alice, but I knew I'd have to write in such a way that what really happened hadn't happened at all. My wife was in San Francisco and Chance's wife was in San Diego. Five hundred miles separated them. Even if they were next door it wouldn't matter, I realized. What possible good could come if the two women met one another? My wife had our baby girl. Did Alice have anybody? I brushed the side of my helmet with the letter inside it like I was brushing aside a cobweb.

"You have to let them go, each and every one, like prying bad teeth out of your mouth," the Gunny said, turning his head slightly so only I could hear him, as we walked.

I grimaced at the image. The captain didn't fit into it. It was a terrible analogy, but I understood exactly what the Gunny was saying in his rather crude and brutal way. Prying the bad teeth out would end that never-ending pain and replace it with a duller throbbing thing that would eventually go away. But would it go away? I knew the Gunny was telling me, because he was so much older and more experienced, that it would. Was he saying it to make me feel better in the moment, or was he telling the truth about the way life would be if I made it? There was no way to know, other than the simple fact that the Gunny never seemed to say anything at all to make anyone feel better.

The Gunny stuck one hand behind him, holding out a dull metal object. I automatically reached for it.

I held the object up in front of me, as I walked. It was a climbing tool, although I'd never climbed or been around the serious technical equipment. Climbing during training had involved obstacles, rope nets and thick hawsers with knots, but no equipment.

"It's called a carabiner," the Gunny said. "Used for clipping on to ropes. Found it down at the bottom where they fell. You can use it as a key ring back home. Remember the ring and the climb and the fact that you did not die, and let him go."

I slipped the strange oblong object into my right thigh pocket where I'd kept the morphine I was blessedly out of. I didn't like the thought of replacing the captain's memory with a ridiculous keyring object. I was already a walking museum of the dead. I carried Tex's Colt, wore Keating's watch and a previous company commander's damaged helmet. My boots were from someone else, identity unknown, who'd died, courtesy of Macho man, and now I had Chance's carabiner, for keys I didn't have.

"They've got three Prick 25s up there. There's no way they can be out of communication with us," I mused to myself, knowing Fessman, close behind, was hearing every word I said.

"Dealing with recon is that way, sir," Fessman said, keeping his voice as quiet as he could, given the sliding thunder of the nearby river and the irritating patter of rain impacting on our helmets. "They don't communicate unless it's deemed vitally important. They don't want to be spotted or triangulated or have their transmissions translated."

"Brilliant," I said, not bothering to turn my head. "Like the enemy does not know where they are. Like they had at least a tiny chance of staying alive before. Now they get to die in silence."

Fessman didn't respond again, or if he did I didn't hear him.

It took only half an hour to reach the fork where the tributary running down into the Bong Song slanted and curved around the promontory of the plateau that all of us referred to as Hill 975. The tributary had been waist deep, and although running strong enough in the days before it had still been fordable without equipment or assistance. The monsoons had changed that. The level of the water, as we hunched down and back from it to keep our exposure from the hillside rising up behind us to a minimum, had risen about two feet. Fast moving water traveling at armpit level was no longer fordable, as before. Whether the Ontos could enter the water and serve as a mid-point stepping-stone to get everyone across was questionable, at best. We could not afford to lose the Ontos, or even have it out of commission once we got across the water. The only security available would be digging in just beyond the jungle line on the other side of the tributary. Even that would provide more camouflage than a true cover. There was no reason to believe the NVA weren't set up in force further back inside that thick, nearly impenetrable, jungle and it was a given they were established in force inside the tunnel complexes they'd dug into the side of Hill 975. The drums continued to beat, as they had since the dramatic execution of Captain Chance earlier, somewhere up and just over the lip of the cliff face.

00:00

00:00The Gunny, and his radio operator made his way through the light scruffy cover to my side. We peered down at the moving water together, the wind picked up and was now blowing the rain nearly sideways down the tributary and out over the Bong Song it joined nearly in front of us.

"There's that," the Gunny said, nodding out toward the moving water before lighting one of his cigarettes, the tinny snap of his lighter sounding familiar but out of place in our exposed position.

"We'll be trapped between two forces again," he said, mat-ter-of-factly, "and how in hell are we supposed to get up that hill again to claim another crop of dead bodies, much less back down should we accomplish the mission?"

"Lightner and Kilo took off north, I presume," I said, having no credible answer to the Gunny's questions.

"Yeah, they headed north," the Gunny replied, and then laughed a derisive laugh before inhaling again. "Those lieutenants sat the non-com platoon and squad leaders down and gave them an hour of the five-paragraph order. I stayed for five minutes. It was just too funny not to have missed."

"A whole five paragraph order?" I asked, in surprise.

The ornate battle planning presentation, drilled by memory into every Marine Officer, detailed every bit of an attack operation. It was effective in training, especially when delivered to other officers who were acting like grunts. The reality of combat was way different.

"BAMCIs and SMEAC, and the whole Kit-in-Kaboodle," the Gunny laughed, taking in and blowing out more smoke. "You should have been there. Never seen so many living Marines with unblinking round eyes and nothing at all behind them."

"Who are they attacking?" I asked, not being able to quite take in what had occurred.

"Who the hell knows?" the Gunny said, not as a question. "They're headed north, attacking a direction, the river, the crocodiles or maybe a water buffalo or two. The NVA are down here, comfortably living among us, and they don't give a shit about those lucky bastards led by those young fools while they jabber on meaninglessly."

I waited and watched the Gunny smoke his cigarette down with-out offering it to me. The Gunny was mad as hell. I knew he wasn't mad because he'd stayed behind. He was mad because Kilo was going north and it had no chance of making it on its own. The smallest un-der-equipped NVA forces would take it apart piecemeal, probably in one night, unless there was a Gunny-type among the non-coms and un-less those four matching second lieutenants were somehow taken out of the equation. The Gunny had stayed, I realized, not because he was loyal to me, or the company, the Gunny had stayed because his chances were better with the racially divided, embittered and embattled elements of our company, and he had someone he could mostly control who called accurate artillery (most of the time) and could read a map.

"You have a plan for all this?" the Gunny asked, his tone indicating that he knew I didn't.

"You won't like it," I answered, knowing my wispy idea of about the only thing we could do to survive had about as much chance of being implemented as it did of being successful if it was undertaken.

"I haven't liked any of your plans," the Gunny replied, his voice flat and seemingly filled with bitter truth.

"The company crosses the tributary using the Ontos," I said, thinking fast. "The Ontos is set to fire up the slope with plenty of rounds to reload. The beehives at maximum range adjustment of the fuses can scour that whole hillside. Two or three Marines go up the chute we slid down. They move wearing cut down trousers, and nothing else, not even boots. We carry our boots around our necks for the trip back down and if we have to move up there to get the bodies. The chute doesn't look like it but it can be climbed. Just under the ferns and tealeaves is thick tough mud, interlaced with sticks and debris. We dig in with bare feet and toes and climb, with any slip being, of course, a nearly instant sleigh ride to the bottom again. We reach the top of the hill, grab the Army idiots and toss them down the chute, dead or alive. You and the company grab them and us at the bottom, and then we make it across the tributary. After that, we get the hell back down to the airfield and get ready for the assault."

"That's it?" the Gunny asked a slight tone of awe in his tone, however.

"Jungle Junior and the Lost World. Where do you come up with this shit? What then, we still all end up back here in the same shitty old airfield. We make an assault on what after that insanity, if anybody's alive, I mean."

"The assault on the river," I answered. "The old bridge is probably still there. The tanks gotta be there. We cross the river again and retake about the most secure area we've been in ever since we've been down here. We hold the area under the lip of that cliff. I use the 175s red bag, up and down the valley, plus Cowboy and his Skyraiders pack a lunch every day and orbit our small world. And we wait, taking every bit of heat the NVA can throw at us."

"What about our orders?" The Gunny asked.

"We wait for new orders, I replied.

"They're not going to put up with this make-our-own-rules bullshit much longer," the Gunny forced out in frustration.

"What about the plan?" I countered.

"So, we're going to do the usual and ignore battalion," The Gunny said, unable to let the formality of our command situation go.

"Like this is becoming normal? That can't go on, you know."

"We get the Army guys off the hill, and maybe even save their lives," I replied. "Then we hold up and survive. They'll want us to go back down the valley at some point, and at some point, we have to decide on that. But we'll be alive."

"The Army gives its own orders to those guys," the Gunny said, trying to poke holes in my plan, "and those recon types may not want to abandon their post no matter how much trouble they're in … that they may not know they're in … until they are dead, anyway.

"They stay up there and die, or they're dead already, or they come down with us," I replied. "Three doors. Pick one. The rest flows from there. We do the same thing no matter which door they pick. We make contact and get the fuck out of Dodge as quickly as we can."

"You think they're going to let you come down that sluice again?" the Gunny asked.

"Hell, they probably don't know where we went or how we got down," I replied. "That hill is a rabbit warren of holes and tunnels carpeted over with a jungle almost too thick to move around in."

"We can't get the Ontos across the river and we can't leave it unprotected unless we spike it," the Gunny said as if that was a deal breaker.

"Really?" I said. "How about if we use the Ontos to drag a bunch of trees and bamboo across the bridge and dump it between the far bank and the bridge. The Ontos drives across the dumped debris and there we are. The Ontos serves as our base of fire to protect resupply coming in on that open area between our protected positions at the base of the cliff and the river."

"This whole thing is beginning to sound way too complex," the Gunny said, scratching his head before pressing his hair and brushing the collected water from it. "We don't have any clue about the deadly silent Army teams on top of the hill, we have no idea whether the Ontos can ford the river, and what's the NVA supposed to be doing while we're trying to pull all this off, not to mention that battalion is going to want us to return all the way down south to welcome another bunch of idiots they're no doubt planning on sending in from An Hoa."

I hadn't missed the small part of his presentation wherein he'd used the word 'you,' instead of 'we' when it came to coming back down the sluice. The Gunny wasn't going back up the hill with me. I had no choice in the matter if anyone was going at all. I was the only one who knew how to navigate up the twisty slippery mess of layered debris, using the semi-solid mud just underneath to dig into with bare toes while staying so low anyone viewing the scene would think they were seeing thick brown snakes creeping up the mountain.

I didn't need the Gunny for the hill. Fessman and Nguyen would do. Zippo was just too heavy and thick. There was no way he could sinuously imitate a sidewinder to get up the muddy mess of 975's sluice.

I looked over to where Fessman sat, fiddling with his private radio, a very low version of Proud Mary coming from its ridiculously inadequate speaker. My wife's name was Mary. The song had to be a good omen.

"What do you think?" the Gunny said toward Fessman, lighting yet another cigarette in the rain by cupping both hands over it, as he somehow used the Zippo to ignite the thing.

I couldn't believe the Gunny was asking Fessman anything. The kid was way old beyond his teenage years, but generally, radio operators and low ranking enlisted were only ever asked about things that directly related to any specialty they might have.

The Gunny waited for the few seconds it took Fessman to turn his radio off, indicating just how important the kid felt it was to be asked his opinion about anything by the Gunny.

"I like that part," he finally said, after taking a few moments to rub his chin and give the appearance of thinking very deeply.

"What part?" the Gunny asked, as perplexed as I was by Fessman's answer.

"The Three Doors Plan part," he said with a big smile, before going on, "Jungle Junior and the Lost Word is cool but too long."

The Gunny made no reply, and neither did I because there really wasn't one to make.

The drums beat on, and only at that moment did I realize I'd gotten used to them. The powerful deep jarring vibrations through the air and coming up from the ground didn't bother me in my very center anymore. The drumbeats had become like the leeches. They were just another part of my strange dangerous world. The grunting whiney sound of the Ontos moving slowly toward us from upriver, the tracks being carefully supervised so they wouldn't bog down in riverbank mud, was also becoming part of my life. I didn't' have to turn to look at it. I knew where it was and how it was doing in the mud just by the sounds it made. I pulled my canteen out for a drink of hot water, and for a brief few seconds, the fetid liquid washing down my throat, I thought of home. I didn't think of my wife or our baby, or even my used up, so precious, GTO. I thought about a coke. A cold coke, in one of the hour-glass-shaped bottles. No ice, the dark liquid just so cold it was almost ice.

I snapped my canteen back into its holder, hearing the second distinct snap at the same time as the cry of "incoming." I heard the thud-ding 'thupe' of mortar rounds being launched against me for the first time. I'd been very briefly trained in our own sixty mm mortars and also the 81s Kilo had earlier, but for some reason, the sound of the cheap light munitions launching into the air was much more threatening and foreign when it was heard from a distance, and you knew the rounds were intended to kill you.

My body hit the Gunny's side as I went face down into the mud. I bounced slightly back up and then a bit away from him. I hadn't count-ed the launch sounds, as they had been very rapid and the rushing fear again was scattering my brain. Everything was silent except for the beat-ing of the distant drums and the rushing waters of the Bong Song. I pushed my face into the mud, not caring about leeches or anything else. The mortar rounds were coming down and death would be dealt out mercilessly from above.

"They're only eighty-two millimeters" the Gunny whispered al-most jauntily from nearby. "Not the shitty 120s."

I didn't have time to evaluate just how that was such seemingly great news. The Ontos, before the explosions, began to rip across the unprotected course of our travel.

one-hundred-four

THE TWENTY-FIRST NIGHT : FIRST PART

It was an impossible mission but there was no other way. Nobody in the company was going to make it up the backside of Hill 975 without getting blown to smithereens no matter how it was done. The first time they'd gone up the back side of the connection plateau had probably worked because NVA forces occupying the outside and inside of the tip of the plateau never dreamed there was a rapid, nearly impossible, way for anyone up there to get back to the bottom unscathed.

I could not take Zippo with me because he was simply too big, and Fessman wasn't going to be able to move up through the muddy, slippery, dark and forbidding chute wearing a radio, and the other junk he needed to stay in communication. Therefore, he wasn't necessary. There would be no communication. Nguyen and I would go alone and we could wear nearly nothing. When things were slippery then only slippery worked. Slippery, with plunging fingers and digging toes. No boots. No Colt. No M-16. Not even a K-Bar. My biggest worry, after the gnawing fear of going up that chute in the dead of night, was making sure the Army reconnaissance teams located at the top, if they were still alive, would not shoot us on sight, or even without seeing. There had been no fire from or on the top of the hill since the RPG incident claiming Captain Chance's life, however. It was likely that the force at the top was following radio silence, or only keeping their radios on in a receive mode.

"What about my getting hold of the Army and then the frequency," Fessman had asked earlier before darkness began to fall. "I can let those guys up there know you're coming."

"How?" I'd responded. "In the clear? In some kind of screwy code revealing the chute and our climbing up it in the middle of the night looking like goblins from some bad movie? Radio isn't going to work and neither is any other form of communication I can think of."

Fessman had no further comment, but I knew my own answer disturbed him a lot.

We would have to take our chances, and possibly the biggest

chance would be in trying to make contact in the middle of the night without getting killed by our own men.

I remembered the base of the chute wasn't climbable. Nguyen and I prepped for the assault in one of the holes dug and left in our earlier time at the bottom edge of 975. The tributary of water was more swollen than it had been but the elevation of the holes just above it was plenty sufficient to keep the holes fairly dry. Maneuvering the Ontos into a position where it could face the slope sweeping up to the north while remaining close enough to back into the water and allow Marines to cross without rappelling or swimming over was critical. The rain kept its solid-seeming fall onto everything that wasn't covered while that was going on. The noise of the rain, the mild wind that accompanied it, and the NVA's own incessant drumming might well be all the cover from passing noise we might need in making the difficult climb.

I used the two different camouflage sticks the Gunny had handed me earlier. One was green and one was dark brown. I used them on my face, neck and then the tops of my hands and arms. Mud would have to do for the rest of my night disguise. Nguyen wore his ancient issue trousers and me my own, stopping short of cutting off the legs simply because I was unlikely to get another pair in short order from one of our most dependable, but strangely laden, resupply flights. Neither of us would wear boots, which was also a difficult decision because I wasn't climbing up Tantalus Mountain in Hawaii with my old school friends. When we came back down the chute, if we came back down the chute, we would not need boots, as long as we impacted into the rather deep pool at its base.

But up on the mountain? And if circumstances demanded a different descent from the peak, then what? Coming down in bare feet didn't seem to feel appealing, as I considered the complexity of the whole thing. But, I also knew there was really no consideration to go through. There was going to be no climb up through that messy flowing muck in boots. Nguyen and I were reduced to our primal states. Toes and fingers would dig in and allow slow constant advancement up the hill or they wouldn't. There was no chance that flat-soled boots, or even if we had the new cleated jungle boots, would allow for the depth penetration it was going to take to dig and move upward, repeating the process all the way up.

"This is a stupid mission and an even dumber plan than the ones you've come up with before," the Gunny hissed into my right ear. "They have Army back up, Army air and Army units up and down this forsaken valley."

I picked up my web belt, wrapped into a ball around Tex's .45 and handed it to him, followed by my damaged helmet. My insides weren't quaking but I was filled with inner terror. My hands were shaking but it was thankfully growing too dark to see them. It was the curdling fear that ate at me. I knew the Gunny was right, but there was no alternative, except pulling what we'd pulled back in my first days of combat. We could violate our orders and say we went up the hill, and then sit at the bottom and wait it out. Even that, given the fact that we were almost totally surrounded, wasn't viable. The Army guys were up there in silence and in deep trouble, they didn't have a clue about. We could not do anything. Assaulting the hill with the full brunt of the company would cost us half of the company, or more, and that assault could not be done at night. Only the Ontos could provide any supporting fire on the surfaces of the slope, and it was limited in range for its mightily effective beehive rounds, not to mention it was the night. Chance's death weighed heavily upon me, and my shoulders slumped slightly in the dark, as I stood there. The movement was almost imperceptible but not to Nguyen.

The slight, but whipcord tough Montagnard leaned into me, and then pushed something harshly into my mouth before I grasped what he was doing. I choked and would have spit the substance out except Nguyen had his left hand covering my mouth and his right behind my neck.

"Chew," I thought he said, followed by some Vietnamese words I didn't understand.

I chewed slowly, and then almost wretched, as some of the bitter liquid squeezed out from whatever solid Nguyen had shoved in my mouth, flowed down my throat.

"Don't do that shit," the Gunny said.

I wasn't sure whether he was talking to Nguyen or me. My hands grabbed Nguyen's but he held on for dear life, his reflecting, but otherwise invisible, eyes eating into my own, only inches away from his face.

"Chew," he commanded.

"That's Betel Nut," the Gunny said, with a sigh, letting me know that he was talking to me, and not the seemingly crazy Montagnard. "That's what the villagers chew. Turns their teeth purple before they all fall out. Crazy shit."

Nguyen released my mouth and neck and backed away. He

pointed downward. I understood immediately that he meant for me to spit whatever it was out on the ground. I did so, only then realizing that I could spit. Only minutes earlier my mouth had been so dry with fear that spitting would have been impossible. I spit several times, saliva flowing like mad. All of a sudden my body was infused with an energy I hadn't felt since landing in Vietnam. I breathed deeply in and out, the night seemed to come alive around me. And then it hit me. I was afraid of what we were about to do. However, I didn't have that core of terror running up and down my center anymore. It was just gone. And I had energy. I wanted to move, no matter where that movement took me. I had to move.

The Gunny, Zippo, Fessman, Nguyen and I made our way back where water fell down from the falls that indicated the bottom of the chute sticking out above us. There was plenty of thick plant growth along both sides of the sluice coming down. I chose the eastern side to begin working up through simply because it was closer. I said nothing to anyone because there was nothing to say and also because I was suddenly consumed to get to the top of the hill. Without boots the early going was hard. I had to make sure nothing penetrated the skin on the bottoms of my feet. I'd been in wet boots for a long time, and I lacked the thick calloused pads I'd enjoyed from running around the Hawaiian Islands barefoot.

The climb wasn't so much of a climb as it was a sinuously winding upward digging crawl, back and forth, from one side of the denser jungle growth to the other. We had to take the rather narrow chute as an off-road vehicle would switchback up a slope, to lessen the degree directly in front of it. The movement wasn't nearly as laborious as it was slow. The constant rain provided plenty of noise for cover, beating down on the upper parts of the foliage like tiny feathering beats on a million snare drums. Nguyen was there but it was too black to see him, and my own movement dampened almost any chance for external sounds penetrating. Could the NVA be so well positioned and alert enough that it could observe our entry onto the surface of the chute, just above the drop-off, I wondered? If fired upon, and not immediately hit, there would be no defensive return fire from Nguyen or I. There would only be one course of action if we were attacked on the way up, and that course was very obvious. Back down the chute would be the only choice we had with any chance for life in it, only this time the transit would be with the likelihood that grenades would accompany our wild ride down.

I knew I was going to be covered with leeches all over, but I didn't care. In fact, I noted almost absently, as I carefully climbed until I could move over onto the surface of the chute itself, I didn't care about much of anything except not writing home enough. Was I losing my distant touch with the only thing in the world that mattered? Had I written earlier and was that letter in my pocket as I climbed? I didn't know. I hadn't even checked. Once I'd chewed the Betel Nut everything had changed. I dug into the mud just to the side of me and made my entry out onto the very surface of the chute. And then I smiled with what I knew was one of the few genuine smiles I'd generated in all of my time in combat. I was suddenly in a bit of home.

My feet sank down inches into the muck and my toes curled to gain traction, while my fingers reached out forward and just above me. I moved upward in a catlike spider sort of animal wending motion. My feet and hands took over, as I traversed back and forth across and up into the chute, the limits of the foliage on either side of the thick leaves and mud and my movement ever upward were my only directors. I cared if Nguyen was behind me, but I didn't care at the same time. The climb was a personal thing. I was climbing for Chance. I was performing a climb with a bit more sense than his own actions had demonstrated and I was climbing up to get his men. The three yellow rope ends played back and forth in front of me, not real, but then nothing except the mud, leaves, and rain were real. The distant drums, still barely audible, were sounds made, as if by some distant Hollywood special effects outfit. They beat to spur me on. They beat to assure that my own heartbeat was still beating with them.

I'd decided to keep my watch. I knew that the mud covering me might not be effective at blocking every glint of light that might glint from the watches more reflective surfaces, but I felt it was a vital tool Nguyen and I could not do without. We were on a night climb and dawn was our worst enemy. I made twenty sinuous slithering moves, and then looked at the face of the instrument. The tiny luminous hands, gleaming gently through the crud on its face, told me that the moves had taken about five minutes. The hill was, based on that guess, a five-hour climb, and that's if we didn't tire from the continuous energy-consuming effort of having to move every second of every minute while in the chute.

I finally stopped, my breathing coming slow but deep and hard.

The work was suddenly almost too much. I didn't look at my watch because I didn't want to see what it showed. The top would be the top and we'd know it when we got there. There was nothing else. Nguyen pulled his way up to my side. I didn't turn my head to look directly at him, although I knew the glistening rain made him partially visible right next to me.

This time he didn't force the Betel Nut into my mouth. He held the drug to my lips and I immediately grasped it in and bit down. The bitter juice flowed once more. I didn't spit. I chewed and chewed until the energy came back. And it did. Whatever was in the nut had a magical power that I knew had to be illegal and addictive back home. Not only might I become an addict but my teeth might turn purple and all fallout, according to the Gunny. Finally, I spit the remnants of the nut husk down into the mud only inches from my face. I wondered if Nguyen was chewing the Betel too but I wasn't interested enough to attempt to find out. I went back at the mud with my talons extended and biting in. There was no smile this time, even though the idiocy of worrying about my living long enough to become a drug addict deserved one.

The top end of the chute didn't end with any drama. The mud just seemed to dry up and my fingers and toes dug into bits of bracken but then bit into the hard ground. I uneasily and weakly got up on my hands and knees. Nguyen pulled me back down. I had to think clearly, I realized. We were a long way from being in any safe position. The most dangerous part of the plan was upon us. How to make contact with a very deadly, but horribly inexperienced, unit of special forces troops on guard against attack in the middle of the night. In a jungle. In a jungle filled with beating drums, blowing triple canopy tree growth and densely falling rain.

Nguyen and I both began to inch forward together, threading our way through a loosely held bamboo thicket. There was nothing on the other side, but there was almost no visibility to see anyone, friend or enemy if there was anybody there. I wanted to whisper out and identify ourselves as Marines, but I knew that was beyond foolish. The one known element of our mission up the hill was that the mountain was run through with tunnels and alive NVA troops filling those tunnels.

We lay still, trying to catch the slightest of sounds or recognize anything familiar, only inches ahead of us in the night. But there was nothing. I rubbed my hands up and down my arms, leeches falling away immediately as I did so. I marveled. Was it the Betel Nut coming out of my skin, I wondered. Leeches never just fell away. Leeches bit instantly and hung on. It was what they did to survive. But there was no time to consider. Nguyen punched me on the right shoulder, before sliding one of his hands to take mine. He pulled me toward him, and then placed my hand on something soft, with wet clothing on top of it. My mind recoiled slightly but my hand did not. I was touching part of a human body. We had to know more. I moved closer and began exploring upward until I got to the body's upper chest. I felt the "T" shirt under the blouse just under its neck. The body was one of our own. The NVA didn't wear undershirts, and neither did seasoned American combat troops. Undergarments simply didn't work out in the field, not in the jungle, anyway. I rolled the body slightly. The man was wearing a Prick 25 radio. There were no lights to indicate it was functional, or on. I didn't have Fessman to operate the thing for me and, even if I had, there was no way I was going to say anything out into the deadly night we were in.

Nguyen and I moved forward coming upon more bodies. Whether all of the army units that had been flown in were dead at the top of Hill 975 was unknown, but it was obvious to me that all the Americans who'd landed had been taken care of, just like the even larger force before. I caught hold of Nguyen's arm and squeezed. I motioned my head back toward the entrance to the chute. We had only one chance to get down. My watch said it was three in the morning. There was nothing to be accomplished by remaining on the summit. Chance's men had followed him into Valhalla, or wherever death had taken them. There was nothing we could do except try not to go and join them. Without light and some understanding of what had happened, it was impossible under the conditions to tell what had killed them.

Slowly we both turned and began a slow crawl back the way we'd come, or as close as we could tell in the night. We moved slower than when we'd come in. It was more important than ever not to be detected. We were in enemy territory and that had been fatally proven over and over again. I felt immense relief when I crawled through the loose bamboo thicket. I knew it had to be the same one. Most bamboo clumps or thickets were too dense to move through at all.

I stopped, and Nguyen instantly stopped with me. We lay flat and unmoving together. Something had been added to the elements that had subtly changed the area we'd come through earlier. I couldn't make out what it was at first. I pulled Nguyen's bare arm closer until his body was only inches from my own. When I could faintly see his facial features, I sniffed my nose repeated, as quietly and quickly as I could. Nguyen's body stiffened. He smelled it too. The smell of cigarette smoke. American cigarette smoke. The Army guys were dead. The NVA had gone through their things and found America cigarettes and not been disciplined enough to avoid using them.

We both lay watching and listening. There were no telltale red dots of burning ash. There were only the tendrils of smoke drifting by, invisible except to our noses. The NVA were not only there and up, they were all around and among us. I couldn't believe we'd crawled through the Army unit and back without being discovered.

It was also obvious that the NVA knew about the chute and were stationed at its head. But what were they waiting for? To think that they might have thought that two men of the opposing force would crawl up the chute in the middle of the night was beyond comprehension. If that was the case, then where had they been when we exited the top earlier? I couldn't figure it out, but I knew it also didn't matter. If the NVA knew we were there among them, then they'd be doing a lot more than smoking, I realized. Once again there really weren't any options. We had to get into the chute and down. The distance to the softer mud was possibly no more than fifteen yards I thought, but what if I was wrong? I tried to clear my head of the Betel Nut drug and think clearly. It finally came to me. It didn't matter. Nguyen and I had to exit the bamboo thicket, get up and then run forward for all we were worth. The chute would take care of everything else. There was no need to dive into it or onto its surface. Once in the slippery grasp of the dead fern fronds, old fallen leaves, mud and water that would be it. We were unarmed, so there was no need to protect our armament or position

I looked over at Nguyen, wondering what he was thinking, hoping he was thinking what I was thinking. I nodded once and then looked in the direction we came from when we'd climbed the chute. I held up three fingers in front of his eyes. He looked at them and then back at me. I made a fist, looked toward where I hoped the top of the chute was, and then back. I rose up slowly to a crouch. Nguyen rose with me. I held up one finger and nodded, and then my second. On the third extension, I turned and ran like hell away from the bamboo thicket.

The shooting was instant but seemingly all over the place. I saw flashes as I ran, but I wasn't on my feet very long before the chute claimed me. I was down, face first, and plunging back into the terror of night, but not with deeper terror inside me. I was leaving a lot of that behind, as my speed picked up and I began hitting the curves and bumps along the way.

Instead of shooting into the very blackest of the night and trying to traverse properly to get hits at targets impossible to see, I would have presumed that the NVA would have used explosives of one kind or another to hit us. Although the thick leaves and mud of the chute would absorb most of the concussion and fragmentation from grenades, some of the effects might have been telling or even terminal. Sending their own men down the nightmare of some Disneyland ride invented by a sick horror movie character made no sense, but the NVA rode with us, and they'd obviously, from their sounds, never done it before. I felt Nguyen jolting and slamming around just ahead of me in the chute. The noise, grunts, groans and near screams of the slipping and falling NVA troops behind didn't cause me as much fear as consternation. What were they doing? They were no longer shooting and there were no explosions or flashes of fire. What could be their plan in coming down the chute after us? Only the Gunny and our company of Marines waited at the bottom of the chute, and they would be there crouching down, prepared to receive us, as we cascaded from atop the fifteen-foot cliff and down into the pool the chute ended over.

The ride down was longer than I remembered but I knew that might be tempered by the effects of the Betel Nut or the fact that I had no idea just how big the force was plummeting down the chute behind us, or if the Gunny would be able to deal with them when they flew through the air and landed in his lap.

My body remembered each and every turn and drop, as I literally fell toward the fast-approaching bottom of Hill 975. I let the mashed mess of fern fronds, dead leaves, twigs and mud mix possess me like I was a well-massaged larva just popped out and plunging toward the earth from the cocoon of some giant insect.

I'd lost track of the sounds from higher up, or whoever was coming down the slide after I had finally figured out that yelling in the middle of the A Shau night was an open invitation to instant death or they had become used to the frightening high-speed sleigh ride without a sleigh.

I knew the ride was over when the bottom of my stomach dropped out. I was in mid-air, just like before. The wait to be caught by my fellow Marines was longer than I knew it should be, and then I hit. There were no loving arms to catch me or any other kind. I impacted the surface of the water hard and then plunged butt first into the mud just beneath, my panicked lungs bursting out the last of my breath. The water was only waist deep, however, but instead of standing up to get clear I slithered along on the surface using my arms and a frog kick to reach the edge of the pool. I laid under what cover I could that was hanging over the edge of the water, the scene not a scene at all because I was in a stygian dark night under cloud cover with heavy rain. Where were the Gunny and the rest of the company, I wondered, before hearing what sounded like a bunch of logs coming down a timber sluice up above the other side of the pool. Nguyen touched my back with one hand and then pushed me outward and down until I was once again fully immersed under the surface of the water. In spite of the fact that I knew I was in the same mud hole, I'd landed in before, being under the water quieted my heart thumping fear of whatever might come next.

I heard the gunfire from beneath the water. It didn't sound like close in combat gunfire because of the near totally deadening effect of the water. I stayed down; the thump, thump, thumpity thump of fully automatic gunfire impacting inside me more than beating against my eardrums. I surfaced to breathe. The muzzle flashes all around me as harsh as the ear-splitting sounds, immediately taking away any night adjusted vision I'd had. I sank willingly back down, hoping to wait out whatever was going on above. Bodies had followed me down the chute. I believed them to be NVA soldiers in pursuit, and not understanding what they were involved with until it was too late and they were in the chute. My mind swirled with fearful probabilities. What if some, or all of the men who'd somehow gotten into the slide, were Army? There had been no way for Nguyen and me to find, much less count, all the bodies of the Army unit members in the dark up at the top of the hill. Had some of the Army guys survived, and then attempted to follow us down to safety? That the company was obviously firing, or returning fire from whoever had come down the mountainside, was ominous to the point of possibly being terrible, but there was nothing in my current situation to be done about it. I was unarmed and defenseless. I had to wait for the firefight to cease, or very likely die in the crossfire or because of mistaken friendly fire.

Nguyen pulled me up again. The firing had quieted down to a few very short bursts from the M-16s. There was no AK-47 fire that I could discern, although my ears were filled with water and I was night blind. We moved away from the drop off where the chute exited out over the water.

We surged more than swam or walked. The water was much deeper than I'd remembered it from the first time down but the monsoon rain had been pretty continuous.

Nguyen half-dragged pulled and carried me along through the mud until I ended up face down where Fessman and Zippo waited. With shaking hands, and their help, I got back into my gear, the .45 being the only piece of equipment that pushed back the fear at all. What had happened and how far from whatever it was could I get in how short a time and still remain company commander or whatever the hell I really was? There was no running away in combat. I'd somehow gotten away with that on my first night but, in the real world of open combat, it was a quick road to death by fire from either side. There was only survival in sticking together although sticking together was nothing at all like it had been in training or in the presentation by other veterans who I now knew had been to a combat area but very likely not participated themselves. Every vet seemed to have an opinion, and most of those opinions were about being tough and aggressive when in real combat.

I wondered if I survived, whether I would ever be able to listen to war stories like I'd heard before coming to Vietnam, about how that macho crap worked. None of us in real combat were tough. We were all afraid, wet, thirsty, hungry and eaten by insects. We spent most of our hours trying or hoping not to be in actual open combat. Real combat was all nearly the opposite of what I'd thought it to be.

The Gunny followed closely by Jurgens, Sugar Daddy and their three radio operators, slid bent over into our little-cleared area of jungle. The pond, or chute exit, was only meters away, but once inside the outer edge of the jungle bracken it seemed almost over in another world. Sporadic single shots came from where I'd landed but that was almost like total silence compared to the intensity of firefight I'd been trying to survive under only minutes earlier.

"Who in hell came down that chute after you?" the Gunny hissed out, his tone making it evident that I had to have something to do with whatever had happened.

I was stunned. I knew nothing. I'd gone up the mountain under the most difficult of circumstance, performed the grisly reconnaissance, and then exited down the same way I'd gone up. There had been no contact with the enemy and my contact with the Army had only involved feeling around a few dead bodies to unsuccessfully determine how they'd come to be dead.

Still in shock, and trying to let the old snake of fear recoil back to its less painful part of my belly, I took a few seconds to think about the question the Gunny had asked. Obviously, he was speaking for Jurgens and Sugar Daddy, as well. If he was asking who had come down the chute then none of them knew. The company had fired away and whoever was found in the water come daylight would be counted and identified. Nobody was going into the roiling wet pit of death to count anyone or anything in the night.

I hadn't reported to anyone. Only Nguyen and I knew for certain that either all or most of the Army recon contingent was dead. The company had opened up when it heard the screaming and yelling of the men following Nguyen and me down the chute. That was combat typical. Shoot and identify later. The Gunny was beside himself with concern that the men who'd come down had indeed been the Army team, and if that was true then there would be hell to pay. It was one thing to lose or kill your own. Between the Services, there would be a whole lot more trouble over friendly fire directed from a Marine unit toward an

Army one, especially if there were no survivors.

The correct analytical answer to the Gunny's question was "I don't know," but there was no way I was running with that.

"They were NVA," I lied.

"That solves that mystery," the Gunny said, relief in every bit of his tone.

"We've got to move, and move in the night before they get organized up there and figure out what the hell happened to their men," I said quickly. to change the subject

"We're going down into a set-in force with another force in pursuit to join up with them. The Army's probably going to come boiling down this valley ready to kill anything that moves in very short order, and I wouldn't be a bit surprised if battalion doesn't send another company of Marines up from the south at the same time. But that's not going to save us in time. We need to hole up and wait, using air and the 175s to beat the NVA back in the day and the Starlight Scope and Ontos to fight them at night."

"The Army's going to come 'boiling down the valley?' Jurgens murmured.

I realized my mistake in not mentioning that the recon team members on top of 975 were all dead. Maybe they were and maybe they weren't, and the last thing I wanted to do was wait around until first light and find some U.S. Army soldiers among the dead in the pool at the bottom of the chute. There was no requirement that we wait for an NVA body count. That could be hypothecated. I was convinced that the Army unit had been wiped out, just as had the one before. Remaining in the area when the sun came up, even with Cowboy and the artillery for daylight support would cost a lot of Marines lives for little or no return, and probably my own. It had been one thing to go up and try to make sure but I wasn't going to stay around in such a likely kill zone if I could help it.

"There was no way to make contact in the night," I said, inventing a story as I went along. "The rain and wind up there were much stronger than down here. We scouted the peak and, finding no one, realized that the NVA were all around us. That was it."

I glanced over at Nguyen's shiny bright eyes, two reflecting pools in the backdrop of another dark night. He didn't blink. I knew Nguyen understood enough English to know that I wasn't telling the Gunny the truth, and, even if he spoke understandable English, I knew he would say nothing.

"I don't want my people to have the point," Sugar Daddy said, coming from almost nowhere. "We've done enough," he said, finishing into the weather-beaten silence his first words had caused.

"Gunny, I need to talk to you for a second about reporting to battalion before we do anything," I said, getting unsteadily to my feet and walking a bit deeper into the blackness of the jungle.

Nguyen disappeared, as I walked away, and I knew he'd be somewhere nearby, invisible but there. My fear level dropped again.

The Gunny followed my lead. I stopped when I felt we were far enough away from the others to avoid being overheard.

"Give Sugar Daddy the tail end Charlie position," I said. "There won't be much of a threat to the point, because they won't easily hear us coming, although they have to know we're coming anyway. If Sugar Daddy wants the rear, then fine. The Ontos and Sugar Daddy's mess of a platoon. I'll be there to call in fire, although the NVA loves to attack at night they probably don't want to face the flechettes in the dark."

"So, no morning body count," the Gunny mused, as if not inquiring anything of me, instead just making a revealing statement.

The Gunny was smart and experienced. I knew he'd figured out my lie if it was a lie. At least he'd figured out that I likely didn't know anything. There was no question asked, so I chose not answer what hadn't yet been asked.

"If we killed a bunch of Army Special Forces then the 101st sure as hell would come 'boiling down the valley,' as you said, but I wonder who'd they be after boiling when they got here."

"There's the problem of the Ontos," I said, ignoring everything he'd said.

"What about it?" the Gunny asked.

"We're back to the question of losing it or getting it across the river," I stated, flatly. "There's no way we can stay on this side. There's nowhere secure to stay."

The Gunny took out one of his cigarettes and somehow got it burning in the rain. The sound of his lighter trilled through me. The Gunny was all the home in combat I had, and when I was alone with him it was like having a steady, talented father at my side.

"So, what's the plan, Junior?" he asked.

I breathed in and out deeply. He was going to let the whole Hill 975 mess go. He handed me the cigarette and I took it, my hand shaking again. I inhaled one long puff. I coughed, but only slightly.

"We get down to the partial bridge," I said, and then laid out the plan that had come to me once I knew we couldn't remain on the west side of the river anymore.

"We run it along that bridge at full speed and jump the rushing water at the end. The Ontos can run in six feet of water for a short time if it doesn't make it fully across. Although the water's really moving I don't think it's that deep right near the eastern bank where we were. It's going to depend on what's been eaten away since we were there before. With the Ontos on the far shore, dug in just in front of that cliff overhang, we'll be damned near impregnable from any attack, either frontal or from the jungle further south."

"And, if the Ontos doesn't make it?" the Gunny asked, taking his time to finish the cigarette before snapping it out into the night.

"Then we lose it in the river," I replied, knowing he wasn't going to want to hear that possible result but not having a choice.

There were no other viable moves for the company to make without suffering either very heavy casualties or utter destruction. If we lost the Ontos we'd likely lose the crew too.

"Sugar Daddy isn't stupid, you know," the Gunny replied, veering away from the plan I'd laid out. "He's been around for a while and he knows what his men fear the most. It's not the NVA attacking from the rear into the face of the Ontos darts."

"What, then?" I replied, in surprise, not understanding what the Gunny was really talking about.

"Booby traps. His men don't want to go home without their eyes, or whatever. We haven't been plagued by booby traps lately because it's been impossible to figure out where we were going at any given time."

The Gunny nodded at me.

There was just enough light to see the slight movement of his head as he paid me one of his rare unspoken compliments.

"Now they know where we're going and they've had time to get ready," I said, not liking where the conversation was going, although I wondered at the likelihood of anyone getting out of the valley alive, wounded or otherwise.

"You got it," the Gunny said, with an artificial laugh. "Put that bit into your plan before you give it one of those special names."

"Got it," I replied. "Thanks. Sugar Daddy's right. When we get to the old airfield we'll shift split the company down the middle and let the Ontos run through. The tracked machine takes the point, and any booby traps along the way."

I didn't like the idea of anyone in the company, aside from the Gunny, refusing to do anything when the chips were down, but I'd also learned that I was a long way from having the wisdom some of them could show from time to time that I didn't have, and probably would never live to possess.

"Straight through the heart, we'll call it," I went on, wishing it was morning and the Armed Forces Network was playing some song I could use for a better name by stealing the lyrics.

"Your scout team will be most approving," the Gunny whispered, as he passed me heading back to where the platoon commanders waited.

No sooner was he gone when Nguyen appeared not more than three feet from where the Gunny had stood. I thought the Montagnard was smiling in the night but it was too dark and wet to see for sure.

I returned to Fessman and Zippo and got into my pack for the move. The Ontos fired up in the distance and I knew the whole company was quickly preparing to pull out. The invisible communication network of the seemingly broken and fragmented unit was amazing to observe in action.

At some point along the way, I was going to have to get aboard the Ontos and clue the crew in about the details of the move. Taking the point in the Ontos was riskier than many might assume. The armor on the bottom of the thing wasn't thick enough to stop any sizable explosive fragmentation. A big enough booby trap, like a booby-trapped U.S. or Chicom artillery round, set off by tripwire or command, would kill everyone inside the machine. The crew would know that. Also, the run across the bridge Tex had laid down would be fraught with risk. That jump at the end of the bridge would be very risky. If the Ontos went fully into the river and was lost in the current, it would likely capsize and the crew would be unable to easily survive. The crew would know that too.

Backing down the riverbank path, close to the cliff wall didn't give me any sense of security, and didn't seem a bit like the company might be attacking the enemy's set-in position. The old airfield, there but invisible in the night, wasn't going to be used, even as a holding position for the company. The river had risen again and likely eaten away more of the bank that had provided a small haven of safety, only days earlier. Moving in the darkness had proven to have many more benefits for survival that I had been first led to believe. The NVA were night creatures but only because they were generally the aggressors in the dark. They were not nearly as capable of dealing with enemy aggression under such circumstance when the aggressiveness was directed toward them.

Time seemed to have slowed, as I covered ground that I'd been up and down only a matter of days and nights earlier. It seemed like I'd been there before but weeks or months or even years before. I remembered Marines now dead, but mostly the ones I had gotten stuff from. Tex and his .45 automatic. I pictured Stevens and the tank but could not place his face in my mind anymore. I could remember nine place grid coordinates in detail, and direct artillery fire in the dark, but I couldn't remember what Stevens looked like. That I wasn't upset about the stark difference didn't completely unnerve me because the only real emotion I lived with was fear. That fear was felt in my stomach, bones and always eating at the back of my mind. What awful thing leading to death was going to happen next fed the fear like a fireman stoking the coal aboard a cross-country steam train?

The Ontos made its way nearby. I'd decided to remain in the rear, as it was much more likely the NVA up on the hill would come down and pursue us rather than the southern force come up to meet us. I also had to pick just the right time to fill the Ontos crew in on their dangerous part in my plan. Sugar Daddy's men were close in and all around me, as the river bank between the jungle glued up against the canyon wall and the river was fairly narrow. The Ontos took away all surprise just by the noise its engine generated and broadcast. The river was running hard, however, and the rain pretty intense, so the NVA forces further south would only have radio traffic, if they had that, to try to figure out just how far along the move we were.

Zippo and Fessman loved the name of the plan, for their usual secretive and unknown reasons. I wasn't so much pleased by the chattering whispers I heard about the name by the Marines around me, as I was surprised about how simple drama so often worked better to gain support than a solidly strong analytical plan. My plan was a tattered mess, as usual, depending more upon luck than any analytical analysis and deep thought.

I made my way over to where the Ontos was backing slowly down the river. I climbed into the open rear hatch, wondering if I could gain the support of the crew for the mission ahead. They had to be all in, or there was no hope. We had to make it past the airfield without being hit from the rear and we also needed to not encounter any booby traps once past the airfield that might be large enough to destroy the Ontos. After all that we were going to need some real luck to make the rest of the plan work. Straight through the Heart might be the name of the plan but whose heart would remain in question until we were successfully across the river.

one-hundred-six

THE TWENTY-SECOND DAY : FIRST PART

Corporal Mike Riorden was the Ontos Commander, although everyone called him Rio, like the city because his roots were from somewhere down in South America. The Ontos crew loved the Ontos, and I was almost certain their love had little to do with the machine's armor or its armament. They got to ride wherever the thing was going, and they always had a place out of the rain to clean up, dry out and hang together. Rio, and two privates named Panda and Sentry comprised the whole crew. Panda drove, Sentry loaded the 106mm recoilless rifles, mounted three to a side on the exterior, and Rio was the gunner. In spite of my hesitation at how the crew might react to my rather suicidal 'straight through the heart' plan, they took to it like ducks to water. Panda, a strange gangly kid from Kentucky, who chewed tobacco or whatever else he could get a hold of, (I suspected the Betel Nut but said nothing), was also the mechanic because the smallish but dependable GM six-cylinder engine required constant attendance. It ate oil, spark plugs and for some reason, air filters, all the time.

"It's supposed to hit thirty miles an hour," Rio said, "but if Panda takes the rev-limiter off, empties the thing out, and pulls the guns and ammo, he says it'll hit forty or even a bit more. Can this piece of the bridge across the river handle ten tons, and is what's left of the thing flat enough to make the run?"

I didn't know the answers to Rio's questions, so I avoided dealing with them until we had enough daylight so I could tell anything for certain. The Ontos might do forty miles-an-hour, as he said, but it was anything but a dragster, and its run-up approach across the bridge would be short. What speed it could manage in that short distance before it plunged off into the raging water was anybody's guess. The Starlight Scope could tell me a lot before the light of day came on, but the resolution, what with the wind-blown rain, would not be great enough to commit lives to a project that might be doomed from the start. It was still too dark to see much of anything from where we were positioned by the idling machine. The Ontos had to have its engine running to be able to either power and therefore turn its turret or move its tracks to face whatever threat might arise.

Nearly half an hour passed, once we got set in along the side of the river. The machine was pulled back into a few feet of the nearby jungle scrub, from where the Ontos crew could maneuver the tracked vehicle properly to have a commanding view to the south and also out across the river. I climbed inside through the back doors of the thing but realized it would be useless to try to see anything in the dark in its daylight-only scope, so I climbed back down. I noted that Rio had somehow torn out his seat and replaced it with ammo boxes. How many extra rounds the Ontos now carried I had no idea but I liked the way Corporal Riorden thought.

It was uncomfortable to be so close to something that seemed to give away its position all the time, but I also knew that the NVA never seemed to shoot at the machine directly.

I instructed Zippo to unlimber the Starlight Scope. Dawn was not that far off, and the Ontos needed to make its move at first light or not at all. With Feesman laying at my side, I peered through the scope, resting comfortably across Zippo's upper right shoulder. The scene was visible, at least the river part, with the bridge and upside-down tank still resting in the middle of the Bong Song some hundred meters further south.

The river, through the enhanced green light return of the scope, ran as before, possibly at a bit higher level, but not high enough, I noted, to rise up and cover the mud flats on the other side. I studied the end of Tex's bridge, as intently as I could. Visibility wavered in and out with the passing sheets of rain, invisible in their passage except for the Starlight's ability to see in the dark. The rain didn't seem to change much to us, as it fell ceaselessly down upon us. It was just the regular, crummy and mildly disabling rain. The vital area between the extended end of the bridge and the far shore was as it had been before. There was simply no way to estimate the depth of water sweeping through the ten-meter wide stretch at the end of the thing. The Ontos was just short of five meters long. It would not take much in the way of momentum to allow the Ontos to pass through most of the water if it got up to speed. Any depth of that fast-moving water that it fell into, over three or four feet, would be fatal to the machine, however. The current would handle the Ontos even easier than it had when it tossed the much heavier tank around.

The water's aggressive rushing sound made me even more uncomfortable than the rain and mud around me. It seemed to be whispering "come, my pretty…" words like the evil witch had spoken in the Wizard of Oz when she was going to attempt to do Dorothy in.

The Gunny joined me, grunting out "Junior" almost silently, as he slid through the jungle growth to take the position on my other side.

I pulled my head back and removed my right eye from the soft rubber grommet. I looked over at the Gunny, his glinting facial features wet with the rain. I could only marginally see his form through my left eye, the right night blind from looking through the scope.

"Jurgens has his Marines ready," the Gunny said, moving his body around so he could get at his cigarettes. "They're ready to disassemble the Ontos guns and get them tied up for transport across the water."

I watched the Gunny getting set up to smoke. It was comforting to watch him, once again. I came to a decision.

"We can't pull the guns and ammo," I said, going against my own plan. "The guns weigh about five hundred pounds each. That's three thousand. The ammunition, at about twenty-five pounds per round, weighs about fifteen hundred, maybe a few hundred less. That takes the total up to forty-five hundred. The Ontos itself weighs ten tons. Two tons, or so, aren't going to make enough difference, and then how do we get the stuff across the water, mated back onto the machine, and ready to go in broad daylight? We could move the stuff at night but there's no working way to get the guns back on the Ontos in the dark, and we won't have any close in covering fire until it's fully reassembled."

"Jesus, Junior," the Gunny whispered out, cupping and lighting his cigarette before going on, "I thought you had it all worked out. What if the Ontos doesn't jump the water? Then we lose it all, and maybe that's the only thing that stands between us and them." The Gunny waved back over his shoulder toward the heavy jungle in the south, where we knew the NVA were watching and waiting.

"I was wrong," I replied. "The water's not that wide, if you want to look," I said, gesturing to the scope, although I knew it's flat black paint made it completely invisible in the darkness. "If it's too wide then we take up positions without it and take our chances with the 175s and how much air we can get down here to cover us during the daylight."

"What if they don't come, either the Army or our own battalion?" the Gunny asked, between puffs.

I noted that he didn't offer the cigarette to me, which made me feel like I was running through heavy traffic all on my own again. I wasn't worried about the Skyraiders coming. They weren't subject to battalion command and Cowboy had somehow grown rather fond of our messed up tattered company.

"I just got off the radio with the Six Actual," the Gunny said, conversationally, not as if he was building a case for some other plan. "The colonel wants us to hold our position until ordered to move back down there."

"That means somebody is coming, Gunny, because there's absolutely nothing down there except the river, the jungle, and the NVA if you will recall?"

"Yeah, Junior, I sure know that," the Gunny came right back. "And now you know that, but I'll be damned if I can seem to figure out why command doesn't know that. They're going to want an after-action report on 975. It won't be long before they figure out the Army lost another entire unit. We haven't filed a daily report in quite a while either. What do you want me to tell them?"

The after-action report would go out under my name, as ranking officer, but it was good to hear that the Gunny was still willing to write it or be involved at all. Maybe it was his belief, like my own, that we weren't going home alive from the A Shau, but I didn't really think so.

"Tell them that we attempted contact," I answered, after almost a full minute. "Tell them that we could not establish it either by radio or physically. Tell them what we hope is the truth. Pray God that there's no pile of Army Rangers lying dead at the bottom of that water pit."

"No, I don't think I'll bring up that part," the Gunny said, snapping his half-smoked cigarette away. "So, when dawn comes they're going to wind this thing up and let it fly.

"Rio's going to go it alone," I said. "When he gets to the other shore he can run it up to the edge of the cliff, flip it around and be loaded for bear until everyone gets across."

"When it's crossing you should have one more aboard in charge of keeping all six barrels pointed as close to south as possible in case they have to return fire on the fly."

With that, the Gunny was gone. I wondered why I hadn't thought of making sure the Ontos could fire at will while it went through the maneuver, but I hadn't. The Gunny was right. Rio needed to man the 106s while Private Panda, the driver, did what he did best.

The arrangements were made and the Ontos ready. The company was in a line of battle up and down the west bank of the river, although invisible in the pre-dawn darkness, misting rain and low but dense jungle foliage. The Gunny had been up and down the line to make sure plenty of small arms fire could be directed to wherever it was needed to support the Ontos crossing. The Starlight showed no movement, although visibility through the single lens was anything but perfect or clear.

At the vaguest of first light, before nautical dawn, Rio engaged the Allis-Chalmers transmission and eased the small but heavy machine down over the slight berm and onto the hardened mud. It didn't take long for the Ontos to reach the leading ramp canted slightly up onto the main body of the mobile bridge.

Rio revved the small six-cylinder engine up to maximum and took off. Without the scope, all I could see was the dense dark mass of the moving object. The Ontos accelerated as it went, crossing the length of the bridge in less time than I would have thought possible. There was no delay at the other end. I saw no splash of anything, only the dark object disappearing and then almost instantly reappearing, climbing quickly up on the far shore. I let my breath out all the way, only then realizing I'd been holding it. The Ontos had made it. After all the thought, planning and worry, the heavy little beast had performed the operation like it was built for it. There was no cheer or additional sound from the Marines in the company but in my mind, I was cheering madly. The Ontos would be there to cover our own crossing, a crossing that without it might have proven impossible or terribly terminal. The light seemed to increase from second to second, full dawn only moments away. With the light came enemy recognition.

The RPG rounds came in from the jungle's edge, located a hundred and fifty meters south of the crossing. The Ontos was a sitting duck, it's recoilless rifles facing forward towards the cliff face. I watched from the berm in front of the opposing cliff face, a relative place of safety that had momentarily shrunk back my belly full of fear.

I watched the early morning action on my stomach, the Japanese binoculars pressed into my eye sockets. I could do nothing. The plan was playing out with the participation of enemy forces and actions I knew had to affect it at some point but in ways, I could not predict.

The 175 long guns from the Army firebase could reach all the way down into the southern valley where we were, as they'd done before. But the 'red bag,' beyond normal maximum range loading, left so much leeway in distancing the rounds that I was afraid to fire them. Deflection wasn't that great a problem, as the battery was outstanding in being able to keep the highly spinning rounds within very narrow limits when it came to adjusting left and right. It was the ranging distance that was the problem. Over such a long distance, the atmosphere slowed the rounds at nearly unpredictable rates and also, at the 'beyond maximum' range we were at, that slowing caused the fuses controlling detonation to become less dependable. If a round was moving too horizontally it could impact the jungle at some other point than its tip, and then skip to somewhere else close by. Close by to anything, including friendly forces.

Two of the enemy RPG rocket rounds struck the mud just before where the Ontos sat, blowing up layers of mud and fire, but the third hit the Ontos armor like a giant glancing spark. It was a flying hit on the angled side of the turret, quickly followed by the warhead going off. The turret top was covered with only one-half inch armor, I knew, so exactly where the rocket's explosive had gone off was critical. Rio and Panda were inside. The question was, were they still alive?

Half a minute went by before the Ontos rifle turret slowly turned and fired back, to my great relief. The machine had to turn again to start moving toward the cliff, and the guns could not shoot when it was moving toward the cliff because the turret only revolved forty degrees in either direction. Another RPG round went skidding over the vehicles right track guard surface before exploding when it came into contact with the one-inch thick side armor. The Ontos angled around until the front of the main turret was pointing back at the river. Rio then turned the 106 mm barrel turret toward the southern mass of jungle where the rocket rounds had originated and slowly backed the machine up toward the stone wall.

"We've got to cross now," I said to Feesman, who immediately began speaking into the microphone of his Prick 25. I assumed he was on the combat net because in seconds it seemed like most of the company was running toward the closest end of the bridge. I watched through the Starlight scope, as bleached out from the looming daylight as the images coming back to me were. Ropes were thrown and the Marines crossed the short turbulent and very dangerous stretch of rushing water.

Small arms AK fire came out from the jungle, although there were no tracers to give any of their true positions. It didn't matter, because Rio in the Ontos fired round after round into where the NVA infantry had to be. The whoosh of the 106 rounds, first leaving their long barrels and then making triangular penetration of hundreds of yards of jungle debris with their thousands of flechettes in each round, was pleasing to hear and see the results of.

It was light enough for binoculars, and I wanted one last examination of the scene before I brought up the rear with the Gunny, Feesman, Zippo, and Nguyen and crossed the river to join the rest of the company.

I readjusted the binocular lenses carefully for maximum visibility in the early light. What I saw was at first pleasing, and then the import of the scene hit me. And terrified me. Half the company or more was spread out over the far bank, bent over and running. The Marines moved with practiced ease, keeping enough space between runners but not too much to deny room for the rest of their comrades. What I watched just beyond them was Rio and Panda out reloading the Ontos tubes with more rounds. The biggest disadvantage the Ontos had was not thin armor, although it was certainly not thick. The biggest single high-risk feature of the machine was the fact that the loader, or in this case loaders, had to go out the back doors, carry heavy rounds with them, and then painstakingly reload those rounds into the backs of the tubes without cover or concealment. The Ontos was the only real target the NVA had, and the Ontos, the weapon the NVA dreaded most, could not fire while it was being loaded. Neither Rio nor Panda were moving much except to stand and load the tubes on the right side. The south side, was most exposed to the jungle mass where the NVA were held up and waiting.

I reached over instinctively for Feesman's radio handset, but he didn't extend it out to me, seeing what I was seeing without the benefit of the glasses. I slowly lowered my hand. The Ontos radio was inside its body. I wanted to run forward and start yelling for them to get the hell back inside the machine, but the distance was too great and I would have accomplished nothing.

Sudden automatic weapons fire from the jungle opened up with great volume. In seconds, it was over. Both Ontos crewmen were down. The whole company had gone into the mud in order to turn and deliver suppressing fire back into the bush the shots had come from.

"Let's move," I hissed, jamming the binoculars over my shoulder into my open pack. "Strap it," I ordered Zippo, who was working as fast as he could to recover the Starlight scope and get his own gear ready.

My pack had to be secure. I needed the glasses, the maps in their barely protective plastic bag inside my thigh pocket, and Tex's .45. I checked to make sure the automatic was on safe and as secure as I could make it inside the holster. The situation with my Marines was tenuous at all times, and now that resupply had brought in a fresh contingent of black Marines to join up with Sugar Daddy, I expected more interpersonal problems than there had been during the deflective events of the past week.

The image of the two Marines standing with arms raised, jamming a 106 round into a chamber, and then being literally cut down by a hail of automatic weapons fire, was burned into my brain. I could not take my eyes off the small plot of mud they'd fallen on. Their bodies weren't really visible, but I didn't need to see them to know they were dead. Marines were crawling toward them with the main elements of Jurgens and Sugar Daddy's platoons headed for the cover only the berm in front of the recessed cleft at the bottom of the cliff could provide.

I had to get to the Ontos. Sentry was the only crew left. I wasn't sure if I was the only man left in the company who had any experience aiming and firing the Ontos' 106 rifles, but that machine was the company's only thing capable of real close in covering fire that was going to provide any real security for any of us.

I dreaded crossing the water again. I felt I'd die if I entered the river again, although there was no solid evidence for why I felt that way. The river ran down the center of the valley and had come to run right through the center of my life. I hunched over and ran for the bridge. I'd figure out what to do when I got to the other edge and had to face the water. Rio and Panda were dead, but unlike the appearances of so many who'd fallen before them, I could still see their faces in my mind. Both men were smiling inside me, and I dreaded to see what expressions they'd died with.

The bridge was a wet sloppy mess of debris, the river running so high that it seemed to gift upward passing bits of flotsam and plant detritus. That the Ontos had gained purchase and run across the seemingly flimsy structure at speed was almost too much to believe. I was reduced to a crawl by the slippery surface. I heard no further enemy or friendly fire. I could hear only the hungry pulsating roar of the passing water, trying to draw anything and everything nearby back inside to take downriver to some more placid hell.

Jurgens waited at the end of the bridge, with his radio operator and another of his men. He smiled his big fake smile up at me as I crawled forward. I was already wet to the core and slimy from contact with all the garbage coughed up from the river. He pointed down at the bouncing arc of the heavy rope. The water made the line jump up and then plunge down like I would be doing as I crossed. I remembered the Marines we'd lost earlier at the previous crossing and shuddered. I wished I'd ridden inside the Ontos, but I knew that would never have gone over very well with my Marines. The company commander could not run from the enemy and he could never take the safer path. Not if it was safer than the way the rest of the company had to take. Not unless he wanted to face a more terminal danger than that he might be avoiding.

I grabbed the rope with both hands and slipped over the edge. The water was cold, like before, but I'd forgotten. I'd forgotten it all, and the memory of my last encounter came rushing back. My fear fled like it'd never been there. I was inside the rushing cold water and I felt clean and renewed. I didn't rush to move hand over hand. Feesman easily passed me, using the second parallel rope. For all its risk, I knew in the depths of my mind and body that the water was a far safer place for me than the surface of the valley, particularly the muddy surface I was about to encounter and then have to run across. I was about to rise up and then run toward the dead without any understanding of why, if I made it, I was still alive.

I crawled up on the bank's surface but lay low, checking my stuff. The .45 was wet and tight in its holster. I placed my hand tightly around the end of the grip and felt a slight bit of warmth return to my body. I looked at the field of mud in front of me. Some Marines had made it. I could see their round helmets sticking over the edge of the berm. Some Marines were hunched over and moving as quickly as they could in that position, and some were crawling slowly, elbow by elbow with their M-16s pulled to their chests. The Ontos was about fifty meters directly to my front. I got to my knees and then stood to make a run for it when a force struck me from behind, taking my wind and plunging me straight back and face down into the mud.

one-hundred-seven

My chest and face hit the mud at the same time, the impact so hard that water was pressed out of my uniform blouse and sprayed up into a fine mist around me. My helmet and liner landed a good five feet away, but I didn't care, as I fought to take any air at all into my blown-out lungs. If I had been hit then the bullet might well be a terminal blow. A double lung shot with a high velocity bullet was an almost instantly fatal. I'd witnessed the awful damage personally several times. A bullet passing through both lungs left no chance that one of them would ever be re-inflated or repaired in time.

Air sucked back into my lungs in one long inhalation. I breathed again before I could think to do anything. Nguyen's face appeared out of the dim light and through the misting mess of my water-filled muddy impact.

"Nguyen," I squeaked out, looking around for the Gunny. I knew it had to have been the Gunny who took me down. How he'd figured out I was about to make a run for it across the open flats I had no idea, as I hadn't even taken my first step before he hit me.

"The Gunny," I worked to get out, before breathing in deeply again and going on. "My helmet," I croaked, trying to scrabble forward.

Fessman slithered across the mud and retrieved my helmet and liner.

"He's gone, sir," Fessman said, matter-of-factly, "he came in at a run, put a shoulder into your back, and then ran on out across the flats like you tried to do."

"He put me down, and then ran himself?" I asked incredulously.

Fessman worked with his bare hands to clean off as much mud as he could from the helmet, before going to work on the liner. He handed both to me, one at a time, the liner first, before answering.

"Looks like he intended to draw whatever fire you were about to get hit with," he replied.

I looked out over the almost bare clearing, leading up to the front of the canyon wall. There was really nothing to see. I hadn't heard any

AK fire from the enemy or even anything from our own M-60s and M-16s. The Ontos was right where the team had left it, with a few of the company Marines, unidentifiable in the light, looking like they were bent over and working on Rio and Panda. I felt a ray of hope, and then the turret on the Ontos moved to bring the six barrels down a few degrees. The barrels were pointed at the jungle where the damaging small arms fire had come from, but I knew the chambers of the guns were empty.

"The Gunny," I hissed out. "He's in the Ontos. We've got to get there and load."

Two more RPG rounds screamed across the flat of mud, their rockets sounding more like jet engines than rockets. One struck just short of the Ontos, throwing up giant chunks of mud, while the other went a bit high, exploding against the face of the cliff wall, tossing out rocks and debris that rained down all around and upon the machine. I started to crawl forward, getting my helmet shakily back on my head.

"We can't make it without cover, sir," Zippo said, pulling me back easily, with one hand tightly grasped around my ankle.

"Hell, we're no better off without cover here than we are crossing to try to get there," I replied, trying to pull away from his strong securing grip.

"Here, sir," whispered Fessman, thrusting the radio microphone out to my face.

I frowned and then got it. I wasn't thinking straight. We had to have covering fire, and the Ontos wasn't going to provide that in time, not with the disorganized mess of the dead crew, the Marines working on them, and the Gunny inside it and trying to figure out how its controls worked. He hadn't gotten back out of the Ontos to load himself, and none of the Marines nearby had moved to get rounds and do that either. All we had was the Army 175s.

I called Firebase Ripcord, pulling the map from my right thigh pocket and quickly opening it up. I found the grid coordinate number I wanted still penciled on the surface map. The number I had used before but needed again. I calculated our position. There could be no games played, as to letting the battery know where we were, not with the inherent 'out beyond maximum range' inaccuracy of the big gun's rounds. We were on the gun target line and down in the valley. Any rounds that came in might strike the top of the edge of the valley wall and then bounce down if they didn't explode from the impact. And we were right where they'd land. Even if they came in 'red bag' accurate, the plus or minus circular error of probability was more than likely to be about half a kilometer or more. Missing by half a kilometer within the narrow confines of the southern A Shau Valley wasn't something to be taken lightly. But the front glacis facing the jungle on the Ontos was only two inches thick. The armor could handle anything up to, and including, .50 caliber machine gun rounds, but it couldn't handle a direct hit from an RPG. And the Gunny was inside the Ontos. I quickly sent the grid numbers in the clear. The NVA knew where we were and where they were. Using codes no longer mattered. They were going to get plastered by artillery fire and it was best if they knew it was coming, for your needs. Killing them wasn't nearly as important as keeping them down and from hitting us mid-crossing with even a single RPG round.

Instead of continuing the fire mission using the normal formal command structure I spoke in the clear to the fire control officer.

"We've got a tough situation here, Bob," I started. "We're down in the valley near maximum range. Your battery is angled off a bit to the west so you can put some stuff down here, but we're on the 'GT' line at max range. We've got to take the risk. Can you fire three spaced ranging rounds at maximum elevation? If we get the range we need then I can creep back onto the target."

"Roger that, Junior," Bob replied.

I'd called myself Junior at the start of the transmission. Instead of sticking to rank he'd said his name was Bob. From that little bit I knew, he was going to try his heart out to help us if he could.

"We've got a ton of ordnance here, Junior," he said. "Just been waiting for the call. Don't hold back."

"Roger that," I replied, smiling ever so slightly at the Army I'd only heard terrible things about in training but discovered, so far, only wonderful things about.

"Shot over," came over the radio.

I waited the seconds out, counting on my Omega. The time was too great to bother counting the seconds away in my mind. The 175 had a muzzle velocity of about three thousand feet per second, I knew. Three thousand divided into the twenty-five miles we were distanced from those muzzles. I watched the 40 seconds sweep by before the radio came back with "splash over." I pushed the front of my body back into the mud. I didn't have to say a word of warning to my scout team. They'd gone down at the first announcement from the battery. One hundred and seventy-five-pound rounds coming in from distant one hundred and seventy-five-millimeter artillery barrels was frightening.

The four impacts came five seconds later, as if they were one explosion, with three more echoes. I'd asked for three rounds, forgetting the 175s were organized with four guns to a battery instead of six, like the 105s. The fire direction center had fired a battery of one instead of trying to break my request up among the guns.

"Far enough," I breathed out in relief, pulling my muddy face up and hitting the radio transmit button. The rounds had come in much more than a thousand meters down the valley. "Battery of six," I ordered.

"Shot over," came back from Bob. "R.O.T.?" he asked.

"Right on target," I replied, knowing he already knew that his previous shots had hit with accuracy, but wanting to hear it over the net.

"Drop five zero on the GT line and repeat fire for effect," I ordered, even before the 'shot over' command from the first salvo had been sent back to us.

I knew the FDC knew we were on the gun target line but I didn't want anyone to forget.

I waited and watched the skyline over the jungle where smoke and debris still settled well to the south in the jungle where the initial rounds had impacted. There were more than a thousand meters separating our company from the impact area. We had to move under what fire we could call. There was only one way to do it.

The six rounds came in, like explosive layers of cake being laid down. Four, four and then four more. A battery of six took about six minutes, normally, to load and fire that many layers of a 'cake.' Ripcord was doing it in three minutes. The Army artillery grunts were extending their personal care right down into the A Shau with us. I could feel it through the radio, and from the effect of their work.

"We're going to move under your fire, Bob," I said into the microphone. "You can safely drop five zero ten more times and still give us about 700 meters left over by the time we get to cover.

The ground shook as the second series of salvos came in. The white coronas of condensed moist air and shock-advancing sound blew up from the back of the jungle like giant Chinese lanterns. They were brilliant white in their instantly created and near instantly gone existence. Whatever was under those 'lanterns' was living in a deafened and miserable wet hell.

"You're crossing open ground, over?" Bob asked, but then didn't wait for my response, "so how about a battery of two continuous, dropping five hundred first, and then working south fifty meters at a time. On my map, it looks like danger close won't be from our stuff, but from that deep foliage further south of your position.?"

"Roger that," I replied, using his own radio jargon again.

Bob and his battery support team were smart, and they were removed enough to be objectively logical. We had to cross an open area and needed cover since concealment was out of the question. Bringing the fire closer initially would do a better job of immediately getting the enemy down before creeping the big rounds slowly into their most vulnerable positions.

The rain increased, as if attempting to foil our plan, but the 175 rounds wouldn't be much affected if at all, I knew.

We waited for the "shot, over" message. We were the remnant. Half a platoon of Marines and our scout team. It was obvious that everyone else had already crossed using the benefit of the lower pre-dawn light. The light level wasn't low anymore, however, even though the rain might provide some misty concealment. A tiny line of leeches danced before me, their little thin bodies sticking up about an inch from the wet mud, seeming to wave at me.

The 'shot over' message came through the radio speaker Fessman had unaccountably turned on. We waited the length of time for the rounds to leave the cannon muzzles and get to our position. I watched the leeches in front of me, knowing I didn't have to stay attentive for 175 rounds that would be impacting less than a click away.

"One of these days I'm going to leave these clowns," I whispered, paraphrasing some famous movie line or song lyric I'd heard.

I didn't crush myself face down again into the mud, although I wanted to. I had to be ready to jump up and run for the cover of the berm three hundred very exposed meters distant.

I held up my right fist, gripping the radio handset firmly with my left, in order to yell "check fire" if the 175 rounds came in among us, not that I would probably be around to make the call if that happened.

"On five," I ordered, quietly, more to myself than those around me.

"Splash, over," came from the speaker.

I held up my thumb and then counted off the seconds, putting up additional fingers as I silently thought of the numbers. Upon raising my last finger, I jumped up, and then went immediately back down, dropping the radio handset while cringing into the mud, crushing the little dancing leeches in front of me. Then I was back up, Zippo and Nguyen pushing and pulling at me. I realized I was deaf. The aftermath of the first 175 rounds plummeted from the sky all around me. I knew we'd been at least two hundred meters from the initial hits because we were still alive. I found my balance and ran for all I was worth toward where the Ontos sat, ominously not moving, with several Marines lying face down along the unexposed northern flank of its right track.

I felt the following 175s come down, swearing as I ran, that I would never call such heavy stuff in so close to my own position again. I'd received fire from the NVA by small arms, heavy machine guns and even the Russian provided 106 guns up on the ridge, but I'd never had to endure heavy artillery fire what the U.S. military could provide in the massiveness of explosive killing size or overwhelming delivery in volume.

The bodies of Rio and Panda lay side by side, as I passed by, headed for the cover only the armored body of the Ontos could provide. Both bodies looked like they'd been worked over by the corpsmen, and both lay back down with their permanent stares directed up into the falling rain that had effectively taken away the bloody signs of their mortal small arms injuries.

"Junior," I heard, as if from a distance, but it wasn't. Sugar Daddy grabbed my left arm and pulled me behind the Ontos, and then down onto the surface of the mud.

"How long we got? The artillery's pounding the hell out of them."

I tried to clear my head and think. The Gunny. Reloading the Ontos. My scout team. The disjointed mess of where I was and what we were trying to do came cascading back.

The double doors at the back of the Ontos opened fully, and the Gunny stepped out, carrying one tubular boxed round of 106 ammunition. From behind me Sentry appeared and took the tube from the Gunny's hands. He pressed his back into the door, held in place by its hold-open latch, and pulled the long 106 round from its black tubular box. I knew from his facial expression, or rather the lack of it, that he'd passed by the dead bodies of his teammates right after I had.

We began to work like a silent machine, the sound of the distant rushing river, the pounding of every more distant artillery rounds and the constant pattering of misty rain on our helmets the background 'music' for what we were doing. We all worked back and forth across the sloppy mud; reaching in, pulling out, and then stripping the recoilless rounds out of their cardboard sleeves, before moving to feed them to Sentry for loading. Only Sentry was familiar with the guns themselves. The Marines working around me made no move to touch the guns unless at Sentry's instructions.

I eased up onto the whitish floor of the Ontos, it's interior stained with splashes of reddish-brown mud. There was no seat, and the extra rounds Rio had substituted for it had been pulled out the back, so I squatted down, my knees bent just enough so I could press my right eye into the soft rubber grommet of the gunsight. I stared out through the brilliant scene of wet green and yellow jungle to the front of the vehicle. The mud was a hazy out-of-focus brown rug. The motor was still running I noted, with the return of most of my hearing capability. I hit the turret handle and rotated the guns a few degrees each way before adjusting up and down. The range increments were painted into the inside of the sight reticle. Each one I presumed to be indicative of one hundred meters, but I wasn't sure.

I waited, once I'd adjusted the little white sighting lines for three hundred and fifty meters, or so. I thought about the Gunny, and why he'd holed up in the Ontos for so long without moving, not that he could have done much to load or fire the guns by himself. The inside of the Ontos was a complexity of buttons, knobs, and handles, with only the tall white track-braking handles being self-evident for what they did. I couldn't drive the Ontos, or service it anyway, but I'd figure out how to operate the turret and aim and fire the guns. If the Gunny had stayed inside to hide out from the enemy like I had a time or two in holes, caves or under nearby brush, then why had he chosen the Ontos to hide out in, what with the more protective frontal cliff berm just to its rear? It made no sense. The Ontos was total protection against the small arms fire that had killed Rio and Panda, but it was a magnet for much more dangerously terminal hits from the RPG B40 rockets.

I waited until Zippo slapped me on the back. I turned to see him holding up two hands with six fingers showing. The guns were loaded, but I could not fire with any Marines directly behind the machine within fifty meters. Sentry pumped his clenched fist up and down twice from his position behind Zippo. I instinctively knew I was cleared to fire.

I waited. I stared into the large single lens sight, the jungle across the relatively short stretch of open flat mud fully visible in spite of the misting rain. The company's Marines were getting set into the shallow natural cave crease that ran along the crack at the cliff's bottom. We'd made it across the river, and then across the mud flats and, following the end of the artillery barrage, there wasn't much the NVA could do. Except to attack. If I was the leader of the NVA forces, deafened, hurt and angry inside the seemingly decimated jungle density beyond, then I'd be preparing to attack at the earliest opportunity, before enemy machine guns were properly emplaced, field mortars set up, and the Marines focused and ready to receive an attack.

There'd been no fire attempted or delivered onto us when we were reloading the Ontos guns, and we'd been as visible as the earlier crew.

I presumed we'd not been fired upon because the NVA was readying its attack in force. I pulled from the sight briefly to look out the back, through the two open doors of the Ontos. I saw four heads sticking up over the berm, off to the northern side. Zippo and Fessman stared out, with the Gunny set between them and Sentry. Sentry saw my look and held up first six fingers and then two thumbs. I got his message. He was ready with two loads of six more rounds, when needed, for the 106 guns.

I returned to staring through the sight, seeing the jungle and the mud before it, and thinking about the two bodies of the Ontos crew, now staring forever up into a raining sky they'd never see again. They'd accepted the danger and gone anyway, across the bridge, over the mud and then out into it to fearlessly load more rounds. For the first time, I wondered how a company commander wrote up Marines for decorations. The two men deserved big ones.

And then they came. Three broken lines of brown and black-clad bodies, hunched low but moving fast. They moved directly at the position where I sat and then began veering to one side before coming back and to the other. They looked like giant centipedes.

I eased the turret down to hold the range steady at two hundred meters, the stock setting for the flechette rounds to explode. The fuses were adjustable, but I hoped and presumed nobody, in the haste to reload, had changed any of the fuse settings. The enemy maneuvered. No Marines fired. Everyone along the bottom of our cliff was immobile and ready.

I waited, my right eye sealed into the rubber grommet of the gunsight, my left hand poised over the six big firing buttons.

one-hundred-eight

The NVA soldiers moved back and forth in the tufted growth mud distance, like sidewinding snakes across a desert of nearly flat sand.

The numbers, I instantly knew, although it was impossible to see individuals at distance even through the mildly magnified gun sight, were too large to be handled or overcome by firing the six gun barrels of the Ontos. I turned my head and started to move from my seat atop the ammo boxes Rio had substituted in place of the metal swivel chair. I stopped midway because Fessman was there already, holding out the radio handset.

"Ripcord, gun control officer, sir," he said, his tone indicating that he and Zippo had probably been able to come to the same conclusion I had without the aid of any visually enhancing equipment.

"Bob, give me a battery of three, drop one hundred from the first grid of adjustment," I ordered, and then went on, "they're coming from the edge of the jungle across the mud flats at us, fully exposed."

"Roger that contact," Bob replied, his voice flat and analytical. "The depression might be more than we can compute from here though so keep your heads down."

I handed Fessman the handset and went back to staring intently through the gun sight, wondering why they didn't make gun sights that had binocular vision instead of a single lens eyepiece, and marginally worried about what Bob's 'might be more than we can compute' might portend.

The rain was misting gray, with slightly darker bands of it crossing the flats from east to west, moving like the ripple of waves along a stage curtain being opened or closed. I could see through the rain but the sight could not overcome the obscuring effect of the water hitting the mud, causing a mild form of ground steam that was just great enough to make things, like creeping soldiers, nearly invisible within it.

The artillery came in like an express train high above, just as before, except all the heavy rounds didn't land where they were supposed to.

At the first explosions, I grabbed the radio handset back from Fessman so roughly he recoiled back a bit.

"Check fire, check fire," I screamed. The reverberating explosions were still coming through the air, some from the jungle to our front but some from behind us, as well.

Ripcord had tried to adjust for the cliff overhang but missed the exact aim point because of the height of the canyon wall and unpredictable travel of those rounds when they were traveling at the very end of their maximum range.

Some of the rounds hit the top of the cliff and then, as I had worried over, bounced instead of going off harmlessly above us. I listened for Marines screaming because it was unlikely in our position at the bottom of the canyon wall that there was little doubt we'd taken casualties. Marine casualties from my artillery call. Again. I grimaced and cringed, pushing the radio handset back to Fessman.

"Call Cowboy and get some air in here," I yelled over my shoulder without turning my head.

I could not concentrate on the effect of the short rounds. We had bigger problems. I studied what I could see across the mudflat in front of me, and tried to decide where to best expend my six recoilless shots. With what I guessed to be nearly a regiment on the move, I could not imagine, as they got closer, that any of my Marines would be able to reload the 106s, and stay alive, in the kind of small arms fire concentration that would be brought to bear. I had to fire when the enemy was just beyond two hundred meters, where the explosives in the beehive rounds were set to go off. If I fired too soon then the flechettes, traveling initially at twenty-two thousand feet per second from the explosion would very quickly be slowed in the thick rain-filled air and become ineffective. If I fired too late the flechettes would fan out beyond the force I was shooting at.

I wiped my eyes, trying to see through the sight more clearly. I'd left my helmet on a nearby ammo box outside and next to the right track of the Ontos, and, in spite of what I was trying to see out in front of me, I was worried that I would lose the damaged thing. I tried to focus through the fear. My helmet didn't matter.

I stared at the moving mass in front of me, waiting for the right moment. I had to get it right. The range to the nearest four lines of stopping and starting, turning and bobbing soldiers was about four hundred meters, according to the little white marks etched into the vertical crosshair line brightly appearing on my reticle.

Three-fifty, I calculated, trying to home in on any single soldier not going down into the mud and bouncing back up. The NVA was not moving using the Marine Corps tried and true 'fire and maneuver' approach to crossing an open field of fire. The 'fire' part of that maneuver was to suppress enemy fire by keeping the enemy's head down. In reality, the maneuver was only marginally successful in an application, but it was better than what I was seeing the NVA attempt to execute in front of me. Why were they seemingly disappearing and then reappearing? At three hundred meters, I heard several of the company M-60s open up. The sporadic nature of their fire spaced out because the gunners could see what I saw, an enormity in number that if constantly fired upon would overheat their barrels and use up their ammunition.

"I thought World War One proved that mass attacks against machine guns were impossible," I murmured to myself, as the leading elements of several of the snaking attackers got closer.

"Fire the One-Oh-Six," I yelled, to warn everyone who might not have gotten the message that killing backpressure was about to be thrust violently outward behind one of the guns. I punched the ping-pong ball sized firing trigger for the left outboard weapon. The switches for the guns were six flat round circles of metal set in a row to match the placement of the 106 barrels.

The flechette round burst from the gun with a deafening roar, followed by an enormous whooshing sound. I'd never heard any weapon in training or in combat that sounded like a 106 being fired.

The sound, and then instant jolt of the Ontos reacting to the launching of the heavy round, caused me to blink and miss seeing the explosion itself. All I saw was a wispy cloud of gray smoke fast-disappearing in the still falling and blowing waves of mist in the air. The enemy disappeared. Nothing was moving in front of me for seconds, then one squad or group of enemy soldiers bobbed up. I fired the second 106. This time I kept my eye open, but again there wasn't anything to see. One moment the enemy was running back and forth crouched as low as their bodies could get, and the next there was nothing except the dissipating smoke to see. No bodies lay in the aftermath of the round's impact. After I fired the third round I turned to instruct Fessman about reloading before I'd used up the ammo in all the barrels, but Fessman wasn't there. Zippo and Nguyen were there.

Zippo grabbed a tube and slid the black container out. The flechette rounds had been laid out earlier in one large triangular pile.

Nguyen took the second tube. There was no plan that I could tell. Both men disappeared toward the left side of the Ontos. All I could do was stare through the reticle and wait. Minutes later Zippo patted me on the back and gave me a thumbs up.

"Locked and loaded," he said, with a grim smile.

I sighted and fired three rounds, one after another from the right side, and then waited for the reload, keeping the three barrels on the opposing side always loaded in reserve. I didn't keep track of how many flechette rounds I fired until Zippo hit me on the shoulder and said we only had high explosives left.

The first HE round I put near a pack of running soldiers went off, throwing up a huge column of mud. The enemy reacted similarly to the impacting of the flechette rounds, but there was a different effect that caught my attention. Not only were there no bodies littering the mud but the NVA on the field had disappeared almost the instant the round went off. All of them. And then I got it.

"Get the Gunny," I ordered Fessman.

"Air is on the way," Fessman reported quickly, before running off to find the Gunny.

The company had come fully online, I knew, from the near-constant din of M-60 fire, and the crisscrossing tracer rounds traveling in floating high-speed lines across the surface of the mud. But there was no enemy to be seen.

"Junior," what's going on?" the Gunny said, slipping back into the double door opening at the back of the Ontos. "Is air support coming?"

"They're disappearing before my eyes," I said, still peering into the scope. "They get up and run, I fire, and then they're gone, but they aren't leaving the field littered with bodies. What the hell? How's that possible?"

"Shit," the Gunny intoned. "I had an idea when we were setting up the machine guns. They aren't out there trying a banzai charge at all, and they're still out there. Spider holes. They've got holes dug all over across that mud flat. They raised front lip of the holes just enough so we can't see the edge of the holes from here. They haven't been attacking. They've been creeping forward, and now they're sitting out there waiting. They had to have figured we might come back to the same position we occupied before."

"Waiting for what?" I asked, my voice slightly quivering with the fear coiling back up in the pit of my stomach. One of the tenets drilled into all company grade officers at the Basic School was to never re-occupy the same position in a guerrilla conflict.

"To come out tonight," the Gunny replied, lighting another cigarette. "That's why they didn't show their normal fear of the Ontos."

I noted his hand shaking slightly. It was the first time I'd seen the Gunny show any weakness in any situation since I'd known him. My own fear escalated up several levels.

"They wanted to get close and inside the set-back range of the 106," the Gunny continued, no emotion in his deep quiet voice.

"They want to go at it hand to hand in the dark."

"Cowboy couldn't make it so he sent Spooky," Fessman said from just behind the Ontos, the AN-323 headset sticking out from under his helmet.

"What's Spooky?" I asked, faintly mystified but glad any air power at all was on the way. "When are they on the station?" I continued, my nervousness too great to allow me to sit silently and wait for Fessman's response.

"Spooky's the 20mm variant of Puff," the Gunny explained, "but instead of three 7.72 guns like Puff, Spooky has two rotary 20mm weapons. They're new so I have never seen it in action."

"It's here," I said, feeling a sense of relief that I knew might not be justified, but it flowed through me like a swig of hot chocolate on an icy cold day. The unmistakable deep thrum of a four-engine C-130 at low altitude seemed to make the very canyon walls vibrate.

"Give me the headset," I ordered, holding my right hand out to Fessman. There was no point in staring out over the mud flats through the sight. The NVA had played me, and without the daylight and beehive rounds, the company would be sitting ducks in the night for a mass attack from their nearby position. The Starlight Scope would not be able to do at that point except let us know we were being overrun.

I reached the C-130 pilot without trouble. The commander of the aircraft came on personally. I filled him in on our position and asked if he'd first fly over to make sure he understood our problem. He said the name of his plane was Rhythm Rain. I remembered the first lyrics of the famous song by the same name; "listen to the sound of the falling rain." Under different circumstances, I would have smiled at the commander's humorous use of the song, so similar to the names I used for my own plans.

"Got your six, Junior, coming in on a port sliding pylon turn at about one thousand over your six, over."

On cue, the big plane appeared, canted over and then performed a slow turn, it's wings impossibly perpendicular to the bottom of the valley as it came around. I stared at the spectacle, my fear lessening, as the plane completed its full 360-degree rotation.

"I presume that Ontos sitting there has to belong to you fellas, over."

"That's affirmative," I replied, relief that our own position was accurately and uniquely marked.

"We're goin' live my partners and friends, so meld your asses down into the loving jungle mud you got goin' for you there."

The 130 came around, dropped its left wing tip and opened up. It wasn't like Puff, as stunning as that plane's attacks had been to witness. It was different. There was no 'braying' or lashing tongue of yellowish red fire hosing the area, but there was plenty of sound. The sound was like a giant out of control chainsaw roaring.. A chainsaw quite possibly a thousand times the size of the largest one ever made. Puff had not hurt our ears, but I was joined by every Marine around me in covering my ears as best I could. The mud in front of the Ontos wasn't mud anymore. It more resembled a bouncing jouncing giant field of dancing and spraying chocolate shakes. The mud was still mud though because it flew so far and wide through the air that it came blowing back over our position. Mud bits, spray, and other awful stuff rained down. I pulled myself fully into the cover of the Ontos and the Gunny did the same.

The big plane orbited for five more times, each three minute run punctuated with the roading fire. My shoulders began to slump down in relief. There was little or nothing that could survive out on the mud flats, or even lightly dug in, not from 20mm rounds. The three and a half ounces of each small exploding round delivered about ten times the power and penetration of an M-60 machine gun round, and the machine guns ammo had no explosive capability.

"We're going to return to the barn for more ammo," Rhythm's commander said, "but we'll see if we can make a vet call out here in the early hours if you feel you might need some extra care."

The big plane waggled its wings, turned, and then flew up the valley. I sat numb, letting my hands fall from my ears. My left ear ringing but my right somewhat protected from the firing by the microphone. I hadn't thought to respond to the Spooky flight commander. I hadn't even asked his name.

The all-covering and uncaring mist of rain continued marching across the mud flat. The river came back with its rushing current sounds. The sediment, mud, and dirt that had been thrown into the air less than a couple of minutes earlier were all gone.

The artillery had saved us earlier but then hurt us too. Air had come in and done the job. I'd been sucked into firing all the Ontos flechette rounds, but we could survive without them as long as we could hold our current position with small arms and air returning in the morning.

Night was coming and it couldn't come fast enough for me, the day having been an initial series of successful moves but then topped off with the short artillery rounds and the ability of the enemy to work and shoot from holes dug into the mud that were, because of the short scrub around them, unnoticeable unless we were on top of them.

The threat was still there because no one in the company was going out to check what was left of the holes until the next dawn. The Starlight Scope could be used to pick off individuals unwise enough to move out across the mud flats in the night. I had eleven rounds left for the Ontos but they were all high explosive. The flechettes had been put to no real good use, but the air support had been massively effective. The fact that we had no more of the infantry-stopping beehive rounds could leave us in a vulnerable position if the next day was to be a repeat of the one we'd just been through, although with the spider holes churned up like a spring day farmer's field, it wasn't likely.

I climbed out of the Ontos, found my pack and helmet, and then made my way over the berm to where the cliff overhand allowed a cave-like interior to be inhabited with relative safety.

I tossed my pack as far back as I could and then squatted down to wait for the Gunny, who I knew would be coming with a butcher's bill of casualties over the Ripcord short rounds. It only took a few minutes for him to arrive, accompanied by Jurgens, Sugar Daddy, and their three radio operators.

"We can't bring choppers in here at all, even for a medivac, not as long as they control the jungle mass over there," the Gunny said, sitting close in with me, Jurgens and Sugar Daddy. "We've got nine wounded but none critical."

The rest of the company NCOs either avoided me entirely or were never called forward to me for any interrogation or commands.

The Gunny handled the company, as he had all along. I occasionally spoke to battalion but never to the six actual. My main contacts with the outside world in the rear areas was either through using the artillery net Prick 25 to talk to the batteries or the AN-323 to talk to the Skyraiders or other supporting aircraft.

"We can bring them in at the old airfield and hump the wounded there and the supplies back," I replied, having given the situation some thought.

We had the nine wounded, none critically and none dead. My relief was palpable.

If the wounded were ambulatory enough to make the trek it was an accomplishable mission. Worse than the medical problem, however, was the fact that we lacked water, in spite of the incessant rain. Our C-ration supply was adequate, at best, and we needed more ammunition. Most importantly, we had to have beehive rounds for the Ontos, and they were heavy and unwieldy.

"Nobody's going to want to cross that river under fire and hump back all that shit," Jurgens piped in. "We've taken enough casualties since setting in here, but then you know that don't you, Junior."

I looked to Jurgens' right side where Nguyen crouched, just inside the bracken that grew back from the edge of the berm. I motioned him away from the sergeant with a nod so small I didn't think anybody else could notice. Nguyen moved, but not far.

My hand went to my forty-five, casually. I knew where Jurgens was going with his comment and I waited, wondering for the hundredth time whether I should just shoot the brutal, nasty man right where he sat or wait to see how the situation developed.

"You called the arty, not me," Jurgens said, "and that cost us plenty. We didn't lose a single Marine to the attack. That's the second time in days where you cost us more Marines than the enemy."

I waited, like I'd waited for the NVA to come at us, my attitude not much different toward Jurgens than it was those enemy soldiers. If Jurgens was going to continue then I knew I was going to shoot him. It had nothing to do with anger. For three weeks, I'd let the sergeant say things that made it more likely nobody in the company could respect me, not for the things I'd done, but because of the few things I had not done. I had not killed Sugar Daddy when he tried to kill me, several times. I'd not killed Jurgens when the things he said in front of other Marines had nearly the same ultimate effect.

I thought about writing home. I'd missed a day, somehow, what with the critical nature of the move and the difficulty of crossing the river and getting ready for the attack. We were still in the A Shau Valley. I sat, staring blankly at Jurgens, and thought about how long I'd been there. It seemed like years. Maybe my wife was tired of reading about the botany and biology of the verdant valley of great deadly beauty. I couldn't write her about killing Jurgens, or the difficulties that were going to arise when his roughly assembled platoon of white crackers from the south found out.

No one said anything, following Jurgens' comment. The Gunny lit a small coffee fire. He smoked one of his cigarettes but didn't remove it from his mouth to flick away the ash. I noticed the bit of composition B burning blue and white instead of yellow and red which normally it had. The Gunny puffed on the cigarette, his eyes following my own.

"New stuff," he said, reaching behind him to grab a white block about the size of two cigarette cartons taped together. "C-4 they call it. Burns hotter and more bang for the buck, or so the paper in the box said. 26,000 feet per second instead of twenty-two."

I realized the safety of my .45 automatic was on. I would need to snap it off, but such a move would alert Jurgens. I knew it could be snapped off quickly and easily when I brought the weapon up, but I wanted to be certain nothing went wrong. Jurgens' radio operator was nearby, as was Sugar Daddy's. Everything and everyone there had to be taken into account.

"Apologize," the Gunny said, finally taking his cigarette from his lips, his voice so soft it was difficult to hear him.

I looked into the Gunny's eyes but could not tell what he was thinking; his expression was the same as it almost always was. I wanted to ask him who he was talking to but I remained silent.

"He used the Ontos effectively, led us here where we sit in safety, and he called in artillery and air to make all that happen. Some artillery went astray. That shit happens. So, apologize to the lieutenant."

I knew instantly that the Gunny had picked up on my nod toward Nguyen, his move to the side and my placing my hand on the butt of Tex's Colt. I knew his words weren't about Jurgens respecting me. His request to Jurgens was a request to let the man live. He'd called me lieutenant for only the third time since I'd been in country. He didn't take that lightly, and neither did I. He was forcing Jurgens' hand while at the same time holding mine in abeyance.

The Gunny held out his cup of coffee toward me across the little blue and white fire, but I wasn't looking at him. I was examining Jurgens closely like a snake might examine a nearby mouse.

What was the sergeant going to do, I wondered?

one-hundred-nine

THE TWENTY-SECOND NIGHT : FIRST PART

I stared at Jurgens, waiting for an apology I wasn't sure I wanted to hear, and damned well knew I didn't want to accept. The man was the epitome of a phrase I'd never used in my lifetime and had only heard about in occasional passing while I was in college. White trash. The phrase fit, even if only in the A Shau Valley the color part of the insult really mattered. And it mattered because Jurgens made it matter, not me. My own father was a racist, born and raised down in Texas, but the word trash didn't fit at all with respect to him. The only exhibition of his prejudice I'd ever witnessed had been to ask my fourth-grade black best friend to get off our property in Michigan, which was terrible for me, but not a violent or killing move on his part. Trash, however, was a choice of lifestyle, and I'd never been forced to think about the applicability of the phrase until I was dropped into Jurgens' life.

"For better or for worse," the Gunny said, "we are all we have."

"It don't mean nuthin.'" Jurgens said, quietly, his eyes meeting my own with a mirrored distaste.

"Apologize," the Gunny said, his voice rising, but only slightly.

I knew the Gunny wasn't going to let it go, and I knew I wasn't going to let it go either, no matter what happened.

"Why can't we just go back to the way it's been?" Jurgens asked, avoiding looking at me by deliberately turning his head to speak directly to the Gunny.

"Because I can't afford to go back with you in a body bag," the Gunny replied, motioning toward me.

"I apologize," Jurgens finally said, his voice so quiet it was nearly impossible to hear him out from under the mild hissing sound the tiny drops made when they hit my helmet cover. "That doesn't make it right, Junior," he went on, his voice growing louder and more powerful.

The Gunny looked at me, as if asking whether I was accepting the apology, but without saying anything.

There was no way around the fact that Jurgens was a vital member of the company, damaged as he was, racist as he certainly was, and disciplined only in accomplishing what he either agreed to or might serve him best, regardless of the rest of the company. But his value wasn't the issue if I was forced to decide between that and the continuance of my own life. My hand started to shake ever so slightly, which hadn't happened in days, but I noted that my right hand, the hand on the Colt .45, wasn't shaking at all.

There was nothing to be said. My hand stayed on the butt of my Colt. All I could do was remain very wary, intent and prepared for any eventuality, but nothing happened. Jurgens retreated backward slowly and the Gunny with him, both of their radiomen waiting until their principals moved past before following. The Gunny waved both hands low, across one another, as if cutting the air down below him where he walked.

I knew the gesture, which was similar to the gesture dealers in professional gambling institutions used to show when they were leaving a table.

Nguyen appeared out of the bracken and into the darkening mist between us. He'd been there all the time, I realized, just like he'd been very closely around and through every other incident of high threat I'd experienced since joining the company, in what seemed like many months in the past.

Fessman and Zippo worked to set up the Starlight Scope, while Sentry did whatever he did inside the Ontos to ready it for action in case it was needed in the night. The tracked machine was not running, to save fuel, but it could be started in only seconds if the turret needed adjusting or the tracks themselves had to be used to maneuver the small but heavy machine around into a better firing position.

Nguyen closed the distance to me but squatted down before reaching me. He was chewing slowly, and I knew what he was chewing. I didn't want to use the drug again, so I didn't approach closer, instead making for my temporary lair under the edge of the cliff.

I crawled from the berm backward, moving slowly but deliberately under the protection of the overhanging cliff face. Every inch brought more protection until I was finally pressed back into the narrow but manageable thick crease where the rocks came together like the base of two giant clamshells. The advantage of being in the cave-like protection was warmly obvious. Almost nothing the enemy could throw or shoot or launch through the air could effectively reach me when I was inside. The bad part was isolation. The same isolation that protected me also caused most of the remaining risk and fear I was never without since I'd arrived in country. I could not see and observe the outside world. I could not see or observe what might be coming. I was dependent on others to tell me from their own positions outside along the berm, and my trust of others, especially most of the Marines around me, had been nearly terminally damaged. I'd been led to believe that there was almost complete trust forced upon all allied forces engaged in real combat. "The combat band of brothers

. I'd found out that just the opposite was true. People, Marines, the NVA, almost every being in the A Shau Valley trusted in themselves to ensure their own survival, and anything living that stood in the way of that unwavering cold-blooded mission stayed in the valley, forever. Only the survivors lived to tell the story and the story they would tell would have no bearing on any combat truth.

Zippo, Fessman, and Sentry stayed atop the berm, with the armored vehicle backed into the front side of the slope. Although the 106mm recoilless rifles had no flechette ammo left, the high explosive rounds were also very deadly against ground personnel, especially at the close range, they might be called on to fire into or across. I knew I had to go down for a short period. I'd had nothing to eat or drink and, although sleep did not overcome me, I knew I was running on empty when it came to having enough energy to properly and quickly respond to whatever the NVA was going to come up with next. But, above all, I had to write a letter home to my wife.

Once again, I'd lost Marines, and I knew I was going to lose more, and I also knew I was not handling the losses well. I didn't see their faces and that I could not see them was both a deep relief but also a deep concern. I didn't have trouble sleeping because I never really slept. I had trouble trying to feel anything that was not just awful, dark and dead-ended. I needed to go down, even if for the shortest of times.

I rummaged through my pack for Jurgens' flashlight, finding it but also discovering the batteries were all but dead. Again. Would the hazy yellow glow be enough? I brought my tattered stationary pack out of my trouser pocket. The plastic bag had held through the river crossing, I noted, pulling it open and extracting two sheets of the small stationary and one Vietnam envelope. Only the distant rumble of heavy water passing by between the riverbanks and the incessant patter of monsoon rains penetrated back and down into my small refuge.

I wrote my letter about Tex, but I didn't write to my wife about his death. I pictured him, although I couldn't make out his face in my mind, as being still with me, an Army officer of higher rank who served in a lower capacity. It was an unlikely interesting story but one I thought she'd be okay with because she might understand that I had some companionship when, in reality, I had little or none that wasn't made up by my own imagination. Fessman was devoted to me, but he was a kid, and barely a corporal at that. Zippo was older but younger in many ways. Nguyen was like a brother in arms but only like one. It was impossible to have a dialogue with a man who almost never spoke at all or when he did, spoke using an incomprehensible language. The Gunny was like a mix of my father, my mother, some Maryknoll nuns along the way, with maybe a decent demanding college professor thrown in.

I pulled out Tex's .45 when I got to the second page. I inhaled the Hoppes #9 I had massaged into the metal earlier. I had no gun oil so the single small bottle of Hoppes I had served as the automatic's cleaner and lubricant all at the same time. I'd always loved the smell of the solvent, way back to my shooting days as a kid with my dad's NRA team. Now, the Hoppes smelled like Tex or at least brought him to mind. I wondered if I lived, whether it would always be that way. Hoppes was made in Overland, Kansas, I knew because it had said so on the label before monsoon moisture ate it up entirely. The smell was so distinctive, like that of the Safesport mosquito repellant. Attractively awful, Zippo had said about both one morning, and that had been a perfect description. Safesport was made in Denver. Denver and Overland places I'd have to visit one day if I lived, but in that thought crossing my mind I could not fathom why visiting them would mean anything at all.

I wrote of the sand and mud by the river and the beauty of wet bamboo groves, with their individual tubes blowing in the mild wind, like waving strands of stiffening but not hard spaghetti. I finished the letter, writing about Hawaii and how R&R would be there after I'd made it six months in the field, even though I knew I'd never make it that long. There was just no way. Finishing the letter, I backed out of my cave, the flashlight still giving out a slight glow, but not enough to write another letter without new batteries coming in on the next resupply, and only God knew when that event could possibly take place.

Crawling out to the berm where Fessman hunched over Zippo's back looking through the Starlight Scope was quick and easy. The rain and the long exposure to the moisture made sliding anywhere much easier than walking, especially if one was walking crouched over to avoid being hit by an attentive distant sniper. For some very relieving reason, the leeches had retreated back underground.

"It's just getting dark enough now," Fessman said, laying the scope down between Zippo's shoulder blades, and then backing away so that I could look if I wanted to.

"Jurgens is coming back with two snipers to use it," he continued. "He says the enemy is probably going to slip out of the jungle to get their dead and wounded after what the rotary cannons did to them."

I looked through the scope, after settling in and making sure my envelope home was safely back inside the plastic bag I carried in my right thigh pocket. For whatever reason, I thought about the necessity of somehow getting a resupply chopper in at first light just so that envelope could go out, and I could assure myself that I'd made it another night in something resembling the hell often described to me in my Catholic childhood but really more like Dante's Inferno.

It was still too light for the scope to work properly. I had enough light to read the silver letters written on the side: "Night Vision Sight, Subassy. MX-7833/PVS2."

For some reason, the scope had a range focus ring at the front of the thing and then an eyepiece focus ring at the back. I knew how to focus the front ring but Zippo and Fessman both insisted that I not touch the eyepiece focus.

Jurgens was coming with two of his snipers. I'd been with the unit for over three weeks and I remained unaware that the company had any snipers, much less that two of them were in Jurgens' platoon.

"Last song of the day, sir?" Fessman whispered into my left ear.

I said nothing, aligning the scope and trying to see through it. It was still too light, however, so I rested it again wishing I had something dry to take the spots off the shrouded lens. There was no protecting anything for long against the pitiless moisture and rain.

"It's a good song, sir," Fessman said, his voice still a whisper, giving me the decision one way or another.

"What the hell," I replied without whispering. I didn't really care about the song as much as I wanted to listen to Brother John tell me good night.

"Here she is," Brother John said from Fessman's crummy little radio speaker. "The one and only Gracie Slick." Somehow, even through such a tinny filter, Brother John's voice remained deep and that depth resonated inside me.

"One pill makes you larger, and one pill makes you small…and the ones that mother gives you don't do anything at all…go ask Alice…when she's ten feet tall…"

I could not help but smile coldly at the idea of taking a pill for escape, although I knew full well that the only pill I was likely to get from the Marine Corps in my situation was one like the mother gives you in the song. White Rabbit the song was called. I'd first heard it the year before, staring across the street at the beautiful Italian college girl my brother was in love with. White Rabbit we'd laughingly called her behind her back. Now, I reflected, I was the white rabbit gone down the hole in Alice's wonderland.

The Gunny showed up as the song ended and Brother John signed off. Jurgens followed him, with both of their radio operators. Four Marines accompanied them, all sliding into the mud and under-growth to maximize the cover the small berm provided. I noted bolt-action rifles carried by all four. I assumed from training that I was looking at two snipers and their spotters, although the spotters were equally armed. I also knew that the PVS-2 scope came along with a special rifle attachment so it could effectively be attached and sighted in for the accuracy of fire in the darkest of nights. How the snipers might attach our scope to one of their rifles, and then get their aiming dope down good enough to hit anything, I had no idea. But it wasn't going to matter.

"No, we're not going to fire out there," I said, making the decision while I talked. "The NVA's going to come out to get their dead, not us. We're going to let them. I'll man the Ontos with the scope in case they decide to take advantage of the situation. We've got plenty of high explosive rounds, and God knows the kind of bloody nose they took earlier from the flechettes and the gunship."

The Gunny slowly and carefully lit a cigarette into the silence, the sound of his lighter ringing loud into the darkening night.

"Bull shit, Junior," Jurgens said, his voice a more a loud hiss than anything else. "They get no quarter, just like they give no quarter. If those were our Marines out there they wouldn't be letting us get our wounded and dead without giving us more wounded and dead. We're going to hit them and hit them hard."

"We have no supporting fires in the night," I replied, my own voice low and controlled, although my right hand was once again on the butt of my Colt. I knew Jurgens was also trying to recover the male macho image he'd lost earlier on, and therefore felt he couldn't back down.

"The Ontos is all we've got, but it can't do a damn thing if it can't see. We need the scope for that. Also, the enemy gets to collect its dead. I don't care one whit about the NVA sense of honor but this is the United States Marine Corps and Marines let the enemy tend the wounded and collect the dead, or at least this element of the Marine Corps does."

Jurgens moved from his stomach up to a crouch.

"Screw the scope," Jurgens said. "The damned thing only works some of the time anyway. We'll go back to our perimeter and pick off what we can see from reflections in the rain hitting the little gook's backs."

"I wouldn't do that against orders, Sergeant Jurgens, and I'm ordering you to stand down."

"Screw your orders, Junior," Jurgens replied. "Our platoon does what it thinks is best when it comes to fighting the enemy."

I stared at the impossible man. He didn't move, and the failing light would not let me read his eyes. No one moved, so I did.

I rose up slowly, crossed the berm and hopped up into the back of the Ontos, where Sentry sat waiting.

"Start it up," I ordered.

The loader turned the key and the Ontos kicked into life after only a few seconds.

I stepped to the controls, hit the turret swivel and began a slow winding move until the front of the turret and the six guns pointed at our own lines. I turned the key off myself, and then hopped down and re-crossed the berm to where the other Marines all sat or lay waiting.

The Gunny held out his cigarette. I took it, inhaled deeply while managing to avoid coughing before I breathed the smoke out.

"What's that supposed to mean?" Jurgens asked,

"I don't know," I responded, wanting to cough but fighting the reaction back. "What do you make of it?"

"I think you're threatening me and my whole platoon, that's what I think, Junior."

"The NVA get their wounded and dead this night," I repeated. "If they attack then I'll turn my attention back to them. If your platoon breaks fire control and disobeys my order then the chips will have to fall where they may."

"Gunny," Jurgens said, a tone of desperation entering his delivery, "are you going to put up with this crap? Those aren't 'chips' he's talking about. Those are 106 H.E. rounds."

"Nothing's happened yet," the Gunny said, snapping his cigarette out into the mud toward where the river still ran in a noisy flood.

"Let them get their people out of there. It's harder to take care of the wounded and the dead than it is to leave them to rot and die. Make it harder on them, not easier. And Junior's the company commander and battalion hasn't relieved him with any success I've been able to witness. It's for better or for worse down here, and, so far I think it's been for the better."

"So, that's just it?" Jurgens said, his voice rising. "We're supposed to go back to the platoon position with our own 106 guns pointed at us all night?"

"Junior?" Gunny asked gently. "You've made your point. It took five seconds to turn the turret. It would only take five seconds again, if that became necessary, which I don't think it will."

The Gunny turned his gaze back to Jurgens.

"It won't, will it?" he said deliberately and slowly to the sergeant, not stating the question as a question at all.

I slid back up over the berm and re-entered the Ontos. Restarting and returning the gun turret to its former position, aimed at the distant edge of the jungle back from the river, was done in seconds, as the Gunny had predicted. In no time, I was back at Zippo's side, ready to begin observing the mud flat with the Starlight Scope. I knew my night would be one of doing that, again and again, and then making certain the Ontos was ready to fire in the least possible time necessary. The time it might take for a charging enemy to reach across the distance from the jungle's edge to where we were ensconced was less than three minutes at a run. That time period would not leave my mind until dawn finally appeared.

Jurgens said no more, waving his barely visible hand in the growing darkness for the others to follow. The snipers, their spotters, and the radio operator disappeared into the misting rain, leaving Zippo, Fessman, and the Gunny and I alone in a clump. Sentry was barely visible hanging out the back of the Ontos, smoking a cigarette. I knew that I'd be on call all night, moving from the berm to the Ontos and back at the slightest provocation. Sentry could load and fire the rounds on his own but nobody was going to be able to replace what I could do with Zippo and Fessman's help, slaving the Starlight Scope's ability to see in the dark with that of the 106 rounds terrific power. There was no way for the NVA to know we were out of flechette rounds until resupply, either.

Once it was dark enough to see clearly through the scope I began sweeping slowly back and forth across the mud flat. I kept the fingers of my left hand grasped lightly around the big front focusing ring near the very tip of the device. The focus was very sensitive but it was vital to minutely adjust to pick out any detail worth seeing.

Stopping to examine one particular spot I was finally able to see the enemy soldiers. They moved across the mud on their bellies. Right away I saw that they appeared to be unarmed. They pulled small packs behind them instead of wearing them on their backs. It took a few minutes to realize what they were doing. They weren't attacking. They were pulling bodies and parts out of the mud holes or from the beaten surface of the mudflat itself.

I'd been unsure about going against Jurgens in not allowing him to use the snipers to take down any enemy moving in the night out on the mud flat. That it was more cumbersome for the enemy to tend to wounded and the dead had been an accurate statement by the Gunny, I knew, but the Gunny had neglected to mention just how many, and how easily, the NVA would be able to get the wounded and dead underground for care in the many deep clefts and caves they had peppered through the jungle area in front of us. I hadn't made the decision strategically or tactically. I'd made it out of humanitarian necessity. It was personal, I realized. I felt so little like a human being that I was forced to participate in doing something that had at least the vestige of humanity left in it. Jurgens had been right to go after the enemy under any and all circumstance. But what was the ultimate result of doing right, in combat terms? The NVA had honored the company by not violating the packs and supplies left behind earlier up in the highlands. The NVA was capable of proving it could also be humanitarian under combat conditions, even if the NVA unit at that time had to have been a different one than we were facing down here by the river.

Nothing changed for hours. My watch told me the time, which seemed to pass in flickers instead of minutes or hours. I knew I was 'flicking' in and out of consciousness.

I was low on food, water and sleep was some strange mix of messed up consciousness and dreams, much like the weather constantly waving and wafting among us all, exposed as we were. Only the cleft under the cliff face offered any solace, safety and real comfort away from the rain and the real danger of getting hit in the night, but it might as well have been miles away.

The enemy worked doggedly and determined to slide the bodies and body parts back and away from the middle ground between forces. I became more and more satisfied with my decision not to shoot the rescuing enemy soldiers, particularly because they all appeared unarmed, something I'd not known when I'd made the decision. Jurgens remained true to his word, and there was no fire at all from the perimeter. I wasn't certain, if that changed, whether I could muster the courage, rage and insanity it would take to fire the 106 against my own Marines, and the further the night progressed the more relief I began to feel.

Everything suddenly changed. Everything was wrong. I was staring at the working ant-like creatures the enemy resembled out on the flat when the night was broken open with the sound of helicopter blades.

"What the hell?" the Gunny whispered, appearing out of nowhere to throw himself down beside me.

Nguyen had moved just as the Gunny descended, in order to avoid being struck. I flicked my gaze toward the area of the night he quickly disappeared into, realizing I'd not known he'd been right there at my side all along.

"We don't fly choppers at night, not in this pea soup and not with the likelihood of incoming fire," the Gunny said.

But the sounds of spinning Huey chopper blades only increased in volume. There was no mistaking what they were and that there was more than one of them. I glanced back through the scope but the mud was now empty of all humanity.

"What is this?" the Gunny asked, shocking me.

If the Gunny was surprised by the chopper blade sounds then all bets were off, and I had no idea what might be coming. The only reassurance I had was that the enemy possessed no Huey choppers of its own. Whatever was coming in without advanced contact or warning was our own, but what hell was its arrival going to cause to be brought down on our heads?

one-hundred-ten

The vibrations from the low-flying Huey choppers beat the mud, the low jungle debris, and even the pebbled cliff face into a mixed frenzy of anticipation. That state was nothing compared to the feelings of anticipation all the Marines and I were feeling inside our minds and bodies, I was certain. The sound of beating blades was nearly overwhelming, and I couldn't quite take the scene in full because of the darkness and rain-blown particulate. I sheltered myself against the swell of the berm, curling my body gently into its surface while pulling down on my helmet with both hands.

I waited, listening intently. There were more Huey's than I'd ever heard in one small place before. After a few seconds, I picked up on the fact that there were 'inside' and 'outside' choppers in the mix. That meant Cobra Hueys were flying close in circling security while the main transport Hueys dropped down like they landed in the center of a hurricane of their own making. None of it made any sense to me. The only night vision equipment any forces in Vietnam had was the Starlight Scope and that device, only a few feet away, was not designed to be used in the air. It was too short-ranged and its field of view was tiny. What sense did it make for Cobra gunships to fly security around heavy-lift Hueys in the middle of the night if they couldn't see?

The Cobras opened up, and fear lashed through me again, only having eased a bit during the short period of time following the rotary ship making mincemeat of the entire mud flat. The smaller rotary miniguns of the Cobras swathed back and forth across the mud flats again, this time fired by pilots who could not see much of anything except possibly the general area above where they fired. I cringed deeper down into the hardened mud of the poorly protective berm. The rotary fire swept close but not across the company position. Both the pilots were experienced savants of their deadly trade and the company and I had been lucky again. Before thousands of rounds of 7.62 bullets could find us, the attention of the Cobras was drawn to the denser jungle across the flat. The NVA had been taken by as much surprise as we had but finally recovered. They fired their own machine guns at the sources of the red-rope tracers hosing the area.

I heard the Choppers accept the fire and quickly dive to deliver their own hard and killing bites back down into the jungle. They fired while charging toward the target, their sweeping deadly approach invisible in the night but revealed when they fired. I stared out in wonder, part of my attention was on the choppers already landed.

The Cobras, what seemed like a dozen of them, flew, hovered about and then rose up to do more of the strange maneuvering and firing. How they kept from hitting one another was beyond me but it was a show of awesome firepower and wonder almost exceeding the deliberate devastatingly lethal fire the rotary supply plane had delivered earlier. The Cobra rotary rounds didn't explode but their pervasiveness over the entire valley floor was evident and fearfully impressive.

The heavier choppers were down on the mud, their blades still rotating at high speed, but not throwing up so much debris it was almost impossible to look up or breathe, as before. The disturbed tumbling rain returned steady, with slight wind drawn curtains wafting back and forth across the back of my body.

Resupply, a new command, Army engineering, or maybe some sort of selective evacuation was in progress, and I didn't have a clue as to what it was or why it was happening. I knew the Gunny didn't either. Since his original exclamation of shock, he'd done nothing but do the same as me, tunnel face down into the mud for prayerful protection.

I could not keep my right hand from creeping down to my thigh pocket. My letter to my wife was going to get out on one of the choppers even if I had to sprint across the mud flat to deliver it before the choppers pulled out.

"No," the Gunny hissed at me, grasping my right hand with his powerful left. "They're dropping, not staying, and you'll never make it in time. Take the risks we have to, not the ones you want to."

The Gunny's words reverberated back and forth through my mind. I pulled my hand from his grasp, feeling like a spoiled child. The risks I had to instead of the risks I wanted to. What risks did I want to? There were no more risks I wanted to accept, not that I could think of.

Getting my letter out wasn't a risk, it was a cry inside my heart and being for survival, for another chance at a life I'd somehow lost or been convinced to give away. But I knew he was right. There was no risk to be taken because it was too late to take it. The choppers were spooling up and getting ready to leap back into the night.

Maybe whoever had offloaded down onto the mud would have answers. That was, of course, if anyone at all had offloaded.

The birds pulled out, as if on the Gunny's command, their blade pounding whups growing in intensity as they leaped into the air, then they slanted forward and down before pulling out to curve back and fly their return route heading north through up the bottom of the valley. Only seconds later, the gathering of praying mantis-like Cobras formed up and followed.

A great base of fire from down in the jungle didn't start until the Cobras were all nearly out of hearing range. M-60s in Jurgens' and Sugar Daddy's perimeter platoons opened up in return. The mud flat gently sloping down in front of the berm I laid behind was quickly covered in plaid pattern of green, yellow and red tracers, interlacing but not appearing to impact on the mud itself. But it was so dark there was no real viewing of any of it except the blazing neon spewing out, around and down from the tracers. The helicopters had been mostly invisible in the dark and continuing mist, but in my mind, they'd been so plaintively visible that I'd have sworn I could read the Marine insignia printed on their sides. In reality, I wasn't certain of whose choppers they were, however, until the Gunny spoke again.

"They're Marine aircraft and we've got to get down there and get whoever they dropped back up here," he whispered, leaning over while he spoke in an attempt to look through the single big lens of the Starlight Scope. "Those guys don't have a clue as to where we are and it's not likely they can read a compass to get here, in this pudding of a night, even if they knew."

"Who are they?" I asked, leaning away and letting the Gunny stare into the rubber grommet.

"Shit, I can never see a damn thing through this," the Gunny grimaced out. "How does anyone see anything with all that glowing crap going on?" He pulled away in disgust.

The shooting died down. The NVA began firing single sniper shots every few minutes. The Marines on the perimeter didn't bother to suppress with return fire and I'd come to understand why. Until there was proof that the choppers had dropped some ammo supplies then ammo had to be conserved. Mama bear ammo. If there was too much (Papa Bear) then it was too heavy to hump up and down the hills, through the mess of jungle crud and the cloying deep mud. If there was too little (Baby Bear) then there was the very real danger of running out and dying like helpless landed fish. The calculation to arrive at the just right "Mama Bear" amount was ongoing and always argued over.

I wasn't that good in the night, and I knew it because I had Nguyen. He could see in the dark, almost as good as the Starlight Scope. I knew where I was spatially at almost all times. It went along with my gifts for artillery calling and map reading, but the wet blackness of night was confusing if I couldn't see, no matter how oriented one might be down deep inside the valley.

"I'll go," the Gunny said, moving away from me to get ready.

"I've got to get the word out that friendlies are going be out on the mud."

"I would suppose whoever's out there under that umbrella of fire isn't too friendly anymore," I replied, knowing that our Marines had adjusted their M-60 fire for whoever was lying flat as pancakes out in front of us.

Whoever it was that had come in, however, it was unlikely that they were combat vets before this very time and in this very place. Combat vets didn't come visiting in the middle of the night. Marines who didn't know any better came, and I could only imagine what they had to be going through out there in the misting rain with their faces and stomachs shoved as deeply down into the leech-infested mud as they could get them.

I sighed to myself, remembering that it had been the Gunny who'd come for me during my first night when I'd been dumped from my own chopper. It seemed like so long ago.

"I'll go," I said. "Nguyen and I'll go and bring them back." I shifted over so I could make sure that my letter home was secure in one pocket.

As I moved the Gunny leaned in and gripped my arm up high. He shoved a package into my right hand.

"We'll go together," he whispered. "Take this stuff, just in case."

I felt the package with my fingers, almost instantly recognizing the case for what it was. The morphine syrettes could be felt through the cardboard like the narrow columns of chalk in the boxes the Maryknoll nuns of my childhood used to store their own 'ammunition.' I shoved the box into my right thigh pocket, thinking that the Gunny was preparing me for another time of grueling violence and blood until he whispered again.

"I've got a bad feeling," he said. "If things go south then you do what it is you do, and without delay."

I tucked the package carefully into my thigh pocket and buttoned it closed. That pocket also contained my maps in their plastic bags and my compass. Some of the Marines carried the smaller M-33 grenades in those pockets but I had my two in my pack. My trust in grenades was low, having watched how ineffective they were in training except in closed environments. In the jungle foliage, they were little more than a muffled bump in the night unless the proximity to one exploding was only a few feet.

The Gunny crawled away into the night. I knew he was going to Jurgens and Sugar Daddy to let them know he was going out, which pleased me. The Marines would not risk shooting the Gunny, and I would be with him all the way. There was no sound from the area of the drop. I went back to staring through the scope, now fully used to adjusting the tube and focus to make up for Zippo's breathing and fidgeting around, but there was nothing to see. Nothing moved and the misting rain made a muck of trying to define anything out of blurry shades of back and foreground.

The Gunny came back and the four of us, Nguyen, the Gunny, Fessman and myself slithered across the berm and down onto the slimy surface of the mud. I'd decided at the last minute to make sure we had a radio, and therefore we wouldn't be dependent upon anyone offloaded from the choppers for staying in communication.

The mud was slick and also difficult to grasp since the rain had been falling for so long. Muck was a better word than mud to describe it, and it also had a distinctive putrid smell of decay. Whether that was being exuded from all the nearby dead enemy soldiers who had to still be interred in their holes from the rotary cannons aboard the C-130 or whether it was simply a function of the nature of the stuff down close to the river. It was unknowable, not that that made any difference. My .45 remained in its holster. I'd left everything else normally attached to my web belt back under the lip of the cave, marginally dry and waiting for my return. The leeches were everywhere, but for reasons known only to them, they seemed to slide away from my hands as I worked to clear the mud before me before pulling myself forward about a foot at a time. Occasional small arms fire came out of the jungle area downriver where The NVA had stopped firing from their protected positions. I knew that if the enemy had a Starlight Scope we'd all be very quickly dead or severely wounded.

"Marines," a muffled voice called out from just ahead of where I was crawling. I stopped to listen, as did the others. None of us made a sound, although it was still difficult to hear anything over the rushing sound of the river and the constant patter of the misting rain.

"Marines," came again.

I pushed forward, the Gunny with me until I ran into a metal canister. I knew what it was right away. The water bottles came in thick plastic bottles. C-rations came in heavy cardboard boxes. Only ammunition or explosives came in aluminum canisters, and very occasionally, hot food. I didn't think battalion was sending us hot chow.

The Gunny took the lead in pushing through the canisters, boxes and some water bottles. The choppers had been on the ground so short a time that they hadn't unloaded. They'd dumped what they had overboard into the moist mud. Many of the items were half buried by the impact of their fall.

"Marines," came the heavy rough whisper again.

The tone of desperation and fear in the timbre of the voice told me all I needed to know. Another team of Marines had come flying into a hot landing zone and been introduced to combat on the ground. It was night, they didn't have a clue as to where they really were, the enemy was shooting at them and it seemed that the friendlies were too. And they were mired down in heavy mud, it was raining, and the leeches weren't being as kind to them as they'd been to us.

"Welcome to my world," Fessman said to me from a few feet away, no doubt sensing exactly the same thing that I was.

"Marines," the voice called out again.

"We're here," the Gunny said back, keep his voice down as far as possible, but still surprised me.

We were out in the open between opposing forces in the night. The best course, and generally only course for survival under such circumstance was silence. Silence without moving was preferred, and silence without moving in some sort of covered shelter was the ideal.

"Shit," the Gunny whispered, hesitating before moving aside to go around something. I crawled forward onto a body.

"Marines," the voice said again.

"Shut up, we're here," hissed the Gunny, knowing full well we were dealing with a remnant of whatever force had been sent out.

The firing by the NVA had been point specific. When the choppers landed the nearby enemy soldiers in holes had been able to register the position. The earlier fire we'd heard and the company had responded to, was site-specific. And now the four of us were in exactly the same position at the same registered site, although nobody was firing at us.

All firing had stopped and an eerie silence hung over the battle-field mud. There was only the sound of the river and the rain. The NVA knew where we were and they knew we were alive.

I crawled forward to where the Gunny had pulled up short.

"You're going to be all right," the Gunny said, talking to a figure I sensed laying in front of him. "You're not hit. Who were you with?"

"Major Cruikshank, and his command staff," the voice in front of the Gunny said.

"Shit," the Gunny whispered again, before twisting back to face me.

"Battalion command just lost a good bit of battalion command," the Gunny said. "Cruikshank was the XO, and I think they're all dead."

"What in the hell happened?" I asked, in shock. What was battalion doing sending out the XO without any warning or ground support, I wondered?

"They were getting oriented here on the ground, and then they were all dead," the voice said. "Just like that. They were all dead. How could they all just be dead like that?"

"Who are you?" the Gunny said, his voice low and harsh.

"I'm Sergeant Bates, serving as aide to the major," the voice replied.

"We've got to keep quiet or we're going to draw more fire," I whispered up near the Gunny's left ear.

"Not likely," the Gunny shot back, not whispering this time. "You don't get it yet?"

"Get what?" I replied, perplexed.

"You, it's you," the Gunny said, "and this guy's fine but his radio's shot to hell. We need to get back up to the berm and wait until first light and supporting fires to come back for the supplies."

"Me?" I said, with the same shocked tone.

"Like they can't know we're here?" The Gunny said, derisively. "These rear area guys got out of the choppers and wandered around like they were touring a park. The NVA registered the site and then put down a very effective base of small arms fire to take out whoever came out and dropped to the mud. I don't know if our company helped things along, but we can't stay out here for much longer. The NVA commander down there might not do the honorable thing all night."

"Me?" I asked again.

"They're letting us recover our wounded and dead because you let them recover their own," the Gunny said.

A long groan came from somewhere in the near distance.

"How many Marines got off the choppers?" the Gunny said to Bates.

"Six of us," Bates replied.

The groan came again, this time insistently loud.

"Shit," the Gunny said, for the third time.

"Somebody made it," I said. "We've got to figure out who, and then what we're going to do."

"Like we have a real choice here, Junior," the Gunny replied, moving to begin checking the bodies.

"What's he talking about?" Bates asked.

My hand automatically went down to clutch my right thigh pocket.

"Nuthin', Sergeant," I replied, "He didn't mean nuthin.'"

one-hundred-eleven

THE TWENTY-SECOND NIGHT : THIRD PART

I made it back to my cave under the rock wall of the cleft I was holed up in, the one I'd spent some time hoping to get back to. I laid in the darkness, shedding outer pieces of my wet rotting uniform, and wondering about the reality of the combat I was hopelessly engaged in. The moving, moist, noisy and miserable tomb of the A Shau Valley gave nothing back. There was nothing to give. I thought about the movies I'd seen growing up. The troops and Marines in the field had litters and stretchers for the wounded. Cruikshank had come back inside a poncho cover, looking like nothing more or less than a giant moth pupa. In combat, Marines carried everything, and there was no way to order them to carry more, and nobody was going to carry an extra twenty pounds in case somebody else needed to be carried. If the Marines didn't want to carry a load or disagreed with what was in it, then they simply dumped whatever it was into the jungle around them. Punishing them didn't change anything. When a punishment, even as extreme as immediate death, is commonly administered among a human group the members of that group get used to it. The Gunny had been very peculiar and particular in how he'd described accommodating combat weeks earlier. Actual ground combat teaches, with death as its primary tool. It doesn't teach by killing the Marines around you. It teaches by killing you.

"You need to come," the Gunny said, from just beyond the outer edge of my hideout.

I knew why he was there. His premonition, when he'd resupplied my syrettes of morphine, about his own mortality in heading out onto the mud flat in the middle of the night had been just a little off. God had swooped in and taken the battalion executive officer instead, and in exactly the same way the Gunny had most feared would happen to him. I pulled my wet trousers back on, and then my stinky mess of a utility blouse. There would be time for the engorged small leech removal procedure later, or in the morning. The little leeches I'd taken on didn't suck enough blood to weaken my body. It was the big ones in the back eddy waters of the Bong Song river, or those to be found deeper inside the middle of the thicker jungle, that sucked out one's real life's blood. Those had to be rid of as quickly as possible.

I crawled out, running into Fessman instead of the Gunny.

"I would presume the six-actual has been heating up the combat net about Cruikshank," I murmured to him.

"No sir, nobody's told battalion yet. The Gunny thought you had been the one to do that, being company commander and all, sir."

"This way," the Gunny said, keeping his voice low.

The NVA hadn't fired a shot since the recovery effort had been started, but that couldn't last and everyone in the company had to know it. The NVA held the huge chunk of jungle that ran between the cliff face and the river, running at least a kilometer or more down south toward where we'd originally come down into the valley. Hill 975 was loaded with another force, probably of equal size, not far from our position up north. The company was trapped between the river, the vertical canyon wall, and then between two nearly overwhelming enemy forces.

Nguyen appeared nearby, looking like the Gunny, Fessman and myself, the wetness of all of our ponchos glistening in some kind of light that didn't seem to come from anywhere but from the ground and jungle outgrowth itself. I moved in behind the Gunny and headed the few meters north along the cliff face until he ducked under the lip of the rock and disappeared. I went to my hands and knees to follow him. A flashlight, covered with some kind of material to mute the light, gave off a dull red glow ahead. The cave-like cleft was bigger than the one I'd adopted as my own a few meters south along the wall. Jurgens was facing me deep inside by the light, and a larger figure who had to be Sugar Daddy was squatting next to him. One of the corpsmen worked on the battalion XO, who lay back down in the center of the cave. It was difficult, in the muted light, to make out what the corpsman was actually doing.

After a minute, or so, the corpsmen rocked back on his heels, squatting like Nguyen did when he was relaxing.

"Seventeen or eighteen rounds," the corpsman whispered. "Took one of them right through his lights. There's no coming back from that, not out here so far from a medical station. He's alive but there's no way."

At that the corpsman quickly got his stuff together and pulled slowly toward the cleft opening, moving backward, like he was bowing out.

The lights. I remembered the phrase all the way back from a frontier novel I'd read years before. Lights were lungs. The XO had taken a round through both lungs. A double lung shot. Certain, but not necessarily instant, death.

"You'll want this," Tank, the Gunny's radio operator said, moving from the darkness at the back of the cleft to hand the flashlight to Nguyen, who'd somehow squeezed past everyone to press himself bent over into the crease where the floor and the ceiling of the cave came together and ended.

Nguyen grasped the flashlight like it was some sort of diseased object, carefully suspending it in the air by making a web of the fingers of his right hand.

"Battalion command," Jurgens said derisively aloud, moving toward the cleft's entrance. "Just terrific. They send one idiot after another to accomplish what? Our supplies are out there on the mudflat, no doubt shot through with hundreds of holes. Idiots."

I crouched by the side of the XO. Cruikshank lay flat on his back with his arms at his sides. An I.V. needle was inserted into the elbow of his upturned right arm, the bag held up by a C-ration can opener stuck into a crack on the cave's ceiling. I couldn't see his chest rise and fall in the bad light, with the mud all over adding to any ability to make out anything inside the cave in detail. I heard his breathing and I knew, as the corpsman had, there was no medevac that was going to save the major. If the man had been shot through the lungs inside an ER he might have had a chance, but even the severity of the 'lights' injury probably didn't matter that much, as that deadly bullet was only one of many that had gone through him.

I leaned forward and peered into the major's face. His eyes blinked and he gurgled in and out instead of breathing properly. His lips moved as if he was trying to say something but his lung damage was too severe. For some reason, his condition, and the fact that he was still alive and struggling made me angry.

"Get out," I hissed to everyone around me, gesturing for them to exit the cave by pointing with my right forefinger back toward the entrance.

Jurgens and Fessman crawled away, and the Gunny faded out of the light, as well. I swung my arm around to bring my finger to bear on Nguyen but then dropped it, as the gesture was unnecessary. Nguyen held the light steady and stared with his black unblinking eyes over it. He wasn't going anywhere.

I pulled out the packet of morphine syrettes with my right hand, opened one end of the small cardboard container, and very carefully let three of the syrettes fall into my other hand. There was no ceremony to be followed, and no reason to delay. Cruikshank continued to groan and croak softly, and it appeared in the bad light that he was turning his head back and forth slightly. There was no way to interpret anything from his moves, nor any point to it. I punched a needle from a syrette into his right thigh, through his utility trousers, then followed it quickly with two more. I sank back to wait, dropping the empty morphine tubes to the floor of the cave.

Nguyen put out the light, and the three of us sat in the dark, listening to the sounds of life in one of us slowly ebb away until there was only silence. The distant roiling of rushing water down the river came back, and the ever-present sound of the monsoon rain remained where it'd been all along, although unheard over the dying sounds of the major. I recognized the returning sounds as the basal backdrop of life in the A Shau. I looked over to where I couldn't see Nguyen in the dark although I knew exactly where he was. He didn't move, and I knew he wouldn't until I did.

I replaced the morphine packet in my pocket. I had seven syrettes left, and I wondered when I'd be called on to use any or all of them again. My left hand went down to the outside of my left thigh pocket, where my wife's letter was folded inside, ready to go out on any chopper that would stop long enough to let me get it aboard. I breathed in and out deeply and tried to relax. So far, in my thinking, I couldn't come up with one part of one task I had to perform as a company commander of Marines in combat that I could ever tell my wife about.

"Sir," I heard from behind me. The voice was Fessman's.

"Battalion?" I replied, turning about to face the cave's entrance.

There could only be one reason Fessman was asking for my attention.

"The six-actual, sir," he replied.

A six-actual to talk to a six-actual. I was living an even worse version of Catch-22 than Yossarian had.

I couldn't see it, but I knew the Prick 25 handset was pushed out between us. I stood to take it, while Nguyen passed from out of the cave, unaccountably rubbing up against me as he went. I pulled away a bit, and then realized he'd slipped the valuable flashlight into my back pocket as he went. I didn't know who the thing belonged to but whoever it was in the company, he wasn't getting it back.

"Six-actual," I said, flatly into the microphone, going down into a squat, wondering it the conversation would be very long.

"Put the XO on, Junior," the battalion commander ordered.

"He didn't make it, sir," I replied.

"The choppers didn't come in?" the commander exclaimed. "I knew it. God damn it. They had plenty of cover and pretty damned good intel."

"The choppers came in, sir, but the team was lost," I reported, as succinctly and flatly as I could. "The choppers came into a hot L.Z. and if…" but I got no farther.

"If, my ass, Junior," the commander screamed into the microphone, making me pull my own handset back from my right ear a few inches. "Don't tell me Tommy's dead, just don't tell me that whatever you do…" he said, as his voice trailed off.

I waited; knowing now that the major's first name had been Tommy and the commander's use of his first name meant they were close.

"You and that ragtag company out there in God knows where. God damn it! What did you do to him?"

I held the handset out before me. I couldn't think of anything to say. It came to me that the commander himself had concocted the surprise nature of the XO's visit, so he could have a surprise inspection team analyze what was going wrong with a company that lost five to ten percent of its T.O. strength every single day.

"What did he do, Junior?" squawked out of the handset I held. "What did you do, Junior?" the commander screamed after that, each sentence accentuated with my nickname.

Suddenly and impulsively I brought the handset quickly up to my head. "He came down in the A Shau to learn about combat, that's what he did, sir. And he learned all right, just as you wanted him to, sir."

I held the microphone, pushed so hard into the side of my head that my ear hurt, but I could hear nothing. I waited, but the commander or the connection, or both, were gone. I didn't know whether he'd heard me or not. I looked around. Only Nguyen and Fessman were nearby. The others had fled when the combat net exchange with battalion had begun, just like they'd fled when the major had to be put down. I slumped down a bit and sighed. I knew I'd have fled too if there'd been any way to do so that didn't involve lessening my already tiny chance to survive. I was the 'shit jobs' officer and I knew it, and so did everyone in the company, and probably even back at battalion. Sadly, I also knew that my willingness to be just that was helping keep me alive, but it wouldn't be something I could ever write home about or tell to any after war buddies I might make back in the states.

I handed the handset back to Fessman. The Gunny appeared out of the wet raining night. I'd left my helmet behind me in the cave, but as I turned to get it he stopped me.

"I've got it," he breathed gently moving me aside with one powerful but gently applied hand. "There was no way for me to maintain if I took that call," he said with his back turned.

He rummaged in the dark for my helmet. I thought of the flashlight in my back pocket where Nguyen had slipped it but I didn't say or do anything.

The battalion commander had called me. I hadn't placed the call and neither had Fessman. Someone had alerted the commander that there was bad news awaiting him. I also didn't understand what the Gunny meant when he used the word 'maintain.' The sentence he'd obviously and carefully crafted sounded an awful lot like one I'd heard used in humor back at my college; "you've got to go there to get there, and get there to be there."

The Gunny put the helmet gently down on my head.

"You're a Marine Officer, Junior," he said, too quietly for anyone else, even Fessman close by, to hear. "You're maybe the best one I've ever known, or at least the only one who's ever really listened worth a damn. Right now, you can't believe that to be true. If we live, someday, you will."

The Gunny straightened up, and then spoke louder, using his normal gravelly tone. "We've got to get those supplies. We need the ammo, especially the flechette stuff because those gooks aren't going to stay quiet forever. We need you to man the Ontos."

He said the last to me.

Another shit job, but this time there was some relief from the gnawing fear that had come back to make a nest inside the center of my being when I'd been out on the mudflats. I would be staying back inside an armored vehicle the NVA feared more than just about any other Marine Corps weapon, except maybe Puff the Magic Dragon.

"Unless, of course," the Gunny continued, lighting a cigarette and sounding like he was talking to himself, "first light isn't far off and they see Junior himself out there in that distinctive helmet... out there collecting our dead."

I knew I wouldn't be staying with the Ontos, and I almost smiled as a shiver of fear just lingering nearby, invisible to everyone but me, came charging back to entwine my core. Of course, I wasn't staying back. I was maybe one of the best Marine Officers the Gunny had ever known. That was the part that made me finally smile, and coldly. The Gunny was a master player and I was but a pawn. The only good thing I could think of about going back out there on that open field of fire was the number of spider holes the enemy had dug earlier and then been forced to abandon. At least they might provide some cover if the light was good enough to see one or more of the well-disguised things.

I made one last attempt to stay back with the Ontos.

"You know, Gunny, they can't make it at all without one of us."

"Hell," the Gunny laughed. "They can't do without either one of us anymore if you haven't noticed."

"Who've we got?" I asked in resignation, knowing the Gunny would fully understand what I meant.

Getting me to go out there again was a lot easier for the Gunny than getting Marines from any of the other platoons to do so. And there would have to be at least two squads to haul all the junk back, not to mention the four remaining bodies.

Fessman messed with his radio nearby and then walked the few feet over to where the Gunny and I stood behind a stand of bamboo down from the berm. He stuck out one long gangly arm with the hand-set gripped at the end of it.

"Six-actual," he said to both the Gunny and I and then waited.

I looked at the Gunny, but he only looked back at me through the smoke curling up from the end of his cigarette, without making a move. His expression, that I could only barely read, seemed to be one of a question, like what was I going to do? He puffed once more and again made no move to do anything.

"It's Sugar Daddy's turn," I said, ignoring Fessman's outstretched hand. I had nothing to say to the battalion six-actual. The major was dead, and the team that accompanied him was dead too. The Battalion wasn't going to provide any assistance in getting our supplies off the mudflat and everything else in the valley, or out in the world, would wait until first light.

The Gunny grinned grudgingly and walked away into the night. His first objective to accomplish his mission, getting me to go back out, had been very successful. His second objective had been to avoid dealing with battalion directly. He'd accomplished that, as well. Now, all he had to do was convince Sugar Daddy that it was worth it for him to risk his platoon, probably for a healthy slice of whatever was laying out there shot full of holes.

I crawled back into my cave to get ready to go out. I found my pack and carefully pulled out the two M-33 grenades I kept there. They had a reassuring weight and feel to them, as I cradled them in the dark. I placed one in each blouse pocket on the front of my utilities. The grenades would make crawling along over the surface of the mud more discomforting and problematic but they wouldn't cause me as much fear as carrying the small deadly things in my trousers. I wouldn't need the pack for my return to the landing zone and I'd already determined that I'd never again go anywhere without Tex's .45 and my K-Bar. They stayed on my belt. I didn't need anything else.

When I came out of the cleft Fessman, Zippo and Nguyen were waiting. The night was different than it had been only minutes earlier. I knew I was sensing astronautical dawn, although there was still no distinguishable light to see by. Fessman had to accompany me, and I knew I didn't have to discuss the plan with him but did mention that we'd need the AN-323 for air support. Zippo needed to stay with the Ontos and work with Sentry to follow our progress in the night, while it was still night. The Ontos was the only supporting fire we'd have, and there was no telling about air for the following day. Nguyen would do what Nguyen did, which was many times a mystery but was always something that ended up making me feel somehow more secure.

The crawl out across the mud was uneventful. The misting rain, the loud burbling rush of river water nearby, and the persistent presence of the small irritating leeches were quite evident. The Gunny led with his radio operator and I followed. Sugar Daddy had chosen to string out his entire platoon, leaving one Marine every four or five yards, to relay stores back from the zone man-to-man instead of simply load up and carrying as much back possible. I didn't like the idea of having one long line of Marines subject to enfilade fire (shooting straight through one man after another in a line with the same bullet) but there wasn't any safe covering part of the mudflat to provide cover, anyway. The slope was faintly downward toward the thick jungle area, with the violent river to the right. Slipping and sliding along through the mud wasn't much of a problem. I just hoped that getting back, if there was to be a getting back, would not be much more difficult.

Nautical dawn, that first tiny sliver of pre-dawn light was rapidly changing the landing zone from a completely black area into a grayish blackness that revealed not much more, but let me know that a brighter civil dawn was only minutes away.

The NVA didn't open up until the Gunny and I were among the dumped supply canisters. I plastered myself face down into the thick mud, before realizing that the tracers were not intended for us. They were firing high.

As I'd feared, Sugar Daddy's men were about to take some terrible losses, with the rest of us to follow, unless something could be done and done fast. It wouldn't take them long to lower their fire and there was no way we were getting back to the berm before full daylight.

one-hundred-twelve

THE TWENTY-THIRD DAY : FIRST PART

I scrambled, slid and crabbed my way through the low growing debris spread like small islands of living flora all over the mud flat I was trapped on. The NVA gunners had opened up high or were trying to take out the Ontos instead of shooting at a few scavengers trying to reclaim dead bodies and riddled supply boxes and tins. I couldn't see in the miserably low light because, what the lack of light didn't hide, the everlasting misting rain made so invisible that nothing of substance or real form could be distinguished. I moved laterally, turning away from the NVA filled jungle down the river and directly away from the river itself. The river's presence ruled everything because it was a given in the night. The noise of the rushing water could be heard over all else. With the Bong Song at my back, I did what I did best under fire, I tried to get away before the enemy got around to cleaning the mud flat of all living things. I'd taken one quick look over my shoulder to see if the fire was directed at Sugar Daddy's strung out platoon, but there'd been nothing to see in the blackness, which was good for the members of that platoon. But those of us down in the supply area were in a previously registered position, and it wouldn't take the NVA long to go back to playing cleanup, with our lives being what were going to be cleaned up.

I found a spider hole. I hadn't prayed to find one, but I murmured "thank God" when my hands plunged over the front edge of the hole. There was no hesitation on my part. I didn't care what was in the hole, I plunged forward and then dove over the lip head first. The hole was big, much igger than I would have imagined. My body had time to flip over as I fell, which was a good thing because I landed in a pool of water at least a foot deep, with a foot of sucking mud right at the bottom of it.

The water and mud cushioned my fall, although the depth of the fall caused my legs to fully bend, descending my lower body into the water along with my feet and legs. My first thought wasn't the relief I'd expected to be overwhelmed by getting off the deadly mud flat. Instead, I felt fear that I wouldn't be able to climb back out, with the depth and the slippery nature of the mud. That fear was driven from my mind, as

I stood up to my full height in time to be crushed flat by another falling body. I slammed down again; realizing the body had to be that of Nguyen, who'd crawled in after me. There was no mistaking the light ropey feeling of his hardened thin body. He crashed down onto me and then bounced off. There was no time for me to recover because more bodies cascaded down into the water-filled muddy chaos. I knew the Gunny and Fessman had come down but was shocked when I pushed myself violently backward to get away from the crush of their bodies. I rammed my torso right into the chest of another human, and my fear came rushing back. Everyone inside the hole had come across the mud with me. Anyone already inside the hole had to be an enemy. My right hand went down to grab the butt of my .45 as I twisted and turned, but I never had the chance to unsnap the holster and drag it out.

"It's me, Bates," a clear male voice said, into the churning mass of recovering bodies and splashing water.

"Bates?" I repeated, my mind not being able to understand what was being said, but my immediate fear draining away, like water rushing into a bathtub drain.

I cleared my head, as best I could, pushing my back against the open rounded wall of the big hole.

"Bates?" I asked again.

"The major's aide," the voice replied.

The Gunny lit his Zippo lighter, and a wavering yellow light illuminated everything in the hole.

Fessman was working to make sure his radio was okay and Nguyen was direct across the hole from me, behind the Gunny, looking as if he'd been there all along.

But only one Marine had been there all along.

"What the hell?" was all I could get out.

"They're all dead, aren't they?" Bates asked, his voice flat and unhurried.

I knew the shock the man was in. I'd felt it so many times myself. I knew it was obvious that this was Bates' first time in combat. All emotion was gone from him, and it'd be gone for some time to come, if not forever. If men like Bates and I ever made it home, I thought fleetingly, maybe every question that might be asked behind our backs would be "where did their humor go?"

"They're dead," the Gunny confirmed.

I stared into Bates' eyes, trying to take him in. He'd found the hole and did what any sane human did in combat when under attack. He'd taken the rabbit hole to safety and then stayed there while the Marines he was with just a few feet away, and a few feet higher up, were mowed down like wheat in a field at the end of a season. Before the Gunny snapped his lighter shut I saw the depth of regret, fear, and resignation in Bates' eyes. He'd joined the living dead and, with only a few hours of real combat experience behind him, he knew it.

"What do I do?" Bates asked, his voice quavering just a small bit.

"'You're with me," I replied, almost absently, trying to give Bates some confidence where was needed. "You were the XO's aide and now you're my scout sergeant."

"I don't think I can do that," Bates replied, the tone of his voice dropping to a whisper.

"It's either down here," the Gunny said roughly, snapping his cigarette down into the muddy water at the bottom of our hole, "or you can join your friends up there."

"What's the plan," the Gunny said, changing the subject and this time directing his question toward me, or so I thought. It was too dark to see anything, but there was no one else the question could rationally be directed toward.

"We stay," I replied since there were no other options.

Going up and over the lip, and then trying to crawl under fire back to the berm wasn't a plan that had any percentage of being survivable.

"Supporting fires at dawn," the Gunny said, his tone one of a quiet agreement.

I knew what his next question was going to be, and headed it off by answering it.

"The scope," I said. "The Starlight Scope. We call Tank and get your snipers back to the Ontos, and then we call the Ontos and get Zippo to sight for the snipers. Anybody coming anywhere near this hole gets waxed until daylight."

"How will Zippo know where we are, sir?" Fessman asked.

I pulled up my flashlight and hit the button very briefly, illuminating the hole for a second, or less.

"Won't the enemy see that too?" he asked, sounding like he had no confidence in the plan at all.

"They already know exactly where we are," the Gunny replied. "If they can get somebody close then all they need is a single grenade."

"The snipers might not be able to hit someone in this mist and mud," Bates argued, speaking for the first time other than to answer questions and indicating that he couldn't function in a combat role.

"The Ontos is loaded with H.E. rounds," I replied. "Close doesn't count, except in horseshoes, hand grenades, and Ontos high explosives."

"They're not going to send out anybody alone," the Gunny said, squatting down in the hole as if he was going to prepare a canteen holder of coffee.

I wondered if the composition B explosives he carried everywhere would ignite at the bottom of a water-filled hole. I thought about what he'd said about the potential of attack, and knew he was right. The NVA would come crawling across the mud like a herd of spiders, half a platoon in force, or more. They'd be hard to spot, even for Zippo with the Starlight scope, because of the wind-blown rain, and, the Gunny was right, it'd only take one well-tossed grenade.

Fessman asked if he should make the calls to the company, and I could tell he was shaken more than I'd ever known him to be.

"The plan is called the 'Dawn Go Away,'" I said.

"Like in 'Dawn go away I'm no good for you?' Fessman immediately asked.

"I love Frankie Valli."

The tone of Fessman's voice changed, and I almost smiled in the dark at the simplicity of how the boy's mind worked. He had a plan and it had a name. For some reason that was more important than what the details of the plan might entail. That the plan's name made no sense at all also made no sense at all, except the mention of it seemed to have a good effect.

"Terrible name but what the hell," the Gunny said. "Is that dawn, as in the coming dawn, or the Dawn of some girl's name?"

The Gunny didn't stop for more than a few seconds after asking the question, before going on. "We've got to do something. Even the Ontos rounds are not going to stop them. What about the illumination. We don't have to worry about the rounds falling short if they're Illum rounds."

"The 175 guns are all that can reach us here," I replied, regretfully. "175s don't have illumination. They load only high explosive and nuclear."

"Nuclear sounds okay," Bates said.

I knew that if we were back home everyone in the hole would have laughed, but Bates comment was met only with silence.

"Beehive," I said, replying to the Gunny's question. "We need to get the Beehive rounds up to the berm, load a few and then do some demonstration fire.

Beehives scare the living crap out of them."

"How much do the rounds weigh?" the Gunny asked.

"Thirty-seven pounds per round, plus a bit," I replied, remembering my single day in training with the recoilless weapon. I didn't remember the data from viewing the round itself since I hadn't handled any, but I'd read the side of one of the wooden ammunition boxes.

"A better question might be where the ammo is up there in the muck if they were dropped like the other junk," the Gunny stated.

"I know the boxes and Nguyen can transport one at a time back and forth to the berm," I replied.

"There won't be any supporting fire in the morning to any effect without you, Junior," the Gunny said, coming right back at me, intimating the mess I'd leave the company in if I got killed.

"They're scared shitless of the beehives," I replied. "If we can demonstrate that we've got them then they won't attack in a massed formation. We can deal with the individuals, or the snipers can. If we don't suppress a broad attack across the mud before dawn, then I'm not going to be here to direct anything. Not alive, anyway."

"The company can use suppressing fire while you're up there," the Gunny said, and I knew by his saying those words that the Gunny was buying into the plan.

"The distance is enough," I agreed.

Suppressing fire would be M-60s firing over the heads of myself and Nguyen while we worked to get at the 106 rounds and then allow Nguyen to hopefully get back and forth to the Ontos a few times. Suppressing fire only worked if it was fired at an angle in support of Marines in front of the gunners, or if the distance was great enough for the bullets coming from the gun barrels to arc high enough to go over the heads of those directly in front of them. Those in front of them would be Nguyen and me.

I waited to see if the Gunny was all in.

"I can go," the Gunny said, after a thoughtful moment.

There was no sincerity in the Gunny's tone. I understood, and amazingly the understanding made me feel a burst of warmth for the man. He didn't want to go out there either, and he wanted me to find a way to let him stay in the hole. Bates was remaining totally silent. I knew the paralyzing fear he was experiencing. The idea of never leaving the protection of the hole was in his mind like it had been in my own many nights in the past. The night the Gunny had dragged me out against my will.

Fessman talked quietly into the radio, arranging what needed to be arranged up the company line. The Gunny would have to arrange for the suppressing fire, which would also be better because nobody in the company was going to want to see the Gunny hit.

"Tell them that you're coming out of the hole with me," I said, wondering what the Gunny would reply.

I counted off the seconds. At my silent count of sixty, he spoke.

"That's good," he said, softly, and I could tell there was an invisible smile on his face. "That's really good."

I would have smiled back if I could. The single most comforting thing about the Gunny, other than I knew he liked me and thought I was marginally competent, was that he always seemed to get it. We didn't have to say certain 'filler' kinds of things or even complete sentences. The Gunny simply got what I was talking about without me having to detail it out, and it was the same way for me.

"How you going to tell the Montagnard what we need?" the Gunny asked.

"He'll know," I replied, having no idea if Nguyen would get it or not, but my confidence in the mountain man's ability to figure things out hadn't faded a bit since I'd met him.

I heard the Gunny moving around the mass of water and mud in the bottom of the hole. In seconds, he was talking quietly to Jurgens on the radio. Bits of mud fell from the top edge of the hole and I knew Fessman had to be standing up to his full gangly height, and holding the extended blade antenna in his pushed-up hand so it would rise up out of the hole.

"Flash the light, Junior, and make sure it doesn't point in the wrong direction," the Gunny said. "They know we're here but they don't know exactly what hole we might have landed in. Give 'em three quick bursts. I've set it up with six machine-gun teams to open up when I give the signal, or if you start taking heavy fire out there. You and Nguyen working to get the ammo out of the boxes may be less hazardous than the trips back and forth up to the berm."

"My sentiments, exactly," I murmured.

"But never forget he's just a Montagnard," Bates added.

Nobody said anything for a moment, as I reached up to aim the flashlight and press the button quickly three times in a row. Bates' comment hit me like some of the other junk that had been passed on to those of us in combat while the command structure remained unthreatened and unharmed in the rear area.

Nguyen had risked his life, time after time for me, and also offered support when I thought I had none from my own Marines.

"Maybe we need a dependable Marine instead, to ferry the rounds up to the berm and then come back down a few times," the Gunny said, quietly, stating the very thought that had come racing through my own mind. There was only one Marine in our hole capable of fitting that Marine distinction. Fessman had to stay on the radio, the Gunny had to direct action from the lip of the hole and I was the company commander.

"I didn't mean anything," Bates said, naked fear being exposed by the quivering in his voice.

"Because you don't know Jack," the Gunny replied, "but it don't mean Nuthin.'"

I heard and felt the Gunny moving about. He was using an E-Tool to dig into the side of one wall. It took him only seconds. I had no idea that he'd managed to include the E-Tool as part of his own kit when we'd come down, but it was so wet and dark he could have carried just about anything and I wouldn't have noticed. He used his lighter to start some composition B burning. The entire spider hole lit brightly around us, which made my own fear lessen a bit.

"What about losing our night vision?" Bates, asked, the fear still emanating from him like a warming radiator.

"Don't need night vision in the dark and rain," Fessman replied. "Can't see when it's this black, except for tracers, and they don't put out enough light to see anything by at all."

I handed the flashlight to the Gunny. He'd need it for signaling along with communicating using the radio. There was no way that I could use the light once we were out on the mudflats, no matter how difficult it might be to find the ammo boxes among the piles of items strewn around the bodies up above. The ammo boxes were narrow and long, each holding two 106 rounds. My K-Bar would suffice to open the boxes. From there it would be up to Nguyen to negotiate a course out across the mud and up to the eastern berm where the Ontos sat waiting.

I tried to relax into the wall across from where the Gunny worked to produce another of his cup holders of coffee. I breathed in and out deeply, accepting a lit cigarette from the Gunny.

"For the critters," he said.

I nodded and blew on the burning embers at the cigarette's end, before carefully touching them to the backs of my hands. The leeches fell instantly away, squirming in agony, or so I hoped. I handed the cigarette to Nguyen, who'd slipped across the hole to be at my side. I stretched out my chin toward the Gunny and moved it as high as I could. Nguyen went from leech to leech, dropping the little monsters away. I wondered if the 'critters' would live in the mud. For some reason, the leeches didn't inhabit the area in or around the river. There had to be something in the water and mud that was unhealthy. I thought about all the insecticide and herbicides American supply planes were dumping on the jungle we all inhabited. If the stuff was infusing the water with poison, and the leeches couldn't take it, then what of Marines forced to struggle in it too?

Nguyen handed the cigarette back when he was done. The leeches that'd made their way under my utility blouse, and no doubt up and down my trouser legs, would have to wait, while they feasted away. There was no way to remove my uniform and get at them under the conditions we were in. Only three weeks earlier I did not know I'd have had a hard time continuing on, but leeches, like the jungle, smells of sweet death and musty misery were things that could be accommodated over time. The relief I felt from the Gunny's brewing of coffee ran warmly though me while I waited to go over the top. The smell of the burning explosive was of a medicinal cordite sort, while the mix of faint coffee aromas, wafting up and around with the cordite, gave me a strange calming feeling of being among friends, even if there was no 'home' effect to it.

"Ready," I said to the Gunny. "No suppressing fire unless we need it," I said, unnecessarily, knowing I was letting him understand just how badly I did not want to go out on the killing mud flats above, but not being able to stop myself from saying anything.

The Gunny drank some of his coffee from the cup holder in his right hand and then crushed out his small fire with one boot before moving to hoist himself up on the step he'd created, so he could see over the top of the debris near the outer edge of the hole.

"Dawn, go away, I'm no good for you," he intoned.

I heard Fessman trying to suppress a giggle, which made me feel better. My life was in Fessman's and the Gunny's hands entirely for the next short period of time, or what I hoped was going to be a short period of time.

It was dead dark again, and Bates had been correct in commenting on the fires destructive effect on our night vision. I could see nothing. But I knew where the top lip of the hole was and I knew how close and in what direction the dropped supplies and the dead Marines were located. I checked the holster snap for the automatic to make sure I didn't lose it in getting out, and then across the sticky mud. I would let the K-Bar stay in its sheath until I was able to find some wooden ammo boxes to open. The boxes would have been easier to carry than slippery individual rounds but would have required two Marines to carry, and also those Marines would have had to remain vertical while they were moving in order to do so.

I faced the wall of the hole. Its upper lip was too high for me to reach up and pull myself over. I grabbed Nguyen's right shoulder with my left hand and moved to hoist myself up. Suddenly I was out on the mud. I realized the Gunny must have moved behind me to help thrust me up. Nguyen was instantly laying at my side. Both of us lay face down, flat on the surface of the mud. The mildly blowing mist immediately began cleaning my face slowly as I brought it up in a vain attempt to see anything. There were no leeches about so I didn't have to deal with that slimy foreign feeling. My night vision was returning, but seeing anything to make out what it might be wasn't possible. I moved ahead. Each time I moved Nguyen moved with me. I thought of two giant caterpillars making their way across the mud. My fear was contained, partly because I wasn't alone, and the fact that there was no firing from any weaponry on either side.

I pushed into a soft barrier, before realizing it was a dead body. One of our Marines. I felt forward with my right hand. The body was laying back down. Instead of going around I pulled myself right over him, knowing the Marine wouldn't care, and no doubt would have let me even if he was alive. Nguyen made his way around, while I waited for a few seconds for him to join me. I wondered if contact with dead bodies was verboten to his religious upbringing, but I knew nothing of Montagnard religious beliefs. We moved together again for a few meters, the night mercifully silent, except for the sound of the rushing nearby river water and the slight but pervasive whispering of the falling misty rain. The air smelled almost pure, wafting down from the top of the canyon wall. My helmet kept the rain from falling down into my eyes, but I sort of missed the washing effect I'd experienced earlier. I couldn't rub my head at all though, because my hands were once again covered with the cloying mud.

I ran into a hard and low barrier. I stopped to feel it. Wood. I'd found one of the ammo boxes. I quickly explored the surface, back and forth. The box was of the proper size. I reached for my K-Bar and began to pry across the length of the upper crack near the top edge. The blade went in and I worked at pulling the wood apart while also trying not to break or bend the blade of the K-Bar. In less than a minute, the whole top eased up and I was able to cast it aside. I replaced my knife, carefully snapping it back into the sheath on my belt, before running both of my hands up and down the length of the sleek slippery rounds. Little holes ran along the ends of both, which was a dead giveaway that the ammunition was recoilless in nature. The little holes allowed the burning powder to push against the inner side of the barrel before forcing the round to be thrust out from the end.

I eased one round out of the box, then slid it across the mud to Nguyen, who clutched it to his body like it was a pet or maybe a baby. It occurred to me, again, that I had no way to instruct Nguyen as to what we needed to be done unless he spoke more English than he'd ever let on. But there was no need to communicate at all from the instant the thought came into my mind.

A fifty-caliber machine gun opened up from the jungle side. Giant green flaming beer cans came screaming in over both of our heads. They'd brought another fifty-caliber up and on the line. They'd saved it for just the right moment. Nguyen and I tried to squeeze down into the mud behind the useless six-inch height of the wooden ammo box which wasn't thick or strong enough to stop a .22 bullet. There was no place for Nguyen or me to run and we couldn't survive for any time at all staying where we were. The fifty would simply stitch the entire area of the registered zone, back and forth, up and down, until it stitched us.

We would join the other four Marines lying dead on the mudflat.

one-hundred-thirteen

Nguyen was gone into the night with the 106 round. I hadn't given any thought at all as to whether the ammo box was marked with a flechette designation for its contents or not. There was no way to tell by feel, and there was no way I was going to use the flashlight with a .50 caliber firing on us. I'd counted four rounds to the box, which left three of whatever kinds of rounds they were. I lay behind the box, the thing useless as cover but sufficient for concealment, since it was sitting up perpendicular to the enemy occupied jungle to our front. The .50 had stopped firing which was good news for Nguyen, and myself. I heard only a few single rounds coming from a gun I couldn't recognize right away by the sound. Then it came to me, Zippo was trying to suppress the .50 caliber gun crew by giving the snipers locating data from the night vision scope. The guns the snipers used were 7.62 millimeters, like the M-14 I'd trained with, and also the M-60 machine guns, but the sound was just a bit different. I'd loved the heavier M-14 but the 16 had already been issued to combat troops and Marines by the time I was shipped out.

I realized that I could lay where I was or slip and slide my body back toward the spider hole.

The spider hole was safer by far, and the trip to get there would become increasingly more risky with the coming of the light. The .50 opened up again, the sound of its nearby frontal discharge almost enough to make my ears ring. I had no time to make earplugs or do anything else except getting as far down as I could. The .50 was shooting back at the location where the sniper fire was coming from, however, and not sweeping my position. I moved back from the ammo box, pushing directly away, taking my helmet off when I was far enough to angle toward where I thought the spider hole was. I left my helmet behind. It was no protection against anything except the smallest fragments from artillery or grenades anyway. Against the power of a .50 caliber, it would be about as effective as tissue paper in stopping a bullet.

I didn't realize I was lost in the darkness until I'd gone further than I knew I should have. I was in the open, on an exposed flat surface of the mud, and I couldn't find the hole.

Shuddering, near tears with frustration, I stopped moving and lay flat, pushing my face into the mud so it would not be a white beacon in the black backdrop of the night. I breathed in and out into the mud, taking the rotten vegetable kind of aroma directly into my lungs. I tasted the river mud jammed into my teeth. I wondered fearfully whether they'd find my body with my mouth full of mud with a startled look of terror in my cold dead eyes. I had to go back. The only guide I had to get there was the river and the occasional burst from the .50. The big gun was directly to my front. I turned, scrabbling away, with the river on my left and the heavy machine gun to my rear.

My right ankle was suddenly pulled backward. I kicked against the pressure surrounding my ankle but to no effect. My body slid back, increasing my panic until I realized it had to be Nguyen who was pulling me, trying to get me back to some relative safety.

Slithering around to confront him helped my deep level of near-paralyzing fear. I was moving in the right direction. I was doing something to stay alive. Anything to stay alive. Nguyen was invisible in the night mist but I felt his presence like he was still touching me or as if I could see him. I slithered straight ahead, following in trace of him, ashamed of myself. I wasn't ashamed for being afraid. I was used to that if getting used to that was possible at all. I was ashamed because I'd figured out that Nguyen didn't really need me to get him the other rounds out of the ammo box. I could have stayed in the hole and been temporarily safe. Would I have stayed in the hole when he returned? That I'd been thinking about doing just that, hiding out while he was taking all the risk, bothered me deeply. I plunged ahead, so low and close to the surface that my chin plowed through the soft fetid mud like the prow of a tiny destroyer easing across a calm flat sea. I hated the smell but the taste in my mouth was worse. I was glad I'd taken my helmet off, as the mist collected and flowed down my face as I went giving my some sense of cleanliness.

I moved until I plowed into one of Nguyen's boots. I could hear him just ahead, easing another 106 round out of the box. He didn't need me, but there was no way I was going back to the hole. I wondered if he just needed me to be there, like I needed him to be there, so badly. Being all alone under fire on a field of flat mud with no cover was worse than the terror I felt in being in direct contact with the enemy. I didn't want to die alone like Tex had died alone right next to the Bong Song, not that far from where I currently was.

I crabbed my body around Nguyen's legs until I was directly behind the box and close to him. I knew he had a round out and ready to haul back up to the Ontos.

The Ontos, and particularly the flechette rounds, was the only thing that might save our lives. Nguyen had to go but there was no way for me to order him to do so.

My helmet was slipped onto my head, and I felt Nguyen's hand patting it down so it'd stay. The mist had partially filled it with moisture, and the slight pool formed in its basin poured coolly down my face. Nguyen pressed my right shoulder with his left hand for a few seconds, and then rolled over and was gone back into the misty blackness.

I could not return to the hole where the Gunny, Fessman, and Bates hunched down in relative safety. No sappers from the NVA force in the jungle would make it across the mud flat without Zippo, using the Starlight Scope and snipers, picking them off, but I envisioned the force that might easily succeed in killing all of us, the NVA scurrying flatly across the mud just as the earliest rays of dawn shown down over the eastern face of the high canyon wall. Such a force could not be easily or fully identified from a distance, unless the mist diminished, which wasn't likely. Air power would not be on station to stop them until after dawn, or if it somehow came earlier, limited by the same visibility problems as my own company's machine gun teams. I didn't try to look over the edge of the rough side of the wooden ammo box, although I wanted to. Was the enemy coming? I didn't take my .45 automatic out because I knew there would be no point. It was nothing against a .50, and little more than that against attacking infantry across open terrain in the dark misting rain.

I reached in to pull another round of 106 ammo out of the box, then cradled it to my chest while laying on my back, licking the mist from the area around my lips. The round was bigger and heavier than it seemed it should be, but I knew how effective and valuable it was. The APERS round it was called and I remembered, although I couldn't recall what the letters of its designation stood for. Each round had six thousand flechettes jammed inside its warhead with an adjustable fuse for a distant explosion at the tip. Five hundred meters the fuse should probably be set for, I thought, trying to recall exactly how far the jungle area occupied by the NVA was from the Ontos. Five hundred meters and the nearly ten pounds of high explosives would go off when the round arrived, showering the flechettes forward in a cloud moving at four to five miles per second. In the night the moving round would be visible in flight because of a tracer element drilled into the back of the casing.

Nguyen was back so fast it seemed impossible that he'd crawled all the way to the Ontos, delivered the round, and then returned in almost absolute darkness. I needed Fessman and the radio. The standoff distance setting on the rounds had to be close, or the effect on the NVA, whether anyone in the outer layer of the jungle was hit or not, would be too negligible to matter. The enemy needed to know that the Ontos was firing its most fearsome weapon. And, the Ontos needed to start firing soon, as early dawn was less than an hour off.

"Fessman," I whispered, as Nguyen began to take the round from me.

"Fessman," he repeated, in almost the same tone and inflection, making me wonders again just how much English he understood and spoke.

He left without taking the round, barely making a sound. One second he was there and then he was gone. I held the round to keep it out of the mud and wished I'd been able to follow Nguyen back to the hole. Fessman wouldn't have to be exposed with me behind the ammo box in that case, and my own safety would be vastly improved. I breathed out slowly, taking more misting rain into my mouth, my eyes closed, the shell rising and falling on my chest, as I clutched it to me with both hands.

I could not lead the Marines from the rear, and I could barely lead them from out front. However, I had to be able to see. I had to adjust the rounds for the Ontos, even though they would be fired using direct fire. That meant I had to be in constant communication with whoever was operating the Ontos rifles. The mist and darkness were bigger impediments over distance, although Zippo had the Starlight Scope to help slice through the night. What I really wanted to do, even more than adjusting rounds in their placement was to control the rate of fire, holding off the NVA until Cowboy could make his appearance. The box of ammo I'd found held only four rounds. Three of us searching through the flooding mud for any more boxes would be more effective than doing the job by me if there were any more boxes. There was only one way to survive, and that was to get through the remainder of the night until supporting fires would give me the cover I needed to get back to the main elements of the company and the safety of my cave.

All I could do was wait. The fifty would open up every few minutes and then, after only a couple of rounds being expended, it would go quiet again. The rounds were all being directed toward where Zippo's snipers were trying to do their own work. It came to me that I would already have been dead if the NVA had our kind of supplies. The only reason the heavy machine gun had not swept back and forth across the mud flat had to likely be because of a lack of ammunition. Zippo was having an effect.

The snipers might not be hitting anyone but they were certainly drawing the enemy's attention and the big gun's fire.

"Sir?" Fessman asked, from right behind my head, causing me to jerk around so hard I almost dislodged my helmet.

I didn't answer him right away. Nguyen had returned with Fessman. He slipped through the mud to lay right next to me, before gently removing the 106 round from my grasp and taking off again.

"Combat net," I said to Fessman. "I need the Ontos to fire one beehive round intermittently with one round of H.E. on my command. The beehive needs to be set for five hundred meters, but I'll adjust based upon a first-round strike of the H.E."

"Yes sir," Fessman said, laying down flat while removing the thick heavy radio from his back and shoulders.

I felt the boy moving about and getting lower and marveled at how aware and combat proven he'd quickly become at his young age. The radio would stick up over the edge of the ammo box as dawn's early light came upon us, drawing the fifty's fire. He knew that. Fessman turned and pushed the radio handset into my left shoulder. I realized that he needed me to give the orders, as I'd been pretty point specific. I held the handset to my right ear but didn't say anything. There were transmissions flying back and forth on the frequency. I listened to the combat communications between the other two companies and battalion.

Lima company was being ordered to come across from the east and then turn down into the A Shau, until interdicting our own company, while Kilo was being sent back to the eastern edge of the canyon down near the valley's southernmost extremity to, once again, climb down the escarpment and move north to join up with Lima. There was obviously no intelligence available to the battalion with respect to what lay between those two infantry elements or else nobody back in the rear cared. My company was the center of whatever pincer movement battalion was planning, but there were no inquiries flying back and forth, with any attempts or comments about contacting us.

I listened until the back and forth died down a bit. I did not understand the coding for locations being used but what was about to happen seemed pretty obvious. I waited for a few seconds of silence before calling the Ontos, remembering the clear Oscar November Tango Six designation. The 'six' was written under the U.S. Army printing on the sides of the vehicle, it's meaning unknown to anyone in the company so far as I knew. But I didn't make the call because another body slid into the spot Nguyen had vacated. I couldn't see who it was in the darkness and rain but I knew it was the Gunny.

"What about Bates?" I whispered across the few inches that separated us.

"Leave him, Junior," the Gunny replied, "he's dead meat up here, probably like the rest of us, but what the hell, and you can't adjust fire in this shit unless you have something to adjust from. The Beehive's got a tracer but the jungle foliage will eat the explosion up. The Ontos can't see through this crap all the way to where we need to hit them, even with the scope, but we can. It's maybe a hundred meters in the range from where we are right now."

Fessman eased the radio handset out of my hand. "You want me to call them, sir?" he asked.

"Okay, but wait for a second," I replied.

"What do you suggest?" I said to the Gunny, trying to put it all together in my head, also surprised that I could have thought the Gunny was hiding out in the hole that I so wanted to hide out in with Bates. The Gunny was right again. The Ontos was a good five hundred meters from the jungle's edge, but the beehive shots had to be spot on to have the effect we needed. It wasn't their causing death and injury that was important. It was the fear they'd generate.

"You brought those grenades of yours?" the Gunny asked.

"Yes," I answered, moving to pull out the two M33s, understanding what the Gunny was getting at. The grenades, when thrown, would only fly a maximum of about 30 meters through the air, which meant they'd go off just before the edge of the jungle. The Ontos wouldn't need spotting help if Zippos was alert to when the grenades would go off. All that had to be done was wait for the flash of fire from the M33, make minor range and declination adjustments, and then beehive rounds could be placed right on target. The cloud of small speeding flechettes would blast forward into the jungle.

I held one spherical grenade in my right hand, ready to throw. The M26 I'd trained so briefly with had been oval shaped with a smooth curving spoon that ran up over its surface from top to bottom. The M33 felt funny in my clutched hand. It seemed too small, too round, and the spoon had a distinctive bend in the middle.

I began to roll over onto my back, holding the grenade to my chest like I'd held the 106 round.

"What are you doing, Junior?" The Gunny said, the tone of his voice one of quiet bafflement.

It was like I could see him shaking his head, but, of course, I couldn't.

"What?" I asked, not understanding.

"You think you can lob that thing a hundred feet, laying in the mud on your back?" he asked, just before I felt both of his hands, clutching my own right hand with the grenade in it. He carefully pried my fingers loose and took the small weapon.

"Tell 'em to get ready," he said, more to Fessman than me.

I heard the pin come out of the M33, and then the Gunny standing up right next to me. I felt more than heard or saw him rear back and fling the small globe toward the jungle before he fell back onto the surface of the mud next to me.

"Tell them 'splash, over,'" the Gunny hissed to Fessman.

The grenade went off with a sharp crack, like a nearby stroke of lightning might make. That was followed seconds later by a much great crack. The Ontos had fired. I crawled the few feet to Fessman, where he had the microphone waiting for my grasping hand. I knew the first round had been H.E. because the Beehive round exploded with more of a thudding crash rather than what I'd heard.

"Fire the beehive on the same registration, but only fire again on command" I ordered and then laid down flat again.

Although our position was not directly on the gun target line for the Ontos, it was close enough that the smallest error in deflection might be deadly to the three of us. The flechettes flew out from the exploding composition B at over four miles a second in velocity, but the tiny mass of each little dart was so slight that each one decelerated very quickly in the dense atmosphere.

The crump of the beehive round came seconds later. There was nothing to communicate whether the NVA was getting the message I was trying to send or not, except the .50 caliber remained ominously silent.

I tucked the other M33 back into my pocket. I didn't like carrying the small deadly little packages, as the stories of accidental injury and death circulated among the Marines all the time. No Marines I ever saw ever carried grenades clipped to the front of their utility blouses, like they did in old war movies. Only someone in the rear area, posing for photographs to be sent home, might be so dumb or inexperienced in real combat to do a foolish thing like that.

The night was no longer the same night. I peered up over the ammo box we were hidden behind. It was still too dark to make out much of anything. I knew from my high school astronomy club days that late September was an equinox month. The three kinds of dawn would take the full twenty-four minutes or so each to go through. Astronomical dawn was beginning. We were about an hour from full daylight, or maybe a bit more because of the depth of the valley we were down inside.

I figured we had about twenty minutes to scour the mud flat for more flechette ammunition boxes before it got light enough to see.

"Call Cowboy," I whispered to Fessman. "We want him in here with as many of his friends as he can gather, as early as possible."

I didn't mention my great fear that the Skyraiders would be tied up elsewhere. Artillery was so much more dependable than air support, but I could not risk firing the 175s again. One slightly short round on the gun-target line and our own company would be wiped out. I tried to think about all the variables potentially impacting our survival. The company was considerably better off than the four of us were, but it was too late, in reality, to try to crawl back up the slight slope to their position or to send Nguyen back and forth. Even with the misting rain and darkness, nautical dawn, and some visibility was rushing down upon us. The NVA might or might not attack in force, knowing our small unit was a sitting duck, cut off from the rest of the company. Nguyen pushed a wooden box smaller and squarer than the 106 ammo boxes between the Gunny and I. The Gunny worked the latch loose and the lid opened with a metallic sound, unlike the recoilless round boxes, which were latched and also stapled, shut. The Gunny handed me another M33 grenade to replace the one we'd used. The box was filled with thirty, or so, of the compact little grenades.

Something grabbed my foot. I felt hands moving up my leg.

"I'm here, sir," Bates said.

"I told you to wait in the hole," the Gunny hissed down toward the young sergeant.

"I can help," Bates said with his voice breaking.

I realized that the boy was more afraid of being alone in the dark hole than he was of being out on the exposed mud flat with us. I fleetingly thought again how combat teaches by killing. Bates, an FNG, didn't want to be alone in the hole while I, a grim veteran of combat, wanted only to be alone in the hole.

"Shit," the Gunny said, more to himself than any of us. "Here, carry these, and don't do a damn thing I don't tell you to do," he went on, pushing some M33s down toward Bates.

"Yes, sir," Bates answered, his nervousness and fear causing him to break a cardinal rule in the Marine Corps.

Sergeants of any kind were never referred to as sir. Non-coms in the Corps took that designation as an insult.

"What do we tell battalion about Lima and Kilo coming into the valley?" Fessman asked.

Nobody said a word in reply to his surprising question.

"Lima will get taken out by the enemy inside Hill 975 and Kilo will get killed off by the enemy in front of us," Fessman went on.

Once again, I was surprised by the young boy's remarkable analysis of the combat situation.

"They can look out for themselves," the Gunny said, his tone harsh and uncaring. "We've got our own problems. If the enemy comes, then everyone starts tossing these grenades, but not until we call the Ontos and let them know."

I said nothing. My mind raced. Fessman was right. We had to let battalion know what Lima and Kilo were facing, even if the relief we were supposed to get from them wasn't ever likely to appear. The battalion was at least trying to help us out. The colonel's loss of his XO and friend had finally focused attention on our plight, rather than simply our terrible daily casualties. I was reaching for the handset when Bates spoke.

"I've got it, sir," he said.

The distinctive sound of a pin coming out of a grenade penetrated the rain, the dark, and the air between the sergeant and the rest of us, like that of a small Buddhist gong. We all froze.

"Fire in the hole," Bates yelled, coming up to his knees and throwing an M33 over our heads toward the jungle. The grenade thudded into the mud just on the other side of the ammo box.

"You've got to stand up to throw the damn things," the Gunny got out as the rest of us buried ourselves as deep into the mud as we could get.

"I'm standing, sir," Bates unaccountably replied.

"The Ontos," the Gunny said, his last words before the grenade exploded not more than five yards on the other side of the box, blowing pound-sized chunks into the air and then back down upon us.

A second whooshing explosion, like the thunderous clap of a hellishly loud cymbal, followed the first smaller concussion.

I cringed down even deeper into the mud. I now knew what it sounded like to be on the horrid receiving end of a beehive round, but I felt nothing. I moved my shoulders, trying to figure out if I was hit. My hearing was all screwed up.

I thought I heard Fessman.

"He's gone, sir."

"Who's gone?" I replied, trying to unstick the front of my body from the cloying mud while using the heavy misting rain to try to wash some of it off.

"Bates," the Gunny said, "the complete moronic idiot."

The Gunny's voice broke right at the end when he said the word 'idiot.' I wondered if only I caught it.

I crawled to where Bates lay, with Fessman next to him. There was no need to examine him in detail. The back-blast of flechettes had made mush of the boy's entire upper body.

The Ontos.

The Gunny had figured it out instantly, while I'd not been so quick. Zippo, waiting and watching with nervous impatience, must have seen the explosion, thought we were marking the target for the next 106 round, and then adjusted and fired. They were all dead, even the sergeant who'd amazingly cheated it the first time around. What the enemy didn't kill, we Marines did. I also realized that Zippo had somehow ignored the 'intermittent' part of my first order. The round we'd received should have been High Explosive, which would have killed us all.

"They're coming," the Gunny hissed out.

"Who's coming?" I asked, still trying to take in the young sergeant's death, while also trying to get my full hearing back.

"Get all the grenades out, call the Ontos, and make sure the M-60's are fully online with night defensive fires," the Gunny ordered, without answering my stupid question.

THE TWENTY-FOURTH DAY : FIRST PART

First light was almost upon us. I peered around the left edge of the ammo box. What I saw told me that there would be no more pawing around through the supplies dropped by the choppers in the dead of night. Through the misty rain, and what was left of the gently blowing night, I could see a slightly darker wave moving out of the jungle towards us. I also knew that we were all as good as dead if we stayed in our current position. It was either time to attempt to run back to the company lines under what covering fire the M-60s, grenades, and the Ontos could provide us or get back inside the hole and, with air hopefully on the way, wait the attack out and pray our hole wasn't found. Three options, and not one of them was without high mortal risk.

My near constant conclusion to evaluating combat solutions whispered out of my tight grimacing lips.

"We can't go ahead, we can't go back and we can't stay where we are."

The same situation, with all different terrain and other variables, ever-changing but never-changing to come together and arrive at the same three-solution conclusion.

"We can always attack, Junior" the Gunny whispered into my ear, obviously having overheard my depressive whispered admission.

"What are you talking about?" I asked, surprised.

"Let's get back in the hole and make-up one of your plans," he replied, then began to slither toward where the hole was located.

Nguyen followed him and Fessman was about to when I grabbed his ankle.

"Give me the AN-323. We have to have Cowboy or what's coming across the flats will be the end of us by full dawn."

"Talked to him, sir. He's coming at first light," Fessman got out, shaking his ankle to loosen my grip. "First light he'll be here but he can't come with the others because of the support they have to give Lima and Kilo."

Fessman succeeded in getting loose from my weakened grasp

and was gone ahead of me into the night. I crawled to catch up, well remembering my inability to find the hole on my own in full dark. It still wasn't light enough to see well yet, and the mist was thickening into regular monsoon rain. The mist was actually harder to see through, but that wasn't going to make much difference to the attacking force coming out from the jungle unless Cowboy could rain Skyraider hell down upon them.

The Gunny's comment reverberated through my mind, as I crawled.

"Attack what, or who, or whom," I muttered to myself, crawling along in the shallow path through the cloying mud left by the three before me.

The hole was there, but I only knew I had arrived by going right over the lip and dropping inside.

Fessman grunted as I piled headfirst into him. I slipped by him to land in the collected muddy water at the bottom of the hole.

"The plan," the Gunny said across the total darkness.

I worked myself up out of the water to finally stand with both feet spread against the upwelling sides of the hole.

"Shouldn't we be looking out there to see where the hell the NVA are?" I countered, wondering what kind of plan he wanted me to think up.

A plan that could have no foundation in reality that I could think of.

"Lima's coming in from the south and they're going to take it right in the side from Hill 975," the Gunny said, speaking flatly and analytically. "Air is headed there to cover their move, little good that will do them. Kilo is headed across the eastern top edge of the highland again, to drop down the switchback parapet both our companies came down last week. Air is being diverted to cover their move too. That's why only Cowboy is coming and he probably had to argue like hell to do that. Not like we haven't over-used air a bit ourselves lately."

I listened carefully to every word the Gunny said. It was the single longest speech I'd ever heard him give, and by far the most complex tactically. Every word he said was dead on and I knew it. It was his conclusion, spoken earlier up above that had, and still, haunted me. Attack whom, when and how?

"Okay, you've got all the data, Junior," he finished. "What do you have for us?"

I didn't have anything, and I knew we were about to lose whatever time we had to prepare for an advancing enemy. For some reason, the Gunny wasn't worried about the attacking force we'd been able to barely observe moving across the flats toward us. Was the Gunny gambling that heavily on Cowboy's arrival to nail them, or the remaining fire of the Ontos to deter them? It didn't make sense since we were not hot on the radio talking back and forth to Zippo and the Ontos crew.

"It's a feint," the Gunny finally said, when the answer to his question was met with my complete silence.

"Feint?" I asked, dumbly.

"They aren't really coming," the Gunny replied. "I've seen this before. 'The old attack at dawn thing'. They aren't coming because they know air support will be here, and the Ontos will be able to see them before they can get onto the mud flat close to us.

"Why the feint, though?" I asked, still not even partially understanding.

"They're going after Kilo but they don't want us to know," he went on. "They want us to cower here waiting for relief. Hill 975 forces are going to take Lima apart, the NVA regiment in the bush here is going to make mincemeat of Kilo, and then they'll both take their sweet time in mopping us up in a pincer movement when they're done with Lima and Kilo."

My mind suddenly exploded with white light. I got it. I got it all. I thought for a few seconds to get everything he'd told me together.

"The plan is to roll the Ontos to us here, and then move the company south in three prongs," I said. "One of our platoons along the lower ledge of the cliff, one along the side of the Bong Song and the last two behind and supporting the Ontos in its charge. We pick up the remaining supplies in the light with those two center platoons. Our machine guns can be concentrated at the very front edges of our moving forces, firing enfilade flanking fire from the outer prongs while the center gunners use ground fire to cover the Ontos as it moves forward into the jungle and through it while blasting away with flechettes and high explosives. Screw Lima and 975 until we're done crushing this force between us and Kilo."

"Fessman, get Kilo up on the net and fill them in," I continued. "Then call back to the Ontos and the company. Get Sugar Daddy and Jurgens. We move on command at dawn just like the NVA was trying to convince us they were going to do. The Ontos makes all the difference, and finding the additional 106 ammo dumped out on the mud flats here becomes vitally important. The Skyraider is there for punch through power and psychology."

I got out of my pack, pushed it to Fessman, and then climbed my way to the top edge of the hole, standing on the platform the Gunny had fashioned. I could see the jungle as a rotten gray line, thick with moisture and mixed with the slanted rain now falling. Dawn was only minutes away. There was no enemy, as the Gunny had predicted. They'd come out under cover of darkness, absorbing our sniper fire, as a price of doing business, then faded back once they thought they'd put the fear of God into us. I stared toward the jungle and then turned to peer back up where our lines were. The Ontos was still invisible against the dark backdrop of the cliff face, but I knew it was there. I glanced once more down at the jungle area that was now totally quiet except for the thrum of the river's passing and its ever-changing currents and eddies.

"They thought we'd be afraid," I said out loud, to no one but the sodden rainy night around me. "They think we're not a bunch of totally whacked out Marines with nothing to lose. Well hell, we're afraid all right, but we're about to become afraid for them and not of them."

Saying the words made my back stiffen and my shoulders lift a bit. There was no real hope in the valley, but there was some satisfaction to be found here and there, and I just knew this was going to be one of those times where some satisfaction might be found. I canted my head down, listening to Fessman putting the Gunny on the radio with Kilo.

"It's almost light, Fessman," I said, looking down at the top of his helmet. "Maybe it's not too early for your crummy little Armed Forces radio. Turn it on. We're not attacking in silence."

"The name, sir?" he asked, without twisting up from his position in supporting the Gunny while he talked on the short-corded handset.

I waited, looking up again into the rain while trying to gather some of it with my tongue. My hands and the rest of my body were encased in the awful smelling mud. I realized my old leeches were still with me, as I'd had no time to strip and get rid of them. I smiled at that thought, waiting for God's inspiration. Maybe the leeches in the mud were really there, after all, I thought. Maybe the leeches that had to be there simply recognized that I was already taken. I was already owned by their brethren, and I had only so much blood to be equally distributed around.

Fessman fiddled over his tiny transistor radio. I knew the music, if it came on, wouldn't matter in our current situation. The mock attack was over and, in minutes, the machine guns, the Ontos and hopefully the Skyraider fire, would drown out all other sounds. The song came, and I struggled to listen to the words I didn't really know. The song was from the Beatles and it was already halfway through when it played up to the top of the hole. There wasn't enough light to see the Gunny's face when he glanced up at me in irritation, but I imagined his expression, and his patient waiting for what was to come next, and for my inspiration. It came with the lyrics: "Penny Lane is in my ears and in my eyes, there beneath the blue suburban skies, I sit, and meanwhile back…" The song was called Penny Lane and the plan was named. I remembered the only lyrics I retained from hearing the song in college. Something about a nurse and poppies and those lyrics had back then, and right now, taken my mind to the famous WWI poem that had affected me.

"We are the dead," I intoned to myself from the poem, "short days ago, we lived, felt dawn, saw sunset glow…"

"Penny Lane," I said down into the hole. "The plan is called 'Penny Lane.'"

There was no way I was going to call the plan Flanders Fields.

The Gunny surged upward a few minutes later.

"The kid's radio's a bad idea and I don't understand the name of this new plan," he said, moving to lay next to me, with half his body out of the hole to keep his place.

"Kilo's gonna be saved for the third time, which is kind of ridiculous if you think about it," he said. "Lima's gonna pay the price but it's not one we laid on them. And these NVA son-of-a-bitches plaguing us from the beginning are going to feel our bite, as long as they've moved that .50 to help them pick Kilo off the side of that wall like slow-moving flies, that is."

"Attack," I whispered. "Attack. Where in the hell did you come up with that idea?" I asked.

"It was your idea, Junior, but Penny Lane, my ass." He slipped back into the hole.

I ducked down, although there was no incoming fire. I squatted on the small step, my back pressed into the muddy side of the hole, still too dark to see anything but ghostly shapes, and then only if they moved. The platoon moving along the cleft overhang of the canyon face would be in the same situation as Lima Company was going to be in,

THE TWENTY-FOURTH DAY : FIRST PART | 167

as they moved south past Hill 975. Fire from the jungle side would pin our platoon against the cliff, while Lima would be pinned against the raging unswimmable Bong Song. My platoon would have one distinct advantage, however, and that would be the fire pouring into the jungle from the riverside platoon, along with the Ontos plowing through the jungle and dispensing flechette rounds forward and to either side. The NVA would at first believe they were pinning Kilo to the cliff before they would only slowly come to understand that they were the ones surrounded on all sides. The only place they would have to go would be down into their tunnels. Resupply. The word came logically to me, as I thought about dislodging or destroying tunnel works. Satchel charges, large and many would be needed. The shock waves from such underground blasts, as the charges were tossed into any openings that could be found, would penetrate up and down the tunnels, even sending terminal waves through solid ground.

"Fessman, get battalion on the line," I ordered. "I want another resupply to our rear, as we attack into the jungle. We need more flechette rounds for the Ontos and we need satchel charges for the tunnels."

"They lost Marines on that last one, sir," Fessman replied, instead of moving to get on the net and making the call.

"And, so?" I asked, surprised he hadn't simply made the call.

"They won't come into a hot LZ where they've taken casualties," the Gunny replied, "and you already know that. Besides, the 106 ammo will arrive too late and the satchel charges can wait until we've secured the surface to set them if we secure the surface."

The Gunny was right again, I knew, although I was beyond the point where such missing of tactical elements embarrassed me. I had been reduced to needing all the help I could get, and what pride I'd had when flying into the country was all but crushed into non-existence. We were going to use a frontal attack on a most capable and equipped enemy. That knowledge was the only thing I could use in my mind to scrape up any sense of my old Marine Corps pride. I was, once again, hiding in a hole, but I was coming out and I was coming out fighting, and soon.

"We'll let the choppers know the surrounding area is secure as soon as we get into the jungle," the Gunny continued, "and it won't be, but what the hell, we can always call the Army if the Corps pilots won't come."

It was strange to think about the amazing and conflicting belief systems that floated down into the A Shau field of combat and through the rear area surrounding it. The Army thought of the Marine Corps as the ultimate fighting force that it was not. The Marine Corps fought, but when the going got tough defaulted to the Army for help for what the Corps rear area couldn't or wouldn't provide. The Marine Corps delivered in a broken sort of tattered leadership way but delivered. The Army delivered in the following role, but also effectively delivered.

"Besides," the Gunny said, in a lower voice, "the next resupply will also drop another contingent of FNG officers to relieve you, Junior. You are not the best-liked officer ever to land down in this valley."

"The men like him though, Gunny," Fessman said in the darkness.

"The men don't like him," the Gunny shot back, anger in his tone. "The Marines didn't give a shit about anything when he dropped in. Now they want to go home. Figure it out."

"He gave us hope," Fessman continued, in a dogged low tone.

"He made it so nobody wants to be around him," the Gunny shot back. "They want to go home to get away from him."

"That's kind of like hope," Fessman replied, his sentence more of a question than a statement.

"They're ready," the Gunny said, changing the subject. "Where's that extra grenade you had? The company moves out in three columns on that signal. Sugar Daddy is coming high diddle-diddle right up the middle to follow and support the Ontos. The sniper team will do rear-guard because I want them ready, with their weapons aimed at the last location of the fifty-caliber, the only flea I see in this plan of yours. If that thing opens up then they have to shoot the gunners or our goose is cooked, because we'll be fully committed."

I moved down from the step and began rummaging around for my pack, staying as far up from the cloying mud as I could. Fessman pushed it into my chest, as I floundered about. The M-33 was where I'd left it. I pulled it out, handling it gingerly. The 33 had a questionable reputation. The M-26 that had preceded it had been the old faithful of grenades, following the infamous pineapple grenade used in WWII and Korea. The 33 had a temper all of its own. Some said the pin was too easy to dislodge, others said that the timing fuse, supposedly measured to be five seconds precisely at the factory, was not as advertised. I didn't really care. I would pull the pin, or the Gunny would, toss it ten meters away, or so, and then let the thing go off. I eased myself back into the alcove gouged out of the side of the hole, held the grenade tightly to my chest with both hands and waited.

Why was the Gunny sticking to the phony story that the plan to attack was my idea? I had no clue. Why had he chastised Fessman about what my Marines either thought or didn't think about me in such a negative and emotional way? Once more, I had no idea. That the Marines might want to get out of the A Shau, only to escape me, didn't seem plausible from everything I'd experienced. I knew that many of them carried superstition packets around their necks with some of my stuff in them. Superstition ran rampant, like gossip, in a field unit, and maybe in the rear areas too. It was only natural for the men to think my amazing survival from time to time, as opposed to the previous officers who'd come and gone so quickly, might have something to do with magic. That many of those officers had died at my Marines' own hands seemed not to count. Fessman thought I'd somehow given the men some sort of hope of survival, and it seemed that the Gunny was ready to unwillingly go along with that in conducting the current operation while, at the same time, indicating that the men were more interested in getting away from me than anything else.

"Ready on the right," the Gunny whispered.

I prepared myself to climb up, pull the pin on the M-33 and then toss it, but first I strapped myself into my pack. There would be no coming back to the hole once we began the attack. Just as I turned to climb up to the lip of the hole, the AN-323 radio kicked to life. There was no speaker for that radio but the small noise the tiny headset speaker made was very audible in the near silence and dead air down inside the hole.

"Cowboy rolling on in," a small tinny voice said. "You got your ears up and ready for that Flash?"

I climbed back down and reached for the headset, pressing my right ear into the small speaker, as I did not want to remove my helmet and risk dropping it into the muddy water below. I squeezed the grenade in my left hand uncomfortably but wasn't about to part with it.

"Flash standing by," I said, pressing on the transmit button and hoping our position deep inside the hole wouldn't block the signal. It didn't.

"I'll be five by five when you start your run," Cowboy said. "I'm a lone soldier up here, orbiting and waiting out the dark, and for your signal. "I'll make a hole for your Ontos right down the center. I know the area well. I'm loaded for bear with maximum ordnance for the effort. Is it Penny for Your Thoughts or Penny Lane?"

"Penny Lane," I said back, astounded by how quickly and effectively something as seemingly slight and unimportant as a plan name could spread and be totally accepted. "There's enough light to launch, Cowboy, and the line of departure will be about ten meters south of the flash from the grenade I'm about to toss from our hole."

"That's rich," Cowboy laughed. "A flash from Flash. I'll start my roll in from eight thousand and hopefully, singe the hair of the guys riding that Ontos into history and Valhalla. Out."

I pushed the headset back at Fessman, now barely visible in the pre-dawn light. I climbed back up on the step and pulled the pin on the grenade with a bit of difficulty because of the slipperiness of the mud on my hands. The M-33 felt perfect in my right hand, the spoon pressed hard against the pool ball sized round surface of the body of the device. I stretched my arm back, like my Dad had taught me to do when trying to throw a football as far as I could, and then heaved the grenade back toward our own line so the flash would radiate out from the top of the mud in front of every Marine present.

I never saw the flash, as I'd dived back inside the hole when the grenade was still in the air. I heard the small 'crump' of its explosion seconds later. I unsnapped the holster flap covering the butt of Tex's .45 and got ready to climb out of the hole. I was as ready for open combat as I would ever be.

"Wait one," the Gunny cautioned. "Wait until we can hear the Ontos and then gauge its position. Everyone on our side is aiming out front of that thing and the last place we want to be is there."

I tried to settle back, but my pack stuck out too far to allow me to force myself back into the crease in the corner of the hole. I stood, with feet spread to stay above the inches of muddy water in the bottom, like the Gunny, Fessman, and Nguyen. I had run through the enemy before, as I had run from him, but I had never charged forward in attack. Getting ready mentally for the effort was not what I thought it might be. I wasn't nearly as afraid as I thought I should be. I was instead hoping. I was hoping that I would measure up as a Marine in combat and I was hoping my company would be able to do the same. For only the second time since being in Vietnam, in combat and down in the A Shau Valley, I was feeling like I thought a Marine was supposed to feel.

I felt the Ontos vibrate the walls of our hole and suddenly wanted to be out on the mudflat, no matter the risk. My fear of being buried alive in the mud was greater than that of being shot, even if that was to be by my own Marines. I vaulted up the step and over the lip of the hole. I felt the others following me. The Ontos was idling right in front of me, it's left tread no more than a few feet from the hole. Zippo sat atop and just behind the layered armor of the thing, his teeth exposed by a huge grin, about the only thing fully visible about him. I heard Cowboy coming in the background but knew the shape of the valley was also radiating sound well ahead of the fierce lumbering beast of the air. But he was there and coming.

I ran to the back of the Ontos, the Gunny pulling up to my side and Fessman not far behind. Nguyen popped up from under the rear of the machine, having taken the easiest path by sliding right under the hull of the thing.

"Ready," the Gunny yelled into the open rear doors of the Ontos. "Are you going inside?" he shouted in my ear with his hands cupped.

I looked up at the open doors of the beast. There was room. I made a quick decision, following my new feeling of being an actual leader of Marines.

"No, I'm staying with the men," I yelled back.

"Then get two hundred meters back. When the 106s start to fire you have to be either under the thing, inside it, or a hell of a long way from the back-blast."

I turned to look up the mild incline to where the company had been set in. Everyone was on the move, and most had M-60 machine guns carried with ammo belts held by assistant fire team leaders just aside or behind them. Sugar Daddy's platoon I knew, because they were so difficult to make out in the bad light. The Marines of one platoon moved against the face of the cliff. I turned once more to watch Jurgen's platoon heading down to the raging water's edge.

"Move out," the Gunny yelled, as I achieved a position far enough away from the Ontos, with Fessman and Nguyen by my sides.

The Gunny had stayed with the Ontos, squeezing into through the doors. I wondered if he'd done that to build me up more or whether he'd done it for security. The last part of that thought made me smile grimly. The Gunny didn't do much at all for his own security.

He'd done it to make me feel like a Marine Officer and it was working.

one-hundred-fifteen

The Ontos moved forward, with the Gunny swinging both armored back doors of the tracked vehicle closed behind him. I followed, slowly dropping back as the vehicle picked up speed, to stay clear of any back blast. I'd wanted to ask the Gunny if I could use a spare M-16 left over from one of our casualties but hadn't pursued that request. I felt naked on the mud flats with only my holstered .45, even if its leather hold-down thong was unsnapped. There was no enemy fire as the attack began. I watched the dawn bring evermore light through the misting rain, with all the Marines in the company moving forward. There was no crawling and no zig-zagging back and forth to attempt to take advantage of available cover, because there really was no cover. A six-inch high clump of bamboo or other assorted jungle plant growth, would not hide a sizeable raccoon, much less a Marine with helmet, weaponry and carrying a full kit on his back.

The company was properly spaced, each Marine just about equidistant from those around him. Not like in training at all. Trying to get Marines in training to stay out of clumps, or naturally congregate together, had proven impossible for training officers. But down in the A Shau, with the chips all on the table, where winning meant getting to stay alive to see light dim and pass into full dark, the Marines acted like the kind of Marines I'd never known back home. They weren't organized in any kind of orderly fashion and they were so tattered and dirty they were almost unrecognizable for what they were, but they were quietly effective in almost every way, from movement, to fire control, distribution of supplies and more. And the fire they delivered was amazingly accurate since I seldom saw anyone actually stare through the fixed metal sights set on top of the barrels.

The Ontos wasn't mired down, as I'd first thought once it stopped moving through the fairly dense jungle growth. The jungle growth was thick but not too thick to inhibit tracked movement. There would have been no possibility of the small but heavy armored vehicle cutting through or crushing past the kind of triple canopy jungle that existed up on top of the canyon walls and descending down almost all the way to the eastern sea shore. The Ontos had stopped to reload 106 rounds. The team of supply handlers the Gunny had sectioned off to recover the strewn mess of the night helicopter run, were being quickly effective in getting to the flechette rounds and getting them loaded into the empty chambers of the long guns.

The NVA Soviet or Chinese origin .50 caliber firing had stopped after the Ontos had unloaded the last four flechette rounds into the jungle area where the heavy machine gun was suspected of being placed. The Ontos only had 13mm armor, but the front of the small beast was slanted, thereby doubling its stopping power. An armor-piercing heavy machine gun round would penetrate the sides or the bottom of the Ontos easily but not the front glacis, which was the primary reason that, once the NVA .50 opened up, the Ontos went directly at it.

I felt more than I heard Cowboy's first pass. The low giant of a noisy aircraft did not come speeding in, which normally would have had its radial engine blasting and reverberating back and forth between the canyon walls. The plane was almost quiet as it came down. I looked up and behind me, when I felt the plane, and then quickly coming to understand what Cowboy was doing. The Skyraider was dropping down at near idle, it's big beastly shadow descending like some monstrous bird of prey. I ducked down and shivered slightly at the sight, but could not look away from its approach. The plane was descending with its nose higher than its tail, all of its flaps fully extended, moving through the dense air and rain so slow it seemed to be a giant artificial prop being added onto the set of a Hollywood war movie. I understood what Cowboy was doing. He was giving us as much time and cover to cross the mud flat as he could, instead of speeding on by after spraying a few hundred of his deadly but sparse 20 mm cannon rounds of ammunition, and, while doing so, he was able to see us making sure he wasn't hitting us instead of the NVA.

The plane fought to recover itself in mid-air, still dropping, until it was only a few meters off the ground before it leveled off and seemed to float right into the jungle in front of me. The feeling the Skyraider gave me was one of core-penetrating terror. All I wanted to do was smash myself into the mud until it passed. But it was Cowboy, and the Skyraider he flew was U.S. Navy. The enemy had to be feeling the same fear that was running up and down my spine, but even more so since they knew the weapon was intended to kill or maim them. I got up and ran forward, staying low but moving fast. There was no order to run that I heard, but every Marine in the company, not riding in the Ontos, took off with me.

The Skyraider's monstrous radial engine screamed up to full power, as it accelerated to maintain its low altitude. There was still no strafing fire, instead, bombs were pickling off the plane's wings, one after another from each side. They began to explode behind the plane, as it sped directly over the center of the jungle vegetation.

The shaking tremor of the explosions ahead drove me forward toward them instead of down again. Wherever those bombs were going off I knew the NVA would not be quietly and lethally waiting. They'd be down flat or underground inside their snaking tunnels and cave complexes. I was a lot more fearful of being killed by the NVA coming out of their holes than I was by being damaged by the bombs.

Once in among the debris, still filtering down through the morning's moisture and rain-laden air, I slowed to avoid overtaking the Ontos and becoming more of a target or injured when one of its 106 recoilless rounds was fired.

There was no crawling through the kind of jungle we were in. I moved huddled down, my knees bent down as far as I could bend them and still get ahead, while my torso was slanted as far forward as it would go. I could not keep loping or running as the load I carried was too heavy to support anything but short stretches at maximum output. I followed the Ontos in its left track as best I could, although the jungle growth, even at my distance, still snapped painfully back and forth. I realized that the part of my plan that had both platoons opposite one another, one against the face of the cliff and the other moving down the river bank, firing into the center-placed jungle to suppress the enemy, was impossible to implement, not without killing Marines in our element moving up the center. I'd forgotten about the speed of the Ontos. The machine could move through the thickness successfully, but it had to maintain speed and use momentum to make it over and through the heavier areas.

The center attack group, of which I was a part, led the attack and had to depend on the flanking forces not to fire into the center if at all possible, which was the opposite of what they'd been instructed to do.

The whirling Wright engine of Skyraider quieted as it gained distance from our position following its run. I knew it would be rising to gain altitude, make its pylon kind of turn, and then return to dive into another run. Each pass would come in as we moved ever deeper into the jungle's interior, giving Cowboy less and less visibility of exactly where we were because of the weather and the increasing density of the foliage. The jungle had to be fast becoming a roiling messy mantle of concealment, at least from Cowboy's perspective. It also provided concealment from those on the ground, and that meant recognition problems about whether the personnel was NVA or Marines.

Small arms fire, mostly muffled but still loud, sputtered up and then died down around me, as I moved. Brilliant muzzle flashes burst across the area just to my front, the passage of bullets themselves unheard, but their presence so physically evident that my body needed no instructions to hit the ground. My face went into the stinking smelly debris first, the aroma almost welcome because of the gut wrench of fear that had returned, like white-hot lead being poured up and down through my core. The rest of my body wedged down, trying to reach the center of the earth, or something close to that.

I went down soft, however, because there was nothing hard under me. The weird sticky layer of mud cradled the broken, hanging and half-crushed foliage, allowing every obnoxious smell of the jungle to be opened like an aged-out tin can filled with bad fruit or putrid sardines. The firing had come from my left, automatic rounds sounding more like a chainsaw than a machine gun. I knew the NVA were only yards away and I couldn't figure out how they'd missed me moving by. I wasn't moving by anymore. The rain beat down on my helmet. There was no point in looking up because the brush was too thick to see through, and looking up might draw more fire. If I still had any M-33 grenades I knew I'd have thrown them, no matter how undependable the fuses might be or how close the detonations might occur. But I had nothing more than my Colt, which was so inadequate that I still hadn't drawn it from my holster, even in the face of nearly direct fire. I was more afraid of losing the only weapon I had than using it to shoot back at anyone armed with a submachine gun. There was no screaming, so I presumed that nobody nearby was hit. Nguyen came out of nowhere to slip in beside me. I looked at him across the few inches that separated us. His eyes remained black and unblinking. He pointed back behind us. I felt more than heard Fessman creeping forward. Nguyen pulled something from his blouse, fiddled with it and then threw it upward and out in the direction the AK fire had come from. He didn't bother to duck so I didn't either. The muffled whump of the grenade's explosion threw debris back over all of us.

I wondered how to say "tell me when you're going to toss a grenade" in his language, but I knew it was a waste of time. Nguyen had calculated that we didn't need to duck and he'd been right. Again. He motioned me forward. I crawled. I wasn't getting up to my feet again until I was out of the hellish jungle, although I also knew immediately that the Ontos was pulling away in front of me. I didn't want to lose the Ontos. It attracted the heaviest fire but it seemed charmed to be able to kill without being killed. As some of the men carried charms with my stuff inside, I wanted to remain in the close aura of survival surrounding the fierce little machine, even if it was an illusion or based on nothing more than hope.

Suddenly the rain stopped like as if some heavenly spigot controlled it. But there was no sun. With the rain stopping, even with the gray overcast of the cloud cover allowing for only a bright twilight sort of existence down in the valley, I realized I had not seen the sun in what seemed like a week. That the rain was gone, at least temporarily, made two things immediately apparent. There would be no dryness resulting throughout the length and breadth of our move because the jungle was so full of absorbed moisture that anything dry that touched any part of it would instantly become soaked through. Everything, from ferns to the leaves and all around, and on any overhanging bamboo fronds, bled water. The second thing was the smoke. Separate tendrils of thin blue smoke rose twisting and turning in the mild wind from different spots in the jungle around us.

The Ontos stopped its forward progress, and the two heavy armored doors on the rear of it sprang open. The Gunny jumped out and loped toward me. I noted that he didn't carry an M-16 either or anything but his sidearm either, and he had no pack on his back.

"Resupply," he said pointing back the way we'd come. "The satchel charges. We need the charges."

"What?" was all I could manage, my position crouching down in the jungle debris for cover, making my question more of a plea than I meant for it to be.

"There are satchel charges in the resupply," the Gunny indicated, dropping his finger.

"Jurgens," the Gunny said, as the sergeant approached from behind where Fessman had taken up a position just back from me. "The smoke. The smoke is coming up out of their tunnels. The Skyraider pass bombed the shit out of some underground supply cave down there, and its burning. The smoke is coming from the tunnel entrances."

Jurgens disappeared, as I rose up to higher crouch to look around. I could see four tendrils rising, although not exactly where their bases were in the rough foliage.

"Holy shit," I breathed.

Without having the flanking fire of both platoons moving south on each side of the jungle area I'd once again lost hope of making it alive to where Kilo was about to descend to 'relieve' us. The NVA, confronting us directly, could face our small arms fire, machine guns, Ontos fire and even the strafing of Cowboy's Skyraider, and then go right back down underground to wait until one of us, or more, passed by a tunnel entrance. Firing from their hidden entrances would be lethal. We would be defenseless.

Marines came from behind us, carrying green cloth sacks. The sacks were different from the containers explosives usually shipped in. The sacks were about the size of briefcases except made of green-dyed canvas. I looked at one bag closely. The black stenciled printing on the broad side of the bag read: "Large Assembly, Demolition, M-183." The Gunny undid the straps quickly on the side of one of the bags and pulled the top open. I saw white demolition cord sticking out of eight rectangular tubes wrapped in a brownish paper. I knew the sticks were composition B because of the color. I also knew the sticks were probably one pound each. Eight pounds of Composition B was a lot of explosives.

Jurgens re-appeared, carrying more canvas sacks. He set them next to where the Gunny worked. The new sacks were thinner and wider than the satchel charges and they had two flaps each instead of one.

"Claymores," Jurgens said with a grin. "Finally gonna get some with these babies."

The Gunny worked quickly, his hands moving almost too fast to follow, as he opened sacks and adjusted the contents of the satchel charges.

"Forget setting these off conventionally," he said to Jurgens. "Let's use the Claymores and command detonate. Simple and safer."

Jurgens opened a claymore bag and pulled the green plastic device out. It was molded smoothly and curved attractively. I remembered well the look of it from training at Quantico. 700 small steel spheres, embedded behind the plastic face, were driven forward by a pound and a half of explosives. Both sides of the device had raised plastic print with instructions about which way the device was to be placed or pointed.

Jurgens unloaded the Claymores, quickly but efficiently wrapping their attached wires around the body of the satchel charge bags. His men crawled forward, each clasping one of the combined packages in his arms, making no effort to be gentle or handle them like the terminally deadly devices they were.

"All right, get out there," the Gunny ordered. "Jam one package down every hole the smoke is coming out of. Run back ten yards, drop down, and then crush the Clacker detonator twice. If you shove the whole thing down the hole you shouldn't have to worry about getting hit. Then, get back here and get another charge."

I watched from my position flat on the jungle floor. I knew the small lever detonators had to be levered shut twice to set off the Claymores, as a safety measure, but I hadn't known they were called Clackers. The Claymores added to the already significant number of explosives in each pack. I hoped that the ten yards was far enough to be from them when they went off.

"We've got to move fast," the Gunny yelled, standing to be heard by everyone, "that smoke won't last forever. Let the M-60s and the Ontos take care of anyone dumb enough to remain on the surface."

I crawled up to my knees and got to my feet, the fear from my close call with what I assumed to be an NVA trooper above ground, not dissipating at all. I knew my right arm was shaking but I didn't think the effect was visible.

The Gunny came close to my side.

"Get your sidearm out," he whispered. "We're going to move fast behind the Ontos. Those underground rats are going to be coming up, coughing, blind and probably deaf. Shoot at the center of mass, no matter how good you are with that thing."

I pulled out the Colt, my hand closing over the butt as I withdrew it from the wet slimy holster. My arm stopped shaking once the Colt was firmly in my grasp. I caught the Gunny's glance down and realized he'd seen my shaking. He was helping me cover the shaking so nobody else would notice.

"That was AK fire," he said. "The crack and no tracers. Not one of our guys."

I made no reply, remaining silently thankful that the Gunny had bothered to relieve my mind. I knew he was correct in retrospect. The sound of the AK was very distinctive and the NVA didn't use tracers in their submachine guns.

The Gunny ran forward, his own sidearm out, flocked with a small group of Marines surrounding he and his radio operator closely before they almost magically split away to blend individually into the bush.

The explosions from the satchel charges began to go off, each one exploding sharply, throwing mud, water, and foliage high into the air. I walked fast, the sky falling around me. Fragments of the jungle had replaced the rain pelting my helmet. I scanned the area in front of me, Nguyen to my left and Fessman just back on my right. Nguyen's M-16, held out in both hands, pointed wherever he looked, while Fessman's weapon remained under his left hand at sling arms. Fessman's right hand was holding the radio handset in case it was needed, with the headset to the AN-323 spring tensioned to his upper arm.

The Skyraider came in, luffing through the air like before, in the strange flying style Cowboy was a master of, allowing the giant metal monster to get lower and slower so the pilot could see and then drop more bombs. When the big radial engine kicked back in, the noise was overwhelming until the Ontos fired two rounds and more satchel charges went off.

My ears hurt but, for some reason, my frightened insides weren't quaking in terror anymore. Being in the center of the combat I felt like moving through a sunken stage where just around and above me, all different symphonies of raucous music played. It was as exhilarating as it was frightening. I was half blind from the flashing of muzzles, explosives, and particulate in the air. I was half deaf from the booming sounds of coming from just about everything, but I was also moving, thinking and not running away. I hunted for anything I could see that might need my attention, as we worked our way down the peninsula of jungle growth.

I didn't have long to hunt. The Ontos had veered to the east, as we traveled south down toward the cliff face where Kilo had to be considering its descent into the hellish A Shau Valley. A still smoking ruin of a broken messy crater was just to my left, which was remarkable but I didn't give it a second thought because the satchel charge that made it would certainly have killed anything close when it was set off, below or above ground. But that wasn't the case.

A uniformed NVA ran through the shoulder high bracken,

seeming to slip through a crack in the reeds and tall elephant grass that couldn't have been there.

His head was bare and across his chest, he held an AK-47. He stopped suddenly only feet away when Nguyen fired several rounds into his chest. The man stopped in his tracks but was still standing, his facial expression flat and unchanged, as if he'd run into a wall. I brought up my .45 smoothly, slowly squeezing the trigger as the automatic rose in my extending arm. As if by perfect design, the Colt went off just as it came level with my shoulder. The NVA soldier was literally blown back from where he came, his head tossing so far back it seemed to disappear. I moved forward after him into the reeds, pulling them aside with my left hand, using my right to point my weapon downward. Nguyen went low and slid under my extended arms. He leaned in close over the body before pulling back. He tapped his forehead when he stood. I understood. I'd hit the soldier in the forehead. Nguyen nodded so deeply it was like a bow, before pulling back and loping toward the Ontos. I followed because his left hand was pulling me powerfully along. He'd grabbed the sleeve of my right just back from my elbow and would not let go.

For some reason, I didn't want to leave the scene, but I only took one glance back before crouching low again, pulling my sleeve loose, and then picking up the pace to pull even with Nguyen and catch up to Fessman. My ears rang from the M-16 and .45 automatic fire that had occurred so close. I couldn't get the dead soldiers expressionless face out of my mind as I ran, but I also felt that I had done what I was supposed to do for the first time in many days.

The Gunny came up from behind me, moving fast to catch up with the Ontos.

"Nice work," he murmured, as he passed. 'You and Cowboy got lucky, thank God."

I tried to remember whether I'd fired just the one shot from my automatic but couldn't. Did I need to reload? And I hadn't seen Zippo in some time. Was he all right? The battlefield was all blending together and I was having a hard time trying to take in the idea that we had no real visibility of the flanking platoons moving along the valley floor under the cleft of the cliff, and also down by the river. I couldn't see most of the Marines who were attacking with me down the very center of the jungle area either. Quantico training in field combat had been so much easier in the open forest areas of Virginia where almost everything had been visible.

The enemy fifty-caliber hadn't fired another round following the twin blast of flechettes from the Ontos and that was more than just a minor relief. It meant that the NVA was down, probably hidden away until we passed. I moved faster to get closer to the rear of the noisy roar of the Ontos' engine. Cowboy came back for another run but this time he didn't allow the Skyraider to slow and drop bombs. This time the 20mm cannons mounted in the thing's wings poured fire down into the jungle ahead of us.

It was a satisfying sound but even more satisfying was looking up to see that the loitering plane still had what seemed like at least a half a load more of bombs and other stuff hanging from under its wings. Cowboy would be coming back time after time. We might make it to the end of the jungle area.

Small explosions came from up ahead and the Ontos slowed. I moved, with Fessman and Nguyen to flank the machine, fully aware that standing directly behind it could be disastrous if it fired any of its guns again. I tried to peer forward through the leafy brush and bamboo but it was useless. There were no easily visible smoke trails, as we'd passed that part of the burning underground tunnel complex. Marine M-60s opened up from both flanks. The explosions I'd heard had to have been grenades, and those hadn't sounded like American models. The ChiCom grenades the NVA carried made bigger luffing explosions than U.S. inventory, but the weapons were plagued by duds because of their water sensitive friction fuses. The body of the German type "potato masher" Chinese variants were poorly machined and carried no fragmentation wire inside them.

Although I could not see all the elements somehow coordinating in our attack, I knew they were there and the attack was working. The good fortune of the underground fire, the brilliance of Cowboy's single Skyraider performance and the dogged endurance of a tattered but hardened Marine unit made up of many deeply disturbed and frightened men was proving to be overwhelming. The NVA had, once again, underestimated just how tough and determined the company could be when backed into a corner.

The rain began pouring back down as Cowboy brought the Skyraider back down to start another run. I moved into the scattered mess of jungle behind the Ontos, more like an armed predatory spider than a uniformed human combatant.

The third time, I thought. The third time in so few days that our company had been called in to be saved from an attacking enemy, but
in every case having to save Kilo Company, while they were being sent
to do the same for us. The helicopters had flown an unlikely resupply
mission at night and dropped in observers who quickly became dead
bodies, but the intent had been to try to do something about the terrible mess we were in. I could not fault the attempts on the part of the
powers in the rear back at battalion, and maybe above that level. But the
results were proving to be similar in every case. An enemy force nobody
would believe was really there was decimating our Marines and those of
Kilo, and anybody else they sent into the A Shau Valley.

I moved through the waist-high jungle debris. The rain had come
back with a vengeance. Our attack, or push south through the enemy,
since the occasionally smattering contacts on both sides could hardly
be considered classically conducted attacks, continued. I moved slowly but determinedly in the path left by the still advancing Ontos. The
flechette rounds found on the mud flats had been delivered to the guns
and the Ontos was loaded to fire on anything while it moved.

That it moved along the jungle floor at all was a function of its
lightness and how well the tracks gained purchase to climb over instead
of plowing through the jungle. I carried my .45 Colt in my right hand.
I'd changed magazines, even though I hadn't used up the first one completely in shooting the surprising, and surprised, NVA soldier. But it
was dark, wet and a mess of leaves mud and my itching-irritation-un-
der-the-blouse leeches kept me from counting how many bullets I'd
used. It was easier just to change magazines than to try to count what
was left in the used one. I didn't know for sure how many men I'd killed
with the .45, but I was willing to bet nobody back in training, where
the automatic sidearm was considered more a decorative sidearm rather than an effective weapon, would have believed it was more than six.

The company moved for another twenty minutes without taking
or giving any fire at all. The platoons on line along the base of the cliff

didn't radio in any suspicion of contact, much less real contact, and the platoon on line coming down the riverbank of the Bong Song didn't either. I was scared, but my fear was a controllable thing, living inside of me, and a real part of every bit of my being, but it was like the Gunny had told me on that first night. The fear would never leave but it would become something I could accommodate and even perform well while holding at bay. The Gunny had also said that if I stayed in a combat situation long enough then I'd come to massage and enjoy it, and there was no coming back from that. He hadn't said if, given that I somehow lived through it, that there was any coming back from the near continuous deep and core-affecting fear.

The Ontos moved ahead, it's progress slow, while there were no more satchel charges to be set because Cowboy had gone for rearming, and even when he returned it wasn't likely he'd get lucky enough to hit another underground bunker. If only the 105 or 155 batteries could reach the bottom of the valley. The 175 didn't fire concrete piercing rounds. If it did then the safety of calling in rounds, even at red bag distances, would have been assured. The rounds would go off under the mud and higher jungle debris. But there was only the Ontos for supporting fires until the Skyraider returned unless some other air branch squadron was freed up to stop by.

I had no letter home. I had one but it was all in my head. The detail of the muddy river bed, the hole I was held up in, the Ontos and how it moved over massive chunks of the jungle by simply riding up and then grinding away until the body of the beast slid down to work its way up and do it all over again. For the most part, the thing could not fire its guns. Even the marginally useful movement of the turret could not be used to adjust to the steep unstable rises and falls, twists and turns.

Kilo was coming down the glacis they'd descended before, and took so many casualties while doing so. Fessman monitored the radio and it was obvious from overhearing the exchanges that the move was going well. Snipers in its bid to move down the Bong Song had pinned down Lima. I was amazed that the entire company had not been wiped out because of the size of the forces occupying Hill 975. If we could continue our move down the valley then it was possible that the NVA forces between Kilo and us would go to ground instead of engaging.

The night had closed in and full darkness, along with hard rain, had descended on the valley. Moving was not nearly as difficult as it was uncomfortable, to the point of being downright painful. So much of the jungle debris was hard-edged and sharp. My hands and face were constantly suffering from small cuts. With my leeches still sucking on my skin under my blouse I was in a sorry state, but moving determinedly. There would be some solace when we made it and joined up with Kilo. The cleft formed under the edge of the nearby cliff face would still provide cover from the rain as well as from fire that might originate out from the jungle area.

I wasn't commanding anything and that obvious fact bothered me, although I knew that communications were terrible under such conditions. The Gunny was out there somewhere, while Jurgens and Sugar Daddy commanded the flanks in their own limited ways. With Marines moving through the brush in heavy rain at night there was little in the way of instructions or directions to give. But the fact that I simply moved along behind the Ontos, my .45 out and ready, didn't seem to be enough. I had no more M-33 grenades. There'd probably been a box in resupply but, except for the satchel charges and reload of flechette rounds for the Ontos, nothing else has been brought forward to add to what was carried into the attack.

The A Shau Valley was not a quiet place. The river's rushing sound was ever-present; the rain beat down with drops of water bouncing about from everything they hit. My helmet was a constant background buzz of rain strikes and there was no hiding from it. Fessman made his replies to conversations unheard on the other end. And the Ontos ground ever onward toward the cliff face where real combat was likely to take place. The fear in my belly did not dissipate as I moved along, although moving helped to hold it down.

The battle began only moments after I'd been thinking how loud the natural sounds of the valley were to anyone awake inside it at night. Small arms fire began to the front and then increased in crescendo. I went down and then got back up to move forward in a semi-crab half-crawl half-run. I could see the flash of tracers but not the tracer rounds or trails the flaming bullets made. Normally, the AK-47 tracers were green in color, compared to the yellow and sometimes red of our own, but the NVA didn't always use tracers in the combat rifles. Either they didn't have them or they didn't want to give away their position. Muzzle flashes were more dependable targets but they were not distinctive in color, so many times muzzle flashes might be from friendly arms.

The battlefield began to light up, as the Marines on both sides of the jungle fired into the area the rest of us were approaching in the jungle center. The company fired all tracers, except for the M-60, wherein those gunners used one tracer to every three or five rounds. The enemy fifty opened up to my front and I saw real green tracers close up for the first time since making contact. The fifty was firing at the Ontos and getting hits because the tracers would bounce directly upward and then die out as their chemical deposits in the point of the rounds burned through.

I realized that my position, moving not too far back from the Ontos wasn't a safe one. The fear that the NVA had for the little lethal machine caused some of the enemy to avoid it but attracted others like bees to honey. I went down again when several rounds screamed through the air over my head. I knew the rounds did not really scream but the faint whoosh of displaced air was emotionally disturbing enough. The .50 went through everything. There was no cover from it except inside the Ontos and that wasn't truly safe either. The side armor was too thin.

There was no place to run. I got back up and started pushing forward again. There was only one direction I could go and staying close to the Ontos was vital simply because it was our only supporting fire. Without supporting fire being as outnumbered, as I knew we had to be was potentially terminal. That it was night and raining down upon the NVA wasn't something to be ignored, either. Water in tunnels, no matter how well formed in the dirt and rock under our feet, was a bit more than a bother when torrents poured into the entrances. NVA communications had to be as bad as our own, if not worse. The enemy had been in the valley fighting for a long time but our own experience was growing by the passage of every night and day.

The fire poured in from both flanks. The Ontos continued its churning forward motion. Suddenly, several of the guns on each side of the Ontos went off.

The sound overwhelmed all other sounds. I felt the back blast and knew I'd been lucky. I'd not been concentrating on the need to keep quite a distance from the back of the deadly beast. The backblast had reached me but not injured me, except for the fact that I was deaf again. Nguyen was on me, checking me out to make sure I was still alive. He pulled Fessman close. Fessman was trying to clear his ears with wet fingers but I knew it was hopeless. Our ears would clear for normal conversation over time. Nothing else would make any difference. I lay still for a brief few seconds. It was peaceful being deaf and the night flashes of bright light from muzzles and tracers had made me night blind too. I was deaf and dumb and a Marine Company Commander in real combat in Vietnam. The reality of that hit me but the humor, I knew, would take a long time to seep into my consciousness.

I climbed back to my hunched over feet. The Ontos was still moving. The attack was still going on and the fire was changing. I could see it in the distance. The green tracers were being redirected to the south. We'd come far enough in that direction to be close to the glacis where Kilo was attempting to descend down the wall, and they were taking fire from the NVA. I surged forward, as the Ontos did the same thing. I felt it in my core. The NVA were leaving their backs open to attack in order to inflict as much damage on Kilo as they could. The NVA were not covering their six and that meant we could have at them with abandon without taking true defensive fire.

I got up fully and ran, waving my Colt and running right past the Ontos.

I was hoping that others would see me, but I need not have had that hope because I saw other Marines running too. Running and firing their all tracer loaded M-16s while they ran. It was a beautiful sight. Both flanks moved and opened up while on the move. The firing against the unseen wall in front of us subsided. There was no return fire because we were among them. Fessman was at my side; Nguyen was just ahead of him, as I looked for something or someone to shoot. But there was nothing there. I wanted to beat the bracken around me to find the enemy but I knew that would be useless.

The firing from the cliff-face died out but the firing by the Marines coming down the Bong Song on the right flank increased. I knew the NVA; those not down deep in holes turned into dangerous muddy havens of death were making a break for the right flank.

A blasting series of green tracer rounds raced in just above my head and struck the Ontos. I heard the rounds hit, rather than saw them. My hearing was coming back. I went straight to the jungle floor, flying spread-eagled to land flat on my torso. I'd almost been cut in half by the .50 Caliber. It had been a close thing. The NVA were firing it while on the move or I'd be dead, I guessed. It was very difficult, even for a very large man, to fire a .50 while on the move. The recoil was ungodly. A regular hunting rifle put out a bullet that developed almost two thousand foot-pounds of energy at distance. The .50 put out nearly seven tons of that same kind of on-site energy.

The Ontos crept forward again, passing me on the left. I rolled right, even though it wasn't that close, my fear of being run over by a tank in the night nearly overcoming me. Fessman and Nguyen had stayed right with me. The rain continued to pound down and the leeches sucking the blood from spots all over my torso were beginning to cause me pain. My pack was weighing me down. I wanted to strip out of it but I knew that when I finally got to some protected cave under the lip of the cliff I'd need everything inside it pretty desperately, and I'd never find it again come the next day.

The Ontos went by and then turned to face the right flank. The brush was thick, I knew, too thick for the flechettes to penetrate. But then I remembered the fuse settings available on those rounds and covered my ears tightly. The guns went off and the boom of the after-blast shockwave rolled over me, and also drove the rain painfully into the skin of my exposed face. I let go of my ears and plunged my face into the wet mud under me for relief. As I'd guessed, the rounds were set to go off after penetrating the jungle growth. I never heard their detonation but presumed they'd done something to help.

Fessman was right next to me, his ears a mess, I knew because he kept his hands over them while lying still on his side. I could barely see him in the rain filled night without much of any light at all. Nguyen was fine because he was the one pulling my head out of the mud, and then wiping the chunks from the crease that ran between my helmet and my forehead. I knew I was a total wreck of a mess.

The Ontos was stopped, and unaccountably, its engine had stopped.

Although the battlefield was anything but quiet, that particular sound disappearing was unsettling.

The Gunny appeared out of nowhere, leaned over as he passed and then ran toward the right flank where the firing had been most concentrated. I wanted to leap up and follow him, but I could not.

I moved forward toward the rear of the Ontos with dread, the darkness coming over me on the outside but a deeper blackness creeping up to layer itself over my heart. Zippo had been hit. He'd been hit at the start of the attack. One of the enemy armor-piercing .50 caliber bullets had found a way in through some crack or imperfection along the front slanted angled armor of the Ontos' forward plates.

"Zippo's hit, fifty got through," was all the Gunny had whispered as he went by. He hadn't stayed to accompany me, as I moved toward the back of the Ontos, which had started to move again. There was no stopping the attack, so the Ontos would not come to a halt for long unless everyone inside was dead. A stopped Ontos was a target Ontos. The NVA had to believe it was still coming for them for the attack to succeed to the end. There would be no medivac until we arrived at our objective, and then quite possibly not even then depending on the amount of contact we might be under and the potential of a safe clearing big enough.

Zippo was hit. But he wasn't hit in my mind. If he was hit and wounded the Gunny would have said he was wounded. I knew that in my heart, but I still had a small tiny edge of hope in my soul.

I didn't catch up to the Ontos. A hand grabbed me from the darkness of the thick dense jungle I was making my way through. I knew that hand; the grab and I knew why I was being stopped in my tracks.

The strong hand wrenched my suspender strap to the point of breaking. I went down on my chest, to find myself lying next to Nguyen once again. How he'd gotten in front of me, far enough the work his way back and lay in wait for me I didn't know. His powerful stringy arm pulled me close.

"Gone," he whispered into my left ear, his hand still holding my rotting ratty blouse tightly.

The rain pounded down, striking Nguyen's upturned face so strongly that it sent visibly little sparkles cascading away, back into the darkness around us.

"Hit. Before. Did not want you to know. Number ten hit. Gone now."

The words came in whispered gasps, like delayed and individually gaseous expressions of horror.

"He's dead," I said, not framing the phrase as a question.

Nguyen let go of my utility blouse. I didn't move away. I felt again, as in other times of dire danger and fear, like I had nowhere to go.

Fessman fell to my side, twisting his face toward me, only inches away.

"You hit, sir?" he asked the note of worry in his voice so great that I wanted to hug him close.

There was no point, I realized, in telling him that Zippo was dead. I knew by the brightness in his eyes and the expression of his normal exuberance that he didn't know. The two of them had been close, like high school or college buddies, I knew. Or even closer, because that is what combat did. You became brothers or you became dead, and Zippo had become both. The Ontos would carry his body. I wondered if the Starlight Scope had survived undamaged but hated myself for thinking about it with the wonderful, out-of-place, black as night kid now dead. Not wanting me to know. Not wanting me to worry and possibly mess up the attack because of him. The kid who loved my plan names so much, The kid who accepted my plans, orders and everything else without question or doubt.

The Ontos was pulling away. I had to get up. I had to move. I hadn't written my wife. I had to have a letter ready to go when the medevac that would be coming in for Zippo's dead body touched down. I realized that my wife did not know about Zippo, either alive or dead, like she didn't know about anyone else in the company except Fessman and the Gunny who were anything but the characters I'd portrayed them to be. Even Rittenhouse and Tex were well known to her, but I'd never mentioned the black kid who'd treated me like a Dad when his own racial members in Sugar Daddy's platoon rejected him. I hated the race war inside my company and Zippo was a glaring and perfect example of why it made no logical sense whatever that one could possibly exist in such rotten circumstance, but it did.

The Gunny was back. He grabbed me by one arm and jerked me to a standing position.

"Can you hack it, you weak little college wimp of an officer?" he hissed in my right ear, too soft for anyone else to hear.

"Zippo," I tried to say, but he cut me off.

"Did you hear my question?" the Gunny asked, still holding my arm up near where my bicep joined my shoulder so tightly that the pain was palpable.

"Keep moving," he said to the night around me.

I pulled as gently as I could from the Gunny's grip. I knew what he was doing. It was what he always did. He was making certain that I went on, no matter what the pain, the loss or the sentiment. I tried to look into his eyes, to communicate just how enraged I was that he was presuming to somehow manipulate me once again, using Zippo's now dead body as a tool.

I stepped forward, before realizing I'd lost my helmet and liner when Nguyen had taken me down. Nguyen wasn't there anymore when I looked down, but the helmet liner slipped over my head before I could do a search for it. Fessman plopped my war-damaged mess of a helmet on the liner right after the liner settled in.

My .45 was still in my right hand but I'd accidentally stuck that hand into the muddy bracken I'd used to break my fall when Nguyen had dragged me down.

Would it fire? I didn't know, but for the moment I didn't give a damn. If the opportunity rose up then I'd fire anyway and worry about my hand or other body parts later.

I moved forward. The Gunny had disappeared in the night, like Nguyen, but not like Nguyen. I knew the Montagnard was close by, very close. He knew I was hurt badly and he was concerned. I'd felt the emotion radiate out of him like a long slow gust of heat. The Gunny was worried in his way and Fessman in his. Everyone was worried about me, but Zippo was dead. I vowed to write to my wife about Zippo and make certain he was not forgotten in my or her memory. Did he have a wife? Japanese was the rumor, but I had not paid enough attention to know. I had a little daughter who meant most of my world, that part not taken up by my wife, to me. Did Zippo have that? I hated myself for not knowing, and for not checking on him and getting him the hell out of the Ontos, no matter how much he loved the small tracked vehicle.

War machines killed men in combat and they didn't respect one bit which side the warrior was on.

one-hundred-seventeen

THE TWENTY-FOURTH NIGHT : SECOND PART

I'd lost something indefinable, aside from my illegally promoted scout sergeant. I'd lost something like a loyal friend, but it was deeper than that. I moved through the jungle, low and almost on full automatic. How had the young black man eaten his way into my very being? Had it been the innocent acceptance of any plan I came up with, as long as it had an interesting name? Had it been his willingness to do any job assigned without complaint or comment?

I went down at the sound of gunfire just ahead, and to my right. Over toward the river. But I had seen nothing, not even the flaring brightness of tracer fire or muzzle flashes. I waited a full five minutes, with Fessman and Nguyen at my sides, hunkered down flat, the same way I was. We got up, almost as if there had been some signal, but there'd been none.

We moved forward, once again having fallen an uncomfortable distance behind the Ontos. We followed the Ontos, but actually, I was following Zippo, unable to get the boy's lack of presence in my existence out of my mind. I'd known him for twenty days but it was like I'd been with him my entire life. How was I to proceed with that kind of void in front of me? More fire and I was down again. The night was beginning to wear on me. The Ontos stopped and sat in front of us idling. It hadn't fired a round in some time. Was Zippo's body, contained somewhere inside the armor plates, an impediment to firing? The enemy was all around us, and I knew they were taking casualties. There was no way they could have avoided being decimated by the placement of the satchel charges set in tunnel openings only revealed by the smoke released by our most outrageous good fortune.

The night was once again filled with more than just the blowing rain and irritating mist. Small arms fire seemed to come from everywhere. Some of it was laced with yellow tracers and some with green. I moved forward but then went down again into the heavy mangled jungle undergrowth the Ontos was spitting out behind its ever-churning tracks. I was afraid, but not of being hit by any of the rounds crisscrossing the area. I was primarily in fear of not knowing what was going on. Fessman was at my side. He'd said nothing since discovering that his companion and friend had become a casualty. Nguyen, Fessman and I followed behind the Ontos like it was a really odd funeral hearse, but one that could deliver more death than it received. In my own mind, somehow, Zippo fought on, guiding the deadly machine along to face the worst the enemy could dish out.

My misery seemed just about complete, so bad that I finally unbuttoned my blouse, and then twisted over on my back. Pulling the plastic bug juice container from my thigh pocket, I began slathering it all over my torso, My fingers bumped along, over unfeeling ridges I knew were leeches that were sucking my blood and my life away. The feel of their presence on me was no longer tolerable with everything else. I tried but didn't get them all. The relieved feeling of having so many of the reachable ones fall away was not truly describable. The mosquito repellant stung badly, but I was beyond being disabled by that kind of minor pain. I buttoned up my blouse, but couldn't make the attempt to unbutton my trousers and tuck it back in. Not with my slippery fingers, anyway. That would have to wait.

Fessman pushed the AN-323 headset into my shoulder. I heard the static and some broken communication attempts before I could get my helmet off and the headset on.

"Whisky alpha tango six," a deep male voice said, its tone so husky that it made the small earphone ends buzz in an irritating way. "You down there, Flash?" the voice went on. Captain John Rolfing Hotchkiss and my Rio, checking in for the night."

Before I could respond, a deep whooshing roar began to grow in volume, coming from the northern end of the valley behind us. The sound was ominous, and nothing like I'd ever heard before.

The connection between the deep voice and the approaching sounds of doom came together in my mind, as I rolled over and looked up into the mess of a night sky. There was nothing to see. The rain was light and wind even lighter, but the sky was impenetrable when it came to seeing anything.

"What's your call sign, Whisky Alpha Tango?" I asked.

There was no way I was going to talk back and forth to whomever, and whatever was up in the night with that kind of name.

"Peter Pan," came back through the earphones, "and I'm Fireside Joe, bombardier-navigator, not Rio, over."

"Not Peter Pan," followed, almost instantaneously, in the deeper resonating voice.

I would have sighed if I could, trying to roll over into some position that didn't make the raw bloodsucking wounds all over my torso hurt like hell. The pilot and second crewman aboard whatever aircraft had flown in to support us were arguing about what they should be called.

"Peter Pan, and Fireside," I transmitted, holding my finger down on the small button. "what have we got in support from you guys? We're taking fire, as you can see if you look down."

"A-6 Intruder, up here, carrying 24 thousand goodies, sir," Fireside replied, "and we've got about three hours of loitering with full tanks. See you down there through our nighttime T.V., methinks, sir."

I tried to think. I'd heard of the A-6 attack aircraft being the best there was, when it came to support aircraft, but hadn't known it could carry twelve tons of ordnance. That was more than four tons more than the Skyraiders I was used to.

The plane passed over our position, making it too noisy to hear anything through the earphones. The sound was like that of some ungodly collection of hurricane-force blowing torches. Two spears of fire came down from under the craft as it seemed to lazily float through the valley over our position.

"Is your tracked vehicle the lead of your line of attack, sir?" Fireside Joe asked. "We can use that since it doesn't appear you have a beacon along for the show."

"Do we have a beacon?" I asked Fessman, before speaking to the Intruder again.

"Rittenhouse mentioned something a long time back, but I don't know, sir," Fessman replied.

"Shit," I whispered to myself.

A beacon had to be something that transmitted our position up to the attack aircraft, thereby making certain the aircraft knew exactly where we were before dumping tons of ordnance. But the Intruder was passing overhead now.

"The Ontos is our lead, with flank support along the cliff bottom and river," I sent, hoping that the crew could indeed see where we were through the muck of wet blowing atmosphere and the waving jungle flora between us.

I wasn't afraid of radio security. The NVA knew our positions exactly, and that was evident from the direction of their fire.

"Got it," Fireside, sent," How about a selection of mixed 250 cocktails before the main course?"

"Standing by," I said, wondering if I would be standing by after the drop.

The A-6 seemed to move almost as slowly in the air as the Cowboy's Skyraider had, although the twin plumes from its jet engines made it much more visible than the prop plane. The volume of noise increased and the traveling plumes, now well past where the Ontos had to be, shot down like twin narrow torches. The aircraft was accelerating rapidly, I realized, and the reason followed right after my thoughts. Ground shaking bursts from ahead of our direction of travel. I counted eight explosions but there could have been more. The sound of the Intruder began to die away, and I instinctively knew Peter Pan was going around to make another pass.

If Peter Pan had dropped eight of his bombs then he had plenty more. The Skyraiders took ten minutes to conduct a second pass, disappearing from sight and sound as they did so. But not the Intruder. It's raucous jet engines stayed with us and I could track its passage as it evidently had popped up out of the valley, and then dived back in.

"Gotten a little quieter down there?" Fireside asked.

"Roger that," I replied.

There was no fire from anyone in the valley, that I could detect, anyway.

A warm feeling flowed through me. We were not alone anymore. The leech wounds were awash with the painful bug juice hurt but I could handle them. We had to move forward and regain our position behind the Ontos. It was near to impossible to figure out where all of the company's Marines were located, as we streamed down the valley, however. I would have to gamble that they knew what they were doing, even though I had great doubts about that. The Intruder made two more passes but didn't drop anything or fire any of its guns either.

"Whiskey Alpha Tango, rolling on around in the sky above you," Peter Pan transmitted, his voice so low it was hard to make some of the words out. "Keeping heads down. My Rio can see them but they can't see us so they don't know whether we're releasing or not."

I wanted to respond by saying "you've done this before a time or two," but I didn't. That the A-6 was there, rotated back into position so quickly and noisily, and that the enemy could not see it, was everything to the continuation and success of our attack.

The Intruder came in again, like a loud shark, diving in toward a reef filled with smaller hiding prey. The A-6 released a load of 250-pound high explosive bombs, and the jungle near the bottom of the glacis where Kilo was going to make its attempt to scale down, lit up in the wet night. The bombs were not high explosive. They were napalm. The searing heat of that much napalm, beating back from the cliff face and pooling at the bottom, exploded back at the jungle, penetrating so deep that any exposed skin within a distance of hundreds of yards would be singed, and any hair exposed melted away into heated dust.

Kilo had taken the Gunny's warning, and over-ridden battalion's order to descend no matter what the conditions below. Carruthers was the name of the captain leading Kilo, I'd discovered, not by talking to the Six-actual, but through Fessman. The Gunny gave battalion its combat updates. Through the attack there had been no necessity, of the company's elements on both flanks, to be in constant contact. The attack was in the rain, in the dark, through miserable undergrowth populated with mosquitos, leeches and the North Vietnamese Army. Through such conditions, our Marine company either moved or died and moved it had.

I eased forward again. Everyone moved again or kept moving forward. The attack was so unlikely, and yet so simply effective, that it worked. I felt it working.

The arrival of Peter Pan had been the single event that had made it truly possible, however. The A-6's screaming presence, roaring up above the rain in the night, poking its two nozzles of fire downward like evil moving eyes of coming death, had taken out what heart the enemy had left. Silence followed after the Intruders went by. I knew there were plenty of enemy soldiers hidden under the debris, squirreled down into tunnels and holes they'd never be dug out of, and would not arise out of until we'd passed by.

The Ontos had stopped because the jungle had stopped. I couldn't see the solid stone wall, but I felt it up ahead. A huge rising black presence inside a sodden night too black to see. But it was there. I moved past the Ontos, as it sat idling, having churned its treads through the jungle undergrowth to make a full circle. The six deadly tubes of the 106 recoilless rifles aimed back toward the jungle we'd all just come through. But I could not think about the defensive power of the mobile armored beast any more than I could allow myself to think about what was contained inside its thick steel exterior.

"Zippo," I whispered to myself. I would write to my wife. I would. I tried to concentrate and make sure that memory was burned in. And I knew my memory was bright. Since the door had opened in the world of Vietnam, I had not forgotten a single small detail. From the shape and form of bugs, leeches, crocodiles, snakes, plants and more. I retained all my night defensive fire coordinates from that first night. I also knew that wasn't possible and therefore I could not still be alive as a real human. I would go to wherever I was going but if I ever went home it would not be as a human being.

"Zippo," I whispered again, as I moved forward toward the glacis of the wall.

Was he in some better place, or somehow still back here where the only proper phrase describing our circumstance was commonly referred to as 'the shit?'

The company had to establish a perimeter, but first, it had to be assembled in communication to affect that end. Looking upward into the night caused me to note that the rain had suddenly stopped. The clouds above me were slightly breaking. The moon was sending its deadly black and white light to cast down some miserable illumination on my life, and wall in front of it.

The wall was as I remembered it, although the dim moon shining vaguely down through the clouds made it much more foreboding than it had appeared before. The rain glistening down it's huge puffed out, a rounded slab of a side made it seem more like it was from a giant movie set than being real. I stared up at the wall for a good minute before leaning back down to proceed through the heavy brush and remaining jungle growth toward it.

We'd attacked through the enemy from one side to the other. The Marines in the company had taken casualties, I knew, but they'd acted like only trained Marines could do. Without effective communications or anything else to hold them together in the night while they came down the valley in their respective positions, they'd followed orders to the letter. They'd exhibited fire control so we wouldn't run out of ammo in case we couldn't get resupply anytime soon. And, although I'd not been able to see much at all, I knew they'd killed or beat back, with vicious efficiency, anything the NVA threw at them.

Fessman was to my rear, with Nguyen almost up next to me, when I fell forward. I fell because my right foot had plunged down into a hole. I struggled to come to my knees and pull my leg out but it was held inside the hole by something. Nguyen was all over me before I could bend forward to explore the hole with my hands.

Nguyen worked away for several minutes, finally cutting me free. As soon as I could pull my boot toward me I worked to get it off. I knew I'd stepped into a pungy stick hole. I was worried sick that I'd stepped onto one of the feces-smeared and razor-sharpened stakes that were jammed into the bottom. The thought of some feces-powered infection racing through my body was somehow more awful than the thought of what the future results of leech wounds might bring.

A quick examination with my hands found no injury I could detect. In ground combat, mobility was just about everything. If I could not get around then I would be dependent upon the company Marines to carry me to some safer place for later evacuation. It had not taken many days for me to figure out that the company evacuated far more dead than it did wounded. I got my boot back on as quickly as I could, regretting that I couldn't take the time to retrieve the one pair of dry socks I had left in my pack. No dry socks, no letter to send home, no food since early in the day before. The only thing I wasn't was thirsty. The rain would not let up and how the wind found a way to constantly stir everything upside down inside such a deep valley was beyond me.

I moved back from the invisible hole, somewhere to my left, but now gone in the night and rain. There'd be no marking it or anything like that. All we could do was hope that nobody else would step in it and, if they did, that they'd have my kind of luck and stick their boot through the stakes instead of being penetrated by one or more of them.

The Gunny was by my side. Like the wall, invisible in the night but felt all the same. A force of nature.

"They're setting up a perimeter and climbing partway up the wall. There are a couple of clefts we can put M-60 teams in. Plunging fire. It'll take that if they open up with anything when Kilo comes down."

The Gunny was way ahead of me, as usual. When it came to classical operations and tactics the Gunny, and the Marines in the company, young and old and of all ranks, just did the right thing, time after time. I knew part of that was the field experience they'd gotten in living so long in combat, but the bulk of it was from the deeply instilled and hard-bitten training the Marines had burned into them before combat with a foreign enemy was engaged.

There was nothing to be said, so I just stood next to him, trying to absorb some of the man's seemingly superhuman strength and so-ber unemotional delivery under the worst of circumstance. The Gunny took out a cigarette and lit it with his special lighter. I couldn't see the lighter but I knew its existence well, like the Gunny himself. Old, worn and boot tough, stretched and wet leather tough. I was none of those things. But I had the Gunny. I saw his face in the flash of the lighter, and then again when he pulled air into his lungs through the cigarette. A faint red glow reflected off the wet flat planes that formed his facial features. I knew the man was looking at me but there wasn't enough light to see his eyes, or even a faint reflection coming back from their polished black surfaces.

"It wasn't you," he said, holding out the cigarette.

I didn't move.

"Take it," he said, this time his voice going quiet, low and com-manding.

I took the cigarette, raised it to my lips and inhaled deeply. I didn't cough.

I held the smoke deep inside me until it hurt.

"He wanted to help," the Gunny said, accepting the cigarette back. "That was the way he was. Always wanting to help. His marker will read Staff Sergeant. I'll see to it if we live."

"A Captain Carruthers has taken over Kilo," the Gunny said, not knowing that I already knew. It was like we might be having some gentle business discussion back home over a water cooler. "He's bright enough to hold his men back from the descent when I told him, and that's a good sign."

"Alright, what happened to the other guys?" I asked, in shock. It had only been days, and the command leadership of Kilo had changed for a second time.

"You have no clue, do you?" the Gunny said, with a gentle laugh, before delaying for a few seconds by taking one long inward breath of his cigarette. "You're setting survival records down in the bottom of this death valley. A record for length and for brutal bloody success, but no-body's ever going to know. Live or die, this story will never be told."

"What's the butcher's bill for the attack?" I asked, not giving a damn about any records for anything.

"Zippo, and some others," the Gunny replied. "Sugar Daddy and Jurgens are coming in. We'll know more. We've got a bigger problem than covering Kilo's descent. When they get down, there'll be all of us and another whole company, besides. We can't dig in here. Kilo's coming down to join us, but there's no place to go."

I was about to reply when the Intruder flew over low, it's burning engines so loud we could no longer hear ourselves. I still had the headset around my neck.

When the nozzles of the plane passed I heard the little ear speakers squawking away.

"You boys going to play some billiards down there, or what?" Fireside asked in his sing-song voice. "The Marines on the ridge are coming down. They look like little insects on my screen, but then that's how Marines always look to me."

I instantly knew the Intruder supporting us was Navy.

"What's your unit?" I asked, reflexively and coldly, bitten by his comment.

"The One-Ninety-Six, at your service," Peter Pan's deep voice came back. "Don't listen to my Rio. He's an idiot. We're remaining on station till dawn, or till the fuel's gone. That's what he meant."

"Thanks, Captain," I replied, knowing I'd reacted because of Zippo.

Zippo was a real Marine and I wouldn't accept any diminishment of what he'd been.

"Carruthers is coming down with the lead element," the Gunny said, Tank having appeared just behind him.

I noted that Fessman was even closer to me, making sure that I had plenty of wire to use the AN-323 mic and phones. I wondered, fleetingly, whether I could ever have been as capable a radioman as Fessman if our roles were reversed.

"Maybe he's not as smart as I thought," the Gunny said to me, flicking his cigarette away and accepting a radio handset from Tank.

I handed the air microphone back to Fessman and stood thinking. The Gunny could not have been more wrong about our position, in my estimation, but would he see it when I told him? Sugar Daddy and Jurgens appeared out of the jungle and joined us. There was no fire coming from anywhere, and there'd been none since the A-6 dropped its second load of napalm. The smell of burned gasoline and vegetable matter was bitter, but not truly awful. The most amazing thing about the sticky horror-laden napalm was how fast it burned. It was there, burning bright and billowing everywhere, and then, in seconds, it was gone. The flame extinguished almost instantly and the smoke drifted away. The heat flared and then died, almost too fast for it to be real, unless you were too close and then the reality was never going to leave you, whether your life was to be very short or long.

The Gunny finished his radio transmission. I hadn't listened to any of it, squatting down with Jurgens and Sugar Daddy to wait. After a few seconds, the Gunny joined us, taking out another cigarette. There was no time or I was sure he'd have prepared a canteen holder of his instant coffee.

"What's the plan?" the Gunny asked, which surprised me.

If he didn't think I had a plan then why would he risk embarrassing me in front of Jurgens and Sugar Daddy by asking? I let the thought go.

"We're going back the way we came in," I said, watching as the others as closely as I could to gauge their reactions.

I went on. "So then I dropped it in the mailbox and sent it special D, bright and early next morning it came right back to me," I quoted from an Elvis Presley song of a few years back. "We'll call it 'Return to Sender,'" I finished.

Nobody said anything in the ensuing seconds, so I continued. "Return to sender. The A-6 is remaining on station. We attack right back up the river, along the base of the cliff and through the middle of this jungle hell, except we've got two companies of Marines, not one. We make this part of the valley our very own."

Again, there was a silence, broken half a minute later by the Gunny.

"He's a captain, Junior," the Gunny said as if the word captain was an expletive.

"Yes?" I asked, not understanding.

"He's coming down first and he's going to be in command of the whole operation, and you and I and the whole company, when he gets here. We don't know what he is or where he's been, but the chances that he's going to go along with 'Return to Sender' is slim and none."

"Man oh man, Junior," Sugar Daddy exclaimed. "Where oh where do you get that plan material from? "Return to Sender". Now that's classical shit. I mean classical."

"Yeah, well don't fall in love with it," the Gunny replied.

"We're doing Junior's plan," Sugar Daddy said. "It's the only damn thing that makes sense. We kicked ass coming down here and nobody thought we could do that, and now we're going to kick ass all the way back up. I like the idea of having my own valley, anyway.

"Well, what in the hell do you expect to do when Carruthers gets down here and says something else," the Gunny hissed, flicking his lit cigarette into the night beyond us.

"Junior said it all with the plan," Sugar Daddy replied, getting to his feet and shaking himself. "If the captain doesn't like it then we return him to sender."

one-hundred-eighteen

THE TWENTY-FIFTH DAY : FIRST PART

The only 25 series radio military occupational specialty in the company, not already serving one of the platoon commanders, was Hultzer. The only thing I knew about him was that he had been assigned to one of the Project Hundred Thousand privates sent in by special act of the Secretary of Defense. Piper, Hultzer's charge, could not read or write and was very likely slow in other areas, as well. The Secretary of Defense had been in trouble, back in the world, because the draft was catching too many kids from the middle class, and the Secretary had apparently gained political favor by making sure that every class of America had some skin in the game.

Hultzer tried to report in, but I was too pre-occupied with the mud, the rain, the bleeding ruin of my leech-sucked torso wounds, and the fact that Captain Carruthers, the new company commander of Kilo Company, was actually coming down the cliff face first to supply the 'relief' so sorely needed by the supposed ragtag loser company I was commanding.

I was scrunched down against the cliff behind where the Ontos sat, it's small gas engine still idling away, so the turret would move if commanded. The little deadly armored vehicle faced into the jungle toward the direction our attack had taken us through. The trail of its travel was the only part of the jumbled flora mess that was truly visible in the limited light of early dawn. The night had been long, hard and filled with misery, even though the company had taken almost no losses. I looked at the Ontos, knowing Zippo's body was still inside. As long as I didn't make any effort to go look or be present for the removal and placement of his body into a body bag I could sort of distantly make believe he was still alive.

There was little cover or camouflage to my position, shared by Fessman, Jurgens, and Sugar Daddy. They waited with me, as the lead party up on the face of the cliff moved gingerly along the indented crack switching back and forth across it, allowing for a moderately safe passage down from the top. I could see the Gunny making his way toward us. I was certain all of us were wishing the cliff face was more like the one that ran up and down the canyon along its eastern side, with a folded under lower lip allowing for complete camouflage and nearly total cover if you were squeezed well back under it.

"We're here, sir," Hultzer said, again, his voice almost a whisper.

Fessman tapped me on the shoulder to get my attention, as I stared up into the night. The rising sun would still be low enough that full dawn would not reach the bottom of the valley for some time, and even then the cliff face, positioned as it was, would be dark further up for some time.

"The new guys are here," Fessman repeated, speaking in his normal voice, no doubt concluding that the NVA were beaten down into their caves and tunnels with the coming of the light, the presence of the Ontos, and the very obvious A-6 Intruder circling overhead.

The noise of the strange looking ground support aircraft seemed aimed down into the valley. The Skyraiders would come and go in days and nights of earlier support, making runs at any enemy positions on each pass, but the A-6 stayed on station, seemingly able to angle itself around in mid-air, and then to swoop in and drop more ordnance where it felt like it. Only the helicopters were more agile, but their ability to carry sufficient amounts of ordnance was severely limited when it came to real ground support.

The first Marine to finally reach the bottom of the valley, some fifty meters from me, had to be Captain Carruthers himself. The big man didn't wear rank but his utilities were so sharply creased the knife edges could be seen, even in the low light. The man jumped down the last six feet, or so, from an angled-out chunk of hard metamorphic rock. The ground was sodden with moisture, however, and the place he'd chosen to land not covered by any of the normally thick jungle debris. His feet went into the muck with a very audible slap, and before he could move at all the rest of his legs sank all the way up to his knees.

The Gunny appeared out of a nearby bamboo stand and made it to the Captain's side at about the same time I did.

"Not the best choice of landing spots, eh?" the captain laughed out, not bothering to try to lift one foot or the other because any effort like that was obviously useless.

The Gunny grabbed under Carruthers' right armpit while I engaged the other. We slowly pushed and pulled upward. The captain's legs slowly eased from the sucking mud grasp until he was free. The semi-hard muck could be walked carefully upon but would not hold up to steadily applied pressure or the kind of impact the captain had placed upon its surface.

The Gunny guided the captain toward the covering edge of the jungle near where he'd come out of. I followed, along with an entourage that had quickly appeared from the same area of the glacis behind us. Fessman was at my side.

Before we made it to the bamboo stand the enemy guns opened up, as I feared they would.

Although the firing was not directed at us, everyone went down into the muck. The captain stopped, laying down flat. I grabbed one of his mud-covered boots and shook it to get his attention.

"Move to the bamboo stand just ahead," I said, my voice low but with power behind it. "They're firing at the rest of Kilo coming down the rock face, not us," I continued, not certain the captain was fully cognizant of the situation.

We were in defilade from most of the fire, since the enemy had re-surfaced deeper inside the main body of jungle growth. Our attack had been a success, and the NVA had taken casualties, but the main body had had plenty of warning and time to go underground until we passed by. The single most telling characteristic of any Marine attack or movement I'd been a part of since being in country was the very temporary nature of everything we did. We attacked, defended, and then moved on, or back, or sideways. We never stayed anywhere, unless it was at a rare firebase or artillery battery emplacement.

"We've got to suppress that fire," Carruthers shouted out to no one in particular. "My Marines are totally exposed on that wall."

I resigned myself to not saying anything until there was something definitive that might be said to help the situation. Kilo had been in exactly the same position a week earlier and would likely take the same kind of heavy casualties unless providence somehow provided a different result. That it was coming on to daylight and the A-6 was still providing cover gave some hope that most of the Marines would survive.

As if to illustrate Carruther's point, two Marine bodies thudded into the mud at the very bottom edge of the cliff face.

Three heavy explosions came from the interior of the jungle and the enemy fire went silent. I knew the A-6 was working the area hard and accurately.

"We've got to provide covering fire," the captain said, slithering ahead of me through the bamboo and into the open interior of the stand that was about as large as a yard entertainment trampoline back home.

I followed him into the relative cover the bamboo provided, checking everything around me for bamboo vipers. The leeches had found me once more, I knew, because of the mud, but I would deal with the ones that made it to the inside of my blouse later.

"There's no covering fire from the ground that we can apply," the Gunny informed the captain. "The jungle's dense and higher than our position. To engage the NVA in there is to fight on their turf. Our Ontos has the same problem. The jungle will simply eat up the flechettes as quickly as they might be fired. Your mistake was in coming down the wall at all."

"Quite right," the captain replied, after a short delay.

I was caught unawares by his answer. The officer had admitted he was wrong and I wasn't at all used to that.

"My first combat order and I sure as hell didn't want to disobey it," the captain went on, sounding like I'd felt when I'd violated my own first combat order seemingly so long ago.

"Is anybody going to check the bodies?" he asked, "and does anybody have a cigarette?"

"They fell a couple of hundred feet after being hit," the Gunny said, producing a cigarette that he promptly lit, and then handed over to the captain. "They're dead, all right. We're pretty much experts at gauging the living and dead without moving an inch."

"I tried to lead them down as fast as I could," the captain said, between quick puffs on the cigarette.

He didn't offer it back to the Gunny, which seemed like some sort of violation, but I couldn't put my finger or mind on why that was so.

"Who are you?" Carruthers suddenly asked, looking directly into my eyes.

I pulled up and pushed my back into a solid collection of bamboo shoots. I wore my helmet, and although the writing on it hard to read in the poor light, the single black bar was pretty evident, painted on the surface of its cover.

"Junior," I replied, knowing it was probably what he wanted to hear, rather than a formal reporting in comment.

"Thought so," Carruthers replied, finishing the cigarette. "Now that's a helmet, indeed."

Marines began making it to the bottom of the wall, the sucking sounds of their boots becoming a regular series of joining sounds. Sugar Daddy and Jurgens had arranged for them to be greeted and directed into covering positions further down the slope, I assumed.

"What are your thoughts, lieutenant?" Carruthers asked me.

"Your radio man is a few meters away," I replied. "Have him call the highest elements of the company and get them to move a whole lot faster, no matter what the risk."

"I was told that daylight would diminish the fire we might face," Carruthers said. "I was told that the NVA don't fight much during the day because of our supporting fires, and we own the night with the Starlight scopes."

"Were you told to lead the men down the wall too?" I retorted a touch of anger at having to try to train another FNG who knew nothing getting to me. "Don't ever do anything that stupid again. You don't walk the point because there's only one of you. You get killed or wounded and that's it, no officer in charge and the Starlight scope's fun but owns less than a sliver of that night you speak of."

Carruther's called out to Sharky, obviously his radio man.

"You're telling me that my assumptions are wrong, Junior?" he whispered, as the radio man crawled between a couple of the thicker bamboo shoots.

The captain's tone once again surprised me. He wasn't being a smart ass. He was truly interested, or so it seemed.

"Your assumptions are wrong, yes," I replied, trying to gauge the man. "Make the call. Our artillery support is in defilade or out of range. The face of this cliff, the one with your Marines on it, isn't beyond the range of their 120 mm guns, however."

"Damn, how low on the face do they have to be?" he asked, taking the microphone in his hand.

"About where we are," I replied. "The NVA doesn't have Willie Peter or variable time in this area, that I know of, or anything else exotic, but their HE rounds will blow chunks of rock off the face that'll be just as deadly as any shrapnel they might throw from their casings."

Carruther's made the call with urgency in his voice. My own attention was drawn away by the appearance of Hultzer and Piper, my replacement team for Zippo. Both Marines had shouldered past Fessman to grab hold of my right sleeve and get my attention with one hand each like they were indigent children in a Dickens novel.

"We've got your pack, sir," Hultzer whispered, as if there was anyone nearby to overhear that mattered. "Where do you want us to set up camp?"

Camp, I thought grimly, and then I thought of Zippo, even more grimly, and the pain went through me. I knew I wasn't feeling the full measure of his loss, but the shiver up and down my core was real and hard enough that I couldn't shrug it off.

"Get under cover and wait," I ordered, sorry that they weren't Zippo, but gently disengaging their grasping fingers instead of being more abrupt with them.

"What's the plan, Junior," Carruthers asked, "since you know the area and I don't. And, you don't mind if I call you Junior, do you?"

I was surprised again. Nobody had ever asked permission before. I gave it with a nod.

"You stay on as the company commander, and I have Kilo. We both take our orders from the colonel at battalion so you don't have to do what I say down here. The colonel's not a fan of yours so I may be able to help there. We both went to the academy."

I hadn't noticed the distinctive ring on the captain's hand, but maybe I'd missed it in the low light. The Gunny looked over at me, and I noted Nguyen just over his shoulder. Both men's dark eyes delivered the same message I was probably transmitting wordlessly to them. Carruthers seemed to be a bit of all right.

"The plan is to work our way back along the eastern lower edge of the cliff until we come to a place near the river where it indents under that edge." I said, delivering the plan to Carruthers with some trepidation.

We'd stayed in that exact location twice before, and the NVA would know that. Which meant that they might have prepared for a third visit. Raking fire by a single fifty across the beaten zone on the other side of the river could be used to drive our companies into the cleft which might be pre-mined to blow us all to hell.

"What do we do about the Marines we're losing?" Carruthers asked, turning from his position among them to attempt to peer between a couple of the bamboo stalks.

I watched the captain closely. I did not point out that 'we' were not losing Marines, he was. That his decision to obey orders was causing Marines to die had become well understood by me. The rank in the rear gave the orders down to the smallest detail if they possessed the smallest details. The job of an infantry officer leading a company in combat was to give the rear area as few details as possible. The reality at the bottom of the A Shau Valley was not a transmittable package of believable detail. Mythology ruled the belief systems of rear area officers and mythology was something not easily countered or modified.

The NVA opened up again, but this time Carruthers did not hug the muck like the rest of us. He jumped up and ran from the bamboo, motioning to his radio operator.

No one made any move to follow him. Fessman crawled inside the bamboo stand to replace him and nobody said a word about that either.

"Where's he going?" I asked the Gunny.

"He's probably going to try to get his Marines already down to fire into the jungle and suppress the NVA gunners, but then you probably already figured that out. He's not seasoned enough to know that sometimes we have to do nothing, even though it might seem we should.

I knew the Gunny was right. There was no possibility that any Marines on the floor of the valley around us could do much effectively against mid-jungle sources of fire shooting up onto the surface of the wall. I watched the captain quickly assemble a team, made up of two squads plus a few extra Marines. To my astonishment, he began using the ropes that had been laid down the slightly angled face to climb back up. I realized what he was doing, or trying to do. He would get his own gunners high enough to return fire on the NVA sources buried deeper in the bracken.

"Carruthers," I yelled, cupping my hands together over my mouth. There was no time to call him on the radio. He either had not heard what I'd told him or he hadn't believed me. The fire of the NVA machine gunners, interspersed by the sound of the A-6 making a return to the area, was suddenly drowned out completely. A thunderous blasting continuity of explosions rained down from above. The NVA had reached out to the artillery, as I'd described and feared, having watched that same battery work before. The range was registered. The battery knew the target range, which was ninety percent of the game in artillery. A barrage battered the face of the cliff. I tried to look up but the falling rock and smoking nightmare above me prevented me from seeing anything.

Thuds followed, one after another. Screams and yells permeated the air around us, no doubt caused by the fact that most of the company had been much lower than when they were first fired upon earlier. Marines were hit or knocked free, or jumped, and were landing wounded at the bottom.

In seconds it was over, except for the fading smoke and the more subdued cries of the wounded.

The A-6 dropped another load, just as the sound of Skyraiders diving low came across the surface of the triple canopy jungle behind us. Air was coming to the rescue, but it was too late for so many of the Marines, again, in Kilo Company.

We waited, glued to the mud, all of us face down inside the bamboo thicket and all around the area surrounding the outer edges of the heavier jungle growth.

Fessman whispered over to me, his face only inches from my own.

"What's the name of the plan, again?" he asked. "The captain didn't ask the name of the plan."

There was no early morning music to help me invent something good. Zippo would so have hung on every syllable of every word I might come up with, I knew. Was Carruthers among the dead? Was he wounded? The man was the first officer I'd met in country that I liked right off the bat. Tex had been good but he hadn't had the captain's intellect or personality. I looked out at the base of the cliff, fully illuminated in the morning light. Several dead Marines lay where they'd fallen, their blood mixed in with a tiny winding trail of water not big enough to be called a stream. The water wandered around and by them, before proceeding down the valley.

"Red River," I said to Fessman, after some thought. I'd originally named the move 'Return to Sender,' but meeting Carruthers and being part of what happened on Kilo's descent had changed things. Return to Sender was too smart-assed and too cool as a proper descriptor.

"Cool, like the John Wayne movie," Fessman replied.

"Yeah, like the movie," I said back, but my voice so low it wasn't likely he heard me.

A single wailing scream came cascading down the face of the cliff in the near silence, as the A-6 and the Skyraiders coordinated and went around to make a real mess of the central jungle under them.

One of the company's corpsmen slithered into the bamboo stand, although there was no room for him to lay or sit down. He didn't stop, however, simply sliding up and over both Fessman and me as he went. He pushed a package into my hand as he went by. I looked down. The light was improving. I was resupplied with morphine. Fessman looked at my hand, and then looked away.

"Someone's got to go up there after the guy who's stuck, and probably hit," the Gunny stated, flatly and quietly.

"Is it him?" I asked, knowing the Gunny, who'd stayed right with me the entire time, had no better information than I did.

"Lay here, write a letter to your wife," the Gunny said, his voice almost inaudible. "We've got to get everyone back up the valley and fly in a medivac. A big one. You have to wait, like I said. All I need is Nguyen with Fessman on the air radio."

I held the morphine in my right hand, making no effort to hide it. Everyone in the company knew I had it. There were no secrets in a unit inside a combat zone, at least not among the living.

"Tell me about Carruthers," I said, knowing Nguyen would scale the wall like a spider, with Fessman and the Gunny using the air support like an artistic team. "He called me lieutenant and then asked if he could call me Junior."

I looked at the Gunny and then over to Fessman, but they looked away like maybe I was losing it. Only Nguyen stared back at me. He blinked once, slowly, leaving me with the feeling that at least he understood. The Gunny was right. I had to wait or neither company was likely to have an officer. In seconds, they were gone, but I wasn't left alone. Hultzer and Piper crawled in and plopped down right next to me like they'd been invited, although neither looked at me. I had to wait.

"He needs a new helmet," Piper whispered to Hultzer.

one-hundred-nineteen

THE TWENTY-FIFTH DAY : SECOND PART

The red river was a rivulet of bloody water that happened to be running down the valley, back from the direction the company had to head up into. The major problem, as the Gunny pointed out, was not our movement, air support or even hauling Zippo and the bodies that had come falling down from the cliff. It was the Ontos. There was no way the company could tramp back through the same stretch of jungle again, and counter-attack on through, without taking near total casualties. The NVA might have fallen for the first frontal attack but there was no way they would be taken by surprise like that again.

"We can run the Ontos along the edge of the jungle," the Gunny noted, "although it'll be a close fit with the wall hugging the solid debris in some places, but the turret can't be rotated more than about thirty degrees if that."

"Traversed," Hultzer said, surprising both the Gunny and me.

I looked at the boy in question, with a frown. Usually enlisted ranks serving under a seasoned Gunnery Sergeant like our own spoke when spoken to and only answered questions they were asked to answer.

"Traversed," Hultzer repeated. "Turrets on tanks don't rotate, they traverse, and that Ontos turret can only traverse fifteen degrees each way."

The Gunny squatted down, took out a cigarette and cupped one hand over it in order to shield it from as much of the mist as he could, ignoring my temporary scout sergeant's comment. The rain had stopped earlier, but the mist continued, seemingly falling from wispy clouds that, back in the real world, wouldn't have had any moisture in them at all.

"And the damn thing won't have the room to use its tracks to turn either," the Gunny got out, between his first and second puffs.

Hultzer and Piper, like twins that don't look anything alike, crouched near the Gunny, as if it was he that they were the scout team for and not me. Their looks, as they watched the man smoke were the same. I realized that they were looks of adoration. I wondered how they looked when they viewed me, and I was unaware they were doing so.

"I helped operate an Ontos for a bit while at Infantry Training School in Pendleton," Hultzer offered.

I squatted down to join the Gunny, not knowing what to say about Hultzer's comments. Carruthers was trying to get Kilo organized and ready to move. My company didn't need any organization and I knew it. The Marines in my company would simply move when they had to and do whatever they had to do to support it. Somehow, they were able to get ready and move without my orders. I'd never understood how they did that and it wasn't likely, I knew, that I ever would.

After a few more puffs of his cigarette, the Gunny turned to face Hultzer, and looked at him silently, as if measuring the capability of the young Marine.

"Okay, corporal," the Gunny said, his voice low and sort of threatening. "What would you do here, since you're an Ontos driver? We've got to get the Ontos up along the base of this cliff about fifteen clicks, and we can't direct its turret in toward the jungle to protect it or us with the flechette rounds."

Hultzer leaned aside to put his lips closer to his constant partner, Piper. He tipped his helmet back to get close enough to whisper whatever he said. Piper jumped up and disappeared at a run back toward where the Ontos sat idling away behind us.

"I didn't drive, Gunny," Hultzer replied. "I was just a mechanic. There's a cotter pin for the main gear because the turret needs to be able to turn fully around in order to lubricate the ring it traverses."

"So?" the Gunny asked, his voice growing impatient.

"We pull the cotter pin, extract the gear, move the turret around left to face the jungle, and then have thirty degrees traverse sideways while the Ontos moves along right next to the brush."

Piper ran back and plopped down next to Hutzler. He moved his right hand to put something in front of Hultzer's chest.

Hultzer picked it up and showed both the Gunny and I what it held. "It's like I thought. The Ontos vehicles are all the same. I wasn't sure."

The corporal dangled a large cotter pin from his fingers.

"I'll be damned," the Gunny whispered, snapping the remains of his cigarette over toward the stone wall.

The butt struck the surface, flared and then extinguished itself down in what I'd termed the 'Red River' of a slowly moving trail of water just below it.

Moments later, under the Gunny's command and control, the Ontos was backed down from its position facing into the full body of the jungle. With Hultzer's help the turret was modified and turned, and then the Ontos began moving along the edge of the cliff face, the sides of its tracks so close that occasionally they made jarring metal rasping sounds when encountering the rock itself. With the turret manually adjusted to face into the density of the full jungle, there was room on both ends of the Ontos to carry body bags. I counted six, as the tracked vehicle made its way slowly past me. I knew Zippo was still inside, and I wondered if his dead presence bothered the driver and the machine's commander, but I said nothing to anyone about it. Fessman, Nguyen, Hultzer, and Piper moved with me, very close in proximity because the path between the canyon wall and the nearly impassible jungle body was narrow, and also because of the known fact that the Ontos could be used to dive under for cover in case of incoming fire.

Mortar rounds, small arms, and even RPG fire couldn't easily reach through the Ontos armor and kill or wound those Marines who got under it for protection. The Russian .50 caliber the NVA had used before was a different matter entirely, however. I was afraid of the .50 more than any weapon the enemy possessed. I never spoke of that fear, however, and neither did anybody else, although they had to have it.

The Skyraiders worked overhead, diving down and firing a few twenty-millimeter rounds here and there. They positioned themselves on either side of the A-6, which flew marginally lower, it's down-angled jet engines roaring over the normally jarring thunder of the Skyraiders powerful propellers. There was no incoming small arms fire, as we moved back up the valley. There was only one place of any security we might be headed unless it might be to recross the still monsoon flooded river, and that thought was ever on my mind. Would the NVA have mined the clefts? My other worry was regarding the ability of the NVA to relocate a .50 caliber close and well-positioned enough to attempt to take out the Ontos. The downside of following the Ontos closely was the simple fact that, although it might be protective offensively and defensively, it attracted fire of the heaviest kind.

Captain Carruthers appeared out of the grayness of the morning drizzle, as the air support began making turns to orbit the area for our move. His new jungle boots squished in the mud.

"I met one of your platoon sergeants," Carruthers said, the moisture condensing on his helmet cover and dripping slightly down over his face. "I don't think much of him. What's his real name, as Sugar Daddy doesn't quite fit into any table of organization I ever heard of in the Corps?"

"He's all of that," I replied, ignoring any attempt to straighten out the vagaries of Marine Corps rigidity and structure inside a battered unit inside a hot combat zone.

"Your Gunny sent part of his platoon forward to make sure the way isn't mined or anything," the captain went on. "I believe this Sugar Daddy threatened me like it was my idea to risk his men that way, but it wasn't. In truth, I didn't think of it, until the Gunny said you had encamped in that exact area twice before. Makes sense. I've got to write this sergeant up, for that and his lack of discipline, poor attire, and disrespect to an officer."

"Let me look into it," I said, trying not to sigh, as the words came out.

"I should hope so," Carruthers replied, turning in the mud with a swishing sound and making his way back to his company assembling for the move.

Sugar Daddy was angry that his men were being risked for those of Kilo, I knew. Carruthers was way too new to see or understand that the price for his and his unit's security might be considered too high a price to pay by Marines not only seasoned in combat but carrying a deep-felt knowledge that they were never going to live to go home themselves.

The Gunny came out of the brush to approach the moving Ontos in front of my small team. I sent Hultzer forward to get the Gunny's attention, and Piper ran along staying only a few feet from his caretaker. The saddest part of watching them cross the short distance was the obvious and apparent fact that Piper knew how damaged he was, and was depending on Hultzer and the rest of us to get him through. He seemed unaware that all the rest of us around him were struggling mightily just to get ourselves through the day, and then another night.

The Gunny trotted toward me, a look of question on his face. He turned upon reaching my position and walked next to me. With the mist, faint wind, the sound of the Ontos and distant roaring of the air support flying above us it was hard to hear.

"What is it?" The Gunny asked, with his tone making no secret of the fact that he had other more important things to do.

"Sugar Daddy threatened Carruthers and I want to talk to him, now."

"Can't it wait?" the Gunny asked.

"You sent Sugar Daddy's men forward to check out the cleft?" I asked.

"Seemed like a good idea," the Gunny replied. "Little chance Jurgen's Marines would really do the job."

"Good move, but Carruthers can blow this whole thing apart from the inside if we end up with Kilo company as another enemy," I said. "Like we aren't in enough trouble as it is."

"Yeah," the Gunny breathed out, after a few seconds of saying nothing.

"Send your Bobbsey Twins to get him, Junior," the Gunny said. "He's with the other half of his platoon bringing up the rear. Can't count on Kilo for nothing just yet."

Hultzer didn't need an order. He was gone with Piper before the Gunny stopped talking. We walked on in silence for a few minutes. The smell of the Ontos' puffing little General Motors engine reminded me of automobile exhaust back home, although there was no home feeling in the hunching fear I felt. I fought to remain somewhat distant from the back of the protective armored vehicle. The danger of the nearby jungle to my left was like an invisible giant spider web pressing out toward me. I knew in my bones that the first sign of incoming fire would drive me right under the rear of the Ontos, where I'd stay crawling along with it all the way to the protection of the cleft near the river.

I heard Sugar Daddy behind me before I saw him. His big heavy body, moving as fast as it could to catch up with us, didn't allow his boots to ease into and out of the muck with each step. The sound of his boots splashing down and then pulling back out couldn't have been reproduced on a movie set. I kept walking. There would be no stopping until we reached the safety of the cleft.

"What's the problem now, Junior?" Sugar Daddy said, fitting himself squarely between the Gunny and me.

"Captain Carruthers," I replied, getting right to the point. "He's in command of Kilo and we don't know Kilo. I don't need any trouble between our units while we're together. I think the captain's a good shit, so knock off the threats and obvious disrespect."

"Don't treat him no different than I treat you, Junior," Sugar Daddy replied, mildly stressing the word Junior.

I breathed deeply in and out and decided to try one more time.

"I'm not quite right, somebody said a few days back, so the comparison doesn't fit. So, I'm asking you to make an exception."

"This is the A Shau," Sugar Daddy shot back. "Ain't no rules down here."

"Gunny?" I asked. "What's the relative position of the point element headed for the cleft, do you think?"

"Probably approaching the edge of the open field of fire by now," the Gunny replied.

"Fessman," I began, but the radio microphone was already being pressed into my left hand.

"Arty net is up, with the Army 175 firebase on the line," he said.

I glanced over at the old young boy, wondering how he had guessed what I was going to want. The 175 battery was the only one that could reach out far enough to impact rounds near the river and jungle area we'd occupied before, but still, how could the young corporal have known I might need to call them?

"Fire mission," I said into the handset. "Grid one niner six eight five five six two," I read from my mind's memory. I was no longer surprised that I could not only recall all my former night defensive fire coordinates but I could not forget them either.

"Battery of four," I said into the complete silence around me, as we walked. "No spotting round and wait for my command to fire."

"What are you doing, Junior?" the Gunny asked.

"Sure you want to play it this way, Sugar Daddy?" I asked the sergeant, my voice soft and velvety, surprised that I was in a place of complete calm and control.

"He's calling in artillery on my men?" Sugar Daddy asked the Gunny, his voice breaking halfway through.

"Don't do it," the Gunny said to me. "Those Marines are assholes but they're our assholes.

"You certain you understand these will be red bag rounds," the tinny little speaker on the side of Fessman's Prick 25 radio played out. "These are plus or minus four hundred meters or more in range at this distance."

"You wouldn't," Sugar Daddy finally said, recovering himself.

I pushed the button down on the handset, raised it to my cheek and spoke.

"Fire for effect," I ordered.

"No," Sugar Daddy screamed, grabbing my left hand with the mike in it.

"I'll do it, whatever you want."

"Check fire, check fire, check fire," I said hurriedly into the microphone, and then waited nervously while trying not to look like I was nervous at all.

"Check fire confirmed," came through the speaker. "No rounds expended. Standing by."

The march along the edge of the jungle went without incident and Sugar Daddy's Marines welcomed the remainder of the two companies as if they were to be honored for their bravery in taking the point. The Gunny moved to compliment and reward the men while my scout team helped me to get inside the same cleft I'd left in a time that seemed so long ago.

Carruthers was battered, beaten and wet to the bone when he brushed aside the poncho-cover Piper had carefully and uselessly draped over the opening to my slice of cleft dug under the edge of the stone face. The valley wall went straight up, and it made no sense that the cleft should even exist except for the strange nature of the soft but long-wearing stone it was composed of. Bullets and explosives were absorbed when they struck, as opposed to the cliff face Carruthers and Kilo company had come down. The poncho cover gave me a degree of privacy but privacy wasn't something I prized at all with the Marines I was supposed to be commanding. There were no secrets to be revealed, and no place to run away from the awful and brutal life and death struggle we all faced all the time together.

The big man bent down to move closer but upon getting closer collapsed to the hard and rough surface of the stone floor.

I made no move from my prone position to help him. The Gunny had been right, although his timing had been off. I was going to write a letter home to my wife, but I hadn't started it out in the open. I had waited until I could be under cover. The incessant rain, drip, and mist a few meters away were almost impossible to write anything in or on unless using a grease pencil on plastic. The black government-issue pens would lay ink down under almost any circumstance, even running water, but the paper to be written on wasn't nearly so tough or flexible. I made no move because I knew what the captain was going through. It was written all over his shaking shoulders and the expression that had to be on his face I couldn't see because he kept his head bowed down.

"How did you know?" he asked, finally, his voice small and lost.

"I told you, sir," I replied, keeping all sympathy from my voice, "I've been hit by that same battery in that same place before." I looked away from Carruthers to avoid eye contact. He was going to have to patch himself together and I couldn't be his therapist to provide some form of motherly or fatherly advice and assistance. There was no time, and the things I might tell him would only potentially risk my own position or even my credibility. I commanded my company or was supposed to, and he commanded Kilo. We were not companies commanded together. He was an officer FNG and I was not, and I could not maintain his company close in and personal as the Gunny had done with me. The captain had his own Gunny, although I knew nothing of the man.

"No, I mean the Montagnard you sent up the wall," Carruthers got out, surprising me.

I remained silent, but the captain had my full attention. My relationship with Nguyen was special and I knew it. It was also based upon secrecy and I wanted to maintain that.

When I didn't say anything for more than a full minute, the captain went on.

"He came up that face like a spider, freed one of my sergeants from his climbing rope, and then got everybody off that nightmare cliff without losing a soul. And he never said a word. The man's a genius. How did you know to send him?"

I didn't want to admit that Nguyen had been the Gunny's idea, and that idea had come to him because he knew I was contemplating going up the glacis myself to try to rescue what Marines I could.

"Did you call in a medivac, sir?" I asked but didn't wait for Carruthers to respond. "What about a list for re-supply? Replacements? And do you have a company clerk in your outfit that can handle some of the load?"

I peppered the captain with questions. Mission orientation, awareness and then working the objectives to accomplish that mission, I knew, was better than any kind of sympathetic counseling I could provide about the fact that the captain was in the A Shau Valley to live and most probably die, and as long as he stayed alive as a company commander, was going to bleed dead Marines like blood pumping from a major artery.

"We're supposed to move back north toward the Rock Pile, eventually," the captain said, raising his head to look me in the eyes for the first time.

I noted that although he'd answered none of my questions, he wasn't giving the appearance of being a helpless wounded dog anymore. I would like to have told him to 'be a Marine and suck it up', but I'd already realized that I didn't really know what it was like to be a real Marine and there was no sucking it up in the A Shau. There was only remaining low, moving as much and as fast as possible, and finally, avoiding being killed by the enemy or my own men. Avoiding that required a bit of avoiding the enemy and my own men on a regular basis.

I got to my feet, carefully folding my unfinished letter into the Iwo Jima envelope I'd send it in later. I carefully removed my utility top, pulling it over my head rather than unbuttoning all the front buttons.

"Would you mind, sir?" I asked Carruthers, turning to show him my back, while at the same time bending slightly so I could disengage my mosquito repellant from the rubber band holding it to the side of my helmet.

A direct shot of gasoline (not ignited) worked the best to instantly dislodge the leeches stuck to my torso in the places I couldn't reach. A hot match head was second best, but the repellant, if applied liberally, and sometimes more than once, also worked, and we didn't have the two other fixes, anyway.

"Oh, the leeches," Carruthers commented, his voice filled with revulsion.

Then he took the plastic bottle and went to work. "I haven't had any of the painful things get on me yet."

I said nothing. The captain had come through the same mud and jungle I'd traversed to get from the bottom of the glacis to the cover of the cleft we were in now. He had leeches, but he didn't know it. The leeches emitted a deadening solution as they bit into human skin. The captain was accurate in expressing his belief that he had no pain from the leeches. You had to feel for the effect of their weight tugging at the skin. There was no pain. It was a subtle thing that took a while to catch on to. I knew that if Carruthers lived long enough he'd come to be very aware of the symptoms, but there was no point in letting him know that in our current position and situation. The first leeches caused an emotional upset in anyone who dealt with them. I didn't need the captain winging out, just yet, anyway.

"We're going to get hit, probably tonight some time, sir," I said.

"They'll probably have their .50 caliber back, along with a load of B-40s. The resupply and medivac are going to come in a couple of hours from now and the 46 is going to play hell getting in and out of here unless we have suppressing fire and air support orbiting all over the place. Get some sleep and let the Gunny organize the defensive fires."

"How come we have so many dead," Carruthers asked. "I've heard the wounded far outnumber the dead in this war."

"This is the A Shau, and it's not in this war, sir," I replied. "This is a whole different war down here."

"Where do I go now?" the captain asked, and I caught a note of 'little boy lost' in his tone.

"Right here, with me, captain," I said. "This is officer country as long as we're here. Fessman and my scout team are right outside. Where's your RTO?"

"My RTO is in a bag on that Ontos out there. What about that black sergeant?" Carruthers said, settling down into a sitting position on the edge of my poncho liner.

I realized the captain wasn't lost, he was in shock. He'd led his unit down a dangerous cliff and then gone back up to save survivors. He'd lost his radio operator and some others in the effort, and he'd done it all without running or showing any fear at all. He was a real Marine officer and I knew that from that moment I would never call him anything but sir.

"Sugar Daddy has rethought his comments and attitude, sir," I replied. "I think you'll be very pleased."

THE TWENTY-FIFTH DAY : THIRD PART

My small cleft was filled with Marines by the time the day moved into late afternoon. I'd finished my letter home, once again extolling the virtues of the local fauna and flora and how the nearly continuous monsoon mist was such a relief from the harsh pounding of the seasonal heavy rain. I left the leeches, foot problems, rotting uniform, and continuous fatigue out of my correspondence. When I finally met my fate in the A Shau Valley, my wife and any later interested parties might wonder how such a mortal tragedy came to be when I'd been traveling through such a scenic and life-filled valley.

The choice to dig in where we were was made by the Gunny. He didn't even ask my permission or choose to inform me that the Marines were going to make an attempt to stay right where we were for an undetermined time. That news only came to me when I arose from the first real sleep I'd had since I could remember. The mosquitos had eaten me, the leech wounds had bled and there would be more scars. But I'd slept a few hours and I had not dreamt of anything or anywhere. There was no dreaming of any place other than the hell I was in, and I accepted that, but I also welcomed the fact that I didn't dream of the valley, or even worse atrocities than those I had, and was, already experiencing.

Carruthers had returned to my cleft shelter when the sun was almost down. There he'd encountered first Fessman and then Nguyen, both of whom did not want me aroused from sleep. It hadn't mattered to Carruthers and, short of violence, there was no way that either Fessman nor Nguyen could stop him.

"What is it?" I asked, trying to find my helmet, that I knew Fessman or one of them would have half-filled with water from somewhere. I had to shave and I had to wash my face, armpits and then the wounds left by the leeches on my torso.

"It's like I'm dead here, already," Carruthers said, settling down to sit on the edge of my poncho liner. I bent down, having found the nearly invisible helmet inside the darkened cleft. I washed my face first, then swung my head up and shrugged off the fresh water. It felt wonderful. I didn't need or want a towel.

"They don't listen to me about anything," Carruthers went on. "They're digging in like we're staying here, but our orders are to immediately head up the valley to connect with other units coming down the valley."

"They're dead," I said, getting my little Gillette razor out, screwing open the base, and positioning a two-sided blade into the revealed opening. The razor blades were good for two or maybe three shaves, not like back home where I could get four or five.

"Who's dead?" Carruthers asked.

I shaved away, without a mirror or any other aid. I didn't care about growing a beard. Shaving made me feel somewhat clean, so I did it every chance I got.

"The battalion coming down the valley had to pass by Hill 975," I replied. "Hill 975 is rifled through with tunnels and caves. It's also a resupply center for the whole complex of trails that run up and down this valley. The NVA troops there were unprepared for us, even though we hit them twice. The third time around, that being when the relief battalion passed by, would have been it. They got hit and what remnants there probably are, will be evacuated out. Listen to the combat net or ask Fessman, my radio operator."

"Hell, you've been asleep, they told me," Carruthers exclaimed. "How in hell would you know?"

"I live here," I said, washing the lather and whiskers from my face. "I just know. If you live down here long enough then you'll know too."

"So, you gave the order to dig in because we can't go back and we can't go up the valley either?" Carruthers asked.

"Well, sort of," I replied, using the C-rations tiny soap bar to work away at my leech wounds.

It was the night coming. I could feel it. The night was the enemy. We had the Starlight Scope, Zippo's scope, but it was so limited in what it could see that the night belonged to the NVA, and what little we could see was easily blinded by the flares they used, tracers or any other light source, including artillery illumination. The light we got in the night or the night we could see through was all but useless.

We had the Ontos and flechette rounds. We had the never-failing M-60 machine guns with replaceable barrels. We had the Browning thirty caliber on top of the Ontos which was irreplaceable when we could get enough 30-caliber ammunition. The M-60s fired 7.62mm

NATO rounds, which was a bit smaller and a bit less powerful than the 30-06 rounds of the Browning.

The fight into the dark was intense. Air had gone home, the A-6 having used up all its ordnance and the propeller jobs running low on fuel. The transition between coming night and the daylight hours was nothing more or less than a building tempo of what might be expected when full dark came along.

The .50 caliber Russian rounds chewed up the berm on both sides of our position. The rounds were useless when they were absorbed into the strange soft rock of the metamorphic rock of the cliff face, but before they encountered that rock surface they could play havoc penetrating the entire earthen berm we depended upon for protection against the NVA onslaught. The enemy wasn't stupid enough to attempt a frontal assault again. Not against the potential firepower of the M-60s and Ontos together. The company's 60 mm mortars had been out of ammunition for some time, nothing provided by the 'inspection tour' resupply of a few nights before. Kilo Company had brought 81 mm mortars down the face of the cliff but their ammunition supply was exhausted, as well. Everything depended upon the resupply choppers coming in first thing in the morning, but getting to that time of first thing in the morning was going to play hell on the survival of our joined companies.

The early night threat wasn't normal. I had kind of expected that after the Gunny had reported terrific amounts of non-combat seeming movement in the jungle. The jungle that we'd just gone through, shooting and killing so many, and the same jungle we'd skirted once again to arrive back where we had started days before.

Daylight air strikes were impressive and there had been many of them, but in my heart of hearts, I knew that caves and tunnels dug more than thirty feet down into the muddy jungle surface would remain unaffected by the bombing, napalm and more. The movements reported to the Gunny meant that our semi-fortified position was going to be hit in the night, and hit hard. The NVA had not had the time or the ordnance to mine the clefts along the bottom of the canyon wall. But that didn't mean they'd left the area open for repossession on our part. It might mean that they'd registered every square foot of the defensive position to fire B-40 rockets, and fire what .50 caliber bullets they'd caged together straight into our position.

The green .50 tracers had started crisscrossing the air above our position prior to dusk. It didn't have to be dark to see the screaming beer-can size tracers lace themselves from one end of our extended line position to the other. Every Marine, except possibly the newest ones, knew that the rounds weren't intended to hit anyone. They were intended to let us know what was coming in the night. Air support was winding down or gone altogether, and the enemy knew that. There was no artillery that could reasonably reach them without causing as many deaths of Marines as it might of the NVA. Whatever was going to happen between the enemy and the Marines was going to happen one on one, unit on unit, and Marine on NVA soldier. The advantage was to the force that was larger, better armed and with more staying capability through the night. My Marines and those of Carruthers were equipped and supplied through the night, but would it be enough? The supply coming in, along with the evacuation of dead bodies loaded aboard the empty chopper, would be extra, but would that be enough? The NVA .50 had plenty of ammunition or they wouldn't be wasting it by setting up some sort of attitude fire, I knew.

Even with the Ontos, how were we supposed to provide covering fire for the CH-46 on the way? The NVA feared the little beast but it would only take one stitching into the side of the chopper by the .50 to destroy the aircraft and the company's chance for survival.

Normal, machine gun, M-72 or even mortar fire wasn't going to work, I realized. There was only one weapon I had at my disposal that might work, at least for the time we might need to get the chopper in, unload the supplies and get the dead Marines aboard, and then out of there. It was a dangerous weapon but the cliff provided the clefts that should protect them, under the cut in edge near the ground.

Captain Carruthers left without saying anything further. I sent Hultzer and Piper off to find the Gunny, and also to get my letter home to Jurgens so he could get it aboard one of the choppers. If my plan was to work then timing would be everything, not just with the air-dales coming in but with the Marines in both companies. Unless everyone got under complete cover then there were going to be heavy casualties on our side. The enemy could remain dug in, although their ability to direct any fire on the choppers would be severely limited during the entirety of the defensive display.

The Gunny was back from wherever he'd gone in minutes, Hultzer and Piper trailing behind his radioman like sheep following a shepherd.

"More of your plan, I presume," the Gunny said, squatting down and lighting a chunk of the composition B. I didn't reply, instead unlimbering my own canteen holder.

The Gunny had coffee and I wasn't going to be left out if I could help it.

"They're not serious yet," the Gunny said, pouring water from his canteen into his own canteen holder, and then into mine. The coffee came next, the small packets pungent to the nose when first opened. The Gunny had plenty of the precious artificial cream packets, as well, but no sugar. Sugar, outside of morphine, and flechette rounds for the Ontos was the most precious commodity in the company.

"They'll be in place, waiting for the chopper," he said, stirring his liquid mix with his big K-Bar knife.

"Our air's gone home, but the chopper will come in with covering Cobras," I replied, knowing the Gunny already knew all about what I was saying. "I can use a zone fire arrangement and burn up the 175 supply at the firebase. Zone will give us almost sixty rounds, at two hundred pounds each, in an "X" formation all over the bottom of this part of the valley. All we have to do is hole up under the edge of the cliff where we're already digging in."

"Red bag rounds can be four hundred or more meters off," the Gunny said, sipping some of his coffee while I mixed and heated my own.

"Yes," I replied, continuing my work.

"That's it?" The Gunny asked.

I didn't answer, taking my time stirring my canteen holder over the Gunny's small but very hot flame.

"Oh, I get it," the Gunny finally said. "The NVA know about red bag shots. They know where the batteries are. They'll know that we don't have a clue about where the rounds will land, and neither will they."

"Likely," I answered.

"The air guys are not going to want to fly under that shit," the Gunny finally said. "Great idea though."

"True," I replied but saying no more.

The seconds went by, while I drank my coffee and waited.

"You're not going to tell them," the Gunny finally said, his voice low, almost a whisper. "It's an Army battery. They'll be up on the arty net but not the Marine combat net. They won't know about the barrage until they're flying through it."

"Likely," I repeated, beginning to feel as if I was sounding a bit stupid.

"Son of a bitch," the Gunny said, setting his coffee down. "It's pure genius, except for the fact that if the pilots and crews figure it out they won't ever come back to us for the rest of the war."

"That eventuality would take place tomorrow," I replied, knowing I could have said 'yes' or 'likely' again and the Gunny would have gotten the same message but wanting to make sure.

"You're looking for my approval," the Gunny said, after several minutes, finishing his coffee and lighting up a cigarette.

I said nothing. Back in the real world, the world of training and Marine discipline and barracks and marching grinders I wouldn't have needed the Gunny's approval for anything, but down in the A Shau, with the enemy not only out beyond our line of fire but within it, as well, I needed his approval for just about everything. I also knew that part of my talent was to know that, and then get that approval.

"That's the whole plan?" the Gunny asked.

I continued to sip my coffee. The Gunny didn't offer his cigarette, which I'd been hoping he'd do. I didn't care about the cigarette itself, but his willingness to share it made me feel special in his regard, and I knew it always came with unspoken approval. There was nothing in any training I'd received that had taught about needing or wanting the support of a non-com Gunnery Sergeant. They were supposed to provide that free of charge as part of the game. But I wasn't in the real world, and it was certainly no game. I was in the A Shau Valley and the reality of the A Shau was its very own thing.

"The choppers come in and you call the fire mission," the Gunny said, blowing smoke out, ignoring the ever-present mist. "The choppers fly through a possible world of hurt, with rounds exploding all over around them, maybe even hitting one or more of them in the air."

I nodded, very curtly, not looking at him. A strike of descending artillery round into something as small and moving like a helicopter was extremely unlikely, but the chance was still there.

"They dump their loads, our guys throw the Marine bodies aboard, and the choppers are out of there...or the air and ground Marines all die where they are from stray rounds going off too close." The Gunny lit a second cigarette, from the remains of the dying first one.

I'd never seen him do that before. When the cigarette was burning he tossed the first butt aside and then held out the second one toward me.

"I knew there was something about you," he said, very quietly. "You're playing for all the chips. Again. If the chopper gets hit, it'll be gone, along with our guys below and waiting. But we'll be safe and waiting in our cleft pockets until the NVA come back, and then the only target they'll have is us, and we'll be down in forces without sufficient supplies. If the chopper makes it then we're resupplied and fully reinforced. What do we have to cover the bet?"

"The Ontos," I replied, handing his cigarette back.

"When the barrage is over, we fire all the flechette rounds we have left, slowly, one after another until they're gone. That's our fallback position and cover for getting the supplies back here if the choppers were able to offload them and the guys capable of getting them back in short order. The rounds won't do that much damage but it's vital that we redirect the enemy's full attention back to us and not to the Marines humping the stuff back. If the resupply works then we have more flechettes to go on."

"That's if no round hits a chopper," the Gunny replied, snapping away the second cigarette butt.

I got up and tried to stretch, feeling the cracking of scabs trying to form over my leech wounds. The chopper being hit or not hit didn't really matter. It might have mattered earlier in my tour but now I accepted the fact fully that I had to fight to stay alive in the instant I was in. The future had to present its own options. I could only play the cards as they were dealt, and that thought made me sigh and frown at the same time. I was constantly reducing the combat back into a board game, but if the A Shau was to be compared to a board game then it had to be Monopoly, except the board had no names on any of the properties and the price for each piece of real estate was always paid in life and blood, not phony play money.

I slipped back inside my cleft, hoping that nobody would find me before the trouble began. Whatever rest I could find would be inside the cleft. Fessman eased in behind me, and I was glad to once again feel his silent presence. A shot of emotion stiffened me briefly, as I lay down, but I quickly shifted my mind away from the fact that Zippo wasn't there too. I looked over at Nguyen's shiny black eyes, visible like a cat's in the low light. I wasn't alone. I wondered if he felt the same. The Montagnard was as silent, since the passing of Stevens so long ago, as he was mysterious and supportive of me. I had no real idea why, although my thoughts about that never ended.

Carruthers came crashing in, tossing the poncho cover aside, pushing past Fessman. He was forced to his knees by the descending rock roof of the cleft. Nguyen seemed to disappear at the captain's dramatic entrance, although there didn't seem to be enough space for him to disappear in.

"Zone fire with the 175s right down on our own position? Are you crazy?" he yelled. "Those things will tear us apart, even under here."

"They're artillery rounds, captain," I explained, keeping my voice flat and educational, "they're not magical weapons or instruments of ultimate power. The rounds impacting will weigh about two hundred pounds, of which only forty pounds or so in each is composed of explosives. Nothing as marginally powerful as they are can reach us under here, because the one-seventy-five's lack a concrete piercing fuse."

"I knew that," Carruthers said, after a slight delay, rubbing his forehead with his right hand inside the nearly dark cleft.

"Yes sir," I replied, knowing he would not be able to see the slight smile creasing my lips.

"Do you want to be here under the cliff or go on the reinforced patrol to pick up the supplies, sir?" I asked, wishing I had one of the Gunny's cigarettes.

"Who's leading the patrol?" He replied, giving me the answer, I expected.

If he was going with the Marines to intercept the choppers he, the ranking officer of both companies, would be leading the patrol, and he would have stated that.

"Jurgens, one of our platoon commanders," I said, after giving him plenty of time, "unless the Gunny or I decide to lead. The problem with that is, of course, that each platoon responds in the dark better to its own."

"They're our Marines, however, one and all," Carruthers replied.

I inhaled deeply, and then let out one long breath before responding. "I think it might be more accurate to say that we are their Marines, sir."

one-hundred-twenty-one

Captain Carruthers settled into one side of my cleft, which wasn't really wide enough to have two sides, but he wedged himself in anyway. There were clefts like my own up and down under the folded rock and he could, with his rank, have stayed in any one of them, but I understood. He wanted to be alone and somewhere else on the planet. Anywhere else on the planet. But he was in the A Shau, and death was lurking everywhere, with living bodies falling to become dead ones all the time. Captain Carruthers didn't want to be alone, and he wasn't alone inside my cleft. I was wedged deep, where the rock roof slanted down into the dry river sand. Fessman was pushed inside the opening just above me, while Nguyen lay next to him. Piper and his charge, the remainder of my scout team, were half exposed to the outside, just inside the outer lip of the opening. Sardines could not have been fit closer inside one of those roll key cans they came in than we were, and that's only when we could get a can in a care package, which was almost never.

"When's resupply coming in?" Carruthers asked, working to drop his pack and get into it with almost no maneuvering room.

"Fessman will alert us when its five minutes out, sir," I replied.

"You call the fire mission in at that point?" Carruthers continued.

I didn't really want to engage in a conversation with regard to what I was about to do but saw no point in alienating the man further. I just wanted to write another letter home about the wonders of the river sand, the beauty of the metamorphic rock, and how it all had come to form the wonder of the A Shau Valley.

"Timing is everything on this one," I said, speaking slowly, working out the plan once more in my own head, as I delivered it to him. "It'll take the choppers about ten minutes, or a bit less, to drop their loads. It'll take another ten to get the stuff from the exposed landing zone to near where we are undercover. That's almost twenty minutes wherein the NVA have to be kept down. The zone fire will cover about half of that, and I'm depending on the remaining Ontos flechette ammunition to hold them for the second ten. The Cobras will not stay on station after that and they have no night vision capability that might help for air to ground operations. After that, we've got the M-60s, M-79s, sixteens, and grenades. That's the plan. If the barrage starts early then the choppers will wave off because of encountering a hot L.Z."

"So," Carruthers replied, stopping his actions in getting whatever he was trying to get out of his pack, "As the ranking officer between our companies, I'll likely be held responsible if you 'accidentally' shoot our own helicopters down."

"There's no such thing as a 'ranking officer between companies' down here, or anywhere else in the military," I responded, shaking my head in the near dark at the bottom of our cave.

I sighed deeply in frustration, but I understood what he was saying. He was still worried about combat in the A Shau might have on his career after we got back home.

"You haven't gotten it yet," I grated out. "That's why you have the nickname you do. The Marines give you a nickname to fit, and they're pretty good at it."

"They call you Junior," Carruthers shot back. "How's that accurate in any way? Seems to me like 'Little Attila, or Count Dracula' might fit better, and what is my nickname. I didn't even know I had one?"

"They call me Junior because that's what I was," I replied. "I was a kid. I didn't know anything but I thought I did, just like a teenager. So, they named me Junior, and it stuck."

"You shouldn't let them call you that," Carruthers said, althoughthe tone of his voice was more sympathetic than anything else.

"A lot of dead Marine officers have told me that," I said, the words coming out fast and hard, but my voice so low that I hoped the others wouldn't hear.

The cleft fell into a dark silence until I got Jurgen's flashlight out and turned it on. I quickly muffled the bright light with my other hand. What I really wanted was a pinch of Composition B to make some coffee but the stuff burned so hot that it would eat all the air we had.

"What's my nickname," Carruthers asked, going back to rummaging in his pack now that there was some limited light.

"Captain Crud," I said, wanting to smile but somehow not being able to.

His comments about Attila and Dracula had hurt, even though I knew he probably meant them as funny. The fire mission weighed upon me, and I wondered briefly about what or who I was willing to sacrifice to save my own life.

"What?" Carruthers said, stopping dead in his rummaging. "How in hell does that fit me? Crud. I'm the last thing from being cruddy," he argued.

"You can't complain about a nickname or you just burn it in," I replied. "When I saw you scale down that cliff wall the Marines around me saw the same thing. You looked like Boy Wonder on a scout outing in your starched and pressed utility uniform. Down below, we were just a mass of dirt-encrusted urchins compared to you. Hence the name."

"Yeah, but how am I supposed to let them call me that to my face?" Carruthers complained.

"That's up to you," I said. "An old movie called Hondo had it down about that. John Wayne said to another guy who was threatening his dog, which was really a wolf: 'A man's got to do what he thinks is best.'"

"I don't like it," Carruthers continued, but I physically turned to face the bottom crease of the wall next to me.

I pulled out some damp folded stationery and muffled the light so I could write home again. I doubted the Marines would call Carruthers 'Captain Crud' to his face. There was quite a distance between how they felt and regarded second lieutenants compared to captains. Whatever they did, however, it wasn't going to be my problem unless, or until, Carruthers got himself killed.

"I don't much care for it either, sir," I replied offhandedly, trying to concentrate on the letter I was writing.

"Why don't you ask them to stop calling you Junior, then?" Carruthers continued.

"I meant that I don't much like your nickname, I'm okay with mine, sir," I replied, trying to ignore the man.

The weight of the fire mission was crushing down on me. I didn't want to call it in, then wait, tucked deep into my hiding hole, while the air guys flying in to help us took the very real chance of being blown right out of the air because of what I ordered. I wished that I could have gone on the patrol to get the supplies with Jurgens, but I knew that would have been a bad decision. I had to survive to command the unit and the Gunny had to survive with me. I wondered where he was holed up, waiting like the rest of us. Any second Fessman was going to announce that the choppers were dropping and hand me the arty net handset. Meanwhile, I had to listen to the captain being concerned about his future career and how awful his nickname was. The man had taken fire coming down the face of that cliff with his men, so he wasn't exactly an FNG, but still, I felt resentment.

"I'm sorry," Carruthers whispered to me, leaning over until he was no more than a few inches from me. "I'm sorry. I can't stop talking. I've never received artillery before. Will we make it in here? I think I'd rather be out there. I don't like small spaces."

I stopped writing, slowly folded my uncompleted letter up, and place it and my pen back into my thigh pocket. I was reminded of my other thigh pocket, the one with my resupplied morphine. I hadn't had to administer any of that for many days and nights, but the thought disturbed me even more than the fact that Captain Carruthers seemed to be coming apart at the seams right beside me. I turned over to confront him, our faces only inches apart.

"What you're going to do, sir is exactly what I tell you," I said, very low and quietly, but also as forcefully as I could.

There was no way I could let Carruthers come apart inside the small cleft we were all trapped in. Not under the circumstances.

"You can talk all you want, but you're not going anywhere until this is over or you'll risk the lives of everyone here getting out, and then you'll likely be blown apart out there and I'll have to explain that."

"I outrank you, lieutenant." Carruthers hissed back, which made me feel better.

He was showing anger and spine. There might be hope in getting through the mess we were all in after all.

I didn't answer, instead I reached down with my right hand, unsnapping my holster, putting my hand on the butt of my .45 and clicking the safety off. Any murmuring sound from the others in the cleft stopped. There was no missing the sound of that distinctive click. I laid next to the captain, our eyes visible to one another because of the flashlight I'd left on next to my left side.

"Jesus," Carruthers finally breathed out. "Is that it, down here in this horrid valley? Everything is about death, dismemberment or the threat of either or both."

I wanted to say sorry to the man, but I couldn't bring myself to do it. I wasn't kidding and he had to know that, just as I had to reinforce myself to know that. I liked the man, as I had some of the officers that had come before him, but I'd sacrifice him as quickly and harshly as I was about to possibly sacrifice some helicopter personnel. The company lived or the company died, and a whole lot of that responsibility for that had fallen on my shoulders, with almost none of it being the kind that I was trained to expect or be able to handle.

The captain had made no move for his own weapon and, other than venting some emotion of exasperation about the conditions we were in, hadn't come totally unglued, as I'd feared. I clicked the safety back on just as Fessman said the words "fire mission," and pushed the handset down into my left shoulder.

I called in the mission with a good bit of fear and trepidation. The Army firebase had been around for a while, and they weren't dummies running it at the battery's fire direction center, which meant they kept a pretty good record of what was going on in their fields of fire. They accepted the previously planned and prepared zone fire mission I activated without comment. If they knew about the choppers landing further up the valley they weren't saying anything, and they weren't checking the fire, which is what I feared most. Without the artillery barrage bombarding the general region, the resupply and pick up of our dead was doomed to costly failure. Under a barrage of that magnitude nobody in their right mind, no matter how courageous, moved through the area working to deliver small arms fire. That included the NVA soldiers. The air above us was about to be filled with chunks of hot metal screaming through the jungle, and every open area, at twenty-two thousand feet per second.

"The 46 is down," Fessman said, obviously switching his radio frequency quickly from the arty to the combat net as quickly as he could.

I breathed in and out deeply. The choppers had to be down. If they weren't down they wouldn't land because of the exploding artillery below. If the rounds impacting weren't too close, they'd stay down rather than risk getting hit by one flying through the air. If the rounds came too close they'd risk it and lift off. If they lifted off then we lost the supplies and our Marine brethren would never make it back home. I had no control over how the red bag 175s would spread themselves throughout the southern valley area we were inside. The mission was over for us waiting in our clefts even before the words "shot over," came through Fessman's tinny PRICK 25 speaker. Only the results of that mission would come in over time.

I scrunched myself into a ball and huddled against the hard rock surface to my front. I waited for the 'splash' alert. When it came, I held my breath through the five seconds, counting them off, before the first giant explosions would take place. I waited. It took a bit longer. The explosive concussions had to travel at the speed of sound to get to our cleft. But when they came they came with withering blasts of compressed air, from nearby shock waves, and then cindered rock chunks and dust shaken from the roof of our small hideaway. I rolled a bit and the flashlight ominously went out. The explosions and the shocks from them continued to reverberate, closer and then further away. I feared for Piper up near the lip of the cleft opening because the shock waves seemed so strong, even way down near the bottom of the cleft where I huddled.

Nothing was said throughout the barrage. Time stopped, punctuated only with the time indicators of more explosions going off. I knew the firebase was firing just about all the inventory it had. If one of those rounds hit one of the choppers then I would never recover, even if I lived. I would never be forgiven by the battery or the air elements supporting us, or by myself. I wanted a drink of water, and to wash the awful dust from my face, but there was no way I was going to unclench my body. I'd become a rounded knot of wood, the tension so tight that when I tried to unclench one of my hands it wouldn't do anything. I realized I was breathing, but very gently. I tried to breathe harder and succeeded. I concentrated on my breathing.

And then it was over. No more sounds came in through the opening of the cleft. I won control of my body functions again. I unclenched my midsection, turned onto my stomach, and began to crawl up past Fessman.

"Butcher's bill?" I asked as I passed. Fessman knew the phrase, as I'd used it before. I was a fan of old sailing novels about the British Navy in the seventeen hundreds.

Butcher's bill was the term the nautical crews had used for those killed or wounded in a combat action at sea.

"Nothing yet, sir," Fessman whispered back, his voice so low I could barely hear him. I realized it wasn't him. The concussion waves had penetrated all the way into the cleft, and my hearing was damaged. I knew I wouldn't have to ask Fessman again, either. He'd keep his ear stuck to the radio until he knew what had happened, and then get the information to me as fast as he could.

I reached the lip of the cleft. Nobody was visibly hurt that I could tell, although with my hearing not quite right I had to depend on my eyes. Darkness wasn't quite over the battlefield when I looked out.

"Jesus Christ, that was something," a voice, filled with awe, came from behind me.

I turned my head and was immediately impressed. It was Carruthers.

"My first artillery barrage," Carruthers said.

The man had just gone through a brutal barrage that could have easily killed us all if a round had landed too close to the lip of the cleft, and the captain wasn't in the least bit afraid. He was like he'd been coming down the cliff. I was afraid, although my hands no longer shook when that happened. I didn't feel the less for being afraid, and I felt glad to have the captain at my side.

"What now?" Carruthers asked.

"The Ontos," I replied, glancing back at Fessman, who gave me just a brief shake of his head. Nothing yet, that meant.

I crawled out of the cleft and was moving toward the berm that heaped up between the cleft opening the flat muddy stretch that ran out from it to arrive at the always flooded and rushing waters of the Bong Song river. I was immediately grabbed roughly and pulled to the side.

"Fire in the hole, Junior," the Gunny's hot breath and fierce hiss beat into my deadened right ear.

I rolled with the Gunny, hoping the captain hadn't followed me all the way out. There was no warning when the Ontos, sitting just on the other side of the berm, let off a 106 mm round. The whoosh penetrated my already damaged eardrums and I felt the hot fiery blast of the back-blast blow by me on the left. I'd been about to crawl right into that killing blast when the Gunny had come along and saved me again.

The Gunny didn't stay. I was alone on my stomach trying to recover my wits until Nguyen pulled me close to his side, his left arm wound around my right.

"Back," he said, although I wasn't quite certain I was hearing the word right.

I shuffled backward and down from the berm. I'd never gotten close enough to the Ontos to see it but my presence was obviously not needed. The Ontos was firing as had been planned. I had no idea how many rounds we had but whatever it was the limited supply would have to do.

With Nguyen's help, I made it back into the cleft. Carruthers lay on the inner edge, looking out, impressing me again. He'd had the good sense to remain inside. I'd only gone out to make sure the Ontos did its job. There was no need for any command presence inside the torn jungle, where it was fast becoming night.

I moved downward back into the cleft, hoping my flashlight was where I'd left it. Trying to find the damn thing in the very bottom of the wedge that formed the pinched off end of the cleft might be difficult since the light was almost gone.

Fessman caught me by my left shoulder, as I tried to get by, just as the Gunny came sliding in along my other side.

"The 46 got hit," Fessman said.

My breath jerked inward. The CH 46? The big loaded supply chopper? With it gone, that meant we'd taken terrible losses, including the supplies.

"Not by artillery," the Gunny said, speaking into my right ear, so close I could feel his breath. "They lost the hydraulics to small arms, or whatever. They pulled out of the landing zone and pickled their load, but we didn't get our Marines out. They said they'd be back in the morning to pick up the bodies and the rest of their crew. The skipper said they'd come in force, whatever the hell that means."

I could breathe again. But one thing he'd said caught my full attention.

"Their crew?" I asked, "what crew?"

"They lost their hydraulics, sir," Fessman started, but was interrupted by the Gunny.

"They couldn't lift much at all, so they left the crew, except for the pilot and his XO."

"How many?" I asked, wondering what the hell we were supposed to do with men who were only used to flying aircraft and fighting from the air. The ground was another war entirely. "And, what rank?"

All I needed was another captain who wasn't a captain at all, like the one I had already. I looked behind me to make sure Carruthers was there, however, and felt better in seeing him waiting patiently to get down deeper into the cleft past our blocking bodies.

The Ontos fired again, its blasting hot air blowing directly into the opening to the cleft. Dust and jungle debris blew around the inside. Suddenly, I was hoping the little-armored vehicle wasn't carrying as many rounds as I'd thought earlier. But it was firing, and the supplies were being rushed to our position without reported casualties.

The plan had succeeded, with some caveats that I hoped we could live with.

"Three Marines," the Gunny replied when he could talk again. I knew from the way he said Marines that the men were enlisted, and I breathed a sigh of relief.

"I want to put them in the cleft to the north with me, but they won't all fit," the Gunny said. "Your scout team can guard the entrance off to the side of the Ontos back blast, which won't go on all night, although the NVA are going to figure all this out and be pissed as hell, once again. These air-dales aren't ready for what's down here.

"You take the staff sergeant and I'll take the other two," the Gunny continued, not bothering to make the sentence into a question. I caught something in the tone or inflection of his voice when he spoke though.

"Why the Staff over here?" I asked, not certain why I was bothering to ask.

I couldn't tell for certain, but I thought the Gunny was smiling slightly when he replied.

"The Staff Sergeant carries a Thompson," he said, before crawling out of the hole, and then rolling to immediately away to avoid any backblast from the Ontos.

one-hundred-twenty-two

THE TWENTY-FIFTH NIGHT : SECOND PART

❚❚ The colors of the rainbow so pretty in the sky, are also on the faces of people going by. I see friends shaking hands saying how do you do, they're really saying I love you…"

The lyrics gently streamed from Fessman's small radio, the last song of the day, according to Brother John, before the Armed Forces network signed off. Louis Armstrong sang the words, in his strangely awful and broken voice, the tone so warbled and deep that it sent shivers of reality straight into my heart. I felt the emotion and was surprised. I wasn't used to feeling much of anything except fear. Macho Man knelt in front of me, deep inside the protections offered by the cleft, an expression of sadness having replaced his usual fearsome tough expression.

Jurgen's flashlight reflected off the jagged roof edges of my darkened stifling cleft. The rain outside had returned with a vengeance, saturating the hot fetid air of the monsoon season with water, insects and tiny spots of flittering mud. The smell was sweet, with decaying vegetation and the aroma emitted by the bodies of past animal life buried under the shifting sands that formed the floor of the cave.

"They left me, Junior," Macho Man said, the words coming out like the man's life was exiting his body with them.

"Yes, they did, and we both know they had little choice in the matter," I replied, sitting with my back to the curve of the wall, bent forward toward the man.

I wondered about the necessity of leaving the three men for a few seconds. The gross lift-off weight of the CH-46 helicopter had to be tremendous. What difference would three or four hundred pounds make? And then I thought about just how great most of the chopper pilots were. The men had most probably been left because the pilot had serious reservations about ever making it back to the base, or likely going down terminally hard somewhere in between.

"They'll be coming tomorrow?" Macho Man asked, his tone turning to hopeful.

"Not likely," I replied, not wanting to raise the expectations of the staff sergeant too high. "You can hear the rain outside. The intensity has gone way up, which means the visibility has gone way down. Your crew might want to come back but they'll first have to repair their bird, and then get the permission of higher command."

"What do I do here?" he asked.

"You're now my scout sergeant, and these are your men, or your team, so to speak until your own people return to fly you out."

"I've never fought on the ground, ever, sir," Macho Man replied, finally easing from his knees to a sitting position.

"Oh, you'll catch on," I assured him while finding it vaguely comforting that Macho Man called me sir, from time to time. "Nguyen, the Montagnard here, doesn't speak Engish but he's vital to the team and he'll guide you along unbelievably well with Fessman to help to the best of his ability."

I looked at Macho man, who had changed his entire orientation in only a matter of minutes. I was watching him go through that metamorphosis and I felt like the Gunny. I'd been in-country for something under a month, but I felt I'd somehow gained twenty or more years of age. I knew the Staff Sergeant in front of me was older than I was, although there were no records available out in a combat zone, and I wasn't going to ask him, but I felt more like his grandfather rather than just his father or his commanding officer.

Carruthers crawled into the opening of the cleft, soaked through, wearing no poncho cover, a trail of water preceding him down the packed sandy slope to where Macho Man and I sat facing one another.

"Who's he, and where did he get that?" Carruthers asked, sliding down on his belly, his helmet rolling off and his eyes going straight to the Thompson submachine gun held by Macho Man across his lap.

I explained the situation as succinctly as I could to the captain, but for some reason, his main interest was in the Thompson.

"What good is that thing in combat here?" Carruthers asked, but then went right on without waiting for an answer. It and its ammunition weigh twice as much as an M-16, and there's no real resupply of the pistol ammo. What do you carry, a couple of twenty round magazines?"

"The Staff Sergeant's taking over as my new scout team leader," I replied since Macho Man didn't seem like he was going to say anything.

The Gunny appeared at the upper edge of the dim glow put out by Jurgen's flashlight, and I briefly wondered how many more members of the company would show up before I could curl up and catch some more sleep.

"We have two platoons being commanded by Buck Sergeants, Junior," the Gunny said but didn't go on.

What he was intimating, I knew, was that the proper place for the Staff Sergeant was in command of one of those platoons. I thought that until I looked closely at the Gunny's facial expression. There was the faintest hint of a smile on the man's grizzled facial features. He knew Macho Man was straight from the rear area and would almost certainly be going back at some time during the following day.

"What's his name?" Carruthers asked as if the staff sergeant wasn't sitting right in our midst.

"Waldo," Macho Man replied, probably intending to add his last name, but never getting the chance.

"Waldo, now that's a fascinating name, indeed," Carruthers said.

"Fessman," I said, projecting my voice to reach up toward the cleft opening, "get the Staff Sergeant properly equipped."

"Go with Fessman," I instructed Macho Man, wondering if I should at least mention his last name of Vanilli to everyone inside the cleft, but then thought better of it.

Accommodating the field forces, when you were dropped in to visit for a very short period of time wasn't necessarily a good thing I instinctively felt, and giving everyone more information wasn't going to change that. Waldo was an uncommon dweeb name and it was likely, for as long as he was in the field, he'd be known by that.

Macho Man got the hint and scrambled up the incline to follow Fessman out into the heavy rain. Fessman pushed a poncho cover back toward the man. No matter what lay ahead for Sergeant Waldo, part of it was certainly going to see the end of his starched and pressed utilities.

Macho Man turned, as he reached the outer edges of the light. I saw his eyes gleam, looking back at me, unblinking. I read the question in them that he couldn't ask.

The man had delivered plenty of Marines down into the A Shau. He knew what happened to most of them. I knew he was waiting for me. Nobody said anything, Carruthers, the Gunny, Nguyen, and Fessman; all-knowing the question that Macho Man couldn't ask.

"You're going to make it," I said, my voice almost too low to hear over the mild drumming sound of the rain hitting the jungle mud just outside the cleft, and then the deeper more distant sound of the

Bong Song slithering by. "All the way, up the hill," I continued and then stopped. Macho Man blinked.

I blinked once back, and the man was gone, following Fessman outside the cleft to find what was needed to get the man at least through the night and next day. I sat back against my sharply curving cleft wall. I hadn't been able to get my letter home aboard the chopper, which made me feel worse than the lie I'd told to Staff Sergeant Waldo Vanilli. Because the 'airdales' would eventually come for him, the sergeant had a much better chance than the rest of us, marooned down inside the A Shau wasteland, but I was no magician, and, in fact, couldn't even spend much of my time assuring the sergeant he would live if he followed my advice. I advised the company, the artillery, the Ontos crew, and even the enemy, in my way. I had no time to do what the Gunny had done for me, and the kind of core twisting fear Macho Man was hiding inside himself wasn't something that any outside force or advice was going to minimize. You lived with that kind of fear and, in the A Shau, you generally died with it.

"Nguyen," I whispered to the Montagnard.

Nguyen stared into me.

I nodded off in the direction Macho Man had gone.

Nguyen disappeared out into the rain, moving away low and silently under his own poncho like it was a second skin. I'd done the best I could for Waldo, in return for his having taken the time and trouble to get me a decent pair of boots and giving me his own care package from home. And, I had to admit to myself, because he was now one of my Marines, no matter how short his time at that might be.

The Gunny had brought a bag full of C-Rations, care packages from home and some six-packs of beer. The beer was Schlitz and rationed, according to the Gunny, at one can per Marine. I gave my can to Carruthers. The captain drank down two cans in two long swigs, and then promptly arranged himself and quickly fell into a deep sleep. The man was amazing in many ways, I realized, not for the first time. If he could last long enough to learn more about what we were all faced with in the A Shau then he might be the kind of company commander I could follow.

The Gunny moved closer, avoiding the captain's stretched out body. The air was thick with moisture but the heat was strangely bearable. I wondered if it was the cooling of the stone composition of the cleft that made it so. With so many humans in the space, the rock tips along the roof of it dripped small drops of water incessantly, although the sound wasn't as annoying as the sound of the rain beating in from the outside.

"They're going to come at us again tonight, probably well before dawn," the Gunny said, his voice low and conversational. With Carruthers down and Nguyen gone the only ears close enough to hear belonged to Piper and his charge.

I knew the Gunny was right, although I hadn't known it until he said it. It made all the sense in the world, or at least the valley. The NVA had been taking it on the nose for many days and nights and they wanted to strike back. What better time to strike back than after we were resupplied with food, beer, ammo and everything else we needed. Plus, we'd pulled off the resupply without taking a single casualty. The Marines in both companies would all feel the same way I did. Finally, a night's sleep could be had. But the A Shau wasn't going to be that accommodating and that made sense too.

"How do you know," I asked, needlessly.

The Gunny's logic and life experience were enough, but I wanted more evidence if I could get it. Another night of waiting in the rain when the safety of the cleft drew me so strongly I needed more proof.

"They're visible over across the river, with flashlights," the Gunny replied.

I thought about that. The NVA was using flashlights so we'd notice their movements. That meant that they were either developing an attack force and centralizing it or setting up a base of fire. Since there was no way they could attack across the swollen Bong Song that meant they were setting up a base of fire. The base of fire would open up to confuse us and also to pin us down and redirect our attention from wherever the attack might be coming from.

"Where are they going to come from?" I asked, dreading the answer.

The company was, once again, in exactly the same position it had been in two nights before. The inspection team from battalion had died across the mud flats directly out from where the opening to my cleft faced and the Ontos pointed. Only the adroit capability of the CH-46 had permitted the resupply to come in further upriver where there was no room for it to land on the bank and no other open area. The 46, thanks to brilliant piloting, had dropped its rear end on the bank and then hung the remainder of its 84-foot long body out over the river. The craft had been unloaded from the rear ramp. The NVA had been taken completely by surprise again. That trick would not work again, but that left only the jungle across the flats for the NVA to attack from. That was until the Gunny filled me in.

"The holes they dug earlier," the Gunny began. "They filled them in. They dug deeper. They connected them. They're probably sitting only a few meters from our own forces right now. We've got the Ontos, but it's severely disabled in the night and rainy weather. The Starlight Scope can handle the night, but the heavy rain kills its night vision ability."

I wanted to ask the Gunny what we should do, but the silence that fell over our conversation at that point said something else to me. The Gunny was waiting for me to tell him what to do. I didn't know what to do but I had to respond somehow, I knew.

"Get me Fessman back here with the air radio," I ordered. "I want Piper and the Starlight Scope and somebody from the Ontos. I need a count of ammunition. How many flechette rounds and how many high explosives. And you better get Sugar Daddy and Jurgens too."

"Got it, Junior," the Gunny replied, his voice giving away the fact that he'd received what he had come to me for.

I had no idea what to do. I was gathering everyone together with the hope that I'd come up with something before they assembled or after. I regretted that the Marines had all had a beer or more since I had no control over what had come in or how it had been distributed. Carruthers was a perfect example of what the company didn't need in the night, and I'd been partially responsible for that. The Gunny disappeared from my cleft and sight.

My brain kicked into high gear. I pulled out my map and directed Jurgens flashlight to hover over it. Our position was secure as it could be, as long as we could weather a frontal assault from the edge of the jungle, or even up from the holes that had no doubt been dug to act as fighting holes. Only the A-6 Intruder could give us the kind of air cover that might totally wipe out the NVA advantage it might have from the holes and light tunnel structure in the mud. Since our visibility was reduced, the Ontos might serve much better as a counter-firebase element, using high explosive fuses, rather than blowing our limited supply of flechettes across uninhabited mud flats.

I stopped thinking about the plan forming inside my head. I pulled the letter I'd written to my wife back out and wrote the last page.

It was a page devoted to the Marines around me. I wrote of Macho Man and how much he liked and admired me. I wrote of the Gunny's loyalty and trust and how Fessman treated me exactly as if I was his Dad. I made it all up but smiled at how good a job I'd done when I was finally done. If air was able to make it in again, and that would only be possible if other heavy-duty air cover came with it, then my letter would get aboard the chopper and most probably make it home. For some reason, I felt it was important that my wife believes that the men really thought highly of me. That the reality of my life and relationships in combat was a broken twisted licorice kind of thing didn't need to be revealed, at least not to her.

It only took moments for the Gunny to gather everyone and jam them down inside the cleft. It was night and my worry was increasing because the NVA could attack at any time. Commonly, they came at us just before dawn, but there was no reason they might not come sooner since they themselves had been caught off guard so many times. The Gunny's prediction seemed totally valid, but how were we to respond to it?

I realized, from the last plan that had no name that it was important that I give meaning to the new plan by naming it. The cleft I was in, along with the others up and down the lower cliff edge, was grounded in hard rock. There would be no chance that sappers might work their way up into where we were staying, but the company was also occupying a whole lot of jungle and river mud positions out from the clefts. We'd attacked right through the jungle to reach Kilo Company, and we'd done so without taking almost any casualties. But the circumstances had changed. There would be no tying up with the force attacking down the valley because that had been a disaster, as I knew it had to be. We had no orders from the battalion, except to hold our current position. That order turned our companies from attacking Marine companies into statically placed targets of opportunity.

I reached out for Fessman, who extended the radio handset. I didn't need the handset, however.

"The Planet Mars Defense," I said. "We're going to call it that. I want everyone to dig in on the outside to make sure nothing's been dug out from under them. Our objective is to get to dawn and air support. Get the Gunny back."

I waited, Jurgen's flashlight beginning to grow dimmer. I switched it off to wait in the dark for the Gunny's return.

In moments the silence, broken only by the rain and the rushing sound of water going by in the distant river, was interrupted by the Gunny's entrance. Carruthers had nodded off sometime earlier but was awakened by the sound of the Gunny sliding down toward us in the dry but slippery sand.

"Who goes there?" Carruthers asked as if we were in some old war movie standing guard.

The Gunny ignored Carruthers and lay waiting in the near dark.

"Have everyone dig in outside their clefts," I ordered. "I want a couple of Kilo platoons to head back down the path toward the jungle and set up a base of fire from there."

"What?" Carruthers said, fully waking from his stupor.

"What's the point?" The Gunny asked.

"They are moving against us with a plan of attack," I said to both men. "I want to have a counter-plan in action against them. It doesn't have to be something that works.

They just have to be observing something they don't understand. We'll take some heat from being so close to their lines but the result is that they won't just be able to move around at will without regard for what we might do."

"Why my Marines?" Carruthers asked.

"We came to rescue you, remember?" I said, forcefully. "It's time to earn your keep. We went for the supplies and got them. Now you guys go down there and interdict the enemy."

"You can't order that, Junior," Carruthers said, his voice tone flat and angry, and placing an emphasis on the word 'Junior.'

"No, I can't," I replied.

"The Planet Mars Defense?" the Gunny asked, as the silence in the cleft drew out.

"The Clay People, from the Valley of Desolation, come out of the walls of the canyon, if you recall," I replied.

"Flash Gordon?" Carruthers asked. "What in hell does Flash Gordon have anything to do with this? And what Clay people?"

"Got it, the Clay people, of course," the Gunny replied. "I'll need two platoons from Kilo to head down that path. "We'll give you reinforced machine gun fire to establish and support the position."

I knew the Gunny was playing with Carruthers. The Gunny probably had never seen Flash Gordon and knew nothing about the Clay People. It didn't matter. Drawing the attention of the NVA by establishing our own base of fire was sound tactics and the Gunny got that, The best defense was a powerful offense, and the base of fire positioning was a startling offensive move.

"This is crazy," Captain Carruthers breathed out. "There is no Flash Gordon and probably no Clay People. I don't understand any of this but I guess I have no choice. We'll use the first and second platoons. I better get out there and let them know."

Carruthers got his gear together and crawled past the Gunny, exiting up and over the lip that led down into the cleft.

"At least that went well," I said to the Gunny when he was gone.

"Did you pay attention to what he said?" the Gunny asked me, lighting up a cigarette with his special Zippo lighter.

I thought about his question, playing back Carruther's comments in my mind. The cigarette smoke blew across me and I liked the smell. Cigarette smoke, the heat, and the moisture-laden air were becoming home to me, and that wasn't making me comfortable. I knew I would never get used to the fetid smell of jungle decay all around me, however, and leeches would never find any popularity in my psychology, no matter what.

"What did he say?" I finally asked, not being able to recall Carruthers exact words.

"He said 'probably no Clay People.'"

"And that means what?" I asked.

"That means he's as nutty as we are," the Gunny replied, putting out his cigarette and clawing his way back out of the cleft.

one-hundred-twenty-three

THE TWENTY-FIFTH NIGHT : THIRD PART

I had the place and the time but I could not sleep. The NVA had brought its .50 caliber equivalent heavy machine gun up on line. The gun laced our position up and down every twenty minutes or so. I couldn't figure it out, laying curled up in my cleft. What was their point? Keep us pinned down until the morning, and then what? They didn't have supporting fires capable of reaching our position, and they didn't have any air support at all. Why get to the morning? I had instructed the Gunny earlier to stop firing back at them. It was a waste of ammunition and it gave their leadership power in being able to conclude that they were actually getting a response. The Ontos, with one of its high explosive rounds, could have reached out and taken the .50 down, except for the fact that the gun fired, and was then quickly moved to a different location. The night was remaining active and I couldn't sleep through it.

They were going to attack before dawn, I knew. How much before dawn is what caused me to be unable to sleep. The Gunny was right. The NVA was an angry force now, after being bloodied so many times, and they were still very powerful in position and troop strength. That they had no clue as to what and why we were still sitting in front of them, a great immobile target, was apparent, but meant little or nothing. They were where they were and we were where we were and that was it.

The Gunny came into the cleft with Jurgens and Sugar Daddy, as I had requested earlier. The fact that the night was half gone, that Carruthers had taken his two platoons down valley to form an effective firebase, was beside the point. The firebase the NVA had set up across the river remained strangely silent. And why was their .50 caliber set into the main portion of the jungle opposite the Marine positions?

"This is a strange night," Sugar Daddy said, stripping off his wet poncho cover.

The other two men did the same, and I realized my dry sand bottom cleft wasn't going to stay dry for much longer.

Nobody said anything in response to Sugar Daddy's comment, although it had shown that he, and probably the rest of the Marines up and down the cliff base, didn't know what to think either, and that could be very dangerous in a defensive position like the one we'd backed ourselves into.

The Gunny ignited a small chunk of Composition B. The cold white light from it radiated around inside the cleft. I looked at the faces of the men inside with me. Sugar Daddy looked tired, Jurgens looked pissed off about something, and the Gunny was impassive, his facial features impossible to read. Fessman, just above and behind the Gunny, stared over his right shoulder at me, his eyes seeming big and round in the wavering strange light reflections. Nguyen was out protecting Macho Man if such a thing was possible. I hadn't sent Kilo's Marines, along with the captain, to form the firebase, in order to send them on a suicide mission. There were plenty of very protected clefts along the base of the cliff where they had taken up position, and they could fairly easily move back to the main element of Marines up valley, even under fire. That he was so terribly inexperienced bothered me. He had his own NCOs however, and I wasn't about to send Sugar Daddy or Jurgens to be his advisor. My trust in Carruther's experience was near zero, but my confidence that Sugar Daddy or Jurgens would take the captain out if they thought it would improve their own survival potential was nearly at one hundred percent. I thought about the two sergeants, and that I had gone for days and nights not thinking about seriously killing one or the other of them, and that thought surprised me.

The Gunny lit up a cigarette, as he heated his canteen holder of water over the small brilliant fire. I laid on my side, facing the men, my helmet propped up under my ribs instead of letting my elbow and shoulder bear most of the weight of my elevated torso. I kept the sharp chunk of artillery metal still embedded into the steel cover out from me, wondering if, like my Uncle Jim from years ago in the attic, I'd be showing it one day to my nephews like he had shown his war souvenirs to me. I almost smiled at the sudden knowledge that my nephews wouldn't believe any of my war stories any more than I had believed Uncle Jim's. I thought about the company's predicament. Whatever was happening in the night just outside had gone from being under some kind of reactionary control, using my plan, to something that was a complete unknown. Suddenly, the enemy's Planet Mongo Plan seemed to be overcoming my Planet Mars Defense.

"What are they doing?" the Gunny asked, exhaling a long heavy stream of smoke.

The smoke ran down to the very bottom edge of the cleft and formed a small cloud all of its own and floated there. It seemed unnatural, as I considered the Gunny's question. The question had been directed at me, even though the Gunny hadn't looked in my direction. Unconventional. The smoke was acting unconventionally. My own unconventional moves and reactions to the NVA forces opposing us had been the same way. And then it came to me. The NVA leaders were learning. From us. From me.

"Their firebase has never fired a round," I whispered more to myself than to the Marines assembled around me. "The .50 caliber is facing the open area like it's there to support some kind of attack from dug in troops in caves, tunnels, and holes."

I stopped for a few seconds, before going on. "How did the NVA firebase get across the river. They can't do that any more easily than we can. And since they did, why didn't they cross a whole lot more troops than a single firebase would require?"

"And then?" the Gunny asked as if he already had guessed the answer.

"And then, to cross them back," I breathed out. "The .50 isn't there to cover an attack coming at us from across the open mud flat, even if coming up out of holes and tunnels might make it appear that way. "The .50 is set there to pin us down as best it can and draw our attention to it, and having us expend time and ammo taking it out."

"They re-cross the river further up, and then come attacking down through the jungle along the very edge of the cliff we are occupying," the Gunny went on.

"The Ontos is pointed in the wrong direction and becomes useless," I said. "Their firebase opens up on us if we attempt to escape down south along the cliff, like Carruthers and Kilo, or attack back across the mud flat as we did before. They take us on the flank. They're deliberately leaving Carruthers and his Marines be."

"They are getting all set to attack right now?" Jurgens asked.

"No kidding, I have to get with my platoon," Sugar Daddy replied, starting to rise to his knees in order to crawl out of the cleft.

"Stand fast," the Gunny ordered, his voice going low and filled with solid timber.

"What's the plan?" he asked, turning his head to face me for the first time.

"The Planet Mars attack," I replied, almost instantly, my mind racing at near light speed. "There's no place to cross that river except the one place, and we made that crossing possible. We know it. It's our ground. The Clay People attacked out of their caves eventually and Queen Azura was vanquished. Get everyone ready. We're moving out. Call in Carruthers. The Ontos will have to follow us up the path here between us and the berm along the cliff. His two platoons have to provide rear protection. Once we're on the move, the NVA will figure it out but hopefully be committed to crossing that horrid killing river while their jungle emplacements will be to set in to allow them to quickly vacate and come after us."

There was a complete silence inside the cleft for several seconds. I wanted to ask the single word question: "well?" but remained silent, waiting.

"Who are the Clay People?" Sugar Daddy asked, finally.

The Gunny laughed out loud, only the second time since I'd known him that I heard the brief barking sound.

"We are," he said, after a few seconds.

"Jurgens, you have the southern platoon. Move out as fast as you can. They'll be thinking of coming at us not us coming at them. Move light, fast and hard, leaving your packs and gear back in the clefts. Open up a base of fire on the river area where the tank remains, as well as the bridge, as soon as you get to the upper edge of the jungle. There is no other place for them to cross. It's dark and raining like hell."

"I think we got this one covered, Junior," Jurgens shot back, grabbing his poncho and crawling quickly up toward the cleft opening. "That's Indian country and we know it well," he whispered over his shoulder. "We'll use the Clay People attack plan."

In seconds the cleft was almost empty.

The Gunny extinguished his fire, never having heated his water enough to make coffee. The light fell off, with only the weak yellow glow of Jurgens flashlight dully shining against the wall behind me.

"You know," he said, slowly turning to leave, leaving his unfinished cigarette still glowing from the side of his mouth. "If you get this wrong, then Carruthers and his men will be attacked from the rear and left flank by overwhelming force. The Ontos will be moving and pointing in the wrong direction with no ability to help them."

I didn't miss the fact that the Gunny, who'd helped me figure out the likely logic of what the enemy had to be doing, was assigning the entire responsibility for the plan's result to me but using the words 'if you get this wrong'. I was relieved that he'd waited for the others to leave before he'd made the directed comment, however. The Gunny said nothing more before leaving.

"Fessman," I said, deciding to pull all the .45 ammo I had from my pack, while I talked.

"Find Macho Man and get the scout team together. I want him right next to me and Nguyen even closer. We're moving out now, headed north. I need to talk to Carruthers on the combat net and let him know what we're doing."

"He already knows," Fessman replied, "Captain Carruthers, I mean. Everyone knows, even battalion."

Once again, I was stunned at how fast news could travel through Marine units under the most trying of conditions. I pulled my extra box of Colt ammo from my pack.

The cardboard box was falling apart but it would do. It said 'Olin Mathieson Chemical Corporation' on its gray cardboard surface, barely readable, but it might do to help Macho Man stay in ammunition. He hadn't been but a few hours on the ground in the A Shau Valley and he was about to go into direct enemy contact.

I put my poncho on, made sure my own .45 was solidly where it was supposed to be, adjusted my damaged helmet, and came up from my knees to stand in the dense falling rain just outside the cleft. Water glittered everywhere from puddles and jungle debris. I wondered where the light came from to make it visible. I'd remembered to turn the flashlight off. I had my letter home, half-finished as it was, in one thigh pocket and my supply of morphine in the other. I didn't need any maps. The entire area was burned into my brain, from geographic features and distances to the grid coordinates of every registration point I might want to adjust fire from. The 175 mm support was all that we could get and I knew I was going to be very reticent to call that in again unless our attack went badly, or I was wrong about the whole thing. And I would never call the big guns into the area again without both companies being buried deep inside the clefts. I wondered if I was wrong about the plan. Maybe the 175 zone fire effects and terror had been too much for those NVA soldiers exposed near or on the surface. Maybe the enemy was hunkered down and simply glad to be alive and waiting for us to move on. But, I knew I couldn't take the chance. I did not want to die, and have my Marines die, shot to death like rats in caves while we holed up inside the clefts.

The company was moving fast, all of it. I was not so surprised as much as I was pleased. The Ontos was running and working to churn its way along. I knew Carruthers was probably very close behind, coming up from the south, having abandoned his firebase. He had taken my orders more than once without comment, and I thought about the likelihood of that continuing until I considered our real mission. Staying alive until the next dawn.

Macho Man blended in out of the jungle to join me, as I began walking fast up the path, hoping that the space between the cliff and the heavy jungle was enough to allow the Ontos to drive its way through, as the area down further south had allowed for earlier.

"Sergeant Waldo," Macho Man said as if reporting into a training command.

I pushed the box of Olin Mathieson at him but kept walking fast.

"Good stuff, sir," Waldo said, taking the box and putting it away somewhere up under his poncho. I noted that he carried his pack up under the poncho, as well.

"You were supposed to leave the pack back in the cleft," I said, over to him. "We're moving fast and hard and you'll have to maneuver when we get there."

"I'm your scout leader," Macho Man replied. "You're going to need some stuff once we get there, I think."

The Thompson dropped out from under his soaking poncho cover, as we walked, swinging in his hands. I wondered how it would do in the rain and mud. I liked the gleaming little reflections that came off its highly machined surfaces. I was glad I'd given him my extra ammunition as if I needed more than the few bullets I carried in my own Colt. It was probably not going to matter, one way or the other.

The move through the wet night was somehow more invigorating than laying inside a dry sand-bottomed cleft. The cleft offered safety, but at the price of near total blindness to what might be coming at any time. And the jungle air inside the folded under mountain caves was hot, fetid and filled with insect life and floating sediment. The rain was cooler and seemingly cleansing. The poncho covers shed the rain almost completely, but the blowing moving rainproof material could not cover everything. Lower trousers, boots, face, hands and so much else became sopping wet over time, and the move consumed some time, although a whole lot less on my watch then it seemed to.

There was no signal when it came time to stop, or rather the signal was open gunfire ahead. Heavy small arms fire and small explosions filled the air around us, although nothing was close enough to allow flares of muzzle blasts or the actual fire from explosives going off to be seen. I knew the good news is that there had been no fire from our rear.

There was no full-frontal attack that had been sprung on our rear when the NVA had realized we'd up and left. That spoke more about the fact that the NVA was committed to having its main body of troops heading to make the upriver crossing rather than having it sit in the jungle or buried in the mud flats waiting to pounce. If my plan had not been right then there would be nobody at the river for Jurgens men to have opened up on, and that fire was heavy.

The Gunny and Sugar Daddy were suddenly there beside us, down on the packed jungle floor, while Marines in slithering noisy poncho covers flowed by on both sides.

"Looks like you were right," the Gunny said. "Everyone's got to get in and down to the edge of the jungle that approaches the river below the tank. I don't know how fast the NVA are coming but they're probably in such numbers that we don't want to face them in the open."

I heard the sound of the Ontos grinding away, coming up behind us.

"I don't want them to face the NVA at all," I said. "The Ontos can face them. The NVA won't have time to bring the .50 all the way through the jungle and get it to the other side. Under direct fire, the .50 is no match for the 106 rounds, explosive or otherwise."

"Alright, I'm going down with Jurgens to occupy the riverside," the Gunny said.

"Okay," I replied, "I'll head back a little and wait for the Ontos and Carruthers."

"Let's move out," the Gunny said, jumping to his feet and running forward. Suddenly everyone was moving except me. In seconds I was alone, except for Fessman.

"What the hell?" I asked. Where's our scout team?"

"Looks like they went with the Gunny, maybe to scout, sir?"

"To the front line in direct contact?" I said, not stating the sentence as a question. "Get the Gunny's radio operator on the net and get them back here."

I moved slowly back toward the approaching Ontos, with Fessman at my side talking on the radio handset.

"Well?" I yelled at Fessman when he lowered the microphone.

"He's not with the Gunny, just yet, sir," Fessman said, speaking more loudly, as the sound of the approaching armored vehicle began to drown out all other sounds.

"What are you talking about, he's always supposed to be with his principal," I said, anger beginning to force its way into my tone.

Carruthers appeared out of the rain, his own radio operator close by, with several of his Marines surrounding the slow-moving Ontos.

"It would appear that your plan is working really well, Junior," the bigger man said, leaning forward, his poncho cascading and throwing great rivulets of water my way. "The Clay People Attack. Now that's something. Who are the Clay People?"

"Let's get this thing into position," I said, taking him by one arm and directing him back to the machine. "We can't just fire across the mud flat here because we can't see where anyone is."

Just then two huge fusillades of fire opened up, one from across the river and further north, and then the response from closer on our side and lower down. I realized that we didn't have to see very well, the AK 47 pops were as distinct in their way as the sharp barking of the M-16s and then the deeper timbre of the 7.62 machine guns.

one-hundred-twenty-four

THE TWENTY-SIXTH DAY : FIRST PART

A cacophony of open combat fire sent me as deep into the jungle floor as I could get. The sound was pure small arms fire, which at close range, with the Marines around me firing outward, didn't sound so small. I crawled forward, eventually running into the feet, legs, and backs of the Marines laying down the fire upon the exposed enemy. The only explanation for the spiderweb crawling of the enemy across the surface of the roiling water, extending out from the end of the abbreviated bridge ending to the near riverbank, was a knitted mix of rope lengths and knots. The NVA had put together landing nets of rope, effective but nearly impossible to control balanced movement across. The enemy soldiers crawled across the length of cargo nets and were easily picked off by Marine fire. There was no enemy base of fire to suppress the Marine M-16 and M-60 fire.

The Ontos ground its way to the top edge of the forest, the sound of its metallic geared tracks almost fully muted by the rain. It fired as it appeared, driving everyone nearby down into the jungle floor or the sticky mud. The rounds impacted short of the river, but the effect was just as great as if they had approached any moving enemy figure and taken him down individually. For one bright moment there were standing, climbing and running figures and the next instant, with the explosion of another round, they were gone.

I was deafened again, being too close to the muzzles of the 106 guns not to be seriously affected. I waited for my hearing to come back. The guns fired some more but I'd had the time to jam my muddy hands over my ears, the fetid smell of the sticky stuff making my headache. The guns fired some more. I could see the effect down at the river's edge. The NVA was taking tens of casualties, but most of the troops that had been ready to leap onto the cargo nets they'd painstakingly tied and then tossed from the end of the damaged bridge to the shore were running back into the deeper jungle on the other side.

The Gunny had appeared, laying down next to me in the mud, just adjacent from the jungle's edge. From that position, I could see what was going on, although the night and the rain made visual observation extremely limited, at best. I stared into the night, the sound of the rough, wild and roiling floodwaters sounding like there was a living monster just ahead instead of merely a torrential river in flood.

There was a stench of death in the air, as I inhaled, in an attempt to get the mud smell from my lungs and mind. The smell was of real death, which I knew because I'd smelled it before when we couldn't get bodies air-lifted out for days.

Our men, including Zippo, had not gotten out to the resupply chopper. The 46 had had to leave without them because of the hydraulics. The bodies were somewhere nearby. I knew, given enough time, I would be able to place them fairly accurately but I didn't want to think about that. I couldn't think about that.

"Have the company cease-fire," I ordered the Gunny, lying face down on the rutted mud surface of the bare riverbed, my head turned sideways so my words could be heard. My hearing was rapidly returning, I realized, except for a ringing buzz. I wondered if I was somehow getting used to being deafened by gunfire.

The fire, mostly from Marines shooting at the remaining individual soldiers trapped in the cargo nets and trying to get back across the river they'd just attempted to cross, was deafening and nearly constant.

"We're putting it to them sir, and we need to keep doing it," the Gunny replied, laying close in beside me, the pounding miserable rain making his voice, even though his head was only inches away, hard to hear distinctly, as the millions of drops impacted on my helmet and splashed everywhere around us.

"Ceasefire," I ordered again.

"Not a good idea, Junior," the Gunny replied, turning his head to attempt to make out what was going on further out near the very edge of the river.

"Fessman," I rasped out.

"Sir," Fessman replied, crawling up my right side, opposite from where the Gunny lay.

I grasped the wet handset he held out firmly in my right hand.

"Fire mission," I said, loudly into the microphone, pushing the transmit button down sharply when I spoke.

"What fire mission?" the Gunny asked, surprise registering in his tone.

"Zone fire, repeat," I transmitted.

"What the hell?" the Gunny said, his tone going from surprise to shock. "What in hell are you doing? We're fully exposed out here. Artillery now will kill half of the company or more."

I listened to the redirect from the battery, asking for me to complete the order to fire the rounds. It came in seconds. All I had to do was whisper one word into the microphone and hundreds of 175 mm artillery rounds would once again blanket the entire southern end of the valley we occupied. Except for this time, none of us were neatly tucked into clefts folded under the base of the nearby cliff faces.

"Shit," the Gunny said, the word turning into 'shush' by the time the rain finished with allowing it through its harsh falling curtain.

"What the hell," the Gunny followed. "Alright. I'll get them to stop, but there better be some damn good reason for all this bullshit." The Gunny slid away, like an Anaconda working its way across a tidal flat.

"Ceasefire," the Gunny started to yell to invisible Marines up in front of him and located in other positions hidden from my view in the night.

I pressed my face back into the mud, hoping there were no leeches just waiting for such a move. I pulled up to breathe and rubbed the mud and water from every area of my head I could reach without taking my helmet off.

Carruthers slithered up next to me, coming from somewhere in the nearby jungle. I hadn't known he was nearby, and his near hugging touch surprised me. Everything about the captain surprised me, almost without end.

"What are we doing?" he asked, still appearing halfway neat, even though he was exposed to the same devastating weather elements as the rest of us.

"We've got to get back," I said, "and right now." I pulled myself up to my knees, and then slowly rose to my feet. "All we need is to leave a small following force in case any more NVA cross the river using the cargo nets."

"Why are we retreating now?" Carruthers asked, staring out into the night, although the river's waters were just beyond the distance we could see unless there were muzzle flashes from any small arms fire, and those flashes providing only instantly disappearing images hard to make out.

"We're not retreating," I hissed back at him, bending low and making my way into the outer edges of the heavy jungle cover before going back down to my knees.

Carruthers followed, as did Fessman. There was no sight of the rest of my scout team and that fact worried me deeply.

"We're attacking in a different direction," I said, before telling Fessman to let the battery know we were checking our fire and canceling the fire mission. I'd used the threat of another artillery zone attack to force the Gunny to do my bidding immediately.

There was no time to be lost.

"Why?" Carruthers asked, "the direction we're heading is back to where we were? That doesn't make any sense, not with the success we're having here."

"You don't see it," I said, "because you haven't been here long enough. The Gunny should see it but he doesn't either. They're running back from the crossing and racing down the river. Where is this body of the enemy going in force?"

"Back to wherever the hell they came from," Captain Carruthers replied.

"Damned straight," I replied, "in force, where they're crossing back over the river."

"Okay?" Carruthers asked the question in his voice as real as it could be.

"Think it through," I replied, getting back to my feet. "Let's go. We've got to get everyone back. They're running back and what do you think the NVA soldiers are going to do when they get across the river? Take a break? Have some chow, or are they going to attack up into the totally exposed and unprotected rear area?"

"Good God, we pulled the firebase and the Ontos is here," Carruthers said, getting it.

"Yes, we did the job here, but only stopped them and dished out some serious but not huge casualties. Now we have no protection if they get over the river further down and come at us while we're busy cleaning up whatever small change is left here."

The Gunny ran through the debris sticking out and forming an edge against the river's high-water mudflat.

"What now?" he said, joining Carruthers, Fessman and I, huddled together against the heavy fall of rain.

The Gunny's voice was filled with anger, at having his hand forced in such a violent manner, and I wondered if our relationship, whatever it was, would recover.

"I want the Ontos loaded with high explosive rounds and firing to take out the bridge and what's left of the crossing the NVA were attempting to make. Nothing can be behind us when we leave"

I explained the situation as quickly and succinctly as I could.

"Shit," was all he said, before racing away. "We've got to get the Ontos back there as fast as we can after blowing the bridge, or what's left of it," he said as if talking to himself. "They've got the .50 caliber and they can move it right in if there's nothing to stop them."

I waited a few seconds before following. When I reached the Ontos, glad it had not fired another round yet, because I wasn't far enough from the angle of its aim to hope for my hearing to survive, I stopped with Fessman and Carruthers to wait for the Gunny to be done ordering the crew to get the machine around and back down to where we'd pulled it out of.

"Where's your radio operator?" I asked Carruthers, mystified about why he wasn't being as smothered by his Marine's presence as I was by Fessman. As if on cue, a Marine in flowing wet poncho swept up behind the captain.

"Three casualties, sir," he said, seeming to almost salute as he reported in.

"Two KIA and one WIA."

"Kilo?" the captain asked.

"No, sir," the captain's radio operator replied, and my stomach fell.

"Names," I whispered, not in question.

"Waldo's the WIA, and the others I'd don't know," the Marine intoned, his voice dropping as he spoke, reading the depth of my own feelings that I could not hide in receiving the information.

"They're moving Sergeant Waldo back with us," he went on. "The other two will be left here for the next pickup."

I didn't have to ask who the other two were. Piper and the Project One Hundred Thousand Marine he'd been looking after were gone. Macho Man was injured, and probably pretty badly since even a normally non-life-threatening injury was serious if no immediate medivac was available. And no medivac was available.

The makeshift gurney holding Macho Man was placed firmly atop the dry sand of a cleft occupied by no other Marines. An I.V. was supported by a hook some Marine had cleverly embedded into one of the stone cracks just over his head. I eased into the enclosure, snapping off Jurgen's flashlight as I went in. A small fire burned next to the sergeant's prone figure, one of the Composition B fires but without anyone attempting to boil water or any of that. The white light of the hot little fire reflected everywhere, as the I.V. tube gently swaying downward, with the mild breeze wavering, the movement caused by my entry into the cleft. Macho Man's feet angled down toward the bottom of the cleft, but his position was obviously beyond the man's real care. I knelt by his side. The corpsmen had left so I was alone with him. There was no need for corpsmen to be present because there was obviously nothing to be done for the man. He'd been hit through and through with high-velocity bullets in the abdomen. Without immediate surgery, there was no recovery possible in a field situation. Even if the rear area could mount an emergency medivac, it could not possibly come in time to save Macho Man's life.

The little white and harsh fire burned bright but its reflection across Macho Man's countenance told the deathly story without emotion. I gently stroked the man's face to remove the perspiration constantly pouring out of his pores

"Junior?" Macho Man whispered.

"Right by your side," I replied, pulling my wet hand back.

"It hurts so bad," Macho Man said. "So bad."

I unbuttoned my right thigh pocket and pulled my morphine pack loose.

"I brought some morphine," I told him, as I worked to get the syrettes out.

"They gave me some but it doesn't seem to have much effect," Macho Man replied, spacing the words carefully between the waves of pain that were overcoming him.

"It hurts so bad."

"This is the real stuff," I assured him, pulling the cover off one small tube and punching it into his left thigh. I sharply squeezed the tube of morphine into his muscle right through his utility trouser fabric. I followed the procedure three more times, successively.

The drug should not have been able to work as quickly as it did. Within less than a few minutes, as I tried to hug the man's torn up torso closer to me, I felt the effects of the miracle drug. Macho Man's muscles began to relax.

"Thanks, Junior, that's better," Macho Man whispered to me,

never opening his eyes.

I waited, the time seemed to pass in forever seconds. One second and then another went by. I looked at my watch but the bright bluish-white fire of the Composition B made seeing detail almost impossible. I put the remaining supply of the morphine back into my right thigh pocket. I knew the dosage and had studied the effects over time on other Marines before Macho Man. I knew I wouldn't need anymore. I wanted to say something meaningful to the man whom I had so identified with when I'd been newer in the country. He'd seemed bulletproof and ultra-tough. One mistake, of going into the thick of contact, had turned the great tough sergeant into a painfully dying human being with no hope for recovery in seconds…played out over many minutes and hours until I had reached his side.

The Gunny came crawling into the cleft to arrive at my side.

"He gone yet?" the Gunny asked.

I wasn't offended. Macho Man's passing was a foregone conclusion once the severity of his wounds was diagnosed. There was no time for grief, sentiment or consideration in a real combat situation. I knew why the Gunny was there. I was needed outside for some other momentous decision that might involve more Marines dying.

A rasping final breath exhaled from Macho Man's throat and I knew he was gone. The morphine was merciful and brutally quick in its effect if administered in sufficient quantity.

"Yes, he's gone," I replied.

"What about the Thompson?" the Gunny asked, looking at the nearby weapon the sergeant had kept close to his side even in death.

"It goes back with his body," I replied. "It was part of him."

"They don't let you take automatic weapons home," the Gunny argued.

"I know," I answered. "I don't care. What they do in the rear with the gear is up to them. He goes out with his Thompson strapped to his side," I said.

"Cool weapon," the Gunny said, but I could tell from his tone that he wasn't going to give me any grief over my decision.

I reached for the Thompson and pulled it close. I released the magazine from the body of the weapon and then began unloading bullets one by one. There were only twenty in the magazine and I had no box, so I poured the bullets into my left chest pocket.

"For your sidearm?" the Gunny asked, but I didn't answer.

I knew with a fatal certainty that no helicopter would ever land in my life again and have such a supporting and stoically caring person stand guard while its blades whirled above our heads. That man had taken my letters, time after time, and very likely got them through to my wife. The fact he'd had no real understanding of what combat was like had killed him, for all the right reasons. He'd gone into the thick of it, like Piper and his charge, and he'd died. I'd been unable to stop him or them. You cannot charge into the thick of combat and live, but I knew that lesson was usually taught by death itself.

The Gunny withdrew in silence, only the rustling of his utilities against the sand apparent. I knew he would be waiting at the entrance to the cleft, some impossible decision having to be made.

I opened my left thigh pocket and pulled out my small pack of stationery. I usually reserved that paper only for writing letters to my wife. I pulled out a sheet of paper, one of the ones with the Marines raising the flag on Iwo Jima. I wrote: "this was a good Marine," on it. I didn't know what else to say or who might see the notation. I folded the paper and stuck it into Macho Man's breast pocket. Maybe, over time, the inscription might have meaning to someone back home.

I slowly withdrew from the cleft. Macho Man's eyes were open and dilated. I could see no point in closing them. The fire would burn out, as Macho Man's life had burned out, in pain and nearly alone. That was the way of the A Shau and I knew it well.

The drums started immediately upon my withdrawal from Macho Man's cleft, and although I felt their brutal vibrations right down into the depths of my very being, it was nothing like how Carruthers handled the action. He was waiting for me as I came up out of the cleft and into the rain. For some reason, the captain was taking the drumming, as muffled as it was by the rain, wind and external effect caused by the fact that we were all once again ensconced under the protection of the cliff understructure, as personal.

The Drums

[audio   src="https://s3-us-west-2.amazonaws.com/strausss-hortstories/Drums-of-War.mp3"]

"Why are they doing this?" Carruthers asked.

I had no answer for the captain that might make any sense. The NVA was drumming because it was an effective device to upset their enemy. We were that enemy and the device was effective or Carruthers would not be trying to pace up and down an interior cleft space that wasn't high enough inside for him to walk in.

"Because it works," I replied. "Look at yourself."

"I'm not upset by the drumming," Carruthers replied, finally sitting back down, but holding himself with clasped arms like his torso was in deep pain.

"What is it then?" I asked, not fooled for a second about the fact that the deadly thrumming beat of the drums affected all of us deeply.

"What does it mean?" Carruthers asked.

"It means that they're there and that they're coming," I responded, forming the answer in my own mind to a question that had lingered since the last time I'd heard the distant threat.

"I don't get it," Carruthers answered. "It seems like such a waste of time and effort on their part."

"This is their country, their land, and their valley, if you haven't noticed. They want us to know that and the fact that they won't quit, no matter what."

"It's their version of the Marine Hymn?" Carruthers asked, finally unclasping himself and working to control his breathing and emotions.

I lay next to him, considering. I'd never thought of the drumming in terms of what it might mean to the enemy doing the drumming. I'd only thought of being on the receiving end. The captain had a point and it was a telling point. We had the Marine hymn and our own solid standing belief system of honor and combat. They had their own, as well.

one-hundred-twenty-five

THE TWENTY-SIXTH DAY : SECOND PART

The attack never came. We'd rushed back to our positions in the expectation that the NVA would understand that we'd left our rear area totally unprotected, but either the enemy had not figured that out, or there was another mystery that might never be explained. Even with the knowledge that we'd made a mistake and were rushing back to fix it, we should have paid a heavy price in casualties. But, that had not been the case. There'd been no opening of fire from either the heavy jungle we knew to be filled with enemy troops nor by anyone in our own combined Marine companies. The Ontos sat still, its idle brought to a halt for the first time in days. I had no idea of how the thing was resupplied with gasoline all the time, or why it was currently shut off, but assumed the Gunny had intimate knowledge, as well as the means to support it.

The Gunny came sliding down my little incline, shedding his soaked poncho cover as he came. Captain Carruthers entered right behind him. I looked up at the opening, to see the very muted light of early day beginning to radiate through the hanging cover Fessman had erected. Fessman was there inside the cave but pushed into the side of the wall above me. I realized that he, and Nguyen across from him, had been there all the time, but I hadn't paid much attention, trying to curl into a ball and find some solace in any sleep I could get. The relief I'd felt when the attack to our rear had not occurred had somehow sucked some energy from my very core.

"We can't stay here," I said to Carruthers and the Gunny, knowing I didn't have to say the words but saying them anyway. "Our position's registered, and there's only a matter of time until they overwhelm us from all sides, no matter what firepower we can bring down on them during the daylight hours."

I felt more relief when I finished, but not from saying what we all knew. The thrum of the Skyraider, multiplied several times, came up through the sand on the bottom of my cave 'floor.' Cowboy was back, and he'd brought friends. There would be no enemy attack in daylight hours, as long as he and his accompanying friends could remain on station, orbiting the bottom of the valley and looking to 'get some.' That phrase, used to describe killing the enemy, or even civilians, rankled me, but I never said anything to anyone who used it. I had come to know that my nature was anything but timid, but I had also learned that being reserved and accepting of bizarre differences of behavior in combat was a good way to stay alive as a commander. I wasn't going to fight any battles or take any chances with my own Marines over whatever use of language might be in vogue.

"Staying here isn't the issue," the Gunny replied, surprising me. His tone was just a touch acidic. My comments about not staying where we were had obviously bitten into some emotion I didn't fully understand.

"Where do we head out to?" Carruthers asked. "Battalion has a whole lot to do with that kind of decision, and there's nothing on the command net so far about us going anywhere. How long until we get to go to the rear to get a break from all this, by the way?"

I looked into the Gunny's eyes, as he lit a cigarette. I saw the minor irritation he'd displayed toward my earlier comments disappear, and a slight bit of humor appear in his eyes. He made no attempt to answer Carruthers, instead concentrating on lighting his cigarette.

"They do rotate units back, or so I've heard," I replied, trying not to laugh out loud, at how silly my answer seemed to me.

In a Marine Corps unit, particularly one in combat, such things should be a given, or so it had seemed back in training. To discover that nothing was a 'given' out in the field of combat had been another galvanic shock to my core of existence, but no more. I had no expectation of going to the rear alive, and I knew the Gunny felt exactly the same. It wasn't something we talked about. It wasn't something anyone talked about. But there was no sense in telling Carruthers any of that, not under the circumstances.

"We'll tell battalion we're moving out when we move out," I said.

"You can't just tell command what we're doing," Carruthers replied, his tone one of some surprise, and displaying a bit of irritated anger. "It's not like you've done so well out here so far, lieutenant."

I had no answer to that. In my estimation, it was one of the most truthful things I'd heard anybody say since I'd arrived in country. The Gunny handed me his lit cigarette. I took one long drag, trying not to cough, and then handing it back. Almost a minute went by without anyone saying anything.

"Since the lieutenant took over there's been almost no killing be-tween the black and white platoons," Fessman said, his voice almost a whisper, "and they used to kill each other all the time."

"There's that," the Gunny chimed in. "The tracers he dreamed up were a good move, and I think they help suppress the NVA fire too."

"What killing?" Carruthers asked, but nobody paid attention to him or his question.

I hadn't thought much about Jurgens or Sugar Daddy and the extreme problems they had posed in my first days with the company. They were right, and I almost felt a sense of pride, but that feeling was fleeting. It reminded me of a Titanic joke. I was doing a great job of putting together really good musical arrangements for the band playing on the fantail of the ship, as it slowly slipped bow first beneath the cold killing waters of the Atlantic.

"Up," I said, after a few seconds.

"Up?" Carruthers and the Gunny asked at exactly the same time.

"If we can't stay here, then we either head upriver or up to the top of the highlands," I explained. "There's no place else to go."

Downriver was a nightmare of closed in valley walls, flooded and rushing river water, and jungle bracken so thick it was not passable by the Ontos, or quite possibly even Marine infantrymen. And the Ontos was the main problem. We could not take it up to the highlands, as the cliffs were so steep that it was nearly impassable for Marines wearing any kind of gear, much less full packs weighing nearly sixty pounds, or more. Even if we went north there was the problem of getting the vehi-cle across the river. The crossing, coming south, that we'd executed be-fore had depended upon the way the partial bridge extended itself out across the water. There was no way to 'jump' the Ontos back up onto that extended lip of the hanging end of the bridge, and the body of the river was way too deep to permit the thing to ford it without some kind of engineering assistance we didn't have. If the Ontos could not make it to the other side of the river then it would have to be destroyed, and its hulk abandoned. The thought of that made me cringe, as the machine had been so instrumental in the company's survival so many times.

I looked at the Gunny and, for the hundredth time, wondered what he was really thinking. His conduct in letting the scout team walk right into death was something I could not talk to him about. I knew I'd never know what happened. Macho Man was dead, like so many before him. How he died didn't really matter, unless his death impacted on my own survival or that of the company. I also knew that Macho Man had somehow occupied a special place in my mind, and that was not likely shared by the Gunny. The man seemed to demonstrate no feelings whatsoever unless they were those of irritation or anger.

"They know we're not going up the face to the top of the highlands," I said, listening intently to the faint sounds penetrating through the occasional explosions caused by Cowboy and the other Skyraiders.

I nodded upward, so they would stop and listen. Very faintly the sound of the drums came through, distant and muffled, but very much there. I was not nearly so unsettled as when I'd first heard them playing deep into a dark foreboding night. Although it was overcast with monsoon rains coming down, the beating of the drums sounded more like frustrating percussive expression than much of a real threat.

"They have those drums up on the lip of the valley again, probably a good distance from where we destroyed them last time. But, it means they don't expect us up there because it also means that if they are up there in force then climbing directly into them would be certain disaster."

"Those drums sound awful," Carruthers said, "What do they mean and why do they do it?"

"Find out if there's another resupply coming in to pick up the rest of our men," I instructed Fessman, before answering the captain. "They do it because they know how it makes you feel, and you are feeling the fear they want you to right now."

"Yes, sir," Fessman shot back, crawling up toward the opening in order to talk on the radio without interrupting our communications inside the cave.

"Resupply?" the Gunny asked, after slowly grinding out his cigarette stub against the rock wall next to him.

"We have to go back up north, past Hill 975, to get into the clear, where the valley spreads out and our supporting fires can reach us," I said. "The Ontos is vital. We need some equipment and an engineer from resupply to get it back across the river."

Fessman returned, slipping his radio off and sliding into the cave before he went to work carefully setting it up against the craggy stone wall. He'd somehow remained under the cave opening poncho he'd hung in order to avoid getting sopping wet. The rain outside, even from my distance from it, seemed so heavy that I wondered how Cowboy and his guys could see any targets at all below them. The good news was

that we'd been in our current position so many times that the supporting pilots had to all know exactly where we were…just like the NVA
did.

I let the drums beat away into the back of my brain, amazed that
I could hear them so clearly way down inside my cave hideaway. Finally,
Fessman turned his little transistor radio on and Brother John introduced a song I'd never heard of and didn't quite get the name to. But
the lyrics burned into me, the drums up on the crater rim seeming to
play right along in harmony: "Now it's the same old song, but with a
different meaning, since you been gone It's the same old song, but with
a different meaning since you been gone"

"We don't know that they don't know," I said, getting ready to answer the Gunny's question I knew had to be coming before he asked it.

What were we going to do next? What was the plan?

"They may not have rushed back to attack our unprotected rear
area because they didn't have time to get set up for it and also, they may
have figured out that we have no place else to go but back up to the
crossing point at the river's edge. They took a lot of casualties but they
can afford a lot of casualties. They're getting into much more fortified
positions right now."

"We're going back to that killing field of fire, and somehow hold
them off while we get the Ontos across that nightmare stretch of moving water?" Carruthers asked.

"That's the plan, Junior, even if they think we're coming and
they're getting ready?" the Gunny asked.

"Yes, the 'Same Old Song' plan," I replied. "I can use the firebase
to light up the top of the cliff where they've got the drums, and probably a base of fire to shoot down on us, but only if we've got choppers
coming. We need gas for the Ontos, more flechette rounds, about twenty Marston Mats with some four by four timber and rope."

"What's a Marston Mat?" Carruthers asked.

"Aluminum runway mat, sir," the Gunny replied, staring intently
into my eyes. "they're metal slats about two feet by twelve feet filled
with holes. Very light. Very tough."

"Will they have them at An Hoa?" Carruthers asked.

"They have them everywhere, especially at that muddy field, captain," I replied. "We use them to bridge the gap out to the broken bridge
that's already there. We need a few pieces of wood and some rope to
hold it all together. The Ontos is light for an armored vehicle, but not

that light when trying to get it up onto that bridge."

"Fessman," I said, looking up at him in the near dark of the cave's interior.

"They can come this afternoon, lieutenant, but I didn't tell them about the engineer or the Marston stuff. I'll get right on it."

He went to work packing his radio up and moving toward the entrance of the cave. The music went with him. The song playing was San Francisco, the city where my wife waited for me to come back. "Be sure to wear a flower in your hair..." floated back at me, not making me think about wearing one at all, but thinking of her doing so, until the draft of Fessman's departure allowed the subtle sweet smell of death to come creeping back in behind him.

"Have him come back and tell me if we can make this work, Gunny," I said after he was gone. "If we're still here tonight we'll get hit with everything they have unless they're fully concentrated and waiting by the river. They have their own dead to deal with from last night."

"How can we know?" Carruther's asked.

"We can't, sir," I shot back. "We guess. They're not great at reacting quickly because so much of their stuff and people are underground, and they're undersupplied in ammunition and pyrotechnical supporting weaponry. They can't move much above ground because of our air, which you can hear from time to time right now. Not in the daylight hours, anyway, even in bad weather. And they don't have an Ontos, beehive rounds or nearly constant resupply."

"Same Old Song," Carruthers said. "I'm not sure I much like the feeling of those words for your plan."

"It's not my plan, sir," I said right back. "It's our plan."

Fessman crouched at the top of the cleft, pushing the poncho cover aside.

"No engineer, sir," he said. "But the rest will be on the chopper at fifteen hundred hours drop in. They'll give us one 46 with four Cobra gunships to cover and a couple of runs with Puff before they hit the landing zone. They want to know how many bodies are left to be lifted out."

I had no idea how many men we'd lost, whose bodies might be there, what with Macho Man, the team battalion had sent and more, not to mention how many had gone out on the previous medivac.

"Eight," I replied, making up a number.

What did it matter? If there were more they'd take them, and if there were less it didn't matter. Only someone fighting the war from a rear area could come up with such a question, I thought, in disgust.

I checked my watch. It was morning, halfway through and Cowboy was covering our six in the air.

"Start the Ontos, since we'll have more gas later. I don't want the NVA to have any idea that anything is different. Let them think we expect them to attack, but I don't think they will. Not in the daytime, and not with the fact that it's so damned likely they've figured out we can't stay here and north is the only way we can get the hell out."

"They might even let us go, and be happy to be rid of us if we hadn't killed so many of them," the Gunny commented.

"But that's our mission," Carruthers replied, in a tone of surprise.

"It's not, really, sir, but we can discuss that later," the Gunny replied. "Let's get some rest if we can until fourteen hundred hours?

I knew, from the previous attack, that we were from twenty to twenty-five minutes from the area of the river we'd have to take, and I was also starting to believe that it was going to a more contested attack than the last one, even with heavy support from the air.

Everyone crawled up the incline and then out through the hanging poncho cover, except for Nguyen and Fessman. Fessman came back to retake his position just above me. The comfort his presence gave me, a teenager's loyalty, protection, and approval, was way out of proportion in importance to anything I could ever have imagined.

"Get air up and make sure Cowboy will be on station for this," I said to Fessman. "Puff would be terrific and the Cobras too, but Cowboy we can count on. He knows us and he'll have a complete understanding of what we're up to."

Fessman pulled the AN-323 air radio from his pack and began to work at getting it up.

"I've got to go outside for a minute, sir, because the frequency is higher and it won't penetrate these rocks," Fessman said.

I nodded at him, and he was gone. Nguyen moved to sit closer to me, an arm's length away. He leaned forward bringing up one hand. When he opened that hand, I saw the sparkle of metal. Dog tags. I knew without saying a word that he had brought me Macho Man's dog tags. I didn't know why. Dog tags stayed with the body to give positive reinforcement to identity, which led to the notification of survivors as well as the application of religious services.

I accepted the tags, noting a hole in one of them. Nguyen pointed at the hole, his eyes looking into mine and not at the dog tag, however.

I frowned. Nguyen's behavior wasn't quite right. He knew better than to take the tags, and now he was handing them over to me in some ceremony he had to know didn't exist in either of our cultures. Nguyen pulled his hand back and reached behind him for his M-16. Quickly he ejected one round from the right side when the bolt was pulled back. He let the bolt slide home, feeding another round from the magazine into the chamber. He handed me the cartridge he'd ejected.

I took it in my free hand but looked back at my Montagnard scout with a question written on my face. Nguyen slowly took the cartridge from my right hand, pulled the dog tags from the other, and inserted the bullet portion of the cartridge into the hole in the dog tag. It was a perfect fit.

I was stunned. The bullet was a perfect fit. The 5.56 millimeter round the M-16 fired was much smaller than the 7.62 round the AK-47 fired. I breathed in and out deeply, but silently. I took the bullet and the dog tags back into my own hands, and then carefully tucked them into the pocket on my thigh where I kept the letters to my wife. Macho Man had been a victim of friendly fire.

Nguyen moved back to his position against the far wall, his face showing no expression at all. I wondered what he knew of Macho Man's death, and he had to know something because I'd charged him to keep the Marine safe. But we were not in the place, and it was not the right time to try to find out more.

Fessman came back in to announce that Cowboy would indeed be on station for the coming attack. My shoulders slumped in relief. I needed rest, but first I had to write home. Resupply was coming in which meant that I could get a letter out.

The letters to my wife had become, once again, after survival, my only means of coping with getting through another day and on into the coming night. For the first time, I decided to make up a completely fictional letter home. There was nothing I could come up with to write about except what was happening, and I could not write that. I lay in my lair, safe, but knowing I would be leaving soon to go back out into the jungle of unpredictable flying metal pieces. Bullets, shrapnel, fragments, it didn't matter much, outside of my cave. If something hit, then the war was over with God deciding whether I would still be in it, in it with missing parts or in it with an injury that might be a ticket home and still allow for full recovery. That last one would be like winning a lottery, even if it included a lot of surgery and unending pain.

I wrote about making a trip to the rear area to buy stuff I didn't have down where I was. Another K-Bar to replace the one I'd somehow lost. I still had the scabbard but no knife. I wrote that I found one, better than the one I'd lost. Of course, I knew my wife would not know that some commissary in the rear was not going to carry K-Bar Marine knives. Those were the issue out of the rear area armories, but impossible to get. Macho Man might have found one if he was still alive. But he'd had the misfortune to land with a ground-pounder unit in combat, and he'd paid the usual price. For me, that meant no K-Bar. Selfish is for the living. I'd never seen Macho Man smile, but I was willing to bet he'd smile in the hereafter if he could read my letter home. Because I'd thought of him, I also wrote about him but changed history to have him still alive, and also into being my friend, as much as an enlisted man can be an officer's friend back in the world.

I wrote on about how neat the rear area of Da Nang was. I'd never been to Da Nang, the town, and in fact, didn't know if there was a town. Maybe it was only a military presence. But my wife would not know, and if she did, probably not care. I also needed stationery and clear Scotch Tape, as well as any kind of snacks that weren't found in a C-Rations box. I had all the Ham and Mothers I wanted but a Snicker Bar would have been nice every once in a while, to take a bite of when the bitter taste of adrenalin filled my mouth. In my make-believe trip to the rear, I was able to purchase ten candy bars, to bring back to the A Shau and ration out over time.

The cave was a safe place from the rain, my letter-writing enemy. I sealed the single Marine Iwo Jima stationery sheet into the envelope using too much tape, as I was about out. The regular lick seal wasn't effective in my environment but Scotch Tape held everything together. I carefully taped over the delivery address so it wouldn't get washed out and then the "Free" word that had to be in the upper right corner in order for the letter to be delivered without postage. I knew I was getting quite a benefit by writing home every day. First Class postage was five cents, but the real difficulty wouldn't have been financial if I could not use the 'free' benefit. Stamps could not be taped to an envelope and still be valid if they washed away. That meant, with the monsoons in full display, the stamp would be long gone before the letter even got out of country.

I only made one exception to my fictional construct of a story. I could not stop myself from writing about the smell. The aroma of dead bodies had come to permeate the southern tip of the A Shau where we had been fighting in for some time. Some of the bodies of our Marines were stacked just north, and there were never enough body bags, and then the satchel charges we'd used on the enemy caves and tunnels in our attack had added hidden bodies to the mess. The sickening sweetish smell permeated everything, including the food. Only the smoke of cigarettes seemed to push it back. I wasn't really smoking, except with the Gunny, but every once and a while I'd light a Camel (I chose that brand from the many we got because I liked the picture on the pack) and then hold the lit tip not far from my nose. The smoke would take me away, to back home, to anywhere not where I was, and it would also completely replace the horrid smell of something worse than death. Decaying sadness and the outrageous injustice of death in combat. It wasn't the bad luck of dying in combat, that was just luck. No, it was the terrible luck of having come to arrive in combat at all. There were thousands and thousands of men in the rear areas but only rare small groups of us out on patrol and being ordered from place to place without the ability to come back. That injustice never left any of us who were out where I was.

I quickly field stripped my .45 Colt, taking it down to its eight main pieces in seconds. The .45, although tight from accurizing, was not so tight that any tools were needed. When I'd learned to field strip the automatic as a kid, from my Dad, I'd only remember that there were seven pieces. I'd always forget, to his disdain, the eighth piece sitting still held in my hand; the receiver. I had no Hoppes and no oil in the cave. I was sure that somebody in the company did, but I wasn't going to bother to try to find some. I swabbed the parts of the automatic with water from my canteen, and then wiped everything dry with a pair of socks I'd saved. I re-folded the socks and put them back in my pack when I was done. The .45 hadn't taken much water to clean, so the socks would be usable in a few days, although nothing really ever dried down in the A Shau, at least not in the monsoon period I was in.

I lay down to try to sleep, curling up against the rough rock wall. The sand felt soft and good beneath me, but my left hand would not stay away from the pocket. I massaged the dog tags, the M-16 cartridge and the letter to my wife as if they were somehow bizarrely connected. My right hand clutched my cleaned .45 Colt, and somehow there was a balance. I drifted off, the dark thoughts swirling inside of me finally fading into oblivion.

THE TWENTY-SIXTH DAY : THIRD PART

Fessman gently shook my shoulder. I inhaled sharply, suddenly realizing he'd been doing it for a while, but the depth of sleep I'd gone into would not allow me to think that I was in the A Shau Valley of South Vietnam commanding Marines in combat. I awoke slowly, no panicked jerk like I'd heard so much about at home, from guys supposedly returning from the shit and flinching at backfires that never occurred anymore in my sixty's world. Maybe the uncontrolled jerk would come over time, and I wondered about that. I yawned and breathed deeply again, stretching my arms out until the pain of my leech wounds forced me to pull them back in. The wounds hurt in a nasty surface way. Not deep enough to keep me from functioning, but deep enough so that I was never without them at the very edge of my consciousness. I wondered if Morphine worked as a topical. Maybe I could just slather some on and the pain would go away, although I didn't really believe it. Pain is what the A Shau dished out, and if you missed the breakfast of leech wounds then lunch would be served with something truly hurtful and more permanent.

"Puff is going to come down and make four pylon-turn passes, at your command, sir," Fessman said, speaking quietly, his head bent down so his mouth could be close to my ear. "We don't have much time. I let you sleep as long as the Gunny would allow. But you have to decide where Puff will lay down its fire. Here or there?"

My mind roiled and tossed. Here or there where I wanted to ask but instead took a few seconds to clear my head. I wanted coffee, some crackers and maybe part of a cigarette, but knew I wasn't going to have the time, or the immediate availability, to get any of those things.

"Here," Fessman said, patiently, "over what we believe is their current position, or 'there' where we are going to attack up along the river, and maybe into the jungle patch just north.

I looked at my watch. It was 1415, or a quarter after two. The re-supply would be coming in at three. I shook myself fully awake, pulling my hand back from its grip on Macho Man's dog tags and the M-16 cartridge. How was I ever going to solve the mystery of his death in the A Shau Valley under the horrid conditions we were fighting under? One of my Marines killed him and I felt driven to know who. I could not think beyond that because beyond that was a place of bleak dark death. If I knew, then I would act. I would have to act. I reached into my pocket and took out my heavily taped letter to my wife. I handed it over to Fessman. I knew that the likelihood of me actually getting close to the CH- 46 was slim. Fessman would be much more able to take the few seconds to make the run and deliver the letter to one of the crewmen, although there were no guarantees if the chopper came under fire.

"I'll make sure it gets out, sir," he said, folding the letter carefully into his right breast pocket.

"How long can the C-130 orbit?" I asked, knowing Fessman didn't know but wanting him to find out.

The enemy knew Puff, like it knew the Ontos, and it feared the fire-breathing dragon of a monster. The longer I could keep the plane on station, the longer the enemy would keep its head down and remain stationary, but I couldn't wait too long. The 46 would not land in a hot L.Z. and Puff couldn't do its thing if the air was filled with Huey Cobra gunships and Skyraiders under it or too close to the cone of fire it would deliver.

"Give me the arty net," I said, holding out my hand.

Fessman took only seconds to comply. I held the microphone and called in the zone fire mission I'd calculated earlier. The battery would give me 30 155 mm rounds, 6 on target, and 6 on four targets designated as the cardinal points of the compass, but fifty meters (the kill radius of a 155 on flat terrain) out from the target. The zone fire would be followed by the same call, except using 105 mm howitzer rounds two hundred meters left and right of the target as I called it in. I had not adjusted for the 155 mm howitzer weapon before, and I couldn't remember if the bigger guns were set up in a battery circle of four or six guns. The 105s were set in a circle of six. If the 155's were only four to a circle then their zone fire volley would be less than what I had planned, but still devastating. I timed the opening of fire to be at 1500, or 3:00 p.m. exactly. The resupply chopper would be on final approach, coming down in the flat L.Z. by the river, while the protective swarm of Huey gunships would be swarming well away from the gun target line where the artillery fire the battery was about to deliver would, hopefully, take out any forces on the eastern ridge where the still-beating drums had been relocated to.

I wouldn't be adjusting fire on the barrage. It would come in on terrain I'd already registered, and the battery was fully capable of hitting that particular spot using only half the maximum load of powder bags. There were other issues I had to deal with, however, and once the artillery rounds were fired and then laid down I could always do a quick adjustment up or down the top of the escarpment, as long as the shells did not strike too far west, and encounter the face of the cliff again. Two companies of men and a crewed Ontos would be down from the top of that cliff face, I among them.

Fessman worked with the AN-323 air radio while I got into my gear. I had to take everything, as we would not be coming back to the caves again, not unless disaster struck and we had no choice. I would miss the total security the many feet of solid rock gave me in the cave. I hoped the days of paralyzing fear were behind me, for the most part, although the coiled snake of fear that could curl around any internal organ at will, never left my insides. The cave had gone a long way toward giving me much needed sleep and a feeling of security enough to allow me to carry on. I knew I would miss the cave badly and wasn't likely to have the gift of such a fortified position protecting me again.

The beating of the enemy drums became more physically present, as I crawled up out of the cave, pulling my pack behind me until I was clear of the hanging poncho cover. Even with my experience and knowledge, I hated the sound of the drums. It wasn't just the sound, somehow reverberating right through the joined drops of falling rain. It was also the naked intent the drums dully transmitted. The NVA wanted us dead, with myself very probably at the very top of a short list.

Drums

[audio   src="https://s3-us-west-2.amazonaws.com/strausss-hortstories/Drums-of-War.mp3"]

My own poncho cover rustled and sparkled as it became almost instantly wet. I settled my helmet firmly down to cover the back of my neck. The rain was going to be both a help and a hindrance in the coming attack. In the very inner sanctum of my mind lived the hope that the NVA had taken a beating so badly at the river the night before they might have gone underground to lick their wounds. I let out a sigh, as I moved out, knowing in my heart of hearts that the NVA was not built that way. Their soldiers thought they were fighting for their families and country, I knew. I was fighting for my country and family, as well, but in reality, I was actually fighting as much for the men around me as anything or anyone else. I didn't love all my Marines. They were like my arms and legs and other body parts. I didn't love my body parts either, but the sum of them made up who I was and how they obeyed my commands and moved determined how I moved through what I knew of the universe. I could no longer imagine what it might be like to move through the A Shau Valley without the Marines who surrounded me at every point. If by some bizarre turn of fortune, I made it back to the world, then I wondered what it might be like to move through that world without them?

The drums beat right on through the deep-throated, but the distant roar of what I knew had to be the turbines of the C-130. The Skyraiders were up there in the clouded-over sky, as well, and, in spite of the fact that we'd soon be engaged in unpredictable and bloody ground combat, I felt a strange warmth for the amount of firepower that was being brought to bear on our behalf.

Fessman pushed the small headset of the air radio toward me. I pulled my damaged helmet off, put the headset on, and then replaced the helmet to keep the water from ruining the electronics and dripping down my face.

"Flash, is that you?" A scratchy voice asked into my ear.

"Affirmative, Cowboy, over," I replied, a small smile creasing my lips.

"Man oh man, but you've got some crap flying around up here, with more coming I presume."

I knew Cowboy had to know about the choppers coming in, but he'd never say anything other than what he'd just said.

"Amen to that," I replied.

"Where are you going to want us for the Thanksgiving feast?" Cowboy said.

"Up and down the alley," I replied, the alley being the river, which I also knew he would understand.

The landing zone was going to be congested in bad visibility and heavy rain. The Skyraiders would provide cover and fire from a few feet above the raging water, running up and down the river, but they'd only able to remain directly on station for very brief periods. The Huey gunships surrounding the CH-46 like a cloud of bees would have the higher air, but not much higher. Puff would fire and then move on before much of any real action began if any real action began. Would the

CH-46 come in on time? Everything was targeting the arrival time of the resupply chopper to be exactly on time. What if it was early or late? There was no way to communicate with the machine while it was on its way. Any communication at all with the choppers would immediately tip off any listening NVA troops that the birds were coming in.

We moved through the edge of the jungle, retracing steps I'd taken so many times I had stopped counting. We moved along the edge of the berm that was set out about five to ten meters from the front face of the eastern cliff wall.

The jungle was to our west, or on my left hand as we moved, and would only draw away as the huge mud flat below where the Bong Song slithered and roared expanded outward. The water hit the wall's flat bottom somewhere below the old airport and well downriver from Hill 975. In the past, the company had jammed itself into the slight clefts that were formed further downriver and within full visibility of the flats, but this time would be different. The companies had to cross the river after the resupply and they had to cross immediately, or the NVA would be able to bring up their .50 Caliber machine gun and a load of shoulder-mounted RPG rockets.

Finally, a good distance from the river, and snuggled in against the outer edge of the heavy jungle growth we came to rest. I knew other Marines were swelling out and up the base of the cliff where we'd taken up defensive positions in the past. Their movement and setting in bothered me, the thought of just how much damage and death a few short artillery rounds, impacting near the top of the escarpment, might generate as they had before.

The chopper came out of the south, dropping in from high up to avoid as much risk from ground fire as possible. The cacophony of engaged combat filled the air around me, although the misting rain was so heavy it was almost impossible to make out any details of the river in the distance, or what was really happening there.

The Skyraiders, three of them, didn't need to be seen because they were so loud. Their thunderous engines bit and plowed through the mist, making mincemeat of the rain and mist, as they made pass after low pass over the river. Somehow the big CH-46 was able to drop onto the river bank without hitting or being struck by one. Each pass of the Skyraiders, several minutes apart was punctuated by staccato strafing runs as they sprayed the sides of the river with their 20 mm cannons. Higher above, split into two revolving groups of three, were the Huey Cobra gunships.

The artillery barrage started after Fessman confirmed the 1500 target time to the battery for the zone fires, and then repeated the order to fire. The crump and blast of that zone fire exercise began less than a minute later, with the noise and feeling of heavy explosions reverberating across and down into the valley area where the companies lay waiting to attack, unload the chopper and then build a temporary ramp over to the remains of the bridge still extending most of the way across the raging river. Everything seemed to slide way into the distance, however, when Puff opened up with its rotary guns. Flying the first rotation of the pylon circle tightly, the rotary guns sticking out of its side roared out their superior death-dealing firepower, and the tongue lash of the concentrated bullets poured into the jungle just to our south, and a bit inland from where the river bank extended up to become a heavy jungle.

I cringed down, although I was not as close to the dragon tongue of fire as the last time I'd been on the ground nearby to observe Puff's effect. The last time my face had been buried too deep in the mud for me to see much of anything. I peered upward, even though my body remained hard-pressed into the fetid stinking mud. I tasted the aroma of the dead, which was strong, it's sugary bitter smell never leaving my awareness, even as I tried to take in the sweeping combat scenes all around me, as I tried to see what was going on. The Gunny lay on my left side and Fessman on the other, both doing the same thing I was. The play of weaponry, the chopper dropping in, blasting debris everywhere, and the flitting in and out nature of the giant wasp-like and heavily firing Huey gunships was overpowering. I heard the Skyraiders begin another run, this time from the north, and I prayed that the CH-46, touching the mud not more than a few meters from the river, would not be so close as to have its whirling rotors strike one of the passing aircraft while it was making a run.

An M-60 opened up to my left, set back up higher on the berm near the cliff wall to our backs. Then another opened up, both appearing to fire ten or twenty shot bursts several seconds apart. I'd ordered the fire and was relieved to hear other machine guns joining the first two. There was no margin for error in bringing all of our weaponry, ground, air, and artillery into play at once in order to assure that the CH-46 did not take rounds and either abort the resupply or be destroyed. The NVA could still fire at it from their hidden positions deep inside the jungle, especially if they'd brought their fifty to be set up for just such a target of opportunity. But would the fifty crew, and individual NVA troops, come out to face the kind of fire they were receiving from all quarters? A few solid hits into the body of the big helicopter and that would be it. There was no alternative plan to crossing the river and moving as rapidly as possible to the north. It was vital to hit Hill 975, in passing, as quickly as possible before the burrowed in soldiers there could be ready to receive us.

The Ontos was the key to our attack on the ground, just as it was the key to our survival while holding off the NVA while the ramp was constructed to get the armored vehicle to the other side of the river. I heard its motor straining as it negotiated the last bit of path along the side of the cliff and then climbed the berm to begin its travel toward the resupply chopper.

The artillery barrage played out and not long after the last pylon pass of Puff was made and the C-130 disappeared downriver so fast that it was like it'd never been there at all. But the gentle wind, blowing upriver brought the smell of burned jungle debris, and it also helped blow the smell of the dead to some other place, at least for a while.

There was a brief respite while the big double rotor chopper began to set in. the noise that usually accompanied it was somewhat muted by the heaviness of the misty rain. I turned to the Gunny at my side, rolling slightly over.

I removed Macho Man's dog tags from my thigh pocket. I did not have time to write my next daily letter home so there was nothing to interrupt the passage of the dog tags and the M-16 cartridge between the inner pocket and my hand. I handed the dog tags to the Gunny without delay or any ceremony. He dangled the two identical tags from the cheap government issue chain. I watched him stop the tags from swinging. He gripped the one tag with the fingers of his right hand. I held out the cartridge but he waved my offer back, as he stared at the tag. I knew then that he didn't need the cartridge to compare. There was only one weapon in the A Shau theater of combat that fired a round even close to that as illustrated by the hole in Macho Man's dog tag.

"Who," I asked, my voice flat and without emotion, my eyes fixed on what I could see of the landing chopper

"Don't know," he replied, replacing the dog tags back into the open and extended palm of my left hand.

"Who has it?" I asked, my voice a whisper.

"Who has what?" the Gunny replied, lighting a cigarette and

then blowing smoke up into the rain and mist, out from under the lip of his helmet.

I caught something in the delay of his answer, however. It was indefinable, but there. I could tell he wasn't looking at me either, instead of concentrating and working to get some bit of tobacco from between two of his teeth and then spitting it out. I watched him closely out of the sides of my eyes, and purposely waited, without answering his question.

"Jurgens," the Gunny finally said.

The Thompson submachine gun had found a home, and I was not surprised at all to understand where, or with whom, it had found that home. The question was, had that new home been made for it at the expense of Macho Man's life? I had real reservations about a weapon so heavy and so difficult to resupply with ammo, but those feelings, I knew, were not shared by most of the Marines around me. The Thompson was cool, and although it wasn't built to perform well in the jungle circumstance we were all in, the fact that it felt good to carry and be seen with, outweighed pure functional capability for most Marines who saw or encountered it.

"Look into it," was all I could think of to say.

Of all the men under the strange command I provided to the company, Jurgens was the most dangerous, murderous and yet combat effective Marine I had, outside of the Gunny and possibly Nguyen. The Gunny made no response to my instruction, but then, I didn't expect one. The Gunny had been dealing with Sugar Daddy and Jurgens long before I had come to the company. Somehow, and through a course where many Marines had died directly because of it, he'd found a way to straddle a hyper-sensitive course through a racial and cultural minefield to survive. I knew there would be no resolution in the death of Macho Man unless I applied it, but I could not apply anything unless I had the tacit approval, if not the direct participation, of the Gunny.

The plan was for everyone to stay down and provide whatever suppressing fire was necessary without exposing themselves to the open flat surface of the mud bank.

The chopper crew tossed stuff rapidly out of the CH-46 rear cargo ramp. I wasn't close enough to see individual items but I knew the unloading was going without incident. Unfortunately, our combined force of Marines would not have the services of either Puff or the artillery when it became necessary to get the supplies to the water and then the ramp somehow designed and built to hold the Ontos' weight.

The attack wasn't directed toward where the chopper was coming down, or the supplies were being offloaded and piling up. The attack was set to be a clone of the attack we'd made nights earlier when the company had been forced to move downriver to rescue Kilo and cover its descent down the cliff face into the valley. As before, except with the addition of Kilo's support, the company had to take the whole length and breadth of the jungle and hold it. Unlike the previous time, where the company had merely swept through it, this time both companies would have to secure and hold the difficult enemy-held terrain in order to effectively suppress fire so the ramp could be built and the Ontos driven up and across the bridge.

The "Same Old Song" attack began silently, the Marines, including those of Kilo Company, almost automatically eased into the shocked jungle as one continuous force, using the rain and mist drifting over the area as cover. The air over the jungle was still filled with tiny bits of debris blown into the lower atmosphere by the rotary strafing power of Puff's orbiting attack.

The Ontos motored down toward the river, making no effort to direct any of its recoilless rifles toward the jungle. Initially, I'd calculated that the applied mass of air power would provide all the suppression necessary to allow us to reach the end of the bridge. Once there, the Ontos was to serve as cover, since there was no other cover available at all, and provide its own considerable suppressing fire across the river. Taking the jungle on our side was one thing, but there was no way the high ground on the other side of the river, a bit further south, could hope to be successfully attacked or its fire suppressed. Carruthers and the Gunny were leading the attack into the jungle, and small arms fire began to rise in volume once the covering fire of the M-60s began to lessen. I climbed to my feet and, with Nguyen and Fessman at my sides, ran to get out in front of the advancing Ontos. No fire seemed to be directed at us, although it was almost impossible to determine whether that was really true or not because of the lack of visibility. The sound of the rushing river overpowered most other sounds, even those of high-velocity gunfire in the distance. We passed by the chopper, not stopping, and avoiding the twin stacks of supplies already offloaded. At some point, Marines from the company must have gathered the bodies of our fallen brothers because I noted those being loaded into the side of the chopper closest to the river as the supplies were still being offloaded from the rear ramp.

The Skyraiders came in over the river just as we reached the area I knew we had to somehow fortify in order to build the base of the ramp. The Marston sheets and the Ontos were all we had, as other Marines began to assemble, no doubt the team the Gunny had selected to do the actual work.

I went into the mud right at the water's edge, where the stuff was solid but wet and messy. My body slipped into the stuff like it had been waiting for just such an intrusion. My helmet and eyes were all that was above the surface, as I thought about my .45, which I'd failed to get out of my holster. Was it better off inside and clean or out with me and filthy?

The chopper's turbines went up to maximum, as the huge helicopter lifted off, rising up and then dipping its nose and heading straight down river, in the trace of the Skyraiders. The noise was deafening and the feeling of being stranded out on the mud flat with only the Ontos as any kind of cover and protection was frightening. My coiled snake of fear, so common to my interior was no more. I was a living, breathing and shaking body of fear, wondering how I'd gotten myself into an even worse mess than I had been in before, and how to command and direct the Marines around me to do what they had to do without the Gunny being there to back my every move.

one-hundred-twenty-seven

THE TWENTY-SIXTH NIGHT : FIRST PART

I moved across the surface of the mud, with what was left of my scout team just ahead. Fessman and Nguyen trailed just behind. We crawled low, the light of the day beginning to die and provide some sort of camouflage, if not cover. The Ontos lay ahead, sitting like a big solid Sphinx of a thing it so didn't resemble, but could be imagined to be in the bad light. The Gunny was already there, as I came around the side of the Ontos's right track edge. I noted immediately that the six recoilless rifles of the armored machine were directed off at an angle back toward where the jungle was heaviest on our side of the river. The river's rush blocked out what sound might have otherwise penetrated the area, only the overpowering beat and thunder of Skyraider propellers got through. But they were on their last run with the coming of the night, I knew. The Skyraiders were not equipped to fight effectively in the dark, at least not to provide the kind of pinpoint support an infantry company like our own had to have.

The mist had converted itself back into a hard rain, and the leech population had approved. I realized I'd picked up some more 'friends' when the pain of the previous wounds on my torso lessened. The new leeches were leaking a deadener into my damaged skin surfaces, acting more like symbiotes than the parasites they truly were. It was a bad deal, I thought grimly, trying to adjust myself to some position of partial comfort on the mudflat. I was uncomfortable but it was okay for the time being.

I crawled forward, sloughing my way through the top layer of watery mud, swirling loosely atop the deeper harder mud base of the river's wide-flattened edge. The rain was ceaseless, and beat down upon my helmet like God was playing me as some sort of weird percussion instrument. I slithered around the back edge of the Ontos's right track and then along the distance of its right side. The Ontos was facing the river directly and it took a few labored seconds to get all the way to the front of the track. The mechanical beast vibrated its dangerous existence through the mud, to let me know it was alive and idling, waiting to deliver whatever kind of awful death needed to be delivered.

The problem we faced was one that seemed to be a dilemma without a possible solution, given the tools and conditions at hand. The Ontos had to go with us if we were to cross the river, survive and keep the NVA from pursuing us. We had to cross the river because our welcome had worn so thin that the Gunny and I both knew we could not possibly survive the night, much less the next day, or longer, where we were. I lay in the mud, looking out over toward what I couldn't really see well, but knew was there in front of me. The heaping waters of the fast-moving river, encountering the poorly laid portable bridge, shown shadowy white, as the moving water burst out over its surface. The river's rush, and the rain coming down on my helmet, prevented me hearing the crashing sound the plunging water had to be making.

Another sound penetrated through all the rest, but it was felt rather than heard. The drums. The NVA had remounted their drums, probably up on top of the cliff to our rear, and the drums were intent on sending their message of doom. The Mexicans had played the Deguello outside the Alamo until it had fallen. Twenty-four hours a day. The effect had to have been similar to what I was feeling now, from the drums varying, but never-ending, vibrations of evil.

DRUMS
[audio   src="https://straussshortstories.s3-us-west-2.amazonaws.com/Drums-of-War.mp3"]

I knew Nguyen was just behind me and was surprised when he surged forward to pull himself up to view the river from right next to my shoulder. I turned my head but didn't see Nguyen. It was Gunny. He stared outward like I had been doing, looking for something that might offer a solution to our life or death problem. I waited, hoping he'd see something, anything, but he just continued to wait and stare.

I looked back over my shoulder, feeling the achy sting of the voracious leech bites when I moved. The smell of the river was a relief from the fetid aroma of the jungle, mixed in with tendrils of sweetly sour stuff coming up from the mud. I felt that if I could just get clear of all of it, stand on some high rock somewhere naked, the rain would wash me clean, but I knew that was not to be.

Some small arms fire opened up from downriver, but I couldn't see the tracks of any tracers, although the body of the Ontos blocked most of my view in that direction.

"Can't stay here long, Junior," the Gunny cautioned, needlessly, from my right.

I pulled myself forward until I was able to see around the right front track edge of the Ontos. I reached up with my left hand to find enough purchase to raise my torso so I could peer over a slight berm that lay between our position and the jungle, where the enemy fire had to be coming from. I knew, unless the A-6 Intruder was somewhere above us, that there would be no air support in the night. I called back along the edge of the Ontos for Fessman, and was surprised when I heard his reply come upward from someplace under the Ontos.

"Yes, sir," came his muted response.

"Front and center, Corporal," I ordered, wanting him out from under the armored vehicle, just as fast as I could get him out of there..

The Ontos could only rotate its turret thirty degrees in either direction. That meant that to aim the 106 recoilless rifles beyond that short arc, the Ontos would have to turn using its tracks. The last time we'd had the same problem, the crew had been able to release and reset two pins, allowing the turret to be rotated and set to swivel in a different thirty-degree arc, but the pins, once the turret was returned to battery, dropped and sealed into place. There would be no removing them from the thick armored metal without heavy duty drilling or torch equipment, and there was none fo that available in the valley, or even anything close. The left track since it would have to power the turn, would churn in reverse while the right would be moving forward. It was the only way the Ontos could turn left to face incoming fire if the driver and gunner felt it necessary, like if the .50 came back online. If the Ontos turned with Fessman underneath it then his remains might never be found, as they'd be so deeply ground into the mud.

Fessman surfaced and crawled around the right track to get to me. I ordered him to call in air support if we could get it. Whatever effort we made to get across the river would have a much higher chance of success if the enemy was either wholly or partially distracted by being forced to try to burrow back underground to survive.

I was about to let go of whatever I'd grabbed on the front of the Ontos when I felt the bar in my hand give and sway. I pulled and released, then grabbed the bar and pulled again. It took a few seconds for me to realize I'd grabbed onto a link of heavy chain. I moved to the front of the machine and ran my hands back and forth across the swinging arc of the chain. The front of the Ontos was covered in chain, but I'd never paid enough attention to notice. I slunk back down in order to avoid being a target, although the small arms fire from the jungle had abated. I stared out across the short distance toward the gray whiteness of the water rising up and then cascading down from the front area of the bridge.

I laid down flat on my stomach and eased over where the Gunny still lay, unmoving.

"How much can it pull?" I asked, in a heavy whisper, although there was no one to hide anything from.

"How much can what pull?" the Gunny replied, not whispering at all.

"The Ontos?" I said.

"How much can the Ontos pull?" the Gunny repeated, more to himself than to me. "How in hell would I know? It's a tracked vehicle with some pretty low gears for getting out of tough situations. I'd imagine it could probably pull ten or twenty tons, depending on whether what you want to be towed was on wheels or not."

I lay thinking. The idea had come out of nowhere. I'd held the chain in my hand and it was like it had spoken to me.

"The bridge," the Gunny said, whispering loudly this time.

"Yeah, if we got enough chain," I replied.

I smiled in the night, at about how quick the Gunny was. He'd figured out my plan as I had been developing it. If we could pull the bridge the rest of the way across the river then there might be a chance.

The Gunny moved, climbing to his knees, before calling Nguyen forward to help him. Nguyen was there like he'd been hovering above, just waiting to be dropped in when invited. Both men moved to the front of the Ontos and began to work the chain loose from the Ontos.

It took several minutes for them to get it free. I spent the time getting closer to Fessman and listening to his dialogue on the air radio. The back and forth went on for what seemed like a long time, although I doubted it was more than a few minutes. I didn't need to wait for Fessman to tell me the result. The tenor of the conversation had been all one way. There would be no Puff, no A-6 Intruder, or any of that. Air Support was down for the night. The artillery 175's could reach us, as I'd called them in before, but with us on the gun target line, fully exposed, receiving red bag rounds was more likely to assure that the company would be fully wiped out more quickly and effectively than if the loom-ing NVA regiment was confronted in direct engagement.

"There's enough, I think," the Gunny said, moving low, back to my position flat on the mud. "I think the Ontos might be able to pull the bridge but I'm not sure, and then there's the problem of the other end. If we pull too much then won't the other end be caught by the current and swing around and over to our side?"

It was a rhetorical question, I knew. There was no way to know what might happen when the chain was attached and physical events were brought to their own conclusion.

"Getting it across…" I began, but the Gunny cut me off.

"We use a light line," he said. "There's one inside the Ontos, but somebody's got to swim it over, and then pull the end of the heavy chain up onto the body of the bridge."

My mind went instantly to the alligator I'd encountered earlier out in the center of the river. That one had gotten quickly dead, but there had to be a whole lot more lying down at the bottom of the rush-ing water waiting for prey. I also knew there was nobody else to make the swim whom I would trust, and I longingly wanted the cleanliness that the fast-moving water would provide, along with the cooling ef-fect I knew it would have on me. I wasn't worried a bit about going up-river, diving in to swim and then encounter the end of the bridge as I was being whisked downriver. I also wasn't worried about getting up on the bridge from the water either. There were plenty of holds and torn away line segments left from previous crossings to alleviate that concern. Getting the chain pulled across and then up onto the flat deck was going to be a problem, however. It was heavy and the current was powerful. I mentioned the situation to the Gunny.

"Nguyen," the Gunny replied. "Once the line is there, instead of pulling the chain we send Nguyen hand over hand using the line to join you. Both of you together should be able to manage it."

My relief at hearing the solution was palpable and my breath-ing slowed, as I began to strip my uniform off. Nguyen I trusted. I also wondered why I had not thought of such a simple and effective reso-lution. I stayed close to the Ontos, realizing that my white skin would stand out in the night with the rain glistening its way down from the top of my head to my feet. I wasn't going into the river with my uniform on. That was a recipe for suicide if the slightest thing went wrong. As soon as I was down to my underwear I pulled my boots off. I didn't want to lose the boots but I could not swim with boots on. I had to count on Fessman to protect what I was leaving behind. My confidence was high, although the .45 Colt I'd promised never to be parted from again lay folded up in its holster inside my blouse, giving me a bit of uncomfortable pause. I would be basically naked and unarmed for the whole operation.

I was about to take the end of the line the Gunny was holding out when Nguyen grabbed me. He began rubbing the worst kind of river mud all over my body. The mud was so awful the rain didn't wash it away, and the rancid smell of it was terrible. I had to keep blinking my stinging eyes, and breathing through my mouth. The Gunny gave up trying to hand me the line, instead squatted down to tie it about my waist.

"Hope we have enough rope, Junior," he offered, the tone of his voice not at all convincing. "If you don't make it on the first go around we'll pull you in and you can try again."

I didn't answer, instead began moving upriver, staying as low as I could while still making good speed. I didn't have far to go. The rope around my waist went taut after about forty meters. That distance upriver would have to do. Nguyen stayed right with me until I was ready. Without warning, I sprang fully erect, ran the few steps to the river's edge and dived in. I didn't go deep. The current was just too great. I flopped onto the surface of the water, and then was grabbed by it and dragged away. The speed of my travel was frightening. I didn't have time to swim at all. I could only reach out as the end of the bridge seemed to rocket by. I caught a bit of ragged old rope right at the very last second when I thought for sure I would fail and be making a second attempt. My right arm was almost pulled from its socket, but I held on, the water tossing me back and forth, and then up and down. I held on for dear life, finally gaining enough strength to pull myself into the lee of the current behind the side of the bridge structure. I fought to find purchase on the metal edges and against the downpour of white rushing water. I was worried about cutting my bare feet up, but I made it up without injury. I got aboard the bridge and lay flat, gasping huge amounts of air, in and out of my lungs. I stayed flat on my back until I could roll over. I looked down at my body. I was totally white again. The river had taken the mud off like it had been a mere layer of water-color paint. If I stood I would become fairly visible, depending upon range. Laying there, I pulled the line firm, and jerked on it three times, before untying it from my waist and securing five loops and using a couple of half-hitches, around a nearby stanchion.

I lay and watched the water where the bent rope was dragged to form an arc by the downriver current. I could see nothing of the shore. The wait was short, however. Nguyen came across the water almost atop the rope, moving more like a giant water spider than a human. I didn't have to help him, as he leaped upward and seemed to fly onto the surface of the bridge and catch hold unaided. We lay together, side by side. I wondered if I would ever be around a man like Nguyen again, attached to me in his strange way, in whatever I might have left as the existence in life if I was to have a life. The thought of my own mortality jarred me into action. I grabbed the rope and began pulling. Nguyen joined me on the other side of the line. We pulled slowly but strongly, feeling the weight of the chain, along with the jarring jerky resistance the current induced. The oscillating grew worse as the end of the chain came closer.

I finally saw the end of the chain surface and move toward us. I was relieved to see a D-ring shackle attached to the first link. I had begun to worry about securing the chain to the bridge, but the D-ring changed everything. The stanchion I'd used to tie off the rope had to be welded solidly to the bridge structure, possibly it could to take the kind of load we were about to put on it, but there was no guarantee.

Working as hard as we could, and trying not to have our hands lacerated by the bouncing jerking chain, Nguyen and I were able to get it wrapped once around the stanchion with some difficulty. While I held on for dear life, Nguyen unscrewed the shackle-bar and then inserted it between the first link and one further down. In seconds, the loop of the chain was secured. Only then did it occur to me that we had no communications with the Gunny, or Fessman, or anyone in the company, and they could not see what we had done. We waited together, but nothing happened.

I looked at Nguyen and nodded with a frown. There was nothing to be done for it, we had to use the chain to get back across to tell them the chain was on, but there was no sense risking both of us. I pointed at myself, and then the chain, and then across the water into the night. I crouched, slithered outward and went down the chain head first on the upriver side of it. The water secured me to the bouncing chain so solidly that I knew I wasn't going to be torn loose, but moving down the chain, while still keeping my head above water proved difficult. After a few seconds, I relaxed, however. The cool water rushing over me was finally having the effect I'd wanted so badly. I was cool. I was clean and it seemed, at least as long as I clung to the chain, that I was safe. The going became easier as I slowed and got closer to the shore.

The Gunny and Fessman grabbed me and pried me loose from the chain.

"Nguyen?" the Gunny asked, looking out in the wet night toward where the bridge had to be.

Rather than respond, I crawled to the side of the Ontos, and worked to get my uniform back on, relieved that everything was just as I'd left it. I strapped the .45 to my waist and got my boots on. Each move gave me more comfort, although it also distanced me from the wonderful cooling freedom I'd enjoyed while in the grip of the river's current. When I was done I went back down to a low crouching position.

"Nguyen's on the bridge," I said. "I told him to stay there and wait, or at least I think I told him that."

"Let's see if this thing's going to work," the Gunny said. "I let the men inside know about what we're up to. None of them could tell me anything about our prospects."

The Gunny moved to the back of the Ontos and worked on something. I checked out the attachment of the chain to the front of the Ontos. The vehicle had a huge ring welded to the very center of its hull. Nothing could have served as a better attachment point for the chain. Slowly the chain pulled up from the mud, as the Ontos clattered into gear and ground it's way backward. The chain grew taut. Soon the chain was so taut that the part I could see was a straight line into the night. The Ontos stopped, although its small engine continued to roar. Nothing more happened.

"Can't do it?" I asked, turning back to face the Gunny.

"Wait," the Gunny replied, blowing out smoke from a cigarette he'd somehow found time to light.

He took two more hits from the cigarette before anything happened.

The Ontos moved backward very slowly, the movement so slow it seemed almost imperceptible.

"Mud," the Gunny said, laconically.

Slowly the Ontos continued to move, faster and faster until it stopped again. I turned to the river, and then got to my hands and knees and crawled forward, feeling the enemy drums beats come up through my hands once more, and regretting the mud that I was again covering myself with. I crawled until I ran into the edge of the bridge, noting in amazement that the body of the thing had plunged slightly downward, as it had likely encountered some eaten-out portion of the bank. The Ontos would be able to drive right on board.

I crabbed myself backward to where Fessman waited, got my pack on and prepared for the crossing. One of Jurgens' Marines came running up to tell me that the Gunny was holding a command post meeting. I thought the use of the phrase strange, as formalities had all but disappeared in the combat at the bottom of the A Shau. I kept my pack on but headed a bit upriver to where the Gunny was squatting and waiting for me to appear. I got down and pulled my helmet off, the rain now light enough to not be such a torturing bother on my skull, and wanting to hear what it was the Gunny had to say.

"Junior's plan is for the company to cross the bridge first, and then set up a base of fire up and down on the far bank," the Gunny said, while Sugar Daddy, Jurgens and then I, crouched in front of him. "There are still plenty of fox holes left over there so we shouldn't have to dig in. Kilo crosses last, leaving it to us to make sure they have plenty of protection to make it on such an exposed run. The Ontos crosses right after us and before Kilo, to add to the base of fire from the far side."

I was surprised at the plan, particularly the part about where it was seemingly my idea, since I'd gotten used to being the one to deliver my plans to everyone around. I was also a bit uncomfortable that the plan seemed too smoothly set up and delivered like the details had been pre-planned earlier. A tingling sensation stayed with me when the men broke apart. The plan sounded good, almost too good.

"What was that?" I asked the Gunny, once everyone was gone, preparing to make the crossing.

"What was what?" he asked, getting his pack on with the assistance of his own radioman.

"Why isn't the Ontos crossing first, and then everyone just following as fast as they possibly can?" I asked.

"The enemy knows what we're doing," the Gunny said. "There's no small arms fire anymore because they're getting ready to attack. The NVA figured out what we're up to and they're coming, and right now."

The Gunny turned and loped off toward the bridge without another word. His pronouncement that the NVA was coming had instantly brought my own fear bubbling up from the abyss where it had been waiting all along. Something was wrong, but whatever it was didn't register on me. I ran toward the bridge and to escape to the other side, closing fast on the Gunny's back. Fessman ran with me, Nguyen joining in as we ran by. I was happy to see the Montagnard, yet sorry that I hadn't had another thought about him being left alone on the bridge since I'd left him.

The run across the bridge was without incident, except for the six-foot jump down onto the surface of the far bank once we were across. The mud and sand softened the fall, but once again, I was covered in mud and debris when I got back up. The platoons crossed and spread out, as the Gunny had laid down in presenting 'my' plan, although going back down on the jungle matting and wet surface of the more substantial ground beneath me, allowed the tingling feeling that something was wrong to rise again to the surface. I heard the Ontos. It creaked along, invisible at the other end of the bridge until it was more than halfway across. It slowly came across out of the night. Near the end of the bridge, where the drop-off was too severe to allow it to continue, the machine stopped. I noted that the crew had turned the armored vehicle around before they'd come onto the bridge, so that the flechette-loaded recoilless rifles pointed back toward the other side of the river.

Small arms fire on the other side started almost immediately, with green tracers streaming up from the downriver part of the jungle. Taking in the scene, marginally illuminated by the tracer fire, the situation came together in my mind. The Ontos could not traverse to fire at that part of the jungle where the firing came from. The supporting fires the company had set up on our side could not see across the river to provide fire support of almost any kind. The Ontos could not complete its journey until some sort of short supporting structure could be built to support its descent to the bank below. And the Ontos was blocking the end of the bridge, quite effectively, for the Marines in Kilo Company who would be attempting to run across and around it.

"You son of a bitch," I whispered, my voice so low nobody could hear.

The Gunny was sacrificing Kilo to save our own company and the Ontos. Not only that, he'd known what he was doing, as had Jurgens and Sugar Daddy when he'd laid down what he'd called 'my' plan.

I got up and ran downriver, in the direction the Gunny had taken. I ran calling his name out loud. I got more than thirty meters before I was pulled down.

"Shut up, Junior, you're just making a target of yourself," the Gunny whispered intently into my right ear, while his hand pushed harshly down over my mouth.

I relaxed, as best I could, breathing deeply through my nose until the Gunny's hand eased away.

"What have you done?" I asked, not knowing what else to say.

"There was no other way," the Gunny replied. "The Ontos has to stay on station to prevent the NVA from crossing. Most of the guys from Kilo should make it. What did you want me to do, sacrifice the company instead, or maybe everyone?"

"Why didn't we all just cross immediately?" I replied, trying to control my voice.

The NVA .50 caliber opened up, firing enfilade fire up from the jungle and straight along the line of the river, sweeping across the bank of the far side. I saw the stream of the green stuttering line before I heard the steady staccato roar of the thing.

"How are they supposed to get through that?" I said, my voice rising again.

"I don't know," the Gunny said, refusing to look me in the eyes.

"We've got to do something," I said, finally watching while the enemy had to be inflicting massive losses on Kilo.

"Why didn't you tell me?" I asked, my shoulders slumping, trying to will the .50 to stop firing.

The drums beat, their sound now able to be heard as the rain had lifted somewhat, the sound of the drums and the drumming of the .50. The running abandoned Marines of Kilo had to be taking a terrible terminal beating.

"Because you'd still be over there, and dead," the Gunny replied.

"What can we do?" I asked, but the Gunny was gone.

Fessman looked at me, as did Nguyen, as if I might have some magical plan to save Kilo, but I had nothing. I stared into the green tracer-tarnished night. There were no yellow tracers being fired from our side of the river. There was no point. I shivered, experiencing a kind of pain I'd never felt before. It went beyond and right through the cloying ache of white-hot fear that had once more risen to paralyze and terrify me, to the point where I didn't think I could handle it anymore.

one-hundred-twenty-eight

THE TWENTY-SIXTH NIGHT : SECOND PART

I crawled to the lip of the berm and fell straight into an empty hole that had to be six feet deep if it was an inch. Fessman cascaded down upon me with Nguyen slipping down next to him. The sound of the drums and the NVA fifty followed us right down into the bottom of the hole. The Ontos was not firing because it was set up with its flechette loaded rifles aimed to cover the bridge, which meant it could not fire at all until the area was clear of whatever survivors there might be from Kilo company trying to get across the bridge. I could not ignore the rapid thumping of the fifty-caliber. It was like each explosion, powering each round, ate into my very being. I climbed to see what I could see from the top of the hole, but the night consumed almost everything except the ceaseless arc of green tracers coming from the 50.

I ached to call in a 175 mm howitzer mission. The company was dug in, but the material of the bank consisted of soft and loamy dried mud. Even dug in, the protection the fox holes provided was next to nothing when pound-sized chunks of hot torn metal would surely be flying around. All of I could think of was how to stop the .50 caliber from decimating Kilo even more than it already had. I could see nothing of the far bank. Even the water heaping up and flying over the top of the upside-down Russian tank was invisible, although I knew it was still there. The scene burned into my mind, almost as if it was lit by huge Hollywood Klieg lights, although there was next to nothing for me to really 'see.' I stared into the dark, listening to the machine gun fire, the horrible drums, and feeling a sense of loss and guilt so powerfully that I could not move. I was not frozen in terror. I'd been frozen in terror before. I was frozen by something else I couldn't understand. I was frozen by a raw cloying agony of not wanting to be alive anymore. I'd been in the A Shau Valley for about three weeks, and I'd retreated up, down and back and forth through it more times than I could count. I had not planned or provided for this, the worst retreat of my life, with any kind of an active or passive thought at all. I realized that I'd thrown myself into being too busy working out a technical problem to pay attention to the fact that the stupendous size and potential effects of the overall situation needed to fully occupy me, and not the detail. Anyone in the company capable could have made the swim out to the bridge, but I'd wanted to do it myself. Anyone could have worked with the Gunny to secure the chain, and then supervised the Ontos bridge operation, but I'd enjoyed the brush blocking avoidance and temporary escape it gave me instead of paying attention to what was happening on the larger scale. I'd led nobody anywhere, instead I allowed myself to be diverted, or in reality, diverted myself from what I should have been doing, and consequently, nearly a whole company of men was having to pay for my potential failure to pay attention with their lives.

I stared fixedly out at the end of the bridge, where the Ontos sat, not twenty feet from the rear edge. Twenty feet. My mind rolled the number I'd come up with out of the blue, around and around in my head. The distance I was approximating for the Ontos to reach the end of the bridge was about the same distance that the bridge was wide. I knew the Ontos was a bit less than ten feet wide itself.

"Get the Gunny on his radio," I commanded Fessman, without turning, my mind running at top speed, calculating distances and measuring the potential for effects if my formulating plan was to be implemented.

"The Gunny," Fessman said, holding out the microphone.

"We turn the Ontos on top of the bridge, right where it is, and then take out that fifty," I said into the mike, without introduction or preamble.

"Interesting idea, Junior," the Gunny transmitted back, "but I'm not sure the surface of the bridge will tolerate how much gripping friction the tracks will put down in the turning. The surface of that thing is wood and not that thick of wood either. The Ontos weighs ten tons, or a bit more."

"It's not an idea, Gunny," I shot back. "We're not going to leave those guys to die over there. The .50 has them pinned down so the NVA can take them out one at a time. They'll all die slowly on that river bank and that's not going to happen unless we lose everything, including the Ontos. Turn the Ontos or I'll take my scout team back onto that bridge and make it happen right now."

As if to punctuate my order, the .50 opened up again, after being silent for a few seconds, the gunner probably having to put in a new ammo belt.

"If the bridge comes apart then there'll be real hell to pay," the Gunny replied, "and the Marines in the Ontos are not going to want to turn it, even when you order it. They're sitting up on top of that bridge staring into that moving current they won't survive falling into, and they know it. They have the Browning mounted on top but all it will do, if they use it, well draw fire from the .50."

I let the exchange fall into silence while I thought. The Gunny had said that the Ontos crew would be reacting to my order, which meant that either he had merely been using a figure of speech or that he was not intending to force or back my order if it came to that. The crew was also likely refusing to man the Browning, which made sense but still did not improve the situation at all, or make me predisposed to feel anything but more anger. I wanted to get to the bridge, climb up the back and man the Browning myself, but that would simply be more of my avoidance in trying to handle the overall nightmare myself.

"You know where I am, come," I said, then handed the handset back to Fessman.

"I want the Starlight Scope back up and operational," I ordered, for the first time truly missing the fact that I had no scout sergeant or any real scout team members left.

That lack illustrated just how I could not do without the constant attention, and even companionship, that Fessman provided. I could not afford to be sending him out to perform necessary administrative details or on missions to assemble equipment or personnel.

"I need somebody to operate the scope and I need that Marine able to mount that scope on his rifle and provide sniper fire across the river." I turned to make sure Fessman had gotten the gist of my message, but he was already gone.

The noise of the combat going on across the river penetrated everything and everywhere, along with the beating of the drums and the variations of sound the nearby rushing waters constant made in the foreground. I had not heard Fessman climb out nor the Gunny slip down into the hole with me.

"I need a scout sergeant and some men for the team," I said, once I realized he was there, making no mention of what I saw as our cowardly debacle of a retreat across the river. We were committed, and there could be no going back. The only thing to be done was to lend as much support to Kilo as was possible with what we had. Kilo was a Marine company, and Captain Carruthers commanding it was no slouch himself, so there was hope, but the company could not move under fire in the open with a .50 having a complete and total field of fire between the trapped Marines and firing across an entire expanse of the open flat bridge deck and the mud flat extending out from it. Kilo could do nothing about the .50 but I felt we could.

"There was nothing else to be done," the Gunny unaccountably said. "No plan of yours, no matter how brilliant some of them have been, could have saved the situation here. Without the Ontos we can't keep the NVA from crossing the river, and losing it would be the end of everything."

I stared at the man, although I could not see the Gunny's eyes because the poor light was insufficient to make out any of his facial features.

"How long is the Ontos?" I asked, ignoring the fact that the Gunny had not responded to my previous order.

"Around thirteen feet, I think," the Gunny answered. "What's your point?"

"You know damn well what my point is Gunny," I responded right back. "That leaves about five, maybe six, feet for the men of Kilo to move past it on the bridge when it is turned to face the jungle."

"If we lose the Ontos, we lose everything, Junior, and I don't want to risk it," the Gunny said.

"I'm not leaving Kilo over there to die," I replied. "They can't make it through the night. The .50 will keep them pinned down, and the NVA, probably not long from now, will simply crawl across the mud flat and take them out one by one, or in small groups."

"You don't know that," the Gunny said, his voice low but even and well- modulated. He lit a cigarette I hadn't seen him holding, or getting from his blouse pocket. "Jurgens' Marines alone won't let you get up on the bridge and force the crew to make that potentially deadly turn. The top of that the bridge is wood, and the wood's not exactly new. I don't want to see the men of Kilo die any more than you do, but saving the company has to be our first priority."

I unstrapped my pack and rummaged around in the dark, finally pulling out Jurgens' flashlight. I hit the button on the side, and a very slight illumination filled the foxhole. I looked into the Gunny's eyes.

"Jurgens," I replied, my voice nearly a whisper. "I noticed Jurgens was carrying a weapon slung over his shoulder at your little command post meeting over there. I've never seen him carry anything but an M-16. I wonder about the 5.56 mm hole made in one of our Marine's back, back when Jurgens carried an M-16.".

The Gunny smoked for almost a full minute, the puffs coming at about fifteen-second intervals. Jurgens' flashlight dimmed and then brightened. I knew the batteries were on their last few seconds but held it steady at my side, waiting.

"There's no autopsy in this valley, you might have noticed," the Gunny said between puffs. "There no Uniform Code of Military Justice, either, and the Rules of Engagement we were all supposed to be given were somehow missing back in the rear with the gear. Jurgens has served faithfully and we can't do without him. What do you want to do? Ask for his sidearm? What about the Marines that follow him? Are they supposed to turn in their weapons too? You'll get your scout sergeant, and probably from Jurgens' platoon but the Ontos should not be turned. The survivors of Kilo can get by it easily where it is. If the Ontos is pointed downriver its gun will not be able to traverse to cover the other end of the bridge. The Marines of this company all know that."

I waited to see if the Gunny was done. I noted that he wasn't offering his cigarette to me. Cold blooded murder of 'friendlies' continued in the company, although somewhat lessened by the introduction of all tracer ammunition for the M-16s. The Gunny was right. There was nothing I could do about what Jurgens, for reasons unknown, had done to Macho Man. I'd suspected Jurgens and the fact that his motivation to take out Macho Man was ridiculous, and probably only about his getting the Thompson. I no longer had any doubts, following the Gunny's tacit admission, without any real admission. The .45 Thompson had turned up, slung from Jurgens' shoulder, as I had been certain it would turn up in the killer's hands. The company was in deep trouble, however, and I knew the Gunny was right. I also knew that he knew that I would not let the matter rest when and if our situation grew less dire. I noticed Nguyen crouched down in the farthest corner of the hole, almost blending completely in with the mud. His dark inscrutable eyes stared up at me, unblinking. I stared back. Nguyen nodded slightly. I didn't know what the nod meant, but I was willing to bet almost everything that Jurgens would soon pay for the acquisition of the Thompson he'd killed to get.

But Kilo was in worse trouble than we were and something had to be done. Fessman was back, sliding into the hole alongside the Gunny.

"Get Captain Carruthers on the combat net," I ordered.

"Hold on," the Gunny interjected.

"Hold on for what?" I asked, in surprise.

"What are you going to tell him?" the Gunny asked, and I knew right away that he was really asking me what I intended to do.

"If that crew won't turn the Ontos, then I'm going to tell Carruthers to dig in as deep as he can. The NVA are probably very exposed, as they get ready to assault across the mud bed. When I call in the 175s Kilo will have a much better chance of surviving than if we leave them at the mercy of the fifty and coming attack."

"You mean if I don't turn the Ontos you'll call the artillery, don't you, Junior?" the Gunny asked, flicking his cigarette down into the mud at the bottom of our hole.

"I guess it really is your call Gunny," I replied, taking my helmet off and brushing my matted down short hair with one hand.

"What in the hell do we do, even if the Ontos turns and takes out the fifty, about the fact that we won't have it to stop the NVA from crossing the bridge?" the Gunny asked. "You expect that thing to grind its way back into battery and face the mud flat again once it deals with the .50? One turn it might make. The wood might hold, but it won't hold for two maneuvers like that. It weighs ten tons."

"Sir, Corporal Dobbs is just outside waiting," Fessman said. "He's got the scope and he says its working fine with a new battery. He's got it attached to his M-16, but he's never fired the gun with the scope on it so he doesn't know how long it will take for him to get his dope down to be at all accurate."

"He doesn't have to be completely accurate," I replied. "The range is fifty meters or less, and he can adjust fire as the NVA come onto the other end of the bridge."

"You think that's enough?" the Gunny asked, although I detected a slight tone of derision in his tone. "One M-16 on select fire, and you think it can hold the bridge through the night against a regiment?"

"The Greeks did it just fine thousands of years ago," I replied, wondering if the Gunny was familiar with the battle at Thermopylae, where 300 Greeks had held a narrow-controlled pass against thousands of gathered Persian soldiers.

"That's the name of your new plan?" the Gunny asked. "Thermopylae? You need a better name. Our Marines will giggle all night long if you use that Greek shit on them."

"So, you're going to order the Ontos to turn?" I came back, surprised that the Gunny might be giving in too easily and too soon, although his comment giving away the fact that he was angry and irritated to his core.

"We can't take a heavy hit from the 175s and you know it. If the Ontos turns successfully, and the flechette rounds can take out the .50, or at least shut it the hell up, and Dobbs and that damned science fiction scope can stop the NVA, then we have a chance."

"You believe I'd really call in the 175s?" I asked for no good reason I could think of.

"I believe that you're not the kid who dropped out of the night a month ago," the Gunny replied, bitterness in the tone of his voice. "I believe you're not quite right, and I think you damn well know it, so I don't know what you might do."

"Are you going to call the men manning the Ontos?" I asked again, trying to take in what the Gunny had said, but having some difficulty.

"You're plan seems idiotic to me," the Gunny said, "but then, half your damned plans have seemed impossibly idiotic to me. Admittedly, some of them worked, but I don't trust that damned scope, along with the known fact that Dobbs is as nutty as you, but then what can you expect from a Marine who's been in the valley half a year? He might do great or he might be terrible. I hope you just may be wrong about the bridge being able to hold when the Ontos turns. Everything rests on that turn. What makes you so sure the bridge won't just break apart and fall into that abyss of a rotten river? If the Ontos tears the thing apart, then Kilo has no chance at all, although it would certainly leave no way for the NVA to cross the water."

"Tex," I replied, the flashlight dying as the word left my mouth.

The dark was stygian and I could see nothing.

"Tex," I repeated. "I can't do better than that. It's built Tex tough or he wouldn't have brought it this far down the valley in one piece." As I said the words, I reflected on the Gunny's last sentence and understood why he was giving in. If the bridge was lost the company was saved. The Gunny wasn't just willing to sacrifice Kilo, he was also willing to sacrifice the Ontos crew.

"Right," the Gunny said, his exasperation reaching out through the darkness toward me. "This damned well better work is all I have to say."

"Bring Dobbs down," I ordered Fessman.

"Yes, sir," Fessman replied, "and I think it's a good plan sir, and Thermopylae has a neat sound to it."

Fessman took only a few seconds to climb out of the hole and bring Dobbs back with him. The darkness was broken only by the weak rays from the dying flashlight so I could barely see the corporal.

"You think you can use that thing to hit anyone trying to come onto the far side of the bridge, corporal?" I asked.

"Yes, sir," Dobbs replied, in a gravelly voice that sounded much older than his young years had to be.

"Good, get set up on the lip of this hole and draw a bead on the other end," I ordered. "The weather's bad and I know that effects how good the scope can operate, but we have to try."

"Nah, the scope's affected alright, but not a whole lot at that short distance," the man replied, reassuringly. The rain is there but not that heavy. Just trying to keep the glass clear at this end is more difficult. I got a couple of boxes of regular ball ammo though, and I know you don't like us to shoot that."

"Why ball ammo?" I asked.

"I don't want to give away our position if I start dinging their guys," Dobbs came back. "The NVA's mighty crafty and they catch on real quick."

The more Dobbs talked the better I felt, at least about that part of my plan.

"Get the scope set up on its tripod before you transfer it over to the barrel clamps," I ordered. "I want to be able to see the Ontos on the bridge just as quickly as you can get set up. And I think using tracer rounds is a better idea. The hits will register the end of the bridge. If I direct four M-60 fire teams to concentrate on the end of that bridge, then every time you fire a round they can open up. You might not be able to stop a mass charge, but they sure as hell can. It will expose us to fire when the NVA figures it out, but we're pretty dug in here."

It took almost no time for Dobbs to get the Starlight rig set up. He stepped backward until I felt his body squeeze on my own.

"Have a look, sir," Dobbs said, and I didn't miss the uncommon use of the word 'sir' he used to address me.

I peered with my right eye pressed into the rubber grommet protecting the rear lens of the device. The objective lens out front, near the other end of the scope, had a tube extending out from it to prevent the rain from destroying any chance of seeing anything. The field of view, when looking through the scope, was pretty narrow, as I'd experienced in the past. Unless you knew where you wanted to look with the thing, then you were likely to sweep all over the place and see nothing of consequence. But, in this case, Dobbs had sighted the tube in so when I looked into the magnifying lens I was staring at the other end of the bridge. I could not shake the feeling that I should be looking at the scene with the scope resting on Zippo's gently heaving back.

The green image of the end of the bridge was not clear but it would do for using as a sniper scope. There was no one trying to get on the bridge as I looked because the .50 was still active, although its volume of fire had dropped considerably, probably in preparation of the infantry attack. The .50 was there to pin Kilo down, while the soon to be attacking troops would attack to kill them.

I moved the scope slightly to guide the view back along the bridge toward the near end where the Ontos squatted without moving. I was surprised to see a tendril of smoke coming up out of its rear end. The Ontos was idling. The scope picked up the strangest things that were entirely invisible to the unaided eye. I saw three crawling Marines approaching the machine from the rear. I wondered whether the Gunny had had to send a convincing squad up onto the bridge to convince the crew to turn the thing.

The enemy had spotted the movement, as well, because the .50 raked the water and the side of the bridge with a pounding spray of fire. I watched the lead Marine rise up and open the back doors of the Ontos and then disappear. The other two Marines lay flat. I wasn't sure how the NVA had seen the team at all, but they somehow had, which meant that they also had someone very close to bridge or on it and in communication. The NVA did not have a Starlight Scope or an equivalent if there was such a thing. The Marine who'd gone in leaped out and then went down to join his companions, lying flat on the wood surface. The armored back doors of the Ontos closed, no doubt pulled shut from the inside. I sucked in my breath at what I saw next. The lead Marine brought his weapon up, as all three began to slither backward toward the drop off to the river bank at the back edge of the bridge.

There was no doubt that the weapon was a .45 Thompson. Jurgens. Jurgens had led the effort to get the Ontos to turn. I breathed in and out deeply, watching their rearward movement until they went over the lip one by one, Jurgens going over last, looking out for his men. I sighed to myself. Every time I wanted to flat out kill the man, he did something of extraordinary merit or valor or saved my life.

The engine of the Ontos revved up to the point where I could hear it while staring through the scope. Slowly, the machine turned to allow its 106 rifles to point downriver. The turn was smooth and without sound. I wondered if the wet wood was serving as a good lubricant for such a maneuver. I had expected some drama, but there was none. The .50, and all small arms fire from the enemy stopped completely. Except for the sound of the rain and river, nothing came back from across the river. Suddenly, I jerked back, turned and climbed from the hole, yelling at Fessman to get the Gunny on the net. All hell was about to break loose when the NVA realized they could rush the Marines of Kilo while also coming at the other end of the bridge. The Ontos might shut down the .50, which it obviously had, but that left open the gate of hell that could lead the enemy across the river.

I laid down immediately on the flat muddy surface of the berm, my movement bringing the pain of open leech wounds on my back. I grimaced but reached for the handset Fessman had already extended out to me. He wisely kept his body down in the hole, only the very top of his wet helmet and extended arm showing at all.

"Tell Dobbs to get the scope mounted on top of his sixteen," I ordered, before talking into the handset.

I quickly informed the Gunny, using the radio, of the change in the plan, to have Dobbs mark the spot, indicate when there was enemy movement and then let the M-60s do the real work. The crews had to be told what was happening and what their job was, however.

"Call Carruthers and tell his radio operator what's going on. Kilo has to be ready to move and move fast," I ordered

In seconds, Marines of our own company began moving around me. I wanted two of the machine guns to be angled in from upriver positions and the other two from downriver. Four M-60s could rain down 2400 rounds per minute on the end of the bridge if they all fired at once.

The Gunny crawled up next to me. "I was right nearby, all you had to do was whistle," he said. "It's Thermopylae all over again."

"I think you mean déjà vu all over again," I replied, waiting to hear that Dobbs had his rifle ready and ready to fire.

"What's Deja vu?" the Gunny asked.

I made no reply, mildly wondering why I had said what I said at all.

"I'm going over to the upriver gun emplacement and Jurgens is coming here to join you," the Gunny said. "Communication is going to be everything on this because only Dobbs can see anything."

"The Ontos made the turn," I whispered across the few feet separating us.

"The risk was too great," the Gunny replied, also in a forced whisper.

"The Ontos made the turn," I repeated, this time without whispering.

The Gunny was gone, I realized. I had not seen or heard him leave, but I knew he wasn't there anymore.

one-hundred-twenty-nine

THE TWENTY-SEVENTH DAY : FIRST PART

Picking out who was who or what was what from the cluster of men who hit the end of the bridge was impossible.. I worked the focus knob on the side of the Starlight scope to no avail. I couldn't get a decent enough resolution to allow the green wispy moving creatures to have any identity. I prayed that Jurgens, being as close and highly positioned as he was atop the Ontos, would have a better ability to determine friend from foe. The flashlights screwed everything up because the diffused light blanked out key portions of the scope's ability to reproduce an image. The image I was looking at was not reality. It was an interpretation and then enhancement by the addition of interiorly generated photons to make a picture on a very small television screen. The flashlights waving about created a bunch of what seemed like giant fireflies batting around all over the place. The Starlight Scope, probably without enemy intent, had been rendered all but useless.

Jurgens opened up with the Browning, firing one long continuous stream that had to consist of a complete belt. How long could Jurgens maintain that kind of fire, if it was Jurgens, I didn't know? I wasn't fully convinced that the totally self-serving man I'd had to deal with, to the point of sociopathic action, was capable of standing to face down the enemy and then stick it out. Could the unrecognizable Marine on the Ontos be someone Jurgens had paid off with the Thompson to stand in for him? It would be just like him.

At first, the volume of fire was spattering until the enemy .50 Caliber opened up, and then the Marines began hammering the entire area, from the end of the bridge to both mudflats on each side. A minor berm would allow for just a bit of cover on the other side if someone laid totally flat and pressed himself into the soft mud. I'd done it several times myself.

The M-60 fire streamed yellow tracers, with the first four dedicated 60s opening up, and then just about every automatic weapon in the company. The M-16s fired all tracers to the point where there was almost enough light to see the other side of the river without the Starlight Scope. I wondered about a cease-fire to save Kilo's men but there was no stopping anything. Kilo still had men over there, including Carruthers. There was no ability, with the confusing, near carnival strangeness, of the whirling flashlights, the beating of the big fifty and then all the supporting fires from both sides. The AK-47s didn't fire tracers, for the most part, except for the special ones the NVA used that had drum magazines. Their white streams were crossing the river, but not many of them.

The Ontos opened up, firing three rounds, all together, into the position occupied by the .50 caliber. The range was nearly point-blank and the initial blast of all three timed distant explosions, setting loose the many thousands of flechettes they carried, allowed for a flash of light that illuminated great fan-shaped furrows that ran out from where the flechettes did their work. It was hard to see what was going on, as the AK fire was beating up the entire face of the much higher berm on our side of the river.

Jurgens opened up again from the Ontos, the Browning's red tracers distinctively different from the other weapons.

I reached for the scope and studied the end of the bridge. The Gunny had told me earlier that one of the Marines had found a letter on the dead body of an NVA soldier, and that we were facing the 206th Sapper regiment, one of the most elite units in the entire North Vietnamese Army. The word sapper had caught me then, and I tried to think about it. Explosives. Sappers carried satchel charges everywhere, like the ones we'd used to clear the tunnels so many nights earlier, not far from where we were fighting this night.

I studied the other side of the river, but it was hard to make out anything. The flashlights were gone. Most of the men were gone. What had been the route of Kilo to get across the bridge, combined with a full-frontal attack by the enemy was over. The intensity of the fire from both sides had been so high that nothing could live in that maelstrom of a nightmare that the bridge end of the area had become. I could not see them but I knew many men had died in the last few minutes. I could only hope that not many of them were from Kilo Company and that Carruthers was not among them.

The drums still beat, as if to let everyone know that the action wasn't over. What more was coming? What had the flashlights been for? A force attacking at night did not use flashlights. It was almost entirely suicidal, given the modern weapons of warfare that everyone on the battlefield was well aware of.

"Get everyone off that bridge and move the Ontos to the very edge of the back of it," I said to Fessman, wrestling the Starlight Scope around to look upriver.

Fessman got on the radio, calling the Gunny and the Ontos crew. It took no time for the Gunny to reach the hole. He dived right in, causing my leech bitten back to arch in agony. The leeches were still there but their pain-deadening symbiotic serum was fading away in effectiveness.

Where and when was first light, I wondered. Cowboy might come with friends at first light, and the enemy would know that too. So, what were they doing? Why the near-suicidal attack? Unless the attack was a diversion. Unless the sappers had not been trying to cross the bridge at all but hauling heavy satchel charges to blow the thing up? The NVA wasn't trying to come across and kill us. The enemy was trying to deny us any place to retreat to when the attack came from the forces ensconced inside Hill 950.

I explained the situation to the Gunny.

"Why didn't I think of that?" the Gunny asked, but not in a tone that called for a reply.

"They're sappers," I replied, "that's what they do."

"What kind of force can they have up there?" The Gunny went on.

"They brought a tank down here before," I noted. "They have to have some pretty extensive infantry units holed up, spoiling for a fight.

Khe Sahn and Tet had come and gone. There was no firebase left where Khe Sahn had been, and the Tet offensive, although a failure tactically, had only made the resistance of the NVA that much stronger. Plus, the troops dedicated to taking Khe Sahn had to be roaming around the upper part of the A Shau Valley, as only about twelve miles separated the upper flattened end from the valley, where the hamlet and now closed base were located.

"They're not in the jungle behind us," I said, trying to think my way through the problem. "They crossed the river to attack us on the other side. When we moved, that left them over there with no way to get back, not without going a whole lot of kilometers south and then crossing. If they pull that off then they have to come upriver again and attack across that high ground or use the narrow gap between that and the river. The Ontos will eat them alive if we still have an Ontos."

I could see nothing to the north, so I swung the tripod back around to stare at the bridge. The Ontos had no choice but to turn again, which meant that if it had not taken out the fifty it would be exposed to that fire and not be able to fire back. With armor-piercing bullets, it was not inconceivable that the Ontos might be taken out with that weapon alone. But there was no choice. It was either go along with what I thought the NVA was up to or likely lose it all and not have the Ontos to hold off any enemy soldiers when and if they came down the river.

The Ontos turned. I heard the ripping of the boards that were layered over the top of the bridge rather than saw it. After only a few seconds there was nothing. The noise had penetrated through the sporadic fire still going on, the sound of the drums and those of the river too. But the bridge was still there. The Ontos backed slowly, its rifles again pointing across the river. Jurgens was done with his frightfully effective work using the Browning and was directing the machine so it could get as close to the lip as possible. There was just a little bit of light. Enough for me to tell it was indeed Jurgens doing the directing. I wasn't sure about whether I was happy or angry about that fact. Jurgens was the easiest man to hate I'd ever known.

Marines were running the length of the bridge, back and forth, to carry wounded men who'd been hit by either the M-60s, the Browning or enemy fire. I watched through the Starlight scope, wondering if Carruthers would be among the wounded. There had to be bodies on the other side, and how many of the wounded would die was anybody's guess, what with medevac and resupply having to come in on our side of the river, and with an imminent attack expected to flow down through that very position. We needed air, as fast as we could get it, and then we needed more suppressive air to halt any enemy in its tracks from attempting a daytime attack.

The small arms fire died out completely. Jurgens climbed off the back of the bridge and made his way back. I wonder what Fessman had told the crew of the Ontos because they were obviously staying with their tracked vehicle. The Ontos could be protected from being taken by the enemy by the M-60 fire on our side of the river so there was no need for the crew to be inside when and if the sappers set off their charges.

The drums stopped beating.

"What's that mean?" the Gunny asked, taking out a cigarette and lighting it.

"We've got to get to the dawn," I replied, which was really no reply at all.

If I was right, then the drums had stopped because the NVA were going to blow the bridge. There was likely no time to get the crew out of the Ontos, and I couldn't imagine how big an explosion we might expect. Until it came. The bridge was clear of Marines, bodies and just about everything else when the far end blew sky high. The entire bridge could be seen with the unaided eye as the end rose up into and then immediately fell back into the raging waters. But it didn't go anywhere. They didn't wash it downriver where the tank still lay upside down. The Ontos was still on the close end, although the bridge had been pushed backward by the force of the explosion, to the point where the top of it was only a few feet from the edge of the berm. The Ontos would not need a ramp or any propping up of wood to get off the thing.

I studied the Ontos with the scope.

"Get them on the radio," I said, without turning.

The concussion wave would have been stopped by the armor, but spalling might have occurred, where everything inside the tank that was not welded or screwed down could fly around and kill or badly injure the crew.

"They're okay, but they want to know what you want them to do," Fessman said, holding the microphone out.

I didn't take it. "Just tell them to back off the bridge and reload. I can't see what kind of a mess the other end of the bridge is, although I no longer expect company from that direction."

I studied the other end of the bridge through the scope. It was a blackened torn up mess, with metal peeled back and broken boarding everywhere. I was amazed that the whole thing stayed together. Once more, thanks to the pushing effect of the explosives and the severe damage to the end of the thing, there would be no equipment or men transitioning from the far bank onto the end of it. It was a pleasure not to have the drums, although it was more likely that the coming of dawn caused them to stop rather than to put an exclamation point on the sapper job. The drums had to be located up on the cliff somewhere, and it would be a turkey shoot for either Puff or the Skyraiders, or anyone or anything else we could raise to help, so they would need to hide and abandon them until nightfall again.

"Have you got the AN-323 up?" I asked.

Fessman went to work without answering

I noted that the Gunny remained quiet, and had been since the drums had gone silent.

"You going to talk to Jurgens?" I asked, waiting for Fessman to reach our air support.

"More to the point, are you going to talk to him?" the Gunny said back.

"And say what?" I replied. "Tell him he did his usual great job of mowing down Marines and enemy alike… a sort of 'one for all and all for one' Browning murderous magician?"

"There was no choice, and I know you know it," the Gunny replied, blowing a puff of smoke out into the night. "You just can't stand him as a person."

There was no argument from me. He was right. I was being unreasonable because it was Jurgens, and I did not want to praise him at all.

"The enemy of my enemy is my friend," the Gunny said, his voice very soft.

I'd read Sun Tzu while at the Basic School. It was impossible not to see the brilliance of the old Chinese general, and how he'd neatly laid out not only how to use war tactics and strategy but also how to apply a philosophy of life. I understood, but I could not take Jurgens into my heart and soul at all. What did it mean if we were merely animals ripping and shredding each other to death so that we could live for another day?

Was I going to end up the way the Gunny had talked about me during my first day in combat? I'd conquered the terror, as the Gunny predicted I would. I no longer felt the paralyzing fear up and down my interior when the enemy fire came pouring in. I could function. Was I nearing the point where I would grow to like it? I felt that Jurgens had. And the Gunny himself had said that there was no coming back from making that adaptation or passage.

"Cowboy's coming and he's bringing friends," Fessman said.

"ETA on target?" I asked back, instantly.

"Twenty-three minutes," Fessman replied.

I smiled sincerely for the first time since I could remember. I would never see or hear a propeller plane again in my life, I knew, without a great welling-up of gratitude and joy. We were going to get to live, at least for another while. We could make it through the twenty-three minutes.

"Get the Ontos swung around, loaded for bear and aimed up the river, just in case," I ordered.

"You want me to get down there?" Dobbs asked, "or stay with the scope?"

"You're a sergeant now, Dobbs, so get down there," I replied. "You're my new scout sergeant. Let the men know that we're expecting an attack from up north while you're at it."

Dobbs didn't move. He stood staring at me.

"Well, you just got promoted corporal, so you might celebrate a little," I said, looking at the Gunny, who wore one of his enigmatic almost nothing smiles, with his signature Camel sticking out the side of his mouth.

"Your scout sergeants don't seem to do too well, think the new sergeant means," the Gunny responded, wryly.

The first light of dawn was beginning to slowly brighten the gloom at the bottom of the valley. Jurgens appeared out of the darkness and knelt by the side of the hole. He'd unstrapped the Thompson and carried it just like Macho Man had before him.

I didn't get a chance to comment, however.

"They're bringing Captain Carruthers up on a poncho liner," Jurgens said.

I climbed out of the hole without saying a word. I could see the four Marines, each at a corner of the poncho cover, hauling their load.

By the time I reached Carruther's side, it was too late. I didn't need to examine Carruthers, because the corpsmen had quit working on him before he got to me, more likely to move to triage and help those badly wounded who might have a shot at making it. The expressions on the faces of the Marines around me were also telling. Carruthers had not been like me. He'd garnered some sort of strange respect from his first day in combat. He'd also led Kilo company, a company not so seemingly ferocious, inbred, and racially charged as my own.

"He took one in the lights, Junior," the Gunny said, approaching me from the side. There's no way any evacuation can get him to a lung surgeon in time."

I knew the 'one in the lights' meant that the captain had been hit in both lungs. There was no hope for survival after such a wound, as there was not enough time to reach a surgical unit, even if the captain had been aboard a chopper at the time of his getting hit. But he was still laying in the mud alive, refusing to give up, to die or to even admit that there was no hope. His blinking eyes told that story, as I bent down over his prone body. His eyes focused and drilled into my own.

I leaned down, somehow knowing he wanted to say something, but lung shots didn't allow for much in the way of verbal communication.

"Get me back to a hospital," he whispered, "and it hurts so much more than I thought it would."

I looked at his left lapel. One morphine syrette was sticking out of the material, its short needle buried in the weave of the tight cotton. I knew he'd received one syrette. There were no markings on his body that I could see, however. If he was going out in the coming medivac then the corpsmen who'd given him the shot would have written down a time, probably on the back of his hand or right across his forehead.

Suddenly, the captain and I seemed alone, as all the other Marines had pulled back, including the Gunny. Only Nguyen knelt by my side, looking slowly around instead of at the captain. I pulled the single syrette from his collar and tossed it away, before reaching down to the cargo pocket located on my right thigh. I hadn't gone into that pocket for some time. I made sure the captain could not see what I was doing, even if he might no longer be able to understand.

I got out two syrettes and took no time in punching them right through his trousers, just below his hip. I squeezed twice and then threw my own empty syrettes after the first one.

"I'm taking you all the way home, captain," I whispered, leaning down so my lips were only inches from his right ear.

"Thanks, Lieutenant, you're a good man and I wish I could stay to do my part," Carruthers murmured, but his eyes were already closed.

I waited. There was nothing else to be said. I didn't know where the captain was from, who his wife was or whether he had children or not. I assumed from his wedding ring that he was married. I felt a great loss and a sense of guilt for not knowing. The captain had treated me with respect and friendliness while I hadn't had the time or inclination to spend any time with him. I was all about trying to survive myself and for those who might help ensure my survival.

I placed my left hand on Carruthers gently moving chest. There was no drama. His chest simply started to move less and less, each breath just a tiny bit smaller than the one before. I looked around me. The Marines were there, Fessman among the closest, but they paid no attention at all to Carruthers or me. Before coming to the Nam, I would never have believed that most humans die alone, even when they are doing so among other humans. I wondered if there was a natural, likely genetic reaction, that almost all humans have about death. My 'taking care' of Carruthers, and others mortally wounded, no longer bothered me. It was simply something that had to be done, as the occasional cleaning and oiling of weaponry, and it was one of those rare jobs that was my own and no one else's.

I looked over at Fessman, the morning light just bright enough to allow me to see his features from ten meters away. The scene was uncomfortable and strange, even by A Shau standards. Fessman pointed at his private radio, the one he'd taped to the Prick 25, and then carried everywhere we went.

I nodded at him. The battle was over, at least for the time being, and we had to try to move on. I pulled my hand from Carruther's unmoving chest, feeling like I was pulling what life was left in him with me.

Fessman's little transistor radio immediately came alive. Brother John's comforting deep voice introduced a song 'coming at you' from Nah Trang, a place I knew I'd more than likely never see or ever hear of again, should I survive, but it didn't matter.

The song that began playing was 'Don't Worry Baby' by the Beach Boys. I'd heard the song for the first time when I was having coffee in the student union of St. Norbert College in West DePere, Wisconsin. The Beatles were a really big deal at the college but I loved the different surfer groups better. Back then, and all the times prior to landing in country, I thought I'd worried a lot. I worried about tuition, about whether I'd ever get a date, about my appearance and more. After less than a month in Vietnam, all I could do was to wish fervently that I might get home to have such ridiculous worries again. A single line of song lyrics seemed to leap across from the tiny speaker to where I'd risen up to stand over the captain's body: "She makes me come alive, and makes me wanna drive, when she says "don't worry, baby, don't worry, baby, don't worry, baby, everything will turn out alright…" and my mind once more went back to thinking about my own wife and small daughter.

I looked for one last time down at the body of Captain Carruthers. Two Marines from the company stood nearby with a black body bag. They waited for me to move on, which surprised me. I took only a few more seconds to wonder about the song lyrics. Was Carruther's place now, where there was no worry that anyone knew about, not in fact the best place to be?

There was no answer forthcoming to that unspoken question, and I knew there never would be.

one-hundred-thirty

THE TWENTY-SEVENTH DAY : SECOND PART

The Skyraiders broke the dawn, and everything else, apart, as they came in over the river at an altitude that had to be less than a hundred feet. First light was upon the valley, and the smoke coming up from the still-burning dried mud of the river bank could be seen, its pungent smell able to be inhaled all the way across the water. The four Skyraiders had come down from higher altitude to arrive almost soundlessly until their giant thundering radial engines became the only thing any animal could hear up and down the valley. Cowboy's plane had to be among the four, but it was impossible to tell in the low light by trying to see through the canopies of the fast passing planes. And then, the sounds grew even louder with the roaring fire that came out of the Skyraider's 20mm cannons.

I knew the pilots could not see any activity below them. The light was simply too bad for that. I also knew why they were firing anyway. The NVA would not only be diving for cover in the jungle beyond, but they'd now be fully on notice that airpower had arrived, and it was of the kind that was going to remain on-site for some time to come. Cowboy was merely giving the enemy a taste, and letting everyone know that nothing would happen in the valley that escaped any notice from the huge deadly aircraft constantly overhead or within seconds of being called to be overhead. That the enemy threat was no longer from the jungle mattered little, until I could get on the radio and advise Cowboy otherwise. There was no missing or ignoring the Skyraiders when they were down in the valley, and that applied to both sides and just about everything else wanting to stay alive.

Medevac and resupply were coming, I knew. Battalion could not have missed the frightened and emotional communications made on the combat net during the battle. I hoped they sent a CH-46, or preferably two of them, along with plenty of Cobra gunships. Hill 975, the hill that had so frightened me, to the point of never wanting to get near it again, was back in play. The hill could not be attacked and taken because our forces, even with total air cover, heavy artillery support and plenty of resupply, were not capable of penetrating deep down into the earth to root the NVA out. Aside from nuclear weapons, nothing in our current inventory I knew of could penetrate that deeply into the planet. There would be problems later in the day with the landing zone because of where it had to be. The only clear place for the choppers to put down was near Hill 975, not far downriver from where the old airstrip had been allowed to go fallow.

The Ontos backed through the remainder of mud and sand that was piled up behind it, almost up to its armored double doors. The raised and angled front tracks were much more effective in plowing through debris, and almost anything else, rather than the very low single follower wheel rear tread. Once fully backed into the outer layer of jungle behind us, the machine stopped, rotated toward the upriver area where Hill 975 rose in the far distance, and then came to a complete stop, although the engine continued to idle. I heard the rear doors slam open, and watched as Hultzer, its new self-appointed crew chief walked around the Ontos' front edge. He saw me, although the light was still fairly dim and not very diffuse, bent low, and sprinted across the thirty or forty meters of distance to the top of the hole I was perched.

"Sir," he began, making a move to salute but not following through. "We've got to have fuel and more flechette shells by the end of the day. Air can only hold them back so long. Fessman said the enemy would be attacking from upriver by the time nightfall hits. If we have gas and about twenty more rounds, we can hold the night." Hultzer stopped talking, yet remained breathing hard as if he'd held his speech inside for some time before being able to let it all out.

"You got a gas can?" I asked, working to unbutton, and then get my blouse off. I slunk down a bit made sure I wasn't exposed to potential sniper fire from across the jungle south from the damaged bridge.

Marine snipers were able to pick off individuals almost as far away as a kilometer, or more. I wasn't certain, but I suspected the NVA had such long-range weapons and accurate death technicians, as well.

"Gas can, sir?" Hultzer asked, his face screwed up like one big question mark.

"The leeches," I said, turning slightly to show him an angle of my back. "Gas is best and immediate," I went on, although I wasn't certain of the conclusion I'd presented.

I'd never used gasoline to get rid of the creatures before.

Hultzer didn't reply, instead turned to run back toward the Ontos.

Fessman's radio belted out another tinny rock and roll song, no doubt introduced by Brother John, although in the euphoria of being alive and sadness of the loss of Carruthers my usual reaction to night combat, I hadn't heard him. The only improvement I'd recorded in that respect was that my hands didn't shake as much anymore.

The song lyrics crossed the short distance from where Fessman lay next to Nguyen, not far from the hole: "You once thought of me, as a white knight on his steed. Now you know how happy I can be. Oh, our good time starts and ends without all I want to spend, but how much, baby, do we really need?"

"Daydream Believer," I whispered, thinking again about my wife, as I looked back out over the now very evident damage to the bridge. It seemed too strange to think about sitting in a battered hole on the edge of raging river, not wearing a shirt, back covered with thumb and wrist-sized leeches, and waiting for a high school kid to come back with a gallon of gasoline I wanted to use as a beach tourist back home might use a container of Coppertone.

I slunk down in the hole and pulled out my stationary. The folded pack was secure inside the plastic bag I kept specially for it alone. My cheap black U.S. government pen still worked, as I pressed it into the Marines raising the flag on Iwo Jima envelope, intending to address the letter to my wife and home. Resupply was coming, which meant I could get an envelope aboard a chopper if I was aggressive and persistent. But I didn't address the envelope to my wife. My hand moved across the blueish military envelope, but the address I put down was that of the colonel, our battalion commander, and not that of my wife. The effect Carruthers had on me could not be simply laid down like a second corpse next to the bagged one I knew was only yards away. I had to write something about him for whatever record might exist about him on into the future, even if it was unlikely that I would survive to see any of the effects. And then there was the company's greatest enigma, after the Gunny. Jurgens. I hated him and wanted him gone, but I could not ignore him or, in truth, take action to get rid of him.

I pulled out one single piece of my precious stationery and began to write.

I wrote short passages about both men. I detailed Captain Carruthers' decision to remain on the other side of the river to assure that all of his men were able to cross over under fire. I went so far as to state that the captain had no intention of crossing if even one of his Marines was down or disabled. With Jurgens I was not as generous, although there was no way to disguise the fact that the man had stood and fired under great danger, at great risk and without flinching or retreating to great success, possibly saving most of what survived of Kilo company, and also possibly preventing a much worse sapper-planted explosion that would have cost us the Ontos and its crew. The after-action report was my first ever, in training, or in actual combat, and although I was uncomfortable with doing it, I simply could not go on without responding to a certain sense of justice in life that I was afraid that I might lose forever.

I folded the amateur after-action report into a shape that was about the size of my right palm. I pushed it toward Fessman.

"See that this gets on the chopper and back to the battalion," I ordered, making sure that the colonel's name and identification were printed on the outside.

I hunched back over and went to work writing a letter to my wife. I wrote of Carruthers and the fact that he didn't make it. I gave her no details, however, and also wished that I was strong enough not to have to mention him at all. But there was no avoiding the loss of the captain, and I knew part of that was because I now commanded Kilo company again, and also that there would be a new officer crew coming in with the resupply. What would that new crop of inexperienced company-grade officers bring, as far as my own survival and that of the company was concerned? I wrote on about the weather, the river and let the rest go. I finished and got the sealed envelope safely tucked into my thigh pocket.

I sat for a few seconds to think about our situation. My discomfort at constantly returning to the same positions we'd vacated not more than days and nights before had begun to bother me to the extent that I called the Gunny over to discuss it.

"We keep taking up in positions where we've been before," I began, but got no farther.

"Yes, like we've had a choice," the Gunny responded, lighting a cigarette and hunkering down by the side of the hole to begin lighting a chunk of Composition B with the same match he'd lit the cigarette with.

"My point," I began, trying again, but getting nor further.

"Your point is that it's dangerous," the Gunny finished.

"I had a captain who taught me about what happened in other

modern wars, like a couple you've been in. His name was Hrncr, and he was a real combat vet, as I've now come to understand. He said that to return to the same position was a form of willful and accepted suicidal behavior. No enemy, no matter how seemingly dumb, inexperienced or ignorant, would long miss the opportunity to mine or place charges under the ground or inside the redoubt of a key position likely to be reoccupied by a returning enemy force."

"Like I said," the Gunny concluded, blowing out a great puff of smoke toward me but not directly.

The Gunny was making his point in his usual way. Indirectly, without embellishment or wasting time.

"Yet, we keep doing it," I replied, my voice showing some of the frustration and irritation I felt.

"Like I said," the Gunny repeated, maddeningly.

Hultzer returned, lugging a five-gallon jerry can at his side, dragging it more than carrying it.

I climbed out of the hole, went down on all fours, and exposed my back. "Pour it over them," I instructed the Ontos' crew commander, "and Gunny, you mind getting rid of that cigarette?"

"You can't kill them with gas," he murmured but snapped the lit cigarette off toward where the river ran.

"I don't give a damn if they live or die, I just want them off of me," I replied, cringing with the pain, as he poured the gasoline liberally onto my back from my neck to my butt, and then from side to side.

The pain was so great that it felt like my entire back was burning up, but I held the screaming gasps inside.

"Man, sir, but you've got a case of them," Hultzer whispered.

I slowly climbed to my feet, the fiery pain beginning to fade into an almost unbearably deep ache. I grunted and then coughed, but I began to feel the leeches dropping away. I stood erect, and the things feel in numbers, bouncing on top of the packed mud, but making no move to crawl away, stupefied by the gasoline, as I'd been told they would be by Zippo, seemingly so long ago. Next to the smell of the earth, mud, and mist, the sharp gasoline aroma almost felt healthy.

"We've got to provide a perimeter and ground support for the medevac and resupply," I said to my small scout team, with the Gunny remaining standing nearby.

It wasn't necessary to inform or instruct the Gunny about such things, although in looking at his languid relaxed state, leaning half-propped up by a thick bamboo shoot by the side of the hole, he was probably relieved not to have to order every Marine around that he encountered.

Hultzer came back, after returning the gas can to wherever it was stored aboard the Ontos. He squatted down in a manner that was almost identical to the Gunny's usual resting position.

"You're the crew commander of the Ontos," I said to him, needlessly, but then went on. "You're also now a part of my scout team, the one that Sergeant Dobbs is leading. I want your radio up on the net at all times."

I had to pause for a few seconds, as the Skyraiders came down the valley low over the water once more. Cowboy was doing a flyby every twenty minutes, or so, and the effect was evident. No drums, no small arms fire from the NVA, and certainly nothing in the way of rockets or the .50 caliber, if it had survived the onslaught earlier by the Ontos salvos.

"Let's get to a position closer to Hill 975, where we can see what's happening when they come in," I ordered. "How much time do we have?" I asked Fessman.

"Just about any time now," he replied.

We moved, but we didn't move far. The edge of the jungle was pretty much of a straight line along the western side of the almost non-existent path. A thicket of heavy brush with a bunch of bamboo shoots sticking fifteen feet out of it served as our new position.

Without any warning, other than that of a turbine's piercing whine, a small OH-6 Hughes helicopter, called a Loach, came down fast, seeming to drop out of the air more than angle in, as was commonly done when arriving at landing zones, particularly those considered to be 'hot' or compromised by enemy fire. The Loach hovered ten feet off the deck, its tail slowly moving around to complete a full circle before starting the rotation again. All the choppers had a frequency on the PRICK 25, so I asked Fessman what the evacuation and resupply plan was since there'd been no pre-discussion before the mission. That they were coming with two CH-46 helicopters were coming was welcome news but I still had no clue as to their intent or the detail of any plans.

"What's the Loach doing, sir, and where are the big choppers?" Fessman whispered

I watched the Loach rotate, and reflected about what I knew of it. It was very fast, able to hit over a hundred and seventy-five miles per hour, and it was very agile too.

But the thing was made out of very thin aluminum and had no armor at all. It was for observation only, no real combat.

"It's waiting to take fire," I replied, looking up into the cloudy sky that still bled moisture but now, in the thick cooler heat of the early morning, on misted down upon us. I could not see the Huey Cobras up inside the cloud cover, but I knew they were there. The Loach was their stalking horse. If it took any fire at all then a whole flock of killer Cobra attack choppers would descend and blast away. My admiration for the courage of the two men piloting the Loach made me think of Carruthers. I brushed the thought aside as best I could.

Hultzer had positioned the Ontos to aim its six weapons at the landing site, which would allow for short-range shooting at a gentle downslope that tailed off south along the river. It was a compact LZ because the rivulet that forked into the river wasn't far down that slope either. At one time the company had set in that position for the night, but the looming enemy stronghold of Hill 975 had brought about a pre-dawn departure and a necessary move further south.

Small arms fire came from somewhere ahead, but the source of it wasn't identifiable. The Loach jumped back, seemed to almost turn over on one side, and then took off so fast it was low and level cross-ing the river rapids before there was time to even blink. The blast of its single spinning rotor blew up dirt, dust, mud and then water spray as it flew under maximum power. I heard the Skyraiders thundering down the valley again but saw the Cobras first. Six of them came out of the clouds surrounding Hill 975 and went right at the southern face of it with their nose-mounted rotary cannons.

The Skyraiders dropped five-hundred-pound bombs on first the area right next to where the Cobras were working and then, minutes later, down on the jungle area across the river where the 206th Sapper Regiment had to be ensconced, as deep down under the thick jungle matting as they could get, without a doubt.

The two CH-46 choppers flew in low, not visible in the northern distance because of the low down-in-the-valley morning light, and also the heated mist that made everything beyond a distance of ten feet blur-ry and drearily depressive. As the two double rotor, big choppers came in, just over the top of the Bong Song's rushing waters, one veered off to land on the planned landing zone just down from the old abandoned airstrip. Surprisingly, the second chopper headed toward the river until it reached the bridge. There it turned gently left and eased down onto the mudflat just beyond the blown up end of the structure.

The choppers had split up. One to deliver the supplies further north and one to pick up the Kilo dead across the river. The Cobra gunships split with them and very quickly four of them circled the resting chopper, it's blades still whirling at a furious rate, but the aircraft going nowhere.

I reached into my pocket, not thinking about the clever resupply and medevac moves made by the airmen, but only of getting my letter aboard the only chopper that was reachable, and it would not be in position long.

"Let's go, I said to Dobbs, Fessman, and Nguyen. I knew Hultzer was inside, commanding the Ontos, and making certain he had a flat enough field to turn and fire in the direction of either landing zone, with only seconds notice of incoming from either. He wouldn't likely need any instructions or orders.

The run was relatively easy and quick, as the path was clear and we had dumped our packs back into the hole behind us at the berm. I'd replaced my blouse after Fessman had rubbed Weapon Oil, Number 01-58 all over my back. The green plastic container he'd found somewhere had "do not handle around food or keep in constant contact with skin" printed in yellow, on the reverse side of the green bottle. My back, after the heavy application, felt better immediately, however, just as Fessman had said it would.

The chopper sat there. No Macho Man stood by to stand guard. Two-door gunners, with hard-mounted M-60s, performed that chore. I pushed my letter into the hand of the gunner located on the choppers least exposed flank. After the few initial bursts earlier, however, and then the overwhelming reply by the Loach and the Cobras, there had only been silence from the hill.

There was no point in remaining in such an exposed position so the four of us ran back to where the protective hole waited.

The Gunny had come by, a cigarette dangling from his mouth, as Fessman was convincing me to try the healing properties of the gun oil.

"He's just a teenager, you know," he stated, between puffs, and wearing one of his smiles that wasn't a smile.

"I suppose it's probably as dangerous as smoking," I fired back.

The Gunny had ignored my comeback, then, but reappeared a short bit later. "You put Jurgens in for the medal," the Gunny said, without any preamble. "Sugar Daddy wants his shot at a medal too."

I couldn't believe what I was hearing. Only a few weeks back both men, and their units were killing each other without warning or mercy, and the only whispered talk there was about anything was concerning the fact that we were all going to die. I stared out across the river through the mist, barely able to make out the CH-46, located less than a couple of hundred meters distant. Was it a good thing that some of the Marines were actually coming to believe they might make it home, and a medal or two awarded for heroism might help them in some way or other back there?

"I sent that son-of-a-bitch out there to die, which he richly deserved," I squeezed out, my voice very low so just the Gunny could hear, however.

"I know that, Junior," the Gunny replied, puffing out more smoke. "He doesn't know that and neither do any of the rest of them. We can send Sugar Daddy out on the bridge with an M-60 fire team, and then write him up, even if nothing happens. None of this has anything to do with truth, justice, and the American way."

"Alright," I said without bothering to give the matter deeper thought.

The only real Marine Corps thing I was doing in combat was beating the enemy while struggling to survive my own Marines and myself. The rest of it, and how it was playing out, was more akin to a single bad novel combining the most brutal and lying elements of Lord of the Flies, Voyage of the Damned and Dante's Inferno. I could not conceive of getting any medals, having that might help me in any way, or caring about having one or more of them, if I was so awarded. We were going to risk exposing a small group of Marines, by putting them out in an open position to cover a landing zone that was easily covered from the positions we held across the river, and by overwhelming air and fire support. I wasn't going to deny the Gunny, however, and I still had not forgotten or forgiven Sugar Daddy's attempts to kill me.

"If they take fire of any kind they need to get into the river on the north side and hold on for dear life so they don't get sucked under the bridge," I said, keeping the exasperation and frustration out of my voice.

"Baby I need your lovin, got to have all your lovin," belted out from Fessman's transistor radio speaker. The words were welcome until less comfortable lyrics strung themselves along: "Some say it's a sign of weakness, for a man to beg, then weak I'd rather be if it means having you to keep, 'cause lately I've been losing sleep..."

I breathed out deeply, too long for it to be merely another sigh. I asked myself why I always felt like a beggar and weak, but there was no answer. It was just a song, I told myself.

The Gunny went off to inform Sugar Daddy that his fake medal expedition was on, and, no doubt, that I was aboard. Less then two minutes later, Sugar Daddy led the fire team out along the bridge, the sergeant himself carrying the M-60 with two bandoliers strapped across his back and chest, which no machine gunner in the company ever did. The dirt, rain, mist, and debris would jam a dirty brass cartridge quickly, and the jam, without special tools, was almost impossible to clear.

The team reached the blown apart end of the bridge without incident, giving me the idea that maybe the plan wasn't so bad, after all. What was the harm? And then the NVA .50 opened up. A line of green tracers swept across the bridge from left to right. Sugar Daddy reacted instantly, and with the ammo belts still strapped around his body, leaped backward into the river. The fire team was neither so quick to react nor so lucky. The three Marines went into the river backward but not because they leaped. The power of the .50's two-ounce bullets, traveling at more than half-mile a second, tore the men apart as they literally blew them off the surface of the bridge.

The Ontos was in motion behind me, making its turn. I only had time to press both my hands over my ears before the giant explosions of the rifles going off shook the ground, and blew debris up into my face and everywhere else. I uncovered my ears, hoping there would not be more rounds coming from the 106 barrels.

"Get Cowboy on this right now," I yelled over to Fessman, as I crawled down over the top of the berm to move toward the end of the bridge.

Sugar Daddy was going to need help getting out of his current situation, and nobody was going to want to cross that exposed bridge with a .50 caliber registered in on a target less than a few hundred meters away. I wondered, as I moved if what had happened would mean that I would not have to write Sugar Daddy up for a medal unless maybe it was for the Purple Heart, which I knew the other Marines who'd had to accompany him would be getting.

The Ontos blew a hole in the jungle where the NVA fifty caliber had opened up from. With the resupply chopper down, Hultzer pulled all the stops out, firing both flechette rounds and high explosives. Two of the Cobra gunships slowly approached the edge of the jungle, moving just fast enough to keep their noses down and their rotary cannons firing on target. My thoughts about Sugar Daddy's survival were mixed, about probability and also about concern, but my thoughts and concern were not as great as my surprise that the penetrating .50 caliber had not gone for the CH-46, a target so big, loud and nearby that it could not have been ignored or missed without deliberation. Why had they not fired at the chopper?

Sugar Daddy had gone over the northern edge of the bridge or been blown over that edge because of being hit with rounds from the fifty, but it had all happened in just a few seconds. The only certainty was that there were Marines laying dead or severely wounded in the water near where the Ontos had recently sat.

There were no orders necessary to give, as a team of men was already crawling along the muddy approach to the near end of the thing, but they didn't move out onto the exposed surface, instead entering the rushing water and using the upriver side of the bridge to slowly head toward the other side of the river.

"He's alive," Fusner whispered to me, across the few feet of the open hole that separated us.

"Is he hit?" I asked back, knowing Fusner was on the command net with what had to be the Gunny's radio operator.

I could see nothing of the rescue operation that had to be going on, as somehow Sugar Daddy, even with the for show ammo belts weighing him down, had managed to hold on until help arrived.

Slowly they worked together, a clump of men, no individual distinguishable among them, as they eased their way back to the near bank. They then crawled toward the nearby fox holes. I realized that they'd basically stripped Sugar Daddy, because the dramatically crossed ammo belts were gone, and except for his great size and black skin, would have been impossible to tell from the others. Fusner was right, the sergeant was alive and moving to safety, although small arms fire had stopped after the firing of the 106 recoilless guns mounted on the Ontos.

There would be no writeup for courage under fire, nor would there be an after-action report, unless someone other than I wrote it. Sugar Daddy had made an uncommon mistake in judgment and the result was three more dead Marines. The penalty for that would be paid through his continued service in the company, and the ultimate result for every Marine in the company was very likely going to be the same.

The new officers assembled and moved toward my position, their new poncho covers glistening in the waning light, brief shafts of sparkly flashes penetrating the misty winds generated by mild temperature shifts created by the coming of night. The Gunny had sent word through his radio operator that they were coming, having been offloaded by the supply chopper that had landed up near the old abandoned airstrip. That the chopper had come in, dropped its load, and then be able to pull out without being destroyed was a likely function of only two causes. One was the surrounding beehive of Huey gunships battalion had sent to accompany it and the other was the ominous ever-present threat transmitted throughout the entire expanse of the valley by the deep beating thrum of Cowboy's Skyraider force.

"They're coming," Fusner needlessly warned.

At least Sugar Daddy was about to become someone else's problem, as there seemed little doubt that I would be relieved, I thought. I harbored a tiny hope that the new ruling officers of the companies would require that I be somehow sent to the rear in disgrace, to either be repatriated home like a coward or sent to Okinawa for trial.

I watched the three officers proceed down the informally beaten but muddy riverbank path. Each officer had a personal RTO. The three radiomen trailed behind, the officers were probably unaware that the many meters of separation of the two groups was of no purpose. The radio operators were allowing their officers to be the point in their movement. I sighed, waiting for their arrival, now long experienced in the fact that in real close combat men did not help other men. They used them. If helping other men allowed for better survival odds, then help was provided. The officers were FNG's, revealed by the tiny nuance of their oblivious conduct alone. Their radio operators wanted as much distance as they could get from the FNGs. I knew I was not going to be so fortunate to avoid them, as all three would no doubt outrank me.

"Junior," the lead officer yelled, from some distance away, performing another function, raising one's voice in a jungle combat situation, that indicated what he was, but the tone of his voice was filled with mirth and I could not help feeling a positive rush course through my mind and body.

I had become inured to the deadness of emotion combat had induced within me.

"Captain," I responded, assuming his rank because he wore none visible anywhere on his helmet or uniform. I expressed no emotion and made no move to climb from my hole to greet him.

"I know the story about your helmet," the big officer said, his two associate officers having fallen back as if to give the captain sufficient room to dominate the scene.

The three stood looking down at me, their poncho's dripping. Somehow they'd found little sprigs of jungle material to stick into the webbing laid over their helmets, and the ends of them dripped small drops in different directions as they moved their heads while talking or looking around. Most of the Marines in the A Shau had long ago dropped such attempts to be in disguise or hidden from the enemy's detection.

In fact, I was one of the few Marines in either company to wear a helmet at all. There was little point. Helmets were most effective for using as a water basin or keeping harder falling rain from directly contacting one's head. They did not stop bullets or artillery shrapnel or much of anything else. Combat Marines wore rough bush hats or rags tied with four knots to form a tight strange-looking skull cap. They wore the coverings against the rain, bugs and to keep their hair flat. There was no hiding from enemy detection in the A Shau. The NVA always knew where we were but their own limited availability of ammo and weapons supply and their constant fear of our massively killing supporting fires kept them from overwhelming attacks.

"There's a story about my helmet?" I asked, surprised, resisting the temptation to take it off and examine the damaged thing.

The chunk of shrapnel still stuck out of the front of it, accumulated by its previous owner, not to mention a plethora of other dents and scratches I'd managed to add. I stared at the three men, the light waning from day into misty dusk, making them look like they were apparitions from some Christmas movie shot in all black and white.

"I'm not a captain," the lead officer said, brushing aside my question.

"Okay," I replied, assuming the three were lieutenants, "who's senior?"

My serial number in the Corps was 0104328, which meant that I was the officer commissioned who was the hundred and four thousand three hundred and twenty-eighth since the beginning of the Marine Corps. Officers of the same rank demonstrated seniority by date of rank but the serial number comparison was more definitive because everyone in the Corps memorizes that number for life and the lower number is always senior. However, no recitation of serial numbers was required.

"You are," the officer responded. "We came out to assist you, since the casualties from this area have been so high, until such time as both companies can be retired to the rear area for necessary rest, recreation and retraining."

I had a hard time believing what the man was saying. The Gunny appeared out from a position below and behind me, up from where the river ran nearby. He spoke without introduction or preamble.

"Why are your RTO's laying on the deck?" he asked, as all three officers looked around to where their Marines lay sprawled behind them.

"Did you fail to hear the fire that was just directed back and forth across this river?" the Gunny went on, his tone flat, low and hard. "Get your asses in the hole and drop those packs."

"Yes, sir," one of the officers replied, not understanding that the Gunny was not a superior officer, and also letting me know, by that lack of knowledge, they didn't have much idea of what the companies were composed of in personnel. As upside-down as everything was it didn't seem too out of place that the Gunny was addressed as sir while I was Junior.

I wanted to shake my head in wonder, however, over the incongruity of what I'd come to know about sending Marines down into the valley. No experienced ranking company-grade officers could, apparently, be coaxed or sent in, so three brand new officers, officers like I'd been, were quickly ushered aboard choppers and sent out, with some flimsy excuse that they were being sent to help in a difficult situation.

Nguyen and Fusner immediately emerged from the hole, as the officers approached, the opening of the hole being plenty large enough for them to get by me without any problem. They listened to every word said around them I knew, and usually without comment. How Nguyen understood so much and so quickly I had no idea, but the look in his eyes was always the same. He backed me to the hilt, all the time and at any time, and that look sometimes was what kept me going. The three officers gingerly climbed into the hole, also taking great pains to not touch or disturb me. I turned back to the river to take in the scene before me as it was beginning to slowly dim in the waning light.

The supply choppers had come and gone from both sides of the river, as had the Cobra gunships and the Skyraiders. It was the approach of night, with mist and more rain on the way to be delivered from above in the darkness. One moment the sky had been filled with screaming turbines and propeller blades and the next it was quiet except for the ever-present rush of the river's raging waters and the patter of falling raindrops coming down on the surface of my helmet.

There was no fire coming from the jungle or anywhere else and, at first, that seemed ominous until I realized why. The NVA hadn't left a firebase or rear guard. They were headed downriver. Downriver was the only way they could get to us, and there was no Marine force across the river to pursue them, so they had no need of a base of fire or rear guard. It would be a hammer and anvil situation. Our companies would be driven upriver and then trapped up against Hill 975 in the night, with no supporting fires available except from the Ontos. Somewhere downriver, further than I'd ever ventured, there was a place they had to be able to cross the raging waters. They would cross and come up on our side, flanking us as they came into a full attack because there was no way we had the personnel to saturate the heavy jungle that lay between the river and the eastern canyon wall. That flanking attack would cause us to have to move upriver one step at a time. But there was nowhere to go upriver unless we could somehow get past Hill 975, and their troops that had to be filling it like bees in a beehive, knowing that we were coming.

"We're going to need the Starlight Scope again," I said, needless-ly, to the Gunny, briefly thinking I'd need someone special to operate the device, and hoping we had someone like that.

Night was coming and it would be another dark night, with heavy monsoon cloud cover and the ever-present rain or drizzle coming down. Penetration of what light would be available would be amplified by the scope but would it be enough? In order for the plan developing in my head to work, we had to be able to see in front of us, and then also be able to peer into a part of the jungle I well remember from weeks before. Where I'd holed up hiding in a slot into the jungle growth next to the river, where the Gunny had found me, there was a sort of clearer area through the single canopy that extended all the way to the canyon wall. I'd not thought anything of the clearing in the quick glance I'd taken in recognizing it as different from the dense jungle area all around it. It was almost like a big bulldozer had gone through the debris and beaten down a flat track through the jungle floor.

"They're going downriver," the Gunny replied, ignoring my comment. "They're going to take maybe three or four hours, or a bit more, and then come up our side and I don't see any place for us to be. Dug in here, even with the Ontos and resupplied, we can't hold against a regiment on the attack, much less a sapper regiment below and another regiment, no doubt, inside that hill."

The Gunny took out a cigarette and began lighting it with his special lighter.

I hadn't seen the Gunny look or sound quite so glum before and it shook me. I waited, trying to think about the developing plan in my head while at the same time getting it together so presenting it might make the Gunny feel better.

Fusner turned his little transistor radio up, to catch the last tune coming out of Na Trang over the Armed Forces Radio Network. Brother John introduced Del Shannon's Runaway, by saying that everyone listening should pay attention to the lyrics. The song played. I listened, not being able to associate or make sense of much of what Brother John had meant until the middle of the song: " I'm walkin' in the rain, tears are fallin' and I feel the pain, wishin' you were here by me, to end this misery…"

All I could think of was my wife. I wondered if my letter had gotten aboard the chopper. I wondered how long it took letters to get all the way back to San Francisco from where I was. I wondered after I was dead, whether the letters continuing to come in would be a good or horrible thing. I suddenly snapped out of my reverie. The plan illuminated in my mind from out of nowhere.

"We're going to move downriver in the shallows, low, light and fast, using the Starlight Scope to make sure we're running in the clear," I explained to the Gunny. "The Ontos will follow, moving real slow and noisy, with Sugar Daddy's platoon strung out in layers between the bank and the jungle. The NVA will assume we're gathered with and around the Ontos for protection, but we'll be running out front, nearly naked, except for our small arms and the M-60s. No packs, no extra ammo, nothing. We blow right by them, and then hit that drift or break where you found me about three clicks down. We cross to the canyon wall and attack right up their rear. The Ontos then turns and heads straight back upriver, preventing the NVA from doing anything but running toward Hill 975. We have a ton of Prick 25's to stay in close communication, what with our new officers. And that's where it gets interesting. We pin them against their own hill and hold them there for the night. We'll have our full ammo supply back for the M-60s and the Ontos. Hill 975 is a few clicks north of us. I'll call in a series of fire missions to cause a diversion, firing well short to avoid taking rounds ourselves. We wait for the dawn and then call in all the airpower we can get."

I stopped talking, realizing that some parts had come to me only as I had been laying it all out. The Gunny blew several puffs of smoke while I'd been talking, inhaling and exhaling fast and steady.

"What's the name of the plan, sir," Fusner broke in from my side.

"Walking in the Rain," I shot back, pulling the name out of Del Shannon's song lyrics.

"Where in the hell do you get this shit from?" the Gunny breathed out, snapping the remains of his cigarette toward where the river ran noisily nearby. "Sugar Daddy's platoon?" he went on, "that because those guys are black as night?"

"No," I replied, it's because I don't like or trust him, but there's no quit in him, or Jurgens either, for that matter, and he deserves the danger exposure for what he pulled on the bridge. If he wants to earn a medal, as unlikely as that might seem, then he's going to really earn it."

I waited then, unintentionally holding my breath. A full minute seemed to pass.

"I like some of it," the Gunny finally said. "Walking in the rain? More like running in the rain. And what if they move to the river, behind the Ontos, as we come down, and then turn to attack back up? All of our stuff will be tucked into these holes, just waiting for them. What are our other options?"

I was taken totally by surprise. What other options? The one I'd thought up had come in as if inspiration from God Himself. That I had remembered the pathway from the river in toward the canyon wall was astounding, even to me, as I'd just glimpsed it in the misting rain at night. The wall had reflected back what little light there was at the time.

The path or narrow clearing gave the companies a shot at making it all the way to the wall and then proceeding north with speed and the ability to take the enemy from the rear, or at least drive the NVA regiment to run and then take a stand. The enemy might figure, once the rout was successful, if it was successful, that the Marines would hunker down for the night and wait for coming massive air support the next day, but it could not know that. Stopping a night attack in the rain by a well-equipped Marine force would likely cause as much fear as the Marines receiving the same kind of attack by a full NVA regiment.

I also wondered about the fact that the Gunny had said nothing about my choice of Sugar Daddy and his men to isolate themselves as targets in order to make sure the Ontos was defended, not taken or destroyed. The Gunny's inability to harness either Sugar Daddy or Jurgens to any kind of real disciplined existence had never really been there at all. It had taken me some time to figure that out. If it involved the Gunny risking himself over the loss of a few Marines then the Marines would be lost and not him. I'd somehow stopped a great deal of the friendly fire slaughter that had been going on in the company, but I had not done that with anything other than the Gunny's approval, not his open participation.

And, in the final analysis, was I any different than the Gunny. The night the three Marines had come for me I had not hesitated to apply fatal force. There'd been no attempt at communication and no warning. One second they were alive and a few seconds later they were dead. And, I was alive.

The officers clustered inside the hole with me had not said a word, although all had remained erect and paying attention. Their conduct surprised me, as I was used to Marine officers almost always interjecting opinions or 'assistance' in some verbal form. I turned to them, noting that the Gunny had lit another cigarette and was preparing hot water using a chunk of Composition B. The acrid smell of the burning explosive reminded me of the physical nightmare we were all living, except for the FNG officers who were about to join us in our shattered and disheveled state. My back had stopped hurting where the leeches had bitten long and deep. Now it just ached, like it had been beaten with a baseball bat. The wet heat was awful and the mist did nothing to cool it. Somewhere there were C-rations because everyone had to eat in order to have the strength it would take for the attack.

"Who are you?" I asked the men just a few feet from me, using the diversion to avoid answering the Gunny's question.

"Lieutenants Smith, Russell and I'm MacInerny, reporting in, sir," the one nearest to me replied.

"You heard everything?" I asked, but not one of the three said anything. "Your first night in combat," I went on, "and you're in the A Shau and with a functional combat company of Marines. You don't call me sir. I'm a lieutenant like you. You call me Junior since everyone else does. If you live you'll get your own nickname. All I can assure you is that you might want to let everyone call you by it and that you won't like whatever name they have chosen for you. Astronomical sunset is at 1830, which is about now. Full night down here in the valley begins a bit early because we're at the bottom of a canyon so we'll be crossing the line of departure not long from right now. All three of you will be taking over Kilo. Our company is used to working without officers but Kilo is used to them, but not this night. This night you're with me."

"Why are we staying with you if the companies are attacking and we're going to command Kilo?" MacInerny asked, his tone indicating that he was fearful of asking the question, or probably of saying anything at all.

"So you'll be alive in the morning to take over," the Gunny said, before taking a swig of his coffee and then a deep inhalation from his cigarette. "I'm the Gunny. You can call me the Gunny. If you do what we say, then you'll stay alive until tomorrow, otherwise, you'll be like the rest of the officers that leave on the next medevac in body bags."

"Yes, sir," MacInerney replied.

The Gunny sighed. "Not sir. Gunny," he said, although his voice was almost too soft to hear.

"This is all happening right now, then?" MacInerny asked, shock in his voice, "we just got here."

I looked over at the Gunny through a small cloud of smoke he'd breathed out, the little fire in front of his squatting figure tiny but burning bright, drops of collected mist collected on his dark forehead. Slowly, his mouth curled into the coldest smile I'd ever seen it form.

"Just going for a little walk in the rain," the Gunny finally said, snapping his cigarette away and then grinding out the burning explosives with the boot of his right heel.

one-hundred-thirty-two

THE TWENTY-SEVENTH NIGHT : FIRST PART

Wet muddy foxholes rapidly became repositories for almost everything the combat company Marines usually carried on their backs. There was nothing to effectively hide or cover the holes with when they were abandoned, as they'd been there so long that both sides of the conflict knew their locations down to minute detail. There was little choice in leaving the gear behind, however. The only success the rapid maneuvering of the companies, and then their attack into the rear of the NVA regiment could possibly hope for, was based upon speed, a good bit of deception and then surprise.

I watched the three new lieutenants prepare for their first contact, none of the three appearing to show any fear or real trepidation. I wondered if they were made of sterner stuff than I was like I thought Captain Carruthers had been. They were wearing the new jungle utilities only recently issued, along with the lighter jungle boots that had special triangular metal pieces in their soles to avoid being injured by punji sticks. The boots and the utilities also, supposedly, dried a lot faster as well, not that it mattered much during the monsoon season when there was no such time, period or state known as dryness. I noted that the new utilities were a whole lot more noticeable against the jungle backdrop than the tattered remnants and dirt layered skin the other more seasoned Marines sported, like myself. The A Shau Valley would, however, tailor everything to its own design in almost no time at all. Mud, mosquitos, mosquito repellant, herbicides sprayed from the air, leeches, rain, and more mud would take their toll soon enough.

Try as I might, I could no longer remember the name of the third new officer, and that omission bothered me.

I waited with the three officers by my side, their radio operators redistributed by the Gunny to Jurgens' and Sugar Daddy's platoon squad leaders. Squad leaders didn't rate radio operators, but heavy communication in the jungle, on the attack and on the run in the rain, might be the difference between victory and death during our attack. Sugar Daddy would have his own RTO's Prick 25 accompanying the

Ontos and the armored 106mm recoilless rifle carrier would have its own, with Hultzler buttoned up inside. The Starlight Scope had been retrieved from where it was kept inside the Ontos. Upon receiving it, I handed it to MacInerny as one piece, without its normal accompanying tripod.

"You learned to handle one of these in Basic School?" I asked him, as he gingerly accepted the heavy black tubular 'gift,' encased in its thick plastic box.

"Starlight?" MacInerny said. "Don't we have some enlisted personnel capable of handling one of these? Yes, we used them on patrols in Virginia, as you must have, but it's supposed to be Op/Con to an NCO or even a Marine of lower rank."

"Dead," I breathed out, somewhat lying, as Hutzler was capable but necessary to have commanding the Ontos. I continued to breathe in and out heavily, working to reduce my fear and get ready for the hard physical task ahead. I checked both hands to make sure they weren't shaking. I'd not had a return to the shaking for many days but still feared to show myself to be weak in front of any of the Marines, much less the three new officers.

MacInerny worked the scope out of its case and then extended the tube out to take in the scene downriver in front of the assembled companies. Nguyen stood at my left side with Fessman poised right behind me. The Gunny had moved up to stand a few meters away, with Jurgens at his side. The Ontos idled in the background, although I knew Hultzer would be applying plenty of revolutions to the small motor and riding the clutch to give the enemy the idea that it was there and coming at them as soon as we pulled out.

"We only have sidearms," the lieutenant named Russell stated, almost in a whisper from just beyond where MacInerny stood.

"That's correct," I replied, between breaths, wondering if I should ask the name of the third lieutenant. I decided that it didn't matter.

"How are we supposed to shoot anyone without proper weaponry since you won't let us lead the men?" MacInerney asked.

"I don't want you shooting anyone," I replied.

"He doesn't want you getting shot, even more," the Gunny said, across the few meters in distance from where he stood. "Leave your .45 holstered with the flap open.

You're here to observe, this first time out, and your life's about to change along the course of this move."

I knew the Gunny was trying to prepare the new officers for being shot at for the first time. There was no preparation that would suffice, that I had figured out, anyway. The terror of facing immediate and painful death delivered with intent and malice by an unforgiving enemy at close range wasn't something that could be trained for.

I felt sorry for Fessman and the other radio operators, carrying their Prick 25 radio gear, on top of M-16s with some extra ammo. The going was to be hard, with the mud, normally not difficult to negotiate if one stepped lightly and slowly but cruelly demanding physically if run through. I began the attack by running forward.

The only command I gave was a very short "come on," to MacInerney. The other Marines would need no orders or instructions. I couldn't run on top of the mud. Each boot plunged down at least four to six inches into the slimy, sticking muck. Withdrawing the boot to make the next plunge was harder than the plunge down in the first place. I ran, the rain grew stronger as if to let me know that it was siding with the mud.

"There's nothing ahead," MacInerny kept whispering until I told him to shut up unless he saw something.

"This is harder than the Hill Trail back at the Basic School," he got out, "and back there enlisted men carried the equipment like this."

"No more talking," I gasped out, still working hard to control my breathing and stay with the Marines around me. There was no sound of the poncho material rubbing against poncho material because the ponchos had been shed and left back in our foxholes.

"Some of those enlisted men will be dying for you tonight. In the future you might want to refer to them as Marines, now shut up."

I knew the first three kilometers would be the toughest because the field of mud and shallow water was wide open for running. The jungle would be tougher to move through, and therefore the going slower, but not as physically demanding as the mud run. Would we be fast enough, quiet enough and really fool the NVA was the question I wondered? The Ontos groaned and moaned away to my rear, the sound rapidly dropping back the further I ran. The move itself was being made in near silence when it came to anything the enemy might hear, as the sound of the river rushing by, only a few meters to the left, covered my own sucking boot steps and those of the Marines running with me. I was running the point with the three new officers and the Starlight Scope, which was more than uncommon in any combat move a Marine unit might make. The Gunny's last words, before we'd taken off, had been ominous.

"When you're running the point just go for it since there's no way you'll be able to see if there's a tripwire or some other device to impede you. I'll be back a bit making sure everyone's following and maintaining as much silence as possible."

I had no misgivings about leading the attack until the Gunny's words settled into the forefront of my mind. I'd not thought about being the point or booby traps, punji sticks or any of the rest of the exposure being out in front as the point entailed, but there was no turning back.

We ran the distance, a little less than two miles, without incident, other than that the rain continued to increase in density, becoming more penetrating as a strong wind sweeping across the river also kicked up. The weather was a two-edged sword, however. The rain covered any noise the companies were creating as we moved down the riverbank, but the wind would carry what noise got through would make its way in reduced form through the jungle and over to the far canyon wall eventually. The rain began falling so hard that the sounds made by the Ontos disappeared altogether, and I felt better about the noise.

"That small cave entrance you wanted to know about is coming up on the right," MacInerney said, his own breathing being nearly as forced as my own.

I staggered the last few meters to where the nearly hidden cave entrance I'd once taken cover in was supposed to be, although without the benefit of the scope I could see nothing through the curtain of rain that fell in front of me and also poured down and off the front lip of my helmet.

I finally stopped, putting out my right hand to let MacInerny know we'd gone as far downriver as we were going to go. The other two lieutenants moved in closer until the four of us were clumped together, while I considered crossing up and over the berm to reach the open stretch leading to the far wall that I knew had to be there. The rest of the Marines had also stopped, I knew, using their learned ability to predict what was going on in the combat zone they occupied, an ability I didn't understand but accepted as part of my physical existence in the A Shau.

The Gunny moved up from the rear, as Nguyen came down over the berm, almost falling into our presence. He pointed back over his shoulder, somehow having been able to perceive what I was looking for, and the vital part of the plan that had to be there for the plan to succeed.

"He has, apparently, learned more English than anyone gives him credit for," the Gunny whispered, his own breathing a bit labored, as he stood recovering with the rest of us.

He took out a cigarette and bent over to light it, his back to the wind, his body guarding against the rain which was falling harder than it had since I'd landed in country. I was beginning to think that the plan I'd devised probably was remaining effective and ongoing mostly because of the cover that rain provided. With their superstitious natures, I wryly figured, the Marines would probably come to conclude that I had something to do with the rain falling so heavily at just the right time.

I recovered enough to turn and climb the berm Nguyen had slid down from. The mud and jungle debris were so slimy that I had to dig the tips of my boots deep into it in order to gain enough purchase to actually climb over the upper edge. I gave no orders to the three new officers, so they followed, gaining the top after me much quicker than I had. I waited for Fessman, the Gunny and Jurgens, squatting down as best I could in the muck and rain. The three officers did the same.

"Help Fessman up," I ordered the lieutenant named Russell.

"Fessman?" he whispered, crawling back toward the lip of the berm.

"My RTO, he's got that heavy radio on," I replied, wondering just how much the FNGs were really paying attention to anything.

It was hard to think only four weeks back when I was in their exact same situation. Nothing had made sense at all and without direction early on I would have been a month dead.

The Gunny, Jurgens, and Fessman came over the berm and joined me, although I could only feel them in my presence. There was almost no light at all that was perceptible through anything other than the Starlight Scope.

"MacInerney, can you see the path and the canyon wall at the other end?" I asked, holding my breath against the answer.

Without the existence of the path to get all the Marines on line and strung out in an attack formation, there was no way the plan could effectively work. The companies could not drive the attack home if they arrived near Hill 975 as a bunch of disconnected small pockets of fire.

"I see the path in front of me, as you described, but the rain is blurring out everything further on," MacInerney replied, " but I can't see any wall, or anything else, really. Are we going to order the men to fix bayonets?"

I almost couldn't believe my ears, MacInerney's comment coming from out of the blue, and seemingly so bizarre. I sighed, but not so anyone could hear.

"We don't fix bayonets," I whispered over to the lieutenant. "We don't use bayonets in combat and neither does the enemy. You go at someone in the bush with a bayonet and all that will happen is that you'll get yourself shot dead on the spot."

"Jurgens," I said, partially to change the subject and keep anyone from knowing what the lieutenant had said. "You take your platoon, with the extra RTOs, and move all the way to the wall and report back on the combat net. Run your squads north in line of the file. The rest of us are going in lines to filter through the jungle, making sure nothing remains as we move until we encounter the enemy. Everyone has to remember to fire only forward because we're not going to be seeing much of anything in these conditions. Even the Starlight Scope is all but useless. If this works, then it won't matter, however. The only time we've surprised the enemy is when we've moved, and right now in this night and rain I can't see that they'll be expecting us."

"If this works?" Jurgens asked in the short silence that followed.

I didn't reply. The silence stretched on while I waited for what might be next, once again wondering whether I should move my hand to the butt of my Colt.

I'd unstrapped the weapon when we'd stopped to climb the berm, but had not drawn it from its holster.

"What if your 'Walk in the Rain' plan doesn't work?" Jurgens said as I guessed he might.

"We couldn't stay where we were, and what's more, you know that," the Gunny said, smoke from his cigarette reaching my nostrils.

The smell was a pleasant relief. For some reason, I felt the smoke was a sign that the Gunny was with me all the way.

"I'd like to accompany Jurgens to the wall," MacInerney whispered into the dark center of our informal group, his voice barely audible through the beating of the rain on my helmet.

"Don't need company," Jurgens hissed back.

"Lieutenant MacInerney will accompany you on his first combat patrol," I said, understanding that MacInerney had somehow guessed the situation, with respect to Jurgen's lack of loyalty to me or the plan, and was willing to do what he could to make sure Jurgens complied.

"In fact, all three of you should go."

MacInerny had no idea, I knew, of the danger he was placing himself in should he actually come into opposition with Jurgens in a combat situation, but his, and the other officer's presence and movement at the wall, was a better possible resolution than my having to take out Jurgens, and then attempt to deal with a platoon of Marines dedicated to the sergeant and angry as hell. At the same time, I felt a slight shiver of guilt and fear course through me. MacInerny reminding me of Carruthers earlier bothered me. Could I have done more to save Carruthers? What was I doing to MacInerney now, and what would I have to do if Jurgens killed him? I thought of Macho Man, and how I knew what had to have happened, and then I'd taken no action.

"Take them," the Gunny said, "and see if you can bring them back in one piece. This outfit has a pretty crummy record when it comes to surviving officers and if we get through this that could be more troublesome than getting written up for any decorations might buffer. And I want you to leave a couple of your best scouts behind, moving slowly north behind us in case we somehow got it wrong and the NVA regiment isn't ahead of us at all."

The lyrics to the song "You Keep Me Hanging On," that I'd heard earlier in the day through Fessman's radio kept rattling around in my head. "Set me free, why don't you babe…" I couldn't remember the rest of the lyrics except "you keep me hanging on," but somehow, they seemed to apply to my situation. What was I to do with MacInerney and the other two new lieutenants? The A Shau Valley was an awful teacher and I had little time to be their guide. I was using them instead of guiding them and I knew it. I wanted to be free but I didn't even know what I wanted to be free from anymore. And I hadn't thought about the timing of the enemy's move. I'd presumed that the regiment would move at first dark to flank us and then drive us north into the waiting force at Hill 975.

"Junior?" the Gunny asked.

I snapped back. I'd drifted off, trying to figure all the angles, and so tired I could barely stand. The rain was hypnotic, and thinking about the conflict with Jurgens, and the coming combat, those issues seeming so old hat that they were becoming weirdly comfortable instead of terrifying and fearful.

"Let's move out," I ordered, coming to my feet with difficulty. "Everyone's tired and we've got three clicks to move south through heavy jungle, and then encounter the NVA if we're lucky. We push all the way to the stream that runs out into the Bong Song at the base of Hill 975 if necessary, although I don't think we'll get that far. They've got to dig in at some point because I don't think a whole regiment is going to fit into the rabbit holes dug into the sides of 975. Get ready for another salvo of 175s. We may not need the diversion but I'm not taking any chances."

Fessman handed me the radio handset when I was done talking. I turned my back on the collected group, even though it was too dark and miserably wet to be able to see much of anything about them. I listened to their wet squishy movements as they moved away. There was no need for further commands. The Gunny would have the companies feeding into the path from the river bed, and then filtering into the jungle in organized files for the brutal jungle consuming hump to chase the NVA down from the rear.

The previously planned zone fire mission, firing red bag, was approved and the first rounds on the way before I was able to hear the Ontos again. It was closer, although moving very slow. There had been no small arms fire that I'd detected, which meant that Sugar Daddy and his platoon were as yet unencountered, and that was good news. Sugar Daddy had survived his grandstanding stunt on the bridge, losing two of the three Marines with him, no doubt causing him some grieving guilt if he was still human, but otherwise leaving him physically fit and able to remain in command of his platoon.

Marines swirled in the dark around the Gunny, as he organized them for the attack. The extra radios on the combat net had to be properly distributed to make them an effective advantage. The first rounds of the five-minute artillery barrage started coming in. The hard rain was no buffer to the sound of the big 175 mm round explosions. The jungle shook and the ground seemed to heave with every blast.

"Stay on the combat net," I ordered Fessman, "and let me know what's going on at the wall and out at the Ontos. We need to get the Ontos turned around and headed back just as soon as we pass parallel to its position."

"What does parallel to its position mean?" Fessman asked, standing by my side.

"When we can hear it next to us as we go by, then it's time to turn it around," I replied.

Hultzer and Sugar Daddy wouldn't really know where our force was but the Ontos could be heard so we would know where it was.

I tried to run into the black of the jungle to my direct front but that effort ended in only a few meters. The explosions of the big artillery shells seemed to draw me toward them. Their diversionary cover wouldn't last for very long. But the jungle was not going to be run through by anybody. I began working my way through the nearly three-foot deep debris, around the currently invisible stands of impenetrable bamboo stands and bumping into and then around the bigger trees holding the main canopy of the jungle above.

Once into the jungle interior, it was good to have the guidance provided by the distant exploding artillery rounds. The direction was straight ahead, but with the wind sweeping the tops of the jungle all over the place, the rain pounding down, and the dead blackness of night, the direction was neither easy nor automatic.

A hard fast and forced walk with bent knees, already fatigued from the run through the mud, drove me forward. I'd heard no shots from the direction of the wall so I presumed that the three FNG lieutenants still lived.

"Turn the Ontos and start it back," I said to Fessman after a while, "But keep the speed down so it's not running with only Sugar Daddy's defensive fires if the NVA figures out what we are up to."

I felt Nguyen at my side and then ahead of me, clearing what brush he could, bending branches and then moving on when I passed.

"Are they moving along the wall?" I asked Fessman.

I'd thought about staying right on the radio with the earphone and headset while I moved but then realized there were no orders I could think of to be given to the Marines as we moved, other than the Ontos. Fessman could tell me what was going on.

"Yes, sir, they are," Fessman said back. "There's a trail right next to the wall and it is easy-going, according to the lieutenant, sir," Fessman finished.

MacInerney had managed to get his RTO back which also meant that Jurgens was likely being pushed to his limit when it came to commanding a platoon with three lieutenants surrounding his every move and judging his every action.

"Tell them to move just aside of the path," I ordered, thinking about how the NVA could so easily mine or place booby traps along such an easy access.

"I told them, sir," Fessman said, "but nobody is answering on Jurgens or the lieutenant's frequency."

There was nothing further I could do. I moved forward with Nguyen's clearing help. I'd had no food since the day before and my water supply was running low. I'd stripped off my extra canteens for the run, and I knew I'd be dehydrated by the time we got back to those supplies if those supplies were still there.

Bamboo vipers didn't hunt at night, so there were some benefits to the long slogging attack and the mosquito population, usually so prevalent during night hours, had gone wherever the vipers spent their nighttime hours. The wind was noisy, scary but also refreshing, as it blew the falling rain coming down against every part of my body. The heat, generally so oppressive, was lowered to a tolerable, almost comfortable level.

I knew I was nowhere near the most advanced party in making my way toward the enemy's rear, as I could hear the movement of other Marines ahead of me off to both sides. The Marines who'd survived in the valley for long periods of time were in unbelievable physical condition. All wiry, thin and tough as nails when it came to humping heavy loads or gutting through tough fast movements like the one we were on. The Ontos continued to run through gears and engine revolution changes off to my right, no longer dropping away in distance. If all things went as planned, then the Ontos would arrive near the inlet stream, or just short of it, at the same time the main elements of both companies did. The presence of those six barrels pointing right at the enemy would be intimidating, at the very least.

It felt good to keep moving, as the fear level dropped inside me, as I moved. There was no logical reason for that drop in terror because at some point we had to make contact with the enemy regiment in front of us. There'd been no reports at all from the scant rearguard we'd mounted, just to make sure that we had not somehow ended up in front of instead of behind the NVA sapper regiment, and that was a relief, the closer we got to Hill 975.

I was relieved to hear the first small arms fire, radiating back through the windy rainy jungle in front of me. The small arms fire was instantly identifiable as M-60 fire, which was also somewhat satisfying. The enemy was there, in front of us, and we were Marines on the attack once more.

THE TWENTY-SEVENTH NIGHT : SECOND PART

The M-60s had opened up from in front of me, but I could not estimate the distance or the true direction the machine guns might be firing from, what with the sound of the nearby rushing river water and the incessant beat of the rain down upon my helmet. I knew all the Marines understood that there was no alternative to a full-frontal attack that would take us to the very edge of the forest line. Digging in, and then holding that position would take every bit of supporting fire in the night that the Ontos could provide and then every bit of fire support from the air to hold the position during the next day.

I pushed forward, with Fessman at my left shoulder and Nguyen breaking the jungle in front of me as best he could. The rain beat away the mosquitos and cooled my skin a bit, although the pain from the leech bites all over my back would not retreat as much as I would have liked. I knew the three of us had to be within five hundred meters, or so, of that front edge of the jungle. From there we would command a full view of the waterway cutting into the side of the Bong Song, and also the southern exposure of Hill 975. The Starlight Scope would once again become very important in sighting in to suppress fire, if we could get it into position.

More M-60s opened up and I was momentarily heartened until I head the distinct 'whooping' sound of mortar rounds leaving their tubes. Our 60 mm mortars had been left in our foxholes alongside the river because we hadn't had ammunition for them until the resupply came in. I realized before the mortar rounds struck, that I had not checked thoroughly to see who had gone to pick up the supplies, or even if anybody had. I burrowed into the floor of the jungle. I hadn't been counting but I knew the mortar rounds would only stay in the air between fifteen and twenty seconds, depending upon what charge they'd been loaded in the tube with and how far they were from us. The mortar charges going off, driving the seven-pound projectiles had sounded very close. The only fuse the Soviet weapon, also manufactured in China, was capable of firing was either a dummy training round or a high explosive anti-personnel shell.

The muffled explosions from the mortar strikes rattled through the jungle in front of me, followed by more intense M-60 machine gun-fire. Somehow, the NVA had been able to set up one or more mortar tubes, or those tubes had been at the ready all the time near the base of Hill 975. High explosive anti-personnel shells were not very effective when impacting into the kind of dense jungle we were worming our way through.

The old fear returned with a vengeance, as I tried to insert my body under the thick matting of the jungle. I felt the tiny animals moving under and around me as my larger anthropoid body displaced them. I didn't care about being bitten or anything else. My fear wasn't logical, I knew, but I could not shed it. I could only imagine some speeding chunk of hot metal plunging down and through my body.

I felt a hand reach down to grip my left shoulder and I shrugged it off. But there it was again, pulling me upward. The mortar explosions had stopped, but my fear had not.

The sound of more mortar rounds being loaded into tubes and being launched struck deeper fear into the center of my torso. I pushed down until I realized that the sounds of the mortars firing were different. The mortars launching were 60s, which meant that they were ours. Somehow, Sugar Daddy had gotten the supplies, set up the mortars, and then was no doubt aiming in the night toward where the brief flash-es of muzzle blast from the 82s were coming from. The 60s fired on and on until a rainy, river water rushing sort of conditional silence returned to the jungle battlefield. I had no idea about casualties on either side, but there was little doubt that the resupply had brought in plenty of 60 mm ammunition and the enemy would now know that. The 82 mm en-emy mortars would not be firing from holes, caves or other openings in the mountain. Mortars needed bare air to fire, almost vertically, up into.

"Monday morning you gave me no warning," whispered into my left ear.

"What?" I whispered back, wondering why I was whispering, ex-cept to maybe avoid being targeted by the not too distant enemy mortar team.

It was Nguyen. I could not deny him. I let him pull me out of the mucky debris like the Gunny had so many weeks before. Nguyen was repeating the words of one of the rock and roll songs he'd no doubt heard coming out of Fessman's radio. Monday, Monday, by The Mamas and Papas

I almost laughed in my misery and fear. A Montagnard who was not conversant in English in a place thousands of miles from the USA was quoting me song lyrics to try to help me overcome my fear. I came erect, sitting, preparing myself to go forward once again. I realized that we needed the 60 mm mortars. We had to have plenty of ammo, after resupply. The sixties could fire upon the 82s at the direction of MacInerney using the Starlight Scope, if he was still alive. Getting to my feet, I reached toward Fessman in the dark and rain. The handset was slapped into my hand like Fessman somehow knew I'd be asking for it.

"Gunny," I said into the handset, knowing everyone was on the same combat frequency for the attack.

"Junior," came back out of the radio, but it was the radio operator's voice, not that of the Gunny. I didn't care.

"We needed the sixties, which somehow Sugar Daddy's platoon got up and working. The Ontos isn't even up to our position yet, however, which means its got to go up to maximum speed to cover Sugar Daddy's forward element now occupying our old position."

There was no reply. I pushed the handset back at Fessman. I knew the message had probably gotten through, as there were many ears listening to the transmission.

I knew that Sugar Daddy had his own radio operator and had to be up on the combat net like we all were. There was no response from him over the radio, and the Gunny didn't say anything either, but there was a distinctly different sound in the distance. The sound was an engine, working at maximum RPM, it's noisy staccato exhaust not overpowering but definitely loud enough to be heard over the sounds of the river's waters and the rain. The Ontos was moving and moving fast. I realized that I might have to write up Sugar Daddy for a decoration like I had Jurgens. I wondered if that was what it was like with guys coming home with medals on their chests from being involved in real combat on the ground. Were they all scumbags who somehow managed to be able to fight, kill and survive, in spite of their lack of any identifiable moral compass?

I tried to remove as much of the mud and jungle bracken from my body as I could. There were no leeches, which surprised me. But the rain was unending. The mud, beneath the jungle matting, was sticky and darkly smelling of earthly burial and death.

I called for MacInerney on the net. Although he'd left the scope to be carried by Fessman, along with his radio and battery gear, he was crucial in any attempt to use the device to sight in on launch points or bases of fire in and around Hill 975, if our occupation of the adjacent jungle was to succeed and we were able to push the sapper regiment into the hill fortifications.

There was not much further to move, as I quickly came upon Marines lying in prone positions, their faintly shiny and water covered weapons thrust out before them. I knew there was only open area to the front so went down in a prone position, as well.

I stared out where I knew Hill 975 had to be in front of me. I wanted to look at it through the Starlight Scope that MacInerny once more possessed. He had gone down to a prone position near my right side. The three lieutenants had come back as one, and I had to admit the presence of them nearby gave me a feeling of relief and strange warmth. There were other living officers in the company perimeter and I didn't have to follow any damaged orders they might give.

"The Three Stooges return," I heard Fessman whisper nearby, no doubt talking to the other RTOs he secretly maintained communication with.

I knew he had probably intended for me to hear him, although I didn't have a negative enough opinion of the corporal to believe he wanted the three lieutenants to hear, as well. I ignored the snarky comment, as I presumed he knew I would.

I decided that I didn't need to look through the scope. There was nothing but the hills' outline to be viewed, and I knew that outline pretty well from memory.

I'd climbed that deadly peak twice and many Marines had died on top of it and around its base, and here were two more rifle companies likely to part with a few more.

The hill emitted no light in the stygian murk created by a monsoon overcast night and a densely falling rain that would not let up. The sound of the water flowing through the inlet to wedge its way into the Bong Song penetrated the darkness, and I realized that that body of water might also be a problem. Earlier, we'd been able to move the Ontos across it because it hadn't been that deep and the water, not that fast-moving, but with the hard rain coming down for some time that stream-like thread of water running hip-deep could be considerably deeper and running much stronger. How had the NVA regiment we pursued crossed the water since there was no fire at all coming from the positions they'd fired their mortars from in the jungle area we now occupied? If they had a way to cross the water then so our Marine rifle companies might have that same way, given it was natural and not some sort of temporary bridge they could destroy or takedown.

Our two companies were in line, according to Fessman's whispered reports, from the canyon wall to the west all the way to the river's edge on the east, a distance of about four hundred meters. One Marine for just about every meter if stood shoulder to shoulder, which they were definitely not. Resupply contents had been rescued out from under the nose of the NVA occupying Hill 975, with the Cobras and the Skyraiders providing heavy murderous cover during the daylight hours of the day before. Our stuff had not been disturbed, when Sugar Daddy's platoon returned for it, which was the greatest godsend of the whole operation. The company's ammunition, water, food and the 60 mm mortar rounds we'd used to suppress the 82s had been there and were intact. I ate a full can of Ham and Mothers in four big gulps, and then consumed a whole canteen of freshwater brought in from the rear area. My energy level skyrocketed. I hadn't been near as tired from lack of any decent sleep as I had been dehydrated and starving from only taking in small amounts of water and no food at all.

The Gunny settled down into the newly dug foxhole that Nguyen and Fessman had been kind enough to dig. It was a poor excuse for a foxhole because the 'hole' part of it only reached four or five feet down through the packed jungle floor. Any attempt to penetrate the mud underneath that dense debris only ended up with water completely filling the hole. The water table was too close to the surface to do anything underground unless there was a mountain like Hill 975 above to block the rain and let it run off to lower elevations.

"It's not going to stay this quiet," the Gunny said. I took in the strong aroma of the unfiltered Camel cigarettes he smoked.

Most of the other Marines in both companies smoked, from time to time, but none of them did so as consistently and as close to me as the Gunny.

The rain muted everything, the sound of its heavy patter becoming unnoticeable to me, except when other sounds penetrated through, other sounds that were not the river's water rushing by, which was always there, as well.

"The 175 artillery was more accurate than in the past," the Gunny went on, "and that made the 60mm's a whole lot more effective. Got the Ontos into position, finally, and it can sweep the whole base of Hill 975, or even the hillside itself, if necessary. They're regrouping in their holes, but they'll be back well before dawn. They know what our plan is now and that the key to it is holding our position until daylight. I don't think they have tunnels coming under the stream or under the bed of jungle we're in. Too much water at this time of year, so I'm not worried about that."

I wondered what was on the Gunny's mind. He almost never went into a conversational mode, even where it involved the enemy, and what that enemy might be up to.

"We need the Starlight Scope with Hultzer and the Ontos crew," the Gunny said, adding to my level of discomfort. "When the attack comes that's about the only way we'll stop it, or at least funnel it over to the canyon wall where we've got plenty of M-60 firepower online and still a load of ammo for the three mortars."

"Fessman, have Nguyen hustle the scope over to Hultzer," I ordered. "They won't need MacInerney. Hultzer's pretty good all by himself with it."

In seconds Nguyen was gone, the scope, case, and tripod whisked away like they were made of some light Balsa wood.

"I agree," I finally said, turning to face the Gunny, but staying as prone as I could be half inside a foxhole dug too shallow to do much other than allow me to pull my poncho over the edges and fight back the rain. But I couldn't get to doing that and talk to the Gunny at the same time.

"I want a full platoon online downriver," I continued, "about half a click to make absolutely sure we don't get hit from that direction, and I want the three lieutenants here to go over to the Ontos and get some OJT on it. None of them are artillery so they didn't go through Fort Sill to meet up with the little beast in training.

"Yes, sir, Junior," MacInerney replied as if I'd been speaking directly to him. The three lieutenants were gone in seconds. I realized that I was liking MacInerney more and more, and that made me uncomfortable too. We'd never done the seniority proof thing so I simply presumed that the other two lieutenants, Russell and the one I couldn't remember his name, who acted as his assistants, were junior to him.

When they were gone, with only Fessman remaining outside, and the Gunny closer, right near the edge of the hole, I asked the question that had come to the forefront of my mind.

"What is it?" I asked. I was determined to not speak again until the Gunny answered.

He didn't answer. Instead, he snapped his cigarette off out into the rain, moved closer and began helping me get my poncho arranged so I'd be able to duck down under it, curl up best as I could, and then get what little sleep I could manage until whatever attack had to be coming showed up.

I got under the poncho and took off my helmet for the first time in hours. My neck was sore from the weight of the thing. I rubbed it, still not saying anything, but I made no attempt to curl up under the waterproof poncho. I sat and waited, holding the edge of it up so I faced the Gunny, laying on his belly atop the jungle debris, his face less than two feet from mine.

"Jurgens," the Gunny whispered, his voice seeming clearer because the rain made less noise hitting my poncho than it had the metal of my helmet.

I waited some more.

"He didn't do anything to the lieutenants, even though they're the usual idiots they send us," the Gunny murmured. "He didn't do them and won't do anything else because you've got him. He knows you know about the helicopter guy."

"Macho Man," I whispered back.

"Yeah, that guy," the Gunny continued. "The guys in the company didn't like it, any of them. He knows that. He doesn't want them to be with you. And he knows you put him in for a decoration. He doesn't understand you at all, but he'll do what you tell him from now on. I need you to promise that you won't kill him or put him out there to be killed."

"You're negotiating for him?" I asked, in shocked surprise. "Like you're his representative?"

"I'm the Gunny," the Gunny replied. "I represent everyone in these two companies right now, like I have for some time, and that includes you."

At the end of his comment, the last few words hissed out, much different than his lighter whispering tone had been in delivering what came before. I flinched inside at those words. The Gunny had saved my life. He'd represented me a number of times, most of them I still probably knew nothing about. For some reason, he was requiring that I verbally, and in reality, promise that I would not finally give Jurgens the justice he so badly deserved. I thought about lying to the Gunny, my mind racing, but I knew I couldn't do it. The Gunny, in his twenty-seven days of eternity with me, was more a father to me than my own father had been for the earlier twenty-three years of my entire life. I didn't reply. I breathed, knowing I had no way out, but not wanting to give in or say the words. The Gunny read my mind.

"Say the one word, Junior," he said, the patience in his voice surprised me.

My promise was important to him for reasons I'd probably never know, and he was willing to wait me out to get it.

I didn't know whether to say yes or no. Yes, I'd kill him, or yes I wouldn't kill him, and there was also the two 'no' possibilities.

"Yes," I finally said, guessing that that meant I would not kill the man.

The Gunny's right hand appeared out of the mud, his arm extended.

I was taken aback. Marines saluted or followed orders. They didn't shake hands, especially not in a combat situation.

I took the Gunny's hand, realizing we weren't shaking hands as officer and non-com, or even as Marines. We were shaking hands man-to-man. The Gunny's grip was muddy but very firm, and then it, and he were gone.

"Sorry Macho Man," I whispered into the raining night, before pulling myself under the poncho and curling up as best I could. I tried to close my eyes and think of any good things. There seemed to be no leeches in my hole in the jungle and the mosquitos could not fly in the heavy rain, but that and the Ham and Mothers were about it. I finally closed my eyes.

But my mind would not stop running at full speed. The artillery might possibly save us again if it could be finely adjusted. The Starlight had to be used in such a way that an attack could be visually spotted instead of simply and violently felt when rounds began being exchanged on the ground. I opened my eyes and came up out from under the lip of my poorly constructed shelter.

"Fessman," I said, the rain beating down upon my unprotected head and flowing back behind me down into my marginally protective hole. "Get me the 175 battery on the arty net," I ordered.

"Have you got the last fire mission registered, with bag weight and the same range approximation?" I asked the battery fire direction officer, as soon as I had the microphone in my hand and the transmit button depressed.

"Affirmative on that data, Junior," came back.

"Circular error probable?" I asked, waiting tensely, hoping the FDO could give me anything at all. The CEP was the likelihood, in meters of radius, that half the rounds of a salvo would strike in that zone.

"Two hundred meters," the FDO replied, sounding like he was fairly certain.

The barrage I'd called in earlier had been exceedingly accurate, given that the distance was beyond the 175 mm gun's table-rated range. The rounds would drop from the battery, passing Hill 975 on its eastern face while coming down into the valley just beyond and over the lip of the A Shau's western canyon wall. Our position was just under two hundred meters from the stream of water feeding into the swollen Bong Song. It was another two hundred meters to the base of Hill 975. Deflection, the rounds aim from side to side, would not be affected much by the extended range. Calling in another 175 fire would be a bit of a toss-up but our situation was tenuous without that fire, and without that fire coming down where it was needed the most.

"What is your position, Junior?" the FDO asked.

I'd called in the previous mission from across the river. There had been no 'rules of engagement' to consider. But now I was calling for fire, from an artillery battery firing beyond its effective range and the rules of engagement might be strictly adhered to. I was calling for a mission that would not doubt be closer than the 'danger close' limitations allowed for. The battery would not fire if we were too close to where the rounds might be expected to come in. No artillery officers in the battery would risk their careers by firing, not if it was likely that those rounds might kill friendlies and should not have been fired in the first place according to the rules of engagement.

I backed our position up five hundred meters down the valley from where we really were, and then called that fictitious position in.

"You want to adjust using the gun target line?" the FDO asked back, almost immediately.

I understood that the FDO knew I was lying. He was agreeing to fire, however, and wanted to make sure that I would not have a problem adjusting fire by having to adjust from a position I wasn't really occupying, which would be damned difficult, especially at night. An Army officer, a battery FDO was taking a potentially massive risk in helping a Marine unit in trouble. I knew if I lived, that I could never say a negative thing about the Army again.

"Affirmative, and I'll need adjusting and battery fire," I replied, while silently hoping that the heavy rain would cause the rounds to reach out a little less further than they otherwise might. Zone fire would be too dispersive and potentially much more dangerous to have an impact than directing the battery to fire at targets registered in real-time by using single round adjustments.

"Do you have a request for a fire mission, over?" the FDO asked.

"Stand by, as we'll be in a danger-close attack situation sometime before the dawn, over," I replied, handing the headset back to Fessman.

"Call Hultzer in the Ontos," I ordered. "The Starlight is going to be everything when it comes to letting us know when they attack, and where."

I wondered if the NVA was on top of the artillery potential of the situation to be smart enough to attack only along the western-most part of the canyon wall, where artillery rounds coming in from the firebase located way up the valley would be partially blocked by the bulk of Hill 975's eastern flank. "And tell him to aim and concentrate six rounds loaded with flechettes, with fuses adjusted to set the rounds up close to where the stream moves by the western face of the parapet."

"What's a parapet, sir?" Fessman asked, "Hultzer wants to know."

I frowned but understood. Parapet wasn't the right word to use, even if Hultzer had understood. The canyon wall was the canyon wall and not a fortification or breastwork to hold off an attack or protect from incoming fire.

"The wall of the canyon below Hill 975 and as east in the distance as the fuse range will allow," I answered.

If the artillery could handle sixty to seventy percent of the forward area we were facing then the Ontos might be able to handle the remaining area, even though the distance and the likely density of attackers would be much greater if the enemy calculated properly.

I crawled back into my hole and pulled the poncho cover back over the opening. I curled up to get some badly needed sleep, realizing that there had been a time in the very near past when an impending attack wouldn't have let me sleep at all.

Seconds later, I felt the cover of my poncho eased upward and someone sticking his head inside.

"I'll do my part," the man said, his voice quiet but clear.

The crease between the poncho cover and the mud lip of the hole disappeared and I was in complete blackness again. I closed my eyes, only recognizing Jurgen's voice as sleep overcame me.

one-hundred-thirty-four

THE TWENTY-SEVENTH NIGHT : THIRD PART

My eyes snapped open, and I took in a quick deep breath. The sound that had awakened me was that of a fifty-caliber machine gun firing at close range. The crack of it, with following cracks and echoes, assured that I was downrange from the muzzle blasts and the shockwave reflecting off of the projectiles exiting that muzzle at supersonic speeds. I was downrange. It could only be enemy fire. I came alive, jerking my sleepy slow body upward, the adrenalin beginning to kick in, as I pushed aside the water streaming mess of my poncho cover to face up into the pouring night.

"They've got their fifty-caliber set up," Fessman said, needlessly, his face only inches from my own, like he'd been there waiting for me to come out all along.

"The Ontos," I replied, my mind coming fully online. I held out my right hand in the dark. "I've got to talk to Hutzler."

The Ontos was our only protection against something like the fifty. I grabbed the handset and transmitted. Hutzler came back over the radio immediately, as I turned, crawled to the other side of my hole and stared into the night. The fifty opened up again but there were, unaccountably, no tracers visible. The Gunny plopped down on the squishy matted jungle to my left.

"They're not using any tracers," I said to Hutzler. "What can you see with the scope?"

"They're using pre-registered fields of fire," the Gunny said, "so they won't give away the weapon's position."

"They're firing from inside the mountain itself, sir," Hutzler replied, "but I can see the muzzle flashes faintly anyway, from the angle I'm at."

"Can we hit them?" I asked, controlling my voice and breathing.

One well-placed fifty caliber machine gun could make the coming attack either an overwhelming success or at least cause heavy casualties on my two rifle companies.

"I'll never hit the opening with a single H.E. round, but with our own .50 spotter I might be able to get a flechette round, fused just right, to go off just at the entrance to the opening."

I imagined what it might be like to be inside the cave behind that opening if a fifteen pound 106 mm flechette round went off only a few feet inside that opening. Thousands of tiny darts would be showered at twenty-two thousand feet per second throughout the interior cave complex.

"Okay, fire one of the spotters and see if you can get a tracer round into the opening," I ordered, as the enemy 50 Cal fired again.

I held the microphone to my ear, Hultzer was leaving his own handset with the transmit button depressed. I heard the short-barreled fifty caliber spotting gun go off and then watched the streaking 'burning beer can' of a tracer round arc over to Hill 975. Three more rounds followed until I heard the command "fire the one oh six," and then a giant explosion went off and I knew the 106 main round was on the way. There was no tracer attached to it, however, the fiery boom of its detonation was readily apparent, lighting up the entire southern side of the hill, when it went off. I was surprised to hear screaming coming all the way across the open area, right through the dense rain, as the night returned to full dark. Hutzler fired another 106 round into almost exactly the same spot, and then another. After the third round, there was no more screaming, or noise at all, radiating out of the mountainside.

"We might have affected them, sir," Hutzler said, into the radio before the line went dead.

"Yes," I breathed to myself, "we affected them, all right."

Fessman and I stayed huddled under my poncho, the rain blessedly coming down hard but channeled away by the small creases around the hole Nguyen had made with his E-Tool. That he was outside, without the benefit of a poncho liner, was discomforting to think about, but I understood it was his way. He was native to the valley, not going native. The A Shau was his home territory, and the weather in it was the home weather he'd endured for a lifetime.

I tried to reach the radios through the operators I'd pried loose from the lieutenants, but there was so much chatter on the combat frequency that there was no getting through. The enemy fifty-caliber had been silenced by the Ontos, but I knew the attack we were expecting had to come. It would be along some path or trail very close to the western canyon wall where I'd sent the extra radio operators to, in order to act as constant communications nodes back to my command.

If the enemy didn't make its attempt near the wall, then the fire mission I had on hold with the 175 battery would wipe them out, as well as maybe some of our own Marines. With only a two hundred meter range safety margin I knew we'd have to be really lucky to avoid friendly casualties.

The Gunny stuck his head under the poncho cover. I knew it was him from the cigarette smoke on his breath. Fessman's Prick 25 gave off a small bit of light but not enough to make out facial features.

"Stop," the Gunny hissed across the short distance.

"Stop what?" I asked, truly surprised by the comment.

"Stop trying to lead from the god blessed rear," the Gunny said, louder this time. "You led them this far. Now let them be what they are. You can't see a damned thing anyway, but you've gotten into the command habit, and field command isn't your talent. So, stay off the net and let them go at it. The Ontos can't see that far in this rain hell of a night, even with that magic scope, and it can't use flechettes against attacking infantry because they'll hit us too. This is going to be hand to hand stuff and you're no good at that either. I've pulled you out of some holes, but now I'm telling you to stay in this one and stay off the combat net. Here, get your energy back. We'll need you later."

The Gunny was gone before I could collect myself enough to answer anything he'd said. He'd tossed something that hit me in the chest and then fell to the bottom of the hole. I pulled it up. It was a box of C-Rations. I knew it would be Ham and Mothers.

"Command isn't my talent?" I whispered aloud, trying to understand what the Gunny was talking about. "How does he know I'm no good at hand to hand, and what the hell is hand to hand combat in the jungle, anyway."

"I don't think he wants you to get killed, and I don't think hand to hand means what it sounds like," Fessman replied, although I hadn't spoken aloud to elicit a response.

The poncho cover edge was lifted once more, but there was nothing said. I knew it had to be Nguyen. Fessman had given me new batteries from the last supply run for

[caption id="attachment_35791" align="alignright" width="200"] Montagnard Kon Tum Fighting knife[/caption]

Jurgens' flashlight. I pulled the little device out and turned it on, muffling the light with my free hand. Nguyen's expressionless face appeared. A sparkle of light darted off something he held in his left hand, dangling over the lip of the hole until he quickly withdrew it. I knew the item had to be his special Montagnard Kon Tum Fighting Knife. The knife looked like a large American butcher knife but was handmade and the steel polished with sand and dirt instead of any special solution.

Nguyen had been right behind the Gunny and maybe had not known who it was in the dark and rain of the miserable night. I wondered briefly about that until I looked into the shiny blackness of the man's eyes. That flat unemotional stare back into my own eyes filled my center with warmth. I was being looked out for, against all enemies, even if that included the Gunny. I wasn't certain, but the feeling was there and I was going to go with it. I turned my flashlight off and curled back up. The Gunny was right, and I knew it. There was nothing I could know from my current position, not yet, and there was little I could do in attempting to actually engage the enemy personally. I closed my eyes, trying to think about a coming time when there was no rain and the sun would beat down between scudding clouds. I briefly wondered if my teenage radioman ever slept, but consciousness left me before I came to any conclusion.

I awoke once more, this time with no doubt about what was happening. Heavy small-arms fire came from the west where the wall was situated. Contact had been established, the M-60 fire mixed in with M-16 and AK fire. I pushed the poncho aside and stared out over the battlefield. The fact that the Marines in my company all fired tracers the direction of fire was easy to determine, and that direction extended much further down toward me than I had guessed.

I reached for the handset Fessman had already pushed into my shoulder and called in the fire mission, wishing the 175 ammunition had either illumination rounds or white phosphorus. I asked for one round, paid close attention to the 'shot, over' reply and the 'splash' indication. Five seconds later the round went off with a flash that was so strong that it showed like a very temporary beacon through the dark night and hard rain. The round had impacted somewhere on the other side of the water, not far from where the base of Hill 975 climbed upward to form the southern tip of the western canyon wall. The mountain was blinking. I realized I was looking at small arms muzzle flashes from AK fire being directed all along our front from holes exiting up and down the outward curving expanse. I decided to start with the exposed eastern side of the mountain's slope.

"Drop two hundred, right one hundred, a battery of four," I requested.

The "shot, over," came only seconds later. The battery was prepped and ready for whatever I was going to call in, and that rapid response improved my confidence and reduced my fear considerably.

The sixteen heavy rounds began impacting up and down the side of the mountain. Even though the battery could not reach the southern part of the slope facing us, the 'firefly' blinking coming from that slope stopped completely.

I adjusted the artillery fire to add three hundred, allowing another battery of four (16 rounds, fired one after another from the four big guns) to traverse over the mountain's flank and strike down into the area over the water but short of our jungle line.

The small arms fire generating so many tracers slowed to only occasional single shots or short automatic bursts. I realized that nobody on the battlefield had any good idea of where or when the big artillery shells were going to land. I called for more fire, trying to continue the suppression of fire from the mountain and also hold off an inevitable decision by the enemy to proceed with the attack because the artillery could not reach back as far as the western wall.

"Get me Sugar Daddy on the net," I ordered Fessman, handing the microphone back to him, my eyes never leaving the open area in front of me that was almost completely black, except for occasional small bursts of brightness from small arms fire.

The detonation of the 175 mm rounds coming in had been hugely explosive, their quick flares of yellow light ending with sharp lightening-like cracks of thunder, transmitted back to me in seconds but still with noticeable delay in covering the distance to me.

"I can't get through," Fessman said, with disappointment in his voice. It was the first time, while in a full radio coverage area, that I had not been able to reach a combat command radio.

I turned around to study the area behind me, the incessant rain beating down on my bare head. I reached down for my helmet, but instead pulled the poncho cover back up and over both Fessman and I. Nguyen, whom I'd been seeking, appeared by slipping onto the matted jungle surface next to me, squeezing under the other side of the cover and looking outward, like I was, and likely seeing the same lack of a recognizable vista.

"Sugar Daddy," I said to Nguyen, "bring him to me." I pointed at my own chest.

Nguyen rolled out and left at a run.

"You're bringing Sugar Daddy in, while this is all going on?" Fessman unaccountably asked.

"A walk in the rain," I replied, "the whole line has to shift massively toward the wall. The enemy's going to figure out the artillery can't reach them there and the Ontos can't fire enfilade fire into that mess without taking out our own Marines."

I couldn't read my watch in the rain, although I tried. I estimated that it took Nguyen ten minutes to return with Sugar Daddy in tow simply because I knew that's how long it took to adjust and bring in two more 175 battery of fours. I could not keep firing the big rounds endlessly, although I was getting no 'check fire' indications from the army battery. The night was going to be long and even the U.S. Army's supply of 175 ammo had to be limited.

Sugar Daddy knelt by my side, with Nguyen behind him, not leaving, again seeming to guard me against the possibility of one of my own Marines attacking me. I looked at what I could see of the big man, thinking about what the Gunny had said about my staying out of the action until it was over. I was not the 2nd lieutenant who'd arrived that first night in totally mindless terror. I was Junior now, and I was in combat with everyone else in the company. I could not hide in a hole, as I'd been so willing and wanting to do in earlier days and nights.

"I need MacInerney, those other two officers and the Starlight Scope back here now," I said to Sugar Daddy, and I've got to have you shift most of your platoon and then successive platoons as you encounter them while you proceed through the jungle and across the open path toward the wall. The enemy's not going to attack on this flank. The artillery is too accurate and too pervasive, plus they're going to figure out that I can't depress the rounds enough to reach them. Those guns aren't howitzers so the western side is protected by the elevation of the hill."

"What do I get out of this?" Sugar Daddy asked, making my hand automatically come to rest on the exposed butt of my Colt.

I breathed deeply in and out, and then it came to me. Sugar Daddy wasn't interested in disobeying orders, or me. He was still bitten by the fact that he knew Jurgens had been written up for a valor decoration and he had not.

"The Silver Star," I replied. "Not for stupidly getting your men killed on the bridge though. I'll write you up for getting to the gear and supplies on your own while also bringing the Ontos into position without orders. And now you are going to mass toward the wall and bring all the units together as you go, so that enemy force is met with overwhelming Marine force when they come at us again."

"A Silver Star?" Sugar Daddy breathed out as if he was thinking about it, although I knew his mind was already made up.

I could almost see the wheels turning in his head through the blackness of the rain and windswept night. He was thinking that, although Jurgens had been written up he probably had been written up for a lessor decoration. The Silver Star was a big deal, just below the Medal of Honor and the Navy Cross. I remembered the Gunny shaking my hand when we'd concluded our deal with respect to Jurgens. I took my right hand off the butt of the Colt and waited to see if the handshake thing would be repeated, but Sugar Daddy merely grunted.

"You're okay, Junior," he finally said, "and your word is good."

I felt a thrill of satisfaction and acceptance flow instantly through my body and mind. I couldn't believe that I was deeply affected by Sugar Daddy's words of approval.

My hand did not stray back to the automatic, as Sugar Daddy got to his feet, turned around and disappeared into the night. I put my helmet back on and called in the next battery of four, bringing that adjustment as close as I could to where the wall attack had to be in the planning and forming stages. I kept my head out from under the poncho cover. I wanted to get up and move toward where I knew the Gunny had to be, right with the Marines waiting for the worst the enemy could throw at them. But I waited where I was. I wasn't in my hole, hiding, and waiting for the combat action to be over, but I was also not at the point of contact with my Marines because I knew that part of what the Gunny said was true. I was the company commander and the only time I might be engaged in hand to hand combat was if I wasn't being the company commander.

MacInerney and his two junior lieutenants arrived just before the Marines I'd ordered, or negotiated, Sugar Daddy to move began infiltrating and then snaking through the jungle around and behind us.

"Good idea to project our force forward to the line of departure," MacInerney said, sounding as if he was in some sort of Basic School exercise with people around him who understood such language.

Regular Marines in combat simply moved to where they were ordered or where combat survival might serve them best while giving as much hell as they could to the enemy. There were no five 'paragraph orders' prior to an attack operation, as there had been in training, and the extensive planning I'd been taught, using contraction reminder words like BAMCIS and SMEAC, were all but useless in real combat. The Marines moved as silently and efficiently as possible, humping almost everything they had with them. Packs would be dropped when they went down to a prone position on the matted jungle floor, so they could operate and adroitly and rapidly shift positions later when needed.

"Set up the Starlight Scope so we can tell what the hell's going on at or near what we can see of the wall where the inlet water comes through," I instructed, ignoring the lieutenant's compliment.

For some reason, Nguyen wasn't visible any longer. I wondered if the three new lieutenants got a pass when it came to the Montagnard's suspicions about what the potential danger my own Marines might be to me. It was either that, or I was imagining the whole thing.

Once the scope was set up, and the Marines had completed their move through our position, I put my eye to the rubber grommet and looked into the inlet area down from the flat bottom where the mountain's slope ended, across the water and then over toward the wall. Mercifully, there was some open muddy ground between the water and the jungle's edge.

"Get me Hutzler on the net if you can," I ordered Fessman.

I could not have the Ontos move forward out of the jungle in order to get a clear direct fire position to hit the open area the scope had revealed. If it moved out of the camouflage the jungle provided it might become the target for any RPG rockets the mountain might have a supply of. It would also become exposed to the undependable range of the 175 mm rounds I was calling in to make sure most of the attack area could not be used.

"Take the Starlight Scope back to the Ontos," I ordered MacInerney, who hadn't even had time to lay down, much less dig a defensive hole in the matted undergrowth.

"But we just brought it here," MacInerney complained, not moving.

"You can either take that back like I'm ordering lieutenant," I said forcefully, "or you can go back to the wall with Jurgens, fix your non-existent bayonet to your non-existent rifle and prepare for hand to hand combat."

MacInerney and the two lieutenants took only seconds to disassemble the scope and take off. None of them said anything.

I reached for the handset Fessman was holding out.

"Hutzler, the scope's coming back at you right now," I said. "When it gets there, take it and crawl forward until you can see. I want to know if you can give me a tracer spotter round from one of your fifties every minute or so until further notice. The NVA knows how the Ontos works. If you can lay a spotter round near that flat area between the water and the wall to the west, then they'll think twice before they attempt to launch their attack over it.

"They're coming, sir," Hutzler replied, "I'll get right on it."

I waited impatiently to call in the next artillery set, not wanting to expose Hutzler who would be laying too close to any incoming, and totally unprotected on the flat mud. I knew I couldn't wait too long. With a regiment to throw at us, which meant about six times the men we had, the enemy could have two companies run across the open area in less than ten minutes. I knew, if I waited too long, they'd take the risk and try it. If they attacked, I wouldn't be able to see since I'd sent the only scope we had back to Hutzler.

In minutes Hutzler was back. I felt like I could breathe again at his news. He could fire through the bracken of the bush the Ontos was idling behind. That also meant the 106 recoilless guns could be fired through the same overhanging leaves and branches since their fuses had a hundred meters of set back before the fuses were armed. I called in another battery of four from the army battery. The Starlight Scope would be useless again unless someone else was risked to crawl out again and view the area through it.

"Hutzler," I called, having had Fessman get him on the radio again.

"Junior?" he replied, which almost made me smile.

Hutzler had been surprised by my call, as he was one of the few men in the companies, except for Fessman, who always referred to me as sir.

"I need someone to go check out the view to that free fire area every ten minutes, or so, and when he goes you need to tell me, and then when he comes back."

"Aye, aye, sir," Hutzler shot back, "I've got just the man."

I wondered who he had that he felt was expendable, but I didn't have time to let my mind dwell on that subject. I called in the next round of battery fire without changing the adjustment. The rounds might not cause death or injury to any of the enemy soldiers but they would certainly keep everyone in or around the mountain on edge and afraid.

I wished that I had spent more time with the Gunny when he'd angrily stuck his head under my poncho cover. The hand to hand combat comment had not gone down well with me. I wasn't upset about the part about my own participation at all. What bothered me was our mission. It wasn't to defeat the enemy in close combat. It was to hold it in place or roll it back until real firepower from the air could be brought in at first light, which wasn't that far away. The only visual we had on the 'beaten zone,' where the NVA regiment had to cross in the open, was through the Starlight Scope, which was being operated sporadically by someone I didn't even know. I had Fessman call the Ontos and relay my order for MacInerney to return to my side. I didn't need to lose any more officers, and the ones I had were too new and green to have to lay out in the open trying to observe what such a cagey and natively savvy enemy might do.

I heard the fifty caliber spotter firing just before the next salvo of artillery rounds impacted. The rounds were not as well placed as the previous ones had been. The concussion from their landing only a hundred meters, or so, away bounced me out my hole, made my hearing go out again, and then sent a wave of compressed rain showering over into and over our position I rolled onto my back, trying to clear my ears.

Finally, I heard something, while I was trying to get my helmet back on and return to what cover and concealment the poncho-covered hole provided. I heard the 106 fire from the Ontos, then two more rounds. The enemy had to be attacking. Worry and fear claimed me again. Would our combined infantry forces, the nearly sightless Ontos and the badly controlled artillery be enough to stop a full ground attack from a seasoned sapper regiment?

one-hundred-thirty-five

THE TWENTY-EIGHTH DAY : FIRST PART

The engagement with the enemy began while it was still full dark. The Ontos fired into the general area near the western wall at its base and flung flechettes across the open exposed area in front of it. With the artillery still coming in, responding to successive fire missions I was calling, in spite of some errant projectiles that might have caused casualties in our own ranks, the single mudflat just in front of the cliff face was the only viable place the enemy could cross to reach our combined companies. The mudflat was also very likely to become the deadliest field of fire I had ever been a witness to and part of since I'd arrived in country.

"There's no point in me staying here," I said to Fessman. "Get your stuff."

I worked my body around so I could strap my own pack to my back.

My torso ached like it had been beaten with baseball bats. The 175 rounds that had flown long had continuously displaced me from my foxhole, and in the process the near-visible shockwaves resonating through the air had struck me time and again, like light wafts of a vicious little collection of wind. But the waves had not been winds, they'd been condensed packets of air and water. The packets struck, as I was bounced from my hole, my poncho cover only retrieved because I'd tied one corner to my right boot with the bootlace. Only after resting for a few minutes did the pain begin. The leech bites were bad enough, I thought, but the pain was diminished by the mortally potential effect caused by the bruising strikes of the artillery shock waves.

I tried to listen to Fessman. His hearing had been spared by wearing the earphones to the Prick 25 radio, but my own was damaged again. My ears rang and Fessman's voice, although it came through, was tinny and partially shredded. I tried to point at my ears but it was still too dark to allow Fessman to see that I was pointing at all. Finally, after getting my pack on and leaning in close, I was able to make out what he was saying.

"We can't go to the wall and help, sir," Fessman was near yelling, I could tell.

"If we do that then it'll mess everything up he's trying to do," Fessman went on, making no move to strap his radio to his back.

I pulled back slightly. It was the first time, I realized, that Fessman had not sided with me, and then gone on to resist my orders.

He was right, I knew, but I had not been thinking of joining the Gunny where contact with the enemy was now imminent. I delayed for a few minutes in responding, by untying my poncho cover from my boot and then getting it properly situated over my head to cover my damaged torso and lower body.

"We're going to the Ontos," I said, cupping my hands and yelling.

I was still unable to properly gauge the full volume of my own voice. "I've got to be able to see or I'm no use at all," I finished.

"Sometimes, maybe, sir, doing nothing at all might be the right thing to do," Fessman replied.

I noted, as best as I could make out, that Fessman, however, was getting his radio onto his back and preparing to abandon our hole.

"The Gunny didn't think to have the majority of our forces move together to meet the enemy where it has to attack. Nobody can think of everything, corporal."

I knew it was foolish and not very leader-like to explain myself, or the reasons for my decisions, but my feeling that I needed the teenager's full support would not allow me to do anything else.

"Sorry, sir," Fessman replied, moving so close to my side, as we'd risen to begin the move, that our shoulders rubbed together.

I looked over but what I noticed was Nguyen, just to the other side of Fessman. I could not see his eyes but I knew he had to be looking at me. What might he have done if Fessman had refused to move, I wondered. I tried to shrug the thought away, but I knew it would lay in the back of my mind for some time to come.

I hunched over, easing the shockwave induced pain in my back and shoulders, and then I moved forward, trying to avoid falling on my knees or face because it was so dark. I felt Nguyen positioning himself so close in front of me that he partially blocked the blowing rain, the wind seeming to have risen with each of my successive artillery barrages. I had forgotten MacInerney and Russell, the two lieutenants that had returned from the Ontos. I stopped and said MacInerney's name into the darkness.

"I'm right here, Junior," he replied, from off to my left. I thought of the other nameless lieutenant.

"Where's the other lieutenant?" I asked, knowing he'd been left back at the Ontos but not knowing why.

"He's spotting with the scope for Hultzer," MacInerny said as if he was surprised I didn't know.

Suddenly, I was moving faster, pushing into Nguyen's back. The one particular battery of four that I had called, the one that had landed so close that it had thrown Fessman and me out of our foxhole time after time and injured my body with following shockwaves had come close. Quite possibly we'd only been saved by the density of the jungle. For the hearing injury I'd suffered, the rounds had to have gone off fifty meters away or less.

The small arms fire began to build to a higher level. There was no response from the Ontos, which I knew had to mean that Hultzer was afraid of running low on flechette ammo. The resupply had brought in plenty, but plenty was a diminished term in this kind of outnumbered attack situation we were in, I knew. I pushed harder through the mess of the water-covered and rain-drenched massed floor, driving Nguyen forward. I heard screams behind me, the screams I knew of Marines and enemy dying together as the attack became fully joined.

For the first time ever, in making a movement under fire, I felt bad from moving away from the fire instead of toward it.

I stared into the eyepiece of the Starlight Scope, the rubber grommet feeling good, pressed all around my right eye socket. The scene in the distance was easy to home in on, as the open area from the edge of the jungle all the way to the edge of the water that ran around the base of Hill 975 ended at the cliff face. That face protruded slightly out over the area just below it, the bottom part covered by thick lichen and plant matter of all types, while above that the cracked rock face was barren and unclimbable, as well. I studied the scene near the cliff base, understanding that that particular small stretch, from the water to the jungle, was the only available area that could be crossed to allow the NVA regiment access. When would the full-scale attack come, the one that my Marines holding a tenuous but tough line just inside the jungle, might only get on to too late? I could see, but they could not. How could we get to the dawn, wherein no suicide attacks, with swarms of men, no matter how well-armed, could possibly succeed? I shuffled backward, pulling the scope with me. Fessman was there with the radio handset out and waiting. I called Hultzer inside the Ontos, located not more than thirty meters from where I lay.

"How many rounds of high explosive do we have?" I asked once he came on the line.

"Twenty-four, sir," Hultzer replied, "We don't use that stuff up as fast as the flechette rounds."

I knew that last part, of course, as flechette rounds were so deadly and effective that it made little sense to call in anything else unless the enemy was dug in, or it was impossible to see where they were. The enemy, in this case, was dug in all right, inside a currently impregnable mountainside. But it was the visibility that was the real problem. I could use the Starlight Scope to study the area from where I was, and hope to report that to the platoons defending the jungle area where the NVA had to strike, but I could do little to be completely effective in that pursuit, as the ground was too broken and the debris all over it allowing for just enough cover to fool me from the angle and distance I had to view it from.

The last problem was the one that I was trying to overcome with Hultzer. How could we best slave the Ontos to the scope in order to fire at the right time and aim at the right place? The key to ranging the 106 mm recoilless rifle rounds was the fifty caliber semi-automatic guns the rifles had to spot where the charge would land with tracer rounds. The wall was a long way in the distance. My idea was to use the same effect that had been tried on us by the enemy when we'd been holed up under a fold at the bottom of the cliff on the other side of the river days back. We'd also had the effect of the cliff face exploding down upon our own Marines when the artillery rounds had fallen short that night not so long in the past. We could magnify the effect of the high explosive rounds by ten times or more, simply by having the 106 recoilless rounds explode against the face of the cliff, up above the growth line visible in the Starlight Scope. The explosively broken and crushed rocks of the face would cascade down onto any troops unprotected from above. And that would be any and all of the sapper regiment attackers.

Hultzer crawled up to me, but he wasn't alone. I huddled, lying flat, my poncho cover extended over me, more worried about the leeches I might be exposing myself to by laying on the jungle floor itself, but still conscious that I could not long survive being exposed to the full effects of the monsoon rains without expiring or falling ill in some fashion or another.

First Hultzer, then Fessman, and then the Nguyen forced their way under my small poncho. Fortunately, we'd all been living under the same circumstance for some time, and the blossoms their own open poncho covers began to layer over my own in a cluster.

I ordered Hultzer to take the Starlight Scope and set it up at the front or facing side of the Ontos. At least he would be able to see something of what was going on in order to properly and effectively place fire on the enemy.

"Where's McInerney?" I asked once Hultzer was gone, noticing his sudden absence among the Marines surrounding me, but nobody said anything in reply. Nguyen motioned ever so slightly with his chin, his face angled and directed toward the wall where the enemy force if it was going to attempt the assault, would have to cross the clearing underneath.

The two junior lieutenants joined our group, building the cluster of poncho covers into a larger, almost interconnected tent.

"Fessman, what the hell is McInerney up to?" I asked, my voice low and concerned, rather than angry at the inexperienced lieutenant's independent action.

"He headed toward the cliff, sir, following in trace of Sugar Daddy," Fessman replied.

My stomach clenched with tension. I'd sent Sugar Daddy off to lead or supervise the Marines who would bear the brunt of the coming major thrust of the attack, and I'd done so with the ridiculous offer of a combat decoration I had no power to award. I could recommend it, but that was it. Now, one of the new lieutenant's was going into the thick of things with no background at all to modify his actions. The phrase 'combat teaches by killing you,' reappeared in my mind. My 'walk in the rain' title for the plan might very well turn out to be a walk in the blood of my own men.

The Gunny was at the wall, now likely joined by McInerney and Sugar Daddy. I was almost certain that Jurgens would be there, as well, waiting for the coming attack.

With this one defensive plan, I was risking almost the entire command structure of the assembled companies, save some other sergeant platoon commanders and the two junior lieutenants whose names I could barely remember.

"Now we wait," I whispered to the Marines around me.

I ordered Fessman to have Hultzer fire at the first flash he might see of the enemy fifty caliber, but wait to fire at the side of the cracked rock cliff face until ordered.

"The idiot," I heard come back through the small radio handset, even though I was several feet from where Fessman lay nearby.

The expression of frustration and anger could only have come from the Gunny, I realized.

"What's he saying?" I asked, my voice a whisper.

"Apparently, Lieutenant McInerney, sir," Fessman replied, "has placed himself under the slight lip of the cliff and is going to blink his flashlight when the enemy attacks so you can fire. He must know we can't really see that well through the rain and over the distance."

"Nguyen, get forward," I commanded, motioning with one hand toward the invisible wall out in the darkness. "Go get him back, if you can."

Nguyen disappeared, almost as he'd never been there in the first place. The man's ability to move in such silence through the bracken and mud was unnerving, as it was now. I could feel what was happening rather than witness it.

I'd sent Sugar Daddy forward to chase his medal, the good news being that Sugar Daddy had come to feel he might live under my command. The bad news was that he was still Sugar Daddy. Somehow, the sergeant wasn't going out to expose himself.

Somehow, he'd convinced the McInerney to expose himself, after which, no matter what happened, he could claim that he'd kept his part of the deal.

"Get me the Gunny," I ordered Fessman, hearing a slithering nearby.

Two of the poncho covers were gone. The new FNG lieutenants had pulled back, probably to the Ontos, I thought, but could not know since they'd said nothing.

"Gunny, get him back," I ordered, once the Gunny was on the combat net.

"Too late," I heard before the enemy fifty opened up, and then a single round from the Ontos whooshed by, in response, without any order coming from me.

I switched my attention to the wall and saw immediately that a flashlight was blinking dimly through the rain, coming from down at the bottom of it. The enemy fifty wasn't shooting at the ignorant officer, however. Its green tracers arced into the line of Marines set in to defend the only possible approach the enemy could use to penetrate our defenses. McInerney continued to blink his flashlight every few seconds until Hultzer, back at the Ontos opened up with a spread of semi-automatic fifty caliber tracer rounds of its own.

I could do nothing except hold on tightly to the radio handset and grimly stare into the distance where only McInerney's lonely light blinked away. Hultzer was doing what had to be done and there was no point in discussing it with him over the radio. The Ontos tracers impacted the wall, sending sparks in all directions, as the unspent phosphorous tips of the bullets splattered into tiny fiery parts, not more than twenty feet above where McInerney's position had to be.

There was no time to order Hultzer to check or hold fire. The giant whooshing noise of six 106 mm recoilless rounds passing by sucked the air from around us as they headed for the wall. At the same time, the Marines manning their M-60 machine guns opened up almost as one. Tracers crisscrossed the entire flat crossing, turning the slightly depressed jungle area into a cauldron of hot burning phosphorous and lead. The enemy fifty was not suppressed, as it sought to penetrate the inadequate cover my Marines would have thrown up when trying to adequately dig in. I knew the fifty would go through at least twenty feet of unpacked earth, mud, and debris. The enemy had to be attacking, as fire control was so ingrained into the experienced combat Marines in both companies that their combined fire would have dropped off in mere seconds if it had been just a reaction to receiving fire from the enemy.

The recoilless rounds hit the wall in a spectacular night display of fireworks and slightly delayed sound. There was no more indication of McInerney's flashlight signals following the first salvo. The Ontos reloaded and fired again with fewer rounds, all impacting the same place on the rock wall. The fifty caliber spotters then trained in on the opening the enemy fifty was firing from, and three of the big rounds went out. The angle was such, toward the base of Hill 975, that they went right over our heads, causing temporary deafness in my ears, once again.

I crouched down, feeling totally helpless to control the events I'd deliberately, and then accidentally, set into action. The firing from the M-60s raged on, becoming more sporadic as time slowly passed. I kept my head up, peering out from under my rain and windswept poncho cover, no longer caring about the misery of the cloying wetness or the risk of being host to more leech predators. The enemy fifty had apparently been silenced by the three-round salvo Hultzer had directed into its burrowed lair. The 106 fired again and again until I thought that the guns must have run out of ammo before it quit. The machine guns stopped firing at almost the same instant. I heard distant chunks of the cliff walling falling to strike the mud below with sickening thuds. I had no idea of just how deep the inset that usually ran along the base of the cliffs might be. I could only hope and pray that it was deep enough like it had been for the rest of the company so many days and nights in the past.

The enemy attack appeared over, and it also appeared to have failed, as the Marines along the line of defense had seemed to quiet down all on their own. I still held the radio handset and was about to call the Gunny when I changed my mind, rising quickly to my feet and gathering my poncho cover in to wrap about my standing figure. I tossed the handset to Fessman and then took off at a loping run, back to where the open area extended all the way to the wall. I ran the entire distance to the cliff face, noting Marines dimly set in around me and hoping that they did not take me for some enemy apparition in their midst. I had to get to the wall quickly and I had to get there personally.

In seconds I was down next to the Gunny, his radio operator moving quickly to make way for my falling body. I hit prone, not more than a foot from the right side of the Gunny's body. I breathed in and out deeply, to recover from the run and to control my emotions.

"Where's the lieutenant?" I finally got out.

"I don't know," the Gunny said, his voice quiet and uncharacteristically gentle. "They didn't get through or even come close to it. Under the tracers I watched the cliff face collapse among them. There must be a hundred men under that mess of rocks and debris."

I looked out but could see nothing in the darkness, the rain still beating down while the wind had begun to abate somewhat.

"He didn't come back," the Gunny offered, understanding why I'd rushed so quickly to his side. "Nice work, sending him out there, though. There was no better way to pinpoint exactly where and when they were coming."

That I had not sent McInerney, nor would I have sent anyone to do such a ridiculously suicidal mission, I kept to myself.

"Where's Sugar Daddy?" I asked, the tone of my voice changing to the point where I observed the Gunny's head turning to look over at me.

He lit a cigarette, the small Zippo light burning tiny but bright

374 | THIRTY DAYS HAS SEPTEMBER

for a few seconds. We stared at one another, as he inhaled, and then the moment and the light were gone.

"Where's Nguyen?" the Gunny countered.

I remembered having sent Nguyen only in that instant.

"Where?" I asked, knowing the answer.

"Don't know", the Gunny replied. "He went out there to do whatever it was he was supposed to do, I guess. He passed by, like the ghost in the night he is, and then moved on without comment or slowing."

"Damn," I whispered.

"You sent him to get that new lieutenant back in when you saw him blinking his flashlight, didn't you?" the Gunny said, puffing on his cigarette and syncopating the smoke between his few words.

Sugar Daddy crawled up, to wedge himself between my legs and Gunny's, his broad shoulders pushing us both aside.

"I couldn't stop him," Sugar Daddy said. "He just took off and ran and I sure as hell wasn't going after him, Silver Star be damned."

"What Silver Star?" the Gunny asked.

Neither Sugar Daddy nor I answered the question.

"What now, Junior?" Sugar Daddy asked.

"We wait until dawn," I replied, hoping the ache in my mind and body was not being transmitted through my voice. "There's no way to prove their fifty is out of commission permanently, no way to tell how many more men they are willing to commit to another attack and we can't see in the dark to dig through the rocks."

"A bit more than a walk in the rain, wouldn't you say, Junior?" Sugar Daddy asked, after a few seconds.

"We took no casualties, except for maybe the FNG officer and Nguyen," the Gunny replied. You can't knock that kind of success under conditions like these, now can you Junior," the Gunny replied.

I said nothing in return, moving further to one side and curling up into the poncho cover I'd kept with me. For the first time, I was truly angry at the Gunny. He'd saved my life, time and again, but what kind of cold-hearted beast was he, anyway. The dawn would come. Hutzler probably had more ammunition on hand and the Marines up and down the line of defense would remain fully on guard. We'd held the position, but to what end and the seemingly small losses would never be counted that way with me, no matter what we found at first light.

one-hundred-thirty-six

THE TWENTY-EIGHTH DAY : SECOND PART

I slept in my scooped out small spot atop the mud, dug down through the normal couple of feet of debris that covered those areas of the jungle not occupied by bamboo groves, trees, lianas and tubers, not to mention the vast dense thickets of ferns and other ground-hugging vegetative matter, that made parts of the area almost impossibly impenetrable to man. I slept until I felt a strong hand grip my right ankle, an ankle that had errantly gotten out from under my protective poncho cover and was soaking wet. I opened my eyes, but under the cover could see nothing. I felt instant relief. I didn't need to see. The hand I knew. It was the hand of Nguyen, my guide and interpreter, but who was much more than that, at least to my imagined characterization of him because he seldom spoke at all. An interpreter who did not speak should have been someone who was either sent to the rear or held up as the butt of some strange war joke that only the A Shau Valley might regurgitate up.

I pushed the poncho cover aside, welcoming the first glimmer of sun I'd seen in many days. The dawn was just breaking. I craned my head around and looked at Nguyen. The man was impassive but I could tell he was energized, no doubt by being caught out in the open during the massive firing of weapons all across the mudflat where the attack took place.

"McInerney?" I whispered hope in my early morning and half-broken voice.

One quick and small shake of the Nguyen's head told me all I did not want to know. Nguyen was not saying that the new Lieutenant wasn't there. He was saying, with that one head slight head shake, that McInerney had died in his efforts to successfully direct the Ontos fire that had broken the back of the enemy attack hours earlier.

Nguyen sat in his usual crouch, his bent knees protruding upward and his butt scrunched down to the point where it almost, but not quite, touched the jungle matter under him. His elbows rested on his knees, as he waited patiently for me to come fully alive and begin planning for whatever the day might bring.

I pulled myself into a sitting position, a bit chilled from the wet night that had been unseasonably cold, once full darkness had set in. I could smell the cordite from the powder that had been expended hours earlier. It seemed to stick to the leaves and fern fronds as if to remind me that our weaponry was just another form of early Chinese fireworks, now refined over generations. The sun and the day would fix my slight chill in mere minutes, I also knew, so I had to do nothing to warm myself except wait.

I pulled my helmet off, took the liner out and then filled the steel shell part full with water from my canteen, making sure to keep enough back to make coffee, should I be able to borrow some of the Texico (made by Coca Cola) powder from the Gunny. I took out my Gillette, checked the over-used blade and shaved without the benefit of real light or a mirror. The razor didn't work well, but time was not an issue so I moved slowly, repeating each stroke many times, not pressing hard in order to avoid being cut by the over-used blade. I'd heard of the new stainless steel blades in training but those were not yet government supplied.

I thought about McInerney. There would be no likely recovering of his body, I knew. Leaving him out there under the rocks after what everyone had seen him do in the night would not go down well with anyone in the company, including me, but there was nothing else to be done. The section of wall the lieutenant had chosen to spotlight was fully exposed to Hill 975. Any attempt to dig through the tons of stone that had fallen to form piles of rip-rap at the bottom of the cliff wall would take time and continued exposure to sniper fire, machine guns and quite possibly the fifty-caliber the enemy likely had saved by pulling it further back into the hill's tunnels when Huntzler had opened up with multiple high explosive rounds from the 106 mm recoilless rifles.

I glanced at Nguyen, but his face gave me back the usual expression he had become known for. Nothing. Nguyen had the ability to show no emotion and deliver no message by being able to have no expression on his face, whatsoever. I'd heard of American Indians who supposedly had that same ability but had never met any to see if it was true. I finished shaving, feeling half human again. I checked my body completely, Nguyen watching with his same impassive expression. Amazingly, no leeches had attached themselves to me in my sleep, or even in the exposed movement and jostling in the mud from the night before.

I turned to stare out along the bottom of the cliff, the area not yet coming into full view, as the light moved from astronomical dawn to nautical dawn. It would be some minutes until real light, civil dawn would overcome the valley. I turned to look back at Nguyen once again.

"Night," he said, distinctly, waving gently toward the bottom of the wall with the loose fingers of his left hand.

I looked back at the piles of rip-rap. It took a few seconds for me to get it. The NVA did not have a Starlight Scope or anything like it. A man, or two men, working quietly, would be able to go out and pull back one stone after another until the lieutenant's body was revealed. The only thing it would require was knowing exactly where in the tons thick mess the body was, and a good deal of patience and hard work.

"The place?" I asked, knowing that we could not pull up all the rocks that had fallen. We would have to have a pretty good idea of where the lieutenant had fallen in order to retrieve his body without getting ourselves killed or working all through the night.

Nguyen looked out toward the bottom of the cliff and then nodded once, very curtly.

Retrieving the body would require that the companies remained where they were, but then there really was no other place to go. The enemy occupied Hill 975 in force, no doubt had significant elements downriver on the side they were holed up on, and then there was the passage back across the river which would not serve at all. Whatever NVA outfit was across the river was there in force, as it had proven when the companies had made our escape to be where we were. No, there was no place else to go unless things changed.

The lieutenant's body could be recovered in broad daylight, given the Skyraiders, Puff the Magic Dragon and the A-6 Intruder. The problem with air was, however, that it could not stay orbiting right over one small area in order to fully suppress any enemy fire. Airpower moved, all the time and everywhere, only helicopters could stay in one place to deliver fire, like the Huey Cobras, but they then became sitting targets for any enemy fire that might come at them. And there was never a guarantee at all that any air would be available. Other units demanded air cover and some might even be in worse circumstance than our own. I could not call artillery again, not with us in our current position, not unless we were completely overrun and we weren't going to make it anyway.

I reflected on the ignorance and waste of the conflict I was in.

McInerney need not have gone to the wall and illuminated it for the purpose of directing fire. The wall was almost a thousand feet high. What would it have mattered if the Ontos had fired higher up against the cracked and broken stone that formed its face? There would have been little difference in the outcome. The wall was hard to miss and Hutzler also had the Starlight Scope and the fifty-caliber spotting rifles. McInerney had acquitted himself with honor and heroic bravery, however, unaware that his demonstration of those things was total without operational necessity or rationality. FNG meant what it meant for a reason. There was no regular peacetime logic that existed or worked down in the A Shau Valley. The A Shau, for me, had become my world, but to a newcomer, an FNG, it was a foreign as it might have been to someone entering Edgar Rice Burroughs The Land that Time Forgot.

The Gunny appeared, as I got my helmet back on and prepared my canteen cover to make coffee. He slunk down in a squat as Nguyen retreated back into a place just inside the higher jungle growth, his eyes never wavering or leaving my own when I checked to see he was there. The Gunny's callous disregard for the lieutenant's life earlier had left me a bit lost and feeling alone. I waited, without asking the man for the coffee fixing. He supplied the small packet, along with two packets of the powdered cream. There was no sugar but I didn't require any. The Gunny started the Composition B fire and we waited, each of us sharing the small intense flame, our canteen cover holder bottoms long stained black by such practice. The Gunny lit a cigarette while we waited for the water to boil.

"We walked in the rain, so what do we do now?" the Gunny asked, his tone mild but with some stiffness in it, almost as if I'd made the comment about McInerney.

"What does battalion say?" I asked, since I had not been in contact with command for more than twenty-four hours.

"The six-actual says to wait while they assemble a combined forces attack to sweep down the valley," the Gunny replied, his tone flattening out into a matter-of-fact analytical bent.

"We don't need a plan to stay where we are," I replied, watching civil dawn come and go as the sun began to rise toward overcoming the top of the distant cliff fact to our east.

"What we need is resupply. We need more 106 ammunition of both kinds. We need to have air hit Hill 975 unremittingly all day long and quite possibly on into the night if they will."

The Gunny sipped his coffee slowly, and then took another hit from his Camel. The strain in the air between us was palpable and I could think of no way to reduce it or cut through it. I wanted to say that I had not sent the lieutenant to his death, that I had no idea of where he'd gone off to until it was too late. I didn't ask why the Gunny had not stopped him from going out into such a suicidal position.

I sipped the scalding hot coffee slowly, being careful not to burn the sides of my mouth on the exposed lip of the wide metal opening. The silence dragged on while the sun worked to climb over the distant edge of the high cliff and illuminate the night's fields of fire. We'd only lost the lieutenant, apparently, from what was said around me. I didn't ask about that, my concern was more personal as I had no plan to go on in opposition to the Gunny or without his support.

Fessman motioned gently toward me with one hand, the sensitive teenager no doubt absorbing the tension apparent between Gunny and me.

Once again I watched Nguyen move to be in a place almost directly behind the Gunny, and that move made me uncomfortable. I did not want Nguyen, my imagined protector, to hurt the Gunny or be his enemy, any more than I did, but I had no plan to deal with the current situation.

I looked over at Fessman. He was tapping his little transistor radio. It was time for Brother John to begin broadcasting over the Armed Forces Network. I nodded my head. There was to be no hiding from the enemy. Every part of their three-pronged surrounding force knew exactly where we were. Only supporting fires from the air, artillery and the Ontos preserved our position along with the miserable open fields of fire the NVA had crossed in order to get to us.

The song that came out of the radio, mid lyrics was called Guantanamera. I'd heard it many times but the Sandpiper's version, the English translation of the famous poets' words put to song, had never penetrated me before, as they now did.

"My verses are light green, but they are also flaming red.

My verses are like a wounded fawn, seeking refuge in the mountain."

I looked off into the distance toward Hill 975. I was the wounded fawn and there was no refuge. McInerney would have been the wounded fawn only hours earlier but he was wounded no more.

Guantanamera repeated with more verses in Spanish. I didn't understand the name of the song as English was my only language except for pretty bad college German.

"I'm sorry," the Gunny said, quietly, but well heard by me and Fessman.

I didn't know what to say so I made believe I hadn't heard him and took another sip of my too-hot coffee.

"I was out of line," the Gunny went on.

I wanted him to stop talking. I didn't want the Gunny's apology. I didn't want the Gunny to treat me as the classical straight-backed officer leading the Marines. I was so much more comfortable with the role that had been assigned to me as Junior.

The wonderfully terrible song played on, seemingly without end: "And for the cruel one who would tear out this heart with which I live. I cultivate neither thistles nor nettles. I cultivate a white rose." Guantanamera.

I knew if I lived that the words would remain burned deep into my mind and body.

"It's okay," I finally replied to the Gunny, knowing that the lyrics of the song were probably not reaching inside him at all. "These are difficult times."

"I hate seeing the officers die," he went on, "one after another, no matter how it happens. I don't have any children. I don't have a son. I'm getting old. If I make it back I might still have time. If I have a son I'd want him to be a Marine officer."

I noted in shock that the Gunny had bitten something back. He'd almost said, "like you." I just knew it and had no reply to any of what he'd said so I went back to sipping the coffee, not noticing that I was burning my lips.

The last stanza of the song played, holding my attention in the silence after the Gunny's staggering admission:

"With the poor people of this earth, I want to share my lot.

With the poor people of this earth, I want to share my lot.

The little streams of the mountains please me more than the sea."

I looked back to my right, down the length of the open area that ran all the way to the Bong Song River. The little streams of the mountains I reflected for a few seconds.

All I had was the Bong Song, and it would have to do.

"The plan is called Candia," I said to the Gunny, as once more silence settled over our small plot of mud, rain, and debris. I crouched under my poncho, only my hand and lower part of my face under my steel helmet exposed.

"The Knights of Malta held out for twenty-two years in that siege," I said. "Time is on our side."

"I'm not sure our Marines are going to understand that one," the Gunny replied, after a delay of a few seconds.

"It's okay," Fessman piped in. A great siege and the Knights of Malta. Everyone's heard of them."

Even the Gunny had to laugh at that one, and I along with him.

I waited for Brother John to introduce his next song and what lyrics of depth they might reach inside me. I too liked the officers that came and went so quickly, none of them wounded, and all of them dead. I even liked the ones I hadn't liked much at all. They'd been here with me and trying their hearts out like I was. Warmth spread through me as I thought about what kind of hard courage it had taken the Gunny to say to me what he'd said, and in front of Fessman, as well.

The first Skyraider came in without much warning. A deep growl in the distance and then it dropped out of the sky to pull up and zoom over our position, more toward the river than right over the top of where we sat. Then two more came in. Cowboy was on station and he'd brought friends. I reached out my hand but not fast enough because Fessman already had the AN323 up and the small headpiece ready for me to clamp on to my head. I pulled my helmet off and slipped into the device. Cowboy was instantly alive in my ears.

"Flash, wake up, coffee's on and it's time to play," Cowboy intoned in his unbelievably upbeat and expressive tone. "There will be joy in this valley, and we brought lunch to stick it out. Puff will lift off in an hour and he's loaded for bear with armor-piercing everything. That Hill is going to be an anthill when we're done with it."

I knew that armor-piercing rotary cannon fire could only likely pierce forty or fifty feet of solid ground, and less where there were significant rock deposits, but I could not help smiling. My gloom, one of feeling like I was going it alone, was completely gone. The resupply would have an excellent chance of success with the kind of supporting fire that the battalion had mounted to finally bring us home. The United States Marine Corps and the U.S. Army Cavalry were coming to get us and there was no way I could be depressed.

The Ontos would still remain the key to our survival, and so resupply that would have to, once again, cross the river would be just about everything. I was certain that Hultzer had fired just about everything he had during the night before. There would be no real air support in the darkest hours of the night and the M60s

along could probably not work alone to stop a hugely determined and sizeable NVA force. Getting the supplies across the bridge again would also probably entail losing more Marines. It was Sugar Daddy's turn to try to earn his Silver Star once again. In spite of the games he'd more than likely played to get McInerney to go out into the field of fire instead of he himself, I didn't want to lose more Marines doing the re-supply, including Sugar Daddy.

Fessman's radio played and Joe Cocker's raucous rough voice began to sing. My smile grew larger. The song was "With a little help from my friends."

There would, indeed, be some joy in the valley along with a great mass of help from our friends.

one-hundred-thirty-seven

Puff came in for the third time, orbiting Hill 975 and pouring what seemed to look like liquid fire into the mountain, while it sounded for all the world like the place was being chewed up with a giant out of control chainsaw. The way the big cargo plane tilted and then orbited was eerie to watch as if the low-flying airplane was being restrained by some invisible guiding string hanging down from high up in the heavens. The sun peeking out of the clouds, as mid-day came and went, added another strange element to the scene, and the Skyraiders, lurking around and around as if waiting for their chance to strike at anything that moved below added an additional odd element of impending doom for anyone under them.

Once Puff was done the Skyraiders took over the attack, slowly flying up and down the valley as if waiting for any surviving prey to show its head. The day wore on without any further fire until mid-afternoon, when Cowboy decided the time was right all on his own without any communication with me. I'd been in communication with him and let him know that we would be out on the exposed flat after dark to recover one of our own. Even the suppression of fire the mighty thundering Skyraiders might supply would not allow us to make the retrieval of McInerney's body without likely and significant losses of our living Marines. The resupply was also being planned and scheduled for early evening so the greater the damage to the fortified and tunnel-riven mountain during the daylight hours the better.

The Skyraiders passed once more down the valley, and then everything changed when Cowboy's lead plane plunged low, dived in toward the middle of Hill 975 and dropped two of the huge canisters of napalm from under each wing. The tanks hit the mountain. The jellied gasoline the tanks contained lit and rolled down the mountainside, spilling out and burning at a rate that caused the heat to be felt all the way behind our lines and beyond. The other two Skyraiders dropped their tanks, each one selecting a different part of the mountain to burn. Once more they circled, and then came in again, except this time higher. All three planes dropped their remaining napalm supplies on the very top of the mountain, causing the torrid liquid to ignite and flow down the sides of the mountain to overlap the areas that had been hit and burned in their earlier runs.

The Wright radial engines quieted, as the planes headed back to base. Through the afternoon they returned three more times to repeat what they had done earlier. Whether the fire on the outside of the mountain, some of which had to reach into the tunnel complex that riddled the mountain, caused a lot of destruction nobody could know, but the mountain that was once green with lush jungle ferns and other growth, was a smoking black cone when they were done for the day.

The Skyraiders finished their last pass. There was no point in aircraft remaining on station to fire their twenty-millimeter machine guns because there were no visible targets for them to shoot at. Whether the withering fire of Puff and then fiery burning effects of the napalm were enough to deaden or quiet the forces holed up inside Hill 975 could not be accurately guessed. There had to be some traumatic shock effect, but the NVA troops were notorious for being tough and enduring punishment, no matter what punishment was thrown their way.

As twilight began to expand the moving shadow thrown down by the western cliff's great height, I prepared the small team we would use to encounter the particular pile of rip-rap and torn apart rocks where Nguyen, who'd been out there with McInerney, indicated his body was likely to be found. The Gunny lay next to me as I surveyed the scene, the particular pile of rocks so close that no binoculars were needed to study the approach or the indicated area. The main problem that became apparent, as the light began to wane, was the presence of enemy soldiers. The mountain had been deadly quiet since Puff had rained metal rain down upon every square inch of its surface and the Skyraiders had gone back and forth to their base to pour at least sixteen giant burning canisters of napalm down upon its sides.

The troops creeping out onto the heavily contested mud flat field of fire weren't even in uniform if they were troops at all. Furtively, they crept out to retrieve their own dead or wounded, which appeared to number in the hundreds, if not more. There had been no notification, no request for a cease-fire or mercy of any sort by the implacable North Vietnamese sapper unit occupying the mountain. The crawling natives, only half-clothed, looking almost exactly like slowly moving parts of the landscape itself eased out from the brush surrounding Hill 975, and then moved out onto the flat to drag bodies back toward the hill, always positioning the bodies so they could drag them by their wrists and not their feet.

Not one Marine along the line fired a shot at any of the visible men. Neither the Gunny nor I and certainly not the platoon commanders had given any orders to shoot or not shoot. Everyone did the same thing. We all watched intently, and with some mild discomfort. The NVA had paid a huge price in attempting to overrun our position, and it seemed poised to repeat that same experience, but yet the small moving creatures out atop the mud moved with furtive but steady deliberation, seeming to disregard the deadly position they were placing themselves in.

Fessman, Nguyen and I, along with the most unlikely of volunteers, Sergeant Jurgens, would make the attempt to dig through the rocks and dislodge and return McInerney's body to our lines.

"Go now," the Gunny whispered urgently into my left ear.

My hearing had finally recovered from my body being placed directly under the trajectory of the Ontos 106 mm rounds when they left their tubes earlier. For physics reasons unknown to me the recoilless explosions when the charges were let off to send the rounds out were almost twice as loud, then those of the 105 howitzers, yet they packed a smaller less powerful punch upon arrival.

"It's not dark enough yet," I said back.

"That's not the point," the Gunny rasped out, his voice nearly a whisper. "They won't fire on you retrieving the lieutenant's body, any more than we are firing now at the retrieval of their own dead."

"But what if they do?" I answered, in frustration.

I not only didn't want to go out onto the mudflat, but I also didn't want to be out there with the enemy creeping around claiming its own.

"They left our belongings alone up on that plateau a few weeks back, if you will recall," the Gunny intoned, this time raising his voice to a more normal level. "They aren't monsters and they do play by a set of rules. They didn't send their men out onto the field to be mowed down by our Marines. Somehow, they depended upon a similar code we might honor as they do."

"But we can't be sure," I replied, knowing his argument had real gravitas while mine sounded a bit nervous and skittery.

Then again, the Gunny wasn't going out there. The companies could not afford the loss of both the Gunny and I and we both knew it, and Gunny was the most influential and important among the two of us. No discussion had taken place about that issue, and there needed to be none.

"It's your call, Junior," was all the Gunny replied.

Suddenly another body flopped down into the mud along my right side.

"It's Russell, sir, and we want to go out with you."

I looked at the young lieutenant, and then over at his clone. Both looked to me like they were grade-schoolers, and I wondered how I, after only a month in the A Shau, appeared to them for both to refer to me, a fellow lieutenant, as sir.

I nodded once and then turned back to face the Gunny, the right side of my face almost in contact with the leech riddled mud.

"No, it's your call, just as it has almost always been," I whispered. "We're going out. If we don't make it, then in the write up about us would you please not tell anyone that we were this stupid?"

Only the second smile I'd ever seen from the man swiftly flew across the Gunny's face before it was gone as it had never been there.

one-hundred-thirty-eight

THE TWENTY-EIGHTH NIGHT : FIRST PART

The six of us moved on our bellies, out toward the jumbled remains in the killing field of the mudflat, as one, without any signal. The ability of Marines in combat to need a whole lot fewer signals and orders than the guys doing all the training back home thought they needed amazed me, once again. We had become homogenized into one thinking and feeling entity by bitter and brutal circumstances.

We moved just like the almost shimmering gray images of the other recoverers of the dead from the enemy side. We crawled, chests touching the mud, and then slid along until encountering some of the rock debris that had been scattered about by the impact of the recoilless rounds against the face of the cliff.

In my mind, as I moved, I thought about the futility of retrieving a dead body while risking the living bodies of six more, but in my heart, I was a Marine, and I was being watched by hundreds of other Marines with the same kind of beating hearts. I could not fail them. I could not fail them even if I died in the attempt. After almost a month in constant combat, the fear of death had still not left me, but the prospect of its eventuality had seeped into every pore of my body. I had learned that one day, and quite possibly this day, I would die. That concept had been taught to me since I was a young boy but the reality of it had never truly entered into my belief system, and now it was part of every fiber of my physical and mental being. Death was not an 'if' thing. It was a 'when' thing.

Nguyen crawled past me, still making almost no noise, as I squished and plopped behind him. He came to the spot he'd indicated and began to toss rocks toward the enemy side of the pile. All five of us then worked to perform the same operation, being careful not to move too fast or hit the man next to us with what we threw. I became oblivious to the enemy troops retrieving their comrade's bodies. It took almost a full hour to reach the lieutenant's body.

We pulled McInerny from the debris. I noted, that he had no penetrating wounds. The Ontos 106 fusillade had killed him, while his finger was still on the button of his flashlight. I tried to pry the flashlight loose from his grip but it would not come, so I left it in his steely grasp. Once we had him flat on the mud we rested for a few seconds.

"We'll carry him, sir, if you don't mind," Russell said. "He was one of our own, after all."

"No," I replied, instantly, understanding that they considered McInerney special because he was an officer. "We'll all carry him back. He was one of all of our own. He was, and remains, a Marine."

There had been no shots fired on either side while we were out on the mudflat, and there were none, as we slowly made our way back to our own lines. Once back, the corpsmen worked over the body to make certain the lieutenant was officially dead, before wrapping him in a poncho cover and spiriting him off to be readied for evacuation aboard the coming resupply chopper.

I lay down in the same small depression I'd left earlier. The Gunny had not moved from his position.

"You were right," I said, breathing in and out deeply.

The work had been exhausting but the fear and trepidation had been even more sapping of my energy.

The Gunny lit a cigarette and offered it to me without taking a puff himself.

It was a small gesture, but not one I missed.

In the silence that followed I thought about the strange behavior of the NVA, an enemy I'd been taught was without honor, mercy or care toward the enemy it fought so fiercely. The fact that the NVA had not fired upon us, or our firing on them, also gave me pause. I had come to find that the NVA was a much more capable opponent than I had been led to believe in training. It was almost as if they were Marines, but smaller, and with a whole lot less technology and equipment. That thought made me uncomfortable. I did not want to be impressed by them or what they might believe.

"You don't lack for guts, Junior," the Gunny whispered, so softly that nobody else could hear him. "I'm not at all certain I'd have gone out there under any circumstance. I've come close so many times I keep getting the feeling that each time now, when the going gets tough, that that's going to be it."

I drew deeply on the cigarette and then handed it back. In the space of only a few hours, the Gunny had offered me more of his inner feelings and thoughts than in all my past time with him in the field. I knew I was in no place to reassure the Gunny. He'd have gone out there, and I knew it, and I thought he knew it too. He was saying what he was saying to lift me up and keep me going, and even knowing he was using that device as a tool, it was okay. I felt uplifted and would keep going.

We both smoked the cigarette together.

"Where the hell was the siege of Candia, anyway?" the Gunny asked out of nowhere.

"The Ottoman Empire," I replied, automatically reciting what I'd learned in a European history course during my college years. Candia hadn't been much discussed in class, but the fact that a surrounded city had lasted twenty-two years under constant fire, attack and deprivation, had gotten at least my passing interest.

"Okay, then where was the Ottoman Empire?" the Gunny went on, pursuing the nonsense subject just to be talking about something other than living miserably and possibly dying in even worse conditions.

At that, I coughed the smoke from my lungs and then had to laugh briefly out loud. "You know, Gunny, I studied that stuff and passed the tests but, in truth, I don't have a clue as to exactly where it was. Europe, somewhere."

"They're coming in hot, high and dry in about half an hour for the resupply," the Gunny said, his voice matter-of-fact like we might be talking about picking up groceries at the neighborhood store. "It won't be dark yet, but it's going to be close. I didn't see any other way we could cross that river again unless it was in the dark. We took a hell of a hard hit last time, and we can't exactly move the Ontos out of its current position to support us over there without being overrun here."

"We'll still have air up, if Cowboy can keep his guys on station that long," I added, hoping I was right.

"Yes, there's that, but from up there they can't see through the dark any better than we can down here without the scope."

"What about the Intruder?" I asked. "It has night vision capability and can carry twice what a Skyraider can haul."

The Gunny didn't reply, taking his time to finish the cigarette, and then tossing the crushed butt into the brush nearby.

"I'll get on the air and see what we can scrape up," I finally said, knowing Fessman was already fumbling with the radio to hand me the headset, as I spoke the words.

It would play hell trying to get the A-6 on station in time to cover the chopper's pull out and our own flight back across the broken bridge with all the stuff that would have to be carried.

Sugar Daddy, Jurgens, the Gunny, and the other platoon commanders assembled minutes later at the foxhole I'd had dug earlier, and now designated as the command post for the resupply operation. I'd had the position dug in order to better view the area that rose upward slightly and a bit back from the river.

Sugar Daddy's platoon would make the crossing while Jurgen's platoon would provide the firebase on our side of the river to suppress fire that we knew would come up out of the jungle just downriver, across another mudflat that had already claimed the lives of so many men on both sides of the conflict.

The best news was that Jim Homan, whom everyone that knew of him called the 'Whole Man,' was coming in, navigating the Intruder and loaded for bear. His A-6, with its uncommon nozzled jet exhaust, would be able to loiter and see through a night that promised to be the brightest any of us had witnessed in weeks. The monsoon season was upon us, but that season was not one that allowed for complete predictability. At any moment the entire sky could cloud over, and then the rain would resume and with it the loss of almost all visibility, even for a high tech airplane that could normally see through stygian blackness. The A-6 coming out, all the way from Da Nang, was using the call sign 'Ring Neck Seventeen,' which I would later discover was not the pilot's or the radar intercept officer's call sign. It was the call sign for the aircraft itself no matter who was inside it, unlike the Skyraider designations that were more personal and comforting.

The supply chopper would be carrying tons of Ontos ammunition, a squad of 81 mm mortars and ammo for them, as well as plenty of water and C-rations. The battalion had hooked up with the regiment, and then the division, for the coming operation, and was apparently, from the radio traffic, in my stated opinion to the Gunny, not about to have our companies overrun or wiped out before they came down the valley to rescue us. That special attention would finally be paid to our dire situation gave almost everyone in the units hope, and a feeling of warmth, as the word spread. But it would all come down to the A-6 flying cover, the resupply landing without serious mishap, and then Sugar Daddy's outfit getting the stuff across the difficult crossing presented by the raging monsoon swollen Bong Song while under fire from the enemy.

At the same time, the rest of our company's firepower had to be directed, once again, at the mudflat extending out from the wall that we'd retrieved McInerney's body from. The Ontos would not have full resupply of its ammunition provisions until Sugar Daddy's unit got the stuff over, and Hutzler had fired everything he'd had, with the exception of only six high explosive rounds, in holding off the enemy during the night before. The situation was precarious, and success seemed to depend upon too many variables, but there was no other plan I felt we could fall back on to accomplish what had to be accomplished.

Sugar Daddy's platoon assembled and lay in wait for the first sign that the resupply chopper was coming in. The A-6 came in first, but at high altitude, the pilot and his navigator bombardier no doubt wanting to get a feel for what was about to happen below before they came in on a firing and bombing run. There was no missing the screaming sound of the A-6 turbines, however, and that sound gave everyone a lift.

The CH-46 dual rotor chopper didn't fly down the valley, as all of us waiting, had expected. It came dropping straight out of the nearly night sky, barely preceded by the Huey Cobra gunships protecting it. The Cobras flew in low, turning and circling like flies surrounding an outdoor light bulb. How they missed one another in the poor light conditions was hard to believe, but they did. They didn't open fire on anything because the enemy remained silent as the supply chopper came in, hovering for only a moment before touching down.

Sugar Daddy and his platoon moved out at the run, the decision to hang back being my own. There was no point in exposing the Marines to fire on the exposed bridge surface by having them lay there in wait. Getting off the other end of the under-extended bridge, still reaching short of the far bank, was going to be the real problem. Sugar Daddy's Marines would take the gap at a run and bull through to mudflat beyond, but it would take a prodigious effort to get the ammo boxes, water, and food supplies back across and up onto the lip of the bridge. It was there and then that I expected real trouble from the NVA force waiting further down in the jungle, dug in and fortified against the kind of firepower they knew would be supporting our resupply effort. McInerney's body would accompany the last part of Sugar Daddy's force, but that bundled poncho wrapped package was on the minds of everyone on the scene.

The platoon surged out across the river bank and onto the bridge without comment or orders, moving almost invisibly to mount the near side of the bridge butted into the riverbank on our side. The Marines wore their poncho covers in order to enjoy the maximum amount of concealment the moonlight wetness, from the rains of earlier in the day, might allow.

I was settled into my hole near the Bong Song river, it's rushing sound magnified by the canyon walls rising up on both sides of it, once more dominating everything in the vicinity. The sound could only be slightly suppressed by crouching deep in the hole, my third hole in nearly the same spot since my descent into the A Shau Valley.

This hole was not dug down below the water table so it was nearly dry, except for the dampness the earlier misting monsoon rains had left as they'd pulled out. The night was nearly upon our position. I could not use the Starlight Scope as Hultzer had to have it back at the Ontos. Hopefully, the NVA occupying Hill 975 would not figure out that our recoilless rifle ammunition was low. The last thing I wanted was to have the sapper regiment attack again after we'd split our forces to hook up for the resupply. They would know, of course, as soon as the chopper was recognized for being what it was. The twin-rotor CH-46 was the resupply chopper for a very particular reason. It didn't necessarily lift much more than a Huey, but it had a cavernous interior for packing boxes and containers of everything and then off-loading the entire load in seconds. The distinctive twin-rotor sound the blades made in beating against the low humid atmosphere down in the A Shau made it instantly recognizable once heard.

Sugar Daddy's Marines were strung out, covering nearly every open space on the bridge's surface, and then everything changed.

The bridge moved. It was impossible to miss what was happening. The end of the bridge, extended from the near bank, and almost all the way over to the far bank, and angled slightly downriver as it hung back from that far bank, shifted. The movement changed the way in which the rushing water was encountering the landed portion of the structure on our side. A huge white spray gushed upward into the night air, reflected out and back under the half-moon's dim but glistening light, and then the bridge moved again. I watched it shift toward the far bank, the spray changing in angle and diminishing in amount, as the entire heavy metal platform speared into the far bank.

Sugar Daddy's platoon was stretched across the length of the bridge, small dark, but shiny lumps, laying as still as they could under their poncho covers.

I knelt inside the foxhole, peering out on the scene from under the lip of my helmet, stunned to the point of being shocked. We'd fought back and forth across the seemingly permanently settled bridge so many times it didn't seem possible that it had moved, any more than the upside-down tank, just downriver from it, might have changed position. It was like those artificial human artifacts had become natural parts of the landscape. I'd never considered that they might move or move at a particularly sensitive and crucial time.

I pulled back and crouched down a bit to think about what had just happened. Fessman pressed against my back and I knew instinctively that he was pushing the handset of the radio into me to respond. As I turned to take the microphone I felt Nguyen slip out of the hole, more like a thick snake than a human. He twisted around and then lay with only his eyes and the top of his uncovered head peering back down. I knew he knew, as I had come to know when I took an instant to conclude something that could not be avoided. I was going to have to get down to the close end of the bridge, now isolated out in the raging water, as the other end had been earlier. Sugar Daddy was going to have the same problem of getting himself and his Marines back as he would have had only seconds earlier, except in reverse.

I pulled the handset to the side of my head, pushing my helmet off to press it closer into my ear. The Gunny was going back and forth with Sugar Daddy on the combat net.

"Six actual," I transmitted, pushing the transmit button down hard and holding it to send interference for a few seconds.

The Gunny and Sugar Daddy went silent.

"I'm coming down with my scout team and I want Jurgens and his whole platoon securing our end of the bank. The bridge moved, and it's likely it's going to move again soon. We've got to act fast, but the crossing has to be held at all costs. At all cost, Gunny."

I knew the Gunny would want to come to the river. He was a man of action and command, but if the enemy crossed the mudflat under the cliff we'd brought down, with the Ontos too short on rounds to repeat its last performance, we would all be lost. I'd left the Gunny with the remnants of Kilo company two of our own company's weakest platoons. The Ontos had six rounds. They would have to make do. Once the Bong Song lit up with fire I was nearly certain the sappers would rush forward from Hill 975 and mount their second assault, especially with the coming onset of darkness to cover them.

"Affirmative," the Gunny replied, his tone flat.

I knew he knew that neither of us was in any position to do anything else. Sugar Daddy didn't respond at all, and I was guessing that he'd simply signed off to lead his men off the bridge to the other side as quickly as he could. The bridge was where he'd almost died only days earlier, confirming that it was the worst possible attractant, with total lack of cover or concealment, that might be found anywhere. The problem was going to be getting the supplies and Marines back on our side, and I had no idea, from my position in the hole, what the new gap between the bridge and the riverbank might be like now.

I put my helmet back on and eased out of the hole. Nguyen was already gone, and I knew where he'd be much before I got there. Fear had started to rise up deep inside my core again, and it felt good to be moving, as I made my way upriver a bit and then low crawled and ran down toward where the end of the bridge had to be, somewhere on the other side of the blocking and irritating wet ferns and brush. I had forgotten about the Intruder altogether.

The A-6 came screaming in on its first run before I got to the river's edge, much lower than its observation runs high up earlier. The Intruder's advanced radar system allowed it to almost see in the dark using radar waves instead of the enhanced photons the Starlight Scope worked on. Our scope was very limited by weather, and then it only gave a small field of view compared to that of the radar return system in the Intruder, which produced fine images of what was below on a large cathode ray tube that sat in front of the Navigator Bombardier. Homan was up there looking down at us I realized, and that thought gave me a jolt of energy and hope. I got to my feet and raced forward. I came upon the scene to see the end of the bridge a good fifteen feet from the bank, with a heaping deep current of racing river water rushing by between the end and the bank.

The howling Pratt and Whitney turbine jet engines of the special ground support aircraft penetrated over and above the sounds of the river, as the machine flew so low that it only cleared the CH 46 over on the far side of the river by what seemed like tens of feet. At that point, it began a steep climb just before it encountered the northern edge of the jungle where the enemy had to be lying in wait, and ready to open up. The plane's engines went to full power and it pulled upward sharply, vaguely visible only because the moon was half full and peeking through the scudding clouds.

Twin explosions followed, and any attention given to the plane was gone. I was used to the five hundred pound bombs dropped by the Skyraiders. They were called Snakeye bombs because fins snapped out behind them to slow their fall allowing the low flying A-1s to get out of range ahead of their detonation. A twin ripple set of explosions sent concussion waves across the river, blowing spray and condensed air over everyone on the river bank, including me. I knew instantly that the bombs were not the normal five hundred pounders. The explosions were huge, so huge that I saw the white curtain of a shock wave, compressing the water out of the air, as it rushed toward me across the river at the speed of sound. I ducked down only a bit too late, and my helmet was ripped from my head, along with its liner, and sent blowing through the air behind me. I went down and deep as hard as I could, and then pulled up slightly out of the six inches of mud I'd forced myself into. I looked up at the end of the bridge, just as Nguyen replaced first the liner, and then my once again damaged helmet, onto my head. I had to squeeze it on. The front of its normally round dome shape had been slightly pushed in.

There was nothing visible following the A-6 bombing run. The river raced on by with all its noisy might. I knew from hearing the water that my hearing had survived the tremendous effect of the bomb's expended energy. I also knew there would be silence and shock spread out through most of the jungle target area where we feared small arms and possible rocket fire had to come from. The A-6 had given us time, but when would the Whole Man and his pilot rotate back?

I looked across the water toward the opposite mudflat, where the big dual rotor chopper sat, its blades still whirling at high speed, as if the helicopter was flying on the surface of the mud but standing perfectly still at the same time.

I crawled on hands and knees to where a small clump of men had risen up out of the muck following the attack.

"Jeez, Junior," Jurgens said, staring at the bulk of the end of the bridge, now fifteen feet across the deadly flood driven water.

The blunt end of the bridge, unlike the other flat blade end on the other side, was a wall of flat iron that rose up a good six to eight feet above the river's passing surface.

"How we going to get them back?" Jurgens asked.

Two Huey Cobras dived down and then screamed over our heads, forcing all of us to duck down. The lead Cobra circled back, the one I'd heard was piloted by a man using the name Turk. The sleek fast chopper repeated the same sweeping move. I knew the big chopper was unloading the supplies out onto the flat. Things were happening too fast. The Cobras were circling to isolate any threats and provide their own threat to any would-be machine gunner located in the shattered jungle. Sugar Daddy's men had to be across and hopefully loading McInerney's body into the body of the chopper, but what then? The chopper was leaving, the Cobras would fly with it, leaving a whole platoon of Marines to get back with all the stuff, and then somehow cross the twisting cauldron of deadly water from much higher up and further away than anyone had planned.

I took in the situation as best I could. I had no plan. Even acting at top speed there seemed to be no way to perform the mission. Sugar Daddy and his platoon would likely be lost no matter what we did.

I turned to Fessman. The kid had read my mind. I pulled off my mess of a helmet with both hands and planted the AN 323 air headset quickly onto my head.

"Whole Man," where the hell are you?" I squeezed out, keeping my voice down but pushing the words out forcefully and hard, as I jammed my finger down on the transmit button.

"Radio etiquette," came back through the little speaker in my ear.

"We're in deep shit down here," I said, ignoring the man's out of place humor. "When is your next pass, if there's to be the next pass?" I asked.

"Should hear us in one zero seconds, coming in hot low and wet with another deuce of the same…and then five more in rotation, and that's in the clear for the little people to hear."

Homan had figured out that the entire mission was fire suppression and he was sending a message to the enemy. If that first run had not reached many of them then five more runs might do all that we needed, keep their heads down and any fire from coming from their weapons.

I heard the whistling sound of the two powerful A-6 engines, as Homan knew I would. It had been about four to five minutes since the first run. With luck, we had twenty to twenty-five minutes to get our Marines back, and then there would be no air cover or anything else unless I pasted together another 175 mm artillery strike that would likely kill us all, anyway.

"We'll make it fine," I said to Jurgens, standing at my side.

He didn't reply, merely turning to angle slightly toward me. He pushed something into my side. I grasped the tube-like object in surprise.

"The Gunny said you'd want this," Jurgen whispered.

I felt the object. It was a Navy issue flashlight. McInerney's flashlight.

THE TWENTY-EIGHTH NIGHT : SECOND PART

I slipped McInerney's flashlight into my right side pocket, its end sticking out a bit and rapping back and forth against the hard leather of my Colt .45 holster.

"Fessman," I whispered, turning back toward the foxhole I'd left, but making no move to retreat there.

"Sugar Daddy," I ordered, and then waited.

Fessman quickly moved the dials he needed to move in order to isolate Sugar Daddy's frequency on his PRICK 25.

"Six actual," I stated, and then went on when he responded by using my Junior nickname.

He was in a bad spot with his platoon and I could hear the tension in his voice just by reading it in the strained tone of his single word reply.

"We need the ropes you intended for the other side and we need them now. Have your men string one single long linked line along the side of the bridge that's upriver. The only cover you had at all, the last time we did this, was from getting into the river and moving along low on the other side of the bridge. The 106 rounds mean everything," I added.

"How long do we have?" he asked, rushing the speed of his words as he'd never done before.

"About twenty, maybe twenty-five minutes," I replied, knowing I was probably going to be caught short.

If the A-6 made its last run sooner than that then the cost would be in Marines taken down by machine-gun fire from the jungle area that Jurgens' platoon, unloading, and the running supplies to the company, would be in no position to suppress. The supplies had to come first or all was lost, and the only men to facilitate and receive the supplies, from the more dangerous position of the bridge since it'd moved, were Jurgens' Marines.

"I'll do my best, Junior," Sugar Daddy said in such a way as I'd never heard him before.

It was almost as if he was transmitting a message of respect toward me, as well as a deep measure of fear. I stood for a few seconds, surprised and holding out the handset before me. I didn't reply. There was no reply necessary. All Jurgens and I could do was to wait for the ropes and then go to work building a makeshift cargo net to get the heavy supplies down and across the deadly gulf that had formed between the river bank and the rear of the bridge structure. And we had to move as fast as humanly possible, given the short suppression period the Intruder could give us and the likely continued and unpredictable movement of the structure.

Marines appeared at the top of the metal wall that was the back of the bridge, visible from the reflected moonlight suffusing up and out from the thickness of whitewater the fast-moving liquid threw into the air all around us. I was drenched, and I hadn't come within feet of the river water itself, which I didn't mind because the fresh feeling of the river water did a lot to revive and keep me going. The Marines began throwing coils of rope across the distance. Fifteen feet was not a great gulf between us, but the coils were wet and heavy. Many made it, to land in the nearby mud, a few others were retrieved as they struck the near edge of the water and about to be swept away. A few were lost altogether.

"Knots, we need knots, and fast, and we won't have time to make a proper net either," I said quickly to Jurgens. "Any of your men who can tie knots I need right now."

My mind raced back to my time aboard the Daniel J. Morrell when I'd served as a deckhand before it went to the bottom of Lake Huron. I'd spent two summers between college years spending most of my off time learning seaman's knots and lore from the other sailors. The running hitch was about the fastest knot anyone could tie that was secure and could be continued, one knot after another, without having to cut the rope to build the lattice, and it was easy and fast to tie.

I gathered a small group of Marines Jurgens had 'volunteered' and showed them how to tie the simple knot, using an arms-length distance for the placement of each knot at the crossing point where the ropes were brought together. It was too dark to show much of anything, however, so I pulled out McInerney's flashlight and lay it on the mud. Its angled head pointed sideways and provided enough light. I took the chance that it also could attract fire if the enemy wasn't crouched down in holes or hiding in tunnels waiting out the Intruder's deadly explosive runs.

I finished my quick course in the showing the Marines how to tie the lines together to form nets that had squares of about three feet in size, way too big to haul or rest cargo on, particularly as it came across the round racing water. We had no time, and the wet ropes were cumbersome and difficult, but they'd probably serve for the Marines to climb onto and haul the supplies over themselves without ending up in the river, either being spirited downriver to some gloomy ending or drowning outright.

The results of the second of the Intruder's runs blew us all into a moment of frozen inaction and silence. The concussive waves crossed the river almost instantly but were partially blocked by the steel corner of the bridge itself. We plunged back into the knotting work after they passed. We finished most of the net before the fourth A-6 bombing run, just as Sugar Daddy's Marines began arriving at the bridge's upper rear edge with all manner of boxes, bags and uncovered mortar tubes and plates.

We were out of time, so I ordered the knotting work to stop. Just as I was about to have a line thrown across the distance to attach what we had of a cargo net, a coiled rope landed right in front of me. I looked up to see a dark figure waiting to haul the end of the net up. It had to be Sugar Daddy.

A single gunner fired a line of green tracers from the jungle area we all feared. The tracers came in well over everyone's head, but still forcing everyone down.

"The light," Jurgens hissed, brushing by and knocking me out of his way. He didn't turn off the fire attracting light, instead, he buried the flashlight deep into the mud not far from my left boot. He said nothing, immediately turning to tie the thrown line to the cargo net, and then yelling for the Marines on the bridge to haul it up.

I eased the flashlight loose from the mud by feel, getting the sliding switch on the side to the off position before I brought the waterproof lens up from the muck. I wasn't willing to give up the flashlight. The light had proven that the enemy would survive the bombing runs and eventually direct heavy fire upon anyone left in the open while they would be making the supply move attempt. I had wished at one point that we could use the old runway further upriver, and also a bit down from Hill 975, but the river water had done its work as it had increased in volume and speed with the increased rainfall. The old runway was all but gone, it's great concrete squares eaten out from underneath by the racing water and then broken up as they failed in pieces instead of being plopped down to rest flat on the river's underwater bed. Two of Jurgens men had bravely gone upriver earlier to check it out.

The Marines worked to get the net up and secured with three of Jurgen's men assigned to hold the riverbank edge down and tight. I watched them work, no orders or instructions being necessary. Somehow, none probably ever working as a merchant seaman other than myself, they knew instinctively what to do. They didn't talk, they just got the job done.

I waited for the next bombing run, hoping that Homan would make sure to hit further down in the jungle area. The Marines crossing the exposed flat surface of the bridge carrying the supplies would be at real risk from the concussive waves of the bombs if they landed any closer at all to where they'd come in earlier. I thought of calling Homan on the radio but then realized he and his pilot knew exactly what they were doing, and very likely their advanced radar could take in the situation we were in as they made their runs.

I carefully replaced the flashlight back in my pocket, this time freeing up my left front pocket so the head of the light wouldn't whack against my automatic. I watched the Marines work, as supplies began to flow first to men struggling to balance as best they could on and in the net, and then as other Marines grabbed the supplies and ran back toward the open area running all the way to the cliff, not far from where my foxhole had been dug. The makeshift cargo net allowed for the transfer, although almost two squads of Jurgen's Marines had to be stuck among the knots and ropes to ferry the stuff down.

The flashlight incident brought a lot of stuff rushing back to me, as I waited to see what had to be done next, and also for the return of the Intruder.

I wasn't made up of anything of my own. I was the creation of others. My helmet was a bruised and battered relic from officers who had died before me. My gun was from a dead lieutenant I'd shared so little time with that I had to concentrate to remember his name. My used boots came in from a chopper crewman who felt sorry for me, and then died hours after being stuck on the ground, and then going immediately into combat. My watch was taken from another officer who'd passed on earlier. The flashlight I'd lost had been owned by one of my platoon sergeants and then replaced by the flashlight owned by another officer killed because he was too new to understand the near-instant mortality of combat to men exposed without any experience. I was like the scarecrow from the Wizard of Oz, a collection of bits and pieces, although different from that fictional character by being gifted, or cursed, with a great memory. There was no making any mistake in my own mind, however, that I was as entirely fictional as that movie creature. I had made myself up, with the Gunny's help, to become something I could not look twenty-eight days back and recognize at all.

I realized that the 106 ammunition was coming across the water first, with Sugar Daddy's large presence visible up on the bridge's end to make sure. It was that touch and understanding that burned deeply into me about the man. I would write Sugar Daddy up for the Silver Star he had somehow come to crave. I wouldn't do it for his heroism in any action or activity he might be performing. I'd do it for his knowing and doing the right thing at the right time to save two companies of Marines from annihilation.

The flat wooden boxes, each with two 106 rounds inside, came over quickly. Although weighing about fifty pounds per box, the wooden crates handled easily when a rope was run through one of the hemp handles and then tied to the other. They bounced easily across the shaky net, guided by the Marines over the holes in the net and the rapidly moving water below. The ropes on the boxes were untied with great speed and the rounds spirited away into the night. I knew they were being run to the Ontos at top speed. In only minutes the Ontos would be fully resupplied with both high explosive and flechette ammunition.

The next run of the Intruder came in, low enough to see the exhaust plumes from its strangely angled turbine engines. The Marines on the bridge all went prone on the deck when the explosions took place, and then popped back up almost instantly when the shock waves had passed.

The C-Rations were difficult to work with. They were easy to toss across the distance but then had to be reassembled on the riverbank because the cardboard boxes were immediately soaked through by the water. They broke open easily upon impacting the shore and the dozen smaller meal boxes had to be piled into poncho covers to be transported.

The 81mm mortar barrel and plate assemblies came over the lip, carried by hand, with no coverings. The mortar ammo boxes came next. They were made of soldered tin, unlike the boxes of the 106 recoilless rounds. The tins were a good bit shorter but just as heavy. Everything about the mortars was heavy, and each element weighed about the same. The tin ammo boxes of three rounds each weighed fifty pounds, while the tube and base, individually, weighed somewhere in that neighborhood too.

I knew the Marines loved the power of the mortar rounds but they also hated to have to carry the ammunition or the mortar body parts. The normal pack load carried into combat weighed between forty and sixty pounds, depending upon when resupply provided more or less stuff, and how much water was necessary to get by on. Two mortars and a dozen boxes of ammunition amounted to six hundred pounds that would normally have to be redistributed among the men for humping up, down and across the devilishly difficult terrain of the valley.

The good news, in our current situation, was that we were in a static position waiting to be relieved. We weren't going anywhere the mortars would have to be hauled. Their passage, as I watched the mortars go by, gave me an idea.

"Set up the mortars and get ready with two teams to register, and then fire on that jungle area when the Intruder is done with its work," I ordered Jurgens, grabbing him by the arm and pulling him back from the river. "Act fast. We don't have that many runs left. Have them fire one round every thirty seconds until half the ammo's gone once they are set up. We'll save the other 18 rounds for another enemy attempt to cross the mudflat."

The mortar round's ten pound loads of highly fractured metal shrapnel and high explosive would be window dressing in the jungle but it might give an additional nine minutes, or so, of additional cover before the enemy resurfaced and really became a destructive threat.

I noticed Nguyen at my side. His presence was closer than he'd normally chosen to accompany me, in combat or otherwise. I noted that his shiny ebony eyes were not on me. His attention was on Jurgens. He didn't trust Jurgens, for reasons that I thought were already buried in the past, but evidently the mysterious but deadly Montagnard didn't agree. Nguyen's impassive and nearly inscrutable facial expressions were such that it was hard to tell, but since Macho Man's murder at Jurgen's hands, the small deadly warrior treated Jurgens as if he was a hand grenade rolling around with the pin already pulled.

The A-6 made its last run, as McInerny's bagged body was sent the other way up our jury-rigged cargo net and onto the main deck of the bridge. The huge explosions came as before, and everyone on the bridge and behind it was ready for them. The enemy was ready for them too because light fire began to come from the jungle in spurts of short automatic fire. How the enemy somehow knew how many of the big bombs the Intruder carried was beyond me, but somehow they did. The first mortar round was launched from its tube with the characteristic 'thup' in the distance. A mortar launch comes with a delay that can be from twenty to over sixty seconds long, as the round climbs high in the atmosphere, and then plunges back to earth in its very steep arc of descent. The round didn't explode in the jungle itself. It exploded like a 4th of July fireworks above the jungle, and then a big swinging light descended down from the cloud of smoke surrounding the explosion. Somehow a few of the rounds that had come in were illumination rounds. I watched the 500,000 candlepower swinging light slowly float on down into the jungle, where it still burned for a while, generating a yellow glow up from the place it had gone down.

At first, I was surprised and then delighted. The small arms fire had died out again, while Sugar Daddy's Marines made their last run to the chopper, and then began returning carrying the last of their load, the big plastic water bottles we needed so badly in the heat. Thirty seconds later, another illumination round came in.

The Marines were not using the high explosive ammunition. They were saving that for using when the sappers would make another assault. I smiled to myself.

The Gunny. He had to be there. Only the Gunny might guess that the illumination rounds would likely be taken by the enemy as a targeting designator for even more powerful airstrikes than the A-6 could deliver. And he was right. The enemy was keeping its head down while Jurgen's remaining Marines raced as fast as they could to get back to the bridge. The 81 ammunition could not last, however, and soon there was again a silence, except for the river's great beating deluge of water passing by, and the sound of the chopper's whirling blades and the constantly passing Cobra gunships.

The CH-46 went to full power and pulled upward, tilting its nose down, and then flying off at top speed up the valley, barely staying more than ten or fifteen feet above the river's fast-moving surface. The Cobra's disappeared with it, never having chosen to fire a round at the enemy, even when some assault rifles had opened up briefly. The tracers crossing the distance had not been directed at the supply chopper. The

Cobra's sole mission was to protect the chopper.

The choppers weren't gone more than a minute before the enemy's .50 caliber heavy machine gun opened up. The enemy hadn't cared to fire on the resupply helicopter, as might have been imagined. They were after wiping out our entire force, and they had more than one heavy machine gun. There was the 50 in the mountain, and now the one located near the center of the jungle area. I retreated back to my foxhole, crabbing up the bank and then standing vertically to run the last bit of distance over the curve of the berm. I went straight down into the hole, followed nearly instantly by Fessman and Nguyen. I reached for the radio handset, propping myself once again against the side of the hole facing the river. I stared out at the occasional bursts from the fifty. It was shooting at the bridge. I knew Sugar Daddy's last Marines, and probably Sugar Daddy himself had to be in the water and on the other side, trying to move toward our side of the river by working hand over hand along the distance of the rope.

"Bring the Gunny up," I ordered Fessman. After some adjustment, I was about to transmit my usual 'six actual' when the Gunny replied, using my name.

"Junior," he said.

"Load one round of high explosive," I said low and slow. "From your last position with the illumination round, drop one-five-zero, left one hundred, over," I said, and waited.

"Roger that," the Gunny came back, understanding that I was adjusting fire for the mortars. "Not certain," he went on, "the light's so bad."

"Prepare four rounds for effect," I followed up a few seconds later, wondering if anyone in the hastily assembled gun crew had a flashlight.

The 'thup' came only seconds later. I waited, counting. Twenty-four seconds went by. The gunner was no doubt using one charge for the short-range since the weapon was capable of firing well beyond two miles. The round landed short of the fifty's position, but the machine gun's firing stopped with the impact.

"Right five zero, add five zero and fire for effect," I ordered.

I couldn't use bracketing, the most accurate way to pinpoint a target under fire, because we didn't have enough ammunition. I had to use 'creeping,' the favored artillery observer tool before Brewer came along in 1931 at Fort Sill's artillery school, inventing the fire direction center and bringing bracketing into effect as the artillery's best aiming tool.

Four 'thups' came from the two tubes in rapid succession. I waited the twenty-four seconds of their flight through, understanding that the Gunny knew so little about adjusting artillery that he didn't use any of the correct radio jargon or back and forth communication usually required for accomplishing an accurate fire mission.

But the mission was very accurate. The four rounds impacted exactly into and closely around the machine gun's position, or what I had gathered was its position from my viewpoint. Without the mortars, I knew we'd have lost a lot more men than we already probably had. Only the fifty was powerful enough to shoot right through the thin but sturdy steel that covered both sides of the bridge. Without the .50 caliber online, the enemy could only aim at those Marines who hadn't made it to the other end of the bridge or who might expose themselves at our end.

Drums of War

[audio   src="https://straussshortstories.s3-us-west-2.amazonaws.com/DrumsJungle.mp3"]

The rain had passed temporarily, and the relief we all felt was palpable. Maybe, somewhere in the resupply goods, there'd be dry socks and underwear around, for those Marines who hadn't given up the issue boxer shorts some time back. Any relief was short-lived, however, because the rain was replaced by the horrid beating of the enemy drums. The NVA never beat the drums in hard rain, probably because their low-frequency sounds didn't penetrate the heavy moist thickness well enough. The drums began their distinctive, and endlessly repetitive and distant, yet close, pounding. The drums could not be ignored, at least not by me.

I reached for the AN 323 headset, poking Fessman in the side so he'd know I didn't want the PRICK 25 for either the combat or artillery net.

"Whole man," are you out there?" I asked. "Do you have any more ordnance left or are you guys done for the night?"

"Roger that," Homan replied, strangely.

I sat for seconds in silence. Did that mean the Intruder had more ordnance available or not? I shook my head in the darkness. Sometimes the air support people were more inscrutable than Charly Chan in the old movies.

"One of those big bombs would be nice," I said, neither of us bothering with the normal radio etiquette in using the monotonous word "over," all the time.

"Roger, One," Homan replied.

That had to mean that the A- 6 still had one of the huge bombs left. I knew the day/night and the all-weather plane had no machine guns or cannons and I couldn't understand how the A-6 might carry an odd number of the bombs since it seemed to have the racks for the bombs under its wings. But I wasn't sure of anything about the unusual plane, as I'd only seen it vaguely in passing when it had supported us in the past.

Up on that eastern cliff, about halfway south down along the jungle area, they've set up drums again," I said. "Is there any chance your radar might make out what are probably stacks of old fuel drums, and then place something down there to quiet their effect?"

"The eastern rim of this God-awful valley, I presume you mean, and 'quiet their effect,' I like that," Homan replied.

"Affirmative," I transmitted back. "Maybe you can take a pass, and if you see what I'm talking about, then send them a message."

"Drop them a message, I think is more to the point," Homan shot back.

The A-6 completed climbing and curving out of the valley from its last pass, and came down the valley, but this time flying low over the eastern rim. The plane continued on down the valley without dropping anything.

"Tiny collection of something down there looking like a bit of a wasp's nest," Homan said.

"That's got to be it," I replied, hoping even a near-miss with one of the big bombs would silence the things.

"Coming back around," Homan noted.

I waited for the whistling scream of the Intruder's twin turbines to become audible, making no attempt to look up into the almost complete blackness of the new night.

Once the plane flew over, if it came close enough, then the exhaust would flare yellow and red, but even that would be almost impossible to make out unless it was very low. The bomb would not have to be delivered from a very low altitude, unlike the bombing of the jungle hit so effectively only a few minutes earlier.

There was nothing visible, as I watched the area where I thought the top of the canyon wall had to be, just across the river and then partway down the lower portion of the jungle area.

A great flash went up, followed by a crack of thunder. Showers of red hot sparks flew outward from the partially illuminated cliff wall and it hit me instantly what was happening. The bomb had been dropped close enough to the side of the cliff to shatter and blow much of the material from the rim down into the valley below. Great staccato rattling, thudding, and breaking branch sounds rolled across the river from the jungle area. If the big bombs hadn't done their job when they'd been dropped, run after run, then the rock shrapnel, not dissimilar from the debris we'd blown from the other side of the canyon, might just have done the job.

There were no drum sounds, following the attack.

"How's the music down there?" Homan asked.

"Thanks," I sent back, not being able to describe how good it felt to have the A-6 do what it had done, from beginning to end.

"We'll be back in a jiffy with a reload and carrying a box lunch," Homan said, his dry humor there, but nearly undetectable.

The A-6 would take hours to reload, refuel and make the round trip to Da Nang I knew but it was still good to know the Intruder would be returning.

one-hundred-forty

THE TWENTY-EIGHTH NIGHT : THIRD PART

Whole Man and his A-6 Intruder were gone, and the jungle below was silent, as well as the drums mounted on what was left of the upper lip of the cliff. The lack of the mind-numbing drumbeats was balanced by the emptiness I felt over losing what air support we'd had until the Intruder might, or might not, return later in the night. How many had been lost of Sugar Daddy's platoon to accomplish the resupply, and getting McInerney's body back to the rear? The enemy fifty caliber machine gun had to have taken an awful toll in being able to penetrate both sides of the bridge's metal structure. The river's depth and flow almost assured that some Marines likely hit had been lost in its waters. The firing had been very extensive, and directed only at the crossing Marines and not the resupply chopper at all. Whether the NVA leaders had determined they wanted to avoid the withering fire of the Cobra Commander Turk, and his squadron of Cobras, to preserve the gun, or whether their reasoning was about something else I couldn't know. There was also no way, particularly in the dark, the enemy could have known about the addition of the 81 mm mortars to our inventory. They had to know the Ontos was pinned down, and the dangers we ourselves faced in calling in another 175 mission. The accuracy and murderous effect of the mortar fire had to have taken them completely by surprise.

Had the fifty caliber been neutralized, and if it had then why was there no RPG rocket fire that might have accompanied the machine gun attack, or even come blasting in after? Another unanswered and unanswerable question.

The moon was gone. The clouds were gathering and a pre-misting wind was blowing across the river from the other side. It was only a matter of time until the monsoon rains began to fall again. There was no point in my moving to the stern, or rear, of the bridge, as the bodies would come over, those that were recoverable, the wounded and the dead. I was not needed for that operation, as Jurgens would remain where he was. Another medivac chopper would have to be called in for those survivors who were still alive and could survive into the next day.

I instinctively felt the small bulge in the right thigh pocket where my morphine supply was located. It was then that I realized that I hadn't thought to get my letter home to the chopper I'd been able to rough out earlier. Two days earlier. I felt bad that the actions at the bottom of the A Shau had taken all of my attention away from any thoughts about home and my wife and daughter. I'd been able to write home almost every day of my stay in Vietnam and wanted my track record to be perfect. It was possible that she, after twenty-eight days, was only now receiving the first letters I'd written. There was no way to predict what happened to the mail any of us put on the chopper. Was it delayed in delivery at some point of departure from Vietnam, or somewhere else along the way? Was the normal damaged envelope and soggy paper available used as an excuse by the military, or even the U.S. Postal Service to toss the letters, or what remained of them?

I could not wait for the butcher's bill on the bridge action. The Gunny was covering the mudflat beneath the wall we'd used for fragmentation the night before. That area was from where the next attack would have to be launched. There was no way to safely cross the river using the bridge. Two M-60s could easily defend the fifteen-foot span of rushing water racing around the displaced rear of the bridge. That was, of course, if the bridge didn't move again, which it was bound to do at some time soon. I knew Jurgens was experienced enough to have pulled down the makeshift cargo nets.

My place was spotting for the Ontos, as I had done before. There were no real commands to issue, as the river covered our eastern flank, and the flooding inlet connection to it kept the enemy from charging across the distance from Hill 975 (except for the shallows that ran thinly over the area near the wall everyone had come to call the mud-flats). An attack from the rear, through the jungle below in the south, was fairly easy to defend because of the difficulty of moving through it, the open area and the ability of the Ontos to turn and fire flechette rounds down the open area nearly instantly also secured that area from any large scale attack.

The expected night assault came without warning, other than a line of green tracers coming out of the lower part of the mountain to begin working back and forth across the edge of jungle both Marine companies were set up to defend. I checked my watch again, trying to somehow force, or at least urge, the dawn to come faster.

There had been no report coming from the river on casualties, and that fact alone meant the results were probably not good. That, plus the fact that I was growing ever more uncomfortable with our position. We had defended the nearly undefendable for some time. How long would it be before the NVA forces downriver attacked from the jungle they were no doubt spending plenty of time and energy digging through and under? A coordinated attack from all three sides, north, south and from across the bridge would spread our defensive fire capability way too thin, even with the 81s, the Ontos and the M-60s laying down heavy fire from the load of ammunition that had been unloaded from the resupply chopper. There was one other factor that the A-6 had reminded me of. The ridges running nearly a thousand feet up along both sides of the canyon on both sides of the river. If the NVA accessed the western ridge, up and above the face we had used to rain rock shrapnel down on the mudflat, then they would have a fourth element of raining plunging fire into our totally exposed position below. There would be no surviving such a four-pronged attack. The attacks on two fronts could not be repulsed forever, even if resupply came in almost every day or night, and that was simply not a possibility unless there was some other way to funnel in massive ammunition supplies I'd never heard of.

The Gunny had the mortars targeting the mudflat, and when the first wave of attackers came their fire was murderously effective, but I could not help but count the rounds expended. There would be little left in the more than likely event of another attack. The Ontos cut the remaining attackers to pieces by firing six of its remaining flechette rounds, under my direction. The enemy attack failed again, and I wondered about the seemingly inexhaustible number of soldiers the enemy had. It was disconcerting, with an added touch of fear. I had Hutzler reload with high explosives once more and then got the Gunny up on the command net. The mortars needed to cover the eastern edge of the next attack and force the enemy to get closer to the wall. The Ontos fire would use the wall to be even more effective in reaching down to kill the exposed crawling soldiers attacking thereby saving as many flechette rounds as possible.

The Gunny surprisingly asked me to come to his position at the wall, which at first I was hesitant to do. That was until a few minutes later when the battery in the Starlight Scope failed.

"Where's the extra battery?" I asked Fessman, who normally carried several for the scope.

"That was the extra battery," he replied, disappointment evident in his voice.

I breathed in and out deeply. Resupply could have easily included more batteries if they'd been ordered. The batteries were small and weighed next to nothing, but they were special and there was no replacement for them. The instrument that had been so decisive in helping us direct our fire at just the right time and just the right place was now useless. We were as blind as the enemy, but with about three thousand, or more, fewer men.

The Gunny called. The fifty had opened up from its mountain burrowed lair again, which was evident without the Gunny's report. The gun crew of the mortars could adjust fire but they needed a forward observer who could call and adjust precision fire without wasting rounds.

I hadn't been exposed to the fifty's fire in some time. My position in my foxhole at the river had been completely protected by a berm of earth and mud even the Soviet fifty rounds could not penetrate all the way through. The Marines crossing the bridge had had no such protection. My current position did not allow for the mountain-positioned heavy machine gun to traverse east enough to angle toward me. I didn't want to move to the wall and become a target of the gun's direct fire, but I knew I had no choice. The Marines manning the mortars didn't want just any forward observer. They wanted me, which under any other circumstance would have made me feel some warmth and pride, instead of dread and fear.

I moved, crawling through the clearing on my belly, with Fessman trailing close behind and Nguyen off to one side and just ahead. There was no moving fast anywhere along the route, open or not. The enemy fire could come at any time from the jungle edge that ran along on the downriver side, not more than fifty meters distant. By the time I reached the Gunny's position, guided in by Nguyen, the fifty was no longer firing.

"We need to shut that thing down, and then fire on the eastern flat to push them into the wall when they come," the Gunny said.

I said nothing to the Gunny about the fact that my conclusion, made earlier, was exactly the same as his own. Instead, I squatted down next to him and went to work to dig a little hole to heat up some water and make coffee. The coffee wasn't to slake any thirst but to make a place in time to talk. The fifty was temporarily quiet, but my hands still shook, while unlimbering my canteen holder and then pouring some water into it. The Gunny, as I hoped, provided a chunk of the composition B explosive for the fire, and then took out a cigarette and lit it with his Zippo.

My crawl up the open space, bare from the river to the cliff face, had been tiring but also strange because there was a certain unsettled silence that had seemed to radiate out from the Marines I'd passed. The Gunny wasn't being as open as he usually was, either, I noted. The re-supply had been a success, but there had to be something going on.

I got the explosive lit down inside my small hole in the jungle floor. There was plenty of brush between our position and that of the NVA force out across the killing field of the mudflat, and the small inlet of fast-flowing water, to make it nearly impossible for the enemy to see either the Gunny's cigarette glow or the small reflection of the fire burning up against the bottom of my blackened canteen holder of water.

"You going to tell me?" I asked, noting that this time the Gunny wasn't in a sharing mood with his cigarette.

"We took a bad hit at the bridge," he replied, the tone of his voice flat and unemotional.

"The fifty, as they intended," I came back, not knowing what else to do other than wait for the report of casualties he possessed. It seemed everyone else had that information too, except for me. I'd hoped for good news there, although I'd suspected that the numbers might be high.

"Twenty-seven," The Gunny finally said, his voice almost too low for me to hear.

"How many KIA?" I asked, afraid of the answer.

Twenty-seven was more than half the table of organization personnel called for, and Sugar Daddy's platoon hadn't been fully up to standard in size.

"All of them," the Gunny replied, "They were all behind the bridge, using it for cover as they crossed, and they're gone. No need for a chopper recovery. The fifty rounds lanced on through the thin steel, taking them out one after another, like it was made of waterproof cardboard instead of solid steel, except for Sugar Daddy. He was up top running all over trying to do something to save his men, but there was nothing to be done. The mortars worked great, finally, but you couldn't get them up and adjusted in time to save those men."

"Sugar Daddy?" I asked, a shot of adrenalin going straight

through my body, from top to bottom.

"Sugar Daddy?" I asked again, but already knowing the answer.

"Dead as a doornail," the Gunny went on, in his same flat tone, one that seemed uncaring. But I'd come to know something of the extraordinary sergeant over time, and I knew he was covering up his own loss by layering an analytical coat over everything he said.

"Jurgens got his body off the bridge, which is a story in and of itself," the Gunny droned on, finally offering his cigarette to me.

I took it in my shaking left hand, but didn't inhale, trying to hold the lit thing in one hand and balance my heating water in the other. We'd just lost almost one-eighth of the Marines we had in both companies, which amounted to the worst night of KIA loss I'd experienced since coming into country.

"They blame me," I finally said, placing the canteen holder on the ground.

I inhaled from the cigarette and then handed it back.

"It was your plan," the Gunny replied. "Funny, it was one of the rare ones that didn't have a screwy name. Maybe we could call it The Night of the Living Dead now, except there's no living about it."

"They blame me," I said again, this time my fear rising like a thick ropey mass moving from my lower gut on up to my chest.

I could not survive the Marines blaming me and I knew it in my core.

"No, that's the funny part," the Gunny replied. "They feel sorry for you. Even the survivors of his platoon think Sugar Daddy thought you saved them all from Jurgens' platoon and then from the enemy. There's no logic in this horrible valley."

The Marines didn't blame me. I felt able to breathe again. I played the Gunny's words back and forth in my mind, once more heating my coffee although I had no coffee packet or creamer, for that matter. The Gunny wasn't offering any. I decided that it was too dark for him to see my predicament, although the glow of my still burning explosive fire sort of blew a hole in that explanation. The Marines didn't blame me. The Gunny blamed me. How could I have predicted that they'd get the damned fifty-caliber up and operational again, or that it would take aim at the vulnerably positioned Marines instead of the heavily defended supply chopper? How could I have had more control to get the mortars set up faster and then adjust fire with Marines if I had no idea might even be able to accept and understand fire direction orders? I closed my eyes and took a swig of the too hot water, with about as much substance in it as was in my own heart.

I thought of defensive arguments to come back at the Gunny with. We had to have the supply mission and it had to land where it did, and then we had to have Marines get over to it and lug the supplies back. None of us could have survived the night without that resupply load of ammo, water and more. But, I knew it was useless. For the first time in my month in-country, and combat, I started to understand and deeply feel the terrible burden of inescapable responsibility, accountability, and also the guilt of commanding men who then died performing their very best to obey those commands, no matter how misguided or misplaced the rationality forming the decisions to make the commands might be, or in this case, might have been.

"Where's his body, or did it go over the side too?" I asked, pushing my hot canteen down next to the expiring fire to fry and squish some emerging leeches from the muddy runnels that squeezed up between the leafy and crushed fern material of the beaten-down jungle floor.

I assumed that there were no bodies to transport because the men had been hit with not only the fifty ammo but with the shrapnel it would have created in penetrating both sides of the bridge, and then hitting them with splashes of molten steel and small razor-sharp bits of whatever else the bullets were comprised of. Some of the Marines might even have lived, at least until they were swept under the bridge and then downriver to drown alone in the middle of the night.

"The body's in your foxhole back at the river, where I instructed them to put if for safekeeping," the Gunny replied.

I turned to look around me. Fessman's eyes were glistening, and I wondered if he was crying. Sugar Daddy had been a Marine piece of work but he'd been such a force of nature in the company that it was hard to imagine the company going on without him. Nguyen was just next to and back from Fessman. I looked into what I could see of his eyes. He nodded ever so slightly back toward the river. I knew instantly what he was communicating. I nodded back by lowering my chin slightly. The Montagnard disappeared in the night, as was his habit. He was going to recover my pack and other belongings I'd left in the hole. If it was the Gunny's plan that I be shamed by having to return and displace Sugar Daddy's body to get my stuff, well, at least I wouldn't have to face that.

"I wrote Jurgens up for a star and sent it off on a chopper to the battalion," I said, to make talk, but also to try to openly discuss rewarding Sugar Daddy for the bravery he'd demonstrated time and again, once he'd come to accommodate me as the company commander.

"I don't trust battalion to give him a damn thing," I went on. "I don't want to send Sugar Daddy's recommendation there. Is there another solution?"

"Send them to Headquarters Marine Corps," the Gunny answered. "Send it to the commandant himself. Chapman."

"I don't know the address there," I replied, not knowing what else to say, and not having expected the Gunny to reply at all.

"Eighth and I, the postal service will do the rest."

"Eighth and I?" I asked. "What kind of address is that?"

"It's the oldest Marine post on the planet," the Gunny said. "He'll get it. It's where Eighth Street and I Street intersect in Arlington, Virginia. You'll find, if you ever make it back into the world, that the United States Postal Service is the Marine Corps of postal delivery. They'll get almost every one of those strange letters you send home all the time, and they'll for damn sure get the citation to the commandant."

"Will he award the decorations if he gets them, at that high level?" I asked, more to keep him engaged and talking than because I wanted, or needed, to know.

"Hell yes," the Gunny replied, the flatness leaving his voice, "because no officers have the balls to go all the way around the chain of command to do such a career-ending thing. But we don't have careers to worry about anymore and God knows you have the balls."

It was still dead dark minutes later when the fourth attack began, but this time everything was different. We had no Starlight Scope to see in the dark. I could not direct the Ontos fire and from our position near the wall, none of us could see anything across the blackness of the mudflat. The attack gave itself away because the soldiers running and crawling were firing their AK assault rifles. The fifty remained silent, as it could not fire blindly through its own attacking force.

The difference was that the Intruder was back, and along with it, 'Whole Man,' our bombardier and navigator. Homan did all the talking on the radio, but without Thompson flying the controls, the plane would never have been able, time after time, to save me and the Marines around me. The rapid turn-around the Intruder made from the carrier was just another proof of that. I knew the plane, some called the flying drumstick, could not stay up as long as the Skyraiders, and I missed Cowboy and his fellow pilots whenever they could not be overhead. But the Skyraiders could not be there at night. They were not day/night all-weather ground attack aircraft like the Intruder. In order to be back overhead in less than three hours, the A-6 had no doubt set some sort of record in loading ordnance, and then flying both legs of the trip at maximum speed. Homan and Thompson cared, as the men on the carrier had to care, and without any of us talking about it on the ground under them, I knew it. That knowledge injected hope and warmth through the core of radiating fear and pain I had come to live with. I could only hope the Marines around me felt the same way.

Homan didn't bring the plane in at high altitude, dive down and then pull up steeply to unload the huge bombs the plane had carried in its earlier runs. These bombs were the smaller ones, but the delivery of them was entirely different. The Intruder came in down the river as the Skyraiders had done in many of their previous raids, but the Intruder seemed even lower than the big radial powered propeller aircraft. The first run was across the lower jungle on the other side of the river, and the plane seemed to drop six or eight of the smaller, but still violently concussing weapons. The ripple effect of the explosions and muted but brilliant fireworks of their effect was undeniably spectacular. The enemy had a disadvantage when it came to trying to deal with Thompson and Homan. They were in a fixed position, even if dug in fairly securely. The constant rearrangement of the jungle above them had to be disconcerting, if not wounding or killing. The second pass of the Intruder was entirely different after I got on the AN-323 and let Homan know in detail about the mudflat just south of the mountain running on our side of the inlet feeding inlet water between our position and that of Hill 975.

Somehow the A-6 was able to fly low across the top of the canyon lip in the east and then drop right down to scream in about fifty or sixty feet above the mudflat. The break in the cliff face, allowing the water to flow from deeper in the canyon complex walls into the Bong Song, proved to be wide enough to let the Intruder fly through.

The string of bombs that came down proved to be much larger and longer than the string dropped to level the lower jungle area. The bombs exploded so much closer that, once again, all of us waiting and watching only a couple of hundred meters away were forced deeper into the muddy jungle surface by the sweeping concussion waves. Jungle debris scattered and fell down upon everyone anywhere close.

How long could the Intruder stay and why could God not let the light fall down into our cursed and killing valley sooner?

I lay in the muck of oozing mud seeping slowly up through the packed, cracked and broken debris of jungle and aging decay. The smell was of the damaged sort I'd come to know as my home away from home down inside the A Shau Valley expanse. I wondered if the smell would ever leave me, should I somehow have the good fortune to survive my experience in actual combat. I'd come late to discover that I, inadvertently, had built the confidence of the Marines around to such an extent that they had gone from being 'dead men walking' to believers that they might make it through the Vietnam war experience and one day go home without serious disfigurement or injury. I had, however, not built up that belief system inside myself. No matter what I did in the few moments of rest or reverie that I had it was impossible for me to believe that I could survive another year under such conditions.

The dawn came creeping up and over the far eastern wall of the canyon rim, with the first tendrils of light visible only like a faint glow across the clouded sky that had to signal a return to monsoon rains. The respite through the night had been too long and too good. The enemy would be able to use the monsoon rain during the next night to cloak another of its relentless attacks, and very likely a fully coordinated and successful one. I peered upward, toward the top of the western lip of that canyon wall but could see nothing. It was time to move from our position, I knew, and a plan was beginning to form in the back of my mind for our next survival attempt.

I knew also that the upper edge of the western face of the cliff that hung over us could not remain out of the building series of coming attacks for long. Supporting artillery fire could reach up to, across, and deep past that rim, but not accurately. Once the 175 rounds were fired they did not have the arc to go over or to one side or the other of Hill 975. The rim was basically untouchable by artillery. Air support was only truly available in the daylight hours, and then only if the monsoon rains were not at their heaviest. The enemy had time on its side. The NVA commanders could wait for the rain, risk the inaccurate fire of the

175s, and then take and settle onto the top of the rim. From there, all night long, they could fire at a high angle downward into our position. That kind of uncommon fire was called 'plunging fire' in training, and it was to be avoided at all costs, at least being on the receiving end of such devastating fire. The enemy wouldn't have to be able to see well in such a position. All the machine gunners had to do was point down at the darkness of the jungle below and fire away.

Our ability to truly dig in, as the enemy did so well, to prevent getting hit, was actually non-existent. We had neither the equipment nor the time to get deep under the jungle's surface. Since the rim would eventually fall to the enemy, or they would decide to risk high losses in acquiring it at some time, that meant the only way out was to attack up the valley until reaching either friendly forces or the DMZ itself. Surviving such a charge did not even bear considering. It wasn't an option unless suicide was a part of the bargain. No, the only way out was in crossing the Bong Song once again, while the bridge was still there, and then preparing and executing a plan to move from the relative safety from under the lower lip of the wall, climb the difficult but scalable cliff further downriver, and then return to the area of Go Noi Island whence we'd come. At least there, and possibly only there, could our advantage in having artillery always on hand and on target allow some of us to survive until we might finally be relieved. Our orders were to remain where we were and wait to be reinforced, but it wouldn't make much difference if the enemy continued its current buildup with its concentration on us in our trapped position.

We'd not only lost Sugar Daddy in the night at the bridge, but we'd also lost twenty-seven more Marines from his platoon KIA, as well as six wounded. We needed another medevac and resupply. If we made it across the river once again, then we'd need more beehive ammo for the Ontos, which brought up the Ontos subject front and center into my thinking.

When night fell on the 29th of September there would be no supporting fires able to be of much assistance, save the A-6 if it came in to bomb the hell of the same jungle it had become accustomed to bombing. But, even recurring flights up around and back into the valley by Homan and Thompson in the A-6 were not going to prevent the NVA from attacking in force across the open area. The NVA had shown no resistance at all to facing machine gunfire out in the open, no matter how suicidal such attacks might seem. At night, everything was changed. Without a Starlight scope on every M-60 covering the mud-flat, the machine guns could only approximate where the enemy might be as they came at us.

I brought Nguyen and Fessman in close and let them know we were headed back toward the river. I hoped that my protected foxhole there was still undamaged and available. The move was uneventful, as we crept low past the Marines who'd emplaced themselves in jerry-rigged foxholes made from gathering the jungle debris and surrounding them-selves with it. The Skyraider's early first pass had shut down all fire from the enemy and their fifty caliber machine gun had not been heard from since the last strike of the Ontos against it. The foxhole was dry and Sugar Daddy's body was nowhere to be seen. I was unsure of what I would have done if it was still there.

I called for the Gunny and Jurgens. Sergeant Trath had imme-diately stepped into Sugar Daddy's overly large shoes, or so I'd heard. He was the senior Buck Sergeant in that platoon and, although I could over-rule the decision promoting him, I was not about to.

The jungle did not offer anything resembling cut timber, or the ability to make such from the wood of the many species of trees grow-ing around us. The Bishopwood was our best hope, I knew, as it was the dominant species in our area of the A Shau. The trunks of the trees, referred to as 'bitchwood' trees by the Marines around me, due to its nature of splitting after being felled over a period of time, were our best hope to build a structure strong enough to allow the Ontos to climb up on the high end of the bridge and then cross over into its new position. The work of gathering enough fallen trunks, since we had no chainsaws or even conventional manual saws, had to be undertaken immediately, since there was no guarantee that the bridge, in its current precarious position, would stay where it was until the work was done, the Ontos was moved, and then the remaining two companies crossed onto the other side.

My foxhole was as it had been and I felt the first relative comfort that I had felt in some time.

"We need another Starlight scope and batteries on resupply," I murmured to Fessman, my eyes raking back and forth across the river, and then up and down its length, that was barely visible in the astro-nomical dawn that was taking place. It was hard to make out what was real, and I was left wondering if I was adding things I could not see but could remember from my former views of the river scene, a scene that changed but that I could never seem to completely escape from. The Bong Song was not only running up and down through the middle of the A Shau Valley, but it was also running up and down through the very center of my being.

"Get Cowboy up on the AN 323," I ordered Fessman, knowing that I had to somehow bring the Skyraiders in on my plan. It would take their relentless suppression in the coming daylight to not only make it possible for us to build a bridge to the bridge but also to prepare enough cover for the resupply chopper to come back in and deliver what we needed, as well as take out wounded and the dead. I wasn't sure where Sugar Daddy's body was. As the company commander, I was supposed to certify that he was dead, and then sign off for identification and his body's removal from the field of combat. Since we'd lost Rittenhouse, so many days ago, however, the responsibilities for clerk-type activity had fallen to Fessman and some Marines in the individual platoons themselves.

Fessman removed my helmet and the liner under it. The Cowboy's voice came through the tiny speaker from the left side of the headset, as Fessman gently pushed the device down to cover my left ear.

"We've got to do the Mersey thing with the beast while we prepare to build a way for it," I transmitted after Cowboy and I exchanged our normal strange greeting. I did enjoy being called Flash, and I waited for that. I could hear the Skyraiders orbiting high above, and I presumed they were orbiting waiting for us to contact them to let them know what we were doing and for the light to improve. The NVA were not going to miss our attempt to build a ramp to the bridge end but the longer it took for them to figure that out, and then to weigh their own survival against delivering full daylight fire against our effort, the more chance we had in successfully completing that part of the plan.

I waited for a reply from Cowboy. It came in seconds.

"Flash, gotcha, in this place I'll always stay. I presume Godzilla to be that many tongued dragon thing. There will be three of us on station with twenty sorties each if we manage the system. I am also presuming the target as long as you can keep the other end of the deal."

I smiled to myself. Cowboy had gotten it all. He knew the Gerry and the Pacemaker's song so well he'd quoted the first line following mention of ferrying across the Mersey in the song. And he was also saying he couldn't adequately cover the mudflat leading toward where Hill 975 lay toward the west while his planes lined up and delivered near-continuous fire on the jungle where we needed suppression the most.

"Roger that," I replied. "Give us full dawn support and we'll go to work."

"Busy little beavers down there," Cowboy answered. "Standing by to cross the line of departure."

I pulled the headset off, breathing a sigh of relief. Cowboy was using infantry jargon, as there was no 'line of departure' for air support. The Skyraiders could stay in the air for three to four hours without refueling and, if they were judicious, they carried enough ordinance to keep any intelligent enemy's head down. Cowboy was telling me that he would wait for word on when to begin their runs. With three planes they could be overhead, moving down the valley, about every five minutes.

"Get the Gunny, Jurgens, Trath, the other platoon commanders, and the new lieutenants down here," I ordered Fessman.

The Marines on the line guarding both our rear area and the mudflat, where another attack was bound to come from, wouldn't need any leadership or supervision to do what they did so well. With daylight coming, the NVA was not about to rush willy-nilly across a flat open surface area covered by several machine guns. Only soon to be dead people charged machine guns in the real world under such conditions.

I listened to Fessman calling in for the medevac and the resupply and was surprised by the detail he was able to give off the top of his head. There was no mention of Sugar Daddy or the identities of anyone being Medevaced, although the black sergeant's entire being was resurrected before me in the near dark. If I lasted through the years I wondered how I would come to consider the man or any of the Marines around me, and still live. Humanity was a term that could only be applied loosely to any of us, I realized. Training, and even my college major in anthropology, did nothing to explain the descent of modern man and all of his social values when placed in the circumstance we had come to know in the A Shau Valley. Humanity wasn't the proper word at all. The phrase 'wounded, agonized moving protoplasm of the walking dead' was a better fit.

The Gunny was the first to arrive with Jurgens at his elbow. They descended into my expansive foxhole and crawled forward to where I was wedged up against the narrow wall that faced the river. I brought myself down and then turned to face them. Trath showed up but didn't enter the hole, instead choosing to rest up on the bare ground, where Nguyen and Fessman were already ensconced. I began laying out my new plan, hoping that some solution as to how the downed trunks of the bitch trees could be found, somehow hewn to fit, and then transported to the river bank for installation. It was going to take a lot of tree trunks to make it work because the Ontos could only be expected to climb a certain grade, and although I didn't know that maximum grade I presumed it wasn't too great, given the weight distribution of the tracked vehicle.

"We're going to have to move a lot of dirt here," I said, without any preamble.

The Gunny stared at me, making no effort or sound in response. I could barely make him and the other men out in the poor light, but I knew I had their full attention. I breathed in and out deeply. I had to bring them into the plan, not just order it I realized or we'd never make it by the time the light of day came and then went into the next deadly night.

"We can't stay on this side of the river and live," I began. "They're going to eventually take and hold the top of the rim. We can't survive plunging fire from up there and I don't have accurate enough artillery to destroy them. Airpower works in the day but this next night might be our last unless we get across the river, hold up under the cliff, as before, and then fight our way back to the glacis downriver and beat our way back up to the top of the cliff. From there we return to Ga Noi Island and move toward An Hoa. There's no relief coming down the valley that's going to get past Hill 975. The NVA has had too much time to dig, fortify, supply, and then dig and fortify some more. Today we build a buttress to get the Ontos up onto the bridge and across. The Ontos is the key to our night time success on the other side. Resupply and the medevac are coming in this afternoon."

"How do we build this buttress?" Trath asked.

I looked up at the sergeant intently. There was the glint of intellect in his eyes, and I realized he was not going to be any Sugar Daddy in leading the platoon, and the platoon had lost so many it was also little more than two squads, way down in number from what it had been when I'd joined the company.

"We use Bitchwood fallen trees to form a lattice platform frame. We fill that with dirt. Eight feet by eight feet by three. Then we build a second platform just beyond the first, this one six feet high. The bridge edge is about eight feet off the riverbank. We can lay trunks from the bottom up to the edge using the two platforms to have an angle the Ontos should be able to power up and over."

I waited when I was done. The AN 323 headset was still on my head but there was no radio traffic.

"You think there are enough fallen trees in this jungle?" the Gunny asked into the silence.

"We have explosives to make more," I replied, hoping we had enough and hoping the Gunny would buy into the plan.

The two lieutenants finally appeared, moving to lay next to Trath at the edge of the hole.

"You know," the Gunny said, "if we just blow down a bunch of these trees and then dragged them to the edge and packed them down with the Ontos we might not need to haul any dirt at all, particularly since the dirt is really more mud than anything else."

I pictured the Gunny's solution in my mind for a few seconds, not nearly so happy with his variation of the plan as I was that he appeared to be all-in when it came to crossing the river again and making our way back to An Hoa without any orders to do so, and likely orders that would be coming to not do so.

"We can drag the trees with the Ontos and we've got plenty of Marines to manipulate the things into a great growing pile near the end of the bridge," the Gunny stated, obviously thinking his plan through.

I pulled the headset off and handed it up to Fessman. The light was good enough to see everyone.

"Let's go to work," I said, hoping that the Gunny's plan would be at least as good as my own when it came to getting the Ontos across the water, given that the bridge didn't move again and the enemy could be kept sufficiently suppressed to allow the Marines doing the work to survive while they did it.

"Call Cowboy," I instructed Fessman. "Tell him to begin his runs in half an hour. "And you two," I said, pointing at the two new lieutenants with my right index finger. "One of you get back to the Ontos and let them know what's going on and the other one go to the wall and make sure that end of things is not coming off the rails."

"I'm not sure about this crossing of the river, Junior," Jurgens said when the lieutenants were gone, his voice almost too low to hear.

"Other than I need you to go over and provide security at the other end of the bridge and for the coming resupply, what don't you understand?" I replied, with an edge to my voice, wondering what was going to happen without the strange balance of Jurgens and Sugar Daddy fighting over just about everything.

Jurgens simply glared at me, his eyes tiny shining pools of light coming out of the near darkness.

"You get over and dig in at the other end of the bridge," I went on. "No more using the bridge for protection, and dig in well enough so that fifty, should they get it up and operational and should we be unable to suppress its fire, can't get to you."

"What's the name of this plan?" Fessman asked, hanging over the lip of the foxhole, hanging onto the headset of the air radio.

"Ferry, Cross the Mersey," I replied, thinking of Cowboy and how easy it was to communicate with him, and he wasn't even in front of me.

"What's a Mersey?" Fessman asked as if reading my mind.

"Think of the Bong Song and the rock and roll song," I replied, patiently, but wanting to move on as quickly as we could. I had little confidence that we would be able to build what was needed to get the Ontos to the other side before nightfall, and I had a bad feeling about the coming of night.

One single thump and then radiating vibration came from across the river. It was a single drum beat. The NVA was rebuilding its drum base, although not likely in the same place the old location had been. The single thump was followed seconds later by another identical thump. It was going to be a long day, I realized.

[audio src="https://straussshortstories.s3-us-west-2.amazonaws.com/JungleDrum2.mp3"]

"Gunny," I said, between drum beats. "I want every bit of fire we take today answered by M-60 fire of our own, so distribute the man accordingly. The NVA is

going to figure out what we are up to and that's going to make them pretty mad since I'm certain they have an extinction plan for us they can't wait to apply tonight."

"Okay, that's it, let's go," I said.

Gunny and Jurgens didn't move.

I didn't move either, having expected some blowback on my decision to get us out of our current situation by changing positions again so dramatically.

"Call battalion and tell them what we're planning," I said to the

Gunny.

"Can we talk about that, Junior?" the Gunny replied, although his tone wasn't argumentative in the least.

"Talk," I said.

"That glacis, the cliff, just how in hell are we supposed to get up there without losing half our Marines?"

"The 175s," I answered, before going on. "The 175's cannot fire down along the face of the eastern wall, so we can't take any hits there unless an errant round impacted all the way up on top of the plateau. I'll rain a zone fire down into the valley while we're climbing out and that ought to play hell with any concentrated sniper or machine gunfire."

"I don't like it, Junior," Jurgens said.

"You know they're coming tonight," I replied, trying to keep the tone of my voice unemotional. "And you know they're coming in force. We have no Starlight Scope and our mortar ammo supply is extremely limited. We get across and then get resupplied and wait for just the right moment to go downriver. They're not going to be expecting this since they've likely been listening to the promises of battalion along with us. There is no way they'll think we might disobey orders and go the other way or fail to hold our position. If you call battalion it's up to you, but I wouldn't say anything about our plan over the radio."

"I didn't think of that," Jurgens murmured. "Everyone knows what happened and nobody wants to cross that bridge, including me," he went on.

"We're Marines," I replied, not knowing what else to say. "Tell your Marines about the attack were going to put together, and how we're going to go through that jungle-like shit through a goose."

"We're going to get even for Sugar Daddy?" he said, some level of strange hope in his voice.

"That's right," the Gunny joined in, "now get your Marines ready. You need to go now before its full light. Take them by surprise. The enemy knows full well it hurt the hell out of us last night and they won't be quite ready."

Jurgens climbed out of the hole without saying another word.

"Get even for Sugar Daddy?" I asked, total disbelief in my tone, once Jurgens was out of earshot.

"It works," the Gunny replied, "not that I'm at all certain that Ferry Cross the Mersey will. How confident are you?"

"About the same as you," I said. "But we can't stay here and we can't move up along the side of Hill 975 anymore. They're ready for that, in spades."

I pulled out MacInerney's flashlight and turned it on, getting a 1-25,000 map of our area from my thigh pocket. I leaned close into the Gunny and then pointed down at our position, which I'd marked with a small black "X" days before. "We don't leave our position tomorrow until we have plenty of air support. We attack down the river, through the jungle and along the lower base of the cliff, but this time we have almost four hundred Marines instead of what we had before. And we have the 81 mortars too, after resupply."

"Is resupply coming?" the Gunny asked, which surprised me. Usually, the man was totally up on all radio traffic, especially on the combat net. Fessman had called it in, I was certain since I'd heard a good part of his transmission.

"You think they'd say they were coming and not show?" I asked, in shock.

"It's happened," the Gunny replied. "Our mortality rate has to be about the worst in this war and who wants to come to that party?"

I stopped talking and waited for more, but Gunny had stopped talking also. There was no way I was going to believe that the air guys, chopper pilots, the Skyraider team or even Homan and Thompson would fail to show if they said they were coming. They would have to be dead not to show. I wondered where the Gunny had been and what had happened when he'd somehow failed to get the promised air support he thought was coming, but I wasn't going to ask.

The Gunny pulled out a cigarette and lit it while I waited in silence, the light increasing ever so slightly down at the bottom of my hole. He took a couple of deep drags and then handed the cigarette to me.

"For Sugar Daddy and his men, and for the success of the Mersey thing," he unexpectedly said.

I took the cigarette and puffed a few times without coughing. The Gunny climbed out of the hole, what was left of his cigarette snapped sparking up into the dim morning light.

I stood and motioned Fessman to me.

"You put the order in for resupply and getting the wounded out and received a positive response?" I asked.

"Yes, sir," Fessman shot right back. "I would have told you right away if they weren't coming at 1400 sir. Can I turn on my radio?"

I replied in the affirmative, wondering what my next step was to be or if the Gunny was going to implement the taking down of the trees and the stacking process that would have to take place down near the end of the bridge. If the plan didn't work to get the Ontos across the bridge then the rest of the plan would fall to pieces since we could not hold the clefts under the face of the canyon wall against overwhelming forces coming at us from every direction in the night without the Ontos and night vision gear.

"You have a letter that came in, sir," Fessman said, handing me a folded over white envelope.

"What" was all I could say, taking the envelope in my shaking right hand, hoping it was from my wife, but it wasn't I realized instantly. I switched on MacInerney's flashlight once more. The letter was from the Department of the Army.

Fessman's radio began its tinny play. Brother John introduced one of the first songs of the day. A song called The Letter played, and as the first words came through the air, driven with power by a strong melody of guitar chords I almost shook my head in weary disappointment: "Gimme a ticket for an aeroplane, ain't got time to take a fast train. Lonely days are gone, I'm a-goin' home, my baby, just wrote me a letter."

I pulled the single sheet of yellow paper from the envelope. The letter wasn't a letter at all. It was a telegram placed inside an envelope. Tersely, the letter explained that my brother, a second lieutenant in the Army, serving down in Bien Hoa much further south in Vietnam, had been badly wounded and was in the hospital in Yokohama, Japan. Condition Serious, Prognosis Fair.

The song played on, as I sat, leaning against the side of my foxhole, vaguely listening to lyrics that told me I had to get back, but there was no going back, not for me now, and quite likely not for me ever.

The drums beat again, the reverberating vibrations rushing through the air and down into the valley where I sat, pushed against the foxhole wall, alone in a world of hurt and loss, my hand clutching a cold uncaring telegram against my chest. My own letters home would be on the resupply chopper or I would die getting them aboard. It was all I had left. The drums beat again in the far distance and then again inside my foxhole.

one-hundred-forty-two

THE TWENTY-NINTH DAY : SECOND PART

No fewer than fifty Marines worked to drag the downed trees and jungle foliage up to the end of the bridge, and then secure it to the structure using the ropes that had been tied to make a cargo net for unloading the last resupply chopper and getting the supplies across the bridge and onto the near bank. The Gunny guided the Ontos, while small explosive sounds came across from behind my foxhole position, in one staccato run after another. There would be plenty of trees, but would the wildly chaotic structure that was being assembled be enough to allow the Ontos to ride up on the bridge itself, and then cross to the other side?

The twelfth Skyraider sortie was coming down the valley. Each of the giant-engined beasts flew as low as possible over the churning floodwaters of the Bong Song.

The rain had begun coming down in a steady series of sheets, with a mild wind driving the sheets over the lip of the eastern wall and then down into the valley and right across the river. It was hypnotic to watch the sheets approach. Fessman and Nguyen had worked to get our poncho covers linked and pegged down, with shallow runnels of water tracing their way around the foxhole to make sure the mildly flooding mud bank did not fill the bottom of the hole.

There had been no fire from the jungle, nor had any fire come out of the dug-in tunnel exits of Hill 975 across the free fire mudflat near the canyon wall on our other flank. First light had come and gone an hour earlier, although the sun had not risen high enough above the dense cloud cover to allow great visibility down in the valley. The rain sheets came and what light there was seemed to lessen appreciably when they struck. The hard-working Marines were fully visible to me but would most probably remain still unseen by the enemy filling the jungle area just downriver from our position. The NVA would know by now what we were doing, but possibly not why, and it was still unlikely, I felt, that they would have figured out we were about to come back across a river we'd crossed only a short time earlier.

The Gunny rushed up the small berm from the back of the bridge where the Marines worked with the Ontos to my foxhole. Both he and his radio operator slipped under the poncho tarps. With Fessman and Nguyen already occupying the hole, along with myself, it was decidedly crowded, and the Gunny and his radioman were both sopping wet. I motioned with my eyes toward the back where Nguyen was pressed against the far rough surface. He caught my look and was gone in seconds, his departure only noticed by Fessman and me.

"This part may work, as long as the Skyraiders can stay on station pounding them down," the Gunny said, unloading a dry towel from his pack and then wiping his neck and face.

"It's got to work and work pretty fast," I replied, peering back out to try to take in the mess of piles of trees and other debris that seemed to heap up and cover the back end of the bridge.

"What about the water rushing three feet deep around the back of the bridge?" I inquired.

"We intertwined a lot of the smaller tree trunks into the cargo net you made," the Gunny replied, working to light a cigarette and then hunkering down to the bottom of the hole to go to work and make a cup of coffee. "When the Ontos goes up the pile, which is going to be higher than the lip of the bridge, it'll press down everything. It weighs almost ten tons."

"I worry about the center of gravity," I replied. "The guns weigh about three hundred pounds each, not including the fifty caliber siting rifles. That's a ton of weight added to the turret. If the Ontos goes over, then it is lost and we may be lost with it."

"It's your plan," the Gunny said, finally getting his cigarette lit. When he began heating his water the explosive we all used in place of heat tabs gave off its smoke and odor. Between the cigarette smoke and the burning Composition B fumes, the foxhole was almost uninhabitable.

"It's my plan but you're working hard to implement it," I replied, trying to be as diplomatic as possible. "Will the modification you made, of simply heaping all that jungle trash in one place, serve to allow a ten-ton vehicle to climb up and reach the back of the bridge?"

"There's no telling," the Gunny replied. "They're working away at it. We didn't have the time to build platforms and then lay down carefully cut tree trunks for the Ontos to drive up on. The riverbank mud would never hold anyway, even with what forms we could fashion. Either this works or it doesn't."

"What if it doesn't?" I asked, at wit's end.

"Then you'll come up with another plan," the Gunny replied, sipping his coffee, puffing on his cigarette between swigs.

I had no other plan, as was generally the case. So far, in my time in the valley, there'd usually been just one way out or at least the chance of one way out, and we'd been lucky. Now we had almost a full complement of two companies of Marines, run by three junior lieutenants and a salty war-experienced Gunny, but with very little room in which to operate. Battalion had little knowledge, that it would accept, about our situation. What's more, it didn't seem to care what we did or where we were. Only a little less than a month earlier I had terrible trepidation and fear of not obeying battalion's orders, but now I really never even took the time to think about it. The battalion command post was in the rear with the gear area and its sum total of understanding had been well illustrated when the six actual had sent his best friend, with a delegation, to check on us. The body bags he'd received back had been credited to me personally. The Gunny, and all of the other Marines, save maybe Fessman and Nguyen, didn't understand. We were never going to be relieved, nor taken back into the rear area for rest and recovery.

The Gunny was true to his word, as I watched the Marines work right on through the onset of new waves of heavy rain coming down. The pile grew and lengthened. I realized that the plan might work if the current didn't destroy the base of what was being built before the Ontos could press down hard enough on the whole thing to gain traction and climb the distorted mess of a pile.

The Ontos finally began its run, Hutzler hitting the gas. The tracked vehicle ground its way into the pile of tree trunks, stumps and other jammed together debris the Marines had so painstakingly blown, pulled or scraped from the jungle area near the river. The ten-ton tracked vehicle, powered only by its small 145 horsepower GMC engine, moved very slowly, as it began to climb the mess of the pile that was supposed to act as a ramp.

A Skyraider flew low through the rain, the air misting when it was between the heavy wind-blown sheets. The Skyraiders huge radial engine grew louder and louder until the Ontos motor could not be heard at all. There was a pattern to the Skyraider sorties and this one, whether it was piloted by Cowboy or not, was impossible to ascertain without getting back on the radio, followed that pattern precisely. It let go with a brief shattering stutter of 20 mm cannons mounted in its wings, and then dropped two five hundred pound 'snake-eye' bombs. Then it was gone back up above the thick clouds. The Ontos fought to remain upright as it climbed the pile of wood-studded debris while I literally held my breath.

A line of tracers came out from the jungle. The bombs had fallen, their detonation causing a minor seismic disturbance in the valley, but leaving no following trace that they had gone off at all. The blanketing rain crushed whatever smoke or flying bits and pieces of the jungle, or men there might be, dragging it all back down onto the jungle floor. The NVA were finally figuring out that the Ontos was attempting to cross the bridge. The small arms fire wasn't from a fifty caliber, however, meaning that the Ontos armor could easily handle any rounds that struck its angled surfaces.

Another sortie of Skyraiders came in this time involving two of the aircraft. They seemed to follow one another at an altitude that could not have been more than a hundred feet off the surface of the fast-moving waters of the river. Cowboy had either seen or had reported to him, that the Ontos was at the most critical part of its journey. Once atop the flat steel surface of the bridge, it would transit to the other side of the river in seconds, where it could turn and direct its deadly 106 mm recoilless rounds against anyone, or thing, that fired upon it. The threat of the beehive rounds would do more to suppress enemy fire than the launching of the missiles themselves, I knew.

The Ontos rocked back and forth near the top of the woodpile that I could not consider, even using my imagination, as any kind of ramp. Chunks of jungle spit backward from its grinding treads, Hutzler was keeping his RPMs at maximum so as not to lose what momentum the ungainly vehicle had. There would be no opportunity for Hutzler to escape the Ontos if it plunged into the river and was lost to its fast-flowing and deep currents.

"Another Silver Star," the Gunny had murmured before the Ontos had begun its run. "I wouldn't drive that thing anywhere near that damned river."

To me, it wasn't a Silver Star performance. It was Medal of Honor stuff, but that kind of recommendation would die on some officer's desk somewhere in Washington. The Medal of Honor was awarded politically, and we all knew it. The greatest thing about the award was that the person receiving it was immediately pulled from combat, although the processing of such an outrageous decoration probably took longer than anyone might have left on a combat tour.

It was nearly high noon when the Ontos crested the top of the pile and then lurched forward onto the end of the bridge. From my foxhole, I heard the cheer from the Marines gathered at the river bank. The Gunny came back to my hole at a run, his radioman trailing a bit behind. Everything seemed to be happening at once. The enemy opened up with a serious barrage of small arms fire, two more Skyraiders screamed down the valley and the Ontos built up speed as it crossed the bridge in order to jump the small gap it would need to cross at the other end.

"Idiots," the Gunny hissed out as he slithered under the poncho covers and crawled on hands and knees to my side... We knelt together, taking in the scene before us.

"There's nothing for the NVA to shoot at except for our cheering Marines, but I could not stop them from exposing themselves and cheering. The Ontos is impervious. The enemy might as well be shooting BB guns at it."

I didn't reply, as none was necessary. I presumed that Jurgens and his platoon were dug in on the far side of the bridge, as they'd been ordered to do. Once he and his men had crossed the bridge near dawn, they'd simply disappeared. There was no point calling them on the combat net because there was nothing to say, except wait, and they were already doing that. Their mission was to remain inactive unless the enemy stupidly chose to mount an infantry attack on the Ontos, and then to provide as much counter-fire and boots on the ground support to get the supplies from the expected chopper and up into the clefts under the face of the far canyon wall. Jurgens would also have to provide machine gun coverage for the crossing and arrival of the remaining Marines in both companies.

"I don't want to wait," I said to the Gunny, who had taken out a cigarette and was lighting it. I noted for the first time that his hands shook a bit. The project had taken a toll on him, I realized for the first time and his slightly shaking hands had an effect on me that ran deep. The Gunny was my rock and it didn't feel good at all to think that he might be scared, or deeply affected by what was going on.

"Yeah" the Gunny replied, "Sugar Daddy and the wounded have to be over there when that chopper comes in. There's no way the choppers are going to linger around on such a hot landing zone,"

"What is it?" I asked gently, not looking at the Gunny, concentrating on the final run of the Ontos as it came up to speed, and then quickly drove across the bridge to jump to the other side.

The Gunny hesitated a few seconds, blowing out a puff of smoke into the rain, which was now coming down hard.

"I don't want to cross that damned bridge again," he eased out, the words coming slow, "and I don't want to hole up in those caves like a rat waiting to be ferreted out and killed."

I glanced over my shoulder to see Fessman and Nguyen pressed against the back wall of my foxhole. I was uncomfortable with what the Gunny was saying but I was even more uncomfortable that not only were Fessman and Nguyen hearing it but that the Gunny didn't care that they were hearing it.

I knew it wasn't the Gunny's fear that was bothering him. He'd been very close, in his way, to Sugar Daddy and was most assuredly so with Jurgens. I didn't know about myself, but it was difficult, in spite of his distant attitude and sometimes insulting behavior to ignore the fact that he had taken me in, guided me and taught me everything he could to help me to survive. I sensed that there was no solace or succor I could give him that would not cause even a worse reaction. We had to get back to the plan and we both had to endorse it enthusiastically, or none of it would matter.

"Fessman ordered a hundred rounds of the 81 mm mortar ammo, which should stand us well at the clefts," I said, changing the subject completely.

We were all going over the bridge and we were all going to hole up on the other side until we were ready to once again take on the NVA in a full-frontal attack. We had never failed when attacking them. We took most of our casualties when we were on the run or exposed, like with Sugar Daddy and his Marines at the bridge. Under the curl of the canyon wall, the enemy could not reach us even using the sparse RPGs they had or their version of our fifty caliber machine guns. The 175s from the Army firebase couldn't reach us under there either. With luck, we would be able to draw on Puff once more, lay waste to the jungle with one zone fire after another with the 175s and then attack while the NVA was down, hurt or at least in complete shock. Our attack would be to pass through them, not wipe them out or engage, except where they engaged us.

"When?" the Gunny asked, finishing his cigarette and snapping the small remainder out into the open air, which was mostly falling water and not air at all.

"Resupply comes in at 1400," I replied. "We cross over at 1300, and then get our defensive fire positions set up during the ensuing hour."

"Fessman told me about your brother," the Gunny said, pulling the subject out of mid-air like it had been floating there all along, just waiting.

I didn't know what to say, so I just stared at him.

"Who was he with?" the Gunny asked.

"The Big Red One, and I presume he's still with them," I replied, not liking the past tense being used on my brother, at least not yet.

A prognosis of 'fair' was not good, I knew, but, according to Fessman, such assessments were invariably written as worse than the reality might be. I knew nothing about Naval or Army procedures or actions at their military hospitals. Mostly, we sent the wounded out on choppers and that was the end of that. We never got them back and never even got to know if they survived or not. The Army hadn't notified me about my brother. They'd sent the telegram to my parents and my parents had forwarded it to me with an address change.

"You get along?" the Gunny asked, no emotion in his voice.

I was growing increasingly uncomfortable but could not avoid the Gunny's direct questions, and at least it took us away from the fears he had mentioned, although I knew those were just a substitute for his not being able to grieve openly over the loss of Sugar Daddy.

"Not all the way along the line," I answered, truthfully. "Only my senior year in college when both of us had to move home to save money. At that point, I think both of us agreed that we were really pretty good brothers compared to what was out there. Yes, we got along." I only realized as the words left my mouth, that I too was referring to my brother in the past tense.

"We get along," I added, knowing the words sounded weak.

"I'll get everyone ready, and I don't want to wait either," the Gunny said, suddenly energized as if the talk of my wounded brother had somehow done something to pop him out of his depression.

"Fast. We have to move fast. Call Cowboy and see if all three Skyraiders can come down the valley one after another, about three minutes apart and tell him to drop plenty of ordnance. That will give us nine to maybe twelve minutes to cross and get under cover before the enemy recovers and pays attention. And we have nine flechette rounds left for the Ontos. When the Skyraiders come in the Ontos can stand by to take out anything that opens up if we're not fully undercover in time. Then it can back its way up to our position, like before."

The Gunny got up and climbed out of the foxhole without another word or waiting for a response. Nguyen followed him out into the rain for no good reason I could think of. Fessman turned up his little radio as I went back to my position against the rough hardened mud wall of my foxhole that faced the river.

Brother John introduced a new song that he said was going to be an international hit, whatever that meant. International because it had come from some sort of Russian folk song. I waited for the song to come and watched the Ontos reorient itself carefully on the other side of the river, its six deadly tubes aimed directly at the jungle area where real trouble always came from and probably would always come from.

"Once upon a time there was a tavern, where we used to raise a glass or two.

Remember how we laughed away the hours, and think of all the great things we would do…" came out of Fessman's radio.

I knew in seconds that the song would be a big hit. There was something longing about it, longing for a younger more positive past. When the chorus hit "Those were the days my friend, we thought they'd never end…" I was convinced. Whatever the melody, the lyrics were about all of us serving in the war, particularly those of us not likely to survive.

The Gunny reappeared the two newer lieutenants at his side, with all three radio operations behind them. He didn't enter the foxhole, instead, he went to one knee and sticking his head under the tarp.

"You're going over with the first wave before the NVA truly grasps what we're doing. The planes are due in five minutes. Get your stuff together and go for it. Jurgens is waiting on the other side. Get his men up to the cleft with the Ontos. We won't come until you let us know the defensive M-60s are in place and the Ontos ready to open fire." He pulled his head out and was gone.

"Okay, Fessman, it might be my plan but the Gunny's running with it. Let's do our part and get the hell over there. At least the makeshift mess of a ramp will let us run up and right over."

I scrambled for my helmet, liner, and pack, having already checked to see that my letters home were securely in my thigh pocket, along with the supply of morphine I hoped to never need again. I felt more than heard the Skyraiders in the distance, so I knew they had to be racing toward us down the valley. The one sound that never left, and immediately came to the forefront, even though the murky misty rain, was that of the lone drum, beating its single solitary sound every half a minute or so. Sometimes it could be tuned out, but it always came back to all of us living under its implied threat. I wondered if maybe the Skyraiders might save one bomb to dump on the top of the ridge again.

The Gunny had left the two lieutenants behind. I climbed out of the hole, detaching my poncho from the others, as Fessman and Nguyen sought to do the same thing. The lieutenants stood like lost children in the rain as if school was out and they had no idea of where to go.

"Follow me," I said, waving one arm toward the river as I moved out.

I almost smiled at the ridiculousness of the command. Seldom, if ever, in real jungle combat, do officers physically lead their Marines. The point is simply too dangerous a place to be and, aside for officers thought to be so incompetent that they are removed by their own men, generally, officers are too valuable to risk by having them right out front as fully exposed moving targets. Nevertheless, I moved fast down the berm and right up onto the pile of wood and debris with the lieutenants, Fessman and Nguyen being trailed by a massed group of Marines. I looked over my shoulder as I climbed the pile. I was finally leading Marines in combat.

The crossing was fast, low and without incident. There was no fire from the jungle, but then we'd lain down on the hard steel surface of the bridge to await the arrival of the first Skyraider. When it passed rapidly overhead, I got up and ran for the other side of the river. When I exited the bridge by jumping across the three-foot opening between it and the bank, although at the same level, I was no longer leading anything or anyone. The Marines went by me as if I was standing still, each of them carrying packs at least three times the size of my own. The second Skyraider was coming in. How could it have been three minutes I wondered. I felt like I'd left the other bank only seconds before. The Marines ran full out toward the far wall across the hardened mudflat. I passed the place where the battalion delegation had died, the holes where the NVA had set in to surprise us. I ran on toward the canyon wall at a trot, ridiculously hopeful that none of the Marines passing me would take my particular cleft, the one that had been the most comfortable and safest place I'd spent time in since being in country.

The mudflat, and then the berm before the wall, became a hot-bed of activity, as the Marines went about setting up machine gun positions against the backside of it.

The Ontos moved slowly toward us, backing, with its six deadly tubes always pointed at the jungle. No fire came from the enemy, but it was only mid-day and our air support was at its most effective and forceful. '

My cleft was deserted and I felt great relief, tossing my pack inside the cave and then turning to lay against the berm and consider what might be done, if anything. The third Skyraider came in. There were still Marines crossing the bridge, I realized. The crossing was taking more time than either the Gunny or I had planned for.

"Get Cowboy and have him swing back right away," I yelled over my shoulder to Fessman, still unloading his gear inside the cleft.

"He's coming back for another run anyway, sir, but they're running low on ordnance," Fessman yelled back.

I breathed in and out deeply. The Gunny still had to make it over and the enemy was going to be rearing its ugly head at any second. The two newer lieutenants joined me, laying down with their chests resting on the berm, like my own.

"What do you want us to do?" one of them asked. I didn't bother to look over at the man. The two lieutenants were proving to be compliant and willing to do whatever they were told. I could not fault them for that. But the Marine companies, particularly my own, ran almost automatically, and I feared that the lieutenants might attempt to make modifications to procedures long-established and get themselves killed in the process.

"There's nothing to be done here," I said, my full attention on the bridge and the Marines crossing, worrying about how long it would take Cowboy to swing back around. The Ontos was there, idling away nearby, but every round we didn't have to expend on the crossing we would have available for protecting the resupply choppers and then getting on through what was going to be a difficult night.

"Go on up and down the line and check the M-60 positions. Let me know how many we have and whether they're set up or not."

The lieutenants didn't move.

"Now," I hissed at them, still not taking my eyes off the bridge.

I saw the Gunny start across. I was shocked to see Nguyen with him, just off his right shoulder and a little behind. I hadn't seen Nguyen in the crossing and now I knew why. He was looking after the Gunny as he looked after me. I wondered if the Gunny knew or even cared. They both ran, their bodies bent over, keeping them from running at top speed but offering a bit more security from getting hit from flying shrapnel blowing back from the Skyraider's bombs.

Cowboy was back. I heard his plane beginning its run further up the valley.

I pulled myself from the berm and moved fast on hands and knees to where the Ontos sat. I crawled up to the back and opened the hatch.

"Hutzler, give me one round of flechette and put it right into the outer edge at the center of the jungle. I want them to know you're here and loaded for bear. When that's done then back up to the face as close as you can get while still keeping your aim point."

"Yes, sir, Junior," Hutzler replied. "Get away from the rear and make sure I'm clear."

I pulled back, closed the double steel doors and then raced back to my former position, wondering if I should have shared with Hutzler the coming 175 artillery barrage.

I covered my ears just as the 106 went off, the round tracking straight to the edge of the jungle and then exploding with a great fireworks display, as the tiny flechettes interacted with the falling rain at extremely high speed. Trails of vapor were everywhere. The Skyraider came in. The Gunny was crossing the mudflat with Nguyen at his side. The plan was working, at least so far.

If we made it back to Ga Noi Island I wondered if I would be able to get some sort of emergency leave to visit my brother in Japan. I doubted it but the idea gave me some hope. I'd only come to like my brother lately but since I had I now didn't want to lose him in the worst way. The Gunny crossed the berm and disappeared up the trail that ran along the back edge. Nguyen came toward me. I didn't have to signal him. I simply turned and headed into my part of the cleft structure that ran along under the cliff face edge. The Skyraider dropped its bombs. We'd made it and not lost a Marine in the process.

A great explosion came from the river area. I raced to the opening of the cave and ran back to the berm. A cloud of debris had risen right up through the falling rain. The bridge moved. I then knew why the Gunny had waited until everyone else was across. He'd blown the bridge. Ever so slowly the bridge moved downriver until it disappeared past the edge of the jungle area. There would be no going back. It was hole up, batter the hell out of the jungle. and then attack toward the glacis and escape up into the forest at the top of the wall. As with so many of my other plans, there simply wasn't one other course of action to be taken.

one-hundred-forty-three

THE TWENTY-NINTH DAY : THIRD PART

I huddled in what I had come to consider my cave, a dry place in a wet world of drizzling misery. The bottom of the cave, although consisting of sandy dirt rather than stone, like its walls, was mildly dusty from going many years without being touched by outside moisture, other than the heavy water-laden air always present everywhere in the valley during the monsoon season. I wrote. The stationery, if I could still call it that, was almost too wet to allow my poor quality government pen to write on. The imprinted blue image, in baby blue ink, of Marines raising the flag on Sarubachi, ran if I brushed my hand over it, and the paper itself came apart if I pressed down too hard with the tip of the pen. I wrote about my cave. I didn't tell my wife it was a cave. I referred to it as my quarters, and my lying descriptions about it were complimentary. I glanced out toward the entrance, nearly hidden by the low light inside the cave's dusky interior. That portal became a window, for my descriptive purposes. My poncho, thrown across the few inches of dry dirt, was my sheet and the sandy dirt my mattress. I didn't mind writing the lies at all because, if I made it, however slim my chances, I would be able to make humor of my attempts to not tell her about the reality of life and death down in the A Shau Valley.

I carefully enclosed the somewhat soggy letter into a drier envelope, although simply addressing that paper caused the ink to run a bit, once it was exposed to the moist air. Mailing home for "free," the word has to printed in the upper left corner of the envelope, had one other undiscussed benefit. I had only written half a page so I'd have to finish the letter later if I had a chance. There was no stamp to attempt to affix to paper that was in no condition to be able to hold it. I placed the envelope in my thigh pocket, buttoned it, and then sat back to consider when the next resupply might be planned and then when it could be arriving.

I carefully withdrew my last two sheets of stationery and one of the remaining Iwo Jima envelopes from the plastic bag I kept it and my wife's letters in, before resealing it. The moisture could not be avoided in the air but at least the rain itself, when I went back outside, would not destroy the only writing materials I had. My brother had been sent to Yokohama, which probably meant that there was a U.S. Army hospital there. It might not work but if I wrote him a letter and sent it in care of the hospital itself someone on the staff might get hold of it and get it to him. His outfit, the Big Red One, would probably have no further contact with him if the Army was the same as the Marines. Once one of my own men left through evacuation for wounds he was never seen or heard from again, no matter how mild or serious the injury. In movies, I'd seen back in the world that had never been the case. It seemed that Hollywood always portrayed combat units as tightly integrated and the men like brothers, never to lose track of one another again. Once more reality bit deep down in the rain, leeches, Bong Song River, and the North Vietnamese Army inhabiting the bottom of the A Shau Valley. If I was somehow to make it back to the world, then I knew in my heart of hearts that I would never see or hear of any of the Marines I was with again.

I thought about the next resupply, if we could get it, and how it would have to hold us until we were firmly in place up above the escarpment. Without another resupply, what the choppers had brought in previously in ammunition, food and water would have to serve as the only tattered foundations we had for our retreat downriver. Without another resupply, the success of the attack downriver would be more problematic. The Gunny's act of blowing the bridge, although assuring that the rest of the main body of the NVA across the river would not be able to attack from the flank and be a factor, also assured that there would be no ability available for the companies to go back if some situation called for it and that there would be no relief coming down the valley that would be any use to us if it arrived from that direction. Battalion had been completely deaf to protests about how the only relief likely to have any success in saving us would have to come from the direction of An Hoa and Go Noy Island. My requests, that the companies retreat up the canyon face and back toward the security of An Hoa, had been denied.

Darkness was once again coming. The cave had grown dim, almost too dim to look across its short distance to where the entrance was and see Fessman fiddling with his radio equipment. How the Marine Corps found such young boys, trained them, set them loose in combat, and then had them act like knowledgeable men of technical wisdom time and again under the very worst of circumstance astounded me.

"I need the Gunny, Jurgens, the lieutenants, and Hutzler," I ordered, not having to raise my voice because the only sounds that reached to the very back of the cave where I'd tossed my pack and spread out my poncho liner were those of river. The water moved in the distance and I could feel its flow through the rock and ground more than I could hear it.

Fessman didn't use his radio, instead, he leaned half his body out over the edge of the lip of rocks that made up the entry to the cave, and speaking to someone. When he pulled himself back inside he went back to working on his radios.

"Who did you send for them?" I asked, not really caring, but wondering.

"Nguyen, sir," Fessman replied.

"I thought he didn't speak English, and you don't speak Vietnamese, much less the Montagnard dialects," I said, not entirely mystified but still curious as to what Fessman would say in response.

"I don't know what you mean, sir," Fessman came back after a moment.

I sighed out loud. "There's stuff you know you know, stuff you don't know, and then there's the stuff you know you don't know," I said, with resignation in my voice.

Talking to Fessman about communications of any sort, I'd decided early on, and that had not changed over time, was like talking to a jittering box of rocks. Sounds came back from the corporal but they weren't interpretable as any kind of cogent or understandable communications on the subject.

"Yes, sir," Fessman replied, his expression from across the cave leading me to believe that it was similar to the one of befuddlement I myself felt.

Nguyen returned, his arrival marked by his quickly sticking his head and upper body into the opening Fessman had used my poncho cover to close off. Then Nguyen was gone. He'd said nothing, which was his custom, but I'd gotten the message from his look, which was confirmed when, seconds later, the Gunny, Jurgens, and Hutzler crawled under the poncho and adjusted themselves along the bottom of the cave, only a few feet from where I sat with my back pushed into the relatively smooth rock wall. The pungent smell of ages-old moisture contained inside the body of the rock surfaces surrounding us was faintly bitter but not totally unpleasant. The fact that the leeches didn't live inside the dry sandy bottom surface of the caves, and mosquitos didn't like it much either were two more benefits of the place.

The Gunny squatted, pulling out a cigarette, while Jurgens and Hutzler both sat down on the dry loamy surface that made up the floor, the cave being too low to stand inside. The two new lieutenants crawled in next, both going to their knees and pushing a bit back into the poncho cover to avoid being in direct contact with the others. The poncho pattered, its rain-induced sounds somehow able to be heard over the gurgling of the Bong Song River in the distance and between the continuing beats of the mean-spirited drums that had begun sending their dark message as the day turned into night. "There won't be another resupply," I said, having come to that difficult conclusion only moments earlier. There was no sense trying to schedule a resupply that could never be put together in time to help. The companies had to move and they had to move quickly.

There was no reaction from the collected group in front of me. I waited a few seconds, the cave lit dimly by the flashlight I carried, with its lens buried partially in the sand to allow us all to have some ability see without any of us being blinded.

"We don't have the time for any choppers to come in, and we probably couldn't defend them in such a free fire open landing zone, not to mention the likelihood that command wouldn't allow them to undertake the mission anyway. The bridge's been blown so that avenue of retreat if we might have chosen to use it, is closed forever."

I didn't mention that the blowing of the bridge had been done by the Gunny in an action made out of his own volition and judgment. The blowing of the bridge left both companies revealed for what we were; sitting ducks or trapped rats.

We only had one direction to go, and although I'd never have planned to travel back over the bridge I'd rather have had the option, or at least let the enemy assume we had the option. That the enemy units on the other side of the river might attack over that bridge had been unlikely, at best, since one M-60 machine gun, aimed down the length of the bridge would completely decimate any force on the trying to cross over the bare expanse of its exposed superstructure.   "What's the plan?" Jurgens asked.

"I don't like it," the Gunny whispered, between puffs of thick smoke he'd been blowing toward the side of the cave where Fessman lay with his radio hugged into his side.

"You don't like what?" I asked, in surprise. I hadn't even mentioned the plan, much less, and details about what it might be.

"I don't like the fact that we've been ordered to stay here by battalion, to await relief, although no relief can possibly reach us, and we've been denied permission to do exactly what it looks like our only option is to do," the Gunny said.

I was baffled by his comment. He'd blown the bridge, assuring that any relieving force coming down the valley, even if it survived getting past Hill 975 in one piece, could not get to our side of the river to relieve us, or even help us without a lot of heavy equipment to rebuild a crossing or a whole fleet of helicopters to transport the number of Marines it would take to reinforce our position.

"Okay, then what's your advice?" I asked, splaying out my hands in front of me.

"I'm worried that we'll attack down this damned valley all over again, make it up to the top of the rim, get back to the island, and then get court-martialed for disobeying orders if we make it."

I was surprised. The last time the Gunny had mentioned being court-martialed we'd laughed out loud at the possibility of such an event happening. Neither then, nor now, were the forces in the rear with the gear; battalion, regiment, or even the division, going to pull anyone in the unit out to be sent to Okinawa for a general court-martial. I knew the Gunny was serious, however, and I also realized that things had changed significantly over the course of only one month. We'd beaten the enemy back time after time, under almost hopeless circumstance each time. The Gunny, like Sugar Daddy and Jurgens, had demonstrated with their newfound interest in being nominated for personal decorations, was beginning to believe that he might live, after all, and if he did, what the ramifications might be for his career or reputation.

"Moot," I replied.

"The question doesn't call for an answer unless you want to stay right here until we're worn away, run out of ammo, food and everything else until finally we get overwhelmed by who and what you know is out there and coming to do that." I put my arms down, my shoulders slumping a bit while I waited for a reply.

"We have two companies," the Gunny said, choosing to ignore the issue he himself had raised. "If we're going high diddle up the middle then what do we do with Kilo company?"

"We did the middle last time, although we came up both sides of the jungle before that," I said slowly, realizing that I was not going to be able to logically lay out the plan I'd formed, so much as distributing it piecemeal in answer to questions that, although relevant, were all covered by the plan.

"We're not going up the middle. We're going downriver under the cover of the eastern lip of the wall, with the Ontos in the lead, its rifles pointed over into the thick of the jungle. Kilo's going to attack along the river as they go, moving fast more than attempting to contact or respond to contact with the enemy. We ourselves will move down about four or five hundred meters along the path and then act like a firebase to suppress fire while Kilo makes its transit. The 175s will soften things up before anyone moves, and then I'll hold them in reserve to fire when Kilo's down and hopefully climbing the glacis, and we're working our way along toward it, hugging the lower edges of the wall."

"What happens to us, once Kilo's down there, the NVA realizes that, and their full angry attention shifts to us?" Jurgens asked.

There was a brief silence. I waited.

"The 175s again," the Gunny answered finally, his voice low, before flicking his lit cigarette against the side surface of the cave wall. "While we move along the bottom of the cliff the 175s drop in on the jungle, and, if we're lucky, none of them get close enough to us to cause casualties, which gives us about twenty minutes to make it all the way downriver. That's not enough time."

"I have two-zone fire applications planned and ready to go," I replied. "The firebase has the rounds and will red bag us all the way, including repeating another zone once we make it up the glacis in the morning, and that's just before Cowboy comes back with reinforcements and Homan roams overhead to get us all the way back to the island."

"Okay," the Gunny replied, his tone one of mollification. "That might work. What do we do to prepare to support Kilo? Our firebase will have to move along with them once they get to the river."

"We make a brief run along the cliff downriver and then stop to provide as much accurate fire as we can. Then the 175s do their first bit of work. Kilo crosses to the river the instant the last round comes in. The enemy will take a bit to recover. Once Kilo's across the open area, and they're a good distance down along the bank, we move on our side continuing to draw the enemy's fire."

"Have you got one of those cute names for this operation?" Jurgens asked.

I'd been waiting for the question, although I'd expected to have it asked by Fessman.

"Hopalong Cassidy," I replied.

"What's that?" Jurgens came back.

"Who is that, sergeant," Fessman answered, from behind him. "He's a great cowboy hero on Saturday morning television."

"Figures," Jurgens replied.

The Gunny nodded his head.

"Complicated," he said. "Simplicity usually works better, but then I'm the one who blew the bridge. I thought it'd make things simpler but I was wrong. I should have let you know first. Let's get to it."

I was shocked.

The Gunny had never admitted he was wrong about anything before, much less doing so in a backhanded sort of apology.

"Can you jury rig a round to take out the machine when we go?" I asked, knowing what his answer would be, but still, I felt the question had to be asked.

"Aye aye, sir," Hutzler said. "I'll miss the little beast, though."

"Yeah, me too," I replied, relieved that by saying what he'd said that there'd be no problems from him or his men in abandoning the vital piece of equipment that had helped keep the company alive through so many contacts with the enemy.

Only Fessman and Nguyen were left in the cave with me. I had hoped the Gunny would stay and we might talk. I missed the time he'd spent helping me to survive to the point I'd survived but I also knew, with a sinking sensation, that he was coming to treat me like a real company commander. And that meant I was to be left alone.

I had Fessman give the signal to begin our movement downriver. The first part, the part where we moved forward and then stopped to establish the firebase, would be touchy, and if it failed Kilo company would be cut down before it ever got to the river. I knew from the past, however, that the NVA, for whatever reason, did not act quickly after being hit. Their counter-attacks were always slow in coming although ferocious when it came to risking and expending men when it finally came.

The Ontos churned forward with its usual grinding growl, getting in position to head downriver, it's small engine laboring mightily as it acted more like a combined blender and lawnmower, eating up the jungle gathered under it as it pushed through pile after pile of old and new leaves, fronds and branches of floral debris. The path located alongside the cliff wall wasn't wide enough for the full width of the machine's compact but stodgy girth, leaving one track to pull smoothly on the bare path while the other ground away at the very edge of the jungle. The six barrels of the recoilless rifles weren't pointed straight ahead, instead, they were angled over toward the body of the triple canopy jungle, ready to strike any position the NVA chose to fire from because fire they certainly were going to before the company reached the lower part of the canyon wall that was scalable.

In the attack downriver I would move behind the Ontos with Jurgen's platoon out in front. There were no FNG replacements in Jurgen's platoon, so each and every casualty, if the platoon took casualties, would consist of vital combat veterans who had been with the company for some time. I, like the rest of my Marines, would be tucked in as close to the overhang that ran along the bottom of the rock wall as possible, while being out from under the lip enough to make decent speed in getting downriver as quickly as possible.

The drums played from atop the eastern rim of the ridge, and the deep beating sounds would follow us through the night, I knew, since there were no supporting fires I could call that close to the lip of the cliff's edge that might not end up falling into the valley down where we were exposed and moving.

There was no point in covering or supervising the laying down of the base of fire. I waited in the cave for our real attack downriver to begin, fearful that this attack would be much more about taking hits rather than giving them.

I took the time I had to finish the letter to my wife, as I waited to call in the artillery. Midnight, without a moon, and in the never-ending mist, would be the time to execute the call, giving me about half an hour. The firebase would open up in minutes. The artillery zone fire would last about twenty minutes, give or take. When the artillery fire mission was over Kilo would make its rush to the river, and then head down along the eastern bank of hard mud, while, at the same time, our company would begin its initial attack before setting in place to lay down heavy machine gun fire and blow as many rounds of 106 millimeters recoilless into the jungle as we could afford, leaving only a few to make a stand at the base of the glacis later in the night. The Ontos

would have to be blown to pieces never to be used again, although neither I nor any under my command, I was certain, would be wanting to
return to the A Shau under any circumstances. The enemy wasn't likely
to have any kind of a supply of the very specialized recoilless rounds the
rifles required, but still, the Ontos would have to be destroyed.

I wondered, in the writing of the letter, if it would be the last letter I wrote home. I'd wondered that so many times, but in writing along
the way I hadn't been a veteran of the conflict. My terror had subsided
over time, with respect to confronting the enemy, but a colder analytical reality of tempered fear had set in to replace it. I paused in the writing, only getting as far as jotting my wife's name down on the damp but
serviceable stationery. What could I write? I put the pen back to paper
and wrote about the valley in the night. I included the drums, knowing
that she would not get the deadly intent that drove the enemy to beat
them as continuously as they could, but that was okay. I wrote of the
river, it's high-speed current passing, making sounds disturbing but also
vaguely comforting. The Bong Song was the core artery that passed
right through the center of the valley, and no life, fauna or flora, could
ignore it or fail to depend on it for life and sustenance. The rains would
come and go but the river would always be there. I finished the letter by
indicating that I was leaving the field of actual combat and heading to a
rear area where I would likely remain for the rest of my thirteen-month
tour. I stopped, as I came to signing my name. A year to go. How could
I possibly spend another full year in such a place? How had soldiers and
Marines spent four or more years going from one conflict after another
in Europe, and then across the ocean to fight in the orient?

I sealed the letter and tucked it away in my thigh pocket, my hand
accidentally grasping the container of morphine I carried with me. I
hadn't had to use any of the opiates for some time, but somehow I felt
that that time might be over. There was no way the companies could
go through the kind of gauntlet the enemy had to have prepared for us
without taking heavy casualties. So far, the company's actions to survive
against superior forces reminded me of what Joe Louis had said about
engaging another fighter who was more adroit and quicker than he was:
"He can run but he can't hide." We had run but we could not hide forever, and that included staying in the same place where we were right now.

"Ready with the fire mission request, sir," Fessman said quietly,
as if not wanting to disturb me. Even Fessman was treating me like a real
company commander and it was making me uncomfortable.

I nodded once, then closed my eyes and breathed in and out deeply while I waited. Of all my plans, this one had to work or we were all dead.

"Shot, over," Fessman intoned, waiting into the silence, as the rounds left the barrels of the guns, and crossed the more than twenty miles through the air to strike the jungle down in our part of the valley.

"Splash," Fessman said, and then both of us counted off the five seconds to impact in our heads, waiting for the explosions to begin. I knew all the Marines under my command, or the command of the other two lieutenants would be okay, as long as everyone was safely tucked under the bottom curl of stone that lined the lower edge of the canyon wall. The 175s were inaccurate at the distance they were firing but there was no way an eastern deflection error could cause much in the way of damage to anywhere we were. The Army firebase, so far away, was firing across the distance using an arc that had to intersect the top of the ridge if the rounds were too low, which meant only the enemy drummers, beating away on their fifty-gallon drums might be at any real risk, and that thought was not unsatisfying.

The explosions shook the floor of the cave and brought hidden dust and small bits of stone and embedded shells down from the ceiling of the cave. Nguyen, Fessman and I crouched low, knowing the rounds, and their terrible shrapnel and expanding concussive envelopes, could not reach inside the cave, but fearful nevertheless. The 175s were no-where near as powerful as the thousand-pound bombs either the A-6 Prowler or Skyraiders could drop, but in the night, with nothing but the drifting mist, no moonlight and the beating drums playing their short but deadly sounds, they seemed just as mighty and dangerous as the bigger ordnance the planes delivered.

The rounds continued to come in. I'd spent some time letting the two new lieutenants know what they had to do, which was almost nothing. Kilo company was made up mostly of combat veterans, with a small supply of FNGs, like our own company. The two lieutenants fell into the FNG classification, although, having lasted a few days and still being alive, would become veterans if they made it only another week, or so. The existing veteran Marines in the company would catch on extremely quickly to what had to be done and would take no time at all in moving downriver, even under fire, and they'd need no direction or leadership to do so.

It was time. Fessman and Nguyen waited at the opening, Fessman having rolled the poncho cover back up neatly and reattached it to my pack.

I looked around the cave, sweeping my flashlight all around the interior. I would miss the cave, no matter where we ended up as a company. Having private and safe quarters wouldn't be something I'd take for granted ever again if there was to be an 'again.'

I stepped out into the wet night, the rain coming down lightly in the night, the drums beating their deadly intent and flashes of fire coming from the cracking automatic discharges from our M-60 machine guns. Kilo had to be making its rush for the river, although nothing could be seen. I drew the sweetly putrid smell of jungle into my lungs, made my way behind Fessman and Nguyen down the path to where the Ontos waited, wondering fleetingly how the wildly brutal 'stage play' of shattering life around me had come to be my home.

one-hundred-forty-four

I examined the great stone wall, the wall that rose up from the bottom of the valley for a full thousand feet, vertically rising without big enough cracks, hand-holds or other features to allow it to be climbed without serious mountaineering equipment. The 175's had done their job by blowing the hell out of the jungle portion of the valley nearby but what worried me was the amount of debris that had impacted against the lower part of the canyon wall, along its lower edge, where the company would be strung out and moving. I'd examined the wall before we'd pulled out with my flashlight (muffled using a pair of socks over the lens). Calling in another fire mission on the jungle, what with the inaccuracy of the rounds fired beyond the gun's effective range, had resulted in plenty of blown bamboo, fern and tree trunks being driven into the side of the lower cliff with such force that much of it had struck at speeds that left bits seemingly glued into the stone itself. Much of the debris, if I fired another zone while the company was pressed against the wall and trying to move downriver, might cause serious injuries, if not death, to many of our own Marines.

The Gunny was there, and he was close to me, but not saying anything.

I felt that he was looking up, but the only visible thing in the night was the red tip of the cigarette he held down at his right side. I didn't like that he smoked when we were so close and exposed to a hidden enemy, but I said nothing. Some 175 rounds had fallen short. I'd felt their explosions down through the thousand or so feet of rock all the way into the cave. It was too much to hope that the drummers had been killed and their barrels blown to pieces, but whatever damage had been done had at least caused them to pause, maybe long enough for the entire company to get far enough down the river to never hear them again.

"It's not your fault, it has to be done," the Gunny said, taking a hit from his cigarette. "It's a good plan and you're going to pull a lot of Marines in this company through."

"Thank you," I replied, hoping the Gunny wasn't talking about what I suspected he was talking about.

"Kilo's over there and beginning to move downriver," the Gunny went on, filling me with a sense of weary trepidation.

"They're going to be hit on their left flank from the jungle, no matter how much firepower we put into trying to suppress that," the Gunny said, waving the burning tip of the cigarette close to me. "They're going to take heavy fire from the NVA across the river I helped prevent from coming over. And you can't call in any more 175s for them because the fire mission would likely kill everyone in the company rather than protect them."

"That's one analysis," I said, but my voice had gone to a whisper all on its own.

"You sacrificed Kilo to save us," the Gunny continued, his words beating into me like the strokes on the drums from above had but with much more agonizing force.

"Nobody else is going to thank you, and not too many will be around to even figure it out."

I couldn't say anything. I looked and listened over my shoulder for Fessman but he was too far behind me to have heard what the Gunny said, and Nguyen, was as close as the Gunny was on my other side, gave no indication he'd heard anything.

"Thank you," I replied to the Gunny, again.

I hadn't planned to sacrifice Kilo company. Two companies of Marines, strung out along the base of the cliff, would have taken a terrible beating, even with the ability to call in 175s for covering fire. At the very least, the blown bamboo stalks, blown off branches from the trees, and other shrapnel-related debris would have taken a terrible toll. Splitting our forces made all the sense in the world to me, although I had to admit I hadn't considered the NVA across the river who would be able to set up and fire across the water and right into Kilo's right flank.

The artillery and the volume of machine-gun fire sweeping the smoking remains of the jungle had done their work. The Ontos had fired some high explosive rounds but had no target for the flechettes. The southern end of the A Shau had fallen into a silence unbroken by high-velocity weapon fire or exploding pyrotechnics. Only the sound of the misting drops of rain, falling on the stiffly brittle material of ponchos, and the faulty cushioned metal of combat helmets made any noise at all. That and the General Motors six-cylinder puffing and pouting its way along - half on the path and half in the jungle just in front of me.

How the Gunny had come to his conclusion, that left me as the coldest killer working to save some remnants of the company, I had no idea, and I was cut to the quick that he would arrive at such a result in his thinking. My hand swept briefly to the outside of my thigh pocket where my letter home to my wife was securely and safely tucked away. I was a good husband and a good man, no matter what had happened or what I had done. I had to gamble that somehow, the tattered, dirty and nearly unprincipled officer I'd become was not descriptive of the man I really was, and hoped to one day be again.

The volume of fire was too significant and continuous for the artillery to have been truly effective in providing suppression, and that small arms fire was flowing almost exclusively toward the river, where Kilo, having made it to the mud bank, was trying to move down and arrive at the glacis near the bottom, where the jungle ended.

Our company's base of fire was ineffective, as the M-60 7.62 mm bullets could only reach into our side of the jungle's interior before being absorbed by the mass of the triple canopy jungle. The radio contact I'd thought to have with the lieutenants running Kilo was there but communications were heated, disjointed mostly broken and many times not really there at all. Kilo had to be partially pinned down on the far riverbank, and there was no way we could relieve or even reach them. The jungle was too thick, and the ages-old fallen debris that served as its floor was impossible for the Ontos to get through or over. I pushed my back carefully and with light pressure against the brush gathered in dense but thin stalks alongside the path that ran close to the undercut face of the cliff. The vertical bracken was taller than me but not by much. Fessman and Nguyen came through the opening I made and quickly squatted down near me as I forced myself under the lip of the lower cliff. There was no deep cave. like I'd inhabited higher up and closer to the river, but my position would have to do for what I had to do.

"Call Kilo and let them know they need to get down, and possibly dig in a bit, as support is coming in," I ordered Fessman. Tell them that they've got to move and move fast once the firing is over. Then call the battery and give them the second fire mission. It'll take about ten minutes for the battery to be up and firing though."

"Unless they're waiting by their guns to pull the lanyards for you, Junior," the Gunny said, as he wedged his way through the hole

I'd made. "They don't have time to dig in and that's not the call they can make and live. They've got to run for it down the river while the barrage is coming down, and we have to give them as much covering fire as we can from over here so the enemy keeps its head down. It's the only chance they have."

"You're right," I replied, as soon as he was done talking.

"We go down our side when the fire mission is over," the Gunny said. "Kilo will still command most of the attention of the NVA, and they're still afraid of the Ontos, so we should have an easier time of it making the transit."

I wished I could turn the flashlight on, even in its most muted state, so I could read the Gunny's expression or look into his unflinching black eyes. Kilo was being sacrificed, just as the Gunny had predicted, and just how he'd described the awful sacrifice as being something I intended and planned from the beginning.

The fire mission rounds came in, on and off-target, and they came in after only a delay of about three minutes. The Gunny was right, again. Some rounds struck the top of the rim above our position and rained small, and not so small, broken off pieces of stone down on much of the valley below. Some rounds also struck the Bong Song river, unseen in the night, but the sound of tons of water rising up and then plunging down again had a certain eerie quality all of its own. There was no longer any understandable radio traffic with Kilo. Our company was on the move, Fessman, Nguyen, and I following the Ontos, its guns angled in toward the jungle but not firing. With the artillery going off everywhere to our right flank there were really no targets to shoot at and the ability of 106 rounds fired on a flat arc from so low wouldn't have enough of a shocking effect to accomplish anything.

Parts of the jungle debris splattered everywhere, forcing every Marine in the company to hunker down low as we moved, use the limited cover of the lower eaten out complex at the base of the cliff, and count on ponchos, poncho covers, and metal helmets to stop whatever impacted on them personally. For the first time since being in country I sorely missed the flak jackets that had been issued in the rear, but quickly discarded by one and all, including me, because of their weight, the heat they held in close to the body, and their ineffectiveness at stopping any kind of personal weapons fire.

The small hundred and forty-five horse engine of the Ontos puffed away, its double muffler system making the machine quiet enough but the baffling, or the design of the 302 cubic inch GM engine itself, made the moving sound of the small but vicious tank a bit eerie and threatening. The NVA seldom fired on it directly, preferring not to have the 106 rifles fire flechette rounds back.

I took in the bluish exhaust through my nose as I walked behind the slow-moving tank, able to move along quite easily at an angle because of having one of its tracks atop the hard narrow path and the other pressed into the soft vegetation the jungle's edge offered under the other track.

The Gunny appeared from behind me.

"Drums have quit," he said.

I hadn't noticed, my mind on other things, but in noting his words I was relieved. One small thing, but it was enough to make me feel better about the whole, nearly hopeless, mission we were engaged in.

"You're right," I whispered out, but then realized the Gunny was gone.

All three of us immediately behind the armored vehicle worked at not coughing from its fumes, while at the same time blessing the same fumes for covering the obnoxious sweet-sour smell of rotten river-bottom mud, old plant matter and also, vaguely, the sharper copper smell of human blood. That aroma revealed to me that the NVA had not all gone down into their tunnels and caves to avoid the barrage. Some had stayed up to man weapons and fire into the left side of Kilo's unprotected flank.

The Gunny showed up again, from somewhere in the night, and grabbed my left arm at the bicep.

"Over here, Junior," he said, making no attempt to keep his voice low.

He pulled me toward the cliff face, through the brush beyond the very low berm it grew up on, and then alongside the Ontos.

"Keep the Ontos between you and the fire, artillery or otherwise," he said. "They don't shoot at the Ontos at all."

The Gunny was gone as soon as he stopped talking. I moved with the Ontos, like I had done behind it, the exhaust aroma gone and a bit of a relief for that being the case, but the torn dead and dying smell of the jungle fully replaced its discomfort. Fessman and Nguyen were right along with me, I knew, in spite of the fact that I couldn't see or hear them. Blind, with hearing only for obnoxious overpowering sounds, having a sense of smell so dominated that my sense of taste went right with it, I only had touch left as a contact to the real world. My hands remained free, my map returned to my pocket, and my Colt automatic never having left its holster. There was nothing for me to shoot at, and not likely to be, although in the back of my mind that I had felt that way before and had to use it. My mission was to move and save both companies to the best of my ability. Thinking those thoughts, I realized, and for the first time, it occurred to me that I really was a company commander and not whatever it was that I'd been before.

Kilo had to be moving because the fire that rose up again as the artillery rounds stopped falling increased. There was no fire coming into my own company's right flank at all. The company was moving rapidly down the path along the base of the cliff almost unopposed.

I moved to the side and a bit back in the dark to where I thought Fessman was until I ran into his left shoulder.

"A lot of the fire over there is coming from the other side of the Bong Song," I said, in a forced whisper.

The lowering of my voice was probably not necessary, given the penetrating loudness of the exploding artillery rounds and then the sharp chattering of small arms fire in the near distance, but the ending of the barrage had created a sort of strange shattered silence all of its own. I knew the effect wasn't real but my reflexes responded to it anyway.

"Have Nguyen get into the back of the Ontos and stop the thing for a minute or so."

Fessman scrambled away. Almost instantly the Ontos stopped, although its little six-cylinder motor continued to idle away.

I got down on my hands and knees and eased myself forward. I didn't need to get into the vehicle. I needed to crawl under it. Once there I pulled my poncho over my head, reached into my right thigh pocket to retrieve my map, and then turned on the flashlight. I was ready for the bright light, my eyes slit down to cracks in order to be able to quickly take in the map I spread across the packed wet mess of path mud. The Bong Song River ran down straight from our former position where the bridge had been. It flowed past the upturned tank and then curved toward the east, toward where we were now, before sharply curving back for a bit before straightening out and flowing all the way down to pass the glacis where we were all headed. The quick glance was all I needed. The distances and perspectives automatically clicked inside my head. I turned the flashlight off, pulled back from the Ontos, and then got the poncho situated where it needed to be to allow me to see, although I could see nothing. It wasn't only dead dark blackout but I was night blind, as well, from the effects of the bright flashlight.

"I want another zone fire from the 175s," I ordered Fessman. "I want it put down on the jungle along the other side of the river," I continued when I realized that Fessman was so close we were rubbing against one another. "The battery will have less trouble with both range and deflection since it's more of a straight gun-target line kind of shoot. Have them use a 'right four hundred from the gun-target line' and fire for effect with the zone extending seven hundred meters in range, and tell them to expedite the mission. Ten minutes of prep time to get it going won't save Kilo."

The Ontos began moving again. I knew Nguyen must have given them the word although, with all the noise of everything going on around us the sound of the Ontos armored rear doors opening or closing didn't even make it partially through the membranes of my damaged hearing.

I moved, bent over, even though I enjoyed the protection of the Ontos on my right side. I wondered about the dead and wounded. There would be no evacuation when we finally made it to the glacis. There was no place for helicopters to land. That meant, since there was cleared open areas at the top of the climb, that anything that made it to the choppers from down below was going to have to be carried, and carried while more than likely under fire.

The 175s came whistling by, high in the night. I hadn't heard the "shot, over," or the "splash" warning alerts, but the whistling of the fast-moving big rounds had come through. I cringed a bit as the concussion from the impacting explosions began. They were so far away, at well over four hundred meters, that no debris was thrown through the night, not making it as far away as I was located, anyway. I knew that Kilo wasn't being so lucky. They'd likely had no warning of the barrage, were subject to its effects, even if there were no rounds that accidentally crossed the river, and then the continuation of the fire coming from the jungle into their left flank went on and on and on. Our company was in a mess but Kilo was in living hell, soon to be a dead hell for so many Marines. Hopalong Cassidy, the plan, and its results were certainly not going to be comparable to anything seen or heard on a Saturday morning matinee for kids back home.

"We may have a chance at dawn, Junior," the Gunny said, his voice the only notice that I had that he was again with me.

I wondered, briefly, whether what the Gunny was doing, circulating everywhere up and down our line of travel was something I should have been doing myself.

"Chance for what?" I asked.

"We cleared a good bit of jungle last time we were here, so it should still be pretty clear," the Gunny replied, holding the red sparkling coal of his cigarette in front of my face.

I took a deep inhalation of the smoke, not really caring about smoking or its effect, but rather on simply accepting whatever the Gunny gave me. It was also a way to wait, without coming across as a questioning idiot, before the Gunny continued.

"We get choppers in, and then we get the gunships with them," the Gunny said, taking the cigarette back. "Then we get what we can of our wounded Marines out and stall to keep the gunships rotating while we climb. Cowboy will be coming but he can only be overhead for seconds before having to rotate around again. The gunships can sit there and provide the cover we need to get up that damned rock."

"What about Kilo, since they'll be there climbing before us?" I asked.

"Your plan takes care of that, Junior," the Gunny replied, taking in a breath of smoke into his own lungs.

I wondered if, when it was all done, if I was still alive, whether the plan to get out of the valley wouldn't go down as the Sacrifice Kilo plan, no matter what my intentions had been, and still were.

"Let's get the choppers in for Kilo when they reach the cliff," I said, but with timber in my voice. "We'll take our own chances with Cowboy and Homan. Those guys will work it out."

The explosions coming from across the river finally stopped and the small arms fire died with it.

Was Kilo even going to be an issue? Had the enemy killed many of them and me the rest? There would be no resolution to those questions until we reached the top of the cliff, I knew.

"You heard what I ordered?" I asked the Gunny, but there was no answer. He was gone again. I was alone. With Fessman, Nguyen, Hutzler and the company Marines around me, but, even with that and them, I was alone.

one-hundred-forty-five

THE TWENTY-NINTH NIGHT : SECOND PART

There existed no corridor through the jungle, like the one that cut through the undergrowth located on the other side of the river. There, the night before, it had been easy to move back and forth through that protected passage to communicate, supply, reinforce, attack, and even defend against the opposing enemy. The jungle Nguyen, Fessman, and I crawled through was something else again. The 'floor' we moved over consisted of packed fern leaves, stalks, bamboo, palm fronds, and much more in the way of mashed fetid flora and infesting small fauna. The mass was packed down to the point that it allowed for working across its surface but that surface also came apart in awful rain-soaked handfuls when it was attempted to be grasped or pulled at. The only way to proceed at all was to push one's body forward with legs spread, using that lower pressed down weight to surge in waves, allowing only hard-fought inch by inch forward progress to be made.

My decision to immediately dive into the jungle and make for where Kilo Company was somehow pinned down against the river had been instantly made and without notification. The Gunny would not have approved, I knew, and he'd probably have been right. But I was driven. Kilo had been 'sacrificed' twice before by my actions, and giving them up to save myself, or even my company wasn't something I could live with, and I knew it way down deep. I'd told Hutzler and he'd come up with the idea of giving us some covering fire, as long as we moved in a straight line from the Ontos to the river. There was no let-up from the steady rain. I was reminded of some old writing I'd read in my youth about Chinese water torture, wherein drops of water were beaten steadily down on a victim's forehead until that victim went insane. Was I going insane? Was I already insane? I grasped my muddy wet hand down to my muddy wet pocket, where my letter home to my wife was tucked inside of its sealed and protective plastic bag. I had a home. I had a wife. I had a daughter. I could not afford to be insane. I could not afford to die and let them be turned loose in a world that was much more dangerous and unforgiving than they would ever comprehend. They would never comprehend if I lived. I gave no orders to Nguyen or Fessman. I knew I didn't have to. I simply told them where we were going. Neither man said anything. If I lived, I wondered at that second, whether I would ever have more willing, more loyal, or more trusting men around me in my life again.

Jungle Rain

[audio src="https://straussshortstories.s3-us-west-2.amazonaws.com/RainFallJungle.mp3"]

The non-stop raindrops beat down on my helmet, blocking out all sounds except those of the AK-47 fire being generated all around us. There was no real seeing of anything, in our punishing reality. How some leaves and other debris gave off a bit of sparkle or nuance of stop-action visibility was a product of reflected muzzle flashes that somehow crossed the distance to illuminate them with tiny packets of light. I tried to move as fast as possible through the smelly decaying mess, not to get through to the other side, and Kilo, so much as the distance to us from the guns of the Ontos. Hutzler was preparing to cover our rear and flanks by firing flechette rounds behind us, and getting hit by the horrid tiny darts that terrified the NVA so badly, now terrified me. My body is instantly penetrated through and through by many hundreds of darts, almost too tiny to see, was an image I could not get out of my mind. I pulled at the undergrowth, feeling leeches' slime through my hands. It was like swimming in hardening jello, a slippery jello substance layered with strangely sweet and sour mud, as well as other small unrecognizable creatures.

I scrabbled and 'swam' through the muck of ages old, yet still fresh muck, pulling handfuls of the sludge through my cupped fingers and then casting them aside. The Ontos fired, the blast coming from directly in front of its powerful shells overpowering all other sounds. I buried myself down into the jungle muck as deep as I could, the analytical side of my brain knowing that I was digging down too late because the shells had already gone off. My body reacted on its own, however, digging deeper, as I was more afraid of the flechettes than the enemy or the collected population of mud, old plant matter, and the parasitic animals I was sheltering down among. The Ontos fired again. I had one side of my face pressed down in the muck, my right hand clutching my helmet when I heard the thundering explosion. I pressed down hard-

er, forcing my face deeper before the secondary explosion of the flechette round going off well past the recoilless rifle's barrel cracked the air.
What seemed like a very brief, but fast hard wind passed over me. Only
seconds later, as I surged forward again, did I realize what the sound and
the feeling of that wind had really been. A cloud of flechettes had passed
right over where I'd been laying. I'd heard the passage of the thousands
of tiny darts, traveling well past the speed of sound, as they were delivered to an area just ahead of where I'd lain, trying to hide. I knew I
wasn't hit, however, as there was only the pain of the nightmare muck
in my nose and eyes, and wet misery spread everywhere else along the
length of my body. That pain I was used to, and certainly nothing like
what I would have felt if the little darts had impacted up, down, and
then through my legs and back.

I felt Fessman to my left and Nguyen to my right, both struggling
along on my flanks. I tried to see them but there was almost no light
at all and I was night blind from the faint but steady flashes from the
enemy's rifles and the fact that the night was the blackest night I could
remember in all of my life.

"Fessman, let the Gunny know where we are and what we're doing," I ordered, in a hushed whisper. "We're deep enough in so we don't
have to worry about the flechette rounds anymore but we don't need
high explosive stuff hitting us that Hultzer might choose to send along
to help.

"Yes, sir, but I don't know where we are," Fessman replied, keeping his voice low. "We took off into the jungle with you. We went straight
out from the Ontos, but where are we now? What do I tell the Gunny?"

"Tell him that we're about six to eight hundred meters from the
glacis and proceeding perpendicular to that cliff face on our way to join
Kilo on the river bank. We should be traveling along a direct straight
line from where the Ontos was when we left," I said, not sure of our real
location at all, but wracking my brain as to where we had to be.

How ironic it would be l, I thought, if we failed to avoid being
killed by our own Ontos fire but I said nothing further.

Fessman relayed the message.

"Are we really sure of our direction, sir," he asked when he was
done transmitting, his tone one of trepidation more than fear. It was
obvious to him where we were going, just not where we were in our
course of travel and why we were going at all.

"Kilo's stopped moving," I breathed out, ceasing my struggles against the surface of the jungle for a few seconds, before getting ready to attack the rotten undergrowth once more. "They're all dead if they stay where they are. I don't know why they stopped. The only hope is to get them moving again."

"The new lieutenants wouldn't stop, I don't think. They seemed like okay Marines, for officers, I mean, sir," Fessman answered.

I didn't reply. The new lieutenants were FNGs, which meant that, under fire, they might do anything at all or nothing at all. I would never get past, for the rest of my life, how I had reacted to being under fire the first few times it had happened. The lieutenants didn't have a seasoned Gunny with them to get them, or Kilo Company, through, however, all they had was me, trying to reach them before everyone was dead.

I surged ahead, struggling to get purchase and fighting to gain as much forward momentum as I could. I thought about answering Fessman, but there was no point. If the lieutenants wouldn't have stopped willingly, then there were other factors at play that I didn't know about. I had to find out what those factors were if they existed, and then get the company on the move again. How radio contact had been lost at such a short-range was unexplainable. There were at least a dozen PRICK 25 radios in Kilo, if not more. Those radios were all tuned to the same combat net frequency, yet nobody in the company responded when called. The grim conclusion I'd come to, that had motivated me to do something as terminally dangerous as we were doing, wasn't something I wanted to keep centered in my thinking.

If all the Marines in Kilo were dead when we reached the river, then so would we ourselves be in very short order. Instead of pursuing that set of grim thoughts, I turned to plan the next move we'd have to make once I was in the presence of the officers and non-coms running the company. It seemed to take an hour to reach the riverbank, although I knew it was more like minutes. The sound of the Bong Song's rushing floodwaters finally overpowered the beating of the rain down on my helmet, and the small arms fire all around us, but not by very much. The river had become a personal river Styx, running its deadly but all present existence straight through the very center of my life. I would never come out of the A Shau Valley as the man I'd been; the Gunny was right. In thirty days, if I was able to reach the top of the ridge atop the difficult glacis climb, I would have died and been reborn any number of times. My letters home were written with the hand of a fictional person I'd created so that there might be a home to come back to if I lived. They were not written by me, this new me scrabbling through leeches, mud, and the very stench of the valley life that I inhabited.

We pulled our way onto a mud flat not far from the river's fast-moving current. Kilo wasn't expecting us and I had fears that we might be mistaken for attacking NVA troops, but that fear was quickly dispelled. The Marines were dug in and we found that out by physically running into several laying half in and half out of the mud.

"Who are you?" one of the Marines asked in a whisper, as I crawled right into him, before backing off a few inches.

"I'm Junior," I replied, "where's your commanding officer?"

"That'd be Sergeant Sweet, sir," the Marine answered, "I'm Lance Corporal Tennison," he went on.

There was no point in asking about where the two lieutenants might be. If they'd been still living, or functional at all, the lance corporal would have so indicated, I knew.

"Take me to Sergeant Sweet, Lance Corporal," I ordered. The Lance Corporal didn't respond, instead merely crawling away downriver. I followed, knowing Fessman and Nguyen would be right with me.

After a few minutes, the Lance Corporal stopped. I discovered that by running into his boots.

"Right here," the corporal said, and then turned away to crawl back the way we'd come.

"Sergeant Sweet?" I inquired into the darkness in front of me."Junior?" he replied, "thank God."

"What's the situation?" I asked, buoyed by his spoken relief and welcome but filled with a bit of trepidation about the poignant crying need his words also conveyed.

The sergeant poured out his story. Casualties had been high once Kilo reached the river and began its journey down the slippery but hardened mud bank. The two lieutenants had been 'relieved of command' by a single errant 175 mm shell going off at point-blank range right on top of them. Their radio operator had died with them. There would be no remains to be brought out, according to Staff Sergeant Sweet. Sweet had assumed command over the company until I'd arrived on the scene. His decision to stop and go down to await any help had cost Kilo dearly but the sergeant wasn't far from being an FNG himself. He'd only been in-country and attached to Kilo for a week.

"They never told me where we were going or why," the sergeant said. I couldn't keep going to someplace I didn't know we were going to."

The sergeant's story and the reason he'd stopped the company's progress made sense, and there was nothing I could say to him about the nature or effect of his decision. Over time, I knew he'd figure things out if he lived, and then possibly have to deal with his decision later on in life.

The snipers, two teams, were still with Kilo. Getting them up the face of the wall was vital. The snipers, if properly positioned up on the ridge, would be able to fire at every muzzle flash below them. Accurate, pin-point, and powerfully delivered sniper rounds, plunging down from on high, could be more devastating than what air support brought in. The teams would be set in atop the ridge long before light came with the arrival of civil dawn if they made it up the cliff in the night.

"Why have all your radios failed?" I asked the sergeant, speaking gently, as it was obvious that the man was shaken to his core.

"Radio silence," Sweet replied.

"Radio silence?" I repeated, unable to keep the wonder out of my voice.

"The lieutenants thought that the enemy might be listening in," the sergeant replied. "They thought that our only hope of making it down the river, to wherever we were going, was to move in silence without the enemy knowing we were here."

"Would you please have all your radio operators turn on their radios?" I asked gently, keeping full control over the feeling of total exasperation I wanted to scream out into the night.

The enemy always knew where we were. They didn't always know the direction we chose to move in or when or where our supporting fires would rain down from or on. Radio silence and codes were only called for in order to keep them from knowing where rounds were going to impact where our ground attack planes were going to strafe or bomb and the time and location of helicopter resupply and medevac. I was certain that the NVA knew that Fessman, Nguyen, and I had moved directly through their area of operations to reach the river, but it was likely they had no clue as to why or what we might be up to. One of the main lessons I'd learned from day one, and the Gunny didn't have to teach it to me, was that the NVA leaders were almost impossible to predict in almost every area.

"I want everyone moving as quickly as they can get their stuff together," I ordered. "I want a forced march to the canyon wall that runs across our front about four hundred meters away, or a bit more. We'll definitely know when we reach it."

"The men want to carry the dead and wounded in poncho covers to get them to the choppers coming in," the Sergeant replied. "Is that okay?"

"Affirmative," I replied, not telling Sweet that I had no idea if a medevac could be accomplished once we reached the bottom of the glacis.

In minutes the company was moving, using fire and maneuver, with the first platoon at the point to clear the way for the rest of the Marines, Fessman, Nguyen, and I among them. I waited until the rear elements were proceeding by, like black moving statues through a dark black night before we joined in.

The company's movement through the lighter growth near the edge of the jungle itself was fast and as silent as the Marines could make it. There were few rounds fired, and even fewer received from the bank of the jungle to the company's east flank. The company reached the wall and then spread down along the length of it, settling behind a low berm that ran parallel to the line of rock located along the bottom of the cliff.

The base of the cliff face I called the 'glacis,' was the only part of the wall located anywhere down in our part of the valley that could be scaled, and then only by using a chiseled narrow and angled ledge that rose up, crisscrossing back and forth, across the face as it went up. I scrunched down at the base. In the dark and constant rain, even with the sound of sporadic small arms fire in the distance, I felt relatively safe. The movement down the riverbank had been precarious, although since the last 175 mission was completed, and things had quieted across the battlefield, the exposed transit was made without much of any organized enemy opposition, other than small arms fire that proved uneven, poorly aimed and ineffective.

"Where are you now, Junior," Fessman whispered squatting down to lean in close to my right ear, draping his poncho cover over both of us to fight off the rain.

I knew he was speaking as the Gunny, rather than telling me what the Gunny said indirectly.

"Where we had to be," I replied, as if I was talking directly back.

"Did you make it?" Fessman went on.

"We're having this discussion, aren't we?" I replied, feeling funny talking to the Gunny through Fessman, but making no move to take the microphone in my own hand.

"Why didn't they answer us?" Fessman asked.

"The radios are all live now," I replied, leaving out the explanation, which didn't matter at the moment, but might make an interesting part of the story later on.

"You've got to take what's left of Kilo up in the dark," the Gunny said. "I mean if you're going up with them, instead of waiting for the company."

"That depends on air support," I said back, looking at my watch.

The white slices of hands pointing at the little illuminated dots around the face told me that most of the night was still before us, and the darkness was, and would likely remain, complete. The Starlight Scope would be as useless up on the ridge, if Kilo made it to the top of the ridge, as it was in the high density undergrowth of the jungle. The cliff was too high, beyond the range of the scope to see that far through the rain and also maintain sufficient vision while the muzzle flashes from NVA weaponry would be 'flashing the tube' destroying any ability to make anything out on its tiny CRT screen.

Fessman handed me an open can of C-rations. My spoon was in my pack. I was so hungry I didn't bother to unpack and pull it out. I turned the can up and sucked down the contents. It was Ham and Mothers, my favorite. I felt the energy flow through me even before the thick grease and mushy ham and beans made it fully into my system. When the can was empty I clutched the letter in my pocket, the one that could not be sent because the resupply mission, intended to be more of a medevac mission because of our casualties, was scheduled to arrive at dawn up on the ridge. The decision had been made at the battalion, not to attempt any kind of landing zone medevac until, or if, the companies reached the top of the ridge. The initial decision made by our battalion commander had been for both companies to remain in the valley, and that some modification of that decision, in receiving new orders about the medevac, gave me hope that I might not, after all, be court-martialed for disobeying direct orders while in combat.

Kilo company prepared to assault the face of the glacis. The Marines in the company acted on their own, or seemingly did so, as I'd come to observe in the past.

I tried to nod off for a bit, scrunched up and wet, but the discomfort at being wet through to the bone and the feeling of leeches attached to me in many places kept me awake. My attachment to home seemed to grow more distant with each passing day and night. What sleep I got was occasional, very short, and tossed and turned with emotionless drivel that played the next morning as downright scary. What was I turning into, I wondered. My most common dream was about a road. A twisting road that snaked back and forth down a slope. It was a road, unpaved, that I'd never been on, but it was in Vietnam. Along the road, local Vietnamese men, women, and children sat, squatted, or knelt. I didn't know any of them. I was not on the road in the dream. I was standing below the road and looking at everyone along the road. The people next to the road all stared at me without any expression at all. Their black eyes never blinked. I had expected nightmares about the things that had happened down in the valley, and deep in my mind I knew I wanted the nightmares so I could get through them before I got home, but the one that kept coming wasn't a nightmare, it was just terribly unsettling.

I would carry my letter up the glacis and hope to get it aboard a resupply chopper there. We would no doubt need ammunition, as we fight to gain the top of the ridge

I closed my eyes and stared into my eyelids. I brought the Vietnamese road back from my memory and then wondered, at looking once again at the people I'd never seen, where my own dead Marines were. Not only were they not on or along the road of my dreams but I couldn't even remember their faces from having been with them when they'd served and been wounded or died. The new lieutenants had no faces. The officers that had contributed my .45, my helmet, and other objects, and then died had no faces that I could remember. Macho Man, who gave me the boots I wore, had no face. I tried to shave every day, even in the worst of conditions, but I had no mirror. When I finally got a mirror in front of me again, would I too have no face?

When I opened my eyes I realized that I had come to another decision without giving it much thought. It was a decision like the one I'd hastily made to cross the battlefield in the thick of the dark, rain, and gunfire from the enemy. The space close to the wall was big enough to bring down a Huey.

I got up, moved along the wall to where I thought the open space had to be and then started to crawl. I moved back and forth across the open area, Nguyen and Fessman crawling with me, no doubt wondering what the hell we were doing out in the open on the very edge of a combat zone where it was too dark and rainy to see much of anything.

We'd brought a supply chopper down into the LZ once before, I recalled, and the area hadn't become noticeably more overgrown since that time, at least not to the feeling hands and body I pushed back and forth across it.

I couldn't climb the face of the wall and leave the wounded and dead behind. It simply wasn't in me. The battalion wasn't available to communicate with because the very end of the valley was so wedged in, and the walls so thick and close by, that even the great penetrating power of the PRICK 25's radio signals couldn't get through. By now my own company would be too close to our position to use the combat net to reach the rear either. The Gunny had indicated that our best survival move was to climb the wall and depend on air support coming in at dawn to protect the collected wounded and dead until a supply chopper could make it down in the light. When I'd directly confronted him about that idea, the tone in my voice gave my negative feeling about his position away. To his credit, the Gunny backed down, saying that his evacuation plan was simply an option, and not one that he'd given serious consideration to.

The base of the cliff was not defensible, except by the snipers who were momentarily going to make their way to the top of the ridge, and that was if they made the ascent and stayed alive. Enemy fire continued to die down until the approach of the Ontos could be distinctly heard, as it chugged away along the eastern path, making that path ever wider with its grinding passage.

I had leeches attached to my hands, but only the top of them so it was no real bother to ignore the minor blood loss I was suffering. I knew I had them on my torso under my blouse again but the removal process would have to wait until we were all secure on the top of the ridge above us.

There was no way bodies of any kind could be put in poncho liners and dragged up the carved rock switchback trail to the top. The chiseled and pounded out rock path was only little more than a boot width in-depth and the slightest misstep carrying an unbalanced load would result in a fall, likely to be terminal in the result. The Marines in both companies had been ordered to shed all extraneous weight, especially weight that could be rapidly replaced when the supply choppers arrived atop the ridge sometime later in the morning.

Kilo had to move up the cliff face in the darkness, and there was nothing else to be done for it, as the collected assemblage of two companies at the foot of the canyon wall together would become nothing more or less than a large living target of opportunity. Air support at dawn might minimize that but it still was likely that casualties would be great if not downright terrible. However, with Kilo's survivors on top of the ridge, their sniper and other M-60 machine gun fire plunging down, and the Cowboy, Homan, and then the Turk and his Cobras coming in to add to the suppression attack, our company would have a chance at making the climb relatively unscathed just after first light. Also, once up on the wall and making the climb it would be risky for the company, but worth taking the risk, to fire another zone of the 175s. A round or two might stretch out to reach the wall itself, but generally, shells fired beyond normal limits fell short and not long.

I ordered Fessman to call the medevac in immediately. If the Marines in Da Nang would not accept the uncommon night mission then the Army chopper crews might. I smiled to myself, as Fessman made the first radio call. The Turk, if he knew we were calling and in trouble, would assemble whatever it took to get here and cover us with the extreme and deadly fire of his own and his friend's Cobras.

And then there would be Cowboy and Homan, probably bringing friends.

I waited for word from Fessman, crouched down into the bottom crevice, where the rock face buried itself into the jungle floor. I tried to imagine how I looked. I breathed in and out deeply, listening to the distant Ontos struggling to reach us, the rain pattering against my helmet, and wondering if I had a mirror whether I would be able to see a face in that mirror when I stared into it.

one-hundred-forty-six

The company proceeded along the eastern base of the sheer cliff rising a thousand feet above it. My arrival in the midst of Kilo's Marines, and reaching the base of the glacis changed none of that. The fire from the other jungle inhabitants, the enemy, remained sporadic, muzzle flashes buried in the night, and in the rain and broken nightmare of decaying bracken that made surviving on the jungle floor an exercise in enduring misery.

Kilo company had come together once more, the loss of the two lieutenants with their radio operators, had been taken by the Marines of the company as a welcome movement of the hand of whatever God they believed in. I couldn't watch them moving about in preparation for assaulting the glacis and reaching the top of the ridge some distance in front of us, as the night was one of total blackness. There wasn't a single speck of light that reached my eyes from the moving Marines around me. There was no lighting of cigarettes or hooded tiny glows of hand covered flashlights. Kilo was a rugged weathered company, having been down in the valley without relief for more than a month, just like my own company. It took some time to finish the move downriver. Enemy fire had been sporadic and effective only in slowing our progress trying to assure that no more of our Marines were lost.

Once reaching the face of the wall Kilo had spread out. I'd pushed into the cliff, with my butt forced into the crack at the base, my back pressed into its solid flat surface. I thought about giving my letter home to Fessman to post, or maybe the Gunny, but discarded the idea without giving it real attention. I'd been in combat long enough as a commander to know that each and every move I made was watched, judged, and then shared with every Marine around who might be dependent upon my decisions. If I gave the letter to anyone else then everyone would know in no time at all. The act would be seen as a surrender, on my part, to my lack of confidence in the plan's chance of success. The Gunny had been right so many times in the past. I was the company commander and the Marines, although driven through with fear and terror themselves, couldn't ever be allowed to see or feel my own. Giving the letter to anyone else to deliver would be seen as an act of weakness I couldn't afford to show. I had to be certain of my own survival, in appearance, or the Marines would lose the hope they held for their own.

I was relieved to have one bit of good news. The medevac was on. Homan and Turk were coming through, and they were coming fast.

I tried to keep my eyes closed, to experience at least a few minutes of meditative relief from the awful pressure of command and the equally awful fear of failure, not to mention the physical misery of my body, literally being eaten alive while I waited out the time required to reach Go Noi Island once more. When I'd last stood atop the rim high above me, a month before, I'd thought of the place I looked out upon down below as a cool welcome relief for the stinking mess I knew the island itself to be. I tried not to smile one of my secretive cold smiles at the remembrance. How quickly things had changed my life, my opinions about it, and my circumstance within it. Go Noi Island, if I reached it, would be a place that was heaven-sent, compared to the death-dealing misery I experienced down in the valley.

The Gunny was right, I decided, in finality. Kilo had to go up the wall while our own company waited below with the dead and wounded for the medevac Turk had no doubt arranged. He was called Turk for reasons unknown to me, but Homan, the A-6 bombardier/navigator, a friend of his, had informed me that the man was not 'The Turk," but only Turk, and getting that wrong, which I was prone to do, was a sore point with him.

As if the thought had somehow been translated into stark reality, the Gunny appeared. I heard him crawling toward me, but didn't know it was him until he whispered my name.

"Junior?" he asked.

"Affirmative," I answered briefly, while he centered himself against the wall next to my right shoulder.

The Gunny's face lit up briefly with the guarded release of light from under the cup he'd made of his other hand in lighting his cigarette. The tinkling mechanical sound of his special Zippo I found to be vaguely comforting. His ability to show any light at all in the stygian blackness where NVA small arms could come alive at any time in the jungle area around us didn't so much scare me as filled me with a strange wonder.

How could a man, who'd been through so much combat in his life, risk making such a seemingly careless revelation of our position to the enemy? I knew it was a question that I'd never ask him, however. I'd come to accept my place as a commanding officer, however uncomfortable I was in the acceptance. The Gunny's role, as the 'father' of the company, was much easier to go with.

"Jurgens doesn't want to stay," the Gunny said, his voice low, after taking in and releasing his first inhalation of smoke from the cigarette.

"Stay where?" I replied, not wanting to predict where the strange conversation was going to go. Nobody in his right mind would want to stay where we were.

"Down here, with the rest of us, while Kilo climbs to the top of the cliff," the Gunny continued. "He wants to take his platoon up the glacis in order to fire effectively from above to support our climb when its light since we'll be fully exposed on the full face of that cliff in broad daylight."

Not for the first time over the period of the last month, I felt like I was being sold something. Not something that might cause immediate harm, but something that still wasn't quite right.

"Why?" I asked, ignoring the Gunny's weak explanation of covering fire.

The snipers, with their special weapons, equipment, training and experience, could provide some covering fire effectively. From the top of the cliff, but regular Marines, leaning over the lip and shooting down would be hard put to deliver any accurate fire, even machine gun fire, at targets they couldn't see. Muzzle flashes could be used for targeting at night, but the NVA used the same smokeless powder we did to fuel its small arms cartridges. Their AK-47 assault rifles produced a muzzle flash, but not one that was easily visible from a great distance in daylight.

"He's trying to make it on into An Hoa," the Gunny finally replied, dropping the sales pitch tone he'd started out using. "He's a short-timer, with only about forty days left on his tour."

"I understand," was all I could think to say. I realized I knew less about Jurgens than I'd thought. We didn't need Jurgens and his platoon in our current circumstance.

We didn't need them primarily because of the presence of the Ontos and, I felt, the softening up the 'carpet bombing' of 175 artillery rounds had provided. Small arms fire originating from the main body of jungle, where the enemy was ensconced, remained light, although that could change at any time.

"I say, let him go, Junior," the Gunny recommended, when I didn't reply.

"How the hell did he end up with us in this valley, having that much time behind him," I couldn't help asking.

"How did you end up down here?" the Gunny countered.

I thought about Jurgens, knowing I wasn't going to answer the Gunny's question, and also knowing that he wasn't expecting me to. Sergeant Jurgens, I'd come to know, but only with great difficulty and even more danger. I could see how the man had likely let his mouth get the better of him with the wrong officer in the rear area. I didn't believe for a minute that most of the Marines in the rear areas lacked enough clues about the kind of fatalities and wounded outfits like our company took on a very regular basis, but that knowledge wouldn't, and didn't, stop them from sending Marines they found to be disagreeable out into such combat situations, and, in fact, as illustrated by my own assignment to the company, it probably encouraged them to do so.

"Okay," I replied, after about a full minute of silence. "He goes, but his platoon goes up last, and he last of all. Get them here and ready. Things are going to heat up with the coming of the light, rain or no rain, air support or no air support, and Kilo has to be up there by then."

The sound of helicopter blades cutting the night into supersonically driven pockets of compressed air began to overpower all other sounds.

The CH-46 came in unlike any other landing I'd witnessed, even though I couldn't really witness it with my eyes because of the darkness. It dropped out of the night onto the LZ not far from where I sat, but remained invisibly embedded inside it. It dropped straight down, not coming in at an angle at all, as was almost always the case with helicopters. Blown jungle debris, lifted from the floor by the chopper's high speed whirling blades, combined with the water they compressed out of the air, hit me like small bits and pieces shredded off some tattered nearby wall, swept up and then down, driven into every exposed part of my body. I dug in closer to the wet muddy ground next to the wall, using raw hands that Fessman had carefully removed the leeches from with a series of burning cigarettes, to press my face down. I sheltered my head as best I could under the edges of my helmet. I inhaled lightly, waiting out the chopper's artificially created storm, smelling the strangely clean-smelling odor emitted by the lichen covering the bare rock face.

My image of the medevac hadn't included visualizing the giant twin-rotor machine. I'd thought of a Huey coming in, but a Huey could only carry a very few Marines when it lifted off, especially in the fetid aircraft unfriendly atmosphere existing at the bottom of the A Shau Valley. A Huey would be lucky to get out with three bodies, and maybe three wounded on stretchers, but that would also be only if the chopper didn't fly with two door gunners, which wasn't likely under the 'hot LZ' nature of our situation. The 46 could carry as many as 25 Marines, dead or alive, but it's signature on the ground was much larger, and night landing down into such a small space had to be precarious and terribly dangerous. I pictured in my mind, with my eyes tight shut, the helicopter blades impacting against the trunk of one of the larger nearby trees, or the face of the cliff itself. If that happened, parts of the machine would penetrate every part of the enclosed battlefield space just as effectively as any anti-personnel artillery round.

The chopper reached the ground unimpeded and unfired upon, however, the proof of that being that the choppers turbines were quickly spooled down and the big twin rotors could be heard reduced to rotating slowly, but regularly, as it waited.

Suddenly, there was activity everywhere. In the air, Turk and his cohorts swooped around, their Huey Cobras twin-blade rotors sounding much more aggressive and louder than the CH-46's many bladed propellers and turbines. The Cobras orbited very close to where the chopper was down and waiting, firing occasional volleys of chain gunfire down toward unseeable targets. Although it was still full dark down in the deepest part of the valley, up above, beyond the top of the precipice and to the east, the sun would be starting to reveal itself as astronomical dawn, the early precursor to civil dawn. The coming sun's light would be all but invisible, although it would send a vague hint, more a hopeful feeling, of its coming identity surging up from below the distant horizon.

The chopper's blades whirled nearby, not fifty meters from my position. Suddenly, from high up in the air I heard the strange whistling roar of the only airplane I'd heard with that kind of exhaust signature.

"Get me up on the air radio," I turned to instruct Fessman. I didn't have to turn far, as he was so close, right next to me, that I could have touched him easily, simply by moving my right arm a short distance.

The complete darkness, the unrelenting rain, the sound of the chopper coming in, and then continuing to run its turbines as it offloaded and then waited, made the night so inscrutable that I didn't really know where anyone was without either touching them or having an indicator like that of the Gunny's lit cigarettes.

"He's got his ears on," Fessman said, letting me know that Homan was there.

Homan's A-6 Intruder maintained its dominating whistle overhead. I knew he had to be up there flying low, slow, and making the tightest turns he could while still maintaining a safe altitude.

"You up there, Whole Man?" I asked into the headset microphone, once I got my helmet off and the little batched wire rig over my head. I quickly clamped my helmet back onto my head, the rain so hard that its impact on my bare skull was much worse than the sound of the hundreds of drops impacting onto the surface of the thin steel shell.

"Why do you call me that, Flash, over?" Homan replied, as if we were back in training, and certainly not in a combat zone under fire ten thousand miles from wherever we would have trained together, which we had not. "It's not whole man. It's Homan. I'm not the whole man, whatever that is." He spelled out the word 'whole.'

"No, it's hole, not whole," I replied, spelling the word 'hole.'

"What is it you need?" Homan asked, no laughter in his tone. "Why am I here?"

"Right," I replied. "This entire circus was brought in by you and your insane pal up there in one of those Cobras."

"He can hear you, you know," Homan said.

"How long can the Cobras rotate on station?" I asked.

"With fuel to and from," Turk's voice cut in, "remaining supplies gives us about an hour on the station, maybe an hour and a quarter, but we have orders to depart with the 46 when it lifts off for An Hoa."

"That's what I thought," I said, unable to keep the disappointment out of my voice.

"What's your plan, Flash," Homan asked, hesitantly.

Only the Cowboy, the Skyraider pilot, called me Flash. I assumed that the air units operating across the board in support of us probably communicated as Fessman did with other unit radiomen when nobody was around or listening. I was glad of it this time, as the nickname Flash made me feel like maybe I could live up to such a compliment.

"I need some time to do our mountaineering thing in a bit," I replied.

"That's up to the chopper pilot," Homan said. "Captain Craig Jackman's got this run. He volunteered. Good guy. I'm sure he'll be reasonable if you send somebody onto the chopper to negotiate."

I didn't reply. Homan was telling me that there would be no change of departure orders unless I found something to convince the captain to stay while Kilo climbed the rock face. The combined effects of the Cobras whirling around overhead, the A-6 screaming above them and then the Ontos on the deck with us was all I had to assure that Kilo would have a fair shot of getting up the face without being wiped out.

I realized that my choices were limited in selecting who might be able to accomplish the 'negotiation' with Jackman, in order to keep the 46 on the deck until Kilo was up atop the ridge. I couldn't use the Gunny. He would be needed with me, to plan and defend the base of the wall and prepare our remaining platoons to assault the rockface at first light. The Ontos had to be taken out, as well, although Hutzler was probably perfectly suited to accomplish that on his own. The Gunny might also have his own ideas about what I was planning. In my mind, there was simply no other choice. We had to have the support of the Cobras buzzing all over that face and waiting to blow anything down below to hell and back if the enemy fired at the wall.

Jurgens and Nguyen were all I had. Nguyen spoke little or no English, although his ability to know and understand things without a lot of language was astounding to observe and be affected by. Nguyen was also one hundred percent loyal. Jurgens was Jurgens. He'd do what had to be done if it suited his own purposes, and sending him to the chopper instead of going up the wall with his own platoon was not going to be something he found that fit his idea of 'own purposes,' I knew.

"Stand by up there, my friends, Everest awaits us, over and out," I said into the headset, before stripping my helmet and liner off to give the rig back to Fessman.

Homan and Turk were bright guys, and they'd understand what I was doing, and that we were getting ready to 'leave the line of departure,' as the assault would have been called if we were conducting some combat training mission back in Virginia.

"Get me the Gunny, and have him bring Jurgens," I added, to Fessman, after thinking about the situation we were in for a bit.

I had to have the Gunny in on the plan, I realized. He had to know that Kilo would have every opportunity to make it, and also that

Jurgens had to go along, which might prove complicated if we were not all on the same page. I couldn't go against the Gunny if he opposed me, either directly or indirectly.

I waited for Fessman to get off the radio. "Nguyen," I said, keeping my voice low.

Fessman didn't answer immediately, and I felt the reason why. Nguyen's hand closed on my left bicep. He was there already, like always. Since the arrival of the Cobras and the Intruder, there had been no small arms fire coming from the NVA, so it was impossible to see even the slightest glimpse of the Montagnard so close to me. I felt his support through his touch, however.

"Tell him, that I need him to go with Jurgens to the chopper and make sure that it doesn't leave the ground until Kilo's up the cliff and safe along the rim," I ordered.

"Yes, sir," Fessman said.

Nguyen removed his hand and I sensed his departure. I heard nothing more, certainly no conversation between the two men.

In seconds Fessman came back "He'll be here, there and then here again."

I wondered if Fessman had ever read the Scarlett Pimpernel: "They seek him here, they seek him there, those Frenches seek him everywhere." The quote from the novel prompted to run through my mind by his words.

The Ontos arrived, to be run backward into the wall not far from my position. I listened to Hutzler position the main part of the small tank so that the recoilless rifles, mounted on the moveable turret, could cover the area around the chopper. There was a certain warm comfort in having the dreaded machine so close by. Earlier in my combat experience, I'd thought that the armored vehicle would attract rocket fire, but had since discovered, at least down in the valley, that the NVA took no chances at stirring the beast. But, they would have RPGs, and they' likely attempt to fire several of them, or more, at the naked surface of the rock, where the chiseled path crisscrossed up to the top. Hopefully, the chopper had come in by complete surprise, since helicopter missions were seldom conducted at night, especially at night under the weather conditions we were experiencing. One single rocket, striking anywhere on the chopper, would destroy it. The exhaust smoke from the Ontos' idling engine filled the air around me, making me wonder for a few seconds how smoke particles managed to travel through the pouring rain, and also if the smoke made it through the air all the way to me than what else might, as well? Even with the supporting fires building up to a morning crescendo, we had to be huge targets of opportunity for the NVA, and I could not see them missing the opportunity we were forced to present to them.

The Gunny came out of the dark, although I could not see it was him and had to assume by simple logic that nobody else would be showing up. He was accompanied by another man I assumed to be Jurgens.

Both moved in close, close enough to where I knew it was them.

"What's on your mind Junior?" the Gunny asked.

I could tell, across the short distance between us, that he was taking out one of his cigarettes.

I launched into the foundation for my plan to get Kilo the protection it needed while making its transit up the wall to the top, finally getting to the part where Jurgens would have to remain behind until most, if not all, of Kilo and his platoon were atop the ridge.

"So, you're planning on taking out the crew of one of our own choppers if that crew, or the captain himself, doesn't agree to remain sitting ducks while Kilo climbs the wall? the Gunny asked, igniting the tip of his cigarette.

"Wow!" he went on after a few seconds, the cigarette lighting his face as he sucked in a double lung full of the smoke.

"I don't think it'll come to that," I replied.

The Gunny held out the cigarette, the gesture he'd not made when he'd smoked in front of me only a short time before.

I took the lit cigarette and inhaled, but only lightly. I needed to be totally oriented. Sometimes the smoke from a cigarette made me slightly ill or dizzy.

"Yeah, he's planning that all right," Jurgens said, the tone of his voice close to a hiss, "but I'm the one who's supposed to do the dirty work."

"You've outdone yourself on this one, Junior," the Gunny said, as I handed his cigarette back.

"If the chopper leaves, then the Cobra's leave," I replied. "If the Cobra's leave, then we have one A-6 up there and the Ontos down here, plus whatever the company can bring to bear. Without snipers on the ridge and our inability to see into the jungle at night from down here, that means the A-6 has to carry the whole load of fire suppression. In which case Kilo is likely dead down to its last Marine. They lost 18 wounded and a dozen K.I.A. coming down the river. The chopper has a crew of five. There are about a hundred and sixty Marines left in Kilo. If I have to lose 23 to save a hundred and sixty, then there's no decision to be made."

"First the sacrifice of Kilo to save our own company, and now the sacrifice of the medevac, and the wounded to save Kilo," the Gunny took another hit on the cigarette, once again illuminating his face for a few seconds. "What, or who's next?"

"What about me?" Jurgens asked.

"Think," the Gunny said to Jurgens. "You've taken bigger risks just to get a few silver stars. Think. You stay with the chopper. You never have to risk the climb, or worry about getting from the island on into An Hoa, which is a long way from guaranteed. You ride the chopper on into An Hoa and you're home free. Junior can write you a note, like a doctor's note. He'll write that he ordered you to lead the advance party, awaiting the company's arrival on the ground."

"You'll write that, sir?" Jurgens asked.

With that question and the addition of the uncommon 'sir' at the end of it, I knew the Gunny had sealed the deal. I also knew that if Jurgens didn't live up to his word, or perform the mission acceptably, then I wouldn't have to worry about the sergeant ever again, one way or the other.

"Kilo climbs in thirty minutes," I said, "and Nguyen will back your play at the chopper. I'll get under my poncho right now and write the letter to command."

I covered myself with the poncho cover without saying more. Turning on my small flashlight gave me a feeling of relief, as I brought my little container of stationery from my pocket. My letter home would have to wait. There was no way I was going to entrust its delivery to Jurgens, or even Nguyen. The chopper crew, even if things worked out the way I needed them to, was going to be mad as hell, and not likely to deliver anything from me to anywhere.

The rain beat down on my poncho, the helicopter's blades stirred the night nearby while the A-6, along with the orbiting Cobras could be heard higher up in darkened sky. The noise of all of it was something I could not write home about, as it was simply not believable. I scribbled the ridiculous 'doctor's note' for Jurgens, hoping that when I pulled the poncho back to give it to him everything outside in the nightmare of the night would disappear. The silent road of my dreams, filled with expressionless but totally accusing civilians along its length, no matter how discomforting, was something I'd much rather step out into than that which awaited me.

one-hundred-forty-seven

THE THIRTIETH DAY

had the leg strength. I'd always had the legs. The records that had fallen to me in the obstacle course, running, and other military skills during officer candidate school and the Basic School had all been functions of lower body strength and agility. The glacis was a challenge more of balance than it was strength or agility, however. Each step sideways, face and the front of my torso pressed hard into the flat rock, had to be negotiated hesitantly but with pressing haste. There were Marines higher up than and many lower down the angle of our climb.

Climbing in the night was a risk, since the enemy, once it figured out that we were doing, could fire indiscriminately at the rock face, and be almost certain to hit Marines unable to gain any cover or move much of any distance in any direction from where they would be trapped. However, even though supporting fires would be on station, active, and very effective, a single sniper during daylight hours could decimate the company in a much more devastating way. Plus, hunkering down at the base of the face, which at its lowest point where they were, lacked the cave-like fold of undercut earth that the canyon wall had provided further up the valley.

The firing from the enemy started when I figured I was halfway up the glacis. There was nowhere to go. With the pack strapped tightly to my back and my helmet securely on my head, I could not turn from my cliff-facing position. I had to slither along the angled and chiseled path, hammered into solid stone. It was unforgiving in its thin rough presence beneath my boots. I could only slither upward, inch by inch, flinching when I heard bullets actually striking the rock face but I was unable to do anything about it. Nobody had yet been hit or fallen and I didn't want to be the first. The climb seemed to take hours although I knew it was more likely only a matter of many minutes. I reached the top and was grabbed and grappled up over the lip by many hands. Nobody said anything, as I moved to crawl quickly away from the edge toward where I knew the jungle started.

The top of the cliff was a large open area of jumbled, artillery-shelled and bomb cratered rocky ground. It was as if the entire football field-sized chunk of high ground had been cleared to allow for a sizeable landing zone the largest of the supply helicopters could land on. The helicopters weren't there or coming unless some kind of arrangement could be made to suppress the many avenues of fire the enemy could concentrate on the place. The 105 battery back in An Hoa was again available for fire, which was the best news, although buffered by the fact that the jutting chunk delineating GoNoy Island from the canyon below was also within the range of the North Vietnamese 106 mm guns.

Previously, when the company had occupied the area before descending down into the valley, we'd set up camp just inside the scrubby jungle area between the open flat land near the edge and the double and triple canopy full jungle that covered the entire interior area like a hundred-foot thick and layered layer of shag carpeting, seemingly hanging upside down. Without consulting me, Kilo had made it up the face of the glacis to occupy that same exact position my own company had abandoned so many weeks before. In the back of my mind alarms were going off. Never occupy the same ground twice in a guerilla environment, particularly not in a jungle environment where the enemy has become more expert and faster at tunneling than the toughest and most persistent of moles. I also realized there was nothing to be done for it until the first light. The entire top surface of the ground in and around the outer edge of the area was occupied, or open to fire, from NVA troops located deeper in the jungle. The only safety at all was from fire that might be generated from down in the valley, as up to now the NVA hadn't used the kind of heavy mortars it would take to accurately fire from below and deliver death-dealing injuries up top, while what RPG rockets they still might have, were also useless against such a high shielded target.

I re-established contact with the eleventh regimental battery located just to the east of the An Hoa runway. The maximum range of the 105s was about twenty-five kilometers, using charge 8, which the battery didn't like to use much, as the wear and tear of the chambers of the weapons was much higher. Our position wasn't that far from the maximum range, although that would change as we moved inland toward the firebase on the following day. The 106 Soviet-supplied guns could reach out farther but were likely much closer in range on the top of the other side of the canyon, although it was anybody's guess at any given time just how much of an ammunition inventory they had, compared to the near-endless supply available for the 105s.

I registered five grid coordinates for a thousand-meter stretch of the interior jungle running north and south about a thousand meters inland. I wanted whatever forces were in that jungle, probably preparing to attack us, to pay more attention to their own survival rather than ours. The battery was well supplied with concrete piercing shells, the kind that worked best because of the ability of the fuses to be adjusted to go off just milliseconds after the rounds encountered the very top of the jungle's canopy.

Most of the company, just up from climbing the glacis, were on our stomachs, crawling across the clear but broken area, thankful to be away from the edge and actually looking for some safety inside the jungle itself. Somehow, the Gunny found me in the dark, and stopped my forward progress by grabbing my right ankle.

"This is a mistake, Junior," he said, keeping his voice modulated to a loud whisper.

"We've been here before," I acknowledged and was about to tell him that we'd done the same thing several times before down in the valley and been okay.

"This is all soft ground, not like the stuff along the bottom edges of the canyon wall down there," he said, blunting my argument before I could get it out. "They've had plenty of time to dig."

"We don't have long before first dawn," I replied, knowing I was handing him a weak excuse for my decision but the alternatives to setting up for the remainder of the night in our current position were severely limited. Either we stayed in the open area where one salvo of enemy artillery could take us out, or penetrated deep into the complete unknown of the thicker jungle the enemy was known to heavily occupy. I found both those alternatives unworkable. We could also keep moving right on through except the Marines had had no rest and no sleep for some time, and once again, the companies would be moving right through an occupied enemy position, and there was no surprise the enemy would likely fall for this time. Once again, I felt we had no choice about what we had to do. Every move we could possibly make was high risk.

"I don't like it," the Gunny finished, "okay, let's get the hell off this beaten zone, no doubt registered to untold numbers of artillery batteries."

The trouble brought me awake in an instant. I was crouched into the half-hole Fessman had dug for me, with my pack wadded up between my knees and my chest. I was not truly aware of falling asleep but I was fully aware that I was awake, as small arms fired opened up all around me. The company was pouring out fire. The tracers crisscross over my head everywhere, which caused me some confusion. What was everyone shooting at? There was no direction to anything. It was like the company was being attacked from all around at once.

I tried to raise my head to peer about, but the blackness was complete and I could see nothing. The rain had stopped, which was a great relief but everything remained totally soaked, from the mud lining the bottom of my hole to all the foliage around. I unsnapped the strap, releasing my .45, but didn't move to put it into my hand. I had to know what was going on first. I dug through my pack until I found the M-33 grenade I had kept, pulled it out, and made sure the pin was still in it.

Once more I raised my head, staring out from under the wet lip of my damaged helmet. The tracers could still be seen, racing everywhere but the brilliant white light of them blinded me from being able to see anything else since the hot fast-moving bullets were too distant to illuminate anything close to me.

I needed Fessman in order to bring the pre-planned zone fire online.

"Fessman," I whispered, knowing he would be nearby.

I didn't see or hear him until suddenly the area in front of me lit up and a scene was revealed in stop-action like I'd never seen before or even imagined.

An NVA soldier was half-crouched inside a hole, holding the edge of some hinged cover with one hand and a firing AK-47 in the other. The reddish-yellow of the muzzle flashes lit everything in front of me and to both sides. I heard Fessman scream from only feet away. I turned my head but was only able to marginally see him go down, sideways but almost on top of my position. He continued to scream.

I had to get to him. The firing stopped and the night took my vision once again.

I had to get Fessman into what little protection my small hole offered. I crawled toward his downed body, pushing the M-33 down into the left pocket of my utility blouse pocket. Pulling on his feet, I dragged him toward the hole, the tracers still flying, closer and lower now, allowing me to see more of Fessman's body. He was stitched up and down his torso by so many blood pumping bullet holes that I was stunned he was able to use his voice at all.

"Mom, mom, oh mom," he cried. "I'm hurt mom."

I finally got his feet to the hole, knowing deep inside me that I was wasting my time while risking my own life, but I could not leave him in the open. It just wasn't in me.

I felt the ground suddenly opened again, and immediately fire came from the hinged hole. I reached for the grenade, dropping Fessman's feet as I turned my body to try to avoid the firing coming from only a few yards in front of me. The bullets took me in the right side and I went instantly down, but I didn't fall toward where Fessman still lay, screaming for his mother. I fell sideways into the hole.

In spite of what had happened to Fessman and all my time in the A Shau, the bullets took me completely by surprise as did the level of pain. There was no comparing it in my life. It was like someone had inserted red hot rods through my body and they could not be removed. I am not sure if I cried out, as Fessman had. All I could do was curl up into a ball, the M-33 falling out of my pocket, landing on the side of my right hand. I clutched it, using one of the still working fingers on my left hand to pull the pin. Only then did I realize I was incapable of getting the grenade to the hole, even if it gaped open waiting. A pain paralysis froze my hands and arm. I lost awareness of my surroundings for a period of time. A voice nearby brought me to.

The words "stay with us" burned their way into my consciousness, as I fought to comprehend the awful condition of my body and even my state of existence on the planet. The words kept repeating, as I tried to see through a distorted return of fuzzy imagery, the hot pokers penetrating and rifling into the very center of my being. The pain came in waves that I rode as an unwilling surfer, each wave coming at me intolerably and inexorably, my stuttering breaths fighting to somehow survive by willing the troughs of those brutal waves to be something less than the outrageous unsurvivable pain the waves themselves brought.

"Look at me, Junior, and stay with us," a face said, the being's beady eyes trying to bore their way into, and then right through, my own.

I tried to mouth the single word "okay" back, but nothing would come out. My breathing was only capable of riding the waves of red-hot pain to bring me to seconds of minutely relieving but never-ending pain.

"You are hit bad through and through and you've got to fight it," the moving mouth inches from my face said. "You're going out on a Huey right now. You'll never make it waiting for the big bird."

Some sort of consciousness, real thinking now foreign to me, came over me as the pain attempted to occupy every shred of every bit of any kind of rational thoughts I might otherwise have. I knew I was hit. I'd seen the NVA soldier rise from his spider hole not ten feet from my position. I'd been moving to try to save Fessman's life, when the NVA soldier came out of the earth.

In that instant, when the soldier had opened up with his AK-47 the second time, I knew the enemy was coming out of the earth. They'd been waiting, after digging like fiends to prepare, since we'd sheltered down in the same position prior to coming down the face of the wall almost a month before, and they'd been ready. The fire I was trying to find the source of was their fire, as they killed my Marines from the rear while the unit fought against what it believed was fire coming in from outside the perimeter.

The yellow and white blasts from the AK had been like a string of Christmas tree lights coming at me, much slower than bullets were supposed to go. I'd turned a tiny bit to begin attempting to evade the string, but I'd only made that turn with my upper body before running out of time. The bullets hit my side and then were gone. The soldier disappeared as I went down. I wasn't knocked down like I'd seen in the movies. I'd gone over sideways, but slowly, like a damaged building collapsing from the bottom up.

"I know the pain's bad, really bad," the small moving mouth with beady black eyes that wouldn't leave my own said, "but I can't give you morphine. Your system will simply shut down and let you die. The pain's keeping you alive. We're going to have you on the chopper and out of here in minutes."

I thought of the morphine in my pocket, the pocket that still held the letter home to my wife I hadn't been able to get aboard any helicopter since coming to the end of the valley. As the face moved back and away from my shortened visual field of view I managed to get one hoarsely whispered word out. I had to speak. I had to get the face to understand and then take action. I could not access the morphine the face would not give me without being able to use both hands and in my right hand, I held tightly, uncontrollably to something that prevented that hand's use for anything other than what it was doing. I had to have the morphine and I didn't care one whit about whether I died or not. I could not take the pain. I would not take the pain.

"Grenade," I hissed across the short distance to the face.

The Marine stopped his retreat and leaned back down.

"Grenade?" he asked, his wetly smooth forehead furrowed with a deep frown.

"Right hand," I got out, trying to gesture by nodding my head to the side and down toward my uncontrollably clutching hand, but my head would not move, any more than my hand could or would let go of the M33 grenade I'd pulled out of my right front pocket as I'd gone down from the effect of the bullets striking my torso. Once the hits registered right into the central core of my being, however, my ability to do anything other than pull and discard the pin had been taken from me.

The face disappeared and I went back to trying to ride the scorching awful waves radiating into and out of my shattered body. I was hemmed in. The bullets had to have gone in one side of my torso and out the other because the waves of pain came from those sides into my interior and then seemed to reflect and bounce back to those sides. Time after time, with milliseconds between them.

"Jesus Christ," a voice I recognized but could not place breathed out. "The pin's pulled. Easy, easy, use the K-Bar to pry his fingers loose. He's not going to give a damn about losing fingers at this point."

I wanted to shout that I did give damn, that I wanted all my fingers, but I couldn't say anything as the pain waves stole my voice, my breath and even most of my ability to see.

My hand hurt from whatever they did, but that hurt didn't matter one bit. The waves racking their way back and forth through my body like those of a shaken bottle of coke absorbed that hurt like it was a bit of remote matter too inconsequential to be anything more than being noticed in a minor way.

"Get the lid up and that thing down in the hole," a loud voice screamed.

Through the waves of white-hot heated pain, I felt and heard a loud explosion. I couldn't remember hearing the explosions that had to have been occurring when the bullets came out of the AK and on into me, but the sound of the grenade going off was unmistakable.

The face leaned back in for a few seconds, "Got any more surprises, Junior? By God, you were a piece of work in your time," and then was gone.

My ears rang, but I was used to that. The face's words; "You were a piece of work in your time," ate their way through the pain, and on into some still open recess of my fractured mind. He'd used the past tense. Was my time of being alive over? I felt a familiar sickening bolt of fear rush its way from the bottom of my feet to the top of my roiling and shattered being.

The face was gone, the explosion far back in my somehow time-slowed existence. I was alone. There were no more sounds coming from Fessman. The corpsmen hadn't even bothered with him at all. I knew he was dead. Nobody could live through the number of hits he'd taken at such close range. Taken for me. Taken because of me. Only bitter awful regret could power its way through and between the waves of racking pain that continued to penetrate and occupy every remaining bit of my living being.

I worked my left hand over and down with impossible effort, the surging power of its goal overcoming iron strength of attempted life-stopping power of the surf-riding, nearly overwhelming, force of the pain.

The morphine. I clutched the small box containing the styrettes. The face had said that administering morphine would kill me.

I felt the plastic bag next to the morphine box, as I worked to get it out of my wet pocket, with difficulty. I felt my letter home. I could not die. What would my wife and new daughter do without me? There was no money on her side of the family and my side of the family wasn't likely to share a thin dime. My wife had worked three times in her life during college to help pay tuition. Once in a potato factory, once in a pet store, and once as a recess director at a summer park. She'd done remarkably well at those foundational and terrible-paying jobs. There was little hope that she might find something to support herself and our daughter without me. I could not die, but I could not take the pain. It was simply too awful, and, in spite of what the face had said, I knew, in what was left of my rationality, that the morphine was very likely the only thing that might keep me alive.

I fumbled the package out, shredding the cardboard box as I did so while bringing my freed upright hand over atop my agonized torso to grasp the tiny styrette. I breathed, and then breathed deeply again to get to a near-instantly passing trough between the giant waves of un-bearable pain. I flicked the plastic cover off the top of the tube and then, as gently as my forced, cut and shaking fingers could do it, I got the tiny metal stopper out of the end of the needle, wondering at the same time about the fingers I couldn't see that had to still be there if I was able to do what I was doing.

I punched the needle of the tube into my stomach. There was no way I could bend my torso to get the drug into my thigh. I knew from long experience with the company in combat that one styrette wasn't going to be enough. I pawed with my left hand and found another stuck in the mud covering my stomach. I punched a second styrette into near-ly the same place the first one had gone. I knew that three styrettes was death for someone of my size. If I was to die from taking the two then it was a death meant to be. I would not do the three. My letter home to my wife still had to be posted, and I was duty-bound to get it in the mail. She, and my daughter, were all I had to hold onto and I wasn't about to let them go.

The waves of fire-hardened pain began to come down from their vaulting heights as the morphine began to do its job. My breathing be-gan to change from the sucked and vacated packets of spewing jungle air it had been to a level where my torso no longer beat itself up and down against the jungle floor.

Slowly, ever so slowly, I worked my head up and eased my bleed-ing torso over the edge of the hole, creeping inch by inch to drag the rest of myself toward where Fessman lay. I ignored his body, the fingers on my undamaged right hand searching for the radio microphone. I found it, still clutched in his left hand.

I breathed deeply in and out, knowing that my life was most probably being very temporarily extended only because of the mor-phine deadening everything in my body. I squeezed the button on the mic.

"Fire mission," I rasped into the thing, hoping Fessman had ad-justed the frequency to the artillery net.

"Fire mission" came right back. Fessman had left the external speaker on. I nodded in my misery. If he hadn't left the speaker on then I wouldn't have been able to hear the other side of the conversation.

"Is that you, Junior?" a familiar voice asked.

It was Russell, from my Basic Class back at Quantico. The same one who always asked how I was doing out in the field, and I couldn't tell him.

"On the gun target line, Russell," I replied, trying to concentrate. "Drop one thousand on the zone fire and fire for effect."

I'd set the zone to run along the flank of our position a thousand meters to the east. I had figured out in an instant what had happened to the company and why Fessman was dead and I was dying. The enemy had tunneled under our previous position, in the hopes that one day or night we would return. The Gunny, who was also likely dead, had been right again. All the firing I'd been hearing, much of it died out and as likely gone as my Marines, had been coming from inside our lines. The enemy had been everywhere around us in the night, but only they had known that. It meant they were also everywhere in the night around me at that instant. The occasional shots I was hearing were the enemy performing cleanup. Killing any wounded they found in the night, which also meant they eventually get to me.

"What's your position, Junior?" Russell asked.

I knew he was asking because of the artillery rules of engagement. He had to know the edge of the cliff was not far enough away to allow the fire.

"We're still down in the valley, about to scale the wall," I replied, hoping the battery had not been monitoring the combat net.

"Roger that," Russell said, instantly. I knew he knew I was lying, just from the speed of his agreement and his light feathery tone.

"Bye, Russell," was all I could get out before dropping the mic and beginning the short torturous agony of crawling back into my hole. The hole and my morphine were all I had left in the world, and hell was coming like a series of giant exploding anvils to take even those.

I heard the enemy, and then the rain. The enemy was talking among themselves nearby, which meant the decimation of the company had to be all but complete. The rain began to come down in sheets as I worked to control the white-hot pain, working against the morphine to reach deeper inside me. I heard a few very close shots and closed my eyes to wait. Then, as clear as the sound of two sharp peeling little bells, the words "shot, over," come from Fessman's radio speaker.

The voices of the enemy soldiers became louder. I knew they had to be gathering near Fessman's body. There were more shots, this time deafening, but it didn't matter because the next two radio bells spoke clearly across the short distance to me "splash over."

I counted backward out loud, no longer caring about the enemy.

I never reached the word 'one.' The world exploded around me. Everything went white, then black and then white again and again. I was thrown above the hole and then out of it. I tried to crawl back inside but the morphine, in taking a good deal of the pain, had also taken whatever strength I had left. All I could do was lay on my back, the rain pounding down upon my face. I licked my lips as more explosions occurred around me. I knew I was deaf because I couldn't hear the detonations at all.

The giant bright flashes let me see the many bodies strewn around my exposed position. I didn't know if they were NVA soldiers or Marines, except for Fessman. I could also get glimpses of the hinged cover hanging near the hole the enemy soldier had popped up from to kill Fessman and grievously wound me.

I had to stay awake if I was to survive. I had to ride the pain, as it came in waves. I was a surfer and the areas between the great swells were friends to me. Up and down, agony to bearable misery. I breathed and worked to control my own blood pressure. I had to be bleeding terribly inside. Multiple torso wounds were invariably terminal primarily because of the loss of blood. I didn't move my hands to feel the wounds. I simply lacked the coordination to make my hands react properly. All I could do was hold my sides as if I was holding myself together in some sort of death grip.

The morphine allowed me enough distance from the pain to reflect while I waited. I'd lost my company and probably Kilo, as well. As I waited for the sound of the helicopters that would eventually come, I thought of the Gunny, of Jurgens, Sugar Daddy, and especially about Fessman.

I thought of Captain Hrncr, back at St. Norbert's, and one of his maxims of combat. Never ever encamp where you camped previously. The sin of my violating that inflexible rule would die with me if I died, or live with me for the rest of my life if I lived. There was no more activity that I could sense from the enemy. The rain came down directly on my face. I thought of taking more morphine but then figured that the arriving choppers, if they got there while I was still alive, might overdose me if I was not coherent. I could see no light but I realized my hearing was coming back. I heard the first sound of aircraft approaching. It was not the sound produced by great whirling blades and turbines. I finally recognized the sound as coming from a large supply plane. I laid my head to one side. They knew back in the rear what had happened. They were sending Puff the Magic Dragon to make sure the chopper teams were not encountered by an active enemy.

My war was over.

FROM JIM

Thirty Days Has September is complete, but the effects and results that have continued through life and in the lives of those who survived continue to move along.

There is no epilogue to *Thirty Days Has September*; instead, there is another book. No epilogue could do justice to the aftermath of what occurred down in the A Shau Valley so long ago, as covered in the three novels.

The fourth book, the ending of that beginning, is called *The Cowardly Lion*, the name taken from a character appearing in a movie long before the Vietnam War. The Cowardly Lion is what the survivor of the novels had to become in appearance and presentation in order to return home from becoming Junior and survive in a culture where none of the tools he used so effectively to control life around him and survive had any applicability. Those actions he learned created habit patterns that had to be shed like a snake's molting skin.

The criminal punishments and social abandonment the American culture dispenses on people who use violence to accomplish their goals, or even survival, are draconian in nature. The tools, the habit patterns, and predatory behavior Junior had grown to become part of had to be abandoned, although never forgotten.

To discover what happened to the companies of Marines and Junior himself the book *The Cowardly Lion* must be read from beginning to end.

Visit *JamesStrauss.com* for updates.